PRAISE FOR
YVES MEYNARD

"In terms of both mature craft and originality of imagination, [editor David] Hartwell's major discovery this year has to be the French-Canadian writer Yves Meynard." —*Locus*

PRAISE FOR
The Book of Knights

"An unpredictable, brilliantly imaginative, and very engaging fantasy."
—Ursula K. Le Guin

"A bildungsroman whose closest analogue would be an adult version of Norton Juster's children's classic *The Phantom Tollbooth*. *The Book of Knights* is a tale of self-discovery that will entertain and enlighten both children and their parents." —*The Washington Post*

"A gem of a fairy tale . . . *The Book of Knights* is sheer delight."
—Dave Duncan

"A pleasure to read, reminiscent of but more mature than Michael Ende's *Neverending Story*. Watch for Meynard's name in the future." —*Analog*

"[With] *The Book of Knights,* Yves Meynard has written a novel that is *about* something. From the ancient materials of myth, folklore, and legend, he has fashioned a work that is wonderfully new and wonderfully wise. Here is literary alchemy of the highest order, resulting in seamless art."
—Terence M. Green

"*The Book of Knights* offers a fantasy with a refreshing difference, and wisdom." —*Locus*

"The author's lyrical style accentuates the allegorical nature of this intensely compact tale of self-discovery. Transcending the fantasy genre, this novel belongs in most libraries." —*Library Journal*

"This is an exquisitely well-crafted book written in elegant prose—few writers in English show such mastery of the language, yet Yves Meynard, a Canadian, has already published six novels in French." —*Vector*

Chrysanthe

YVES MEYNARD

A TOM DOHERTY ASSOCIATES BOOK

NEW YORK

CHRYSANTHE

Design by Mary A. Wirth

A Tor Book
Published by Tom Doherty Associates, LLC
175 Fifth Avenue
New York, NY 10010

www.tor-forge.com

Tor® is a registered trademark of Tom Doherty Associates, LLC.

Library of Congress Cataloging-in-Publication Data

Meynard, Yves.
    Chrysanthe / Yves Meynard.—1st ed.
      p. cm.
    "A Tom Doherty Associates book."
    ISBN 978-0-7653-3026-0
    1. Princesses—Fiction. 2. Magic—Fiction. 3. Imaginary wars and battles—Fiction. I. Title.
    PR9199.3.M4524C47 2012
    813'.54—dc22

2011025186

First Edition: March 2012

Printed in the United States of America

0 9 8 7 6 5 4 3 2 1

For my parents

Every man's life is a fairy tale, written by the finger of God.

—Hans Christian Andersen

BOOK I

Far and Away

1. A Make-believe Princess

"Once upon a time," came Tap Fullmoon's voice, "there was a little princess named Christine who lived with her uncle."

Christine burrowed her head deeper into her pillow, cold where the fabric was still wet with her tears. She shut her eyes tight and strove to imagine the princess in her castle. She saw her wearing a gown full of ruffles and ribbons, with stars—real stars yet, not foil cutouts, but actual lights, dazzling bright, silver and gold—somehow sewn to it. She lived in a big castle full of friends and treasures, and everyone had to call her "milady." A tear leaked from beneath her left eye and crossed the bridge of her nose before it was drunk by the pillowcase.

The princess Christine had no mother; her mother was long dead and she had never seen her. She had a father, a tall man with a beard both black and white, but Christine couldn't imagine him as more than a distant presence, a figure seen from the corner of the eye. Still she missed him and wept for him, but so long had he been gone from her life that her tears were more reflex than grief. And though she wrapped the princess dream about her every night, clung to it with desperate energy, she did so as a token of what she had lost, and no longer as a hope of escape.

She cried herself asleep every night, and cried when she awoke. She didn't sob, not anymore; when the tears had run their course she would knuckle the dampness away and rise from bed. Tap Fullmoon would be sitting on her chair facing the desk; he'd smile at her, consoling, his great big front teeth catching the morning light from the window. It gave her the strength to go about her day.

Daddy had been taken away when she was four, one-third of her life ago. She had lived in a different place then, a wonderful place that she couldn't recall precisely; not as nice as the castle in her daydream, surely, but still a source of delight. There had been many people, all of them nice to her. Her memories faded away swiftly as they reached into the past. It was like when she wet a brush on a disc of paint and smeared color across paper; the bright, full tint bleeding away into whiteness. If she closed her eyes for a long time and concentrated, she could bring some images to mind. People dressed in dark clothes bending down to talk to her, somewhere in a vast room full of shiny things, where pale blue marble statues ranked themselves along the walls. A plump woman wearing a wimple; her dress was red as wine, and stray strands of graying hair framed her face with its high cheekbones; but Christine could not recall anything else of her features, nor could she say who the woman was in relation to her. Walking along a cobbled street, the way her ankles flexed at every new stone, so that she found herself climbing up at one moment and down at the next. She had had to be careful, and someone with her, another woman, had held her hand with great care, hovering behind her to prevent her from falling.

One memory that must have been only a dream she'd once had: a landscape covered with flowers, so many flowers, growing bigger than people, in a dazzle of purple and yellow. And a few pale impressions of Daddy. A tall thin man, with a long head, a long straight nose. Being in his arms; the warm wetness of a kiss on her neck and the terrible tickle of his beard.

When she was four, something had happened, something she couldn't recall, a great wrenching upheaval in her life that had come upon her without any forewarning. She had traveled away from the place where she had always lived and she had come here, to live with Uncle. This place was all gray and dull, and very small. She hadn't minded that so much, because she herself was so little still that in a way she preferred a world more to her own size. But Daddy wasn't here, and that was terribly, terribly wrong. In the beginning, she'd asked again and again where her daddy was; every time, Uncle told her Daddy was gone forever and she'd never see him again. She knew what death was, because Mommy was dead, so she'd ask if Daddy was dead. Uncle would grow angry then. No, Daddy was *not* dead. He was gone. Just gone. And Christine should forget about him.

Many of her questions made him angry; especially so when she mentioned the land of her birth and asked why things were so different here. Uncle had had to correct her, time and again, because she kept making things up. Now that she was six she understood better the difference between imagination and reality; back then she hadn't, and had invented things that couldn't be true, angering Uncle when she put forth her fantasies as fact.

She must have conjured up these wild stories because her mind couldn't hold on to the memories of her first few years: They'd poured out, leaving only their dregs behind. Just enough to make Christine yearn for an unattainable past. Most often it was in dreams that she recalled them; she would awake with a start, a scrap of remembrance clear in her mind. She knew with all her heart it was a true memory, and yet it would be a random image stripped of most of its meaning: It might as easily have been a dream. Towering walls of foliage, covered in blooms; a dizzying perspective of receding corridors striped blue and brown; a cascade of shining objects pouring into her lap yet somehow devoid of any weight; an intricate geometric landscape that must have been the pattern of a carpet she had gazed at from very close to the ground. Fragments of a life lost to the dim past of a few years back.

She no longer tried to connect these scraps together, to invent towering edifices of imagination to justify them; she merely kept them as safe as she could in the recesses of her child's brain, and focused on the world where she lived now, which was, as Uncle never tired of repeating, the real world, and the only one that mattered.

She did remember clearly what had come just after the change; she recalled that at first, she'd been terribly unhappy. She wanted her Daddy back, she wanted everything back as it was, with a fierce intensity. She would sob and wail for hours. Back then she must still have been able to remember how things had been before, but soon she must have started to forget, to fill the gaps in her memory with invention. Now that her memories had faded away, now that she had also forgotten the inventions that had so annoyed Uncle, she wasn't as sad anymore. And there was Tap Fullmoon to console her: her faithful companion and succorer in hard times. It felt as if he'd always been there, though there must have been a time when he wasn't. Tap was a little white rabbit who stood on two legs and talked. He didn't look like a real rabbit; he was more like a cartoon in some ways, or maybe a puppet.

No one but her could see Tap; she was well aware of this and made sure not to tell anyone about him. She never asked that a place be set for him at the table, never protested when people sat in a chair he had been occupying. For Tap Fullmoon was clever, and fast, and did not need to eat. He scurried out from under people's rears in the twinkling of an eye; he never talked when other people were speaking, never did anything that might have made Christine betray his existence.

It was mostly at night that he talked to her, when she lay in bed with the lights out, head buried in her pillow. His voice wasn't what one might have expected. It wasn't a high-pitched, accelerated cartoonlike voice, but rather the voice of a young man, a light tenor. He would say, "Don't worry, my princess, one day things will be better for you. Hope and trust, trust and hope. Old magics are at work to free you. Don't despair."

It was nice of him to play the pretend game, that she was really a princess, and not just little Christine whose mother was dead and whose father had been taken away from her for reasons beyond her understanding. She played the game because it made her feel special, made her believe the path of her life would eventually extend into sunnier climes. Sometimes just as she fell into sleep she felt herself enter her princess dream, and it rose about her in a blaze of glory, like the fulfillment of a thousand immemorial promises, like an answer to every question ever asked. But come the morning, there would only be tears left.

❧ Uncle was a balding, stout man with a temper, whose face went an incredible shade of crimson at least twice a week. Now that she was more grown-up, no longer such a little girl as she had once been, Christine was almost never the cause of these flare-ups anymore; and the few times she did get him mad he calmed down almost immediately and apologized. He said he understood she was still a child and didn't know any better. His real flashes of anger were caused by his many conversations: Uncle was a businessman, which meant that he went to work every morning in his office, where there was a telephone. He spent most of the day talking into the mouthpiece, and this made him rich. Every so often people would come to the house and deliver some new piece of furniture, painting, or small trinket she would be allowed to look at once but never touch.

Sometimes, but more rarely, they brought a toy for Christine. She didn't always like the toys, but mostly they were nice. Her favorite was a doll, a thin plastic Jessica with hair down to her buttocks. You were supposed to be able to cut and style it, but she never dared use scissors on it. There was something about its silken length that felt inviolable. She played quietly with it, whispering the things Jessica said to other, invisible, doll persons. Often Tap would play with her too, and he whispered what the other dolls said. They made up stories that Jessica lived out: Sometimes she was an explorer, or a singer, or a scientist inventing exotic potions and eldritch rays.

At first Christine would spend her days playing aimlessly (not outside, though, never outside, except on special occasions when Uncle would go out to "take the sun in," which meant he would lie down on a canvas chair and go to sleep, while Imelda, the woman who came in every day to cook and clean, would watch Christine with a bored expression). Then, not long after her sixth birthday, she was told she would have to go to school in the fall. She was scared of school, and said so. Uncle got angry, not crimson-faced angry, but angry enough, and said everyone had to go to school; he'd done it himself, and it had made him rich. Christine asked if school would teach her to use the telephone then, and Uncle's face started to flush pink. "Don't mock me, child," he said (when he called her "child" it meant she'd done something stupid). "You'll start attending as soon as the school year starts. It's time you made friends; you're old enough by now."

Christine, not wanting to push her luck, just nodded in silence. That night, when she went to bed, the tears came, as automatic, almost as meaningless, as when her bladder voided itself.

"Tap," she whispered. The rabbit bounded on the bed, cocked his head to look at her from closer up. His eyes were big and shining blue, even when the room was dark.

"Don't worry, my princess," he began.

"Uncle said I'm going to go to school in the fall. What will it be like?"

"Why, I think it will be a good thing," he said, surprising her. "You getting out of the house! Isn't that something nice?"

"But what could there be outside? I mean, other people . . . I don't know what they'll do."

Tap was silent a long moment. Then, "What could they do to you that's worse than what's already happened?" he asked in his light tenor voice, and Christine could not find an answer. The next morning, as she woke, she found she wasn't crying anymore.

❧ Come Seventh Month, school was not so horrible as she'd feared. She didn't have to walk there; a man who worked for Uncle took her there in a car and dropped her off in front of the building, which was built of nice red bricks and had wooden trimming around the windows. She had taken Jessica with her in her bag, not telling anyone, hoping for some comfort from the doll. When she entered the classroom and filed to her desk, though her heart pounded from the proximity of so many people, she found she could stand it. And then she felt a silken touch on her bare knee and had to stifle a gasp of astonishment: Tap Fullmoon had followed her to school. He winked at her and whispered from the corner of his mouth, "Surprise! I'll be with you every day, if you need me. Don't worry; hope and trust, trust and hope."

Buoyed by the presence of two talismans, she was able to face the terrors of school after all. Her teacher was a kind woman with long reddish hair and a pointy nose, and Christine soon found she liked her. At recess, she got to talk with other children. She was pretty sure she had never done so before; it seemed to her that in her previous life, she had always been surrounded by adults, had never played with others of her own age.

She was shy, and didn't speak much, but no one was mean to her as she'd feared. Where had she gotten the idea that children were always rowdy and prone to hit each other for no reason? These children looked happy and not at all aggressive.

Standing in the yard, leaning against the dark brick wall, she felt Tap's reassuring touch on her leg—he was much shorter than her, even when he stood on his hind legs he didn't reach higher than her waist—and began to think this indeed might work out.

She still wept in the mornings, briefly, but not at night anymore. It had turned out that she liked school. She liked learning things. It was fun most of the time: There were lessons on the Earth, with the teacher pointing out the seven continents on a big globe; and ancient people (including kings, queens, and princesses, most of whom only lived in fairy-tale books anymore); and how to read and write too. She had taught herself how to read by watching educational programs on television and was astonished to find out other children couldn't yet make sense of the letters.

Her life was changing again, and this time for the better. Tap was happy too: There was an extra bounce in his step and a twinkle in his cartoony eyes, and his voice would sometimes briefly rise up in pitch like an excited child's. Uncle still got into his tempers every so often, but Christine was never the cause of his upset. He was pleased with her, and when he looked at her report card and smiled his praise, she would beam.

And so weeks and months passed. Having learned to write, Christine decided to keep a journal. Day-to-day occurrences swiftly grew boring to relate; then she thought to write down what few memories returned to her in dreams. Whenever she did this, Tap would stay at her elbow, quietly attentive, sometimes nodding. She filled page after page over the months, and for a time grew excited, since it seemed to her she had started to recall more of her past. But after a year, when she carefully reread the contents of her journal, she was chilled: What she thought she had remembered was painfully silly; no more than fluff culled from fairy tales and cartoon shows. Every time she had woken from dreams clutching a priceless piece of remembrance, hurrying to write it down, she must have been still in the grip of the dream. *Daddy ordering three hunters to bring down a stag for the festival*: that was from *The Princess and the Peasant*, obviously. And this next entry, scrawled in the predawn dimness so that the letters slanted across the blue lines on the page: *The woman in red sings about God, a pretty song.* Even now she could bring the scene to her mind's eye, hear fragments of the melody—but no one dressed like that, and no one sang like that. The upper corner of the page bore a scrawled mess of a drawing: She had meant to depict a dress made of feathers, something she had thought to recall, even to the sensation of her fingers brushing across dozens of feathers all at once. But Annika the Magic Girl on television wore a feathered dress, and clearly this was where the false memory had come from.

Yes, to read these penciled notes still brought flashes of impressions to her mind, and she felt something tremble at her core. But she couldn't make herself believe they were true memories; she had been playing pretend too much, had spent too much time wanting to be a princess, and so she had imagined these snatches of dream were meaningful. With regret, Christine went to the latest entry in her journal, wrote "THE END" below it, closed the notebook, and put it at the bottom of her sock drawer.

Months became years; Christine still daydreamed of being a princess, and still pined for her former life, but in a more and more abstracted fashion, as a routine matter, then an intermittent bad habit, the way some people bite their nails.

When she was ten, Tap Fullmoon began to fade away. She didn't notice it the first time, not really: She was at school, and she'd been working on her tasks hard, not paying attention to anything except the book she was reading from and the questions on her sheet. She looked up at one point, once she was nearly done, expecting to see at least the tip of his ears peeking over her desk, but she couldn't sense him. She looked at the clock, saw that she had less than ten minutes to finish, and bent back to the sheet of paper. When the last bell rang, he was there at her side, putting his paw in her hand, as always; she didn't question the situation.

But it happened again the next day, during recess: She was by herself, waiting for her friend Freynie to come back from the bathroom. Tap was chattering to her about unimportant things, and suddenly he fell silent. She looked down and he had gone. This would happen sometimes if someone were about to step over him; but always she would see him somewhere else close by, grinning at his own speed and cleverness. She looked about; he was nowhere in sight. Freynie came back from the bathroom and started telling Christine all about her older cousin Leon who was old enough to smoke. Christine could barely listen, all her energies focused on seeking her absent friend, until she suddenly sensed Tap was back; and he was, perching on a windowsill, batting his big eyes at her. She relaxed, told herself this meant nothing, that it would not happen again. But of course it did, again, and again, for periods of time ranging from five minutes to over two hours. And then, one Seventh Day, she woke up to an empty room, and for all that she concentrated on him, with desperate energy, he wouldn't appear.

The tears came to her eyes, as they almost never did anymore. She was being stupid, she told herself: She was simply growing too old for this sort of fantasy. She knew the difference between real and make-believe. Knew that what she imagined had no intrinsic grounding in reality. She had known this for years, nearly half her life. And yet she couldn't help but miss the imaginary rabbit terribly.

Tap was gone most of the day, but then, an hour before supper, he returned. She was sitting at the desk in her room, doing an arithmetic problem. She kept making mistakes when she had to divide by fractions, and was laboriously erasing her answer for the third time. Then she felt Tap's presence suddenly, at her back, and when she turned he was there. His eyes had lost their twinkle and his cartoonish expression was one of sadness—almost despair.

"Oh, my princess," he whispered in a tragic tone, "I'm so sorry!"

He ran to her, jumped up in her arms—though he had grown along with her, she had grown much faster than him, and she could now cuddle him almost as a pet.

"I didn't want to leave you," Tap said from the shelter of her lap, "but I couldn't help it. I'll try to keep it from happening again, but . . . it probably will. You must be brave. . . ."

"Tap," she said, looking down at him, and suddenly uncrossing her arms so that he bounded onto the floor. "Tap, I'm glad you're here. But don't feel bad. It's okay. I think maybe I'm growing too old to have an imaginary friend. . . ."

The instant after she uttered these words she found Tap was perching on her desk, in front of her. She was stunned: In all the years he had been her companion, he had never done anything of the sort. Every move he made, no matter how swift, had always been continuous—she had been astonished sometimes at her own powers of imagination, more spectacular than any animated trickery on television. But this time, Tap had actually *blinked* between one place and the next. The discontinuity rasped at her nerves, a deep wrongness. And now, compounding the strangeness, he spoke to her in a dead-serious tone, sounding like a priest at First Day confession.

"It isn't a question of your age. I am not imaginary. I was constantly there for you, because you needed me. You still need me now, but something has gone wrong with *me*. I'm not sure what; when I'm not there I'm still there, but everywhere at once. . . . I can't explain it, because I don't understand it. I'm not very smart, really. All I know is I may not be able to stay with you much longer."

Christine felt sadness warring with incredulity.

"But, Tap, I . . . I made you up," she whispered. "I imagined you. Dora at school used to have an imaginary friend too, he was an invisible boy called Tod. . . ."

Tap shook his head and his left hind paw trembled in agitation. "You didn't make me up, my princess. A little part of me may have come from your mind, but most of me does not. In an instant I was made and in the next sent out after you; I flew so fast . . . I think there were more like me at the beginning; many of us, seeking for you. But only I could reach you, and you were fleeing away so swiftly, I barely could keep up. But one of my paws was grasping your hand, and I was pulled down, down, down, along with you. . . . I remember those first days; you were so upset that you had lost the power of speech. You were screaming and wailing, and I was there for you. I let you see me, and feel my fur, and it soothed you. You don't remember, do you? Oh, my princess, I'm old. It shouldn't be possible for me to age but I feel old; something's gone wrong. It's like I'm in a thousand pieces inside. . . ."

Christine felt a shiver go through her at these words. Her imagination was running amok. "This is crazy," she said, and waved her hand through Tap. There was no resistance; her outstretched fingers passed through his presence as through air. "*You are not there*. No one sees you except me."

Tap's cartoonish face was twisted with anger, or despair.

"That doesn't mean I'm not real! If I were made up, would you be thinking to yourself what I'm saying to you? I was sent to you, I was charged—"

"That's enough!" she shouted, loud enough, she suddenly realized, that Uncle could hear her from the living room. She closed her eyes and dropped her voice to a whisper. "Go away, Tap. I don't want to hear those things. You're making me sad. Go away! I don't want to believe in you anymore!"

Tap's voice nearly broke as he replied, "I must not hurt you, my princess. I will not . . . I *will* not. I'm sorry. I love you."

And Christine felt a surge of warmth go through her, an intense tingling in her fingers, a roaring pressure in her ears. She was looking at the ceiling, and pinpoints of light swam in the periphery of her vision; her back and shoulders hurt.

The door to her room opened; Uncle rushed in, saw her and knelt by her side.

"What's going on?" He helped her sit up, an arm protectively around her shoulders. "Are you hurt? I heard you shout, and then a thump. Did you fall off the chair?"

"I . . . I was playing, just playing. I was playing pretend, and I tilted the chair really far back, and then I fell. I'm sorry, Uncle."

"You don't look well at all. I'm taking you to the hospital."

Despite her protestations that she would soon be fine again, Uncle carried her in his arms to the car then drove her to the big dark building over by the river. He had her lie down in the backseat and would frequently look over his shoulder at her. She assured him she was feeling much better, but each time he forbore to answer and returned in silence to his driving.

Was he angry at her? His face was its normal color, so perhaps he was only worried. Christine herself felt shame at her condition; she dwelled on it, tried to drown herself in it. Anything rather than think about what had just occurred. That feeling of dislocation, the rush of strangeness in her . . . She mustn't think about it. Her hand, of itself, moved out to feel the reassuring touch of fur; it encountered only air. Hope and trust, trust and—she was starting to cry, and desperately told herself, *I'm so ashamed, I'm so ashamed, I was playing pretend like a little girl and I fell out of the chair and my uncle is going to all this trouble for me. . . .*

The doctor was kind in an impersonal sort of way. He asked her to focus on a little light he shone into her eyes, to hold out her arms in front of her and keep them steady. Did it hurt when he touched here, or there? She kept her answers almost mechanical throughout, related the stripped-down story she almost believed herself, about goofing off in the chair and falling down.

"What's your sign?" asked the doctor.

"Crown."

"Hmm. This wasn't supposed to be a bad day for you. Do you know your ascendant?"

"No."

"Mr. Matlin?" But Uncle didn't know either.

In the end the doctor nodded his head sagaciously. "Well, there's nothing to worry about," he said to them both. "Christine never lost consciousness, there's no sign of a concussion. She just had a scary fall and bumped her noggin hard."

As if this dismissal was instead an accusation, Christine's tears started again at that point. She tried her best to hold them back, but her entire body was shaken by sobs. "There, there." The doctor held her shoulders as she gasped and wailed. "It's all right, you'll be fine now. You had a good scare, didn't you?"

"No," she blurted out, unable to hold the words inside, "it's Tap, I'm scared for him, he left and I know he won't be coming back, and it's my fault, I sent him away. . . ."

"What was that?" The doctor was looking at her with a frown. For the first time, she felt she had truly engaged his attention. And Uncle was gaping at her over the doctor's shoulder. She was so scared, so bereft, that she sobbed out the whole story: how she'd had an imaginary rabbit friend, how he'd told her he wasn't imaginary, how she had said that was enough, and been so frightened at his words that she'd sent him off and she'd fallen out of the chair then . . .

When she was done, she felt a ghastly relief spread through her like venom.

This must be what confession felt like when one had real sins on one's conscience. After confession came penance, of course, and she knew she was in for some unpleasantness. Uncle would rage and storm, call her names, maybe confine her to her room. But she could look him in the face now, hold his shocked gaze without trembling, now that she had scooped out all her secrets and utterly betrayed her younger self.

"Can you wait here in the chair for a little while, Christine? I need to talk to your uncle; we'll be right back," said the doctor. Christine nodded obediently and sat in the black vinyl and chrome chair for fifteen minutes by the clock on the wall, feeling and thinking almost nothing. Finally the door to the examination room opened again; Uncle came in to take her back home.

He was silent during the whole journey. Christine, sitting in the right front seat, said nothing either. She watched the scenery pass by, slowly in the distance, so very fast close to her. So was her life moving now, her childhood receding in the distance. Tap was gone; why should she think about him any longer?

They reached Uncle's house in the suburbs, parked in the driveway. Uncle got out and opened the door for her. It was as he was helping her up, her hand tiny in his big meaty paw, that he finally spoke.

"I've made an appointment for you," he said—she couldn't figure out the tone of his voice: It seemed to speak at the same time of deep sadness and bleak satisfaction. "You're going to see a Dr. Almand next Second Day."

❧ Dr. Carl Almand's office was all the way across town; Uncle's chauffeur drove her there as he did for school, but it took a lot longer. She guessed, of course, what kind of doctor she was being sent to, but she knew little about them, and had not dared asked Uncle for any details. She wished she had brought her Jessica along, though she had stopped playing with her a full year ago. The plastic doll at least was tangible.

Christine had expected Dr. Almand would practice in a modern clinic, a white square building. In fact it was on the second floor of what had been a private home and had been divided up into apartments and small offices. Dr. Almand himself opened the door to his office when the chauffeur knocked.

"This is Christine Matlin," the chauffeur announced when the doctor peered out.

"Yes, you're right on time. Very well. You can wait in the smoking lounge at the end of the corridor; we won't be more than forty-five minutes. Won't you come in, Christine?"

Dr. Almand had her sit on a chair at first, while he studied a lot of papers, among which was her astrological chart. He was a tallish man, with a very round face and sparse sandy hair. He had on casual clothes, neither suit nor cloak, but brown trousers and a pale violet shirt, open at the throat, without a tie. He wore glasses—why did doctors always wear glasses? The light from the windows was reflected in his lenses, and she could also see tiny rounded images of the papers he was looking at.

"Now, Christine," he said at last, in a soft yet firm voice, "do you know why you were sent here?"

"My uncle didn't say, sir."

Dr. Almand leaned back in his chair. "Well, I'll tell you straight out; you're old enough to accept it. Your uncle asked me to see you because he's afraid there may be something wrong with your mind. I'm *not* saying he thinks you're crazy. He doesn't think you're crazy, and I don't think you're crazy either. We're just . . . concerned that you might be feeling troubled, confused, and I want to help you out."

"Why . . . Why does he think I'm . . . that I have a problem?"

"When you were brought in to the hospital, you told the doctor in charge that you had just sent away your imaginary friend, and that was why you fell out of the chair and fainted."

She lowered her gaze, nodded assent. In a low voice she said, "I used to have an imaginary friend; but now he's gone. Other people have had imaginary friends. A friend of mine had one."

"Was she as old as you are now?"

". . . No."

"You're saying that it's normal for a child to have an imaginary friend, Christine, and it is—but not past a certain age. You are ten years old. How long have you had this friend?"

"Well . . . as far back as I remember."

"I have read many books, Christine," said Dr. Almand, pointing to the shelves on the side walls of the office, which indeed overflowed with them. "And in all of these, it says that past the age of five or six at the latest, a child shouldn't have an imaginary friend. If yours lasted so long, I think it means something has been bothering you. Making you unhappy. That's what imaginary friends are, Christine, they're a way to help unhappy children cope with the world around them. Would you say you're unhappy, in any way?"

"No. I like school. I like learning things. I'm happier now than I was before."

"So you were unhappy in the past?"

". . . Yes. I was . . . very unhappy when I was young."

"In what way?"

"I cried a lot."

"Why was that? Did you feel bad about yourself?"

"No. Not that. I missed my father. I can't remember him, but I know that when I was young I could, and I cried because he had been taken away from me."

"And do you know why your father was taken away?" asked the doctor in a soft voice.

She drew a blank. "Well, I . . . When I was four, Daddy went away; he didn't die—my mom was dead, but he didn't die. I went with Uncle. I suppose I had to. It was . . . It was . . ."

"You don't know. You have no memory of it, do you?"

She found she was breathing very hard, clutching the wooden armrests of the chair. "I know that someone took me away. . . . I know my mother had died a long time before that. I know I couldn't stay with him, even though I wanted to. . . ."

"Those are not answers, Christine."

She was sweating and almost sobbing. "I don't know," she admitted. "I forgot. I think I used to know, maybe, when I was young, but it faded."

Dr. Almand made a note on a pad of paper, steepled his fingers and leaned forward, his round face looking very grave.

"Do you know what 'abuse' means, Christine?"

"Yes, I do. This year we have a lesson on it every week, on Fourth Day."

"Do you understand that you were taken from your father because he abused you?"

Her heart started pounding. She stood up, outraged. "That's not true!" she shouted. "I was never abused! No one's ever . . . I . . . I . . ."

Dr. Almand smiled appeasingly at her. "It's all right, Christine. Please, sit down. I won't keep you here any longer today. I'll make us an appointment for next Sixth Day, after school, and we can talk some more, okay?"

Though he gathered up his papers immediately, she was able to read the word he'd written in capitals on his pad, reflected backward in his glasses: DENIAL.

❧ She came to see him after school four days later. She didn't want to go, she had kept trying to imagine excuses not to see him, but in the end she could not avoid it. Tap hadn't come back; she had tried to will him back into existence a dozen times, but always it was as if she were struggling to overturn a concrete wall: the sense of exertion against something so immovable it was worse than futile. And she was worried about herself. Worried that Uncle was right in his concern; worried that she was indeed having problems with her mind. Worried that even Dr. Almand might be correct.

There was a couch in Dr. Almand's office. This time he made her lie down on it. He sat next to her, playing with a shiny gold coin on a chain. "Look at the coin," he said. "Focus on it. Listen only to my voice. You can hear no sound except for the sound of my voice. You see nothing except the coin. You are feeling very relaxed. . . ." He went on in this vein for several minutes; gradually the outside world faded away, leaving only the doctor's face, the shining coin winking light then dark, and the droning voice.

"Your body remembers, Christine, even though your mind has blocked off memories. . . . You remember what your father did to you. . . . Don't you remember?"

She tried to focus on the period of her life before coming to live with Uncle. It was so hard: That era lay beyond a kind of blurred barrier, or rather at the end of a road grown patchy through disuse. She had to force her way over obstacles, overgrown areas, fallen timbers. . . . She was afraid she would lose the path completely; but the doctor's voice was there to urge her along. And suddenly she found something.

"I remember . . . ," she said. "I remember being with my father . . . on a boat." Warmth filled her at the recovered memory. "On a sea . . . it was so shallow, you could see the bottom; with lots of fishes swimming around. I was small. Daddy held me in his arms and let me look above the rail. I was afraid, because I was leaning over the water, but Daddy held me close, so I knew I was safe. . . ."

In that moment she grasped the memory entire, jewel-like in its translucence and purity. She was held tight in her father's arms; she could feel the warmth of his flesh and the solidity of his bones through the fabric of his clothing. The ship stretched behind her; it was a blur of brown at the corners of her sight, but she could smell its fragrant wood, and mixed with the tangy scent was a wisp of floral perfume from upwind. Below her, a sea spread, a shallow sea, its transparent waters refracting the sunlight. Fish of all shapes moved about the bottom, their bodies glittering, their fins like sequined wings, darting between the fronds of seaweed. Here and there on the seafloor were large pieces of swarthy metal, looking like parts pulled out of a gigantic clock, speckled with marine life: urchins and seastars, in all the shades between incarnadine and deep purple. She was aware of people about her father and herself, though all of them at some distance. There was the murmur of conversation in several voices, a sharp clink of metal on metal that drove into her awareness. But all she really cared about was the water, which lay far below her, what seemed both an exciting and a frightening distance. For all her fascination with the sea life beneath, she felt a dread of falling, some fear that welled up from the core of her mind, as inevitable as drawing a breath would be.

As she marveled, caught within the miracle of this morsel of the lost past returned, Dr. Almand's voice broke in.

"Christine . . . you were afraid that your father would let you fall, weren't you?"

"No," she said, only half aware of him, wishing he would be silent. But he went on.

"But you just said you felt afraid. Why did you feel afraid, then?"

"Because . . . I was leaning over the water. I could have fallen in, if he hadn't held me tight." She was losing her focus on the memory; the sense of immanence had faded.

"He held you tight. Very tight?"

"Yes. I remember his hands on me." She did; she recalled her father's hands, strong bony fingers. But again her grasp on the memory loosened. She found herself wondering where in the world one could take ship on a sea so shallow and transparent, and why it was the fish she recalled were more extravagant than any tropical marine life in the nature books she'd read.

"You are saying more than you realize, Christine. Your daddy who held you so tight; do you think he might have let you fall? Or even thrown you down? Weren't you afraid of being thrown into the water?"

Dr. Almand was looking at her intently; she met his gaze behind the lenses of his glasses, and the sights she recalled dimmed away into wisps of fog.

"Your body recalls everything, Christine," said Dr. Almand. "Your cells hold a perfect memory of every instant you've lived. You must remember. Didn't you feel your father shake you, like he was about to throw you into the water?"

She squinted and drew back her lips. She tried to recall any such feelings. There had been no hint of this in her memory, she was sure. But now it had all grown vague. Still, she persisted in her denial. "No, I didn't feel him shake me. If he held me tight, it had to be so I would be safe."

"But then why were you so afraid? You had to have a good reason. If you had been by yourself, you wouldn't have been afraid of falling, because you would have been able to hold on to the rail. You had to have another reason. Why was your father holding you up so high?"

"I wasn't so high. And he wanted to show me the fishes."

"But why? Don't you think he might have been trying to scare you? Hadn't you been a bad girl? Didn't he call you that? Don't you remember? I am sure you do, Christine. You simply have to try harder."

There was something; some other memory, very dim. She said, "I remember . . . once, I did something bad, and my father called out my name. He was angry at me. He shouted."

"Did he call you a bad girl?"

"I . . . I think he might have . . . maybe."

"Cast yourself back to that time, Christine. Do you understand me? I want you to go back in time to that occasion. You can do it, don't be afraid. You remember."

As Dr. Almand urged her on, Christine focused on the shred of memory; it began to come clearer and clearer. Her father yelling at her, yes. She was feeling afraid of his anger. Dr. Almand asked her if her father had hit her. Didn't she feel pain from that time?

She did not, not at first. But he pressed on, and after a while she did. The memory assembled itself. It was harder to recall than the earlier one, and Dr. Almand had to coach her extensively. He helped her examine the dim memory of the pain; asked her if she had felt it in one place or in another, at long last discovering that it was her face, her cheek, that had hurt. After a while she fully recalled the sharp sting of a blow to the face, like that time she had been struck by a branch whipping back after another kid's passage through a hedge. Yes, she had been struck; but why? It took many questions, but the answer eventually became clear: to silence her because she was bawling too loudly. She remembered it. As Dr. Almand had promised, her body remembered.

Dr. Almand ordered her to wake fully; Christine shuddered once, all over, and sat up abruptly. At the end of the overgrown road of her memories, that one tiny patch had been cleared. A yell from her father, the sharp sting of his hand slapping her face. Crying and fear. She looked at Dr. Almand in dismay.

"Why did you do that? Why did you make me remember that?" she asked him.

"I want to help you, Christine. And to be helped, you need to remember what happened when you were young. Your memories have been repressed—that's a technical term; let's just say you made yourself forget. But you must regain your memories if you're to be healthy."

"Is there . . . Is there more? More like that? Him slapping me?"

"I'm here to help you find that out."

"Are you sure I need to? I'm okay, really, I am."

"Oh, Christine, but you're not. You know you're not. That imaginary friend was just one element of your condition."

"I don't understand."

"You've kept an imaginary friend with you all these years. But this friend isn't the problem; he's a symptom. You know, like when you have the flu. You get a fever, but it's not the fever that's the real problem. What's wrong is that you have a virus inside you, and you need to fight it. Well, it's the same with your friend. He may be gone, but that doesn't mean you're well. You have issues that are going to make you unhappy, maybe your whole life, unless you work them out with me."

Christine found herself crying in fear; Dr. Almand offered her tissues from a box printed with pink flowers.

"Now, now, Christine, don't worry. It's not that bad. The point is your uncle wants you to be well, and you want to be well. And I'm here to help you. You've made progress already. Now I want you to go home and get some rest. I'll see you next week."

And so she returned to Dr. Almand the next Second Day. During that session, her body was made to remember more. Blows. And touches also. By the end of the fifth session, she was screaming as Dr. Almand made her remember all the times her father had hit her, and the other things he'd done. For he had used her in unspeakable ways, which she was asked to describe precisely and which Dr. Almand dutifully noted down on his pad. It was during the tenth session that she recalled her father had killed her mother in front of her. And Dr. Almand sent her back to that time again and again, until she could conjure up every last detail of the horror.

When she got home after a session, she would eat some cookies and then go to bed. Once she had undressed and turned out the light, she would crawl under the covers and start hitting herself, slapping her face hard with her open hand, until the pain became too intense to bear. Five or six blows were all it took. Then she'd curl up into a ball, and she would weep in silence, until sleep released her from the pain.

On the night of the twelfth session she hit herself so hard that she couldn't suppress a cry of pain. As she lay in her bed, her left hand stuffed in her mouth to muffle herself, she heard the door open, Uncle's tread on the floor. He called out her name and whipped off the coverlet, just in time to see her right hand make contact with her cheek as she slapped herself uncontrollably.

Uncle caught her wrists, begging her to stop. He pulled her hand out of her mouth with the utmost care; Christine wailed something incoherent as soon as her voice was unfettered. Uncle threw her arms around his neck, picked her up bodily, carried her into the living room, sat her down in his armchair. Christine curled up on herself in the chair, trembling and sobbing. Uncle picked up the telephone on a little table and made two calls, his face scarlet, his words brooking no denial.

He wrapped a fleece throw around her and brought her water to drink, stroked her hair and babbled at her while she mostly ignored him, sunk in unthinking misery.

Soon the doorbell rang and Uncle answered; Dr. Almand walked into the room. Christine whimpered but lacked the strength to flee. Uncle spoke angrily at Dr. Almand, who was very calm in response. "This is all perfectly normal," he said soothingly. "I'll admit I was taken a bit by surprise, since she seemed otherwise to be coping with the revelations quite well. You must understand that, as buried and repressed traumas rise to the surface, she will necessarily have to work out her stress in new ways. This behavior is a sign of returning psychic health. So there's really nothing to worry about."

As Uncle expostulated, Dr. Almand pulled out a large bottle full of bright orange pills. "Now, now, Mr. Matlin, I'm not saying you weren't right to call me. We want the best for Christine. If you just give her two of these now, she'll calm down. Have her take one every evening before bedtime, two after a session. This should suppress the behavior entirely. If it should recur, there are stronger medications we can use. Also, an extended stay in the hospital might do her a world of good; you should consider it."

Uncle dismissed that last suggestion, but he did bring her the pills. Christine struggled to swallow them with a glass of water, the slick coating of the capsules pressing against the walls of her throat, making her think she would retch. Within minutes she fell asleep. When she woke up the next day, she was so groggy she couldn't attend school, could hardly make her way out of bed. By evening her mind was clearer, but then it was time for another orange pill. She swallowed it dutifully, glad there was only one. On Fourth Day morning she returned to school, her steps uncertain, her attention clouded.

And so the new routine went. Sessions, pills, grogginess. Christine's grades started to slip as she lost a large part of the energy for schoolwork. Uncle talked with the teachers and it was agreed she would retake her year if it became necessary. She was given several books with titles like *What He Did Was Wrong* and *It's Not My Fault: A Manual for Victims of Childhood Abuse*. Uncle told her several times a week how proud he felt that she was facing up to reality with such strength. Jessica the doll gathered dust in a drawer.

⁂ During her fiftieth session, Christine recovered a startling memory: As she focused on a particular instance of rape, she saw Uncle's face leering at her. She related her discovery to Dr. Almand, who immediately corrected her: Uncle had never met her until she had been taken away from her father. It couldn't have been him; rather, someone else, who only looked like Uncle. With Dr. Almand's help, with what her body remembered, over the course of a double-length session, Christine finally came to understand it had been a perfect stranger. A stranger who had purchased the use of her body from her father, when she had been three and a half years old.

Coming out of the trance, Christine was drenched in sweat. Even Dr. Almand seemed tired. He gave her paper tissues to wipe her streaming face, a drink of water from the cooler in a conical paper cup. He congratulated her for her efforts, praised her for achieving this major breakthrough. As she made her way out of his office, he reminded her to take two pills that evening and to get some rest.

Come nightfall, Christine went to the kitchen, poured herself a glass of water, and dutifully swallowed the two pills prescribed after a session. She put the water jug back into the refrigerator, then went to the sink, pulled open the second drawer, which held various odds and ends, and took out a pair of scissors. She opened the blades wide, gripped the scissors firmly in her right hand, laid her left flat on the counter. Then she slammed the blade into her palm.

She hadn't wanted to make a sound, but the pain was so awful she couldn't hold back a shriek. Still, she pulled the blade free and prepared for another blow.

The bright blood pouring out of her wound gave her momentary pause; and then Uncle had grabbed her hand, torn the scissors from her grasp and cupped her bleeding hand in his.

"Child! Child!" he screamed. "What are you doing! I won't let harm come to you; do you understand?" His face was scarlet; he looked scared, far more than angry. *"I will not let you be hurt!"* he repeated. Christine only howled in reply, something rising in her that she could neither explain nor avoid. She struggled in his grasp, her whole body jerking, like a string puppet when the crossbars are snatched up. Another jerk, and she freed herself. She fell against the kitchen counter; her legs gave way under her and she crumpled into a heap. Her screams sandpapered her throat until she started choking and passed out.

She awoke at the hospital, in a bed with leather restraints. Her left hand was bandaged. It hurt dimly, more like an itch. Her eyes were sore from crying. Something was wrong with her throat: Her voice was gone and she could only speak in a whisper.

Dr. Almand came to see her, his round face grave. For once, he was wearing a jacket and tie.

"I'm very sorry, Christine," he said. "I didn't expect the intensity of your reaction. But then, what we discovered took me aback as much as it did you. I failed to realize how much of a turning point this must have been for you. I'm deeply sorry. I should have had you supervised. But now that you're here, things will be easier. They'll take off the restraints soon; this was just a temporary arrangement. You'll be getting a different medication, a newer drug that's better at calming you down but won't make you feel sleepy at all. I know you can't feel very happy now, but trust me: This is an important day in your life. In the future, you'll look back on it as the day you finally began to heal."

Christine wanted to hit him, to stab him with the scissor blade, not in the hand but across the face and through the heart. But she knew she was wrong to feel this. This was the man who helped her; no matter that his revelations brought pain, he was doing her good. She started to weep again, at the hurt she was doing him. "I'm sorry," she croaked, "I'm so sorry." He patted her hand. "Don't worry, Christine, you'll be fine. I'll see to it personally."

The next day her restraints were removed. Instead of the orange pills she had been given white ones. These did work a lot better: After taking them, her feelings were still wrapped in layers of cotton but her mind was no longer fettered as it had been.

Dr. Almand came back to see her and they held a session in her hospital room, with the knowledge and approval of the staff. Armed with the breakthrough, Dr. Almand was able to make her remember other times she had been assaulted by strangers. That day, she recalled two such instances. The day after that, three more.

By week's end, running sessions every day, the picture was at last complete and Christine's story clear. With her mother's passive complicity, her father had sold Christine's sexual services to a roster of pedophiles from the age of half past three onward. The day Christine's mother had finally dared to raise her voice in protest, Christine's father had murdered her in front of their child.

He had not been able to conceal her death, and the authorities had at last stepped in. Christine had been taken from him and given in adoption to Uncle, whom in fact she was not related to. Uncle had tried to give her a life sheltered from all the horrors of her past, as he had told Dr. Almand, but the traumas his foster child had endured had left their mark. It was a good thing she had gone to see Dr. Almand early on: Time would only have worsened her condition. Now the abscess had been burst. Armed with the new drugs, with Dr. Almand by her side, Christine was well on the path to recovery.

2. A Knight in Shining Armor

By her thirteenth birthday Christine had mostly come to terms with her past. Although she still experienced episodes of self-directed violence, they were very rare— and never left any traces. She accepted the fact that she had been sexually assaulted, at last count, over a hundred times, and that this would doubtless make severe difficulties throughout the rest of her life. She attended school regularly and her grades, once bad, were now fair to good. She was weakest at subjects like history and languages—though she could assimilate the basics easily, the details bored her and she found it hard to retain them. She was better at the sciences, though some of what was taught she found hard to accept; in particular she doubted astrology belonged in the curriculum at all.

Socially, she was withdrawn and had made no real friends. Every night, after her homework was done, she'd watch television until it was time for bed. It soothed her. When a show started mentioning sex, she would calmly get up from the flower-patterned couch and change the channel. She had an inordinate fondness for cartoon shows and watched them religiously every Seventh Day morning.

She suffered recurring nightmares, which were vague and formless; though she often woke from them in the middle of the night, she was always dry eyed. She had not cried, for any reason whatsoever, in over two years. Her mental picture of her father had started becoming blurred again, since she did not see Dr. Almand more than once a month now, and mostly then she would talk about ordinary things. He had been writing a book, and her story was material for two whole chapters. She had been asked for her permission and had granted it willingly, as long as her true name wasn't mentioned. Dr. Almand had been on television twice, on talk shows, explaining what it was he did and why it was needed. Christine had tried to watch one of the shows but she had begun retching after the first five minutes and had had to turn the set off. Dr. Almand had asked her if she might want to go on TV herself, her face hidden by a mask so no one would recognize her, and tell her story. She had refused, and he had not insisted.

She had started menstruating a few months before she turned thirteen. It had been a surprise, but it didn't bother her much. The cramps were not particularly painful, especially compared to the atrocious pain she had recalled experiencing at the hands of her father and his customers. She used sanitary napkins exclusively, uncomfortable at even the sight of a tampon. When changing them, she would tuck the soiled napkin blindly into an opaque plastic bag, keeping her head averted or her eyes closed.

❧ Years passed, and Christine found herself adjusting better and better. Uncle remained as protective as ever, and her life was mostly spent at home. She buried herself in books, having fallen somewhat out of love with television. She kept up a few tepid friendships with other girls. Boys she avoided; she had been courted once or twice, but had put an end to it as swiftly as possible. She was aware she had a reputation at school; that the kindest thing said of her was that she was pathologically shy; that some boys called her frigid, or a saphian, almost to her face. She didn't care. The outside world was a dangerous place; she knew that to the core of her being. People could insult her as much as they wanted; words were not blows, they drew no blood and left no mark.

Sometimes she would feel suffocated, it was true. Sometimes the constraints of her life weighed on her and she would slip the reins for a bit. She would go to the ice cream store and order a floater, eat it by herself at a corner table, arrive home late and endure Uncle's recriminations stoically. She knew he meant well; knew he cared so much about her that he could barely stand her being out of his sight.

That, she reasoned, must be the sign of true love, wanting to keep the other person always with oneself. It was embarrassing that she did not feel this way about Uncle; she had to admit to herself she did not truly love him. But then, how could she: He was a man. Perhaps she was a saphian in truth? But she felt rather that she could not afford to love anyone, that the capacity for love had been raped out of her.

❧ One Fourth Day afternoon in the spring of 1981—she was seventeen—as she was walking back home from school, her attention was drawn by a sudden screech of brakes. In the middle of the street, a young man driving a shiny red car had come to an abrupt stop. Christine thought automatically that it was lucky there were no vehicles behind him, otherwise he would have been rear-ended for sure. Then she noticed that there were no vehicles in *front* of him either. He had braked for no perceptible reason. She looked at him and found that he was looking back. Staring at her, slack-jawed. A shiver went down her spine. It was almost as if the sight of her had been what had made him apply the brakes.

It had to be a false impression. It made no sense. Yet all the courses she had taken on abuse and the need for protection came rushing to her head. All men were potential rapists, the teachers had intoned over and over. Not all of them seemed to believe it fully, but they all mouthed the official line. As for Christine, she knew it was the simple truth, and had sometimes wished she had the nerve to tell her teachers and classmates just how dangerous a place the world really was.

She might have believed herself safe at this moment: She stood in broad daylight on the sidewalk of a busy street. But no one was ever safe anywhere. She took evasive action immediately, ducking into a store. From inside, hidden by a rack of clothes, she peered at the young man and his car. His engine had choked; he started it up again and drove down the street, turning right at the next intersection.

Had he been looking at her as she entered the store? She couldn't know, but she felt he well might have. She stayed in the store for a full twenty minutes, glancing at the street constantly, until she found the courage to walk out and scurry home. She saw no sign of the young man in his red car.

❧ He was in her thoughts often after that. She replayed the incident in her head many times. At her next session, she was on the verge of mentioning him when she felt some kind of obscure embarrassment—of all things to feel in front of the man who knew every hideous secret of her past. Still, she kept the incident from her therapist. She promised herself she would mention the young man if she should see him again. She wasn't, after all, in any real danger from him. She knew nothing about him, and not even she could automatically assume all strangers were monsters. Maybe—it was a stupid idea, of course—maybe he'd been stricken by her looks. Maybe, like in the teen movies that were shown on the First National Network, he'd fallen in love with her at first sight. Wouldn't that be a laugh. When Christine's thoughts ran that way, she felt her stomach clench into a knot and her right hand, the one that had held the scissors that night when she had remembered the strangers' rapes, begin to twitch. And so she thought of other things; she chided herself for being paranoid. He might have braked for a cat or a squirrel crossing the street, which she hadn't noticed. Why did she imagine she had to be the center of everyone else's life? She was someone unremarkable; she wanted to be unremarkable, forgettable, forgotten. She tried to forget herself all the time.

❧ There were no further odd incidents. Her life settled back in its accustomed pattern; she started to forget about the young man. At the end of Sixth Month would be the final examinations, to end the school year before their three months of holiday. She didn't like those much, as she never knew what to do with herself. She would go to the library once or twice a week, spend hours swimming in her backyard pool, watch television for half the day sometimes, when tennis finals were on; on occasion, a schoolmate would invite her over. Last year, she'd even been invited to spend three days with the Longs at their cabin, but Uncle had refused. She had not dared put up a struggle and had told Freynie she was too busy to come, a lie good-hearted Freynie had accepted without taking the least bit of offense.

Second Day ended with Practical Astrology 201. She hated that course: something about it offended her instincts. Drawing star charts was easy enough, but the whole matter of interpretation she couldn't stomach. It was a relief when the bell finally rang. She wrote down her last homework assignment before finals, analyzing a famous personality's career in terms of their houses, then picked up her bag and left the classroom along with everyone else. She followed the long corridor to the front of the school and the wide entrance hall, and stopped dead as she turned the corner.

In the hall stood the young man who had driven the red car.

She felt her heart thudding in her chest. What was he going to do to her?

Nothing, she told herself. He could do nothing. They were surrounded by dozens of people, and there was a security guard at the end of the hall. All Christine had to do was to scream, and people would come to her aid. She had never been safer.

He wasn't looking at her. He wasn't even looking in her direction. Perhaps this was just coincidence? Maybe he was the brother of a student. Why was it that she panicked so upon seeing him? He had never done anything to her, never threatened her. He had just been in a car that had braked for no apparent reason. She had seen stranger things happen. He could not be any of the men who had raped her. She had remembered all of them, carefully, had made crude drawings of them, so that she might recognize them if she ever saw them again. None of them had been very young; this man might be in his late twenties at the most; she had never been raped by teenagers. . . .

The flow of students heading out had been pushing against her, with a few muttered imprecations. She was too small and light, especially in her own mind, to resist the shove of a crowd. Christine let herself be pushed forward, making sure not to look at the young man directly. As soon as she had gotten past him, she would know his presence had meant nothing and that she'd been freaking herself out for no good reason. Not far to go now; a few yards, a few seconds, and she would be free. . . .

The flow of people ebbed and swirled; random motions pushed her toward him, despite her attempt to move away. He was not moving; he stood immobile in the crush, like a rock in a stream. She tried to pass him; she had to get to the exit *now*. But a group of loud jocks were shoving their way inside; the crowd flowed back, pressed her, and Christine was almost thrown against the young man.

She nearly lost her balance; she had to clutch at him not to fall. She felt she was about to faint with terror. Stand up, stand up, let go of him, move away!

His head swiveled to look at her. He smiled good-naturedly, cupped her elbow in one hand for a moment as he helped her regain her balance. "Careful, there," he said; and she was riven to her core.

He had Tap Fullmoon's voice.

She freed herself, shoved and pushed with desperate energy, thrust her way out of the crowd, finally found her way outside. She reached the top of the broad front steps and collapsed on the sun-warmed stone.

"Hey, Christine, what's a'matter?" Freynie Long was touching her shoulder, shaking it in well-meaning roughness. Christine saw her blurrily through the tears that filled her eyes. Christine breathed painfully, her chest inflating in a rush, then taking seeming minutes to empty itself.

"Are you sick?" Freynie asked. "You need me to call the nurse?" Other people had loosely gathered around them.

"No . . . No. I'll be okay," Christine said, shivering. "It's just . . . I needed air. Too many people . . ."

"Oh yeah," said Freynie, "the crush is brutal. You got a case of agro-phobia, right?"

"Yeah, something like that," Christine gasped. The onlookers were drifting off. They had all been fellow students, people she knew at least by sight. Safe, safe, she was safe still. "Walk me to the street, please?" she asked, forcing herself to stand up. Freynie held her arm as they crossed the lawn. Leaning on her, Christine looked all around them. But she saw no sign of the young man. She did not dare ask Freynie if she saw him around.

Christine had dried her eyes by the time they reached the sidewalk. Freynie offered to walk her all the way home; maybe they could hang together, watch some TV? Christine wavered at the brink of saying yes, but then shook her head, pleaded she had too much studying to do. She thanked Freynie, went so far as to peck her cheek, and headed home alone.

She felt a vague guilt at doing this, knew someone less sweet-natured than Freynie might resent being rejected this way. She couldn't help it; Freynie was the closest approximation to a best friend she had, but Christine could never be really close to her, never divulge the raw wound at the core of her soul to the other girl.

And she feared Uncle's questions; feared Freynie would reveal what had happened, even if Christine asked her to keep it a secret. Uncle was a brusque man; neither Christine nor Freynie could resist telling him what he wanted to know. If he suspected something was amiss, he would pry the story out of them. And Christine would be taken to see Dr. Almand the next day. She was so sick and tired of Dr. Almand. He had shown her all the nightmares in her past; she had had enough of him, if all he could do was to make her hurt and then congratulate her for it. She didn't need him to make her hurt over this. She was perfectly able to do it by herself.

❧ She stayed home the next day, pleading "female trouble," the mention of which always made Uncle uncomfortable. She even took some pills, to corroborate her lie. As she lay in her bed, she tried to see things as they were and not as she feared they were. Objectively, little out of the ordinary had happened. The young man hadn't looked at her as though he recognized her, had he? Or had he? Her memory of the expression on his face was vague; she had been looking down, trying to keep from falling. She had seen his arms clearly: broad, well muscled. She had heard his voice. . . . *That* was what terrified her. The one thing that made no sense. Maybe, she told herself, she was just imagining that he had Tap's voice. She had never *heard* the imaginary rabbit's voice. She had merely conceived of it; it was like the voice in her head when she was reading, which was a sort of nonvoice, really. She could never have said truly that she had heard a voice that sounded like that one. So how could she claim the young man had had the same voice as one that she had only heard in her mind? It was ridiculous.

She dragged herself out of bed around Eleventh Hour. The postman came around that time every day. She heard his tread on the front steps and the clanking of the box's lid. Once the man was back on the sidewalk, she opened the front door and fetched the letters from the box. She liked to sort mail for Uncle—this was one of the first tasks he had entrusted her with as a little girl, and ten years later she still enjoyed it.

There was a letter addressed to her among the mail. Her address was written in a curved, flowing hand, in bluish ink on cream-colored paper. Who could this be from? When she opened the envelope, she caught a faint scent from the letter inside.

Not perfume, though. A smell spicy and sharp, which reminded her of . . . something she couldn't place. It felt like the sea, yet she'd never been to the seaside.

The letter had been carefully folded in three, the creases flawless in the thick paper.

Lady Christine,

Would you meet me in Telzer Park, tonight at Nineteenth Hour? I should very much like to speak with you.

Quentin of Lydiss

With icy fingers Christine crumpled the letter up into a ball, her whole body shaking. Then she flushed it down the toilet, and flushed once more, in fear that the wad of paper might flow back up the pipe.

She knew from whom this had come. This wasn't like a teen movie; it was like one of those monster films they showed once in a while. There should be screams now, and a flashing blade, and deathblows shown in silhouette. . . . She saw that she'd forgotten to destroy the envelope. She took it to crumple it up—or no, wait, she could burn it, much better—then she paused.

There was no return address, of course. But, although there was no postmark, there *was* a stamp. A strange stamp, in glowing colors, dark gold and vibrant mauve and violet. There was something about those colors that tightened her throat. . . . She shook her head to clear it. She had to think. Too complicated to burn the enve-lope, too messy. She wadded it up in turn and flushed the toilet three times before she'd calmed down.

She delivered the letters to Uncle, dropping them on his desk while he was on the phone, having his usual verbal sparring match with one of his suppliers. She strove to appear calm; either she succeeded perfectly or Uncle was not paying much attention. She spent a few hours in her room, sitting in her armchair next to the window, reading through a passel of books from her girlhood, letting the familiar stories jumble themselves up in her head: boys and girls who were always brave and persistent, who always solved their problems by the last page, overcoming wicked men who repented their ways when confronted by the children's innocence and pure faith . . .

She knew that Uncle would be going out that evening, one of his rare indul-gences. She would be left alone; it had been four years since she'd had a sitter. He checked in on her at Fifteenth Hour, told her he would be leaving a bit earlier than usual, in an hour or so, and coming home late. Did she need anything?

She said no. She was much better now, was sure she would be back at school the next day, enjoy yourself, Uncle. She did a bit of homework, then made supper for herself and ate watching television. On the news she heard about a war in the In-dies, the subject people rebelling against the British overlords, with support from Roman sympathizers. She changed the channel and watched an educational pro-gram about sailing ships from the Renascence. Images floated in her mind, just be-low the threshold of consciousness. She couldn't quite make them out; shapes half seen, at the corners of her mental vision, yet very familiar. Something she'd lived with since she was young, like that picture the word "puzzle" always summoned, a mess of mismatched animal shapes, with a gorilla in the center . . .

At half-past Eighteenth Hour she rose to go out. She was at the door when she stopped herself. She knew where she had been going. But how could she? What had she been doing, telling Uncle nothing, letting him leave tonight of all nights?

I must be insane, she thought to herself. Of course, that was it. Things fell into place with a click: She was insane. Hadn't she known that, ever since Dr. Almand had revealed her past to her? He had said he didn't think she was crazy, but that was a kind lie. Of course she had to be insane. Anyone who had endured what she had must be out of her mind permanently. It all made sense now. She wanted to go meet this anonymous person, who might not be the young man in the red car, but who *had* to be. The stalker who wanted to rape her like all the others. She wanted to go meet him. Like a moth throwing itself at a porch light; or no, not that, because insects didn't understand what was happening to them. No, this was like standing at the edge of a cliff and wanting to throw herself down. To surrender to the terror of heights in the only final way.

She wanted to go to the man, and be raped again. That couldn't be right. Dr. Almand had said she was healing. She was supposed to get better. She *was* better, she had been getting better for years. She was afraid of the young man, as was only proper. But she still wanted to go to him. She wanted to hear his voice again. Tap Fullmoon's voice.

That thought reduced her to tears. She could not cope with it; somehow that very idea destroyed her. She missed her imaginary friend. A stupid rabbit who stood on his hind legs and spoke. Why did she miss him so much? She was a stupid, stupid insane girl.

"I'm crazy," she said out loud, and dealt herself an open-handed blow on the side of the face, so hard she saw flashes of green light and heard a shrill whistle in her ear. But the pain didn't help. It never had. She fell to her knees on the carpet and sobbed again. Hadn't she been through enough already? Her father and all these men forcing themselves into her, the mind-numbing pain, her shrieks, the way they had laughed . . .

Why was it that she felt such burning anger toward Dr. Almand when she thought on that? She was sick. She was insane, crazy. There was no hope for her.

She fled into her room, lay facedown on her bed, shutting down her mind, dwelling only on the swirling reddish blackness in her sight, as if this way she could stop the world and escape from it. Eventually she rose and changed. The clock said 18:50.

She went out of the house, her eyes carefully patted dry, her hair combed, wearing a nice shirt and pants. She had her running shoes on, in case she had to flee. She carried a bag, and inside the bag a big kitchen knife, so sharp you'd slice the flesh of your fingers if you even brushed against the blade.

She lost her nerve when she got near Telzer Park, so she turned around and hurried back to her house.

Once she was in her yard again, she could not bear to go inside; for ten seconds she found herself in balance between contradictory impulses, standing motionless in

front of her door. Then she forced herself to move; she went into the backyard and
sat on the twinned rocking chairs, pushing herself back and forth mechanically. She
was crazy. Just crazy. Crazy Christine: that had a nice ring to it. When she was an
old lady, everyone would call her that. She saw the years ahead of her suddenly, a
wasteland of time, through which she would carry her pain, alone, until the day
came when she was allowed to die. How would it be? She'd be in a hovel, probably,
a stinking place with not even a cat for company, feeling the cold seep through her
flesh. . . . She wanted it to end sooner than that.

"Lady Christine," came Tap Fullmoon's voice.

In an extremity of terror, she looked toward the source of the voice. The young
man stood on the other side of the waist-high hedge that delimited their property.
He was wearing a black T-shirt with the picture of a leaping fish on it.

She rose from her seat, walked slowly toward him. She had unzipped the bag
and the knife glittered inside. Her whole body tingled with electricity. She wanted to
cry again, but wouldn't let herself.

"Who are you?" she whispered when they stood five feet apart, the hedge between them. Her heart was pounding so hard she could feel her throat vibrate in
response to the flow of blood.

"My name is Quentin."

"What do you want? Why are you following me?"

"I have been searching for you for nine years. At first I was uncertain that I had
found you. And I had to be careful."

"If you come any closer, I'll scream. And I have a gun in the bag. I know how
to shoot and I'll kill you."

He appeared astonished by that declaration.

"I mean you no harm," he said. "I have come to take you home."

"No. I don't know what you want, but you have to leave."

"What have they done to you?" he asked, almost matter-of-factly. "What did
they tell you about your past?"

This was someone who had known her father, then. Perhaps he was the son of
one of the rapists, and he was here to take her back to the nightmare.

"Why do you have Tap's voice?"

The question had come out of her without her volition. As soon as she uttered it,
she began to tremble. There would have to be more therapy, wouldn't there? More
sessions, more remembering of horrors. Maybe she would remember this young man
savaging her, like all the others. She had promised herself she would never again
dwell on Tap Fullmoon. She had outgrown him; he was the emblem of a childhood
spent in denial. Now she knew and accepted who she was; didn't she?

"Who is Tap?" he asked.

She clenched her mouth shut. *Don't talk. Shut up, shut up. Go away. Run away, inside
the house, call the police!* Why wasn't she doing it?

Quentin's hair was a light brown. He had a broad face, gray eyes. There was a
faint scar on his forehead, running from the middle of it to his right eyebrow. His
mouth was wide, and had a quirk at the corner, as if it thought he ought to be laughing all the time. But he looked very concerned now.

He spoke again, very softly. "I was thirteen years old when you were stolen away. I took my vows as a knight at the earliest opportunity, four years later, and swore I would know no surcease until I had found you and brought you back to Chrysanthe. I have been seeking you for nine years. Orion had told me there would be a pang when I found you, but even so I was deceived once before. After three years, I found a girl I believed to be yourself. I thought I had felt the pang of recognition. I tried to bring her back to court—but I could not; she was not you. I returned to the quest, sought even deeper. When I found you, then, at long last, I knew what Orion meant by 'a pang.' It was as if a huge bell had struck and I was in the center of it. Even now, after weeks have passed, I can still feel its echoes in me."

She could make no sense of his ramblings. So he was crazy too. It made for a lovely symmetry. She challenged him, unable to resist. *Fling yourself down a little bit, see if the ledge catches you or if you'll fall all the way down to the bottom.*

"You say you're a knight? A knight on a quest? But they don't make knights anymore, they haven't for centuries."

"In Chrysanthe they still do. Who is Tap, Lady Christine?"

"Don't . . . don't say that name!"

"He was someone you knew," said Quentin, the insane stalker who claimed to be a knight. "He had my voice." This was like Dr. Almand all over again, the gentle probing that heralded the outbreak of repressed horrors. She had to stand firm. And so, rather than deny, she must accept the truth, speak it.

"He was made up. A . . . an imaginary friend. A rabbit, who stood up on his hind legs. A silly girl's dream. That's all." She was regaining her sanity. What on earth was she doing here, talking to the man? "You have to go away now. Please leave or I'll call the police."

Quentin shook his head. "I do not think it was imaginary, Lady Christine. When you were taken from us, Orion sent a covey of benisons winging after you, like a flight of curlews. If only one of them took hold and warded you in your descent into the made world, it might well have appeared to you as an imaginary companion."

"Go away. You're insane. I'll call the police, have them take you in. Go away or I'll shoot you!"

"I am armored, my lady, although it does not show. Bullets will not hurt me," said Quentin, with a quiet gentleness. Then he turned his back to her and left, walking unconcernedly. She watched him go for a few seconds, then panic overwhelmed her and she ran inside her house.

She started to call the police, then stopped herself. Her thoughts were whirling inside her head, so that she questioned every decision she made. She could barely make herself get a drink of water, torn as she was by contradicting urges to call for help and to keep the whole thing silent.

She managed to calm herself slightly, reasoned out the thing to do. There should be no doubt in her mind about it. She had to stop blaming herself for not having done it immediately, and do it now! She was about to pick up the phone when it rang. She gripped the receiver and put it to her ear. She heard Tap's voice again, muted and distorted by the hiss of the line, but unmistakable.

"Lady Christine?"

"What?" The question was an admission of defeat. The voice at the other end of the line sounded instantly relieved.

"Ah. I was not sure that I had succeeded in reaching you. This is a strange contraption and I have difficulty twisting the rotator properly."

"You don't know how to use a telephone."

"I never had an opportunity to learn."

She laughed then; this was just too silly. "Where can you come from? Even . . . even Tap knew what a telephone was!" She nearly screamed this last sentence.

"I am a knight of Chrysanthe, Lady," said Quentin's voice over the line. "There are no 'telephones' there."

"Why are you calling me? Where are you now?" Perhaps he'd be crazy enough to tell her. Wasn't there a number you could dial to have your call traced automatically? She couldn't remember for certain; maybe she was only imagining it.

"I am calling because you appeared terrified when you saw me. I wanted to spare you anguish, but I do have to talk to you."

"I'm not afraid of you. I called the police a moment ago. They're on their way to my house now. They know I'm being stalked. When rapists are put in jail other prisoners kill them, you know. When the police catch you, you're a dead man."

"I am no rapist," said Quentin, his voice rising. "I would die before I let anyone attempt to harm you."

"I know all about your kind. All they do is lie, and hurt. The more you talk, the less I'll believe you. Go away, just leave me alone!"

She heard an indrawn breath at the other end of the line. Quentin's voice broke. "Oh, Lady, forgive me. I am young and foolish. I thought the hard part would be finding you. I thought you would know from the start I spoke the truth. I failed to realize the real task would still lie ahead of me. What can they have done to you? They made you forget everything. Now I must convince you to trust me."

"I can never trust you," she said, as if trying to reason with him. "You're wasting your time. Your story makes no sense. Don't you realize what you're doing? I can't believe you come from some country without telephones. I can't believe you're some stupid knight!"

"A thing can be true regardless of your belief in it." She could not dispute that, and said nothing, on the verge of hanging up. Quentin went on: "What would constitute proof, in your eyes? Is there *anything* I can do to convince you I speak truth?"

She exhaled raggedly. "If you leave me alone, I'll believe you. Do you understand?"

There was a pause. Then, in a soft voice, "Yes, I do. If this is what you wish, then so be it. I will not bother you again. But should *you* ever want to see me . . . You can summon me."

Tap's voice, at the end of the line. Christine was dizzied anew. She made a sound, less than a word, but he went on as if she had asked how.

"Any ritual that has some significance for you. Anything at all. Orion's seeking-spell pulses in me still; I can feel your presence with all of my being. However you summon me, I shall hear it. And I will wait for you; all my life, if I must."

She finally freed herself from her morbid fascination with his voice, with his

madness. She hung up, slamming the receiver hard into its cradle, picking it up as
soon as she figured the connection must have been cut. Then she called the police
and told them, trembling and stuttering, that she was being harassed, stalked.
Within half an hour a patrol car showed up at her door. She told the officer about
Quentin, described him, explained she was afraid he would sexually assault her.
The officer took her statement, asked her if she wished to go to the station, and
when she said no, stayed with her until Uncle's return. He repeated the whole story
to Uncle, who demanded that their house be placed under surveillance and was
promised there would be a patrol car making the rounds regularly.

And then, of course, Christine was sent to see Dr. Almand.

❧ She did not want to tell him what had happened; for the first half hour she
walled herself up in silence. Dr. Almand merely looked at her at first, then began
speaking of idle matters. She knew his ways by then, knew his angles of approach.
She managed to remain mute even when provoked. But he was tireless. Uncle had
told him something, and now Dr. Almand dangled it in front of her, distorted into a
near blame. She took the bait and corrected him; and swiftly found herself recounting most of the story: how she had noticed a young man staring at her in the street
weeks before, seen him again yesterday, and then been approached today. She said
the police were watching the house now and Uncle had promised she would not remain alone in the house anymore; if he had to go out, she would have an adult sitter
with her. Everyone was very concerned about her.

"I am very concerned too, Christine," said Dr. Almand. His face assumed an
intent expression that felt wrong to her. This wasn't the blandly pleased look he usually wore these days, to compliment her for getting better and coping with the
stresses of her life. Rather it was the face he had worn at the beginning, when he had
been hunting ruthlessly for the truth.

"This young man, who's been following you, as you say . . . you're sure you don't
recognize him from anywhere?"

"No. I had never seen him before."

"Did he wear any special jewelry? Was there an emblem on his shirt?"

"An emblem?"

"Yes; a design of some sort."

"He had a black T-shirt with a leaping fish on it, and gray jeans. I think it was
gray jeans."

"Black and gray. But no jewelry?"

"No. No jewelry. Why do you ask?"

Dr. Almand frowned, as he always did when she questioned his procedure.
Without a word he pulled out the coin on its chain and began to twirl it in front of
her eyes. She was so used to this that she felt herself going under immediately; she
tried to fight it, she didn't want to be hypnotized just now, but the outside world dissolved away and there was only the sound of Dr. Almand's voice, and the winking of
the coin. Still, she had the will to insist.

"Please tell me why you asked that question, Doctor."

"I have a new theory," explained Dr. Almand. "In recent months, I've pulled data from a number of cases together and I have uncovered a pattern I know to be very important. Yes, close your eyes now. Relax and listen to my voice.

"For years now, several of my clients have mentioned hints of . . . call them ceremonies, associated with their abuse. For a long while I didn't pay any real attention to that, but lately I've come to realize this is an area that warrants further investigation. And I have made some amazing discoveries. I've been keeping them to myself, until I've amassed sufficient evidence.

"You see, Christine, I have discovered that a large percentage, at least sixty or seventy, perhaps over ninety percent, of cases of abuse are accompanied by Arhimanic worship. I think this holds the key to much of the world situation today. It appears there is a worldwide church of Ahriman, whose members practice ritual abuse upon their own children. They are aware, of course, of the dangers they run if their existence should be revealed. This must be why very strong injunctions are given to the victims against remembering. And so, even if the abuse itself is uncovered, the deep reason for it remains hidden.

"Many of my patients, even though they've recalled their traumas and faced them, have remained troubled and maladjusted. At first I didn't understand how this could be; but it makes perfect sense if you assume that they were victims of Ahrimanic rituals. And so I have been digging further; I'm no longer accepting the simple answers. The process is arduous, but what I'm uncovering is so astonishing . . ."

In Christine's mind something began to wail. More pain. There would be even more pain. Now her parents had become devil worshipers. She would have to remember more and greater horrors. She would relive it all, again and again. . . . There would be no end to it.

She pounded the couch with her fists, shouted, "No!", swinging her head from side to side. Her eyes were tightly shut; tears leaked from beneath the lids, were flung off to the sides.

"Exactly," said Dr. Almand in a smug tone. "As soon as the Ahrimanic element comes into play, the subject begins to deny it forcefully. We're going to have to work very hard, Christine, but together we'll set you free at last."

"Please, not yet," she said, "I'm not ready yet."

Dr. Almand's hand was on her shoulder, reassuring her. "Oh no, poor child, not yet. Calm down, now. We won't be probing that area yet. You can come out of the trance now . . . that's right. No, stay on the couch, rest. What I'm going to do is to give you something to read. I'm trusting you with these books because I know you're a responsible young lady."

He was showing her *Occult Influences in the Modern World* and a worn paperback copy of *Children of Ahriman*. "I don't expect you to take either of these seriously, Christine. This novel is trash, frankly, and the treatise is fifty years obsolete. I just want you to leaf through the books. Read a bit here and there. See if there's anything that feels . . . familiar. Will you do that for me before our next meeting? I'll schedule you weekly, every Second Day evening, as we used to do, okay?"

"Maybe," she said, and would not commit herself any further. She strode out of his office as soon as she could. All through the ride back to Uncle's house she clutched the two books to her chest and was silent.

She tried reading them that night, found she couldn't endure it. *Occult Influences in the Modern World* claimed that radio might be used as a tool for demonic worshipers to communicate between themselves via coded sentences, and went on to worry about the effects of "noisy modern music" (by which it meant anything with a rhythm track to it) on contemporary youth. She felt suffocated reading it, as if under a weight of some substance that clogged her thought processes. Yet the novel was far more terrifying; not because it made any sense, but because she could sense that, despite Dr. Almand's words, this was exactly the world he would find out she had been living in all along.

She let the novel drop from her limp fingers. Sitting cross-legged on her bed, she suddenly slapped her face, once, twice, three times, until her left hand took hold of her right and forced it down to the bed. She wished she had some of the old pills left, the ones that knocked her out and made her mind lurch into sleep. She had to stay content with holding one hand captive with the other as she toppled on her side, unable or unwilling to move to close the light, eyes wide open, waiting for hours until she surrendered to exhaustion and fell into slumber.

The next day found her almost as numb as when she'd used the old pills, but this was a purely emotional effect. She moped around the house; glanced out the window occasionally to see a police car cruising by, keeping the officer's promise. Uncle was on the telephone, talking and arguing and shouting and sometimes laughing, which meant more money was coming his way. The door of his office was open, and from time to time he'd peek out, checking on her. He was concerned too, they were all concerned. She was surrounded by people who cared deeply for her.

Early in the afternoon, she went out of the house into the backyard. The pool glittered in the sunlight. The compressor made its usual roar from beneath the porch. She leaned her head out and looked under there before she descended the steps to the lawn.

A few daisies were growing wild next to the hedge. She picked one and sat down in the grass. She took hold of one of the tiny petals and plucked it off. Then another. He loves me, he loves me not. . . . The stupid old phrase ran through her head, then faded. She was so absorbed by the process that she was no longer aware of her other thoughts. Then she realized she was running a different phrase through her mind, every time she plucked a petal. *Hope and trust, trust and hope.*

She kept on plucking. Remembering Tap Fullmoon and the way he had consoled her when she was still a little girl, wetting her pillow with tears.

"Quentin," she whispered, very low, dizzied by her own daring. "I don't believe. It makes no sense. But what Dr. Almand tells me doesn't either. I don't believe in him anymore. So this is your one and only chance. Prove yourself. I will pluck every last petal off this flower, one by one. In this way I summon you. Come to me, and take me home."

She plucked every petal off, as she'd said, one by one by one. Careful never to pluck two at a time. It took a long time, but she kept at it determinedly. And when she was done, feeling both stupid and abashed, she stuffed the heart of the flower into her mouth, tasted the pollen filling her mouth, chewed, and swallowed.

She shivered then, felt sweat break out all over her skin. The sun on her head was unpleasantly hot; its light dazzled her half blind. She stood up, walked back toward the house. It occurred to her that she hadn't bathed yet; she suddenly yearned for the coolness of water.

She went into the bathroom, ran water plashing from the faucet and shed her clothes. In the tub, she soaped herself conscientiously, scrubbed at her face, her chest. Her nipples grew hard under the rough caress of the washcloth. She rinsed herself, did her legs next.

She found herself thinking of Quentin; remembering his arms. The muscles revealed by the short sleeves of his shirt, with the emblem of a leaping fish. She wiped at her eyes with the washcloth, but there was still soap scum on it, and it made them tear even more.

She splashed some water into them for a while, until the hurt passed away. She rested her head against her knees. Her hands clenched and relaxed; she sniffled. She found she was rubbing the hair at her crotch, that what had begun as a reflex movement to scratch an itch was now tickling her sex.

She stopped. She only ever touched her genitals to wash them. She knew about masturbation: The sex education manuals acknowledged its existence, and she had absorbed enough knowledge, more by osmosis than anything else, to know how one went about it. But she had never rubbed herself, feeling that to do so would be to invoke the memories of her rapes—and almost, somehow, to justify those rapes. She was not a sexual being. She would not allow herself to be.

And yet now she felt an urge, rising from her core, something she could not deny. The weight of her existence was bearing down upon her; she felt she must escape who she was. She let her fingers wander down, sighed at the touch. She bit her lip, and touched herself more boldly. "Quentin," she whispered, not truly aware of the name she spoke, and rubbed herself harder, until a brief rush of pleasure went through her and she half relaxed, panting.

It was no big deal; really not. She felt like laughing and crying. Guilt fought with pleasure inside her. She suddenly remembered Freynie wanting to "play doctor" when they were both twelve, teetering at the edge of adolescence, and how she had refused, unable to tell Freynie the truth behind her panicked reaction. The memory brought a load of shame with it. Stuck-up, frigid, saphian, Miss Geek . . . all the nicknames she'd heard or imagined she had been given were echoing inside her.

What if she called Freynie Long and told her what was on her mind? "Hey, Freynie. You remember what Roman Theroux said last year? How I'd never get anywhere if I never let myself get laid? Well, you know how many times men put their cocks in me when I was a little child? And don't you think I've had more than enough sex?"

She flinched, her arm falling into the water with a loud splash. No, no, she was turning this into more misery. She did not want to fall back into that mood. For a moment, she saw herself from an outside perspective; saw how sadness had become almost comfortable for her. How the familiar pain had become something she almost craved, the way an addict craves her drug.

Her left hand had crept between her legs, cupped her sex as if to protect it, an old defensive gesture she often used as she fell asleep. Pushing downward with the heel of her hand, she felt the pressure in her sex and woke sensations in her flesh.

She did not like herself to be unhappy. She did not want to be the same person anymore. She had called for Quentin—God, she had called for him! She would not be sorry about it. She was not insane. She was sad, she had been hurt; but she could not be hurt forever. Not this way.

She wanted to burst out of herself like a butterfly from its chrysalis; wanted to be utterly different from the girl she'd always been. At this moment, she felt she would rather die than remain the same. She wanted to put all her past pains behind her.

An idea, foolhardy and numinous, crossed her mind, and in her current state she acted upon it without second thoughts. She stood up in the bath, stepped out, laying a dripping leg on the bathmat, reached for the sliding mirror-door of the cabinet, took out an implement, brought it back with her into the bath.

She looked at it for a moment, pondering the use she would make of it, which it wasn't intended for; there was a panicky flutter of dread within her, but she was beyond fear.

She checked with a glance that she had locked the bathroom door, as she always did. Then she drew the curtain shut on herself, for she would only dare try this if she were twice hidden. She expected failure at best, a disaster at worst, and yet she wanted to try. She let her fingers move of their own will, letting theoretical knowledge blossom into experience. A little more daring . . . She could barely believe she was doing this.

There was pain, yes. Discomfort scaling up to a burning sensation, which came and went. But not what she had expected. Not at all. She started gasping, not from pleasure, not from any pain, but from a realization that shattered her world.

Uncle called her for dinner at the accustomed hour. She came and sat down at the table, waited for him to serve the dishes. Uncle prided himself on being a good cook, though his repertoire was limited to a dozen or so dishes. This time he'd made chicken potpie, Christine's favorite. He set the Pyrex dish down on a pair of oven mitts to guard the table top, then sat down at his accustomed place. He recited the Blessing before they ate; Christine mumbled in accompaniment, trailed off several seconds after he was done—her mind was elsewhere. Her attention was brought acutely back to the present, however, after Uncle had served them. He cleared his throat and looked at her with a worried expression; for an instant she thought irrationally he must had been aware of what she had done earlier.

"I've been speaking on the phone with Dr. Almand today, Christine," he said. "He told me that he's found a new element to your case. Something which has him concerned."

Christine remained mute, though he seemed to expect some sort of reply. After a moment, Uncle sighed and went on.

"He also said you seemed very upset when he mentioned it. Apparently, you even said you didn't want to go back and see him. Now, you didn't really mean that—did you?"

As a matter of fact she hadn't. She had rebelled pointlessly, harmlessly, know-ing she would be back in Dr. Almand's office as ineluctably as the sun rose into the sky. But now, she found she could decide that she had meant it. She laid the forkful of pastry crust and gravy back into her plate with a *clink*.

"I'm sorry, Uncle," she said, trying and failing to keep her voice firm, "but I'm sick and tired of Dr. Almand. I think . . ." She drew a deep breath; for a moment she dared not say what she meant, but finally words came to her, articulating her feel-ings at long last. "I think he's wrong. I think that he makes things up about people, and hypnotizes them, and sees whatever he wants to see. For a long time he was happy finding out people had been raped and seen murders and all that. . . . But they weren't any happier after he'd cured them. So there had to be something more, right, 'cause it couldn't be *his* fault. So now he thinks there's a worldwide Ahrimanic conspiracy, did he tell you that? There's worshipers of Ahriman everywhere, and they torture their own children, and then the children forget everything that ever happened. . . ."

Uncle's hands were resting on the edge of the table, his broad fingers spread out. He spoke in a reasonable voice. "Look, Christine, I'm not a psychologist, and nei-ther are you. But Dr. Almand has studied for many years, he's a professional. I know that what he tells you is shocking. . . ."

"Not shocking. That's not the word. What he tells me is *insane*. He shapes what I believe; he tells me what to remember. That's how it's always been! Whatever I told him, he would twist it so it fit what he wanted to hear from me. And whenever I fought it, it just proved he was right. The more I fought, the more painful the memory had to be, the more he was right and the more I suffered. If I don't believe my parents were Ahriman worshipers, it's proof that they were, because they must have made me forget. It's just so neat and tidy for him: He can't ever be wrong."

"Christine, please . . ."

"I remember seeing him on TV last year. When they had that girl on with the mask. That would've been me if I hadn't refused to do it. All I could stand to watch were the first five minutes. It didn't strike me then, but it does now. You know what he said? He said every patient he treats has been abused and repressed the memo-ries. *Every* patient. It's not his patients who're the problem; it's him."

Uncle looked deeply scandalized. "Christine," he said, "you know that terrible things happened in your childhood. You can't blame Dr. Almand for that. He helped you remember, but he's not the cause of the pain. Please, my child . . ."

"*I am not your child.*" There was a pause; Uncle swallowed. Christine, her heart beating faster and faster, went on. "And I'm telling you: Dr. Almand is the one who should be in therapy, not me! I don't want to see him anymore; I don't *need* to see him anymore." She could hardly believe she was saying this.

"That's enough." Uncle's voice was now cold, as he stood up. "You are going to go see Dr. Almand again, Christine; in fact, you're going tomorrow morning, first thing. That will be the end of it. You need treatment, and you're going to get it whether you like it or not."

Christine stood in turn. She felt herself vibrating, like a tuning fork that has just been struck. For all Uncle's bluster, she sensed he was hesitant. He was feeling the reins slipping from his hands. His hold on her, which she had never in all her life questioned, had faltered. Because he was wrong this time, utterly wrong. She shook her head slowly.

"Uncle, do you know what I did this afternoon, when I took my bath? I'll tell you what I did. I put the handle of my hairbrush up my *cunt*"—It was the first time in her life she had spoken the word, and it resonated with astonishing power in the room—"to see what it would feel like. And do you know what I found out? I found out that in all my memories of being raped, all of those times, *I remembered wrong.* Having something inside me doesn't feel *at all* like what Dr. Almand made me recall. Not at all. He used to say 'Your body remembers, Christine, your body remembers.' Like hell it does."

There was a moment of silence. Uncle's face had come undone. Christine carried her reasoning to its conclusion.

"You know what that means? That means none of it . . . N-n-none of it ever happened. I was never raped. Dr. Almand made me remember what he thought I had to remember, just like everyone else he sees. I was never raped, and my father didn't—"

Uncle stepped around the table, his lower lip working soundlessly, his eyes wide with alarm. His hand reached out toward her. "Christine, please, my baby, don't do this, you were getting better. I know it hurts, but you can't deny . . ."

His hand brushed her arm; she screamed out, "Don't you *dare* touch me!" and slapped his face, the blow resounding as loud as her obscene word had. They froze in place, a tableau of anger and bewilderment on both parts. Seconds stretched out interminably. Uncle's cheek was reddening, the shape of Christine's fingers blooming into existence. What would happen when the equilibrium broke, Christine could not imagine. And then she heard a car horn, outside. Though she had not believed, she knew the man she had summoned had come.

She turned on her heel, ran out of the kitchen to the front door, yanked it open. There was a red car in the street, in front of the house, its engine purring. Standing beside the open driver's side door was Quentin the psychopath, who thought he was a knight from some mythical land, Quentin the stalker, Quentin who had answered her invocation as he had promised.

She could hear Uncle running after her, calling out her name. Her legs did the thinking for her; she found herself running down the steps and toward the car. At her back, she heard Uncle's labored breathing, and then a shrieked command: "Stay! Christine, I order you to stay!" She had been slowing down as she approached the curb; now she stopped and looked back. Uncle stood on the steps, reaching out his arms toward her. His face was crimson with the sudden exertion; whether through a trick of the failing light, or because of her state, she saw his countenance alter into something indescribable, a mangle of flesh and bone with its own twisted logic.

"Who are you?" she whispered at it, and it occurred to her that she had never asked this question of her guardian before. Never asked it of anyone, save Quentin.

"Lady, get in the car, quickly!" said the stalker-knight. His eyes were open wide, shining fever-bright as he looked at her over the roof of the car. He was poised and tense, as if he hesitated whether to run toward her or jump behind the wheel.

She could still run away. Her old life waited for her. Uncle lumbered forward down the steps, holding out his arms; and Christine turned her back on him, though she felt as vulnerable as if he were a leaping tiger, and took the remaining steps to the car.

She opened the door and slid in. Quentin had already jumped in and closed his door. She heard Uncle shout again, syllables clear and distinct—but the words made no sense to her. She slammed the door shut, turned to look back over her shoulder. Quentin gunned the motor; the car jolted forward, the acceleration pushed her back in her seat. She could not discern Uncle's face through the rear window. He stood on the edge of the curb, still shouting and waving his arms as the distance shrunk him into a doll.

They were already at the corner with Barton Street. "Buckle your restraint!" shouted Quentin, and at that instant all the windows went black. The car's interior was plunged into almost total darkness. Without hesitation, Quentin twisted the wheel hard to the right; the car slewed with a shriek of tires. Christine only stayed in her seat by clutching the door handle desperately. She screamed in alarm, certain that they were going to slam into something and get killed . . . but they didn't. The car raced forward again, Quentin driving blindly. Christine found the resources to draw the seat belt out and buckle it at her side; this way when the crash came, she might have a slim chance to survive it.

Quentin shouted several words she could not parse, and ran his left palm down the windshield. The blackness receded; tendrils of transparency appeared and spread downwards. The blackness rolled visibly downward, squeezed itself along the side, as if it were being wept away.

Now Christine could see that they had drifted out of their lane and were about to ram an incoming car, whose brakes were screeching. She screamed incoherently; Quentin twisted the wheel hard again and they slid back into their lane. He floored the gas pedal; they accelerated with a snarl of the engine and ran a red light.

"You're going to get us killed!" Christine shouted at last. "Stop it, stop!"

"If we stop, Your Highness, we'll get killed for certain. Pardon me; I should say *I* will be. They will never harm you, but if we are caught, I am a dead man."

"You're insane! Let me go!"

"Is that why you summoned me? Because you think I'm insane?"

He swiftly cranked down the window on his side, admitting more light. They passed a car, another. Horns and drivers both screamed. Christine felt her stomach sink each time, but Quentin drove with superhuman skill; she began to believe he might know what he was doing. And besides, should she try to wrest the wheel from him she would surely get them killed. She had thrown in her lot with him, hadn't she?

"Where . . . where are we going?" she asked. "And why did the windows turn black? What happened? Was that paint on them? How did you get it off?"

Events were catching up with her, and she was having a hard time figuring it all out.

"With a little help on my part, this vehicle can repair most injuries. I would like to stop and clear the rest of the windows, but they should get better by themselves in an hour or so."

"But how did they turn black?"

"He cast a spell. Did you not hear it?"

They took a right turn with a screech of tires, and almost immediately Quentin took a hard left. The sound of a siren rose behind them.

"*Spell?* What spell?"

The street gave onto a two-lane road. Quentin merged with the traffic, slowing just enough so that he could fit into the stream of cars; then he shifted gears and the car accelerated again. Christine felt her terror abate slightly, but it still threatened to return, like a heavy object momentarily balanced on an edge.

"The spell your warden sent after us; it was a clever one. He meant to force me to abandon my vehicle, but not in a way that would injure you. If he had exerted his magic in a destructive way, he could have torn it to pieces—but that would have risked hurting you, and that is not an option open to him."

"What? What are you saying? There's no such thing as magic. I don't believe those stories."

"Oh, magic is very real, Lady. Only a very few people can wield it, but it does exist. Glass does not turn opaque of its own will. Princesses do not summon knights to them by simply plucking petals off flowers. Magic permeates the world in all its aspects—both the real world, and this one."

"What's that supposed to mean? I'm lost. Quentin, I—I want to believe you . . . And you did come when I summoned you. But I still don't understand anything. You've got to start making sense; explain all this better."

"Please roll down the window on your side first. More visibility will help me ride." Christine turned the crank handle and lowered the window. Why hadn't she thought of it herself? Quentin slowed down a trifle, so that the car was matching the traffic speed.

"This is not the time for leisurely explanations," he said, raising his voice against the roar of the wind through the windows. "But I can try to clear up some matters at least."

A dozen questions pressed in her mind; she ordered them, asked the most important one—and thus the most dangerous—first.

"Who am I supposed to be?"

"You are the Lady Christine; daughter of Edisthen, King of Chrysanthe; and princess of the realm. You were stolen from your father when still a very young girl, and taken out of the world, to this place."

"A princess? That's . . ."

She was going to say "crazy," but it was no crazier than what had just been happening. Glancing into the mirror on her side, she saw flashing blue lights.

"The police are on our tail; what are we going to do about them?"

"Use some of that magic you do not believe in, milady. Do you see an exit up ahead?"

She did not; and then suddenly she noticed one, barely a quarter mile distant. The road didn't feel familiar at all anymore, though it had seemed so at the start. The police cars were gaining on them; Quentin clenched his teeth, accelerated brutally and darted from lane to lane, slipping between cars. Christine looked over her shoulder, saw the flashing lights vanish, then reappear. At the last possible moment

Quentin swung from the left-hand lane to the right-hand one and onto the exit ramp. He took the curve at such a speed that Christine felt the seat belt dig into her shoulders; her heart rose in her mouth. She closed her eyes and tried to pretend this was a roller-coaster ride at a fair; it didn't help.

She forced the words out: "I know you want to escape them, Quentin, but you're scaring me. Could you go a bit more slowly, please?"

"I am so sorry, milady—it was very difficult to shake off the pursuit, and the best path lay in speed. But I have finally shifted away. From now on, we will have easier riding."

Indeed, they had completed the turn and were now going along a narrow and straight road, utterly empty of traffic. "Driving," Christine corrected Quentin, aware this was the second time he had made the mistake. "Why do you say 'riding'? This is a car, not a bicycle."

"It may look like a car, milady, but in fact it began as a horse. It shifted as I went deeper in. I had time, in nine years, to learn to ride it as well as it could be ridden. It may have wheels and an engine, but it's still a loyal beast at heart."

Christine closed her eyes again. The pavement here had been redone recently; there were seams in the asphalt over which their wheels thudded regularly, like a savage heartbeat. "You don't make it easy for me to believe you when you say things like that."

She felt Quentin's gaze on her, opened her eyes and saw that he was indeed glancing at her, while keeping most of his attention on the road. "I have no wish to frighten you, Lady Christine," he said, still shouting to be heard above the roar of the wind. "I am speaking the simple truth—but I sometimes forget it must sound very strange to you. Did you have any other questions? We may be left in peace for a little while."

Christine came out with her second question. "Where is . . . where is this country called Chrysanthe?"

"It is not a country; it is the world, all there is of it. As to where it lies . . . Outward."

"Outward? What, in space? Are you an Aresian with a flying saucer?"

Quentin frowned, as if puzzled by the reference, then his eyebrows went up. "Oh, you mean a man from another celestial sphere. Oh, no, milady, not at all."

"Well? How is it 'outward'?"

Quentin heaved a sigh.

"It is outward because we are inwards of it. This is a made world, you see. . . . Well, no, you clearly do not. I do not fully understand such things myself, but I can try to explain; Orion once drew us pictures.

"Imagine building a great castle, with walls of stone. There is the country outside the castle, and there is the castle itself. To someone living in the castle and never going outside, the castle might seem to be the whole world. Even if that person were to see outside, the outer world to her might appear smaller than the area the castle encompasses. And to someone else, who had lived all her life cloistered in a single room, the castle as a whole might appear smaller than her room.

"Now imagine that things are truly as they appear. Imagine building a castle that was larger inside than out. Imagine yourself traveling toward the center of the castle; the castle would grow larger the further in you went, so that you would be ever further away from the door, but never an inch closer to the center. This is much the way a made world is. There are openings in the true realm, leading to countries larger inside than out. Some are so small they must be entered on hands and knees; legends speak of one made world whose aperture was so tiny only a young child might wriggle through. Yet inside the made worlds, there are lands and oceans without end. The farther in one goes, the larger the world."

Christine digested this for a moment, then she said, in a voice so low the wind almost took it away, "And you are telling me we're within a magic world like that?"

"We are thousands of leagues down into it; so far from Chrysanthe that I feared the whole of nature would be insane here. But your abductors took good care of you; they did not dare put you in a mad place, as that would have risked harming you. They picked a very strange world for you to live in, but not so horrible as they might have. . . ."

"But the world isn't like that," Christine found herself objecting. "We live on Terra, it's been mapped out for centuries. The world is a round planet with a diameter of twenty-two thousand miles; and there's Luna and Ares and Aphrodite and the other planets and constellations. . . ."

"Yes, of course, milady. This is what it feels like to you, because you have never noticed the door that leads out of the room into the courtyard; and until you have passed through that door, it will seem to you as if the room is the whole world."

"But where is that door? Where do we pass through into the . . . into the outside?"

"As Orion put it to us, milady: There are no walls, no windows, no doors. There is only the made world, growing larger as you go deeper in. It takes a special sort of sight to see *beyond*, to perceive the direction of reality. This is what I mean by Chrysanthe being outward."

"But how do you expect to reach it, then, just traveling on the road at random?"

Quentin, after checking the side mirror, eased on the gas pedal. The roar of the wind decreased as the car assumed a more sedate speed. "We are already traveling outward. Look around you. Look at the trees; have you ever seen ones quite like this? Look at the sky, Lady Christine: What color is it? This is how I lost the constables; I moved outward, away from them in a direction they could not follow."

There were trees growing close to the road; their foliage was a shade of pale orange-yellow Christine had never seen even in autumn—and it was early summer. The sky had a tinge of purple in it that she had never seen before. The sun behind them shone on a great valley in which there was no sign of the city within which she had spent nearly her whole life.

She was silent for a while, then looked at Quentin. Wonder and dread battled each other within her. "I shouldn't trust you," she said. "How can I trust you?"

"I cannot say," he replied. "How does one trust anybody? Lady, I would lay down my life for you without hesitation. I am sworn to return you to your rightful home; I am your servant."

"This just makes it worse. Real people don't talk like you; nobody's willing to die for someone else. . . ."

"I know I am real. And I know what I would do, because I have been raised all my life to be the person I am now."

The car had slowed down still further; the air that washed over them smelled of green things growing, with a tang of some floral perfume she could not put a name to. Christine remembered an imaginary rabbit with Quentin's voice saying, *Hope and trust, trust and hope.* She nodded as if in answer. For the sake of her long-gone friend, she would give it a try.

3. In Flight

Shortly after dawn in a forest of dead pines a man walked, leading a gray horse bridled with silver and pearls, and behind that horse another, black and bridled in dark leather and iron. In the saddlebags of the gray mount were waterskins, a flask of brandy, some food, a suit of clothes, a trowel, and a shovel. The man—his name was Evered—followed a long-haired young woman who strode almost noiselessly on the carpet of fallen needles. He glanced frequently to right and left, trying to orient himself, but he had to admit that he was lost. His guide, by contrast, walked swiftly and without hesitation through the trees.

Their path kept climbing a gentle slope; eventually it eased, and the carpet of orange needles thinned out. Soon they had reached a small clearing amongst the dead trees. No plants grew from the bare soil. The woman stopped, turned her lucent gray eyes to the man. "This is the place," she said.

"I knew that," he replied. "Hold the bridle." He went to the saddlebags and took out the tools, then advanced into the clearing. Near the center of it he finally spotted five stones laid in a cross shape, half obscured by dirt and needles: The passage of a mere six months had already dimmed the sign. "Tie the horses close by," he called to the woman, "then bring the saddlebags."

"How close should I tie the horses?" she asked.

Biting back a curse, he said, "Ten yards from the edge of the clearing!" then began attacking the ground with the trowel.

He dug shallowly into the clayey ground, cautiously, clearing a space about a yard in diameter. The work went far more slowly than he'd have liked. All around him, the dry trees, the petrified sap, the lifeless wood, reminded him of things he would rather forget. The woman had brought the saddlebags into the clearing and stood by them, motionless. Muttering under his breath, Evered continued his task.

After a quarter of an hour's work, as the trowel scraped off a layer of soil at the bottom of the growing hole, there was a different sound added to the rasping of the dirt particles against the metal edge. Evered paused in his work. There was barely enough light to illuminate the bottom of the hole he'd dug. He let his fingers see for him; with their tips he identified locks of dirt-encrusted hair.

He recommenced digging, with renewed energy, spreading out from this point of discovery. Gradually he exposed the top of a head, a large and broad head. Having circumscribed it, he began to dig deep again, eventually freeing the head up to the neck.

He stood up then, to stretch his abused back and hams. He wiped sweat from his brow, reached into the saddlebags and took out a waterskin from which he drank deeply. At the bottom of the hole the head of a man was now exposed, with a fleshy face, its eyes and mouth closed. The hair was sandy brown; a fringe of beard followed the contours of the lower jaw.

Having drunk, he picked up the shovel and began to widen the hole, for he would have to free the shoulders next. The wider blade made the work easier; soon Evered had gotten down to the shoulders. As he plied the shovel, the pit deepened and widened, with a stalactite of soil at its center. Evered turned to the cone of soil with the trowel. Eventually he had cleared the clotted earth down to the paunchy waist. The other man stood naked, unbreathing, at the bottom of the hole, as if he'd been planted in earth there like a sapling.

Evered called for his erstwhile guide to toss him a waterskin, emptied it and tossed it back out of the pit; she did not attempt to catch it. With the trowel he cleared the wrists and hands.

When the hands were free, he rose and pinched the other's nose with his left hand. Plugs of soil fell out of his nostrils. Evered pulled down the jaw, spread the fleshy lips apart with his fingers, scooped out the clay that filled the other man's mouth.

When it was done, the naked man suddenly expelled a wash of air, fragrant with dirt, incense, and some long-steeped human exudation. The next second, he drew in a deep shuddering breath with a sound like a bellows, and coughed.

Evered stuck his fingers in the corners of the man's eyes, and cleaned his lids of dirt. The man's eyes opened, stared blindly.

Sweating, Evered grasped hold of the man's wrists and tried to pull him out of the ground by sheer force. But the man remained rooted in place. A significant amount of his bulk was still interred.

Evered cursed soundly, once, and stopped himself. He called out to the other man, in fairly calm tones:

"Casimir! I could use your help. Are you awake, Casimir?"

But the man he had named Casimir did not stir. He breathed in and out, and his eyes were half open; but he did not seem to see anything. Evered cursed again and began to work around the man's waist, deepening the pit.

After five minutes, he understood his error. He leaned at the man's side and, reaching out with the nail of his little finger—a long, hard nail, for the prince liked to play the mandolin—he scratched out the plugs of soil in Casimir's ears.

"Casimir! Help me pull you out!" he shouted. "Casimir! Wake up, damn you!"

At the sound of his name the man's gaze grew focused, his breathing quickened. He began to struggle with his legs, fighting to free them from the imprisoning soil. Evered meanwhile had taken up the shovel and was digging a trench around Casimir's waist.

Once the trench had reached to midthigh, Casimir's own struggles began to bear fruit. Evered grasped his wrists again and pulled; with a rustle of dirt, Casimir finally came free of the ground. Evered pulled him up the slope of the hole and collapsed next to the saddlebags. He dug within for the brandy and allowed himself a generous slug.

The man named Casimir stared about him, puzzledly. His nude, fleshy body was still dirtied by patches of soil. The woman stood motionless by the saddlebags, gazing at Casimir, saying nothing. With an unnerved sigh Evered rose to his feet, took the clothes out of the saddlebags and threw them at Casimir.

"Dress yourself," he said. And to the woman: "Go put the saddlebags back on my horse."

Casimir put on trousers and shirt, though he neglected to button the latter. Evered had to lead him by the hand to the horses. Getting him to mount up was a chore, and for that one at least the woman was able to help, hoisting Casimir's bulk aloft until he could put his bare foot into the second stirrup.

Grasping the pommel of his saddle, Casimir for the first time uttered a sound. "Wh—Who . . . ?"

Evered had mounted the gray horse. He grasped the black's bridle.

"You are named Casimir. Do you remember?"

"The earth . . . the soil . . . dark, and cold . . . dirt in my mouth. I ate dirt."

"You were in the earth six months, Casimir. Do you remember it?"

Casimir looked at him dully. Yet a tiny flame had started to bloom in his eyes.

"I remember," he said. "I remember all of it."

He said no more for the remainder of the day, no matter how Evered pressed him. The woman walked in front, leading them back; once they were out of the dead forest, Evered ordered her to ride double with Casimir. From here on, he could orient himself.

They made camp when it got too dark, in a tiny clearing. Beasts of the night hooted and called; Casimir listened to their cries as if he could understand them. After one particularly long howl he chuckled the way he might have at a well-turned joke. Evered, who sat facing him across the flames of a small fire, asked no question. Casimir looked at him, moistened his lips, then named his companion, somewhat hesitantly.

"Evered . . ."

"Yes," the other replied after a beat.

"I remember you asked if I should find the king your father . . . I did not see him. There was no sign of him in that place. None whatsoever."

"I didn't expect you would find him," said the prince, his gaze shifting away from the other man's. Casimir's eyes seemed to glow from the fire more than a man's eyes should.

"But in all other respects, I succeeded. There *were* Heroes in the void, Evered. The earth is still stained with their memory. Nikolas Mestech and Juldrun of the Hundred Hands and sweet Ilianrod; they were there, more real than you are to me now. I shared a meal with Felofel and bedded Weoll the Flame. . . . A pity these six months passed by so fast."

He looked about him, a puzzled look on his face. His gaze paused on the woman who stood motionless by the horses.

"Where are my other servants?" he asked.

"They wouldn't come. They said the time was not yet right and refused to budge."

"What? What day is it?"

"Twenty-fourth of Chill."

Casimir's face fell. "A week!" he cried out. "I still had a week left, you fool!"

"I could wait no longer!" replied Evered. "I won't have you risking your life on mad ventures like this when my need is real, and—"

He fell silent, for Casimir had risen to his feet, held out a hand, and with a triad of words had altered their fire. The flames now glowed green and moved as though they were a viscous liquid, molten glass perhaps, elongating and shortening, droplets breaking off then falling to rejoin the mass. The flames rose high, braided themselves, became an eyeless snake that stretched forth and looped itself around Evered. The blind head faced his own, opened a mouth fanged with glittering spikes, and hissed forth a desiccating breath straight from the heart of a forge.

Casimir spoke coldly: "I left precise instructions, Evered. My servants would have come to free me in due time. You have abused your power."

"It was only a week," gasped Evered.

"Time flows otherwise in that realm. Those last few days might have brought a richer harvest than all others combined!"

The snake tightened its coil; Evered felt the heat from its body scorching his clothes. Casimir was risking his own life, to so threaten to harm him, and yet . . . The man might be mad enough to wish for both of them to be destroyed. The eyeless head swayed a few inches from Evered's eyes; he was torn between the urge to close his lids and the terror of remaining blind before the supernatural beast.

"I apologize, Casimir," he said. "I should have trusted you better. I thought of myself rather than you. And yet, I swear I was genuinely concerned for your safety."

His gaze left the snake's blind head, locked with Casimir's eyes. Dazzled as he was by the green glow from the snake, all Evered could see were two points of reflected viridian within a shadowy bulk.

"Touching," came Casimir's voice. The snake's tongue flickered out, licking at Evered's face, the searing-hot points almost, but not quite, causing pain; then the animal not so much uncoiled as dissolved away; and their fire returned to normal. The whole episode might all have been an elaborate illusion, were it not for the reek of singed fabric rising from Evered's clothes.

"Yes," the wizard went on, "your concern is touching, Evered. Well; what's done is done. No need to lose our temper. My harvest was plentiful; that little trick was the least of what I've learned. I hope you enjoyed it. It has an elegance only a fellow practitioner can fully appreciate, but even a layman such as yourself can grasp some of it, no?"

Evered mumbled in acquiescence and nodded.

Casimir sat down again with a grunt. His face had lost some of its earlier feral expression. "Let us be clear with each other, m'lord," he said. "I am still your man, but don't ever override my spells like you just did. You have no idea what some of the forces I work with could do to you if you diverted their flow at the wrong time. Do you understand me?"

"Yes, Casimir," breathed Evered.

"Then I think I'll lie down and sleep a bit. I've been awake six whole months in the ground; the kind of thing that tires a man out."

Casimir lay down on his side, pillowing his head on his arm, and closed his eyes. Within a few heartbeats he was snoring.

Evered remained seated on his side of the fire, gazing at the sleeping wizard. It might have been a trick of the flickering light, but he thought he saw tiny, formless things crawling out from between Casimir's fingers to die twisted upon the ground. His own hands sought each other and clasped themselves.

It was to be expected, he repeated to himself, that Casimir would be somewhat addled from his long absence; the wizard had reasserted his fealty in the end, had warned Evered for his own sake about the dangers of the enterprise they were about, no more. There was no reason to feel afraid, to wish he had dared to bring his own retainers on this expedition. From her post by the horses, Casimir's servant watched him with eyes that never blinked.

For a long moment after the car had vanished from his sight, Christine's warden remained standing in the middle of the street expectantly, certain that at any moment it would return. It wasn't so much that he could not believe his spell had failed; it was that he'd forgotten he'd cast a spell at all, forgotten who he had been a few seconds before. He stood in the street, his mind coreless as a pithed fruit.

Then he shuddered, as his identity boiled back to the surface. For thirteen years he had submerged his true self under the cloak of an assumed life; he had believed himself truly to be Christine's benevolent adoptive father, who had taken pity on a poor victim of abuse. It had been a necessary process, both to conceal his presence within the made world and so that no *deliberate* harm come to the child.

The disguise had taken all too well; in thirteen years his false identity had congealed and hardened, become real enough that now it fought the earlier self as it returned. The warden—he didn't remember either the name he had worn in this world or the one he used to wear before—trembled and fell to his knees. There was a sun of pain in his head, casting shafts of harsh light on everything he looked at. He had panicked in the house; had it all been his fault? He had felt his authority over Christine slip from his fingers, and known from the core of himself that this must not be allowed. But he had panicked, had gone harsh and authoritative, even while he knew that this was not the correct way to deal with the girl.

All might have yet been saved; but then she had run away—run away with that man in the car—a *real* man, real, real, unlike everyone here save Christine and himself . . . The warden had run after her and when she had ignored him, as she rode away in the car, he had recalled a thing he must do, and he had—he had . . . *What had he done?*

A desperate moan escaped the man's lips. Then in a gush of fright that nearly stopped his heart the warden's fake identity was finally rent, and his former self regained control.

He stood up, dazed and still weak from his inner turmoil. But he had been— was again—a disciplined man. His duty took precedence over his feelings. Vaurd had said of him once that he would fight for minutes after receiving a mortal wound, because he couldn't be bothered to notice that he was dead. Vaurd who had been slain by Christine's father a season after uttering those words.

"Mathellin," the man said, at last recalling his name after thirteen years. He clenched his left fist, felt his powers gather, still unsure after lying so long dormant. He cast his sight *beyond*, toward the center of things; his vision was filled with the chaos of the made world, the realm of possibilities converging toward the actual. Through an insane cross-hatching of false realities he could barely discern his charge and her rescuer, traveling at speed, describing an arcanely complex trajectory that drew them swiftly and steadily away.

He had failed. When she made her bid for freedom, he ought to have cast away his counterfeit self in a second, as if doffing a cape, and raised up all the power at his disposal. He had not anticipated the effects of so long a dissembling. And now Edisthen's daughter was too far from him; he had wasted precious minutes recalling himself to himself. And that damned boy was riding a *car* through the made world!

Mathellin ran back into the house. He grabbed the telephone, dialed sevens until he heard a click at the other end of the line and a chill, impersonal voice answered.

"I hear."

"She . . . she has escaped. Do you hear me? The princess has escaped. Send word toward the surface, as swiftly as you can. Everything must be bent toward recapturing her. Concealment is no longer necessary."

"I obey," was the only reply, then the line went dead.

Mathellin dropped the receiver in its cradle, breathed deeply. However Christine's rescuer had done it, Mathellin could not emulate his feat and ride an engined vehicle toward reality, at least not at the speed he had perceived them to be going. If he was going to catch up with them, he had to hope, first that some of the defenses laid long ago would slow down the fugitives, and second that he could get to them swiftly enough under his own power.

His innate magic rose within him and he shed the shape he had worn these long years. He grew taller, leaner, and younger by over a decade. His muscles stiffened, and as they tensed and relaxed he felt his power ascend to a keener pitch still. Rage seeped into him, overwhelming his dismay. This was not over yet.

He ran out of the house; for a fleeting second a remnant of the fool he had been stirred in him, worrying about the house, the wealth inside, leaving it open for anyone to plunder. Mathellin directed a fraction of his anger at this fragment of his old self and felt it curl up and char to nothing. Nothing here was real, save for him; let it all dissolve into emptiness for all he cared.

He ran along the street, heedless of the nonexistent people who stared at him from their front yards. And as he ran, his shape shifted like mercury; it was a huge, pale dog who ran now, claws ticking on the asphalt in a mad rhythm. Faster still, and the dog blurred into a bird, an ivory-white raptor with scarlet-rimmed eyes, which rose into the air with a screech, and in the next instant traveled *beyond*, and was gone from the imaginary world.

For hours now they had been driving along this same road, whose few turns were so gentle as to appear unnecessary. Quentin had increased speed and kept it well above eighty miles an hour; they had overtaken other cars two or three times, but never met anyone going in the opposite direction. They had passed a few exits; Christine had never heard of any of the towns they announced.

She had slowly gotten calmer; the ride was smooth and without any danger, but Quentin's explanations were far more unnerving in the end than his reckless driving had been. The windows had all cleared themselves up now, although dark smut remained caked along their rims. The side windows had been cranked up and only a thin thread of cool air came in through the crack Quentin had left open at the top of his. Christine had stopped asking questions and looked out at the passing landscape, struggling with the revelations she had been vouchsafed.

With the setting of the sun the moon had gained in brightness; its rays, at first tinged with yellow, had now assumed their usual silver radiance. They illuminated the strip of asphalt along which the car sped. There were no streetlights, no road signs anymore. It was as if the road no longer ran from anywhere to anywhere. Quentin heaved a sigh, reduced speed, and brought the car to a halt on the shoulder.

He opened the door and got out, stretching his legs. Christine imagined he would head for the bushes to relieve himself, and at this thought she realized that she badly needed to void her bladder. But Quentin just stood there, gazing at the night sky. She opened her own door and went to join him.

"So beautiful," he said, pointing with his chin at the moon. "At first when it appeared it terrified me: It was like a huge round idiot face opening in the vault of the night. I thought it a sign of the growing madness of the world. But in time I grew to appreciate it; and now, it feels a necessary part of things."

Christine pondered his words for a moment. "There is no moon in Chrysanthe, then," she said. Quentin nodded and said: "There are only the stars. They are bright, far brighter than these, in fact, and some shine with many pretty rays . . . but there is nothing to compare with your moon. I shall miss it when it is gone."

"Excuse me," she said, and went off. She had only done this once before in her life, and hated it; but it was clear she could not wait for them to stop at a bathroom. Away from the road the ground sloped down; she found a scraggly bush that would have to do, dropped her pants and crouched to urinate. Then she noticed Quentin had followed her, stood a few feet distant. "Hey! What are you doing!" she protested.

"I am dreadfully sorry, Lady; but I had rather you did not leave my sight."

"Turn your head away, Quentin! Or I can't go!"

With reluctance Quentin turned around. Christine was still too embarrassed to proceed; she waited for half a minute, until Quentin asked her if she was all right, at which she yelled she would be just fine if he would only behave decently. The pressure in her bladder had become as acute as her embarrassment by then and just as she had started to fear she would be utterly blocked, she managed to let go.

She came back to the car simmering with embarrassment; Quentin gazed at her in mingled apology and defiance, asked her to remain where she was, and vanished on the same errand. Once he'd returned, she asked him: "Aren't we going to stop somewhere to eat, or to sleep? Or are we driving straight through to Chrysanthe?"

"We could not possibly make the whole journey all at once. But I want to accumulate as much distance as possible right now. I am . . . I am sorry that I did not think ahead; I could have located a rest area, with bathrooms. I am used to rougher circumstances, but you naturally are not, and I should have thought of that. The fault is mine."

She sighed, her anger partly deflated. "I know men have an easier time of it on trips. But I need to stop every so often for . . . that. Say, every three hours."

"Very well. I will see to it in future. What o'clock do you have?"

She glanced at her watch. "Nearly twenty-first hour."

"All right. We will ride on for a while, but by midnight I will find us a nice inn."

"Quentin . . ."

"Yes, milady?"

She shook her head, dizzied by the changes in her life. She should be terrified, alone here with a strange man . . . And yet, inappropriate as it was, a measure of excitement at her adventure was swelling within her. But it couldn't be true at all, could it? Quentin looked at her, waiting for her to speak. He could not be what he claimed, yet he had Tap Fullmoon's voice. This might all be a dream, a fit of insanity—logic said it had to be. Or rather no, it did not. Her fear and common sense said this was a dream. Logic argued that she must gather more information before she judged. So far she had pinched herself, and looked carefully around, and made half a dozen inconspicuous tests; it all panned out. So far, logic argued that this was not a dream. How it squared with what she knew of the world . . . that required more thought.

Just as she was about to speak, a weird howl rose from all around them. It sounded like a cross between a wolf's lament and a mechanical siren's blare; a sound to set one's hairs on end.

"What is that?" she asked, a shiver running down her spine.

Quentin's hand had gone to his side, clutching at emptiness. "I have no idea," he said. "In the made worlds anything goes. This might be simply some lonely and harmless animal. Please get back into the car now."

He got into his seat, turned the key in the ignition; the engine purred back to life and they returned to the blacktop, resuming their former speed. "It doesn't sound like a harmless animal," said Christine. The howl ebbed and rose, coming from everywhere and nowhere. "It sounds like an alarm. Oh, Quentin, it couldn't be an actual alarm—for *us*, could it?"

"This deep in the made world . . . anything is possible. Your abductors could have raised help of any sort you can imagine. Given time and a base of operations . . . Perhaps this is indeed a signal that you have escaped."

The howl still filled the night air.

"It cannot be everywhere," said Quentin, and suddenly the road forked, grew a curve where none had been; they took it, and were on an overpass bridging a highway where silvery cars and trucks ran in a dense stream under bright mercury vapor lights. The howl had stopped. The road curved 270 degrees to merge with the highway. Quentin inserted them into the traffic. All Christine could hear now were the roar of the car's engine and the whistle of the wind—though she imagined she could still hear a faint ululation, a whine of a different sort; maybe it was just the singing of the blood in her ears. They sped on through an unknown country, and exaltation and dread mixed in her soul.

BOOK II

Made Worlds

1. Hunted

As Mathellin flew through the made world prospects shifted and blurred beneath his wings. The general direction of his travel was outward, toward Chrysanthe, but the pattern he described was of necessity complicated. The geometries he followed led to a way station, a locus of power raised there in years past against just such a need as his.

Ramparts grew distinct beneath him, lit by the viridian glow of the molten glass that roiled at the bottom of a moat. Mathellin dropped to the ground, resumed his human shape. Soldiers dozing at their post snapped to attention as they saw him approach. He called out the password, and they opened the gates for him.

Through doors and corridors Mathellin sped, until he reached a chamber sunk deep beneath the ground, where quivered a hundred strands of power he had spun himself, over a decade ago. This stronghold had been erected here, worlds away from Christine, in the fear that Orion might be able to discern the concentration of magic and that it might lead him to her. A hundred men patrolled the place night and day, ignorant of what it was that they guarded but able to destroy it all rather than let anyone save Mathellin gain access to it.

Near the center of the room was a crystal of smoky quartz, emerging from a rough lump of white mineral. This Mathellin stroked with his fingers as he mouthed a spell; and slowly, slowly, a picture of Christine became visible in the far depths of the quartz. Seeking-spells do not work between worlds, but Mathellin was using a specific form of sympathy resonance that he had perfected over the years. Fueled by the years he had spent in close proximity to the girl, aided by the net of spells he had woven across worlds, it allowed him at least tenuous perceptual contact with Christine wherever she might be.

He saw her sitting in the right front seat of a car that drove through the boundaries of worlds with the greatest of ease. Her position in the multidimensional reality of the made world he could determine with a fair degree of precision; and his gaze went to a nebulous shape that floated in midair, a swarm of colored clouds threaded with brighter or darker curved lines that served him as a crude map of Errefern. Defenses existed throughout the realities, hundreds if not thousands of them, but any quantity divided into infinity yields a small quotient indeed. The message Mathellin had sent propagated across the boundaries of worlds, a cohort of spells warning their forces of Christine's escape; but it might not be much help.

His attention returned to the depths of the crystal. He sent more of his power through the link and the image sharpened; he could smell the scent of the girl's hair, touch the fake-leather texture of the seat. The young man who drove grew in reality, and Mathellin sensed the warmth of his flesh, traced the line of his jaw as the light gleamed on it. The reek of magic was all about him, but this was not a fellow wizard; the magic he used was borrowed, power lent to him by another— Orion. Sweat beaded at Mathellin's temples and rolled down the sides of his face as he sent more and more of himself through the sympathy spell, until it was almost as if he hovered unseen just above and behind them, a lurking presence within their vehicle.

They were far, and getting farther every second. Damn the boy, how could someone not even a wizard control a *machine* across the boundaries of worlds? Boats, Mathellin could understand; he had sailed through the rivers of Hieloculat often enough, worlds unfurling under his prow like foam as he went down a gradient. But a machine full of moving parts, traveling at such speed of its own power rather than being blown about by the natural impellings of wind and tide, and without benefit of a gradient—this was beyond astonishing.

Mathellin considered the windshield of the car, his perplexity growing by leaps and bounds. Until this instant, still in shock from the resumption of his true identity, he had not recalled what he had done as Christine and her rescuer fled. Now he did: He had sent a spell at the vehicle, to darken all of its windows and force the boy to abandon it—of course, he ought to have disrupted its engine instead, but he had not properly recalled himself yet and had used the first impulse that came to mind. The spell had worked; so why was all the glass utterly transparent now? It wasn't as if he had merely flung paint at the car. . . .

And as he focused all his attention onto the vehicle the answer came to him, and he raged curses at Orion.

After half a minute, the stream of curses ran dry like a faucet twisted shut. Mathellin was not one for losing control of himself. Setting aside his fury, he drew, with the tip of his little finger, a new line of light on his map of Errefern, plotting the course of the fugitives. The representation of the made world everted itself again and again as he worked, until it had achieved a geometry where their trajectory approximated a straight line. Extrapolating this he identified a region through which they were bound to pass if they kept to their present course. Resources his side had in that domain; not many, but some.

Mathellin summoned a messenger from the box where it had lain dormant, filled its embryonic mind with his request. Then he started severing connections, breaking the strands of his web and reabsorbing whatever of their energy he could. His network started to unravel, destroying the patient work of years; Mathellin felt not the least twinge of regret, for his masterwork had no more use for him, and he could not enjoy anything for its own sake.

When only a single strand was left attached to this node, Mathellin gathered all his power and sent the messenger hurtling along the strand, a screaming meteor passing from world to world, bearing his message to whatever of his allies could hear it. The effort forced him to his knees and for a second or two he blacked out.

Mathellin tottered to his feet. His fingers caressed the invisible strand of power, still thrumming from the messenger's swift flight. It would pass Christine and her rescuer, alert his allies up ahead, and give him one chance at least to intercept them. He swept up the quartz crystal into a bag and exited the room without a backward glance. He climbed the winding stairs two steps at a time, and as soon as he had reached ground level he ordered a mount be brought to him.

The horse had canines like daggers and clawed hooves; it stamped and snorted, bred for speed and murderous rage. For a moment Mathellin thought of imitating the young man's trick instead, but the prospect was too daunting in his present state of near exhaustion—and there was no appropriate fuel handy. Damn the boy, and damn Orion. He mounted the horse, which took off at a gallop immediately. The guards were still hurriedly drawing back the gate as Mathellin and his mount passed through, along a winding mountain road that soon ran at the bottom of a dried seabed, then along a linear city whose fifteen-story buildings were a hundred feet wide but no more than ten deep, a row of giant's dominoes set in the powdery earth. And still, with every furious step his mount took, Mathellin could feel the fugitives' lead widening.

Traffic remained dense for two hours, as they sped along the highway; spaced precisely every ten miles, brightly lit rest areas were announced by huge orange-and-white signs. Christine could see trucks of all kinds parked there, and a scattering of cars. Nearly every vehicle was a shade of gray; a few were blue or green, certainly none red. When she glanced at the drivers of the cars that they overtook, they were always men, always wearing wide-brimmed black hats. Several glared outrage at bareheaded Quentin—and one or two at herself. The car doors bore their maker's insignia in chrome letters: *Zelta, Mecheld, Bruschin Matar Jet*. Amongst these vehicles, Quentin's scarlet sports car was a freak. Christine expected the local police to swoop down on them at any moment; but then, Quentin could sideslip out of their world with a thought. . . . Although how exactly he managed to guide his car between worlds he had not been able to explain to her satisfaction.

They shifted to the left lane to pass a small truck. Its door said *Zelte*. Had she read all of the others wrong, or were there two different makers with names a single letter apart? Or did the words mean something else altogether?

Ten minutes later they were passed by a pale-blue *Möcheld* car whose insignia was of dark steel; the driver wore the usual wide-brimmed hat, but there was something indefinably different about him. . . . Had it been a woman?

There were fewer trucks now, and at least half of the vehicles were colored; she saw a burnt-orange station wagon with two children in the backseat.

"This isn't the same world as it was ten minutes ago, is it?" she asked Quentin. "It changes all the time . . . continuously."

"Exactly, Lady Christine. As long as I am impelling us outward, the world changes a hundred times with every heartbeat."

"Then how come there's always a road under our wheels? If the world changes all the time, we should flash across grass and sand and rock, not always asphalt."

"There is more than one direction involved, Lady. I choose a route through the made worlds by virtue of the traveling-spell; it is naturally a route that keeps our immediate surroundings almost constant, by the principle of least resistance. A great wizard like Orion could carry himself instantly from a desert to the middle of an ocean, but it would require immense effort. Far easier, and not that much slower, to find a path in the sand, let it lead you to an oasis, follow its shore to a lake, climb aboard a small fishing boat, let it become a trawler, then a caravel, and you will find yourself where you wanted to be."

"You make it sound so simple . . . ," muttered Christine, again dizzied. A sign announced *Æxit 27A - Clearlake*. Quentin shifted gears and took the curve, gently this time. Barely half a mile farther, they came to a hotel. Quentin pulled into the parking lot and stopped the engine. From the trunk, he pulled a pair of backpacks, their leather scuffed and stained from years of use.

As he shouldered one with a practiced swing, Christine asked: "How are we going to do this? I mean, we're not being sought for, right? In this world, no one knows who we are."

"No one should, no. But we cannot be absolutely sure, Lady. Remember you were abducted by people who could wield magic; I am not the only one who can travel between worlds. I have no reason to believe we are in danger, but still we must not throw caution to the winds."

Seeing her dismayed expression, he bent forward and tried to soften the impact of his words.

"Please do not fear; you, at any rate, are absolutely safe. No one wishes to hurt you; your abductors kept you a prisoner, but they would not have let physical harm come to you. I am the only one whose life is at risk. And we are very, very far from where we were. We will rent rooms here for the rest of the night, and leave at dawn."

They walked to the main doors, entered the lobby. The night clerk greeted them affably enough, though he glanced disapprovingly at Quentin's battered luggage.

"And what can I do for you, sir, madam?"

"We set out too late," said Quentin. "I thought I had enough time to reach the city in a single leg, but I just cannot drive anymore."

"A room, then, for you and . . . ?"

"My sister. I want a suite, though. You have that, do you not?"

"We have one, yes, but it's more expensive. Will you be paying by debt card?"

"Cash."

The clerk frowned. "In that case, you have to pay in advance, sir. The rate for a suite is a hundred thirty-five per night, plus state and confederation tax."

Quentin pulled out a wad of bills from his pocket and counted out the requisite sum; the clerk, his qualms appeased, secured the money in a lockbox, then showed them to their suite: a small parlor-kitchenette with three doors leading to a bathroom and two bedrooms.

Once the clerk had left, Quentin stretched his whole body and yawned, catlike. "I advise you to go to sleep at once, milady," he said. "We must set out again at daybreak."

"All right," she agreed. "But I'll take a shower first."

As soon as she found herself alone in the bathroom, Christine was seized with a feeling of unreality so intense she had to sit down with her head between her knees, gripping her thighs and scoring the flesh with her nails, panting and sweating.

She ran through the now-familiar cycle of thoughts: that this could not be hap-

pening, that it could not *not* be happening, that dreams that masqueraded so con-
vincingly as reality might as well be real, that perhaps she was insane, so badly
delusional that she'd made her own world as a refuge from all that terrified her . . .

In a few minutes the fit passed. She rose trembling to her feet, splashed water on
her face, and after some hesitation proceeded to take a brief shower. She emerged
from the bathroom still damp; Quentin was pointedly looking in another direction,
but for a fact she had put everything on again, even to her socks and shoes. Once inside her room, she started to strip down, but could not bring herself to sleep naked and
so kept her stale panties and bra. She climbed under the covers, left the lamp on,
and shut her eyes, convinced she was too nervous to sleep but trying to relax anyway.

Her thoughts ran over the events of the day, looping back without cease. Again
and again Uncle's face as it had appeared to her in those last moments rose up in her
sight. There had been *something* wrong with it; but the more she tried to bring it out
the less clear it became. She stopped herself then; if Dr. Almand's sessions had filled
her mind with false memories, there was no reason why she could not bring it upon
herself as well. She resolved she would not imagine what she could not remember.

Worlds beyond worlds; an infinity of worlds and Chrysanthe at the end of the
road, or rather the beginning. A princess. She had been a princess in her dreams;
were those true memories, grown distorted by time? Her faithful knight had the
voice of her imaginary friend. . . . She would believe for now: She had no other
choice. She had learned that things were not as she had believed they were, when
she had eaten the flower's heart and summoned Quentin to her. After that day, she
could never have remained the same person, even had he not come, even had she
remained trapped in Uncle's house forever more. . . .

There was a loud crash in the parlor; the sound of a piece of furniture breaking
apart. Christine sat up but then froze, terrified, her mouth open but incapable of
words. Shouts and thuds; the door of her room flew open. A man stood in the doorway, staring at her with a grin of triumph that faded to slack-jawed astonishment.

"Sweet Miriam mother of the Lord, I've found . . . Oh God, what's happening
to me?"

He trembled and swayed and gasped. Christine had time to think of escape,
and to realize there was none save through the door, before Quentin jumped the
man from behind and bore him to the carpet. The intruder tried to defend himself,
rolling onto his back as his hand reached for some weapon in a sheath at his hip;
Quentin's fist smashed into his temple and knocked him unconscious.

Quentin spoke to Christine as he rose to his feet. "Get dressed, milady. We must
leave at once."

"What—?"

"*Now*, please, Lady Christine. Put on your clothes and let us leave!"

Quentin removed the intruder's weapon from its sheath: It was a short knife
with a serrated blade. He looked down at his supine opponent, then at Christine,
who had clambered out of bed but was still gazing at the scene.

"Your clothes are on the back of the chair, Lady. Put them on now, and your
shoes. Hurry."

She convulsively put on her pants, threw on her shirt and buttoned it at random, stuffed her socks in her pockets, slammed her feet and ground her heels down into her shoes. With a sigh, Quentin tossed the knife away, motioned for her to follow.

In the parlor another intruder lay on the carpet, unmoving. The door was wide open; beyond it a fat man in his bare feet, wearing a flannel nightgown and a black peruque, was staring at them with horror and outrage. Quentin ignored him and grabbed their bags.

"Stay where you are!" the fat man declared. "The enforcers have been summoned. Stay where you are!"

"Absolutely," replied Quentin. "This is just what we will do." He took hold of Christine's wrist—a surprisingly gentle hold, more an encircling of the wrist—and led her along as he shoved the fat man out of the way and raced down the corridor. A door gave onto stairs; they went down three floors and reached an emergency exit, which Quentin kicked open without hesitation.

A siren began wailing; Quentin and Christine stepped out into the parking lot. A smear of grayness on the black sky promised the dawn. Christine could not stand even the faintest touch of Quentin's hand; she had been trying to break free and now at last yanked her wrist out of his grasp.

"The car is over there, Lady. Quickly!" He did not touch her, but ran at her back, urging her along as a sheepdog would a lazy ewe. She allowed herself to be hustled into the car. Quentin threw the bags into the trunk, pulled open his door. It was only then that she noticed that the car's doors had never been locked; that in fact, they had no locks at all.

He dropped into the seat, pulled the belt across him and clicked it into place, did the same for her, then turned the key in the ignition. The engine roared to life and with a screech of tires the car tore out of the parking lot and onto the road. Christine saw the clerk in the rearview mirror running after them, waving high in the air what seemed to be a huge scroll, covered with ribbons and seals; then the road took a ninety-degree turn and the clerk and the hotel vanished behind a screen of pine trees.

Quentin was tight-lipped; he stared ahead at the road, frowning. There were no streetlights; the road remained dark save for the yellowish glow of the car's headlights. The asphalt changed to gravel, then rutted earth. The car jounced and sideslipped; Quentin shifted gears savagely, guided the car along a curve, past which the surface improved: hard-packed dry dirt, through which their passage plowed twin clouds of dust. A minute later they were back on some kind of asphalt; the sun was rising beyond the trees that fringed the road, and a watery gray light filled the world. The road was still deserted, only one lane wide.

"I have been inexcusably careless," said Quentin, not looking at her. "I tender my apologies. I failed you."

She had been looking at the ignition key all this while. A tiny bauble depended from it, a wooden bead painted dark red with two bronze-and-black feathers glued to it. There was no slot in the barrel, in which the key would have fit. The bow looked as if the key had been welded in; or rather as if the barrel had been cast with a key's bow sprouting from it. She was trying not to see again the second intruder lying on the rug; trying not to remember the stain beneath him.

"You killed him, didn't you?" she asked, in a trembling voice. Quentin did look at her then, his face reflecting a mix of emotions.

"He would have killed me, milady. I had to dispose of him quickly: You were in danger. I . . . I did not kill the other one. Him I spared."

She looked away from him, clutching at the door handle. Talking to the smear of pitch rimming the window, she asked, "How can a person bring himself to kill someone else?"

She thought he would dodge the question, assuming it applied to his attacker; but he answered, his voice fainter.

"The first time I killed, I was nineteen. It was in self-defense; I have never murdered anyone, nor would I ever. He was a big armsman, pockmarked and stragglyhaired. I did not even want to fight him, but he was addled and enraged. He had a mace that would have crushed my skull like an egg. I stabbed him below the breastbone, at an upward angle. The blade stopped his heart; when I withdrew it, he fell at my feet like a sack of meal. I still see his face in my nightmares."

Her hand squeezed the door handle, white-knuckled; she glanced at him, saw he was looking at her, turned her face away again.

"I do not take pleasure in killing, Lady Christine. I fight when I must. Please do not fear me."

"I'm not afraid of you," she said, unsure whether she lied or not. "I just . . . I've never seen a dead person before. And I'm afraid of what will happen. Are we going to get attacked again like that?"

"I pray we are not. It was all my fault anyway."

She risked looking forward; Quentin had returned his attention to the road. "Why was it your fault?"

"I was overconfident. I stopped while we were much too near your world; I rented a suite and stupidly went into my own room instead of guarding your doorstep, as I ought to have. When they came in, I should have been ready to meet them; instead, I was caught at a disadvantage. Had there been more of them . . . things would have gone badly."

"But who were these men? Who sent them? The one who came into my room . . ." She shuddered at the memory. "He said something like 'I've found her' and then he asked what was happening to him; then you jumped him. What was going on?"

"I cannot be sure of details; but I believe your captors have agents throughout the made world: creatures under their orders, though not direct control. Keeping always in mind the way reality is refracted within imaginary lands, it is hard to say these men were in fact sent by your jailer. But it is fairly safe to assume someone somewhere sent out minions, seeking you. Much the same way sounds in a room can be heard in the one adjacent, orders spoken loudly enough in one world may be obeyed in another. Those men were looking for you; they were primed to detect your presence, in a way akin to the way I was sensitized myself. When the one found you, he must have felt a pang such as I did. I am not sure if I explained it clearly enough. . . ."

"Never mind," she whispered. Her eyes were filling with tears. She began to weep, shaking in a long-delayed reaction. Quentin remained silent; when, after her first bout of sobbing had passed, she wiped her eyes, she saw his attention fixed on the road; yet he looked utterly miserable. Rain speckled the windshield, then increased, as if mocking her tears. Quentin switched on the wipers; for a time she lost herself in the back-and-forth motion, but then the tears came again.

"Lady . . . ," came Quentin's voice, but she shook her head angrily, dismissing him from the core of her terrors. She huddled on the seat, her head in her hands, feeling bereft, until her misery condensed in a hard dark lump at the center of her thoughts and she wept again, silently, wishing her tears could be pure acid and etch through her flesh down to the bone. Such anguish cannot sustain itself indefinitely; after a time, it ebbed somewhat. Christine blinked her sight clear and leaned shakily back.

The rain had stopped; the sun was shining gently in a sky full of cottony clouds. The road wound among shallow valleys and low hills crowned with majestic trees. The view was straight out of a postcard; all that was missing was a flock of sheep or a picturesque ruined church.

"Are we close to Chrysanthe now?" she made herself ask.

"Closer than we were, but still a great distance away, milady."

"What if . . . what if I don't want to go? What if I told you 'Let me off, now'?"

Quentin slowed the car, brought it to a full stop, its engine purring. He turned in his seat and looked at her intently. "My lady," he said, "I have been looking for you for the past nine years. When I set out I was a boy; now I am a man. I swore to bring you back or die in the attempt." She cringed back at this, expecting him to grow furious and scream or strike her. But he was not losing his temper. "I want you to come back with me to Chrysanthe; it is your proper place, and your destiny. But I will not take you there against your will. I urge you, I beg you, to let me take you there. I admit I am not the flawless knight I wish I were; I understand this form of travel is troubling to you, and that you may feel I have not proven I am fully worthy of your confidence. I assure you I do not intend to repeat the same mistake I made last night. I will make sure to protect you at all turns; and any lack you see, you need only inform me of, and I will remedy it."

His face was undone by sadness. "However, if it is your decision not to go, I will respect it. I will take you anywhere you choose. If you wish to return to the world where you were imprisoned, I will direct my mount thither. Or anywhere you bid me go. In a made world, possibilities are limitless."

There was a pause as she wrestled with his words. "If I open the door and leave here, now . . . ?" she said. "If I tell you to leave me here, go away, never come back, would you do it?"

"If you bade me so, I would."

"And after I went away, what would you do?"

"I would very carefully mark this position, then complete my journey alone. Once in Chrysanthe, I would inform Orion and the king of your whereabouts, and let them decide what to do."

"And if I told you not to report anything, not to let anyone know—would you?"

He closed his eyes, shook his head. "No; I would not. I will leave you alone here if it is your wish, but I will not keep your location hidden. It would be wrong."

She nodded, at once disappointed and reassured that Quentin had his limits, that he was not going to obey her every whim blindly. "I want to stretch my legs," she said, unbuckled her seat belt and opened the door of the car. She levered herself out, took several steps away from the vehicle. The grass by the side of the road was impossibly lush, emerald green, dotted with delicate pale-yellow flowers. The wind was warm and caressing; the whole landscape felt strangely new, as if it had just been built, yet the weathered hills spoke of millennia of erosion. Somewhere over the horizon might be a city whose name she had never heard, filled with strangers dressed in extravagant clothes; they would welcome her, let her make a new life for herself. Christine Matlin, from another world, who had never managed to figure out what she wanted to be in the one she had called her own. She saw herself suddenly as her old Jessica, stuffed away in a drawer, forgotten, as if she had never existed. Once this would have been what she wanted.

Quentin still sat in the car, looking at her, awaiting her decision. She went back to it, resumed her seat.

"All right," she said with a trembling bravado. "Let's get going."

Her stomach growled loudly, spoiling whatever trace of panache her words could have held. ". . . And maybe we can stop for breakfast somewhere," she finished.

&. Through the impossibly green countryside they drove for hours, and very little seemed to change—save when Christine gazed at the horizon, where mountains rose and fell as if they were lumps of dough squeezed by a child's hands. Then the road grew more curved and they began to descend from a high plateau down to a semi-desert plain. They had met no traffic so far today but now began to encounter other cars, all going uphill; lumbering, ugly vehicles belching blackish exhaust fumes, most of them packed tightly with two adults and three or four children.

"Why are they all going up the mountain?" wondered Christine, munching on a pastry Quentin had purchased at a traveling cantina, hours ago and worlds away.

"We would have to stop and ask them," replied the knight. "Maybe they are all 'vacationsing' there—that is how your dialect puts it, is it not?"

"I suppose the mountain is nicer than where they're coming from," she said, looking through the windshield at the plains land two thousand feet below. "Do you . . . Well, does it have to be so drab and sad down there? Could you, maybe, make it nicer?"

"Well, yes, but it would be more work. I try to follow the path of least resistance. Once we are down into the plain, I can find a superhighway and get us moving really fast. But if you really want me to shift to nicer countryside, it is not that big an effort."

"No, that's all right. I mean, I wouldn't want you to get lost on the way back. You passed this way coming, didn't you?"

"Ah, no. I did not come by this precise route. There are too many dimensions in the made world; it is far worse than trying to find one's exact way through a forest. Imagine trying to retrace your steps when you have been flying, through a forest in the air, laced with a thousand different paths at every step. . . . I do know where we are, overall. But the exact worlds we travel through on this leg of the journey are in many ways quite different from those I passed through as I went downward."

They were reaching the bottom of the vast cliff they had been descending; Christine, on an impulse, rolled down her window and stuck out her head, looking back at the towering plateau, their road like a gray thread ascending its slopes, strung with beads that were cars, inching their way up. The sky above the plateau was a different color, turquoise shading into jade green, as if some cool aura played about the summit.

A town had appeared at the foot of the mountain; Quentin found a shopping mall and parked the car as close to the corner of the lot as he could. In a restaurant bright with chromed surfaces, sitting on red plush-covered seats, they ate a meal of sandwiches and mashed potatoes smothered in tangy dressing. Quentin drank two huge cups of coffee; Christine tried a fizzy drink that looked like the Sparkle Pop she was fond of, but left a metallic taste in her mouth.

She rubbed her eyes, glanced at her watch. It contradicted the clocks in the diner, which insisted it was well past noon, while the watch declared ninth hour barely reached. She had slept in the car, in fits and starts, noticing half an hour had passed while the sun appeared still in the same spot in the sky. She was tempted to adjust her watch to agree with the clocks, as she had always done all her life; but it would still have disagreed with the next clocks she encountered. And this way she could keep her bearings from the world she had left.

They exited the restaurant by the doorway that led into the mall; there were two women's clothing stores facing them, and Christine suddenly felt acutely conscious that she had been wearing the same clothes for over a day.

"Quentin . . . I would very much like some more clothes. I can't wear the same things all the time, they'll smell. Do we have time to get something? I'm sorry, I don't have any money to pay for it, but I don't want much, I promise."

Quentin waved a hand dismissively.

"Lady, we can buy whatever you want. The expense is . . . immaterial." And he smiled as if at a private joke.

This was the stuff of daydreams for her; she had often wished she could raid the mall back home and purchase whatever she desired. Yet now that it had become reality, the taste of it soured in her mouth, much like the fizzy drink she had yearned for. If she had had all the time in the world, not been hunted by people and things she could not imagine; if she had had a home to come to afterward . . . No, she must not think of this. She was on an adventure, and must take things as they came. Still, she felt little or no pleasure in going through the garments on their hangers. She soon settled on a blouse and a light sweater, a pair of black pants, and a pair of gray-blue jeans. There was a pretty suede jacket on display, which was the only thing she really wanted, but she could not bring herself to ask Quentin for it. She tried the clothes in the dressing room, decided they fit her well enough—she wasn't about to be difficult. As she came out, Quentin appeared before her, holding the suede jacket on a hanger.

"How about this, milady?" he asked. "You seemed to like it."

She felt herself blush, then a disquieting reminiscence crossed her mind, a story of men recruiting young girls for a prostitution ring by first buying them clothes and shoes, and then telling the girls they owed them. . . . But then, she doubted the pimps had the power to take their charges from world to world. She might fear many things, but Quentin's intentions could not possibly go in that direction.

"It's . . . it must be too expensive," she said, to cover her embarrassment. "What does the price tag say?"

"I cannot read the digits in this world," Quentin replied cheerfully. "Try it on; this should be your size."

It wasn't; Quentin insisted he would get one in a smaller size while Christine protested it was too much trouble. A salesgirl appeared with the jacket in a "young maiden" size, whisked it onto Christine before she knew what was happening, and exclaimed at the good fit. In the end Christine allowed Quentin to purchase it because it was too much trouble to protest.

Neither of the stores, however, carried underwear. Christine and Quentin walked to the department store at the end of the mall, passed between two huge columns of fake marble, and entered the wide, quiet aisles. Christine located the lingerie department and rapidly made her choices. Quentin handed several bills to the cashier, who put the purchases in a store bag. At that moment a woman wearing a discreet uniform came up to them.

"Excuse me, sir, madam. I'm store security. Would you please follow me?"

Quentin had spun about to face her before she'd begun to speak; now he took a step forward, shielding Christine. He darted glances left and right, tensed his muscles; Christine saw his biceps swell beneath the sleeves of his T-shirt and experienced a terrifying premonition of imminent violence.

"What seems to be the problem, madam?" Quentin asked in a mild voice.

"I'd like to speak to you in private, please. This way."

"I am sorry, but we cannot oblige you. My sister and I are on a tight schedule and we must leave now."

The woman took an implement from an inside pocket. The next instant, a knife had buried itself in the hollow of her shoulder. She gasped, dropped the object, and staggered back a step. Quentin slammed his foot in her abdomen and she fell to the floor, winded.

Christine was not aware she had screamed. She saw customers and sales staff staring at them. Quentin had picked up the woman's implement: It was merely a self-contained telephone handset, with lighted plastic buttons bearing unreadable numbers. A red bulb set above the push buttons was blinking very fast. Quentin threw it away, grabbed the bags with their purchases, and put an arm around Christine's shoulders.

"Walk fast, Lady, and be ready to run when I tell you."

They stalked out of the store, began trotting as they approached the fake columns at the entrance. Shouts had been rising behind them and men and women in store uniforms were rushing over. "Run, run!" shouted Quentin, and Christine freed herself from his grasp and ran all-out. They exited the mall through glass double doors and had to dash across the parking lot to get back to the car.

Christine let herself tumble into her seat; Quentin ordered her to close the door on her side and she obeyed numbly. The engine roared to life and Quentin's red car jolted from its place, spun on a dime, and tore out for the parking's exit and the open road. Through the rear window Christine could see a knot of gesticulating people, hurrying toward them.

Had there been an automatic gate, like those Christine had seen at some malls, they might have been stopped. Then again, she guessed Quentin wouldn't have hesitated to smash through any barrier in his way. As the car turned into the street, they moved *beyond,* and now the mall behind them was quiescent, all the turmoil they had fled gone as a dream fades in the morning light. Again and again they shifted worlds, and the buildings about them were and suddenly were not. Christine closed her eyes, dizzied by the abrupt changes. The car stopped; Christine opened her eyes, saw that the traffic had halted at an intersection. Quentin was breathing heavily, sweat beading on his brow. He glanced at her, and his tense expression softened with a dash of ruefulness.

"I am sorry, Lady Christine. That must have been frightening for you."

Christine looked down at her hands. "I . . . You must know what you're doing. But that was just a phone she had."

"It might have been anything; especially a weapon. And she had absolutely no business apprehending us. I could not afford the risk."

With a clang, the traffic signs rotated and now displayed *GO* for their lanes. Quentin got the car in motion once more. Christine looked at him again. "I guess you're right. . . . Are you okay? You're sweating terribly."

Quentin wiped his forehead with the back of his hand, glanced at it with an expression of mild surprise.

"I feel fine," he said. "Just . . . very tense, I suppose. All my instincts were screaming at that woman. And with good reason, I might add. You failed to see what else she had on her. Look at the backseat, milady. The folded sheet of paper, next to the plastic bags."

Christine twisted about in her seat, reached for the two bags of clothes Quentin had carried throughout their flight and thrown onto the backseat. She finally found the piece of paper, lying on the floor. She brought it forward onto her lap and unfolded it. She stared at it for a long time, chilled.

It was not the language that disturbed her, though its tone rang false, as if the text had been written by someone who did not truly understand the vocabulary or the grammar of the tongue he used. It was the photograph—slightly blurred, coarsely half-toned, yet unmistakable. She and Quentin, standing together on the seashore. She was wearing a striped bikini top, he a florid, too-big shirt. He had his arm around her, smiling broadly. The faint scar that marked his forehead was very clear in the picture.

She did not say the obvious, that this could not be them. Quentin must know it as well as she did. Instead she stared mutely at the couple in the photograph, who were desired for interrogation by the authorities and must be localized at the earliest possible convenience. She felt sure somehow that it all had to do with a murder, a murder that lay in the future when that photograph had been taken, but not too far in the future. The couple—for they were truly a couple, they were lovers, she had given herself to him without hesitation that summer, in the cheap motel room they rented—had perhaps already been planning it when someone had snapped the picture, yet they had been unconcernedly happy, they had smiled broadly at the lens, secure in the knowledge that they could not fail. . . .

Christine folded the paper again and carefully put it on the rear seat, forced her gaze to return to the road. She was not sure why she had retreated so deeply into fantasy; perhaps it was too unnerving to look at these analogues of herself and Quentin, and she had to convince herself these were two profoundly different people, as different as could be. . . . The girl in the photograph had looked confident, alive; she was someone it was impossible to ignore. So unlike Christine Matlin as she had been and had wanted to be. Christine found that she desperately wanted to be that young woman in the picture; and at the same time would rather die than become her.

"I'm sorry, Quentin," she said. "This is all my fault. I shouldn't have made us stop so long there."

"Do not say that, milady. Staying in one world for an hour will not necessarily bring disaster on our heads. We were simply unlucky."

"I . . . I don't know. I don't feel that way. I mean, it stands to reason we should be moving all the time. It's when we're stopped that people have a chance to notice us and . . . and try to capture us."

"There is something in what you say," Quentin conceded, "yet we remain vulnerable even while we are moving. If in that world our photograph was being circulated, in others it might be our car's. Someone could identify it and attempt to stop us."

"But aren't you changing worlds all the time? That's what you said before."

"True; but I cannot shift us away from a threat I do not perceive. If a person in one world is seeking a car such as ours, a myriad others in a myriad neighboring worlds are looking for the very same car at the same time."

Christine was silent a while; something in what Quentin had said bothered her. Then, suddenly, she had it. She was not used to thinking of the surrounding world as a mutable thing; but Quentin was, surely. Then why had he behaved, not once but twice, as if they were prisoners of a single reality?

"Quentin . . . you said you couldn't shift away from a threat you didn't know about. But you knew about that woman in the store; couldn't you just have shifted us away from her? And even that first night, in the hotel; you might have done things differently."

Quentin sighed. "Yes," he said after a pause. "Yes I could. But I was not willing to lose the car. If we had gone to another world, it would have meant abandoning it. I could have tried to return to it, but it would have consumed effort and time, and unlike in your case, I would not know with certainty if I had succeeded. . . . Please do not misunderstand, milady: Had our danger increased any further, I would of course have shifted us away. You are infinitely more important than . . ." He gestured all inclusively at the dashboard, seats, and hood. "But a knight can get immensely attached to his mount. It has a claim on me I cannot easily deny."

He wiped his forehead, again smearing sweat on the back of his hand. "Still . . . I might have made an error of judgment, milady. Please believe me, I am doing my best."

Christine started to say she understood; but she broke off as Quentin's expression grew more and more distressed. His eyes grew wide and he took in a sharp breath.

"The coffee," he said. "There was something in the coffee. I have not been feeling quite right ever since we left the restaurant. When we met the security woman, I . . . I panicked. I almost lost control when I fought her; I was like a blind squire bashing at random in the lists . . . I did not want to believe it of myself."

"What do you mean, there was something in the coffee? What thing?"

"Intoxicants in made worlds are dangerous; they can have unforeseen effects on a real man. I thought I noticed a metallic aftertaste, but I was only concerned that I remain wide awake as long as I could . . . I am a fool."

The street suddenly widened and Quentin stopped the car in the rightmost lane, just behind a parked vehicle.

"Quentin, are you sick? What are you doing?" gasped Christine.

"Do not be alarmed, milady. I just need this out of my stomach immediately."

Quentin bolted out of the car, knelt by it, and stabbed two fingers down his throat, making himself throw up. He convulsed once, emptying his stomach on the pavement, then twice more, to bring forth the last dribbles of half-digested food in his belly. Then he reentered the car and leaned back in his seat, panting and coughing. Though he had closed the door immediately, the acid stench of vomit tainted the air.

Christine was frightened by the paleness of his face, bathed in sweat. She pulled paper tissues out of a box and, hesitantly, wiped his forehead dry with a wadded-up ball of paper, then cleaned the corner of his mouth, feeling the faint pressure through the crumpled tissues as something not quite a touch, just this side of safety.

"Thank you, Lady Christine," Quentin gasped, taking the wadded ball from her hand, brushing her fingers with his as he did. "I am feeling much better now. I just need to catch my breath. Then we can get going again."

"Quentin . . . *my* drink tasted like metal a bit, too. Quentin, I'm scared. Have we been poisoned?"

He looked at her, frowning in concern. But his words soothed her fears. "Poison? No, that is beyond belief, milady. If someone other than store security had recognized us, why would they put poison in our drinks, rather than call the constabulary? How many people walk around with vials of toxin ready for pouring? No, there could have been no poison in our drinks. The water used to make the coffee as well as your drink might taste of metal; God has seen how often I have drunk foul-tasting water in my travels. That is a likely explanation. And remember: Someone might want to kill me, but no one could possibly want to harm you."

Christine let pass that last statement as the obvious lie it was; she was in no mood to argue about that. In fact she was in no mood to argue anything, as queasiness rose within her in sickening waves. She opened the door on her side, expecting to vomit in turn; but though her stomach threatened to spew out its contents, the menace failed to materialize. And after some painful minutes, she decided she was not after all going to be sick, though she kept the window rolled down on her side, so she could breathe fresh air—spoiled though it was with the occasional acrid whiff. Quentin got the car into motion. He drove at modest speed for half an hour, at the end of which Christine felt her stomach had settled. On his part, he had ceased sweating and declared himself fit once more.

They increased their speed slowly, and left the vast suburban sprawl they had been traveling through. Now the road wound its way through scrublands, with always the hint of buildings ahead, which never grew any nearer. Christine fell into a doze once more, swam out of it when they paused at a gas station. She brought the bags of clothes with her when she went to the bathroom and changed into her purchases. It had been growing cool and she put on the suede jacket; she smiled despite herself at the feel of it. A jacket was the most comforting of clothes; she had always felt somehow armored when she wore a jacket, with its many pockets where the essentials of life could be stored against need.

Quentin was waiting for her close by the bathroom door; she was growing used to this caution on his part, and she was in no position to argue it was unneeded. They returned to the car, got on the road again. They stopped for a meal some hours later. Both of them were nervous. Quentin insisted on tasting the water first, and neither of them drank anything else. Afterward, he took a brief nap in the car, sleeping while still wearing his seat belt. It was late afternoon by the sun, thirteenth hour by her watch. A brief, warm shower wet the pavement, letting the smell of damp cement rise afterward.

They drove on, through a region of rains; the beat of the wipers across the windshield like a listless drummer keeping time to a song long since ended. Christine stared at the passing scenery. Once she glimpsed figures of horror by the roadside: naked men, their flesh darkened by exposure, tied to wooden frames, their limbs set at grotesque angles. But in a blink they were gone. Quentin had not noticed them; for her part, she tried to forget them—how was she to say they had not been something else altogether, that she was not mistaken? Yet she felt certain her brief glimpse had been accurate; and she reflected for a while on the ramifications of an infinite series of worlds.

The light grew worse; Quentin muttered an annoyed curse. "I cannot get us away from this damned rain," he said. "It seems to be everywhere; I cannot impel the car fast enough to outrun it."

"Is something wrong?"

"No . . . It is the state of this region of Errefern at present. To escape this rain I would need to be a mage born and trained. I lack the craft to fight against the made world in this way. We just have to ride this through. Or sleep it out. I am for stopping and resting."

Christine said nothing. She feared stopping for more than a few minutes; yet Quentin could not drive indefinitely. Sooner or later, they would have to find a place to sleep.

He led them to a small town that boasted three incongruous office towers: apparently the satellite of a great metropolis whose skyscrapers might be dimly glimpsed at the horizon, glowing through the curtains of rain. Old-fashioned wooden houses, boxlike structures with red trim and peaked roofs, gave way abruptly to a modern complex of glass and cement. In the middle of the complex was a hotel. Quentin was able to park the car in an underground garage, in a spot very close to the exit gate.

He procured them a suite on the ground floor. This time, without comment, he slid a chest of drawers out of his room and laid it against the door of the suite. He dropped a blanket and pillow on the floor at the foot of Christine's door, and bade her good night.

It took her forever to get to sleep; she lay in bed, listening to the ticking of the clock on the nightstand, the gurgle of water from a room upstairs. Quentin had looked annoyed that all three rooms had windows. He had warned her to call for him should she hear anything out of the ordinary. Now she found herself opening her eyes, staring at the rim of light leaking from around the closed drapes. She rose from bed, drew the curtain back slightly and peeked out. There was nothing to be seen but the rain and the bluish glow of the streetlights. She returned to the bed but still could not rest. She pulled the nightstand drawer open, found the Byblos she had expected. In the near darkness she opened the book, and was astonished to see the pages shedding their own light, the green glow of phosphorescence on which the inked-in letters were gaps of pitch blackness.

This was no Byblos like the one she knew. She read at random, expecting something wonderful, or terrifying. But she found nothing of the sort; rather, lists of descent, recountings of meaningless deeds, exhortations to virtue. There were no mentions of God that she could find. Already the pages were losing their glow—but how could they have stored it, when the closed book had lain in a shut drawer for hours, if not days?—and she was finding it harder and harder to decipher the lines of tiny script. She put the book on the nightstand and at long last slept.

It was morning; Quentin woke her with a knock on her door, and she started, but there was no cause for alarm. She had washed summarily before going to bed; she took a hot shower now, changed underclothes. After Quentin had washed in turn, he pushed the chest of drawers away from the door and they went to breakfast. There was orange juice, which she could not resist, though she waited tacitly for Quentin to taste his first. They refused the waiter's offer of coffee.

They came out of the hotel and returned to the highway without a hitch. Christine allowed herself to relax at last. Quentin's face was no longer lined with fatigue and he offered her a smile, which grew wider as the sun peeked out of the clouds. As Quentin drove, the cloud cover dissipated swiftly and the land became bathed in sunlight. The highway, which had been winding lazily between small wooded hills, now grew straighter and wider, with three, four, five lanes of traffic. The land around them became utterly flat, featureless, barely vegetated. Quentin floored the accelerator and the red sports car increased its speed, comfortably settled in the leftmost lane, with no other vehicles to hinder its swift flight.

Quentin relaxed his shoulders, drew a deep, delighted breath.

"We are well on our way, milady. The shade of the sky is close to what we need, and soon I will be able to get rid of the moon—sorry as I shall be to see it go, still its disappearance is a major signpost. We are nearly out of the peninsula where you lived. There are some very strange worlds ahead of us still, but this road should lead us through them with minimal disturbance."

And so they drove on, stopping only for the briefest of pauses: food and drink and relief. Christine dozed on and off, heedless now of what her watch said, aware that Quentin kept the sun's progress to a minimum, trying to cover as much ground as he could at once, now that traveling conditions were optimal.

"There is no radio in your car," she remarked, aware suddenly that there ought to be music to accompany the drive.

Quentin laughed. "So sorry, milady. It was hard enough getting the wheels and the suspension; evolving a radio was beyond my power. Besides, even if I had one, even if there were broadcasts it could receive, they would change every time we shifted worlds. If it is music you wish, I can sing."

Quentin turned out to have a mediocre voice, but he sang with gusto; he offered her a succession of folk tunes whose melodies seemed both familiar and strange to Christine. For a few hours she found herself amazingly comfortable, joyous even, hugging her jacket to herself, breathing in the pure air that came in through the quarter-open window, listening to the knight of Chrysanthe belt out tunes he had learned as a child, in the world that lay beyond all others, where she herself belonged and to which they were bound.

2. The Munken

The streets were paved with asphalt here, but the sidewalks were nail-studded iron. Palm trees grew along the boulevards where elegant steam-powered cars rolled, and legless beggars sat in ceramic pots so as not to shock people's sensibilities.

Mathellin's mount was dying. Bloody foam dripped from its mouth, and its legs trembled at every step. It had borne him swiftly from world to world, but Christine's lead had only increased, until any reasonable man would have conceded defeat. But Mathellin was not a reasonable man, and he still had a trick up his sleeve.

A five-story building rose in front of him and shimmered slightly as he reached the exact aspect he had been seeking. He halted his mount, vaulted off its back. The horse fell to its knees, saddle buckles jangling. Mathellin spared it one backward glance, then hurried into the lobby. As he passed through the revolving door he heard the beast scream, but already he had entered the green coolness of the lobby, where twin cascades of water frothed at the foot of living palms, framing a large desk at which stood a thin young man, making entries in a register.

"Sir? Are you sure you've come to the right address?" the clerk asked, looking distastefully at Mathellin. "This is a Merionist residence; only members of the Order may lodge here. Is that . . . animal yours? You'll have to—"

"Sybaris," Mathellin said, the proper code word for this place.

"I'm afraid I don't understand, sir," the clerk replied, wrinkling his nose and looking down at Mathellin from his near seven-foot height. For a moment Mathellin feared he had gotten to the wrong place; anger bloomed in him and he grabbed the clerk by the lapels of his jacket.

"I said 'sybaris,' man. Either you know what it means and you act upon it, or I shall kill here and now."

The clerk opened his eyes wide. "Ma—Master?" he gasped.

"The room, you bloody fool, and now!"

Mathellin let him go. The young man groped for a key at the rear of a pigeon-hole, then led him along a corridor and up a flight of orange-carpeted stairs. Mathellin took the key from the clerk. "Tell the others I am here," he snarled. "But let no one disturb me, or people will die. Understood? Now leave me alone!"

The young man fled, tripping and almost falling down the stairs in his precipitation. Mathellin opened the door at the top of the stairs, entered the room.

It looked like every other bedroom the club provided for its members who needed hospitality, but its furnishings were of a different order. Mathellin had woven a knot of magic here, part of the web that pervaded the made world. There was an opticon facing the bed: a cube with a large screen and an opening for slides. Mathellin ignited its lamp, which burned with a crackling purple-white glare and a stench of sulfur. He pulled a drawer open, chose a slide; it was featureless black. He pushed it inside the opticon through the slit, and an image melted into being on the screen.

He saw a map of Errefern again. The fugitives' course burned like a thread of green fire among clouds of lead and blood. Ahead of it shone glimmers indicating outposts; one of them was close enough to the path that something could be attempted.

In a way, this was much easier than spying on Christine and her rescuer; sympathy resonance with one's own substance was a simple matter. Worlds away, there lay a city of people who obeyed him blindly. Had he reached them, he could have raised an army to capture Christine. But he was still much too far. There remained a few individual agents, things less than men but more than beasts, which his magic could summon and control. Mathellin took another slide from the drawer, shoved it into the slot next to the first, then sat down, cross-legged, in front of the screen. A new image bloomed upon it, colors eerily glowing on a black field. Mathellin's vision began to grow dim at the edges, until he looked down a tunnel to the image that burned on the screen.

His power reached out through the worlds. The messenger he had sent out had passed through that place and awakened its denizens to his needs, else Mathellin's efforts would have been for naught. But now the creature in the tank was awake, quivering with impatience. Across distances that could not be truly measured, the wizard felt his mind catch it like a fish on a hook. An involuntary cry escaped him. His eyes rolled back into their sockets and his body grew rigid.

He saw through the munken's eyes now, his vision blurred and monochrome. Arms reached out to the rim of the tank and pulled the munken out. It called out in its child's voice, but the words were Mathellin's, his thoughts transmitted from a remote place through the link he had forged himself.

"Help me," the munken gasped. "Take me where I direct."

The attendant on duty was a pale young man with watery eyes. Without question or protest, he cradled the munken's obscene bulk in his arms and began walking toward the door.

"Quickly," Mathellin thought-spoke at him. Superimposed over what the munken saw, he perceived Christine's trajectory. He wished it could have been a perfectly straight line. It was nothing of the sort—and yet, for all the imprecisions and degrees of freedom the made world's infinity allowed, the trajectory did have a clear orientation. All made worlds had a geography of their own, which transcended the usual three dimensions in much the same way that a mountain range transcends a single line tracing its peaks. Unless Christine's rescuer were determined to follow a perversely difficult path, whatever route they chose would pass by this place within a few hours.

The munken twisted in the young man's arms, sank its hand into his chest. The young man hiccupped and staggered, but continued to walk. Mathellin made him stop, then hop in place. The bond held.

He sent more and more of himself through the link; back in the hostel room, his body's pulse slowed, its flesh cooled. Mathellin's consciousness of his true flesh grew dangerously thin. The munken flowed inside the young man, melded its substance with his. To a born shapechanger, there was little that was disconcerting in the process. Mathellin spread himself out within the young man's body, like a courtier might put on a new suit of clothes. There was a moment of vertigo, then his senses merged with the human body's. He saw colors again, heard a full range of sounds. He could feel a heart pounding in his chest, beating ten times for every time his own heart beat, in that silent room so far away.

&ce; Christine jerked awake. The sun—a dark orange sun, looking like some spoiled exotic fruit—was staining the inside of the car with tawny light. Her gaze went to Quentin, whose face looked curiously slack in the light.

"Where are we now, Quentin?" she asked. There was no answer; she repeated her question. Still no sound from the young knight. Why would he ignore her? "Quentin? Quentin!" She shook his arm; he shuddered, and feeling flooded back in his face.

"I—Lady Christine, I— What we were talking about?"

"I've been asleep, I just woke up! I was asleep for . . . over two hours! Quentin, something's wrong with you!"

Quentin passed a hand over his face.

"I have no memory of those two hours," he said. "It seems to me you just went to sleep—but I trust your wrist-clock."

"What's going on? Is it some spell? What should we do?"

Quentin sighed and half smiled. "Fear not, milady," he said, "it is not a spell, or at least not a magic spell. This is a condition that strikes people who drive for long distances, especially on featureless roads—and this highway is as featureless as I could make it. I have had it happen to me a few times before. Once I woke up from such a trance with no recollection of the past two hundred leagues I had traveled."

"Are you awake now? Really awake?"

Quentin chuckled halfheartedly. "Yes. But this is a sign that I really should rest. We have been riding hard. A few hours of sleep will not put us in danger."

"Yeah, and I'd rather take my chances that way than have you fall asleep at the wheel," said Christine, still concerned about Quentin's mental state. "Do you want to pull over and rest for a bit?"

Quentin glanced at the dashboard. "Actually, I would as lief find a combination refueling post and hostel."

"You mean a gas station and a motel?"

"Depending upon what I can achieve in this region of Errcfern. We have made great progress toward the true realm and no world will look too much like the one you knew. Still, let us aim for something at least somewhat familiar to you. . . ."

The five-lane road still plowed a perfect straight line through a flat landscape; but now signs became visible, announcing a turnoff. Quentin decreased speed, shifted lanes. A minute later, they took the turnoff into a land of low wooded hills, soon found themselves in a quiet little town. Quentin located what he had been seeking for: A large rotating sign, made of wood rather than the neon-lighted plastic Christine had expected, depicted a green shield on which the letters "RP" were blazoned in white. At its foot were a cluster of awkward-looking pumps and fifty feet away stood a two-storied motel, the same logo displayed at the entrance to its office.

Quentin stopped the car at the pumps and let out a painful sigh as he removed his hands from the wheel. "I am more tired than I thought. I believe I should risk three hours rather than two."

Christine shrugged. "We could sleep for the night here, if you want."

"Mmh. Not here; this is certainly not what I would choose for spending the whole night."

The attendant walked out of the office. He was a man in late middle age, short and squat. "Thank you for choosing Ruritanian Petrols," he said automatically to Quentin through the lowered window.

"I would like the tank topped up, please. Also, there are three empty petrol jugs in the trunk. Could you fill those up as well?"

The attendant's expression grew slack, as if Quentin's request had bewildered him. He scratched his head for a moment. Then, much more slowly than he had spoken his standard greeting, he said, "S'against the law, sir. I can't just fill any container, it has to be . . . a legal container, sort of." He paused, then went on at a faster pace, as if his mind had caught up to his thoughts: "But we sell legal and proper containers, sir. So I can still sell you petrol, but you'll have to pay for the jerricans as well."

Quentin frowned for a moment, then shrugged. "Have a look at the containers I have. If they are not legal, sell me some that are."

Quentin opened the trunk and got out of the car. The attendant met him at the rear. He took one look at the jugs and shook his head. "Nah, sir, these won't do. I can't sell you petrol in these."

"All right, then get me three jerricans of the same capacity."

"They cost fifteen rupiah each, sir."

"Not a problem," said Quentin in an annoyed tone, taking a large, colorful banknote from his wallet. The attendant nodded and set out for the office. While he was gone, Quentin tried to work the pump himself but couldn't, and he had to wait for the man to return, carrying three tin containers stamped with the RP logo. He filled these first, set each in the trunk with a thud. Then he topped up the car's tank, named a total price, and laboriously counted out Quentin's change, twice.

The young knight got back into the car looking exasperated. "Ready to move on?" he asked Christine.

"I thought you needed to rest!"

"If I have to deal with this man again, we will be here all day adding up the totals. . . ." Quentin paused, screwed up his face; his upper body swayed slightly. "You are right. I must rest. It is not as if it were real money I am spending, at any rate."

Quentin got back out of the car, squared his shoulders, entered the office, and came out having rented room six for the day. He drove the car into the parking lot, then he and Christine walked along the row of units to the door marked "VI," whose lock protested but finally yielded to their key. There was a smell of damp fabric and stale cigarette smoke in the room, but, for all the shabbiness of the curtains and the faded prints on the walls, it felt bitterly homey to Christine.

And yet there was no television set in the room, only a huge, ungainly radio that should have been half a century old, but appeared brand-new. And a cardboard notice was taped on top of it, warning patrons that *It is illegale to operate wireless receptours in this establishment after nine post meridian.*

Quentin had stretched out on one of the beds. "Please wake me if you need to go out, milady. At any rate, wake me in three hours. We should get going again as soon as is reasonable."

Christine nodded in agreement; she started to ask him a question, then stopped. Quentin had dropped to sleep instantly; his mouth was half-open, and his eyes moving behind closed lids. Christine looked at her wrist to check the time, noticing that there was no clock in the room—no, there was one integrated with the radio set's dial. Christine went to the huge set, turned it on, setting the volume at its lowest so as not to disturb Quentin, and worked the frequency knob, hunting for stations. What she found bewildered her: shapeless music, full of drones and plucked strings in unfamiliar scales; what might have been political speeches referring to events she could not fathom; three different stations devoted to broadcasting the same governmental educational program about civil defense, fire safety, and homemade meteorological stations. Once, in the wasteland of dead air between stations she thought to catch voices amidst the static. One said, "She has gone—" and another one, metallic and inflectionless, replied, "But I see her." The voices vanished; Christine spun the dial backward then forward in diminishing increments, trying to find the voices again. Despite all her efforts, she failed. She looked toward Quentin, who was snoring on the bed. Should she wake him? To tell him what? That she had heard voices on the radio that might be referring to her? Anything was possible in a made world, he had said, and she had to believe him. But somehow it seemed ridiculous that magicians would speak to each other on the radio, rather than using some spell.

Maybe, though, this was an explanation of sorts. Maybe magic spells were really some form of electromagnetic influence, a use of the physical laws of the world. Reality was more complex than she had ever believed in her life, but this didn't entail it had to be meaningless. There was a cartoon show she had watched avidly, all twenty-five weekly episodes of it, through three complete consecutive runs, until she knew every line and plot twist by heart. It was called *The Cosmic Patrol* and featured a crew of brave explorers in a starship that roamed the galaxy. In one of her favorite episodes, the HSS *Constantinople* encountered a hostile alien race that cast it into a parallel world from which it seemed impossible to return. Commander Seldar had used his powers of reasoning and his crew's superhuman competence to deduce just how the alien device had functioned, and to alter the ship's mirror-matter drive to open a portal back to their home universe. She had always wished she could be like Commander Seldar one day, and solve problems as he did, with the powers of logic and thought. This world that Quentin had thrust her in must be intelligible. She had to understand it; it must be ruled by laws that needed to be figured out.

She found the voices again. The metallic one had just finished saying something. Then the other one answered. It said, "Chocolate cake." Then there was only static. Christine shook her head. There had never been any voices. She was finding phantom patterns in noise, like when she heard the telephone ringing over the sound of the shower. She shut off the antique-but-new radio set and went to sit on the other bed, parting the curtain from the window and looking through the slit at the passing cars and people.

For nearly two hours Mathellin had been issuing orders, deploying forces as best he could. The resonance spell was still active, and he could sense his quarry approaching, getting very close. The general trend of the path the young knight chose through the made world was clear, but the details were hard to predict. Mathellin was aware that the task was almost futile; that did not prevent him from attempting everything he could. As he spoke to a messenger in his improvised head-quarters, an iron clock clanged once; he stopped in midsentence, focused his attention on his true body, willing its heart to beat strongly, twice. Then he returned to the munken-possessed man's body, resumed giving orders. His lieutenant, a graying man with four teeth growing from his forehead, saluted and left. Mathellin leaned back in his chair, idle for a moment while he awaited reports. He reflexively checked on the location of Christine, and saw that she had stopped moving. He focused on her carefully: She was definitely remaining in the same world, essentially motion-less. And she was less than fifteen leagues away. Mathellin hesitated for a minute; he would not allow himself another mistake, should the girl and her rescuer begin moving again. But they had truly stopped; they must be resting. He would have checked this with his crystal, but it was back in the hostel room, worlds away.

So be it. He strode out of the makeshift war room. His forces had orders and would do their best to intercept the fugitives; he himself was going to take the fight to them directly. He went down a flight of stairs, emerged from the bottom into a valley floor, where a carriage drawn by four huge hounds awaited him. He clam-bered aboard, whipped at the curs, sending the conveyance rattling along a small stream that gradually grew into a wide river. It developed curves, the odd bridge here and there. Houses sprouted all around him, then tall towers. A six-foot-tall rat emerged from an ale house, chittering and clutching something shiny to its chest with its upper limbs. Mathellin lashed his team, and it was a tall ruffian who fled the inn, pursued by a half-drunken mob. Across a bridge, the houses were shorter and wider, the streets packed earth dusted with crushed quartz. He was getting near.

All this while he held the presence of Christine close to the surface of his mind; the combined exertion of spellcraft and supernatural travel dizzied him, but he steeled his will and brought himself to an even greater peak of function.

Closer still; he had the shape of the town right, the hue of the sky, the lay of the surrounding hills . . . Christine's true location blazed too bright in his mind's eye and he could not orient himself from it anymore. He halted his team, which had been going at a slow walk as he crisscrossed the ever-changing streets of the town. He jumped down from the carriage; for an instant the way his limbs landed on the ground felt horribly wrong. He closed his eyes, regained consciousness of his true body, held its proper shape clear in his mind, compelled its blood to flow, its lungs to breathe. If he forgot himself entirely he would die. He felt a pulse of terror as the intellectual realization decanted from the abstract into the real.

When he was reassured no lasting harm had been done, he stepped down the street. Behind him, the carriage and its canine team ceased to be. There should be a building to his right, should there not? Yes, this was better. Add a bridge over the river bend and lengthen that park. . . . No, backtrack. Biting his lip in frustration, Mathellin wandered back and forth between worlds for nearly half an hour, ever missing his quarry.

And then he had it. The resonance with Christine became searingly intense. This was the right world. He walked for less than a minute before he located the hostelry where she and the young man were staying. He sat himself on a bench, reminded his true body it still lived, and pondered his course of action.

Direct attack was possible, but unattractive. His powers were available to him even as he inhabited this man; he verified this, growing a set of claws on his fingers and shrinking them back into nails. But he was already exhausted, and he disliked physical combat even when he was at his peak. What he wanted was to attack when it was least expected. He rose, passed in front of the hostelry, glancing idly at the façade. One curtain was pulled back from the edge of the window and he glimpsed what had to be Christine's face behind the glass. His heart pounded and he nearly forgot his resolution; he could smash through the wall, grab the girl, and flee worlds away in a heartbeat. . . . But deliberate neglect of Christine's well-being counted as intent to harm: one drop of blood, one bruise, would mean disaster.

In the parking lot he found their car, saluted it mentally like the lesser brother to him that it was. Acting quickly, he cupped his hands in front of his belly, then withdrew himself from the young man's body and emerged. Condensed once more within the munken, Mathellin dropped into the arms meant to receive him. His own will restored to him, the man gazed at the munken he cradled, in mingled terror and ecstasy. Mathellin twisted in the young man's grasp, reached out to the car, and gripped its flank with the munken's long fingers. He felt the car shudder beneath its metal skin; his fingers sank in, his substance began the merging, not resisted but in fact helped by the spell laid therein. He twisted his head to look back at his former bearer. "Once I am merged, leave this place at once. If you are stopped and questioned, you know nothing and were just admiring the car. Never return here."

He pushed with his tail, sank in completely, fused his body with the car. His perceptions altered radically; his hearing remained adequate, but his sight was weirdly distorted, monocular and lacking in contrast. It took him a long moment to understand what acted as his eyes—not the headlights as he'd thought, but the windshield. He had never tried to be a machine; as the munken's substance commingled with the car's, he experienced serious discomfort. His organs mapped oddly to the motor, while his limbs stretched and distorted to correspond to the shafts and axles of the wheels. Yet he felt confident this metal flesh, no matter its strangeness, would obey his will. The car's mind was dormant, not aware that its body had been invaded. Mathellin would not yet attempt to gain full control; it was already bad enough having to maintain his true body without risking drowning his sense of identity into that of a mechanism. For the moment, he could rest. The advantage would be his when the time came to act.

❧ The three hours passed slowly; eventually Christine went to wake Quentin, who bounced up as soon as her hand touched him, fully alert.

"Yes, milady?"

She held her hand over her chest, pressing it against her thudding heart. "Damn it, Quentin, were you pretending to sleep? How can anyone wake up this fast?"

"I trained for years to achieve this, milady. One does not get to be a knight of Chrysanthe easily."

"I guess not. Anyway, your three hours are up. Are you rested?"

"I am much better. Let us go."

The sun was halfway up the sky; traffic on the town streets had increased from nonexistent to sparse. Quentin found a way back to the main road; as he did so, Christine watched the town behind them vanish like a dream. She could not see anything actually fade; even when she fixed her awareness on a particular building, it remained fully visible until suddenly she realized she was no longer seeing it, but had missed the moment of its vanishing. It was like Quentin's road trance: returning to consciousness with only the dimmest memory of the times one had lived through. . . .

The car slipped gears as Quentin accelerated; the transmission clashed and ground for a moment, then Quentin shifted back into the proper gear. "Sorry," he said, frowning.

"How much farther?" asked Christine after a moment.

Quentin looked thoughtful a long moment. Then he said, "Perhaps six hundred leagues."

"That's nearly eighteen hundred miles, isn't it?"

"Fairly close to that figure, yes."

"And where are we, now, in this world? We must have crossed half of Septentrional America by now."

"Oh, the continents have changed shape thoroughly from what you knew. If you would like to look at a map, there is a current one in the compartment in front of you. In a brown leather folder, with a little strap."

Christine opened the little door and took out a pair of brown leather wallets. The one she opened contained an oil portrait of her, as precise as if it were a photograph taken this very morning.

"What the hell is that?" she exclaimed, astonished. "Where did you get this, Quentin?"

He glanced at the wallet she was waving at him. "This is your portrait."

"I can see that! But how could *you* have it? Where did you get it?"

"This is fleshpaint, milady. The pigments for this picture were derived from your flesh and blood; the picture updates itself according to your current appearance. All the knights who went off questing after you owned one; we had to know what you looked like, after all."

"So this was made . . ."

"Shortly after your christening. From the blood the priestess drew from your finger."

"But he . . . she . . . couldn't know I would be abducted."

"Oh no. Fleshpaint portraits are a tradition dating back to Felofel, who discovered the spell for it. Since then, the royal line of Chrysanthe have always had such portraits made of them. From the cradle onward, the sovereigns and their heirs are limned in fleshpaint."

"And what happens when a person dies?"

". . . The portrait is burned."

Christine opened the second wallet; it contained a few pages of very thick, stiff paper—perhaps this was parchment. The pages bore a series of maps, going from a local road map to a world map on the last page; the Earth depicted thereupon was unrecognizable, land filling nearly half the globe's surface with seas reaching arms in all directions, in a tormented pattern, as if some immense beast had gouged out wounds from the land at the creation of the world. Christine studied the maps for a while, both fascinated and repelled. Whenever she flipped a page, the map on the next one wasn't exactly as she remembered it. This map also, like the fleshpaint portrait, altered itself to fit the circumstances. What would Commander Seldar have made of it?

She put both wallets back in the glove compartment and leaned back in her seat, closing her eyes. *The world is intelligible,* she told herself. *It may not be easy to accept, but you have to; that's the way it is.*

They drove on, in silence. The wind spoke at Quentin's window, the same meaningless word it endlessly moaned, and Christine felt it lulling her into a doze.

Suddenly, Quentin pushed her against her seat with great force. She opened her eyes wide and gasped as she realized it wasn't Quentin that held her, but a huge, pale hand, as wide across as her own chest, its four knobby fingers curling around her body. It felt as if she could hardly draw breath to scream, but she managed.

Quentin had been gazing at the road intently; in the instant of her scream, his head snapped toward her and his eyes widened in horror. He screamed in turn and shifted lanes instantly, narrowly missing a collision; as the car made its way onto the shoulder, he shifted gears and hit the brakes hard. The car did not slow down measurably. He shifted again, into neutral, and gave the wheel a violent jab, slewing the car at a forty-five degree angle to the road, then reached for the parking brake and pulled up the handle. For several seconds it appeared to Christine that they were going to turn over, or wander back onto the road and get smashed; but in fact the car slid to a halt, still on the shoulder.

The arm that clutched Christine against her seat came from behind her; sick with terror, she craned her head back to see what sort of thing it belonged to, and saw that the hand emerged directly from the backseat. That its pale, finely grained skin in fact melded with the leathcrette of the seat. There came a screech of metal; teeth were growing from the roof, around the windows, like steel icicles. The floor beneath her feet was flowing and reshaping.

Quentin had grasped the arm and was trying to pull it away from her, to no avail. He glanced at the transformations and his lips drew back from his teeth in a grimace of fury.

"Quentin, for God's sake, help me!" Christine pushed at the hand, beat at it with her fists; it merely tightened its grip. Yet it didn't hurt her; it felt almost as if she was being cuddled, cradled against the bosom of an overcareful ogreish nanny.

The door on Quentin's side flowed into a mouth shape and snapped at him. Quentin slammed at the handle with his foot and the door flew open. He was still wearing his seat belt; but his hand held a wide-bladed knife and slashed twice, freeing him. He jumped out, rolled to his feet on the gravel.

Christine saw him raise his hands to the sky, and he shifted in turn. No longer clad in T-shirt and jeans, he was now armored, head to foot, in shining, black-chased metal. On his breast, the leaping fish of his T-shirt was preserved as an enameled design. A massive sword was strapped at his side. He drew it from its scabbard with a fluid motion and ran back toward the car.

The entire vehicle convulsed around Christine, reshaping itself like wet dough squeezed between the fingers; her seat curled over her protectively, as if to save her discomfort during the car's violent transformation.

The car reared up, its front curled downward; through the windshield Christine saw Quentin rush at the car and stab at it with his sword. The car screamed, like a twisted parody of a horn blast, ending with a throaty rattle. The right front wing melted, reshaped itself, like a rope dragged through treacle, into a spiked limb, and the vehicle swung at Quentin. The knight blocked the thrust with his sword; sparks jetted from the collision.

The car lunged at Quentin, who dodged nimbly out of the way, then struck with tremendous force; Christine saw the point of his sword pass through the side panels, scoring a deep gash in the metal. The car screamed again—its voice more organic now—and twisted in place. The roar of its engine waxed and waned, pulsing. Her seat still cradled Christine, and the ogre's hand kept a secure hold of her. She had been less comfortable in a kiddie roller coaster than this.

The car snapped at Quentin, catching him at the shoulder; but the knight's armor held. One thrust of his sword smashed the left headlight. The car reared up at this; Christine saw sky through the windshield; Quentin struck again, at the exposed floor, and barely rolled in time from beneath the car as it fell down on the ground, trying to crush him.

Next instant he bounded up on top of the hood; his gaze swept across her, but she had the feeling he wasn't seeing her at all. He swung at the windshield. The sword impacted with a ringing sound; the glass cracked but did not break, obscuring Christine's vision. The car bucked, still screaming, and Quentin was thrown off. Christine pounded the monstrous hand as hard as she could, kicked at the floor, twisted in her seat, all to no avail.

The car lunged at Quentin, and again he evaded it. Clashes of his sword against steel jetted more sparks. The car's shape still flowed like mud; its sides were rounding, it was twisting visibly from side to side, resembling more and more some sort of serpent. The dashboard's illuminated dials had gothic-style numbers by now, bone-white indicators swinging chaotically back and forth.

"Let me go!" screamed Christine, desperate. "Let me go, damn you!" The hand only tightened its hold on her in response. Every crack in the windshield had gone bright red, a lattice of blood overlaying her view of the world.

Quentin scored another hit and the car bellowed brassily, twisting about as if in agony; a smell of heated metal filled the interior; the engine's rumble had become a massive heartbeat; Christine's seat cupped around her, threatening to seal itself up completely, enclose her like a leatherette egg.

"Let me go, you're hurting me!" she shouted.

The car convulsed violently; the door on her right popped open, her seat melted away, the belt snapped. The huge hand thrust her outside, deposited her in the grass by the roadside.

And Quentin struck the deathblow. Standing just below the transformed car, he thrust his sword deep into its body and stopped its heart. The machine shuddered, bent back, extending a half-dozen limbs of every description as if to tear Quentin apart—then fell over on its side. A fountain of steaming fluid gushed from the wound; the car screamed one last time, a sound to burst the eardrums, which choked off into a prolonged hiss. At long last it was still, its elongated, segmented body drenched in viscous oil. The arched hood at the forward end had dug a shallow pit in the ground in its dying throes; most of its teeth were snapped off at the base. The feet with their cracked black soles had gone limp, the chromed claws were tarnished and scored.

"Milady!" Quentin had rushed to Christine's side. "Are you injured?"

"Not . . . not a scratch," Christine heard herself saying. The ground was littered with fragments of metal, broken-off gears, smashed glass. Traffic was still going by on one lane of the roadway, cars first slowing down as they approached, then speeding away.

Something was wrong. She felt no heat from the wreckage, yet Christine saw it blurring and wavering, as if burning hot air were rising from it. It was altering, changing shape again. Every fragment was doing the same. She took a step back, afraid it was alive still and about to attack once more.

It shrank visibly as she watched, the air fluttering above it as if an inferno raged there. The machine oil that spattered the ground turned to blood, the smashed gears were entrails; and the body of what had been their mutated car disclosed itself as that of some hideous hybrid, in which she recognized the hooved legs and maned neck of a horse, mixed with something else into an obscene puzzle of flesh.

"I will not let it finish this way," said Quentin; he went to the carcass, raised his sword, and drove it point downwards into the corpse.

This time Christine thought to feel the heat, as if she were being burned merely by looking at the thing as it changed. The air blurred and shimmered again; and the pieces of the puzzle sorted themselves out, made two coherent wholes.

On one side of Quentin was a dead horse, a black-maned roan, its belly ripped open, its legs smashed like matchsticks, its head gashed, its eyes burst. What lay on the other side she could never have put a name to. Half as tall as a man, it had a huge monkeylike head, its features compressed into a tiny pouting face. Its scrawny body bore two long arms ending in four-digited hands; but below its waist there was only a short, segmented tail, with a cluster of gleaming metallic needles sprouting along its inner surface.

Christine shivered uncontrollably. "What . . . what the *fuck* is that?!" she yelled, an obscenity that she had never before dared to utter.

Quentin pulled up his sword, which had sunk into the ground, and came to stand next to her, gazing at the two-limbed horror.

"I have never seen its like or heard of it," he said. "But it is clearly some sort of being that possesses another, merges with its substance and perverts it. Are you sure you are well, milady?"

He raised a hand to her shoulder, in a gesture of comfort. She pulled away instantly, shivering. "Don't *touch* me!" she gasped, and he stepped back, contrite. She took a few steps toward the disemboweled horse, drawn against her will to contemplate the carnage from closer up.

"I am to blame," Quentin let drop after a moment. "This is all my fault; I let my guard down once again and this is what happened. Oh, my poor Thunder."

She turned to him, uncomprehending. "What are you talking about?"

"The man who sold us the petrol containers. I knew something was wrong about it all, but I was so tired, I thought I was imagining things. The containers were infected; they carried the . . . the germ of this being. And they were left in the trunk of the car for hours, time enough for it to thoroughly merge with Thunder and corrupt him. . . ."

"Thunder? Who's Thunder?"

"My horse. I told you my car began as a horse; Thunder shifted into that shape once I was deep enough into the made world to take advantage of powered travel."

Quentin rubbed his chin; there were several cuts on his face and the shoulder-plate of his armor was dented, the black enamel scraped off in long gouges. "They used the same vulnerability again: My mount was my weakest point, since I depended upon it so thoroughly. Your warden tried to blind it when we escaped; this time they corrupted it so that it turned against me. . . ."

He paused, frowning. "But no; no, when I think about it, that makes no sense," he said. "They did not need to kill me. They must have meant to take you away from me. If the corruptor had taken full control, it need merely have fled, with you cradled safe inside, a prisoner. No, Thunder must have fought against the invasion. He fought to stay with me; maybe he knew I would kill him, but he remained nonetheless. . . . Loyal unto death."

Quentin stood next to the dead horse, sank to one knee and patted the gashed and bloody head. "You have done well, old friend," he said in a tired voice. "Rest now."

He rose to his feet, spoke to Christine or to the air, she wasn't sure which. "I used to think how fine it would be to rescue the princess and ride home to Chrysanthe in triumph, on my beautiful horse. Throughout all the years of my quest, often I consoled myself with that image. . . ." He shook his head violently, as if to scatter all the foolishness it contained to the four winds.

"What are we going to do now?" she asked him, still shivering and hugging herself. A car passed by without slowing.

Quentin looked as though he were coming back to himself. "We will have to walk, until I can locate some alternate mode of transportation." A few feet away from him, a pair of torn saddlebags lay on the ground. He went to them and pulled out a few items, including the two leather wallets that had been in the glove compartment.

"May I entrust you with the allmap, Lady Christine? As for the portrait, there is no need for it now, but it seems like a waste to leave it behind. . . ."

"I'll keep it," she said, and put both objects in the inner pocket of her suede jacket.

"Are you sure you are well, milady? Can I do anything for you?" he asked awkwardly.

"You *could* just get me home without any more horrors trying to kill us, maybe," she answered in a trembling voice, delayed terror suddenly rising in her. "I'm fucking tired of this, Quentin." The swear word already seemed to have lost most of its power. Christine shivered again, and coughed.

"I am doing my utmost, milady; but I promise I will be more careful in the future."

She looked at him; discerned not the slightest trace of sarcasm in his tone or demeanor; and was abashed.

"Forget what I said, please. It's just that I'm still scared. I should thank you instead; you killed the—whatever it was, and saved me again. Thank you, Quentin."

"You are welcome. Shall we get moving now?"

They began to walk along the shoulder. When Christine looked back, compelled to glance one last time at the horror they had left behind, the road had returned to its previous state; the gravel of the shoulder was undisturbed and pristine. "There will be a turnoff soon," promised Quentin, "and a sidewalk leading to a town. We will see what we can get there."

She nodded twice, said, "Great," as if to convince herself. After a moment, she asked: "Tell me one thing; this . . . is this your true shape, or are you . . . something else?"

"I am a man," said Quentin. "This is my sole shape. It is only my armor and accoutrements that shift."

Christine heaved a sigh of relief. "In that case, don't you think you should shift them back? We're drawing quite a bit of attention"—she pointed to a passing car whose occupants were craning their necks to look at them—"with your armor and sword."

Quentin looked down at himself, grunted. "I am loath to shift the sword into hiding; I keep expecting another attack any second. But that is a silly concern; I can get it back fast enough."

He closed his eyes for a second and frowned in concentration. His armor shifted the same way the world around them had; Christine did not see it fade, but grew aware suddenly that he was wearing a long-sleeved jacket of some dark gray oily-looking material, white bell-bottomed trousers, patent-leather shoes. His shirt was dark blue, and he wore a wide red tie on which the leaping fish emblem was repeated a hundred times in miniature.

"What is this?" she asked. "You look like a clown."

He shrugged. "Local fashion."

"Couldn't you shift back to the T-shirt . . . on second thought, what does it matter."

"No, of course; you will feel more at ease with the clothes you are used to seeing me in," he said, and the T-shirt and jeans were back. She remembered with a pang the first time he had appeared to her clearly, in the neighbors' backyard; how terror had sung in her bones, yet had been overlaid with a desperate yearning. . . .

"I'm the one who said we shouldn't draw attention," she said. "Change back to that suit, if that's what stylish people wear around these parts. And let's find that sidewalk you promised."

In his sheltered room at the core of the Merionist hostel Mathellin lay thrashing and screaming. His body shifted shape uncontrollably, flesh melting off his bones like tar, then bubbling forth anew within stark gaps. His spine bent and contorted, whipped back and forth; the back of his head drummed against the floor, leaving red circles of blood spots from his cracked skull.

Finally he got a tenuous hold of his agony, stilled his movements and transformations, lay at last blessedly motionless, while the world around him spun mercilessly, as if it were trying to hurl him off. He drew a long, painful breath.

He had gambled, and lost. To reach across the huge lead the fugitives had over him, he had used sympathetic magic, making his very self resonate with the munken. The plan had nearly worked, but his hold on the transmogrified horse had been too weak; he could not control it as easily as he had wished. He might still have won, even though nearly blinded by pain, crippled by the knight's deadly sure thrusts; he might have either killed his opponent or gained enough control over the beast to make it flee. But Christine had said those damned words. *You're hurting me.* In that instant, he had been too wrought to realize she was not being truthful, that it was only an expression of her fear. He had forgotten everything else but the need to keep her utterly safe, untouched, lest he be destroyed—and so had left himself open for the killing blow.

He had managed to break the sympathy resonance and return across worlds to his true body just before the munken died, but it was by then much too late anyway. Every wound Quentin had inflicted upon the mutated car Mathellin had suffered in both mind and flesh. Despite all his control over his own shape and his consequent ability to heal preternaturally fast, he was an inch from death. Pain flared across his body in long waves; though both his eyes were whole, one was now blind and the other saw dimly through a red haze of cracks. A moan escaped his burst lips; his throat felt scoured with acid. Change shape, change now, remember wholeness, a heart beating strongly, well-knitted flesh firm and smooth on the bones. . . . But the part of his mind that still resonated with the munken insisted *You are dead, you are dead and rent,* and Mathellin fought desperately to deny it. He heard blood seep from his blinded left eye; it made a faint crackle as the droplets burst through weakened vessels. He clenched his will and tried to make it stop, to hold it back in, to impose the template burning bright in his mind upon his rebellious, treacherous flesh. Ruby tears dripped from his lids.

❧ Their progress was slow at first, walking along the side of the road. Still they traveled outward through the made world, and the scenery around them kept shifting. Once, Quentin tried to take Christine's hand to help her up a slope that had suddenly appeared before them; she flinched and recoiled from his touch. For a moment he seemed about to say something, but in the end he remained silent. They walked now at the crest of a hill; to their right a grassy hollow opened, with a spinney of birches at the bottom. Orange and yellow birds, their plumage so bright as to appear soaked in fluorescent dye, cheeped from the branches. The buildings of a city could be seen in the distance, wrapped in haze.

Quentin made an "Ah!" of satisfaction: They had reached a widening of the road, marked with a pair of signs. They halted there, and a quarter of an hour later a bus pulled up. Quentin waved a pair of yellow cards at the driver as they climbed aboard and found adjoining seats. Christine sat next to the window, leaning her head against the glass. She was shivering, but maybe it was only from the bus's air-conditioning. The driver sang in a language she couldn't recognize, though the melody was hauntingly familiar.

"I think I have the vectors aligned," said Quentin. When she did not reply, he added, "Our progress is helped if the direction of travel is coincident with the direction of the true realm." He made awkward movements with his hands, trying to clarify. "When we reach the city, there should be a train heading in the right direction within a few hours. That should speed things up appreciably."

Her eyes were closing; exhaustion claimed her and she dozed. She rose almost to the surface of wakefulness time and again, found herself diving back down. Anonymous shapes struggled in her dreams: scraps of flesh, torn ligaments, and smashed skulls swirled around her vision. The shapeshifting beast reached one enormous hand around her waist and clutched her to its malformed chest. At this she awoke, sweat running down her back. Quentin was looking at her, the usual concern on his face.

"We have almost arrived," he said. "If you are hungry, we can go to a restaurant."

She was, and they did. In a large room overflowing with plastic ivy, amidst the buzz of conversation, they sat at a heavy varnished-wood table and ate greasy hamburgers. The buns were pumpernickel and the tomato slices mottled green and black.

With food in her stomach, Christine's mood eased. She looked around them, at the room both recognizable and not, swept her hand at it.

"All this," she said, "an infinity of worlds, one inside the other? I've seen that it's real, but . . . even now, it's still hard to take."

"If it is any consolation, Lady, I needed weeks at first before I grew used to the shifts. I would wake up in the middle of the night, deathly afraid I had traveled in my sleep and would find myself stranded ten thousand leagues away."

"Does that ever happen? Traveling in your sleep?"

"No. One must be awake and exert one's will."

"Just how do you do it? How much of a magician are you?"

"Oh, not at all. I am just a knight."

"What do you call magic, then? What about your armor hidden away as clothes? Is that natural?"

"All the magic I wield comes from Orion. Each of the knights who set out to look for you was gifted with spells. I did not cast the magic that alters my armor and weapons, I merely control it. It is much the same with travel through the worlds. Only a magician can see *beyond,* and will his travel in that direction. Orion gifted me with the ability, as he did the others before me."

"A generous man. I wish he could give me that gift. I'd like to see where we're headed."

"When we get back, I believe you can ask him for anything; he will gladly give it to you."

"You think he'll like me that much?"

Quentin smiled, eyes downcast. "Do not forget he knew you as a small child. Everyone in Chrysanthe loved you, milady. The whole court doted on you. On your first birthday, your father the king decreed a week of celebrations throughout the land. I remember that day very well, as we were let out of school early and I was given a mug of cider to drink, compliments of the king."

Christine shook her head. "Hearing you say that makes me feel unreal." She ran her hand across the table's surface. "Even this doesn't feel quite real."

"Well, it actually is not. From a philosophical standpoint, nothing surrounding us really exists."

Christine frowned, annoyed at Quentin's theory. "Oh, come on. I had a philosophy teacher who used to bore us to death with that nonsense. It's called solipsism. I didn't think you'd be a solipsist, Quentin."

"I was not being clear. You must remember that one can find anything and everything in a made world, if one goes far enough. Made worlds, by their very nature, are imaginary; not fully real. No one here, apart from you and I, truly exists. When we are gone from this part of the made world, their existence will not continue."

"That's horrible," protested Christine, appalled. "It can't be true. Just because we aren't there to see them, they still exist!"

"If I walked to the buffet, turned around and walked back, and took just one step *beyond* in the process, when I returned to my chair that portly lady would no longer be sitting there. No one would remember having seen her. So, where would she be?"

"But you could find her again," Christine objected. "You could walk the same way again and take back the step *beyond.*"

"True. But how could I know she was the same woman, and not just one who appeared identical? Not even if she recognized me could I know; for I could easily find a world where everyone knew us, where any passerby would be our lifelong friend."

"Okay, but what if I stayed behind? If you returned and found me still sitting here, wouldn't you know you had to be back where you started?"

"I am not going to attempt the experiment. I was not willing to take the risk of losing Thunder down in the made world, and I am certainly not willing to risk you, for all that I expect I would feel the pang once more to confirm I had located you.

But even if I did this foolish thing, it would not disprove my point. The woman is adequately real as long as you are here with her."

"I won't accept that." Christine was shaking her head vigorously. "It's a cruel philosophy. I've lived with people like these all my life. You want me to think no one I knew was real? That's just awful!"

"Please, do not get angry. I am not fond of that viewpoint myself; perhaps I am wrong. I would be glad if that were so. . . ."

He took a breath, hesitated, then went on.

"Yet one thing remains. I told you that six years ago, I thought I had found you. I had felt the seeking-spell resonate. The young girl whom I had found matched your fleshpaint portrait exactly. She lived in a large mansion, surrounded by servants, never allowed to leave their sight for an instant. She was a prisoner, even though she did not realize it. I wiled my way into an underservant's post at the mansion; I engineered a chance meeting with her, then another. I gained her confidence; a week later I seized the opportunity and sprang her release. She trusted me with her life, and that to me only confirmed she must be the object of my quest."

Quentin pushed a crust of bread around on his plate. "Servants tried to prevent our escape. I had to kill two of them; they were armed only with kitchen cleavers, but any weapon can be dangerous in skilled hands." He pointed to the faint line that ran from the middle of his forehead to his right eyebrow. "One of them nearly slashed my face in half. But we escaped, and rode away through the made world, and after a few adventures we reached our destination."

Quentin lowered his gaze; his voice grew strained.

"She was all of eleven years old; she had known terror as we fled, but throughout it all she had put her faith in me. She had even laughed a few times, as we spun through imaginary lands and she saw strange things that delighted her. I had told her of Chrysanthe, of the court and of her father. When we came to the opening into the true realm, I took her hand in mine, and held it tightly as we crossed. But when I turned to look at her, I found I was grasping only air.

"She was eleven years old. Where did she go, Lady?"

Mathellin had slept at some point; one of the momentary gaps in his consciousness had grown to swallow him whole. He had feared to sleep, feared that the loss of control over his rebellious body would let it die; even now, as he emerged from the abyss of sleep, he felt certain that to slip back into it would be fatal.

He forced himself to sit up; the world tilted crazily around the axis of his torso and a moan escaped his lips. But his limbs obeyed him. His eyes opened, and both could see, though the left one was still veiled with red. He coughed and nearly fainted from the effort; he worked his mouth and let a clot of blood-streaked mucus dribble out.

He clung to a bedpost and hauled himself trembling to his knees, unable to achieve his feet. His skin itched and burned; as he looked down at himself he saw that it was peeling everywhere, revealing raw pink dermis. He lifted a hand to his face, ran it along the side of his head; his hair came loose in clumps.

He looked around him; he had only a vague recollection of where he was. Close by, on a table, was a strange box with a lamp inside it, whose front was a transparent screen. A feeble glow, along with wisps of acrid smoke, rose from the lamp's burnt-out filament, and torn shadows lay in the corners of the screen. Mathellin could no longer remember what this was for. He had run so long and so hard, he was so tired. . . . He croaked "Help me!" but no one came to his aid. He crawled on his knees, then on all fours, to the door, and reached for the knob. There was a plastic card hanging from it; Mathellin could not read the characters, and this evoked dread in him. Had he traveled so far down into the made world that he had reached a place where the language of Chrysanthe was unknown?

He could not turn the knob. He pounded weakly on the door, called out for help. "Damn you all!" he wheezed. He tumbled away from the door, his vision dimming, the abyss of sleep beckoning him. And then there came a rattle of metal and the knob twitched. The door swung open; a woman wearing a black uniform with gold piping entered, cried out and bent over him.

"Master!" she cried, eyes wide with concern. "Oh, Master, I have come. Are you hurt?"

The cut of her uniform triggered memories in Mathellin. He noted the three buttons on her shoulder and the double-cross insignia. His breathing sharpened, as if the touch of her flesh were healing him. Three pips, a double cross; this meant she was a high-lieutenant. The armed forces she belonged to boasted twenty-eight different ranks, this Mathellin recalled now. He recalled also how their upper officers had been subverted into serving him as the emissary of a Divine Principle, as had the senior members of the supposedly agnostic Merionist Order. His mind cleared; he knew where he was now, knew he held absolute power over that woman, and that she feared him the way a doe fears the smilodon. Yet he was too weak to utter the caustic reply her inane question called for. "Help me stand," he whispered. The woman held him gently and pulled him upright, letting him rest against her once he had gained his feet. She was half a head taller than him, and impressively strong.

"Why didn't you come sooner?" he said, when he had gotten his breath back. "How long did you leave me alone here?" His head still rested against her shoulder; he felt her small firm breasts pressed against his chest.

The woman hesitated. "You've been in the room a day and a night, Master," she said. Mathellin felt her voice vibrate in her rib cage. "Some wanted to come to you, but you had told us you must remain alone and undisturbed. . . ."

Mathellin leaned on her arms, looked at her. "Even when you heard me scream, you didn't think to enter."

"We were afraid, Master. We dared not disobey. We live to serve. . . ." Her gaze avoided his. In a small frightened voice, she continued: "I have failed you. Shall I kill myself in retribution?"

Mathellin levered himself away from the woman and stood tottering on his own. She looked at him guilelessly, her face tight with distress; yes, she meant what she had just said, every word. In his travels throughout the made world, Mathellin had sought out allies, dream-people to serve him. And like all dreams, they sometimes veered into the absurd without warning. Mathellin felt his gorge rise at this woman's devotion; she was worse than one of Evered's servants. Though he ought to, by virtue of the role he played and his disgust at her incompetence, still he could not bring himself to order her suicide.

"No, you shall not. Attend me instead. I need water, and food."

"I will fetch them at once, Master. Do you want a healer?"

"No healer. I am my own healer." Mathellin rubbed the back of one hand; the dead skin flaked off, then the inflamed flesh underneath toughened and grew a new epidermis. He raised his hand, now whole, and showed it to the woman.

She fell to her knees, spread her fingers wide in a sign of worship. "You work miracles, Master," she said huskily.

"Deeper miracles than you know. When I am gone from this place, it will be as if you had never existed," he started to say, but his own cruelty suddenly and unexpectedly shamed him. "Rise," he ordered her. "Just go get me some food and water. Go!"

She left the room at a run, closing the door behind her. Mathellin sat down heavily on the bed. He remembered everything now. He glanced around the room: at the opticon, at the burnt remains of the slides that had channeled his sight and mind through the worlds, at the bloodstains flecking the wooden floor. His strength was slowly pooling back, yet something was wrong: as if some essential spring in him had been broken. Soon, he promised himself, very soon he would be back to his old single-minded self. This unclean aura of doubt and fragility he could feel around his spirit would dissolve, and he would be truly whole.

After a moment he got up, took the crystal out of his bag, sat down again. He tried to gaze toward Chrysanthe, to see Quentin and Christine in their flight, but his sight remained stubbornly anchored to this world, and the effort dizzied him.

"You have to rest," he said out loud to himself, "you have to rest if you are to continue the hunt." He took a long, trembling breath, and as he waited for his insane worshiper to bring him a meal, he picked at the skin of his face; it peeled off all in one piece, and lay like a mask in his hands, his own features blankly looking back at him.

3. Climbing the Gradient

The train was a steam-belching contraption both opulent and ungainly; its cars were floridly decorated, their seats overstuffed, the stewards polite to the point of sarcasm. Christine and Quentin had a compartment to themselves, which Quentin had secured with more bills from his apparently bottomless purse.

"You're never short of funds, are you?" asked Christine.

"For a fact, the money is illusion. The purse is always full because it really contains nothing. Here." And Quentin started to draw bills of all shapes, colors, and denominations from the small leather sack, piling them up on the little table between their seats. Christine picked up the topmost one, as big as her two palms together. It showed the portrait of a man from the Indies, with a mustache and glasses, and a kind smile on his wrinkled face. Across the top were written the words "In Vishnu We Trust." She let it flutter from her fingers and shook her head; when she glanced at the table again she saw all the currency had vanished.

The train started, with a loud venting of steam. The station began to recede from them slowly. Christine was still thinking about Quentin's purse. "Haven't you ever been tempted to just settle down and live like a millionaire? You could have had everything you wanted."

Quentin shook his head, smiling embarrassedly. "The only thing I wanted was to find you, Lady. I will not deny the thought crossed my mind a few times. But . . ."

"You're a devoted man."

"So I have often been told."

They left the station and crossed a maze of intersecting tracks.

"Do you know what this city's called?" asked Christine suddenly.

Quentin pulled out the allmap and after a time said, "Londinium, most probably."

"Well, good-bye, Londinium. Or is it too late to say good-bye already? We've been shifting worlds away, haven't we?"

"Not very much yet. The gradient should steepen once the tracks get into the proper direction, though. Then we shall make real progress."

"You've lost me again."

"There is a natural gradient to the made worlds; some paths through a made world take you deeper into it of their own accord. The made world known as Hieloculat opens at the entrance to a cave, where a stream goes underground. If you let yourself be carried downstream, you will soon reach stranger and stranger realms. Travel back along the river, and you will emerge into Chrysanthe once more; travel away from it, and you might wander the made world forever."

"Just how many of these made worlds are there?" asked Christine, uneasy. "You make it sound like any wrong turn can lead you astray."

"Not that many. I have read there are twenty-eight, all told. The apertures can be sensed by a magician; all those in inhabited regions are very carefully marked off. About half of the made worlds open in remote, uncivilized lands, but even those are indicated, some very clearly indeed. The entrance to Jyndyrys is flanked by two huge redstone statues; they are said to have been raised by the Hero Knaw, four thousand years ago."

"And this made world that we're in; what's its name? Where does it open?"

"It is called Errefern. It opens in the Hedges, about twenty leagues from Tiellorn, the great city at the heart of the land."

"And why did you seek me here, rather than elsewhere?"

Quentin pursed his mouth. "Sheer luck, I would guess," he said softly. "Other knights had gone looking for you in other made worlds. I picked this one because it had not been explored to any great extent. Of course, Orion did explore them all himself first, but he could not search everywhere at once. His first travels brought no fruit; this was when it was decided to send knights questing after you."

Christine pondered this for a while. The train was speeding along the rails, and the countryside spread beyond the window. The grass was a deep, emerald green, and the sunlight that lit up the window and stained the table between the facing pair of seats had a late-summer feel. Christine sensed that they were traveling through the seasons as well, and was not surprised when for a brief spell the trees showed yellow and red leaves, then went back to a pale green.

She said: "If I was going to kidnap someone and take them into exile in a made world, I would go very, very deep, so deep that no one would have a chance to catch up to me. Then I would be safe. Why didn't my kidnappers do this?"

"Because," Quentin answered, "if one goes too deep into a made world, reality starts slipping into nightmare. Orion told me once of reaching a place where the air itself opened mouths to devour him, where thoughts flocculated into white lumps and sounds cut flesh like shards of razors. So there was a limit to the depths to which you might have been taken. But knowing one is safe from infinity is cold comfort at best. I might still have sought after you in vain for the remainder of my life."

She spoke softly. "How did you know, then, to find me?"

"I like to think I felt you calling. I was attuned to your presence, as I told you. Still, I should not have been able to feel it from worlds away. But something impelled me down a certain path, about a year ago. Perhaps it was a hunter's instinct, though what that means exactly I do not know.

"I had come to a world where the people were strange, though they looked very much like those of the true realm. It was their minds that were strange. They had built many odd machines whose main function seemed to belch ash and smoke, and lived all in concrete tenements, like cubical hives. The skies above their cities were palled with soot. Every morning they assembled in large groups and engaged in screaming matches, the winners of which were given alcohol until they grew insensate and slept till morning; apparently everyone thought this a great reward. I felt I was coming close to the limit of sanity, that if I went much farther the fabric of reality would tear into madness; yet I thought I saw an interesting path. The moon was round and bright in the sky, and I guided myself by it. I let the world change as it would, almost, but I kept the moon constant.

"The shape of a made world is not something I can understand; certainly I could not describe it. But there seemed to be a . . . a pocket of sense growing there, a still, quiet backwater of worlds, where the outer madness was abated. Or like a peninsula, if you want. I followed it, very carefully. If I had followed only my desires, I could have found anything I sought, but I would have lost the exact place. And I thought, if I had meant to hide you, I would have hidden you there, where no one would be likely to search.

"It took me months and months. But ever so slowly, I felt I was closing in. For six weeks before I found you, I had gone through cities exactly like yours, or nearly. Always I returned to the gyneceum, riding Thunder. I thought I could sense you, just around the corner. I must have passed that street a thousand times, at every occasion altering something here, something there, getting it into greater conformance with my destination. . . . And then one day, as I was driving along the street for the thousandth time, I saw you. I felt the pang Orion had promised—for a second, I thought I was dying. I saw that you had noticed me, and I drove away. I had wanted to jump out of the car, seize you, and take you away on the instant. But that would have been far too risky."

"I noticed you," Christine said. "You braked the car, but there was nothing in front . . ." She felt some of the old terror creep back as she said this. "I thought . . . You know what I thought."

"You thought I was a rapist," said Quentin diffidently. "I have been wondering . . . No, please forget I said anything."

"I hate it when people do that. If you've got a question, ask it."

". . . Why, milady? Why did you think I was the kind of man who would rape a young woman? Were there reavers in your world, bandits who slay and pillage? I never thought I looked at all conspicuous or threatening; the whole point of the shifting clothes was to fit in. How could Orion's spell fail?"

"Oh, you looked . . . not inconspicuous, with that red car, but harmless enough, I suppose. It was your behavior. A woman must be aware of . . . predators."

Quentin's face fell. "Oh," he said. "Customs in your world . . . You are telling me rape was acceptable—or at least not punished. Forgive me for bringing up the subject; I should have understood the situation by myself. My apologies."

"No, it's not. Rape; it's not acceptable, it's a crime. But it happens. And I had reason to . . ." Her gorge rose and she clamped her mouth shut.

"Milady? Are you unwell? Please, let us talk of other things. I am so sorry."

Christine shook her head. She was remembering rough hands holding her down, an abstract burning, ripping pain; for a moment it was as if she were still in Dr. Almand's office, bringing this very memory into being. "Your body remembers, Christine," she heard his voice say. Her body remembered. She shuddered violently and bent over the table, retching.

"Milady!" came Quentin's cry of despair. He took her by the shoulders; she screamed wordlessly, twisted out of his grasp. "Don't touch me! Don't you ever t-touch me!" she shouted, then collapsed on the seat.

"Lady Christine, what is wrong? What can I do? Let me help, please!"

For a few moments she remained bent double, her stomach heaving but her throat sealed tight; then her torment eased. She drew a trembling breath. The rough, dirty hands, the broken filthy nails and the swipe of fingers on her child's body receded from the forefront of her thoughts. Lies, lies, they were lies. The only touch was the fabric of the seat now; across from her stood a man with his arms open, his face twisted by concern. A man who did not, would not, touch her, now that she had asked him. A man she had chosen to trust; a man she did trust.

"I'll . . . I'll be fine. I just had unpleasant memories. It'll pass."

Quentin scowled. "Unpleasant memories?" Then his eyes widened and he grew pale. "You were . . . You could not have been. That is unthinkable. Milady, are you telling me you were . . . forgive me . . . *forced*?"

She looked away. "Do you have psychologists in Chrysanthe, Quentin?"

"I do not know the word."

"Mind-doctors."

"Some healers treat people's spirits as well as their bodies; a few never treat wounds of the flesh, only those of the soul."

"I was taken to see a man like that; his name was Dr. Almand. He was very concerned about my imaginary friend. About . . . about Tap." This was much harder than it should be; but she did not relent. After what they had been through, she owed Quentin the truth. "Tap was a rabbit," she said in a quivering voice. "A cartoon kind of rabbit, who stood on his hind legs and talked. He was always with me. He began to fade away when I was ten. He . . . he said to me, before he left, that he wasn't imaginary. That a small part of him came from me, but not the rest. You said that he might have been . . . magic."

"A spell, yes. A benison, a kind of ward, attached to you. When you vanished, Lady, Orion was called. He gathered his power and sent out a host of spells after you, to seek you out but also to protect you. You were not found, because you had been taken into a made world, and seeking-spells cannot cross the boundaries between worlds. But I think—I am no wizard, perhaps I am wrong—that one of the wards might have reached you and kept by you all this time."

"Tap said that something was wrong with him; that he felt old, or sick. He scared me; imaginary friends aren't supposed to surprise you by saying things like that. I thought I might be going insane. I told him I didn't believe in him, and I . . . I sent him away, somehow. I passed out then, and when I woke up, Uncle took me to the hospital. I was confused, I talked about Tap, and so they sent me to see Dr. Almand."

"I am sure there was never anything wrong with your mind, Lady."

She heaved out a breath, a single bark of contemptuous laughter. "You have Tap's voice, Quentin. Just that would make me doubt my sanity. . . . Dr. Almand was upset that I still had an imaginary friend at my age. I thought he would tell me I wasn't grown up properly; I was afraid he'd tell Uncle to keep me home, or push me back a year at school, or send me to an institution. Instead, he . . . he . . . I can't say it."

"There is no need to say anything. If you do not want to talk, Lady, you do not have to."

Outside the train, the landscape rolled on, ever-changing. Mountains rose proudly in the distance; their tops, Christine realized with a shock, were carved and pierced with colossal oriels. Moving specks of light swarmed around the summits— flames from the engines of aircars? A cloud condensed behind the peaks, and for a moment of terror she thought it was solid, the limb of some unimaginable entity. Her eyes followed one of the glints of light; she realized the mountains had changed, and the gray mass was only a bank of clouds, and the firefly light was gone. She was not there to see it, and so it did not exist; had never existed.

She brought her gaze to the top of the table, fixed her attention on the grain of the wood. Her fingers ran along the faint scar on the back of her left hand, that had its smaller twin on the palm, the mark of the scissors blade she had slammed through her hand, long ago, because she had to fight back against what had been done to her, and yet there was no one she could hurt, save herself.

"He made me remember," she said slowly, in a half-whisper. "He made me remember being . . . abused. Being r-raped. By my . . . f-father, and by others. I spent years seeing myself like that. It happened . . . nearly a hundred times."

"Lady!" Quentin was outraged. "Lady, this is simply not possible!"

"I know." She was shaking, on the verge of laughter. "Dr. Almand was convinced it was the only explanation. But I think . . . when he put me under hypnosis . . . I think he made me invent it. You can hypnotize people and make them see things that aren't there; why couldn't you make them invent memories? So he made me remember being hurt, because he was convinced I must have been hurt, since I had been taken away from my father. And the more I thought I remembered, the more convinced he was it was all true. So he just pushed me through it; again and again, trying to help me get better. But I stopped believing in it, in the end. When I called you. When I decided his story was just as insane as yours, and I had rather be insane your way than his." She exhaled raggedly.

Quentin was shaking as well, ever so slightly but with enormous tension, like a plucked bowstring. "Lady Christine," he said, "please hear me. It is simply inconceivable that you should ever have been raped. Anyone who did this would not live to boast of it. What your Dr. Almand did to you is unforgiveable. I swear to you, once we have returned to Chrysanthe, I shall go back to your world and—and I will kill him."

Christine felt Quentin's fury like a physical thing, a toothed blade against the skin of her face. "I thought you said you weren't a killer," she breathed, afraid of him yet still hoping the heat of his passion made him speak in hyperbole.

Quentin dropped his gaze.

"I am not. I have never murdered. But . . . For what he did to you, he deserves to be punished. Milady, to avenge you, I would do anything."

"I don't want to be avenged, Quentin. And besides, isn't he dead already? If you're right about the made worlds, then Dr. Almand no longer exists now that we've left him behind."

"I could find him again, or a man who deserved to die as much as he does," replied Quentin, but she realized from the hollowness of his tone he was being stubborn.

"No. Don't talk, don't ever talk, of killing people for me. He didn't mean me harm. Let it go. That . . . That is an order, Sir Quentin. I don't believe anyone anywhere, no matter what, deserves to be killed, and I will not have you kill for me."

Quentin rested his fingers against his forehead, looking both relieved and bereft. "As you wish," he said. "I will spare his life if you ask. But milady, please believe me: Nothing that he said was true."

"I chose to believe that when I called you. But there are times when . . . when it's harder. You can't touch me, do you understand that?"

"Yes. Yes I do. Say no more."

They were silent for a while, then Christine sighed. "I wish I was in my bed, with a book. I wish I could shut out everything around me. There's no place safe, now."

"I am here with you. You are safe as I can make it."

"No place that *feels* safe. Don't you miss your home, Quentin?"

"Seldom. A knight has to learn to make his home wherever he is."

"I can't do that. I've lived all my life in Uncle's house. I can't believe I'll never see it again. All my things are gone." She blinked back tears. "I can't believe I miss my pencil cup, but right now it feels like the most important thing in the world, and it's gone."

Quentin gestured to the purse of imaginary money. "I can buy you a replacement, if you wish. I know this is slim comfort, but I will get you anything it is in my power to procure."

Christine shook her head. "I don't need anything," she whispered. She hugged herself, her clenched hands in the pockets of her jacket, and closed her eyes. Time passed; she was unsure whether she slept or merely imagined she did. It seemed to her that she opened her eyes after an endless time and saw Quentin staring out the window, frowning in concentration. Outside, under a red-purple sky, volcanic cones reared; a river of lava ran parallel to their course and she saw a ship sailing on it, the metal hull adorned with a hundred vanes that fanned out like fantastic wings. She closed her eyes again and dreamed that she slept.

&& The line had begun to run uphill, at a sharper and sharper angle; Christine felt the ground slowly tilting up under her. There were the cries of huge birds, trumpeting across the void, and their train moved on rails of spun gold and sugar. . . .

She came awake; but the reality that surrounded her seemed hardly more comforting than her dream. Huge trees, whose trunks forked very near the ground and whose blackish leaves hung limp like gonfalons, crowded close to the track. The sky was barely lit; she wasn't sure if dawn was coming, or the day almost dead. The line was indeed going uphill; the train's smooth movement had become irregular, and shudders thumped through the carriage as though the gaps in the rails were growing dangerously wide.

Quentin sat facing her; his face was drawn, his eyes puffy and feverish-looking. "Are you okay?" Christine asked him. "You look awful."

The knight nodded briefly. "I am simply very tired. I have remained awake all this while, pushing us up the gradient. We are near its end."

"How close are we to Chrysanthe?"

"I would guess less than fifty leagues remain. I think we can make ten or twenty more on this train, but it is becoming very difficult to navigate."

Just then a jar rocked the wagon, and a series of lesser tremors began to shake them. Outside, the trees had thinned and become smaller. Sweat had broken out on Quentin's brow.

"Don't you think you should rest?"

"Later . . . I want to go as far as I can now. Twenty leagues on foot is a three-day journey at the least for you. We can cover this ground in a few hours as long as I can keep this vehicle stable. . . ."

"I . . . think I need to go to the bathroom."

Quentin closed his eyes for a moment, opened them again. "There is still a toilet at the end of the car. Let us go."

Christine sighed but did not protest. At least there would still be a door between them. They went out into the corridor. Their car was the last one in the train, now. The toilet was cramped, the seat made of wood, and there was no water, just a hole in the floor through which she could see the ground rushing by. She could not see any ties, just sandy soil. The car juddered first left then right, in a complex rhythm.

When she came out, Quentin escorted her back to their compartment. There were no cars in front either, just the bulk of the locomotive. Through the uneven window at the front of the car, she saw the tenders, small dark men in leather clothes, moving swiftly in the cab at the back of the engine.

Quentin was breathing heavily. His face was getting pale. He denied anything was wrong, but advised her to make sure all her belongings were packed. The sun had risen, and golden light flooded the world now. The weird trees had vanished, and a broad plain spread before her sight. Mountains rose in the distance; still the track lay slightly uphill. For the barest flash of an instant, a city came into being in the middle distance, buildings shaped of pure light, heartrendingly beautiful; then it vanished.

The train was slowing. Quentin muttered words under his breath, and their speed increased for a brief while, but then it dropped to its former level. "I cannot keep it going," he said.

"Quentin, you don't have to."

"We can gain some ground still. Every hour we stay aboard saves us a long journey. You must understand, while we are on foot, we are vastly more vulnerable. And in all frankness, I find that my nerves are shattered. I wish to be back in Chrysanthe as soon as humanly possible."

"Is there something you're not telling me?"

His gaze evaded hers. "I cannot be sure. . . . While you slept, for a moment I thought we were being attacked again. A fleet of aircraft dove at us; they were letting things drop from their bellies, like huge eggs. . . . I shifted us away in time. Perhaps it was no more than a coincidence. In my travels, I have had many a chance encounter with danger. Still . . . I cannot afford to be overconfident. I want you brought to safety. The nearer we are, the more urgent it seems."

They went on for another hour, though their speed had dropped lower still. And then the juddering of the car increased. Quentin shook his head in anger. "I cannot push any farther. The gradient has all but vanished." He looked at the all-map, sighed. "Still, it is not so bad. Twenty more leagues. Do you have everything in your bag? We are coming to the end of the line."

The car swayed more and more, and they slowed to a near crawl. A regular thumping came from ahead, in time with the swaying of the car. They ground to a halt. Human wails rose up ahead, whether celebratory or mournful Christine could not say. Quentin nodded to her, and they left their compartment. It was now the only one in the car. The corridor that had led to the toilet now ended a foot beyond their compartment. Quentin opened the door in the side of the car, jumped down, then assisted her.

The line stretched behind them, through the empty plain. There were no ties, only twinned metal rails snaking off through the pale grass. Half a dozen small dark men, clad only in leather harnesses, swarmed around the locomotive, which panted and wheezed. Its pachyderm body was plated with metal that seemed coterminous with its dead-gray flesh. It had six legs, a club-shaped head whose many horns had been polished, draped with ribbons, and crusted with metal and stones. The men, having climbed down from the howdah set upon its back, were jabbing it with ankh-headed staves. One of them looked at Quentin and Christine with such hatred in his face that she felt chilled.

They left, walking at a rapid pace. When Christine looked over her shoulder, expecting the half-metal beast to have vanished, it was still there, surrounded by its distraught handlers. She turned to Quentin, whose face was drawn and whose gaze was almost as absent as it had been when she had woken aboard the car and torn him from his road hypnosis.

"Quentin, we're not making any progress toward Chrysanthe anymore, are we?"

"No. I am sorry. Let me . . ." He staggered, came to a stop. She glanced behind them, saw an empty plain, devoid even of rails. "I cannot go on," gasped Quentin. "Forgive me, but I must rest now. I have come too near the end of my strength."

"That's okay, that's okay," she reassured him, frightened to see his arms suddenly tremble. "We can just rest here."

"No. Not in the middle of a plain. That stand of trees . . . Let us make for it. There will be . . . there *will* be a spring there."

It took them twenty minutes to reach it. There was a small pool of water among the trees, not very clear. Quentin shook his head angrily, let himself fall down in a heap next to it. "It will have to do. You still have water in the bottle we bought at the station? Then drink that, and as much as you want." He bent down to the water, scooped it up in his hands and slurped at it noisily. "It tastes a bit of home," he said with a wistful smile. "We are getting very near. I must sleep now, Lady, I am too worn to go on. Please stand guard. If you find yourself falling asleep, wake me. One of us must remain on guard at all times, it is important."

He was asleep before she had finished nodding yes. She found herself once more contemplating him in slumber, as she had in the motel room, before the shapechanger had attacked them. The memory made her skin crawl and she felt threatened from everywhere and nowhere at once. She realized that Quentin must have felt like this throughout their entire journey, from the very moment he had torn her away from Uncle's wardenship. . . . The time of day felt wrong to her; they had traveled through worlds and seasons, and though her body insisted the sun should be setting, it was not yet noon. She had not known it was possible to be jet-lagged from riding a train.

She walked through the stand of trees, checking their surroundings. If she was to keep watch, should she not make rounds, like a guard? Still, she hated to let Quentin out of her sight. The plain was empty in all directions. The stand of trees was like a tiny room in a vast house, a small country all her own. She walked back to Quentin, who slept in what must be an uncomfortable position. She felt an urge to rearrange his limbs, as if he were a life-size doll she had put down on her bed all tangled up. She picked up the allmap from the bag and studied it. It had far fewer pages now, as if the world were shrinking. And in fact, all the leaves save one were blank; the lone illuminated page seemed to show a single continent, its scale uncertain, bordered by oceans east and west. North and south, the map just faded away; were there pages missing?

Time passed, but she had resolved not to wake Quentin until she was ready to drop off herself. The sky was reddening with sunset when the knight came awake; this time he was slow to come out of sleep, as if his exhaustion demanded days of unconsciousness to be properly relieved. Once he was fully aware of his surroundings, he exclaimed in consternation at the lateness of the hour; for an instant he seemed about to reproach her, then he shook his head. "There is nothing for it; and I did need the rest. . . . We will camp here tonight, and set out tomorrow morning."

Before boarding the train, back in Londinium, they had visited a few shops and made purchases. Quentin unfastened the flap of his backpack and pulled out a pair of blankets, which he laid upon the ground. "A sorry bed, Lady Christine, but the night should be mild in this place. I apologize: With better foresight, I would have aimed for an inn, but I was too tired to think straight."

"There's not much room for two," said Christine, looking at the blankets.

"No, this is *your* bed. I will be keeping watch."

"All night? Doesn't anyone sleep normally in Chrysanthe?"

"Oh, most people there sleep through the night. When I lived at home, I would sleep like the dead. Even while I quested for you, I made sure to take plenty of rest. And when we are back, my first destination will be a feather mattress. . . ." For a moment Quentin was lost in thought, then he looked at her with an odd disquiet in his gaze. She felt the tension, but could not put a name to it. For a moment, she thought it might be sexual, and felt her gut twist and her throat tighten. But no, it couldn't be that: Quentin was sighing and looking off into the distance. It was worry that twisted his features. "As long as . . . ," he muttered.

"As long as what?"

"Nothing, Lady."

"I told you not to do that! Answer my question."

"I was going to say 'As long as we reach Chrysanthe.' But we *will* reach it. I am tired and glum, Lady Christine, and I spoke out of turn."

"You're still worried about an attack." He simply shrugged in response.

After a minute, she asked, "Are you angry at me?"

His face plainly showed his surprise at the question. "Of course not!"

"I did keep watch while you slept. But there's absolutely nothing to be seen out there. I didn't even see any birds. Maybe I can watch some of the night, so you can sleep? I just want to help, Quentin. I don't want to be a piece of baggage."

"That is the last thing you are." After a pause, he added, "There is some food in my pack. Would you like to eat?"

"Only if you eat your share too."

Quentin took a few small bags from his backpack, along with a large tin can offering *Park's Old-Fashioned Hibernian Ragout*. "I've always thought this an incredible invention," he remarked. "A complete meal in its own mess tin. All you need is a fire to heat it."

"I'll get the firewood," she offered. Quentin let her gather fallen twigs and branches, though he kept his gaze on her at all times.

Once she had returned, Quentin laid the dead wood she'd gathered into a tidy pile, in a carefully chosen spot, and took out a lighter from the pack's front flap.

"I wish these things could be fashioned in Chrysanthe," he said. "But one has to go pretty far down into the made world to obtain them."

"Why? It's just a flint on top of a fuel container. It ought to be easy to manufacture."

"Your question holds its own answer, milady. 'Manufacture' is not a real word. Your world had manufactories, great places where people work all in a row to make things. Chrysanthe does not. The very words for it do not exist."

"You mean you're the only person in all of Chrysanthe who knows about factories?"

"Of course not. Through the millennia, hundreds of people have gone down into made worlds, and brought back accounts of what they saw. But to have manufactories, one needs everything that comes before them. A huge population, for one thing, and a will to befoul the land with mine pits and waste matter. No sovereign of Chrysanthe has ever been very receptive to the concepts."

For a moment, Quentin was silent, while he tried to get the lighter to work. "Here is another, perhaps more important reason," he said when he had finally gotten the flame to catch. It glowed weakly, with a greenish tinge. "A made world is not like the real world. In the world of our dreams flight is easy and we can soar into the air simply by willing it. In much the same way, made worlds allow miracles to happen which the Law forbids in Chrysanthe. Things burn here that do not in the real world. Already, since we are close to Chrysanthe, this lucifer is breaking down. I presume the fuel is a petroleum derivative, like that which powers automobiles. This kind of thing will not ignite in Chrysanthe. Wax, olive oil, and resins burn, but not rock oil. In the marshes near the mouth of the Lorvil River in Kawlend, there are pools of naphtha seeping to the surface; five centuries ago, the great chymist-wizard Haraundy tried everything he could to turn it into a usable fuel, and he failed. Can you see the difficulties we face? I am not saying we could never harness steam, say, using wood as fuel, since that does burn in the real world, but I fear its applications might prove much more difficult than they are in the made worlds."

"How do people live in Chrysanthe, then? They don't have any industry at all?"

Quentin had been playing the lighter's flame about the smaller twigs and at last managed to ignite them; he blew on the flames gently before answering.

"Some people are lazy, but most are quite industrious, I assure you. Farmers raise crops and cattle; artisans craft useful items of all kinds; there is commerce, though not much compared to your land. You must understand there are very few people in the real world compared to what you knew: Your world crawled with humanity. We have nothing like your giant cities, like those sterile towers where you pack people like wood in a cord."

"No cities at all? Does everyone live in villages?"

"We do have towns and cities; just of a more, let us say, reasonable size. Tiellorn is the oldest city in Chrysanthe, and it is by far the largest. Each of the three surrounding duchies has its capital, which would also rate as a city—a small one. But most of the population lives in small towns and villages."

The stew had heated up; Quentin poured half of it in a tin for Christine and ate directly from the can himself, his spoon scraping and ringing against the metal.

"This is *really* awful," Christine said after her third bite.

Quentin raised his eyebrows. "I have had worse." He frowned and spat out a piece of gristle into his cupped hand. "Though the less said about the meat, the better."

Christine found herself giggling at this remark. Quentin appeared vexed at first, then grinned apologetically. "Would you prefer some of the other food?" He proffered a cellophane packet of maize chips, which proved acceptable.

"What is Chrysanthe like, really?" she asked after a while. "You said there are few people, and they live the way people did in the Medieva, in my world. Are there castles, then?"

"Many. In early days, people built them as defenses against the wild; now that the land is civilized, there is far less need of them, but tradition insists they be built. No self-respecting baron of the outer marches will consider doing without at least a motte and bailey. The greatest castle in the world is Testenel, where the king resides. This is set some distance from Tiellorn. There is another castle within the city itself, called Perfenel. It was used in olden times, but Testenel is much newer, and immensely nicer. There are few sights the equal of it in all the made worlds, and none in reality. It is a huge building, made of blue stone. It has towers by the hundreds; the tallest is a thousand feet from the ground. . . . Doubt me if you want, milady. When you see Testenel you will know I spoke the strict truth."

"I don't . . . I don't doubt you," she said. "I'm frowning, but not because of that. I felt something, when you mentioned a castle of blue stone with a hundred towers."

It had been like a fine needle in her heart, so slim its sting was barely felt. Perhaps, she told herself, she had imagined it; perhaps it was a memory of stories she had once read, no more. A castle of blue stone. She thought she could see it in her mind, but it was an abstract shape, standing by itself, devoid of context.

"We'll come back to the castle later; I still don't know what the land looks like," said Christine. "Is it very strange? I mean . . . all the things we've seen in the trip. There's no moon in the sky any longer, and the stars look bigger than they were. What else is there that's strange? What do the trees look like, and the rivers? Do people live in straw shacks, or baked earth?"

"The trees and plants appear very much like those you are seeing now and those in your world; there are two main kinds of trees, those with broad leaves that turn color in the autumn and are shed, and the firs, whose leaves are like bluish needles and never fall. As for the smaller plants, I've never paid them much attention. There are many kinds of flowers, usually brighter colored than those I saw in your world. There is the blue thessany, which smells like fresh-ground cardaunce, and all the variants of the goldflower, from the tiny one whose name I forget to the petaled sun, which is almost a perfect sphere; roses, bellinores, aracerulles, and malifoils . . . You will have to see them yourself, I am worthless at describing flowers."

"I've always liked flowers," said Christine. "I liked those from Terra Australis the most, because they were so colorful. Everyone always said they were strange, but I just thought they looked so nice. And some of the memories I kept, even those that I thought were just dreams, were of flowers. . . . What about animals? Do you have dogs and cats? Sheep? Cows? Or stranger things?"

"No, our animals are very mundane, Lady. Save perhaps for the predators of the extreme south. In civilized lands we have quite a few domesticates, though not so many breeds as you have been used to. The breeders in your world were mad, if you ask me. Still, we do have cats, though they are rarely kept as pets; they hunt rats in farms for the most part. Dogs you will find about more often, usually for the hunt and herding, but the smaller breeds are no use except as companions. We have kine that will look very familiar to you, and sheep whose wool we shear and weave into clothes. I hope you did not like goats very much, because that animal is foreign to us. But you might like hogs; they are a kind of bristleless boar, pink and brown. Smart and strong, and their meat is delicious . . . I see I am upsetting you."

"I don't like to think of something I'm eating as having been smart."

"My apologies. . . . You asked about houses, did you not? We mostly build in wood, though the houses of the wealthy are all stone. We do not have that brick your world is in love with. Our houses are straight . . . well, I mean . . . words fail me. They are the shape a house is supposed to be. I have spent my life looking at imaginary buildings and seeing them as different from the proper norm; I find I cannot describe it. But I assure you you will recognize them as houses; and very fine ones, at that."

"Gray-white stone?" she asked, the image having sprung unbidden into her mind. And when Quentin nodded, she added, her heart pounding: "And the mortar is thin black lines, like jam in a sandwich, isn't it? And there is always wood to frame the windows, and the roofs are . . ." Here she stopped, the wellspring of remembrance immediately running dry. But Quentin continued the sentence for her: "Gabled and tiled in red and brown, usually." She could have sworn those very words had been lodged in her own mind beneath the threshold of speech.

Christine shivered; she waited for more shards of memory to surface, and found herself recalling the journal she had kept just after she had learned to write, in which she had written down those fragments that came to her in dreams. "I remembered . . . ," she started, and went on: "I still remember walking on a cobblestoned street. I was very little. I still see the sunlight on the stones; I can't tell who's with me. I think there were many people at a distance. Where could that have been?"

"Tiellorn, in all probability, Lady Christine. You might well have been taken on an outing to the city."

"I used to remember so much more," she whispered. "I wrote it all down, but I thought I had been making it up. Uncle said it so often at the start . . . *Stop being silly, Christine. Don't be such a child. These things aren't real; you're just playing make-believe.* He lied to me; he made me think I was just a silly child with too much imagination. But he knew the truth, didn't he?"

"Please, Lady, you are becoming overwrought. Perhaps you should lie down."

She paid Quentin no heed, her mind having taken an unexpected tack.

"I used to think that I had stolen my dreams from books and television," she said. "Like fairy tales and Annika the Magic Girl on television, who lived in a mansion with her father and went on trips to enchanted countries. . . . Quentin, could it have been the other way around? Could the stories I read have come from my memories?"

"Perhaps, Lady Christine," Quentin said softly. "Made worlds are distorted reflections of the true realm, after all. But this matter is too deep for me: I cannot give you a definite answer."

At these words Christine's momentary exaltation left her. Regardless of the final truth about the stories where she had found such solace, here she was now, worlds away from the place she had learned to call home, nearing the end of a journey she could barely comprehend.

The sun had vanished below the horizon; Christine felt exhausted. She lay down between the blankets and shut her eyes. She could hear Quentin pacing back and forth around her; she felt both threatened by his very presence and protected. It took her a timeless stretch before she could fall asleep.

4. The Hedges

Magic was a series of journeys, Casimir reflected as he spiraled down, down, down. Journeys through the landscapes of one's mind, reflected in the outer world. Journeys through made worlds, which were nothing but efflorescences of power, and thus ultimately of someone else's mind. Journeys through nonspace, through the underside of reality, in search of yet greater power. And now this power made possible a journey through earth and rock, into places long forgotten by mortals.

In the early ages of the world, as the primeval Heroes carved a place for Man within nature, they had battled fierce creatures by the dozens and hundreds. Tlelak of the Burning Spear had kept a roster of the things he slew. Engraved on metal with a quill plucked from the Levin-bird, the list stretched for page after page until it became boring through sheer accumulation of impossibilities. *A Daemon with the Heade of an Eagle and the Bodie of three Joined Serpents, each Scaled in Bronze. A Crab-like Beast with Legs twelve each Terminated by the Heade of a Lovely Girl whose Fangs Spat Black Poison. Seven Eyeless Sisters with Bodies of Chitin and Clawed Handes.*

With the passing of centuries and millennia, these monsters had all but vanished. By the time Hundred-Handed Juldrun had battled her tarrask, humanity rarely if ever caught sight of them. The days when villages in the far reaches of civilization would be terrorized by prowling nightmares were long past. True, the world did grow larger every year, and there were huge stretches of land empty of humankind where fell beasts might still hide; but no one doubted that the age of monsters was gone.

They were, of course, wrong. Hundreds and thousands of demons had been slain but dozens were still extant, far removed from human ken. In the dim past, some beings had proven too powerful or too inconvenient to slay. Instead, they had been sunk into an endless sleep, in places sealed from the upper world. For all intents and purposes, they were indeed dead. But they might still be wakened, by one who had the power, the knowledge, and the will.

Down, down, down, steps forming beneath his feet and vanishing once they were past the level of his head. The rock all about him was lit by a sourceless light that revealed the structure of the minerals. Through great veins of bloodred ore Casimir pushed his way down, through sudden flashes of silver and threads of purest gold, faulted crystals of white quartz the size of whales, clusters of tourmalines, billows of chalcedony, and jagged lines of feldspar.

Cracks appeared in the mineral matrix; presently the stair opened into a huge cavern, a sealed bubble in the rock. Casimir jumped from the last step and plummeted two hundred feet, lightly as a feather. Once he had touched ground, he summoned more light to him, and slowly the far recesses of the cavern, which had not seen light in over five thousand years, were illumined.

On the bare pale rock, a great form lay supine. It had seven limbs in total; though one might have assumed from that number that one had been lopped off, this was not the case. The demon was intact, its gleaming body unmarked by any wounds, untouched by time. Not even the tiniest speck marred its surface, though the floor of the cavern bore everywhere a thin coating of rock dust.

Casimir approached the sleeping demon. In the elongated dome of its skull, in the bulk of its arm, he saw himself reflected as in a puddle of mercury. The air was still, his own breathing barely disturbing it. The demon's chest did not rise or fall; not a quiver agitated its many limbs. The seven fingers of its nearest hand had curled in a complex pattern, as if it had been readying some spell no human mage could ever cast.

Casimir had attuned his senses and perceived the sleep-spell that enmeshed the demon. It was a working of great power, though fundamentally very simple. It would not tax his strength excessively to break it, but that would accomplish nothing useful. Being left alone in a cave miles beneath the ground, facing a newly awakened demon, held little appeal to a sane man. The working could be used to better purpose, however, for the sleep-spell could be cloven in two: a command substrate that gave one power over the demon, and a sleep injunction. The latter Casimir could safely discard; he would be left with a hold over the demon: the ability to compel it to his will. All that this took was knowledge of its name, and a sufficiency of raw power. Casimir had ample supply of the latter; and as for the former, the shadow of Buell the Archivist had proved a trove of information. Seven sleeping horrors Buell had known of in detail, their names and the locations of their tombs.

Casimir spoke a spell, his voice echoing weirdly in the vault. He capped the working with the demon's name, a knotted skein of consonants and glottal stops. The sleep-spell decayed into its more basic form, and the demon awoke instantly.

Its movements were of a terrifying fluidity that no creature possessing bones could equal. It took less than a second before it stood up, less than two before it stretched out its claws toward Casimir. The wizard shouted an order at it, and the metallic claws stopped mere inches from his face. The eyes of the demon had opened, and their gaze bored into Casimir; in his very bones he heard the song of abysses that compels men to jump to their deaths.

"Desist," he told the demon. *"Subside."* The great beast lidded its gaze and huddled down onto the floor like a puddle of metal, coiling its limbs about its body, resting its chin upon the ground. Casimir could barely see over the top of its skull.

"I will go now," he told it. "Bide here for my command. When the time comes, I shall open a way for you to the land above. When you hear my call, come to my side."

The demon showed no reaction, no movement. Asleep or awake, it did not breathe. Casimir turned his back on it and ascended to the ceiling of the cavern, where the stairs still stood. He began to climb, his legs moving him effortlessly upward. Once a good hundred feet of stone separated him from the cavern he allowed himself a shuddering sigh. He had come dangerously close to death. The demon's will strained against the imprisonment of the command-spell, but Casimir held it secure. As long as his willpower held, the beast would obey him.

He climbed still, toward sunlight and air. He grew calmer as he neared the surface, and his assurance returned. This had been the greatest of the sleeping demons; the others would be easier. And he could hold all seven of them, of that he had no doubt. Not only his knowledge, but his power had grown from his long sojourn in the earth. One by one he would gather them, hold them at the ready. Come summer, it would be time for a decisive strike, time to unleash the demons from the Book of Shades and let them loose upon the world.

At dawn they set off again; Quentin set an easy pace. For a time they followed a trail, and made better progress, but soon they left it behind them. "I had rather travel through unpopulated areas now," Quentin explained. "And besides, since our destination is not in a peopled area, it is simpler to reach it this way."

"Can you actually see it?" asked Christine. "I mean, what is it like, looking *beyond*?"

"I cannot explain it well. When I cast my gaze outward, I see, or I imagine I see, all the worlds layered on top of one another. All the hills, all the rivers, everything. It is like a sculpture made of sand grains, all swarming. . . . I can see what little is left of the gradient toward the real world; we are going up it. We still have many choices for the exact path we follow, but fewer and fewer as we approach the aperture."

"How far away is it now?"

"Perhaps . . . fifteen leagues. A bit more. Three days still, at five leagues a day."

"That doesn't seem much. I could walk faster."

"We will try going a bit quicker if you want, but I will not have you exhausting yourself. It is not fitting for a princess of the realm."

After a moment, Christine said, "I keep forgetting it, you know. That I'm supposed to be a princess. Most of the time I just think of myself as . . . as just me. When I'm back, will I have to spend all my time thinking 'I'm Princess Christine'?"

"Since that is who you are, you will not need to remind yourself of it, I am sure. And the people will address you as such; they will remind you."

"I'll have servants. People to do my laundry and cook for me, and everything else. I don't know how I feel about that. It's like being very rich, I suppose, except they'll obey me because I'm the king's daughter." Christine heaved a nervous sigh and they continued walking in silence.

The land became thinly forested. Trees grew in clumps, their trunks gray as cinders, their leaves tiny and round. When a wind rose, the trees shed some of the pale-yellow leaves, which fell upon the travelers like coins from the skies. Christine kept one in her pocket; it felt like money more tangible than Quentin's illusory banknotes.

A bit later Christine tripped on a rock hidden by the grass; she cried out, fell forward, and was caught by Quentin. He held her in a strong grip until she could get her feet under her, then let her go as she shuddered all over.

"I am sorry, milady," he said. "But you were falling."

"I . . . I know. Thank you for catching me." She rubbed at her arms, where his hands had gripped her. She had felt, could still almost feel, the strength in his arms and hands. She saw him in this moment as a figure of power, male and dangerous. His clothes were now a green jerkin and dun trousers, with black boots; he was like an image in a child's picture book, and for some reason this very thought was fearsome. For a few thudding heartbeats, she quailed at the sight of him. Why had he taken her this far, worlds away from the reality she knew? They stood in a land without trace of human presence, all alone. He could do whatever he wanted with her. . . .

"Are you well?" came Quentin's concerned voice, which was also Tap's.

Hope and trust, trust and hope. She wiped her brow and said, "I'll be fine." Then she made herself walk forward, as if the regular motion of her legs were a spell to leach away her anguish.

They paused to eat and drink at midday and late in the afternoon. Toward evening, an inn became visible in the distance, at the outskirts of a forest.

"I am taking a small risk," said Quentin. "But I want us to get a good night's sleep, and fresh food and drink. This will be the last time we shall be amongst people until we return to Chrysanthe. Please let me do all the talking."

Christine felt her nervousness reborn as they entered the inn, which was small and bereft of a sign. Yet the innkeeper proved friendly and his food more than adequate. Quentin rented a single room for them both. Christine had kept silent throughout their meal, which the innkeeper apparently saw as a challenge.

"And what does your wife say, friend?" he asked after he and Quentin had agreed on a price. "Hey, mistress? Spend a good night in my inn?"

"I'm sure," said Christine in a small voice.

"Well, well, she can speak! I'd been starting to think she was one of those Cassinites. . . ." The innkeeper laughed at his joke, and Christine tried to join in.

Quentin and Christine went upstairs, entered the cramped room Quentin's illusory coin had purchased them. For furniture there was a single bed, with straw ticking, and a cracked chamberpot; but the room was clean and smelled pleasantly of wildflowers from a fresh bouquet hung on a nail above the door.

Christine sat on the bed. "What's a Cassinite?" she asked.

"I have not the least idea. I apologize for letting him think we were man and wife, but for obvious reasons I had no wish to go into the details of our association."

"That's fine, I understand. You don't need to apologize." Color had come to his cheeks; she realized she was blushing too. She unlaced her boots, pulled them off, and stretched out on the bed. Suddenly she felt almost dizzy with fatigue. "Quentin, I think I need to sleep now. Can you wake me when it's my turn to watch?"

Quentin had sat down with his back against the door. "Very well. Please do not stay in the bed once I have woken you; you might well fall asleep again without knowing it."

"When you replace me in it, I'll get out."

"It is not proper that you and I should share the same bed!" Quentin was definitely blushing now. Christine felt her voice tremble, yet held on to logic.

"I'm not suggesting we sleep in it at the same time, all right? And even if we did, I thought I could trust you."

". . . Naturally, but appearances . . ."

"To the innkeeper we're man and wife. Whose opinion are you concerned about?"

Quentin remained speechless for a moment; then his mouth twisted in a grin of vague self-contempt as he came up with the answer. "The court's. As if that gossip Bridianne were to be informed of every detail of our trip. Forgive me, Lady, I am not thinking straight. It matters to no one except ourselves how we share this bed tonight. . . . Oh dear, what have I just said?"

His cheeks were flaming, as were Christine's. "I know what you meant!" she said, exasperated. "God, why are we having this ridiculous conversation?"

"I am so sorry. . . ."

"Quentin, shut up! Stop apologizing all the time. You're driving me crazy!"

Quentin started to reply with another apology, which he bit back.

"Look," Christine said, and found to her astonishment that tears were beading at the corners of her eyes. "Look, we're not like two teenagers renting a motel room to d-do it without their parents' knowledge. You're a knight of the realm and I'm, I'm the one you rescued. We're traveling companions. I never thought otherwise. Unless you . . ." She could not go on.

"We are both exhausted," Quentin said carefully. "Please go to sleep. In a few hours, I will wake you, and I will stretch out myself. Agreed?"

She nodded, smearing her tears across her cheeks with a fingertip. Quentin blew out the candle he had carried up to their room. Christine lay with eyes wide open in the darkness. She felt so troubled and confused she could not imagine going to sleep; and thinking this, she dozed off.

It was early morning when she woke; Quentin was still seated with his back against the door.

"Quentin!" she called out in a whisper.

He answered instantly: "I am awake, Lady."

"Why didn't you wake me?"

"You slept too deeply. I let myself doze, but I remained half awake; an old trick. Do not fear, I took plenty of rest."

She wanted to scold him, but the memory of their awkward discussion the night before convinced her to dismiss the matter. Quentin went to rouse the innkeeper and fetch some heated water, so that she might wash, which she did quickly, while he waited outside the room. When she was done, she called him back in.

"The water's still warm, Quentin. You can wash now, I'll just stand outside the door."

"Well . . ." He hesitated, looking at the water and soap longingly. "I probably should not."

"Are you saying there's danger here?"

"No; none that I know of. When I went below, everything was fine."

"Then you can spare five minutes to get clean, can't you? I promise, if something happens, I'll scream."

"Do not joke, milady. But . . . all right, five minutes."

Christine stepped out, leaned on the railing of the narrow walkway that gave access to the inn's three rooms. Quentin had made sure the other two rooms were empty; still, she glanced warily at their open doors.

"Good morning, mistress," said the innkeeper from the ground floor, startling her. "Breakfast now, yes?"

Christine could not find a way to refuse; she went down the stairs to the inn's common room and sat at a table. The innkeeper put before her a platter of roasted potatoes and some bits of lard, with a cup of what proved to be mulled and heavily spiced cider.

As Christine coughed from the drink, he asked her: "How long you've been married, you two?"

"Not—not long."

"Good husband, is he?"

"Yes. Yes, he is."

"Won't let you out of his sight much, eh? Newlyweds the same everywhere. Where you off to?"

"To . . . to his village. We'll be living there together."

"Is it this side of Tellarn?"

Quentin came down the stairs at that moment, carrying both their bags. "A bit beyond it," he said. "I will have some breakfast, please, and I shall settle our accounts directly."

Coins drawn from the bottomless purse clattered on the counter. The innkeeper nodded and brought Quentin his breakfast. Once they were done, Quentin bade the innkeeper good-bye, with Christine muttering along with him. They were already well along the path when the man's bellow reached them. "May God keep you in Her sight and bless your marriage with many daughters! Farewell! Farewell! Farewell!"

Christine turned back at the third farewell, but the inn was no longer to be seen; and the jovial, nosy innkeeper had ceased to exist. If Quentin were correct in his philosophy, then it followed that to travel among the made worlds was to commit murder at every step. Yet should anyone be deemed a murderer for killing dreams?

❦ Quentin had bargained for some additional supplies; at noon they made a frugal meal of fresh bread and some pickled yellow-pink vegetables Christine had never tasted but which Quentin clearly had, and relished. "Abances! They taste exactly like those I ate as a child. We are getting very close, milady."

"They're not bad, but they taste rather weird to me. Are they like cucumbers?"

"No, they grow in the ground. You have to pick them early in the season, else they grow big, starchy, and quite inedible. Late-summer abances are only fit for hogs. When I was seven, my mother put me in charge of picking the abances; it was my first real responsibility."

"If you hadn't become a knight, I think you'd have made a good gardener."

"I doubt it; I care about abances only because I love to eat them. Do not ask me to spend my days hoeing turnips and manuring roses. . . ."

They walked the rest of the day, through brief stands of forests and evanescent hills; the ground was more and more often flat, with here and there a nearly straight ditch full of water, and small poplarlike trees growing in a single row alongside. The sky was a rich blue, the sun strangely pale, with the suggestion of texture in its surface when Christine chanced to glance at it.

When it set, she distinctly noticed a roiling pattern within the solar orb; she drew Quentin's attention to it. "Is something the matter with the sun?"

"Not at all. This is how it looks in Chrysanthe, or nearly."

"It . . . it feels wrong, somehow." They had lost the moon in their travels long ago; now she felt as though they would lose the sun as well.

"It shines like yours did. It is simply more interesting to look at. Sunsets in your land were often nice, but they cannot compare to summer dusk at Testenel, when clouds mass in the sky and it is as if the sun is setting them aflame. . . . And when a cloud gets at just the right angle, it reflects the glow straight at you. Then you can catch every flicker in the corona redoubled in the cloud, and it is like a kind of dance. There is a famous book by Karyss of Dawl, called *Demesnes of Light and Shadow*, which was inspired by one of the most spectacular sunsets in over a century. She writes that it was the sunset that told her the story in the book; she just set it down afterward. It concerns an imaginary land, somewhere in the made worlds; and the last stand of the forces of good against the onslaught of evils out of the Book of Shades. It is a harsh tale that ends in tears. When I first read it, I was saddened, and I felt betrayed by the author; but there are several chapters in it that are so splendid I could not help wanting to read it again all the same."

The night was warmer than the day had been. Setting forth from the inn, it had been early fall, a chilly morning. They were moving through the height of summer now; night lasted a bare six hours before the sun rose again.

The land was not as flat as it had been, but the prominences of the ground were small in all dimensions; to Christine, these small buttes and rolling miniature hills seemed landscaped. Flowers spangled the grass with increasing frequency. Thornbushes sometimes barred their way. Quentin detoured around them with not the slightest sign of annoyance, and whenever they rounded one, Christine could look back and see that the land behind them had altered again. She wondered if they were now so close to their destination that the direction of movement had ceased to matter.

The bushes lost their thorns around noon. They grew so much higher now that the term "bush" felt forced. Their foliage reached up to Christine's shoulders or higher. They blocked sight in all direction, and though there were large expanses between them, still it felt that Christine and Quentin were moving through a vast maze.

This impression only grew stronger after their midday meal, as the bushes became straighter and straighter, and then perfectly linear, meeting one another at right angles. Quentin had been growing more and more anxious; he no longer wore traveling clothes, but the full suit of armor that was his real accoutrement. His sword swung at his side. He set a brisker pace, kept looking back at her as if to hurry her. Christine's legs were getting sore.

And then, toward midafternoon, he stopped abruptly and stood there quivering for several heartbeats, his arm extended as if to prevent her from taking another step. They had been walking along a tall hedge for half an hour; Christine saw that there was a small gap up ahead, less than six feet wide.

"This is it, Lady Christine," said Quentin, his voice strained. "The opening in the hedge. That is the aperture into Chrysanthe."

They approached the gap slowly. Through it, a different vista was revealed. Christine gasped suddenly as it became clear to her. It was another succession of hedges, but these were of a different sort. The bushes were denser, overgrown with purple and gold flowers that grew to extravagant sizes, nearly as big as her own head.

"The flowers . . . I remember those flowers," whispered Christine. Quentin's letter had borne such a flower on its stamp, but it was a pale reflection of the reality. And these flowers, this profusion of them, brought something back to her. A true memory—at least she hoped it was. Her heart swelled at the sight; she felt she was coming home.

"I will cross first," said Quentin. "Just to be sure there is no risk beyond, though I see nothing to threaten us. When I motion to you, you may come."

He drew his sword, pushed branches aside, and stepped through the gap. Christine saw him shimmer in the instant of traversal; and when his image cleared, it had changed subtly. His armor gleamed more brightly; the leaping fish engraved on the breastplate looked more real than any mere picture had a right to. Quentin looked right and left, put his sword back in its sheath, and motioned to her.

Christine swallowed, her throat tight with sudden fear. Then she stepped forward.

She felt nothing at all when she passed into Chrysanthe; she had expected a subtle wrenching sensation, some knowledge of reality finally blooming in her mind. There was none of that. She did feel a sudden drop in temperature, and a very strong breeze. Quentin's face had blossomed into a smile, but the next instant twisted in acute embarrassment. Christine realized simultaneously that she was stark naked.

Horrified, she crouched down, her arms about her. "What's going on?" she shouted, more bewildered than anything else.

"Oh, milady, I forgot! I forgot!" babbled Quentin, rushing toward her and trying to avert his gaze at the same time. "Here, here, wait, I can . . ." He was fumbling with the cape he wore over his backplate, finally managed to remove it and hand it to her.

Christine draped it around herself, tied the thongs together, and clutched the folds of it in her fists. "What happened?" she asked, in the tones of a child confronted with the utter absurdity of the world.

Quentin was gazing steadily at her bare toes, poking out from beneath the hem of the cape. "I told you, Lady Christine, nothing of the made worlds is real. Nothing of them can exist within Chrysanthe. When I brought back the false Christine, we came together through the gap, but on the other side my hand held only air. She vanished utterly when she tried passing through. The same thing just happened to your clothes, since they are not from Chrysanthe."

"And you never planned for this situation?" Quentin's explanation made sense; she could afford to be angry now.

"I . . . Well, that was the least of my worries. I was mostly concerned with finding you and bringing you back. When I pictured myself successful, I always saw you as clothed as we passed through. I guess I never thought about . . . this aspect of things."

His expression was so contrite she started to find the situation comical; and then she remembered the other times she had been naked in front of men and froze in terror.

But those events had never happened; no matter that she remembered them, they had been born of Dr. Almand's meddling. This was in fact the first time of her life she had been naked in front of a man. And he was the last person in the world who would harm her. She trusted him. She did trust him. Her ears were singing and she felt she might faint, but she reached out a hand from within her makeshift cloak and grasped his wrist.

"Help me up," she said, and he did, still keeping his gaze averted. "You can look at me, I'm decent," she added. Quentin looked carefully at her face only and started to apologize again. "No need," she said. She felt light-headed, the blood having fled her head as she rose. She reached out a hand to steady herself against him. The cape opened as she did so; he might have gotten a flash of her body had he not been looking so intently into her eyes.

"Are you all right, Lady?"

"Yes . . . I'm fine." She clutched the folds of the cape with one hand and leaned on her other arm, which shook a bit with the strain. Her thoughts drifted a moment, as if she dreamed. It came to her that she wished to doff the cape; she wished to show herself naked to Quentin, and not feel fear. For a moment she felt she was truly about to do it, then she regained perspective and her insane bravado faded away.

"Sorry," she said. "I got a bit dizzy there. It was the shock, and I'm very tired."

"Yes, of course. I can . . . I mean, I could carry you but I . . ."

"No, I can walk. Just hold my arm, all right?"

She stepped forward. The ground was covered in short grass, which tickled her bare feet; but she felt no pebbles, almost no irregularities. Uncle's lawn had never been this well maintained.

"Where are we going now?"

"Well, in fact, we need not go anywhere by ourselves. One of the last spells left to me will call to Orion. He will come to fetch us."

"Well—do it, then."

"Yes, yes, of course, I am . . . Forgive me, I have been so afraid I had been misled again, that you would turn out . . . not to be yourself, that my mind is numb. I must concentrate a moment."

Quentin closed his eyes, drew a deep breath. Then he spoke five sharp syllables and called out "Orion!" He opened his eyes and gazed into space. After a while, his face fell. He glanced at her. "I . . . cannot hear him. There is no reply."

He was clearly worried, and his mood was infectious. "Maybe," she said, trying to make sense of things, "he isn't at home. I mean, how does this spell work? Is it like a telephone?"

"Of course not. This is no mechanical contraption. Wherever Orion is, even if he should be asleep, the spell would reach him."

"Well, did you cast it correctly?"

"I could not cast it incorrectly: Orion imprinted it into me himself. I am no magician—the words came out the way he put them in."

"Try again."

Quentin tried again, to no more avail.

"I fail to understand, milady," he said. "Whatever the cause, whether the spell has decayed in my mind or something else has gone wrong, I cannot reach Orion."

"And you can't call someone else? Then what will we do?"

"I guess we have no choice but to reach the nearest village. I am afraid it is several miles away. We will have to walk for quite some time."

Christine tried to shrug, but the necessity of holding the cape tightly about her shoulders made the movement near imperceptible.

"Where are we, anyway?" she asked. "Is this a garden?"

"The Hedges are no garden, never have been. This is wild land—there are no human habitations within the Hedges themselves. I am sorry that we will need to walk so far. I had counted on having my mount still with me when I returned. I guess I am a paltry strategist, milady."

"Stop apologizing. You're a brave knight and you've brought me back to my home—" Her eyes had gone blurry with tears as she said this; she blinked, felt two drops form and fall, clearing her sight. "And I'm very grateful, even if I am half-naked."

Quentin bit back a reply—obviously a further apology. Christine looked around them. From this side, the hedge was different: in the shape and the color of the leaves, and mostly in the flowers growing riotously over it all. She recalled a sight like this, that she had believed nearly all her life had been a dream. Had she been taken here, once? Had she seen the tall hedge and the dazzle of its flowers and dreamed about it later? She might have; but she could not claim with certainty that she remembered having seen this place.

She pointed to the flowered wall of foliage with her chin. "You say this is wild land; then how can all this be so well tended? This feels like a prize-winning garden, not a forest."

"It is not a forest; forests are truly wild places. But neither is it a garden; you have never seen a garden in Chrysanthe—I mean, you have not seen one since your exile—but I can assure you this area is a shambles compared to the Royal Gardens."

"But why is it so clean? Who trims the hedges?"

"No one. They grow this way. The land itself shapes them, if you will."

"More magic?"

"So the stories tell. In olden ages, when Heroes by the dozens walked the land, wizards laid spells upon the land that have endured to this day. The Hedges are maintained by very ancient magic, the likes of which can no longer be found. In the beginning of the world, when the realm of Men was yet very small, the Hedges marked its boundary. Beyond them the land was lawless and dangerous. . . . But that was thousands of years ago."

Quentin started walking to their right and Christine followed him. The grass corridor turned left, and just past the bend a weathered wooden gate barred their way. It was an easy task for Quentin to jump over it, as it rose no higher than his waist and was collapsing in the middle besides; Christine had a harder time of it and nearly lost her grip on the cape. There was a large panel set atop the gate. It bore writing on the obverse side, careful hand-painted black letters: *Traveler beware! Beyond lies the entrance into Errefern. Turn back lest you wish to be lost in infinity.*

Reading the words, Christine felt a shiver course down her spine. "Not much of a warning," she said. "If it were me, I'd build something bigger and stronger."

"Bar people's way in with stone? It has been tried, milady. Four hundred years ago, a fort was built in this place by Queen Idanith for just that purpose. But the Hedges that had been cut grew back, split the walls apart, and collapsed the fort. Here." He scratched at the ground, dug up a pebble as big as the end of his thumb. "This is all that is left of the fort. The Hedges crumbled the stone to bits. I will grant you one might put columns on either side of the aperture to indicate it better, as was done for Jyndyrys, but it is perceived as a waste of effort. After all, no one lives close to here, and there is no incentive to travel within the Hedges at random. People pass through one of the gates that lead straight through this area and avoid treading the corridors, which after all lead nowhere."

They walked on, their feet coming down softly on thick, short grass. The sun was hidden behind the tightly woven branches, but pinpoints of light made their way through the interlacing of boughs and leaves: The corridors were shaded but not gloomy. The way they had been following was ruler-straight. They came to a cross-road. The intersecting paths were not quite perpendicular; Quentin took the left-hand one, but it dead-ended after two hundred feet or so. Quentin shrugged and led them back, then picked another path, which grew broader and angled in a direction that satisfied him. Forestalling Christine's question, he explained:

"This is not a maze by any means. Some of the corridors end in blank walls, but the vast majority do not. Except at the gates, following a straight way is impossible, but few detours need to be taken."

"Why make it like this to start with?"

"I do not think anyone knows. If anyone does, Orion would, being who he is. You can ask him when we meet him. . . . When I was little, I was told it was because demons cannot travel crooked ways to reach their goal: The Hedges made it impossible for demons to slip from the outer world into the realm of Men. When I was older, Sir Glenn taught me that was utter nonsense. Why then would there be six gates piercing the Hedges, broad and open, wide enough for an army of demons to pass through? I have decided it is like asking why the sky is blue: There is no need for a reason; things are just that way."

And Quentin gestured at the sky above their heads, a dazzling shade of blue, here and there offset by brushstrokes of white clouds. Left and right, fore and aft, the hedges surrounded them: walls of foliage, sometimes just taller than Quentin, usually far higher, ranging to nearly twice his height. Flowering vines intertwined with the branches, their own leaves delicate and pale, fernlike. The flowers' fleshy petals were sometimes pink, sometimes red, but mostly gold or purple, in numerous variations of pigments. Christine bent over one to smell it, and was surprised at the tartness of the perfume. Quentin walked slowly by her side, looking at her from only the corner of his eyes.

"The Hedges are only about a mile wide," he said. "We will soon be out of them and into fields. There is a road not far from here; we will follow it, and be in Quamerien before nightfall."

He had mostly been looking at the sky rather than at her; suddenly he halted.

"Wait!" he said, and stepped back, looking at a corner of sky the intervening hedge walls had been masking. Then he uttered an exclamation of wonder. "A skyship! Quickly, Lady! They must see us!"

He jumped at the nearest hedge wall and began clambering up it. Branches tore and snapped under his weight, but the trunks were sturdy enough to bear him. With grunts of effort or urgency, Quentin at last achieved the summit of the wall, a good twelve feet in the air. He stood teetering, his legs sinking to his ankles through the branches, drew his sword and waved it about, screaming at the top of his lungs.

He screamed and waved for several minutes, trying to raise himself still higher and nearly falling in the process as branches gave way all at once and he sank to midcalf. Careless of the damage he was wreaking, he stepped along the wall, gaining an area of intact branches that bore his weight for now, and resumed his display.

"Yes!" he finally shouted. "The skyship has seen us! They are coming this way!"

He was looking down at her with a beaming smile, when the hedge gave way once more and he had to bend down and clutch desperately at the branches. Flower petals rained down as he hauled himself upright again.

"You're going to fall!" shouted Christine. "Get down here!"

"As soon as I am sure they know just where we stand . . ." Quentin waved again, but with more restraint, having prudently sheathed his blade. At long last he climbed down, just as sails hove into view above the leafy walls. Then below the sails evolved the body of a ship: a wooden-planked hull with what looked like a pair of outriggers at the end of stubby rods angled downward. Christine stared at it, dumbstruck.

"Ahoy!" shouted Quentin. "Here we are! Ahoy!"

The ship was passing overhead. A gondola with a latticed floor hung twenty feet below the keel at the end of a long arm—a reversed crow's nest. Someone stood inside it, doubtless acting as a lookout.

An emblem was painted on the bow of the skyship, a symbol whose meaning was obscure to Christine; but Quentin recognized it, exclaiming: "It is the *Black Heart,* Lady! I cannot believe our luck. Ahoy, above! Let us aboard! We are on an errand of the highest importance!"

Orders must have been given aboard the ship, for sails were canted or furled, and the craft swerved sharply, reducing speed and altitude.

Quentin clambered down the hedge wall, in a flurry of torn leaves and snapped branches. He reached the ground and rejoined Christine. Vines had tangled themselves around his knees and pink and gold flowers had been bound to his legs. "They are going to land," he said. "There must be an open space in that direction. Let us hurry."

They walked as fast as Christine could manage without the breadth of her strides flapping the cape open. Not far off, a perpendicular way opened across their path. They turned right.

The corridor they were following gave onto a large square area, into which many passages opened. There was a natural pool at the center, irregularly shaped, yet seeming sculpted carefully by human hands. The ship hovered just before the pool, settling closer and closer to the ground. Two slim anchors were dropped from bowsprit and sternpost at the end of ropes; they were shaped like long-fingered hands, and when they touched the ground, their fingers flexed and clenched at the soil. Christine felt a shiver run through her when she saw this. Yet Quentin was urging her onward. Clutching the cape around her, she followed.

"Ahoy there!" called out a man from the railing, a good fifty feet in the air still. "Who are you, then?"

Quentin stopped his advance when they stood close to the bank of the pool. The afternoon sun shone on the skyship, making every surface gleam. The man who'd spoken was dressed rather flamboyantly, his vest a clash of red and purple with here and there a sulfurous yellow attempting to mediate. His raven-black hair escaped his huge hat on one side only; on the other, some sort of thick white plume drooped down, for an odd effect. Crewmen stood to the left and right of him; many more were up in the rigging, adjusting the sails.

"Captain Veraless!" exclaimed Quentin, delightedly. "Such a pleasure to see you again, sir! It has been a long time since our last meeting."

"You have the advantage over me, lad," Veraless shouted back. "Who the hell are you, and who's the chit by your side?"

"I am Quentin—Sir Quentin of Lydiss. You would not remember meeting me; it was years ago. And this, Captain . . . well, this is the Princess Christine."

Dead silence fell, for a heartbeat. Then Captain Veraless said, "God's teeth, I don't care if you're both crazies—I'll have you flayed for that lie."

Quentin drew himself up. "I am telling the exact truth, Captain, no matter that it may be hard to believe. I must request that you convey the Lady Christine and myself to Testenel at once."

"Take them aboard," the captain ordered curtly. A pair of rope ladders were thrown over the side of the skyship; half a dozen men and women went down the ladders and stepped down upon the ground. They were dressed in knee-length breeches and loose blouses; all of them wore gloves with cutout palms.

One of them spoke: "If you please, sir, madam, come up the ropes. We'll go up before and behind you, and hold you tight."

"I am afraid that is out of the question," said Quentin. "The Lady Christine requires a gondola." After a brief argument, a small gondola was lowered on ropes; Quentin and Christine climbed within and were hauled aboard.

As they rose, Christine squeezed Quentin's hand. "He doesn't believe you," she said fearfully. "No one will know who I am, will they?"

"He will know when he looks at you, milady."

"He can't. Even if he saw me before I was taken away, I was four years old."

Quentin assumed a smug expression. "Ah, but milady, we have proof: We have your fleshpaint portrait—" His face fell. "You . . . You do have it, do you not?"

In answer Christine only clutched the cape tighter around herself.

"It was . . . it was in your jacket?" asked Quentin. "But it came from the true world. It must have survived the crossing. Though, if your clothes vanished . . . I suppose we did not notice it."

Christine shook her head; she remembered nothing from the crossing except her abrupt nakedness. Had the pair of leather wallets fallen to the ground as she entered Chrysanthe and her clothes vanished? Had they tumbled back through the gap into the made world? She could not recall.

Quentin shook himself. "No matter, no matter! Wherever the portrait may lie, it is gone now. But we do not need it. I will vouch for you. The word of a knight of Chrysanthe must be believed."

They were set down on deck then, and had to exit the gondola. Christine managed to do so without revealing too much of her naked body.

Captain Veraless faced them, hands on hips. Christine saw that what she had taken for a plume was in fact his hair, which was dyed white as chalk on one side—unless it was the black side that was dyed, for the man was no longer young; his face was seamed, scarred in a dozen places; his nose had been broken at least once, and a large mustache hid a badly torn upper lip. His eyes, a luminous pale blue, glared at them.

"I don't remember any Sir Quentin of Lydiss," he said. "While you, girl, might be anyone."

"I was dubbed nine years ago, when I was seventeen," said Quentin. "I immediately went questing among the made worlds for our lost princess."

Captain Veraless nodded grudgingly at this. "You and a score of others. A waste of effort, I always said."

"But I have succeeded," said Quentin quietly. "I found the princess and brought her back."

"I'd like to believe you," said Captain Veraless with a hint of pain in his voice. "But Christine has been lost to us for over a decade; how can anyone expect her to come back? This is some peasant girl you've found in a hamlet at the edge of civilization and brought back to impersonate the king's daughter."

"Captain!" protested Quentin. "You insult the lady!" When Veraless shrugged, Quentin continued: "I give you my solemn word as a knight—"

"Yeah, your solemn word. That's just what Sir Reivin said," interrupted Veraless. "Five years ago, he showed up at Testenel with a girl in tow, fresh from the hell of the made worlds. He gave his word as a knight that this was the Lady Christine he'd found. People believed him. They went to the king in a frenzy. They were bringing back his daughter. I was with His Majesty when they burst in, all of them insane with joy. We have your daughter, King Edisthen, they cried, we have her! *And I believed them too.* At that moment, I believed them and my heart swelled so much I thought it'd burst. They brought the girl to him; she was beet-red, so flustered she couldn't speak. I was all ready to cry.

"Then he turned to them and he said, he said, 'This isn't her. This isn't Christine.' He wasn't even angry."

Veraless took a step forward; his eyes gleamed with repressed fury.

"Do you understand, lad? *He wasn't even angry.* He corrected them like you correct a child when he's shaped a letter wrong. Then he turned back to me and started talking about the new gardens he wanted planted on the western slopes, and what did I think of purple ansognias instead of evening sweets? Nobody else was making any sound. Then the girl starts to sob, she falls on her knees, screams to the king to forgive her, she was only trying to help. . . .

"He turned to her and patted her head, said it was all right. Reivin was white as a lemure. They left then, all of them, with Reivin and the girl. The king kept talking about his garden, so I couldn't follow them. I was told they hardly said a thing to Reivin. The next morning he was found in the main courtyard; he'd slashed his own throat. No one knows what happened to the girl.

"Now I'm telling you, lad, Quentin, get off my ship while you can and take this chit with you. You mean well, but there's no point: Edisthen would recognize his daughter if he hadn't seen her for a hundred years."

"I do not doubt it," said Quentin. "I always knew he would recognize Christine when he saw her. This is no impostor, Captain, I swear to you."

Veraless looked at Christine with a sneer—but his lower lip was quivering.

"Any reason why she lacks clothes?"

Christine was tired of being spoken of in the third person; she answered him.

"Sir—Captain—I was wearing clothes until I passed through the portal into Chrysanthe. Then they were gone. Quentin said that nothing from the made worlds can exist here. So I was wondering, in fact, if you could lend me some decent clothes; I'm tired of being n-naked under this."

Captain Veraless remained silent for a moment, as if preoccupied; then he snapped, "Clothes. Someone bring clothing for the girl!" Turning to Quentin—he had to tear his gaze away from Christine this time—he added, "I'll punish you personally for this. You won't be allowed to go Reivin's way."

Quentin shook his head. "I am sorry about Reivin. I knew him somewhat. He was—very dedicated."

Veraless turned and stalked away abruptly, leaving his two passengers among a ring of staring sky-sailors. One of them handed a packet of clothes to Christine. Quentin took them, Christine's hands being busy clutching the cape to her.

"She needs a place to change," he started to say. At the same instant, Captain Veraless bellowed orders to cast off and make for Testenel at once. "And put these two into the forward cabin!"

This was done. The forward cabin, apparently intended for passengers, was spacious and fairly elegant. Quentin stepped out and closed the door behind him. Christine, feeling dazed at the change of scenery, studied the furnishings for a few minutes before loosening the cape and shaking out the bundle of clothes. Though well worn, of coarse weave, they were quite clean. Almost the kind of clothes some punk kids back in her world might have worn. Underwear was limited to panties. She put on a dark-red blouse and trousers striped orange and brown. Her breasts swung freely under the fabric, but the blouse was loose enough that her figure would not be revealed. The shoes, more like leather slippers in fact, were much too big, but she kept them on anyway.

She found herself laughing helplessly, in a sudden release of tension that threatened to turn into a storm of tears. Being clothed again had restored a measure of power to her. She had been feeling terrified and not known it: after all, this was a scenario out of a nightmare in many ways.

Thinking this, she felt reality shifting out from underneath her. She couldn't stand to be alone. She went to the door, opened it, for a moment certain that Quentin would have vanished and that everything would go screaming into insanity from that moment on—but he was standing with his back to the door. When he heard it open, he turned his head a quarter-turn only, calling her name.

"I'm clothed," she said, and he turned to face her. His expression fell.

"These are not clothes fit for you," he said in an offended voice. "Captain Veraless is being insulting."

"Do you really think he carries princesses' gowns in his holds, Quentin? I don't care how this looks, as long as I'm decent."

"We will repair the omission as soon as we reach Testenel, Lady."

"Oh, don't fuss, please. You're just doing this because you're insulted the captain doesn't believe you."

Quentin blinked, taken aback. Then he cast his gaze downward, conceding she was right.

"He wants to believe me, milady. He wants it so much he does not trust himself. He is a hero of the Great War, you know. He defended your father staunchly against the forces of Kawlend. He fought in many battles and nearly died more than once. No man in the realm is as devoted to your cause as Captain Veraless."

"Well . . . that's good to know, I suppose," said Christine. She looked to Veraless, who was shouting orders in an aggrieved voice, his back to them.

"Would you like to look at the land, milady? It is a rare sight we have been afforded."

Christine approached the edge reluctantly and only allowed herself to look down once she had made secure her grip on the gunwale. The skyship was perhaps two hundred feet in the air, and flew at a gentle speed. They had left the Hedges behind; as Quentin had promised, the land was now fields, green with early summer's growth. They were approaching a village, the one Quentin had named Quamerien. People on the ground had been moving about their business but now stopped to point and gawk at the ship. Children ran excitedly, shrieking; adults were more sedate but they too waved enthusiastically at the vessel.

"They do not know you are aboard," said Quentin softly. "If they did, the women would be dancing for joy and the men would be fainting with emotion. Once the news has reached them, that you were brought to Testenel aboard the *Black Heart*, they will shout to themselves that they saw you, they will make themselves remember you waving to them. Perhaps you should wave to them, milady."

Christine shook her head. "I don't want to lose my grip on the railing."

"You're quite safe, ma'am," interrupted a young voice. A sailor had come up to them; she spoke quickly, darting a glance at Captain Veraless, who was currently haranguing some crewmen working at the stern. "Really, you can't fall off, the gunwale's high as your chest." She paused, then continued in a whisper: "I heard what your man said! It's true? You're really her?"

"She is truly the Princess Christine," said Quentin.

The girl went down on one knee and bowed her head, then rose to her feet, trembling.

"Oh, ma'am! Oh, ma'am! The king's daughter is back! Oh, this is so wonderful!" Her mouth was slack and her eyes misty. Christine felt compelled to say something, but words failed her. "I've gotta go," whispered the sailor. "I'll—I'll be back later if you need anything, ma'am. Oh, God!" And she ran off.

After a long silence Christine asked, looking at distant clouds: "And this is how people will react if they believe I'm the princess?"

"Of course."

The skyship sailed on, as the day advanced. They overflew several villages: from the air, these appeared unreal, storybook pictures come to life. People tilled the soil, raised cattle and poultry. Quentin named the villages as they passed; one or two of their names sounded familiar to Christine, but no more.

Then the character of the landscape altered; hills rose from the plain, mantled in woods. Again, though, these had a well-tended aspect. There was no real sense of wilderness in them. The road continued on, a ribbon of packed earth flanked by wide grassy swaths. The hills rose, while the airship kept its altitude constant, so that the treetops neared them. Then they fell away, as the ship entered a broad plain.

"This is the heart of the world, milady," said Quentin. "On the horizon, that is the great city Tiellorn. On the left, you can see Testenel."

Christine gazed at the view. Slowly, slowly, the skyship ate up the distance remaining. The city was surrounded by a wall; beyond it, Christine saw small cramped houses, twisty streets, here and there a larger building. She could not see Perfenel, the old castle Quentin had talked about—and besides, her gaze was drawn more and more irresistibly by the new castle, which stood at least a mile out from the city.

As they grew nearer and nearer, Christine found herself in turmoil. She told herself she recalled the shape of the castle: It felt as if an image that had stood, blurred, in the background of her every thought during this journey, had suddenly moved into focus. And yet, she had experienced this same feeling before, when she came across an old book from her childhood and its painfully familiar illustrations that she had managed to forget for over a decade. She might be deluding herself that she recalled Testenel when in truth she was merely reacting to its semblance to a fairy-tale drawing.

For a fact the castle looked much more like an illustration, a draftsman's flight of fancy, than a real building. Logic argued that nothing could defy gravity in this way and yet stand. Testenel was an enormous mass of blue stone, rising from a circular stem and opening up into a hundred turrets, like some monstrous flower. The architecture was fantastically complicated, every wall pierced by a dozen windows, slender bridges spanning the gaps between towers, ornamental billows of stone flowing down walls like dribbles of lava, giving birth to hybrids of gargoyles and angels.

There was a wide terrace jutting out from one of the towers; it was intended for just such a ship as theirs. The hand-anchors were skillfully thrown out and made themselves fast to the heavy metal railing that bordered the terrace. The sailors hauled on the ropes and the ship was snuggled closer to the terrace, until a short ramp could be lowered over the gunwale to the stone of the castle.

Captain Veraless walked up to Christine and Quentin. Behind him most of his crew had gathered, and gazed at Christine in fascination.

"This is your last chance to walk away," said Veraless. "Run down the ramp and lose yourselves in Testenel. Drop from my sight and the court's notice and I won't pursue the matter."

"Please lead the way to His Majesty, Captain," Quentin replied.

Veraless bit his lower lip, then he set his hat at a jauntier angle and trod down the ramp. Quentin and Christine followed. Three crewmen hovered at her elbow to assist her, until Quentin shooed them away. She hesitated, then took his hand as they descended the ramp. She was afraid of falling—the ground was two hundred feet below the terrace—but there were safety nets spread on each side of the ramp, and a pair of ropes to serve as handrails. However, as soon as her feet found the stone floor, she froze, imagining the entire castle was swaying, was about to fall. . . .

Do I remember any of this? she asked herself. *Is there anything in this palace that I'm sure I recognize?* Then with a shock, something within her answered yes. It wasn't the striking architecture that she recognized with certainty, for all that it ought to be unforgettable; it was the stone. The bluish stone of the tower walls, seen closer up, was marbled with faint abstract patterns. Overcoming her unease, she approached the entrance to the tower, where Veraless was waiting for them impatiently.

Yes; she did recall this stone! Veins and clouds of deeper blue over a paler background, and some cloudy patches of near-white, the whole forming meaningless designs, sometimes like faint inverted vistas of distant lands, or roiling storm clouds, or clotting milk suspended in water. . . . This pattern in fact had stayed with her all her life; it was deeply familiar, but for years she had no longer been able to associate it with anything concrete. A memory that had dissolved itself into the mental background of her life. Christine let her hand brush the stone, feeling its texture, though that didn't evoke any new memories. She looked up at Quentin, wordless.

Then, just as Veraless was showing temper, she got into motion and followed him inside Testenel, Quentin at her side.

Guards waited for them in the level below, a pair of tall men in gold-edged black armor. They recognized Veraless and saluted him but frowned at Quentin and herself.

"I'm taking these two to see His Majesty," said Veraless. "I'll be responsible for them."

"You may not carry any weapons in Testenel," said one of the guards to Quentin. "Give me your sword."

"I am a knight of the realm!" objected Quentin, pointing to the device blazoned on his breastplate. "I am exempt from that regulation."

"I don't care if you're a Hero from the Book, sir. Surrender your blade, please."

Christine touched Quentin's elbow. "What does it matter?" she whispered. He looked at her. "Aren't we safe here?" *Can I trust you, or is there something you didn't tell me?*

He nodded. "Of course we are." He unbuckled his sword, handed it, scabbard and all, to one of the guards. Then he drew a concealed misericorde from within his armor, added it to the sword.

"One moment, please," he said. He worked at a catch on his right greave, and withdrew three sharp pieces of metal from beneath it; some sort of throwing knives. They were stained and darkened, as if they had been frequently bloodied. Lastly, he

shook his left arm sharply, and a dagger bloomed into existence between his fingers—
Christine remembered how it had flashed through the air and buried itself in the
shoulder of the security woman at the mall. . . . Quentin added it to the bundle in
the guard's arms.

"May we pass now?" he asked the guards, with an impertinent smile, which
faded at their expressions. Stone-faced, they now forced him to remove every piece
of armor, as well as his boots, and searched him thoroughly. Veraless stood by, looking at the proceedings keenly. Christine felt acutely embarrassed for Quentin, who
bore the investigation resignedly.

Then the guards turned to her. "Put your arms away from your side," one said.

"No!" said Quentin. "You may not! Hurt her and you are a dead man!"

The guards looked angrily at him. Christine had begun to tremble; but she
would not deny what had to be done. She was brave now.

"It doesn't matter, Quentin. They have to be careful, don't they? They don't
know us."

"Milady! There is no reason for you to be treated like this! These fools are going beyond the call of regulations!"

She held out her arms and looked at the guard interrogatively. As soon as he
reached for her, her courage started to melt away. He felt her up and down, patting
his hands along her body. Though the contact was impersonal, her gut twisted inside her and she shuddered. It was almost over, she told herself, almost over. She'd
done it. Then his hand touched her breast through the fabric of her blouse, and with
a cry she tore herself away. Her whole body convulsed; she curled up into a ball,
wailed and gasped. Her gorge rose; she retched, a throaty rasp escaping her lips.

All the sessions with Dr. Almand rose up in her mind, all the memories she'd
dredged up and fleshed out. This had been like the touch of the squinty-eyed man
with his huge cock, almost broader than long; she remembered the way he held her
wrists pincered while he forced his organ inside her, and she thought she would be
ripped apart, she was crying out *Daddy Daddy why?* and her father didn't look at her,
he was counting his gold, chuckling as it poured from his hand and clattered and
clinked onto the table. . . .

Her face was inches from the blue-stoned floor. Though her stomach heaved
violently, her throat was closed tight, and nothing would come out. More memories
were rising in her, but she thrust them away. They made no sense, they never had.
She could not have seen her father so clearly and at the same time have the bulk of
her rapist towering over her. She had made it all up, out of her inchoate child's fears
of sex, out of a bottomless well of imagination, and it had all been molded by Dr.
Almand's questioning into something that fit his preconceptions. She had made it
all up; she had found that out in her bathtub, when she discovered she could give
herself pleasure, when she had found out penetration did not feel at all like what
she'd falsely remembered. Dr. Almand's poison had stained her mind, but she had
resolved to wash it all away.

She lifted her head, grew aware of what was happening in the room. Quentin,
his face scarlet with rage, was scuffling with the guards.

"That is the *royal heir*, you cur! I will see you whipped raw for this!" he was

BOOK III

The Court of Chrysanthe

1. Testenel

Through doorways and down corridors Christine fled, her legs pumping with limit-less strength. She lost herself in flight; the pounding of her soles on the floor annihi-lated all thought in her. People appeared in her field of vision, but most shrank from her path, and those who did not move out of the way immediately she eluded, even the guards in armor. Walls, doors, stairs danced about her, as if she were in fact unmoving and the world itself flowing past at random. Her mind felt broken and stuttering, unable to handle anything but the visceral need for flight.

She saw a woman standing in her way, arms spread, unmoving. A sense of im-minent collision thrummed in her body, like a trio of strings along her arms and down her torso. Christine veered left; her shoes, much too large for her feet, slipped on the flagstones, but she kept her footing and resumed her flight in another direc-tion. Then, insanely, the woman was in front of her again, and this time there was nowhere to go, no option but to slow down, but Christine could not slow down, she must run away, flee the presence of the man from her nightmares, and the woman before her grew closer and closer, and Christine flung herself at the woman, as if she could burst through her with sheer desperation. They collided, yet there was no impact, no pain. All of Christine's impetus somehow drained away, until she was immobile, held tightly in the woman's arms.

With the cessation of her flight, her attention could no longer drown itself in the pounding of her legs; she began to think once more, and as she did she screamed. The woman brought Christine's head into the hollow of her own shoulder; though she gave voice fully, Christine heard her screams dwindle to a muffled whine. She should have been thrashing in horror at this imprisonment; but these were a wom-an's arms that held her, and she had not been taught to fear a woman's touch.

"Hush," said the woman, "hush, you are safe."

Christine sobbed harshly, and felt her manic energy ebb at last. She pulled her head back, drew in a shuddering breath—the woman's gown bore a strange smell, a mix of odors floral and harsh—and tried to speak.

"I-i-it's too much," she stammered, "it's j-just *too much*. I can't touch him; I can't. I remember all the things that happened even if they didn't. It's just too much."

She sagged against her captor, felt the arms that enfolded her move up to her shoulders, felt a hand being run through her hair. No woman had touched her in affection in years, not since the day she'd gashed her knee and the school nurse had stroked her hair like this as she cried in terror at her blood.

"You're safe, Christine," the woman repeated. Christine pulled her face away from the woman's body, looked through tear-blurred eyes at her face. It was terribly familiar. A straight nose, wide-spaced blue eyes, brown hair growing to the shoulders.

She had seen this face before; recalled it in the sessions with Dr. Almand. Confused, disbelieving, still she felt her heart swell.

"Are you . . . are you m-my mother?" she asked.

"No," said the woman. "I am Melogian. You don't remember me, but—"

Christine cut her off. "No. I do. I know your face. I saw it . . . when he made me remember." There had been so many sessions, so many rapes she had recalled, and so few glimpses of the woman who had borne her, who had tried to protect her, who had been murdered for it. And all of it lies, the vomitus of her undermind, that she had vowed to let go. "When I saw my mother in the sessions," Christine explained, "she had your face." She sobbed once. "Is she . . . alive?" she asked, knowing full well what the answer would be.

Melogian looked at her with compassion. "I'm sorry, Christine. Your mother passed away giving birth to you. You never knew her. When you were a little girl I used to play with you sometimes; that must be why she had my face in your memories."

Christine rested her head against Melogian's shoulder, gritting her teeth and moaning.

"I knew," she murmured. "I knew, because Quentin never said a word about her. I knew she was dead, I always knew, but I hoped it was a lie like the rest. Oh, God, Melogian, it's too much. I'm going to throw up. Make it stop, please."

Melogian's arms moved against her. "There's a chair just over there. Sit down and put your head between your knees. You'll feel better."

Christine's legs trembled. Melogian helped her to sit down. Christine bent her torso forward, until her head nestled between her knees. Sweat fell from her forehead in large drops onto the floor. Her breathing was ragged and she felt waves of heat and cold pass through her limbs. Melogian's hand remained on her shoulder, warm and soothing, and she focused on that touch, forgetting all else for blessed moments, until her breathing began to slow and she could feel a measure of calm diffusing through her. Still she kept her head down, gazing at the meaningless patterns within the blue tiles of the floor: here a white ball surrounded by a film of pale blue, like a star aborning in its caul of gases, there an asymmetrical monster with five legs and a nubbin of a head . . . So much simpler to dwell in these flat lands of fantasy than to face the heartache of the real world.

❧ In the moment of Christine's flight, Quentin felt himself finally overwhelmed by circumstance. He called out "Lady, Lady, wait!" but she was past hearing his words. Anywhere else, whether down in Errefern or on the lawns before Testenel itself, he would have run after her. But here he stood in the presence of the king, and the Hero's gaze left him transfixed like an insect stuck by a pin to a corkboard. He looked at Edisthen, slack-jawed, desperate to explain himself, unable to find a single word to say. To the king's right and left, courtiers had advanced: old Benegald, Baron Thorzin, a half-dozen people he did not know. One figure at the edge of his vision he recognized: Melogian the sorceress, Orion's apprentice, who had stood by her master on that well-remembered day the wizard had imbued Quentin with magic and sent him on his quest.

A shocked silence still prevailed; Edisthen's words rang loud in the hush. "Protect her!" he ordered. At that command, Quentin recovered the use of his limbs and ran off after Christine. Behind him, he heard other feet pounding on the floor: Veraless and Melogian ran along, as well as the two guards who'd escorted him into the king's presence.

Christine at first sprinted with such desperate energy Quentin was hard put to follow; then she slowed down and he was able to match her speed. He called out to her again and again, to no avail. She fled blindly, and risked collisions several times. Veraless bellowed, "Stand back! Stand back for the blood royal!" and bystanders shrank away from Christine's mad dash. Down a flight of stairs she pounded, almost losing her balance. Quentin had a horrified premonition of her fall, but she reached the bottom landing and set off once more at a run.

"We have to stop her, she'll hurt herself," came a voice at his elbow: Melogian's. Quentin looked over his shoulder, saw that they had left Veraless panting far behind, and that three guards now followed, weapons sheathed and keeping a respectful distance.

"What has come over her?" continued the sorceress. "Why is she so terrified?"

"It is a long story," said Quentin. "Our journey back was dangerous."

They came to a four-way intersection and Christine continued straight forward. Melogian veered left and shouted to Quentin: "Follow her; I'll catch her from the other side!" Quentin, though he would have said he still knew his way around Testenel, was now utterly lost. He grasped Melogian's meaning soon enough, when the corridor turned left, and left again. After the second turn, Melogian appeared, standing firm in Christine's path, at another intersection. Christine evaded her, darting to the left, back toward the first intersection. Quentin cursed as he followed. Melogian calmly spoke several syllables; as Quentin reached her, she vanished from sight. Turning to the left, Quentin saw Melogian reappear right in front of the fleeing girl, and this time Christine could neither turn nor stop before Melogian caught her in her arms. Quentin gasped at the thought of Christine bruised from the impact; he hurried over, sick with dread for the sorceress. But everything seemed all right; Melogian held the sobbing and wailing princess in her arms and stroked her hair. Quentin stood back as Melogian calmed Christine and finally got her to sit on a chair with her head between her knees, her breathing hoarse and ragged.

Two guards had joined him; he waved them to remain where they were, and was mildly surprised to see them obey. The guard he'd threatened earlier had vanished; perhaps he had fled to avoid the whipping Quentin had promised. . . . But Quentin could not stand to wait where he stood any longer, and took a step forward.

"Is she unhurt?" he whispered to Melogian, who nodded in reassurance, then motioned for him to approach.

"She doesn't fear you, does she?" mouthed Melogian at his ear; Quentin shook his head emphatically.

"Lady Christine," said Melogian softly. "Your friend is here, if you wish to see him."

Christine unbent and looked up at him; her tear-streaked face was twisted with anguish. Quentin felt his heart swell in his chest and he had to contain himself not to rush to enfold her in his arms as Melogian had done. *Protect her,* the king had ordered—as if Quentin had ever needed any man's order to do this.

"I'm sorry," she gasped. Quentin knelt at her side, as close as he dared, but careful not to risk touching her. He knew the fear that gripped her, knew himself to be an agent of it, despite his denial to Melogian; for he was male, and thus to her an emblem of danger scarcely less potent than her own father.

"Do not worry, milady. I am here by your side; I will . . . I will help you," he prattled. "You must not be afraid."

In response, Christine screwed up her face and buried it in her hands. Her shoulders shook, but she remained silent, and after a moment she seemed to grow slightly calmer.

Huffing and puffing, Veraless had reached them. He stood by the lone remaining guard—the other one had left—with his hat in one hand, wiping his forehead with the other and chewing his lip. A trio of onlookers was gawping at the scene; noticing their presence, Veraless shooed them away and ordered the guard to keep all others at bay.

Quentin rose to his feet and went to speak with Veraless.

"I owe you an apology, boy," the skyship captain murmured. "I was wrong. But I'm glad beyond words to have been wrong."

"I need no apologies from you, sir," said Quentin. "Thank you for being here for the lady's sake."

"The guard's gone to inform His Majesty. He'll be here directly."

Quentin shook his head, alarmed. "Captain . . . the king must not come. The Lady Christine is made distraught by his presence."

"But why? What's wrong with her that she should fear her own father?"

"She has suffered too many emotions," evaded Quentin. "Remember, she barely knows him. Most of her life was spent in a made world; and only a few days ago I took her from all she had ever known and brought her through Errefern and into the true realm. In a way, she has been in shock throughout our journey. Her father's presence is too much for her to bear at this moment. Please, Captain, he must not come; or she will flee again."

Veraless yielded. "Of course; His Majesty wouldn't want to cause her distress. I'll go repeat your words to him."

At that moment Christine took her head from her hands and gazed about her. The sight of her tear-stained face brought Quentin to her side as if it had been a summons. Veraless came on his heels; Quentin could not for the moment find the words to warn the man away without further alarming Christine. Yet she did not appear afraid as Veraless knelt before her.

"Milady," said the captain. "My Lady Christine, you are well?"

ॐ Christine's heart gave a little jump of fright when Veraless knelt by her side. But then his voice rose, ever so gentle, asking her if she was well, and she knew that now he believed. The title he extended her might have been courtesy, and he might simply have knelt because she was sitting on a low chair. But the expression on his face, mixing concern with a wild, almost terrible joy, could not be mistaken. His belief warmed her and gave her strength to answer.

"I'm . . . I'm better now." She exhaled raggedly. "I'm still very frazzled, though."

"Frazzled, milady?" Veraless appeared disconcerted by the word.

"She means 'overwrought,'" offered Quentin. "A made world dialect."

"Where am I?" asked Christine. She had been looking around her, found that she was sitting in a chair at the edge of a corridor hung with tapestries and thickly carpeted; a window in the opposite wall admitted some light—the blue she saw through it was not the blue of the sky, but of Testenel's stone.

Melogian answered: "In the corridor leading from the Triune Fountains to the Demmerel Chambers. You led us a merry chase for ten minutes, and I believe you'd still be running if I hadn't caught you."

"I'm sorry," muttered Christine, looking down at her hands. "I was so scared . . . I lost my mind." There were a few seconds of silence, broken by Captain Veraless.

"Milady," he said, "I'll be going to inform your father that you're well, but that you require rest. Melogian, surely there's a room somewhere close by that she could use?"

"Of course. Christine, do you wish us to take you to a room where you can rest?"

The way the invitation was worded reminded Christine of Dr. Almand's smooth manner, his unctuous kindness and what it had led to. She felt a pang of unreasoned fear: What had his legacy wrought in her? She tried to fight against it.

"It's not right," she said. "Quentin, I should go meet my father. Otherwise, it'll mean Dr. Almand won. I have to go see him, now." But she shivered as she said this.

"That would not be wise," objected Quentin. "Take time to rest, Lady Christine. His Majesty waited thirteen years for you, he can wait a few more hours."

She met his gaze, dropped hers after an instant. "I'm so very tired," she admitted. "I guess I need to rest for a while. Maybe sleep. What time . . . ?" She glanced at her left wrist automatically, saw it emerge bare from under the rough sleeve of the dark-red blouse; remembered that all she knew had been left behind forever, within the dream of the made world. She had lost count, sometime during their flight, of how many days had elapsed by her watch. Had it been five days, or six? She guessed, vaguely, that it might be the dark of the night according to the timepiece that had never existed. She surrendered. "Yes, I suppose I should sleep. . . ."

Melogian helped her up; Veraless bowed and took his leave. Flanked by Melogian and Quentin, Christine walked along the length of the corridor she had fled through nearly blind. Melogian opened the third door they reached; it gave onto a suite of two luxuriously appointed rooms, an antechamber and a bedroom, the latter dominated by a four-poster covered with a purple-and-gold quilt. The rooms were impeccably kept but felt disused, as impersonally immaculate as hotel rooms aimed to be.

In the bedroom, Quentin drew heavy curtains from the narrow ogival window, letting bright light in. Christine noticed him surveying the view from the window— a receding perspective of blue stone walls, like a chaos of towers—and realized he was still checking for vulnerabilities.

"Is there some danger, Quentin?" she asked in a small voice. He turned to face her, looking almost guilty.

"No, milady. No danger. The whole of Testenel surrounds you. You will be safe from now on, I promise you. I merely take precautions out of habit."

"It's a wise thing to be cautious," said Melogian. "I will protect you as well." So, saying, she spoke three words and gestured oddly, as if stretching something flexible and throwing it into the center of the room, then brushing a finger down Christine's forehead. "There; the web in this room has been tautened and bound to you. Even while I am away from here, it will be as if I watched over you in person."

"What was that?" Christine asked.

"A spell, milady. I've tied the watch-web to your person."

"You're a magician?"

"Yes," said Melogian in a tone that implied the fact should have been obvious. "I am."

"The Lady Melogian is Orion's apprentice, Lady Christine," explained Quentin. "She is a sorceress of the highest skill, second only to him."

"I do what I can," Melogian amended with an air of mild self-deprecation.

Christine found herself unwilling to believe her. All her life she had known wizards were frauds, exploiters of the gullible. Even in a world where magic worked, she could not put her faith in someone who claimed to control supernatural forces. Quentin's powers she could accept because they did not come from him. But for this woman to claim she could work miracles by waving her hands about . . . Somehow real magic should be different, a drawn-out affair that exhausted the will and demanded arcane reagents and dangerous rituals.

And yet Quentin trusted and believed Melogian, and Christine had known safety in the woman's arms. She was overreacting; her fears had loosened from their source and now fastened upon anything and everything. She had to remember Tap's words: hope and trust, trust and hope.

Captain Veraless came in at this point, hat in hands. He spoke in a formal tone: "Milady Christine, I've spoken with the king your father. He expresses his concern for your well-being and desires you should rest and be given anything you require."

He paused. Christine realized he expected a reply and she stammered: "That's . . . that's very kind of him. I, er, don't need anything right now. Just rest."

"As you wish." Veraless bowed, then turned to Quentin: "Lad, the king summons you to him at your earliest convenience, in the Griffin Room." He then turned back to Christine. "Milady, I'd be honored to be the one to guard your rest. Will you allow it?"

Christine answered almost unthinkingly: "Well . . . of course, if you want."

She was surprised to see a radiant smile blossom on the captain's scarred countenance. "I'll stay at the outer door of the suite," he said, and withdrew.

"You look exhausted, Christine," Melogian said. "We'll let you sleep, now."

There were several fat candles in the room. Melogian went to them and touched their wicks with a finger; flame bloomed at once. This casual miracle performed, she drew the curtains shut again and made to leave, drawing Quentin after her;

Christine felt a lump in her throat. She did not know if she could stand this. From the first moment of her flight with Quentin until her attack of panic, the knight had remained by her side, sometimes on the other side of a door, but always close by. Now he had been summoned by her father the king; how long until he should come back to her? Her panic breathed a warning to her, that she would never see Quentin again. He stood on the threshold of the inner doorway, looking despondent. For a moment she thought to beg him to remain with her, to sleep in the room, his back against the door, to keep her safe still and always.

She fought her panic down, using not only reason but shame. She would not be drawn into a replay of the scene at the inn. Anything but that.

And she was in no danger. Not here, where Quentin had sworn to take her. If he said she was safe here, then safe she was. She must trust him, and grant him time to pursue his own affairs. Still, she could not deny her need wholly.

"Quentin," she asked, "will you be here when I wake?"

He smiled at her then, and she sensed that he too wished them to remain together. "Have no fear, milady, I will come at your call. So will the Lady Melogian."

The sorceress nodded. "There will be people about to take messages to me or Quentin. Just ask for us. We'll come. And if there were some emergency—which there *will not* be—I would know and come before you could think to call out."

Christine nodded. "All—all right."

And Quentin astonished her, bursting out: "Do you want me to stay with you, Lady?"

He blushed as he said this. She felt herself redden too, but had the strength to answer.

"Thank you, Quentin," she said. "I know I'll be safe here. When I wake up . . . When I'm up I'll call for you."

He lowered his gaze, turned to leave on Melogian's heels. The outer door closed behind him, and then Christine was alone.

She looked about her, remembering that this was not her appointed suite, just a pair of rooms that had been available. And yet they were decorated with such richness they might have belonged to a sultan's daughter. She smacked her palm against the bedpost. It was solid; her hand stung from the force of the blow. This was real, no matter how much like some fantasy of power and wealth it was. The quilt's fabric was real, smooth and warm; if she peered closely at it she could count the stitches. She had had, a few times, complex dreams in which she dreamed that she awoke, yet was still trapped within sleep; but the world of her false awakenings was never as solid as this. She was awake now; she couldn't have been dreaming her entire flight with Quentin, not days and days on end. If she felt the familiar sense of unreality creeping in, it was because she was dead tired, because she was already falling asleep. . . .

She sat down on the bed, but her heart kept pounding. She grew aware that she was afraid to go to sleep. Afraid not so much that she would wake up in her room in Uncle's house, afraid rather that she would never wake at all. Sleep is the punctuation of life, putting parentheses and dashes around and within days; sometimes we cannot make ourselves forget it is also the final period.

Christine rose, then padded across the antechamber to the outer door and pulled it open. Captain Veraless was standing on the other side and turned to her immediately.

"Captain," she said, timidly, "I think I would prefer it if you stayed in the suite while I sleep. I would feel safer." *And more real.*

Veraless appeared astonished for a second or two, then embarrassed. Finally he bowed and followed her inside.

"Ah . . . Please take a seat," she said, waving at the three chairs in the antechamber. "Can you sit . . . just outside the room? Where I can see you? I need to know you're close by."

"Of course, as my lady wishes." Veraless brought a chair right by the doorway. "Please go in, Lady Christine. When you're ready, I'll reopen the door." He closed the door behind Christine.

She was too exhausted to think of undressing; she stepped out of her shoes—the woolen carpet felt soft and thick under her bare soles—pulled back the quilt and crawled under the covers.

"All right," she said to the door, which Captain Veraless opened.

"Do you want me to extinguish the candles, Lady Christine?" he asked her.

"No; please no. I'd rather have some light." As she said this, it occurred to Christine with a touch of horror that this would be the only source of light in Chrysanthe once the sun set. She forced out the next words. "Good . . . good night, captain."

"Sleep well, milady." Veraless sat ramrod stiff into the chair. Christine turned her head away, toward the window. Chinks of light came through the curtains, making meaningless patterns of bright dots. She swung her head back, saw by the glow of candle flames the form of Veraless sitting quietly in the chair, his gaze on her. This should have made her afraid, perhaps. Yet it did not. She was safe here, as safe as she could ever be.

And though fear still gripped her at the thought of surrendering her consciousness, she allowed oblivion to claim her.

Once Veraless had shut the door to the suite, Quentin heaved a sigh; he felt a sudden flagging of the energy that had sustained him up to now. He stood staring at the door, unwilling to move away and thus set in motion what had to come next. Veraless had settled himself by the door and looked at Quentin with a frown.

"You don't seem to be able to bear being parted from her ladyship," he said, though not unkindly.

"She is in my charge, Captain; I mean, she was in my charge, all through our journey. No offense intended, sir, but I feel like . . . like I am betraying her by leaving her side. I feel that my duty is not done."

"A good soldier's duty is never done. But now you've been summoned by the king, boy. Go; I'll keep watch here."

"Quentin." Melogian had taken his arm. "You know Captain Veraless can be trusted; and the spell-skein threaded throughout Testenel holds her snug. You mustn't fear for her; she couldn't be more safe."

Under other circumstances the pull of duty would have impelled Quentin to the king's side without question. But now, it was with painful reluctance that he tore himself away from the threshold.

Yet leave he did; Melogian drew him onward along the corridor. At a turning stood a guard who had kept half a dozen people from going any farther in.

"Lady Melogian!" called a tall bearded courtier. "Lady! What has happened? Who was the girl?"

"It was the lost princess!" shouted a blond woman. "His Majesty said it! The warrior's the one who brought her back!"

"Is it true, Melogian?" asked the courtier. "Tell us!"

"She's like her portrait! It *was* her!" This came from a servant boy of twelve or thirteen who held his ground amongst the onlookers as if his status matched theirs.

Melogian put her hands out to quell the others' voices. "Please be silent. I . . . I have no announcement to make. Let us pass."

The courtier insisted. "Is or is there not a young woman in one of the Demmerel Chambers?"

"That does not concern you, sir."

"Why are we prevented from going to see her? And why did Captain Veraless cry 'Make way for the royal blood'?"

Melogian's composure faltered. "That . . . that's his affair. Let us pass!"

As Melogian and Quentin made their way through the small crowd, the courtier grabbed ahold of Quentin's arm.

"You, young man! Say something! Who are you?"

The knight opened his mouth but nothing came out.

"Leave him be!" said Melogian, pulling Quentin along. She darted him a warning look he did not truly need.

"If it's the king's lost daughter, why keep it a secret, Lady?" cried the woman.

"I'm not keeping it a secret!" retorted an exasperated Melogian. "Now let us go!"

"She's admitted it!" said an old man in a mason's overcoat. "It *is* the princess!"

The shouting redoubled; the bearded courtier tried to bluster past the guard, who rapped his toes, perhaps accidentally, with the butt of his spear. As the courtier hopped on one foot yelping, the servant boy ran off yelling excitedly and the blond woman started berating the guard as a mother would her errant child.

Melogian dragged Quentin away at speed down the corridor, through a door into a short, low-ceilinged hall furnished with parallel rows of chests whose cushioned lids doubled as benches. She shut the door behind them and leaned against it.

"I feel," said the sorceress, "that I did not handle that at all well."

Rather than state the obvious, Quentin looked at the floor, and suddenly sat down, feeling a wave of dizziness pass through him. "Do not worry, Lady Melogian," he said, barely thinking upon his words. "Surely things are not as bad as you fear."

Melogian surprised him by chuckling. "That was so insincere I should feel insulted. . . . Bah; I doubt even if I had said nothing that it would have made much of a change. How long could we expect to keep this quiet? In fact, it's a wonder so few people have yet been alerted. There are days when Testenel is a hive of bees; tonight it is sleepy. I guess we should feel grateful."

Quentin had been looking at her; she held his gaze and hers sharpened.

"Quentin . . . Now, I remember you. I began to recall your face when we were in the Demmerel room. How long has it been?"

"Since we met? I took my vows in 'eighty-five."

"You searched for her for nine years. . . . Where was it you went?"

"Into Errefern." His throat was tight. He recalled his passage through the hedge; how innocent he had been, full of the fire of life, immune to doubt. He stood up, unwilling to sit while Melogian stood.

"I have been at fault," said the sorceress. "I put your memory away. You and all those other knights, going off into infinity . . . I didn't allow myself to think about you more than once a season. If Edisthen had asked me to say how much time had passed since I had last seen that knight with eyes like an Estephorin winter, I wouldn't have known what to say. Fifty years or five . . ."

She took a step toward him; put her arms around his neck and kissed him passionately. Her whole body pressed against him; her lips mashed his, and Quentin felt an electric thrill running down his spine. She let him go an instant later. Quentin gaped at her, bewildered.

Her face was split by a wide grin. "Let it be said I was the first one to officially congratulate you on accomplishing the impossible, Quentin. God, but it's only now sinking in. You've done it! You have in truth done it!"

She was laughing now, her eyes sparkling. "You brought her back, Quentin! The entire realm will honor your name! They will make statues of you, paint you on frescoes! If Paucelin were still alive, I'd place an order for a monument!"

Quentin protested: "No, please, Lady. No! I want none of that. You must be joking. . . ."

"Joking? Joking! What did you think would happen if you succeeded? A tea party on the lawns of the Royal Gardens?"

"I . . . I hoped for . . ." Quentin was at a loss. His success had never been more than a bright dream, a few disjointed ideas. He'd imagined the king clasping his hand, some applause, and yes, perhaps a meal eaten in splendid circumstances. He suddenly understood that his quest had not simply borne fruit: it had changed his life utterly. He was and would remain famous—he would be remembered. He did not know whether to be thrilled or horrified. "I just wanted to bring the Lady Christine back home," he said.

"And modest too!" Melogian exclaimed. "The very embodiment of chivalrous ideal. You are quite disgusting, Sir Quentin."

She kissed him again, on the lips, so briefly and innocently that it seemed to apologize for her earlier effusion.

"We shouldn't tarry," she said in a husky voice. "We're keeping you from His Majesty, and he deserves to at least hear the full story from your mouth."

They exited the hallway through the far door; Melogian led the way along a deserted warren of short corridors until it gave onto a flight of much-traveled spiral stairs Quentin thought to recognize. They climbed a flight, Melogian looking straight ahead whenever their path crossed someone else's, and reached a landing where stood a guarded door. The soldier let them pass; behind the door he warded lay a passage guarded by three more soldiers, and beyond them an old door, of ancient stone and wood, crudely carved into the shape of an animal half eagle, half lion. Melogian pushed it open; and finally they stood in the presence of the king.

Edisthen was alone in the room, sitting with his hands in his lap. A low table stood to his left, covered with piles of books and some folded maps. Other seats were scattered here and there in comfortable disarray. There were no windows in this chamber; a multitude of candles cast a flickering illumination upon the walls, which were paneled in dark wood. It was as if the Griffin Room belonged to another castle entirely, from an older and sadder age.

Quentin had forgotten a good part of the protocol he had memorized a decade before, and in his travels he had had to learn so many imaginary customs that for a moment he did not know whether he should abase himself on his belly, cast a pinch of cinders over his shoulder, or hide his face and moan. Then common sense reasserted itself, and he knelt and bowed his head.

There was silence in the room; then Quentin heard Edisthen stand up and approach him.

"Rise," came the Hero's dry voice, and Quentin rose to his feet. "You are Sir Quentin," Edisthen said to him. "Born twenty-six years ago in Lydiss, knighted on the tenth of Ripening, 6085. A week later, Orion bestowed the Quester's Gifts upon you and you left court to seek for my daughter. Your stated goal was to journey into Errefern. I presume this is what you did?"

Quentin's words came out hoarse. "Yes, Sire."

"I want you to tell me what occurred. Please be seated."

Edisthen returned to the armchair where he had awaited them; Melogian, apparently unnoticed, took a seat to his right. With trembling arms, Quentin brought a chair to face the king and sank down in it. Edisthen tilted his head slightly to one side. His long gaunt face showed no expression.

"If it please Your Majesty," began Quentin. "I shall skip over the early years of my journey. Nothing good came of them."

With a twist of pain, he remembered a small warm hand in his, a hand suddenly gone as its owner tried to pass into the real world. No, he definitely did not deserve statues raised to his glory. His mind veered away from those memories, refocused on the recent past. He spoke on.

"I had been following Orion's advice all this while, not seeking for the Lady Christine herself, but for the idea of her. By early 'ninety-three—as near as I could tell—I had gone very deep in the made world, almost too deep. But I found . . . it is hard to put it into words. Like an eddy in a raging stream. A quieter spot, strange to me but not so strange. I thought . . . I remember thinking to myself it would make for a good hiding place. And so I went farther in."

"Continue," whispered Edisthen when Quentin paused.

"After a while, I began to think the made world felt . . . more real than it should have. It could have been imagination. But Orion did say an exile from the true realm living for a long time in a made world would eventually cast a—a glow of some sort. A sheen over the dream.”

Quentin noticed Melogian nodding vigorously at these words. She appeared to want to say something, but visibly held her tongue. He went on.

“So I traveled more cautiously. The world was very large by then; I kept to the area where people spoke our tongue. I doubted the Lady Christine’s abductors would have chosen to travel to a place where they could not be understood. It took me about six months to circumscribe a perimeter: from Amarga down to Amerille, not far from the eastern ocean. Some days I was afraid I was chasing phantoms. . . . But in the end—well, I did find the Lady Christine.”

“And where was she?”

“She was living in a huge city—though not so large by the standards of that world. Attending a lyceum.”

“She wasn’t a prisoner?”

“Not as such, Sire. Though—”

“What?”

“She did have a guardian. A wizard. When we escaped, he cast spells after us. He was trying to force me to abandon my mount.”

“You are leaving much out.”

“I beg your pardon, Your Majesty. My thoughts are scattered.”

“Try again.” Edisthen’s tone was almost flat, but Quentin felt sweat spring on his brow and his throat tightened.

“I first glimpsed the Lady Christine as I rode my mount close to the lyceum she attended. Having finally located her, I spent several weeks learning her exact situation, as inconspicuously as I could manage. She was not, as I have said, a prisoner. She was not even guarded; there was no hint that anyone kept an eye on her when she was outside of the house where she lived.”

“What about spells?” Melogian burst in. “There should have been spells laid on her.”

“You are interrupting, Melogian,” said Edisthen. “But do answer the question, Sir Quentin.”

“No spells, Your Majesty. I did expect watch-magic of some sort, but I could feel none. I thought perhaps Orion’s bequeathed abilities were not sensitive enough. It turned out there was no magic in that world, no wizards except in books and theaters. Some charlatans claimed powers, but their miracles were too shabby to be believable. After a time, I began to think that there was no magic on her because there was no one to cast any. And it did make sense. I had hunted, at first, for a captive princess. And early on I had found . . . someone whom I had thought was Christine. It was a mistake. And I think I learned from that mistake—learned not to seek what I expected to find. I have come to believe that the Lady Christine’s abductors left her there precisely because she was not imprisoned, because she did not dwell in a castle guarded by demons. . . . The way one hides a treasure by burying it in an ordinary spot where no one would think of digging.”

Edisthen prompted him: “You say there were no spells on her; yet there *was* a wizard.”

"I did not know he was a wizard, Your Majesty. The Lady Christine lived with her uncle. I learned what I could about him: He was a high-ranking merchant, mildly powerful in his guild. But there was little else. I suspected he was more than he seemed, but I had no clear indication. I eventually made contact with her, at a time when he was absent."

Quentin drew in a breath.

"There were . . . complications. The Lady Christine did not believe me. I confess I had not counted on this. I did not force the issue; I told her I would wait until she changed her mind."

Edisthen frowned. "You did not return here to inform us?"

"I . . . I would have, Sire, after a while. But I feared she might panic and speak to her guardian. What if he should possess the ability to take her *beyond*? I resolved to wait some time, to see what happened. I would not allow her to slip from my notice and become lost again. And in fact, it was two days later that she summoned me to her."

Quentin looked at his hands, to avoid gazing at his king's face.

"I had told her I would be waiting to take her away, back to her rightful home. When I felt her call, at first I was not certain I did. I am not a sorcerer, and the seeking-spell was slow to convey meaning. Once I grew certain, I prepared myself as best I could and I drove—rode—to her house. I had Thunder give voice . . . I could feel something through the spell, something fierce and burning. Her spirit was crying for escape. I could have rushed in with my sword drawn. But I remembered how it had gone with—with the other, and I waited.

"And she came out of the house; she saw me—she expected me, she knew I would be there. She ran to the car—to my mount, I mean. I had shifted its shape as Orion had taught me: It was a metal vehicle I rode.

"I urged her inside; as soon as she had climbed aboard, I goaded Thunder to flee. Her guardian had come out after her. And when we sped away, he cast a spell to blind us. He thought that from within the vehicle, I could not see where we went once the windows had gone black. But I could still see *beyond*, and I used that sight to navigate the streets until I could repair Thunder's vision."

Quentin shifted in his seat and met Edisthen's gaze once more.

"After that, Sire, we traveled for days. We were . . . pursued, at the beginning. We evaded this pursuit, but the final attempt almost succeeded. Something possessed my mount: a kind of made-world were. Thunder started to shift into something monstrous. I was thrown out, but the Lady Christine remained inside. So I fought it, and killed it. The Lady was unharmed, but it was a frightening episode for her. We went on foot for a time, until I located a train—I mean a self-propelled carriage, running along a metal road—that followed the gradient out of Errefern. In the train, the Lady became very upset. I thought it was the consequence of all she had undergone, but it was something else. . . ." Quentin paused. "What I have to say, Sire, is painful to hear."

Edisthen's face showed no expression. "Speak."

"You see, about seven years ago, the Lady Christine was taken to see a soul-healer. A man who specializes in treating illnesses of the mind. There were many such in that world. She was taken to him because she had had an imaginary companion, and this companion had behaved strangely, and she had confessed to this."

Edisthen's nostrils flared. "Are you saying that my daughter is addled?"

"No, no, Sire! Not at all! She simply had an imaginary friend, a talking animal named Tap, when she was a little girl. Many children indulge such fancies. It is not at all rare." *But he cannot know,* Quentin thought to himself, horrified, *he cannot understand what that is like. What will he think of her?*

"So why was she taken to see a healer, if such a thing is normal?" Edisthen was asking.

"Your Majesty, I believe it was not an imaginary friend. When the Lady was taken from us, did not Orion immediately send out benisons to protect her? I believe it was one of those spells that spoke to her, in the guise of a phantom companion."

Edisthen turned to look inquiringly at Melogian, who said: "It didn't happen quite as you think, Quentin. But it's true Orion did send out magic to help Christine. I don't know exactly what spells he sent out after her; what you describe is conceivable. Magic will often surprise us in made worlds."

"This does not answer my question," said Edisthen to Quentin. "Why was my daughter taken to see a healer?"

"She said it was because she was judged too old to have an imaginary companion still, at the age of ten. And that healer, Your Majesty . . . He was not a competent one."

Quentin's hands were ice. When he spoke next, his voice rasped and squeaked.

"The Lady Christine explained to me that the healer became convinced that she had . . . that she had suffered at a very young age. That she had been, ah . . . I beg your leave, Sire . . . forced. And he, in turn, convinced her that she must have been mistreated."

The king's face showed not a trace of expression. Quentin plodded onward.

"The Lady told me she remembered . . . that she was made to remember . . . many occurrences of this sort. She explained that she rejects this now, that she no longer believes this happened. But those . . . those teachings . . . have made a deep impression. She believed in them for years. It is hard for her to simply forget. Your Majesty, there is one more thing. The instigator of these . . . this ill treatment, himself was directly responsible, in the healer's stories, for . . . I mean that she . . . she was taught her own father had forced her."

The king's lips had grown bloodless and the corner of his mouth twitched. His eyes were the eyes of a corpse. Quentin felt himself wither under their gaze.

"Continue," said Edisthen.

"Your Majesty . . . !" Quentin protested.

"Continue." Edisthen's dry voice demanded his obedience as would a torturer's lash. Quentin gathered his wits.

"The train pulled us out of the depths of Errefern. I had to guide it the whole way, until it grew too shallow for me to sense the gradient. By the time we left the train we were maybe twenty leagues from Chrysanthe. We traveled the remaining distance on foot, over a few days. We encountered no more threats. We reached the exit from the made world, which as you know lies within the Hedges. It was our great good luck that Captain Veraless's *Black Heart* was flying in the vicinity. When we spotted it, I climbed a hedge to signal. The *Black Heart* took us aboard and made for Testenel. We reached the castle, and then we were taken into your presence."

"And after my daughter fled?"

"The Lady Melogian caught up to the Lady Christine and managed to soothe her. We . . . The Lady Christine is resting in one of the Demmerel Chambers. Captain Veraless is guarding her door personally. The Lady Melogian put the Lady Christine under the protection of her spells. I believe the Lady Christine is sleeping at present. The Lady Melogian and I returned here; there was some commotion in the corridors . . . I believe the rumor of Her Highness's return is spreading."

Edisthen was silent a moment. Then he said:

"You have done well, Quentin. The whole land is in your debt. Name whatever you desire as a reward, and it is yours."

"Your Majesty . . . ," breathed Quentin. Looking at Edisthen's countenance, he dared not make the least request. But neither could he throw Edisthen's gift back in his face. He thought for an endless second and found a way out. "Your Majesty, I beg time to think about it. I am exhausted and my wits are gone."

"Granted. You may leave now. Please go to the chamberlain and request accommodations for yourself. Insist on proximity to the heart of Testenel; I do not wish you lodged in a garret in one of the outer towers."

"As Your Majesty commands." Quentin rose to his feet, bowed to the king thrice as he walked backward, until he had reached the door. He turned away from Edisthen's dead gaze, pulled the door panel open as little as he dared, and squeezed himself through the opening, feeling as though he were escaping a nameless peril.

❧ The door to the Griffin Room shut. Melogian had been looking at Quentin's exit. Now she was forced to turn her gaze to the king. Edisthen had been nearly expressionless while Quentin told his tale; now his features twisted into a grimace as he returned her gaze.

The king leaned back in his chair and took a ragged breath. He hid his face in his hands for a moment, then ran them, pressing hard, from his cheeks over his forehead and into his thin salt-and-pepper hair. Tears leaked from the corners of his lids. Melogian felt a shiver run down her spine, but it was more relief than anything else: She had feared Edisthen would keep such a hold on his emotions that it would fell him.

"Do you have anything to add to this tale, Melogian?" the king asked in a broken voice.

"Nothing, Your Majesty. Quentin's recounting is accurate from the time the Lady Christine came into the dining room."

"I do not understand myself," said the king. "I should be happy. I should be dancing about the room. My daughter is returned to me. Why is it I only want to mourn?"

Melogian waited a moment but Edisthen appeared to need a reply. "It is possible, Your Majesty, that it is anger you feel."

"I cannot feel anger; there is nowhere for it to go. Whom can I punish? Whom can I kill?"

"Your Majesty . . ."

"Be silent."

Edisthen was gazing down at his hands. He spoke on in a dry voice.

"She was told that I raped her, my flesh and blood. She was told this at the age of ten. She has spent seven years believing this lie. The first words she said to me in thirteen years were 'I can't touch you.' Her accent is more outlandish than if she were an Estephorin fisherwoman. I lost my little daughter and a stranger has been returned in her place. A broken young woman who blames me for harming her . . ."

"No, my liege. You're wrong. Quentin said she didn't believe this anymore. That she had rejected the lie. She came back to you, she chose to return to you, because she did not believe the lie anymore."

"You seem sure of this."

"I am sure of it. She wouldn't have chosen to come here otherwise."

"But she cannot stand to be near me."

"She has been ripped from a land she thought her home and brought to a vastly different place. She had not set eyes on you in a dozen years. What would you expect a young woman to do in such a situation? She panicked, as anyone would have. Give her time to regain her balance."

Edisthen took several deep breaths, appeared to grow calmer. At length he spoke again.

"If they had nicked her little finger, they would have lost everything. But they didn't harm her, did they? Still they managed to burn her soul to ashes, without incurring any consequences. Really, I'm compelled to admiration for Evered. This is revenge beyond what I could have imagined. And injustice beyond what anyone could accept."

" 'To look for justice within the world is to seek the Law where it is not,' " quoted Melogian, trying to soothe the king.

Edisthen snarled at her in response, his head snapping forward. "Do *not* give me those words! Do you think I could ever forget a single verse of the Lesser Book? Then mock me not by quoting from it!"

Melogian shrank back from his wrath. "Forgive me, my liege," she quailed. "I didn't mean to insult you!"

Edisthen's anger faded as quickly as it had flared. He shook his head.

"No, I should ask you to forgive me. I know you meant well. But don't offer me dead words, Melogian. Give me the benefit of your wisdom. Tell me how we can deal with this. What I can do to set matters right."

Melogian thought for a moment, letting the painful pounding of her heart subside. At last she said, "As far as I can see, at present we are doing what we should be doing and all that we could be doing. The Lady Christine was not physically harmed, and against damage to the soul, time's a powerful remedy. She is overwhelmed by recent events. Her flight out of the made world was enough to shake anyone. But soon she'll be better. If we give her stability again, it will help her recover all the sooner. We must treat her well, make no demands upon her, accede to her wishes when possible."

"And what will happen when Evered arranges to get rid of her once more?"

Melogian shook her head. "You jest, Edisthen. Even forgetting the guards and the magic that protect her, how could Evered think of having her abducted again? She is no four-year-old anymore, to follow strangers out of safety."

"I meant assassination," said Edisthen. "What if Vaurd's get decide to murder her?"

Melogian made a noise of incredulity in her throat.

"Your Majesty, they want the throne, not their own destruction."

"The younger ones, yes. But not Evered. I remember the day I came to Testenel. . . . Once Vaurd was dead, Evered screamed like a darrow let loose from Hell. If Duke Edric had not physically restrained him, he would have thrown himself upon me. The years may have given him better control of his hatred, but . . . he lives only to see me destroyed. What if he should cease caring about the consequences of a direct attack? What can hold him back?"

"His brothers will rein him in. Casimir will. They won't invite destruction on themselves for his sake. And you can't expect Evered to appear uninvited in Testenel with a drawn sword."

Edisthen looked down at his knees. "No doubt you're right," he said. "But I cannot afford to disregard the possibility."

"Of course not, Your Majesty. That is why we have men and spells shielding your daughter as well as yourself. If I can think of any additional protection we could employ, I will inform you of it."

"Enough. You're reassuring me as if I were a tiny child or an old man in his dotage. I don't need this much coddling."

There was a moment of silence; then Melogian said: "Very well, Your Majesty; let us talk of something disquieting then. There is one thing I have thought of that has been bothering me. Has it occurred to you Christine may have been deliberately let go? That Evered's agents might have *allowed* Quentin to find her, to bring her back? So that you would see what had been done to her and suffer?"

The king cawed laughter, once. "No, milady," he said, "no, that I will not credit. If we start double- and triple-thinking, there will be no way out of the trap. That way madness lies. There must be a limit to the depths of plots. Vaurd's sons abducted my daughter and tried to trap her into exile to cut short my lineage. Not even Evered is twisted enough to deliberately allow their prize to go free. They would never let the heir to the throne back into the real world if they could avoid it, no matter how painful it might be for me to see her. This is not some plot of theirs; that young knight really did find and rescue my daughter through his own valor. And it is for this reason I fear Evered may become enraged enough to seriously contemplate regicide."

Melogian shrugged. "As I've said: A thousand soldiers surround us; my magic shields you and your daughter; the Law itself protects you both. And no matter how maddened he is, Evered knows as well as you do that he cannot restore his line by murdering yours. Even if you were assassinated—God forbid—you would be replaced. The throne of Chrysanthe may not remain unfilled."

Edisthen twisted his mouth sadly. "Be careful what you say. 'The Law does not come to our bidding like a dog running to its master,'" he quoted.

"I don't understand what you mean."

"History is clear enough in the matter of Heroes. In the early days of the world we thronged the land; now there are only myself and Orion, and he is lost among the made worlds. If my offspring and I were killed, Melogian, how can you expect a new king would arise *instantly*? How much time might pass before another Hero appeared to sit upon the throne, assuming God were to send one again rather than wait for Men to settle affairs by themselves? The throne may not remain forever empty, but how long is an instant in the eyes of God?"

Melogian found no answer. Edisthen continued: "If I'd had any way of knowing that the people would not have to wait years, I might have acted a long while ago. I have often thought, and very seriously, Melogian . . . ever since Christine was abducted in fact . . . of being the one to strike and end it all. Being the weapon instead of the target."

"Destroy Vaurd's sons?" asked Melogian, incredulous.

"Not all four; just Evered. But him, why not? If I had been replaced immediately, there would have been no harm to the land. . . . As long as it was a clean assassination, not another war to spread blood on the earth, I might have done it. Many times, when I was convinced Christine was lost forever, I came close to ordering it. But then Orion would argue with me, dissuade me, convince me to wait a while longer. . . . He never said it in so many words, but it was clear he would refuse to involve himself in it. That was the main stumbling block; without his magic, no assassin could stand a chance. Now that Christine is back, I might risk going to Vorlok alone, shielded by the Law; but Orion is gone. Without his support, I am helpless. . . . Your pardon, Lady Melogian. I'm belittling you."

"I take no offense," she said, looking down at her lap. "You are quite correct. I cannot match my mentor's strength; but allow me to say, my liege, that I'm glad this gives you a reason for staying your hand. The land needs you; your daughter needs you; don't throw away your life merely to rid us of Vaurd's mad son!"

Edisthen grunted. "In this you are the equal of Orion: You argue with the same words. . . . I feel as if I were in the wrong story." He sighed, slumping in his chair. "As Heroes go, I often think I am a very poor one."

"You are as you were written, my liege, the true king of Chrysanthe. And your long-lost daughter is back amongst us. Remember that."

Edisthen rose to his feet, in one effortless motion. He clasped his hands and ground them together.

"My daughter is back amongst us and cannot bear to touch me," he whispered.

Melogian rose to her feet in turn and took the king's arm, careless of decorum as always.

"She will heal. What has been done to her is not irreversible, I'm convinced of it. Time will cure her. Now smile, my king, smile and go put on your robes of state. Let your people see you joyous; tonight you must announce the return of the princess."

King Edisthen nodded, broke loose of Melogian's hold, and went to his apartments without further words. The enchantress was left alone in the room and for a moment she shivered. This was what Edisthen feared, she thought: to find himself alone, all those he loved vanishing one by one. For years she had thought she might well be the next one to be torn from the king's side. First his daughter, then his court

mage. She had replaced Orion at Edisthen's side, and although her talent was no
match for his, she was one of the very few powerful mages in Chrysanthe. It made
perfect sense to remove her from court—yet no attacks against her had ever come.
Were the king's enemies content with the state of things? Or were they waiting, with
enormous patience, for ancient plots to bear fruit?

Knowledge was what she lacked; and because of the Law and Edisthen's indul-
gence she was not able to act. How simple it was in the made worlds, where enemies
could be escaped by a footstep *beyond* or obliterated by a wave of caustic force. But
the Law protected Vaurd's sons no less than it did Edisthen. And they were too far
away in any case: Edisthen had let them settle in Vorlok, an ancient baronial castle
belonging to Vaurd's line, over a hundred and fifty leagues away. Early on, it had
been possible to spy on them despite the distance, through spells. But Casimir had
unraveled those long ago, then protected Vorlok by talismans and blind-sinks.
Given enough time, her master Orion could have pierced through those protections;
but she lacked the requisite mastery.

All she could do was to sit in the heart of Testenel, aching with the desire to
hold Evered, Innalan, Olf, and Aghaid in the vise of her power and squeeze until
their bodies burst like overripe fruit; knowing she was merely entertaining childish
revenge fantasies, knowing herself as powerless as an untalented waif, all her knowledge and will good for naught.

Melogian swept out of the Griffin Room, returned to the suite where Christine
slept. The guard placed at the entrance informed her Captain Veraless was watching over the princess in her room. Melogian opened the door nevertheless. Veraless
appeared at the entrance immediately, putting an angry face at the opening; he relaxed the instant he recognized her.

"What is it?" he whispered.

"She's sleeping?"

"Yes, but she's agitated." Veraless drew back, let Melogian enter. The door to
the inner room was open. On the bed Christine lay on her back, fretting in her
sleep, muttering indistinct syllables. Her features were drawn, her head jerking from
side to side as if she were receiving imaginary blows. After a moment she turned
onto her side and relaxed somewhat, her breath loud through her half-open mouth.

Melogian recalled the little girl this young woman had been, remembered sitting Christine on her knee and pouring illusions from her hands onto the child's lap
like a cascade of roses, to make her laugh and squeal in pleasure. She found her eyes
were burning. She muttered a good-bye to Veraless, who sat down again in his chair
to watch the sleeping princess. Melogian left the antechamber on silent feet, blinking hard to ease the pain: For her, there were no more tears to be shed.

It was apt that she should come upon Quentin next; as she crossed a gallery on
her way back to her apartments, she saw the young knight stretched out on a bench
against a wall. His head lay back, his arm had fallen over the edge until his knuckles
brushed the floor; he was so pale and drawn that for a moment he appeared dead to
her, then she saw his chest rise powerfully, drawing in air. She went up to him and
crouched at his side. "Quentin? Quentin . . ." He did not react, nor when she shook
his shoulder gently. From his accounting of his travels with Christine it seemed he

had taken almost no rest during their flight back to the real world. He must not have had the time to find the chamberlain before exhaustion overtook him. Melogian stroked his hair, the line of his jaw, roughened by a nascent beard. Then she kissed his forehead and whispered, "Sleep well, brave knight."

As she stood up, ghosts of blue roses bloomed in the air, to swim and circle about Quentin. He could not have been aware of them; but whether because he had sensed her kiss or because he knew in his bones that his long task had ended in success, he smiled then. He looked to her like an etching in a book, a picture of the Hero Gildencaulde who, it was said, had not died but still lay sleeping deep within the ground, kept young by enchanted dreams. Melogian smiled at Quentin and heaved a sigh she herself could not quite interpret.

2. Vorlok

Mathellin the magician beat the air with pain-racked wings. There never had been enough time for him to rest properly, to heal his injured body. The grim fact of pursuit overwhelmed his thoughts, urged him to fly on and on, brought his mind to the gates of madness.

Through forests and mountain passes in the made world he had flown, pausing for rest only when exhaustion threatened to rob his mind of all consciousness. Then he would perch on a branch, catching his breath, claws clenched on the thin wood, feeling the branch sway under his weight. Once a measure of strength had returned to him, he would launch himself into the air, beating his wings hard to achieve altitude sufficient for a long glide through the air and across a thousand realities. His power quivered in him as if it were dying; somewhere in his travels he had lost the crystal, left his few demented allies behind. All his plots had collapsed, all his cleverness gone sour. There was only left to him the raw fact of pursuit, and the knowledge that he would never catch up.

He had passed through the gap into Chrysanthe as if shot from a giant's bow; and in the next instant crashed to earth and broken his arm, for the transition into the real world had compelled him to assume his true shape. For long minutes he had lain naked and bleeding upon the ground, gasping. Then, marshaling the dregs of his energy, he had healed himself and resumed the hawk shape, taken off and spiraled up into the air above the Hedges, headed not north as Christine and Quentin had been, but southwest, toward the duchy of Kawlend and Vorlok.

Through Temerorn he had flown; villages passed beneath his wings, unrecognized, then wilderness, dabs of yet darker green onto the rich summer grass. At last low foothills had appeared beneath him; as he flew on, they had grown taller and steeper, until their crowns burst free of the mantle of soil and grass, their pink granite glowing in the light of the sun. On and ever on, as the hills grew into mountains, he traced the border of Kawlend; the duchy of Estephor lay to his right, beyond the peaks. On and on, toward the end of the world, as the sun coursed through the heavens, until the mountains sprouted huge shadows. Within his mind, crushed into the bird's tiny brain-box, Mathellin heard a man's voice. "Even if you received a mortal wound, Mathellin, I expect you would keep fighting until you could be bothered to notice you were dead. Even if you were killed, why I expect you would fly on and on, until someone told you you were in fact dead. Even if you were killed, on and on, fly on and on, fly, fly, even if you were dead. . . ."

Then, at long last, the low broad towers of Vorlok swelled in Mathellin's blurred sight. The early dusk of these mountain lands had long since arrived and all lay in shadow, though the sky still glowed blue. Mathellin could barely keep himself aloft. He had to reach the ground, but a controlled landing would overtax his strength. Crumpling in a heap on the ground might be his only option; but then, how much more time to heal his smashed bones and crawl his way into the castle? Perhaps he could locate an open window and dive into the room beyond, though he doubted he could aim adequately.

Then he saw light blooming in the rock garden set atop the Low Tower, the glow of burning oil within frosted glass globes. By that light he espied a figure sitting on a bench between the lamps: a blond man wearing the red and green of Vaurd's line. It was more than he could hope for. He veered, beat his exhausted wings against the direction of his flight, twisted his feathers in the air to lose even more speed, and tried to flutter down.

His body betrayed him; he lost control of his flight, tumbled and fell. There came a wet sound as he impacted the flagstones and for a moment everything was drowned in blackish red.

えど Prince Olf started when he heard the impact and the strangled cry. He set down the picture book he had been reading, rose from his seat against the edge of the wall, hurried to the bird. He stopped a pace or two away, astonished. He'd never seen a white hawk before, never heard that any existed. Had someone shot the bird down from a tower window? Olf looked around, but could see no archer in evidence. Yet beads of scarlet speckled the white feathers. He bent down, reached out a hand, only to draw back with a startled oath when the hawk suddenly stirred. It quivered, then shook as if its heartbeat were too strong to be contained within its frame. The hawk grew, its flesh pulsing like boiling dough; within half a dozen breaths its shape had blossomed into that of a man.

The wizard Mathellin, a figure from Olf's youth, lay naked on the graveled alley before him, panting hoarsely. His body was deformed: the arms elongated and too thin, the feet pointed with clawed toes clenched tightly and the heels half sunk into the calves, an incongruous tuft of white down at his crotch. Mathellin's lids rose; his eyes were so bloodshot as to be almost an even red. They swiveled in their orbits, fixed upon him. The wizard inclined his head the merest fraction, worked his mouth until words at last emerged.

"You are . . . Olf? Tell Evered," Mathellin breathed. "Tell him Christine escaped. She is back in Chrysanthe by now."

Olf remained slack-jawed for a long moment as he digested these words, then he regained the power of speech. "Escaped! How?"

"Found . . . by one of the knights of the realm. He took her away. . . . I couldn't hold them back."

Olf clenched his fists into the fabric of his shirt.

"God's sweet eyes," he said. "I can't believe this. How could you let her go? What happened? How did he manage to take her?"

"Go tell Evered," rasped Mathellin. "Go . . . tell him. Now!"

Olf stood indecisively at his side for a second more, questions pressing on his lips, then he turned away and ran down the stairs.

Having reached the third floor, he went along a wide hall to Evered's door and knocked, but received no answer. He descended to the ground floor; at the foot of the staircase one of Casimir's servants was sweeping the flagstones with a broom. Olf called out: "You there! Listen to me." The servant stopped, turned pale-gray, lucent eyes toward Olf. "Where can I find Evered?" asked the prince.

There was a slight pause, then the servant replied: "He might be found in many places. I know of seven hundred and twelve. I can recite the list in order of increasing distance from this point, or—"

Olf cut the servant off angrily. "No, no! Not that. I mean: Where is Evered now?"

"I do not possess such precise knowledge. Do you mean to ask where Evered is most likely to be at this moment?"

"Yes, you cursed imp!"

"To the best of my experience, he is most likely in the West Atrium."

Olf hurried off in that direction, leaving the servant staring after his departing back with unblinking eyes. The prince followed a long corridor, draped in blue against the dark gray stone, like a feeble attempt to evoke the Testenel he and his brothers had been exiled from. He soon reached a high ogival double door and shoved one of the panels open, almost tumbling into the room.

His three brothers and Casimir the wizard sat close to the cold fireplace, seats drawn close together around a low table. All four looked up at his entry; none seemed too pleased.

"She's escaped!" Olf shouted. "Christine has escaped!"

"We know that," replied Aghaid. "Casimir has been telling us. His spy-spells have been relaying turmoil and clamor. He's gotten several glimpses of the girl and Edisthen's reaction leaves no room for doubt."

Taken aback, Olf remained gape-mouthed. "Oh. But then, why didn't you summon me als—"

Evered cut him off, frowning.

"But how do *you* know about it? Casimir cannot have told you, can he?"

"No, no, I've been told by Mathellin!" Olf announced. "He, ah . . . he *flew* back here, in the shape of a bird. Then he turned into a man, but not quite. He's injured, I think, his eyes . . . He could hardly speak. I, ah, I left him on top of the Low Tower."

"Mathellin!" Evered exclaimed. "Well, at least he didn't stay behind to cower in Errefern. Olf, get servants and go to him; have him taken to a room. If he's injured, see that his injuries are taken care of. Tell him I shall speak to him soon."

"Who cares about Mathellin!" said Olf. "I want to know what's going to happen to us. When the princess tells Edisthen what happened, what will he do?"

Evered shook his head and blew an exasperated sigh. "She won't accuse anyone, you little coward. Let her say whatever she wishes. She was four years old, and we were cloaked by illusion. Her father will learn nothing more from her than he already knows. You're quite safe from big bad King Edisthen. . . . Now do as I said, before I lose patience with you."

Olf hesitated for a moment more, but Evered's expression chased him off and he trotted back along the corridor, calling for servants.

❧ Aghaid rose to shut the door and snorted in contempt. "Dear Olf. Even when one tries to keep him out of things, he manages to bungle his way in."

"Never mind Olf," snapped Evered. "I'm concerned about strategy."

"But Olf does have a point," said Innalan, who had borne a gloomy expression from the moment Casimir had informed them of Christine's return to Testenel. "Christine's return has indeed complicated matters; it has damaged our position. Instead of saying this plainly, we've been hedging around the matter for the past hour. I respect your feelings, Evered, but we'll get nowhere without plain talk. Olf has at least that one virtue."

Evered leaned forward in his seat and quivered; then he sat back with an obvious effort and the unhealthy gleam in his eyes died out. "I can listen to anything you have to say, brother. There is no need to spare my feelings."

"M'lords, if I may," interjected Casimir. "The truth, the plain truth, is that our position is still very strong." He shot a glance at Innalan and pursed his full lips for an instant. "Olf was correct that Christine's return is an unexpected setback. But what Olf doesn't see is that it is a minor one. He forgets that her abduction served its main purpose long ago: not to demoralize Edisthen, not to drain his resources, not to cut short his line, but to force Orion's hand. It was because of the huge amounts of power he granted to the knights who were sent questing after Christine that he could in the end be dealt with. Yes, m'lord Innalan, it would have been best if Christine had remained forever gone, but her return at this point is of little consequence. Our plans proceed."

"Still," argued Innalan. "Edisthen will fight with much greater energy now that his heir is present to be protected. And as yet we have no absolute commitment from Kawlend."

"What do you expect, brother? Ambith won't deliver her signature at the bottom of a written contract!" said Evered. "We understand each other: She is on our side. When I ask, I shall have the whole of Kawlend behind me. This is not in question."

Aghaid looked doubtful. "I beg to differ. The duchess hates Edisthen, true; but will her hatred extend to his daughter?"

Evered's face twitched and his fingers clutched at the fabric of his armchair. "I tell you, Ambith is my ally, as much now as ever before!"

Aghaid paused a moment before continuing the argument, his tone very mild. "She backed you once before, and she lost. She may well back you again, but think: These new conditions might weaken her resolve. Ambith may be sympathetic to our cause, but in the end it is her own interests she pursues."

"Her interests align with our own!" Evered pounded the arm of his seat. "The barons of the southern marches are mine for the asking; Kawlend will follow the red and green once more when I challenge Edisthen."

Aghaid was cowed to silence, but Innalan, provoked by Evered's tone, let heat enter his voice. "Listen to yourself! Kawlend will follow you, just like that. It will follow you against Archeled, Temerorn, *and* Estephor."

"Yes! Yes, it will! In the name of justice and reparation."

"Evered . . ."

"Are you a coward, Innalan? We've spent a third of our lives in this dank pigsty: Have you grown to like it here? Are you afraid of losing the comforts of your apartments? The swamp-wood bed, the stinking tallow candles, the leaky thundermug?"

Evered sat quivering in his chair, a drop of spittle on his chin. Innalan closed his eyes for a moment, and the bright spots of color on his cheeks paled.

"I am afraid of nothing on this earth, Evered," he said. "I want Kawlend to follow us. But it is one thing to want something, another to actually get it. I want us to be sure of what we do. It's taken us thirteen years to get to this point. We have to know we're striking at the right time, with all needed force. I would not have us waste all these years in exile."

"Forget Kawlend, then, brother. Let's assume Ambith will stay abed with the flux. It changes nothing, because we do not need Kawlend anymore, do we? Not with Casimir's demons. A hundred men following in their wake could capture Tiellorn in a week!"

Innalan made a sour face and glanced down at the table, where a sheet of paper bore a half-dozen drawings Casimir had made with a fine-point ink pen.

"Well," he muttered, "either those hell-spawn will compel absolute obedience or else they will make the entire army desert. Just their images are enough to loosen a man's bowels."

"So the peeping chick grants I am right! You agree, all of you: These six alone would yield us victory, even if Kawlend should fail to support us!"

Innalan could not hold his brother's gaze; he averted his eyes, and though he muttered some words of protest his voice was too low to be audible. Aghaid, youngest of them all, remained silent. Evered let a smile bloom upon his face.

"Then enough with these discussions; I want us to move now," he said. "Now, at the very moment that Edisthen thinks to see his line restored; I want that murderer's hopes dashed into ruin. We will act now. The barons know my wishes: their levies can be raised quickly. Bring your demons out of the ground, Casimir. Kawlend will follow us when we've assembled our host. We can march in less than a week!"

The wizard scratched his beard, harrumphed. "Well . . . that isn't what I'd advise, m'lord. In fact, I think we should delay a while longer."

Evered gaped for a second, then his voice rose in outrage. "Delay? Again? That is all you ever offer me! Delays and deliberation! Damn your patience, Casimir! I've waited half my life for justice; I will have it now!"

Evered's wizard scowled at his master.

"I spent six months interred for your sake, my Lord Evered," said Casimir in a flat tone. "I gambled with my life to gain us a crushing advantage, and I succeeded. In Snows of last year we decided on High-Summer as the time of our attempt, and all our preparations have focused on that date. Do we rush foolishly now, a month early, because the girl has been rescued from her made world, and spoil our advantage?"

Evered sneered but, perhaps remembering a certain fire, held his tongue. Casimir continued.

"Ambith will not want to be rushed. She knows what we intend and she knows when we planned to launch the attack. If she thinks we're forcing her hand, she may reject us. If only to avoid angering her, we should wait; but I have a better reason. I have been reflecting these past weeks, my Lord Evered, on all I learned underground. And there is one further trick we might play on Edisthen. I'd been pondering it, and with this latest development I believe it becomes quite apt as a countermove against Christine's rescue; a way to turn their triumph to grief."

Evered's eyes blinked once. "Go on."

"As a new wrinkle on our original plan, it is not, I admit, an *immediate* response. But first see how you like it, m'lord."

Casimir bent forward in his seat and hunched himself over the table. With a mutter under his breath he evoked a map of the world on its surface. Vorlok was indicated by a glowing red and green tower close by his side of the table. Testenel was a glowing blue tower at the center of the map. A few roads wandered over the topography, and villages and towns were marked by translucent outlines of rooftops. Miniatures of armored men now appeared on the map, symbols of armies. They were more numerous about Testenel, otherwise sparsely scattered here and there, though a small clump had formed next to Vorlok. The livery of the troops within Kawlend vacillated between the duchy's colors of ivory and brown and the red and green of Vaurd's line.

Casimir pointed at Vorlok: Miniatures of Vaurd's sons and himself appeared, and then, one by one, six eldritch figures pervolved at various places within the world and traveled more or less swiftly to rank themselves around the castle.

"This is the plan so far," he said. "The terrapin moves slowest of all, so I should summon it first; the others will not need more than a few days to reach us. Egrevogn, here—" He pointed to a green figure, which had emerged well within the borders of Archeled. "I can fetch in a whirl, though he will just barely fit; I can do the same for Mehilvagaunt. The others will need to make it here on their own. There are feasible routes in all cases, and I will guard their travels as necessary. Then, once all are assembled, we declare war, Kawlend sides with us, and we throw everything we have at Edisthen."

The demonic miniatures had made their way to Vorlok and now swept forward at the vanguard of Evered's armies. Kawlend's forces, their livery now green and red, joined them and a tide of men and demons flowed north, toward the center of the map. Opposing forces gathered and clashed with Evered's, an indistinct roil of battle that ended with Vaurd's sons in possession of Testenel; then princes, soldiers, and demons all faded away.

"Alarms, battles, slaughter, and the kingdom is ours," said the wizard. "This was always the straightforward part of the plan—but a bit more deviousness can tilt the board further in our favor."

Casimir pointed to the representation of Testenel; three figures appeared, miniatures of Edisthen, his daughter, and Melogian. Casimir reached out with thumb and forefinger and neatly removed Edisthen from the map, then rolled the illusion around in his meaty palm.

"Down in Jyndyrys I learned to play a kind of chess where captured pieces can come back. An important aspect of the proper strategy being that, if the opponent keeps bringing a certain piece back, one should focus on another."

He flicked Edisthen's miniature over his shoulder, and it evaporated before it hit the floor.

"You make it look so simple," commented Innalan with more than a trace of strain in his voice. "Have you learned to stretch your arm a hundred leagues, to pluck him out of his throne and fling him into the ocean?"

Casimir bristled at him. "My magic is a bit more subtle, m'lord Innalan. Or do you want me to undertake research in the direction you mentioned?"

"I want a clear picture of what you propose, not theatrics."

"Enough of your peeps, brother!" said Evered. "Casimir, please explain your idea."

The wizard sniffed and glowered for a long moment before he consented to detail his plan. As he spoke, his hands moved above the map of the world, stretched their shadow over the glowing blue tower that was Testenel. The princes questioned him, and Casimir fielded all objections in an even tone. As the discussion progressed, even Innalan began to nod his approval.

"When?" Evered finally asked.

"I will need time to prepare; this isn't a trivial spell. And the demons should be summoned and gathered here first. Then, even if Edisthen should fail to step into the trap, we will be ready to set the armies forth."

"I wish we could bait him," said Evered. "Is there anything that might entice him there?"

Aghaid shrugged. "Edisthen's legs must itch with all his worries. Sooner or later he'll wander into the trap."

"But Testenel is huge," said Innalan, "and the king is a busy man."

"If he doesn't get caught, he doesn't. We lose nothing by trying this."

"Save that we tire Casimir for days on end."

The wizard snorted in contempt. "You never knew my strength, m'lord Innalan. And I am far greater than the man who went underground last spring."

Evered saw Innalan lean back involuntarily, so menacing was Casimir's tone.

"It's settled, then," he said loudly, to catch the wizard's attention. "It shall be done as you suggest, Casimir. If you wish to inscribe a schedule for us, I would be grateful. I will go see to Mathellin now—no need for all of us to be present. Casimir, I trust you will want to question him?"

Evered rose, went to the door. The wizard fell in step at his side as he walked down the corridor. From behind him, Innalan called for wine in a peevish voice.

Two burly servants in leather armor, part of the token guard force Vaurd's line had been allowed, waited at the door to the room where Mathellin lay abed. One of them opened it at Evered's order; Vaurd's eldest son and his wizard entered. The room was lit with three candles, casting a yellowish glow on the recumbent Mathellin. Casimir muttered an incantation and made a pass in the air; gleaming motes drifted from his fingers to hover above the bed, to shed a better light upon the scene.

Mathellin's eyes were closed, his face drawn. A bead of blood rolled from beneath his right lid. His breath hissed in his throat.

Casimir drew back the covers that had been pulled up to Mathellin's shoulders. The shape-shifter's arms were revealed, twisted together like branches a negligent gardener had allowed to interweave. The flesh of his abdomen and chest swelled and contracted in slow waves, the bones of his rib cage flexing.

"Mathellin," Evered called. "Mathellin, awake!"

Mathellin shuddered and came awake with a gasp. His arms unwove, thrust back against the mattress and half lifted him. His skin goose-pimpled as if from a cool breeze—then the hairs thickened into translucent needles and the skin into armored scales.

Evered stepped back, alarmed. Mathellin drew in a hoarse breath and his shape melted back to that of a man.

"I . . . ," he said, his eyes focusing on Evered with many a blink. "I am back."

The words seemed to have exhausted him; he sank back down and closed his eyes once more.

"What happened?" asked the prince. "How did the girl escape?"

Mathellin half opened his eyes, reached out for a flask of brandy set beside the bed on a nightstand. He swallowed three mouthfuls and shivered. Gritting his teeth, he sat up, leaning against the headboard.

"I need food," he said. "Meat—uncooked—and sugar. I am so tired. . . ."

Evered ordered one of the guards to fetch those, and the other one to get them two seats.

"I want to know, wizard, how it is that you failed," he said once a chair had been brought for him and he had sat.

Mathellin blinked at him. "Evered . . . My Lord Evered. You've changed."

"Answer your liege's question," said Casimir.

Mathellin looked at him, lowered his gaze. "Yes . . . Yes." Mathellin took another swallow from the flask. "I was . . . I was very careful, my lord. I took care of her. I lived as her warden, kept her as removed from the world as I could. She . . . She hurt herself, when she was ten . . . that would have been seven years ago. Fell from a chair and in the healing house she babbled about an illusory companion. I took her to a . . . 'psychologist.' We don't have that word. A soul-healer. I was concerned about the companion. I feared magic, some spell of Orion's that might have found her. I couldn't feel anything about her myself, but that damned Hero knew things no other wizard did. . . .

"The healer was concerned as well. He said she had evidently been mistreated in her youth and that she badly needed his arts. What was I to do? I could hardly refuse him; it was the story I told everyone, that I'd had to take her away from her father. So I sent her to him, regularly. But the little cow got worse and worse, until in a fit she stabbed her own hand. God's eyes, royal blood spilled . . . I thought I would go mad when I saw it."

Mathellin drew a ragged breath.

"But the Law doesn't prevent self-injury; and it was her own hand that had done this, not mine. Still, I had her treated most carefully. That world had powerful drugs, much harsher than the strongest poppy juice. She was given those, for her own good. For days she moved about like one of your golems, Casimir. I cried myself to sleep every night with worry. I was . . . I was devoted, my lord Evered. I *warded* her."

"What does any of that have to do with her escape?" asked Casimir.

Mathellin was gazing down at his hands and was a long moment continuing. When he spoke again, it was a near whisper.

"I couldn't prevent her from growing up. I would have had to imprison her once she was a woman. . . . You yourself were the one who rejected that idea, Casimir. I remember it . . . so clearly. As if it were yesterday. No fortresses, you said, no adamantine walls around the bereft princess. Too obvious; Orion would hunt for such nodes of circumstance across infinity.

"I thought, instead, she might be made to imprison herself. She withdrew from the world; I did not let her have close friends, kept her by me whenever I could. I had dreams in which she slit her own throat . . . I cried when I woke up from those, and went to check in on her . . . I remember feeling so disappointed, and so horrified at myself, when I saw she was sleeping soundly.

"But then, after many years, something happened. She . . . she said something to me. . . ."

The guard sent for food had returned, a slab of raw meat in one hand and a bag of sugar in the other. Mathellin lifted his gaze to the meat and a rope of saliva fell from his lips. Evered contained his impatience and disgust while the shape-shifter ate, tearing at the raw meat with hooked teeth, stuffing his mouth with handfuls of coarse sugar, washing it down with slugs of brandy. When all the food was gone, Mathellin extruded a liver-dark tongue and swept it around his lips, mopping up the crystals of blood-soaked sugar stuck to his face.

"*What* happened exactly? What did Christine say to you?" Evered asked when Mathellin at last lay back, swallowing the last dribbles of his meal.

This time the wizard's gaze met his own, but only for a heartbeat before it dropped.

"The soul-healer . . . had made her recall rapes, my lord. Dozens."

"What?"

"It was the fashion. To treat people by bringing forth memories presumed dormant from their childhood. Such stories were frequently reported: Adults recalled having been raped by their parents as children, or forced to sacrifice to demons from the Book of Shades. Some told tales where they were taken away in flying chariots by beings from spheres hung in the heavens, and then brought back, no one else the wiser."

Evered felt a shiver go down his spine, an emotion he could not name. He asked, his voice thin: "You're telling me Christine was made to recall Edisthen *raped* her?"

"Yes. And sold her body to others as well. And murdered her mother."

It was more than Evered could bear. He burst out laughing, forcing the explosions of noise out of his throat until it grew sore.

"Edisthen's daughter grew to believe her own father was a murderer and a procurer? Oh, that is too rich for words!"

He laughed for a minute more, wringing every drop of bitter humor from the revelation, bursts of hilarity rising afresh as the idea showed its various facets in his mind. It was joy he felt, he decided when his laughter had subsided and he lay back in his chair with tears in his eyes; joy so strong it tasted like gall at the back of his throat. What else could it be?

Casimir had waited for him to calm down; now he turned to Mathellin and prodded him. "None of that tells us why or how she escaped."

Mathellin blushed, in symmetrical patches over his face like butterfly wings. "It happened like this," he said. "She . . . she began to doubt the memories the soul-healer had made her retrieve. She confronted me about it. She had . . . well, practical proof that she had not been forced. I knew what to say to her. I believed it myself. Her body had changed over time, hadn't it?" He chortled briefly. "I had been a woman enough times in my former life. . . . I knew firsthand how our senses are shaped by our flesh. But there was more to it than that. She had never rebelled before, and I sensed something . . . I felt fate move at that moment. The hand of God reaching into the book of our lives. She struck me. She said 'I am not your child.' And then . . . I heard a car horn outside. I mean a mechanical vehicle's noisemaker. She rushed out, I followed . . . I knew it then. When I saw the man in the vehicle. The knight of Chrysanthe. He blazed with reality, the way only Christine and myself did.

"I was thinking with two minds at that point. I had buried myself for so long into the other man. . . . I cast a spell to stop them, the first thing that came to me. . . . But it failed, I don't quite know how. And then they moved *beyond*."

"In a *mechanical vehicle*?" Casimir seemed outraged.

"It wasn't a machine. It was a shape-shifted horse. Orion gifted the damned knight with a shifting spell for his mount."

Casimir sneered. "I see. So that is how she escaped."

"It isn't!" wailed Mathellin. "Don't accuse me! I won't let you accuse me!"

"No one has accused you of anything, Mathellin," said Evered.

Pointing to Casimir with a trembling hand, Mathellin cried out: "*He* has! I know what he thinks! That I just let her slip through my fingers! But that's a lie! I fought them; every step of the way!"

Mathellin bent over, clenched his teeth and pursed his lips as he shook with the force of his retching. "God's teeth, get him a pan to vomit in!" Evered ordered. Mathellin shook his head in denial. He mastered the convulsions of his stomach and sat up, opened his mouth and exhaled a scentless gust of air.

"I fought them, my Lord Evered," he repeated. "I was helpless for a moment only; and then I was myself again, and I knew what I had to do.

"I sent out an alarm, so the outlying posts would be aware of what had happened and be able to warn Casimir if he were down in Errefern. Then I traveled *beyond* to the nearest strongpoint. Once I had fetched a mount, I rode through Errefern, as fast as I possibly could . . . and I reached them, in the end, I did reach them—at least in another's body. I tried. . . ."

He drew a breath, his gaze vacant.

"I cast myself closer to the surface, into an infectious were. From that vantage point I intercepted them as they rested. I merged with their mount, I took control of its shape. But it fought me; such stupid loyalty in that beast. . . . I had to keep the blood royal safe. The knight got out. I almost had her then. All I needed was a moment of clarity, to step *beyond*. . . . But it was so hard to juggle it all. I did more than anyone could have done! I had to fight them both, the knight and his mount, one without, one within. . . . He struck again and again; God's eyes, the pain! And then she said, she said, 'You're hurting me'! I couldn't . . . I couldn't think. I had to let her go. The Law . . . And then he killed us. Our eye was smashed and bleeding, and he thrust into our heart, and we *died*. . . ."

Mathellin began sobbing, covering his head with his arms. Evered looked at Casimir briefly, returned his attention to Mathellin. Though the wizard's story was lacunar, Evered did not doubt its essential truth.

"Get rest," he said after a moment's hesitation. "You have pushed yourself hard. Rest for now; I will see you again soon."

There was a knock at the door, a light rattling the Lady Veronica knew well. "Come in, Sylviane," she called out. The door opened and her maid trotted in, her fat cheeks flushed in excitement.

"M'lady, m'lady, you'll never guess what!"

Veronica smiled, always ready to be entertained by the girl's enthusiasms. "What is it?"

"The princess! Princess Christine, she's back! His Majesty sent word throughout the land! She was found and returned by a knight of the realm!"

Veronica felt a shiver course through her; it seemed as though her head was weaving on her neck, and a great shout was caught in her chest. The emotion was deeply familiar and yet strange. . . . Then, before the girl could finish drawing breath to continue, Veronica understood. She had felt like this exactly twice before: the first time on the day of her wedding, when she had sensed the wheel of the world turning, things falling into place, the sun rising after a nearly endless night, a yawning void filled. And the second time, when her husband had died, for all that it was personal tragedy. She had always known that she was not important in the scheme of things, and she had learned it anew as she saw her husband dead in the arms of his successor. Though a scream of torment was about to rise from her throat, still she had known, had felt in her bones that all was right with the world.

And now a third time, this sense that might be akin to what a warrior feels as the blade is withdrawn from the wound: relief so intense it was pain.

Sylviane was already prattling on— she would repeat herself happily over and over until one cut her off—but the Lady Veronica shut her up in her customary manner, by laying a finger on her lips.

"Where was she? Who had taken her there?"

Sylviane's face fell. "I don't know, m'lady. I know who brought her back, it's a knight named Kevin, Kevin of Lydiss—"

"Yes, you've just said that. Is that all that the message said?"

"That's all I heard," conceded the maid. "Oh, isn't it exciting? I've never seen her, I'm too young, and now she's back at court I hope I can get a glimpse of her, you know, and I'll tell you all about it. . . ."

"Sylviane, will you please take a message to His Majesty the king?"

That brought the girl up short. She blushed, and curtseyed in acquiescence. "What do I say, m'lady?"

The Lady Veronica considered writing down her words, but they were not important words; certainly they would be nothing like the fancy speech of the courtiers. For all her years at court she had never learned to speak in the manner she was expected to. But Vaurd her husband had never minded; he had always been that, loving and understanding, forgiving of her faults.

"Just tell His Majesty Edisthen that I'm very glad his daughter has returned. Go right now, please."

Sylviane curtseyed again and went off on her errand. Veronica locked the door and went into the endmost room of her suite, which was littered with personal possessions of every kind: instruments she could not really play; pens and inkpots she rarely used; jewelry and fine garments she had no reason to wear. At the back of a heavy cupboard a painting hung; she had to shift ranks of dusty dresses to bring it into view.

For the first few years after his death she had kept Vaurd's fleshpaint portrait well hidden, knowing what sight would greet her if she glanced at it. When she'd judged enough time had passed, she had risked a glimpse; and though it had brought her pain, there had been no horror. Now she would gaze at it once or twice every season, a ritual of sorts, more satisfying than laying flowers on his grave. The statue of him that stood by his headstone was fine and lifelike, but it did not look down at her, there was no kindness in the features. It was a statue of the deposed king; not of her husband.

The painting showed Vaurd from the waist up, one hand on a marble desk, the other lightly gripping the pommel of the sword at his side. The great crown of Chrysanthe rose from his mane of black hair, its twelve points each topped with a gem of a different hue; yet it was translucent, ghostly, as was the sword. By now the fine clothes had decayed to rags; through the tears in the fabric earth-browned bones peeked out. The face had rotted away, but flakes of the scalp still clung to the grinning skull and snarled strands of hair fell to Vaurd's skeletal shoulders. This was no more her husband than the stone statue by Paucelin, but she would have said it was closer to the truth. Vaurd her husband, the man who had chosen her for no reason she could ever fathom, the man who had loved her, the man who had been slain by a Hero from the Book, had lain dead in the earth for twenty years. Sometimes when she woke her side was warm as if from his presence; sometimes some part of her would think *Oh how he will laugh at this when I tell him*. Yet seasons turn; the world goes on and what is right is right. The dead king's widow drew the dresses before the painting as drapes masking a window, then shut the cupboard doors.

3. Audiences

The voice in Quentin's dream was loud, somewhat nasal, singsong. "There you are, dear boy! The hero of the hour! A prince amongst men, the flower of knighthood!"

Quentin started awake. He was lying in a comfortable bed, stripped to his underclothes, with not the faintest memory of how he had come to be there.

The voice had not been a dream. A courtier whom Quentin vaguely recognized stood at the foot of the bed. Dressed as if for the hunt, the courtier made expansive gestures as he praised Quentin, holding a silver flask in one hand.

"I trust you're rested? What folly to lie abed still, when you could be lording it amongst the rest of us! I'll take you directly to the feast, shall I?"

"What?" mumbled Quentin.

"A feast, my boy! A feast in your honor! I've spent half the night organizing it, and the other half finding out where they'd hidden you. All of us are just *dying* to hear your musical voice, to see your handsome face, to kiss your warrior's hands! Hurry now, get dressed and come with me!"

"My lord . . . Ah, my lord . . . ?"

"Laschan, dear boy. Surely you know me?"

"Forgive me, my Lord Laschan. I've been away from court for nearly a decade." The name meant nothing to Quentin, but the man's face, now that he reflected, was definitely one he had seen at Testenel in the past.

"Oh, but of course!" said Lord Laschan. "No offense taken, none at all! How could I begrudge such a hero as yourself anything whatsoever? Of course, in all your travels, I'm sure you've had precious little occasion to think of us! But that is just the point, you see. We are all so eager to hear everything that's happened, straight from your own mouth!"

Quentin had sat up, drawing the covers up to the middle of his chest. He noticed his armor carefully hung on a support in a corner of the room. His sword in its scabbard was not with it—he spotted it leaning against the wall beside the headboard.

"What is it precisely, my Lord Laschan, that you wish to hear from me?"

The courtier affected an astonished air. He shook his head in wonder, then took a quick swig from his flask.

"But, my boy, the story of how you rescued the princess, what else?"

"How . . . ah . . . Why do you think I did such a thing?" stammered Quentin.

"Oh now, do *not* play that game, it doesn't suit you. The king himself has sent messengers to Tiellorn to inform the city that his long-lost daughter has returned. As we speak, envoys are on route to Korunn, Aluvien, and Waldern with the news."

Quentin shut his eyes briefly, but he could not retreat back into sleep, tempting as that was. "Very well, my lord," he said. "I shall get dressed. May I have a moment of privacy?"

"Of course, of course," said Laschan, and withdrew from the room, pulling the door shut behind him.

Quentin clambered out of the bed and knuckled his eyes. He had no idea of the time; his room had no windows from which he could guess at the sun's position. An oil lamp provided the light in the room; Quentin took it up and investigated what lay beyond the door facing the one Laschan had left through. He was surprised and delighted to discover a small water closet at which he was able to perform his ablutions. A chest held some clothes in his size, including bright yellow hose. He put it all on, looked at himself by holding the small shaving mirror at arm's length. An overdressed peasant boy looked back at him. With a sigh, he went to pick up his sword—his armor he would chance leaving here, but he'd be damned if he were parted from his blade—and buckled the straps around his waist and shoulder.

As soon as he opened the outer door, Lord Laschan exclaimed at his handsomeness and urged him onward to the reception. "A moment, my lord," said Quentin. "I must know where exactly I have been lodged."

"We're on the eighth floor, dear boy, at the edge of the Chalcedony Atrium. You just need to find the statue of the Three Sisters—see it way over there? The huntress's sword points right at your room."

A guard came up to them. "Everything all right, my lord?" she asked Laschan.

"Yes, yes, it's fine, dear," replied Laschan, looking slightly annoyed.

It suddenly became clear to Quentin just how Laschan had located him. He addressed the guard. "You know who I am?"

"Yes, sir, I do." She dropped her gaze after an instant.

"Who brought me here, and when?"

"Last night, sir, the chamberlain had you carried to your room."

"Right. And your name is?"

"Madrin."

"Madrin, I have left my armor in my quarters. I did not dare expect a lock on the door, but I do expect to find my possessions when I come back."

"Yes, sir!" she retorted, looking up with an outraged expression.

"So long as we understand one another," said Quentin before following an increasingly fretful Lord Laschan.

Their way led them across a goodly part of Testenel; once they had reached corridors lit by sunlight Quentin was able to ascertain it was very early in the morning. Throughout their journey, Laschan twittered about trivial matters, referring to people whose names Quentin had never heard, alluding to scandals and adventures he cared not a whit for. Finally, they reached the promised feast. Quentin had hoped for a small gathering, had feared a vast assembly. The reality was worse than either possibility: A score or so of courtiers were gathered in a torchlit hall, where tables laden with food and drink had been thoroughly ravaged. Half of the courtiers were deep in their cups, the other half were well on their way. At Laschan's arrival, they all raised a thunderous cheer.

"There he is, my loves, there he is! Quentin of Lydiss, the hero of the land!"

The courtiers rushed upon Quentin, eager to touch him, clasp his hand, thump his back, kiss his cheek. Half a minute of this mauling left Quentin's hand itching for the sword at his side; Laschan came to his rescue, extricating him from the crush and taking him to a dais against a wall.

"Loves, loves, let our hero breathe! Here, Quentin, have something to drink."

Quentin swallowed from the goblet Laschan had put in his hand; it was claret, no doubt an excellent vintage, but the slug of alcohol on an empty stomach burned him to his core.

Several courtiers were clamoring for him to tell his story, seconded by Laschan. Quentin discovered a profound revulsion at the thought of telling his tale to these people: They had not earned it from him, nor could they be expected to appreciate it. He took a deep breath and began a recounting so truncated as to border on a lie.

The courtiers appeared not to notice; his least remark was cause for cheers, and toasts to his health, and more cheers. After two minutes Quentin realized he could take a tangent and expand upon his early travels in the made world, which were strange enough to excite the crowd. So he told the tale all crooked, and no doubt left most of the audience with the impression that he had spent the better part of his nine-year search fighting two-headed giants and exploring sunken graveyards.

At long last he drew the story to a close; by this time only Laschan was still following the thread, and since he had kept swigging from his flask throughout, he was in no shape to complain that it stopped rather than ended.

To general applause and huzzahs, Quentin stepped down from the dais. The courtiers let him make his way to a table where he grabbed some lukewarm scones and finally settled his growling stomach. As he ate, various courtiers introduced themselves and babbled at him. Servants had come in and were cleaning the tables and, alas, restocking the drinks.

One courtier now approached him; Quentin had noted her amongst his audience, but had not yet seen her clearly. Now that he did, she fairly took his breath away.

"Quentin! My dear Quentin, it's so delightful to be in your presence! I am Lady Alicia." The courtier pushed herself so close to him they were nearly touching, her eyes almost level with his own. Her face was painted with the utmost skill; the strokes of the cosmetics brush were barely noticeable even from this proximity. Her mien was lucent as an icon's and her flesh gave off a piquant scent.

"We owe you more than we can ever repay, Sir Quentin," she said. Her eyes were swimming in moisture, her lips glistened as if she had just lifted her mouth from a basin of water. Quentin had always told himself he felt a vague contempt for heavily made-up women; yet in Lady Alicia's presence his mouth went dry as if he were a stripling lad.

"But I for one have vowed to see you rewarded as much as is possible for me," she continued. Her slim, long-fingered hand found his and raised it. Quentin for a moment thought she wanted a baisemain from him, a greeting that was only proper between closely related nobles, unless fashions had changed in the past decade. Then she slipped their hands into her clothes through a hidden slit at the waist and laid his hand on her left breast. He felt her naked skin under his fingers, and the swelling of her erect nipple.

"Meet me at your convenience, in my apartments," she whispered. "You may do what you want with me. If you wish, my friend Miltella will be present as well. We will pleasure you beyond your wildest expectations, I promise it. I am lodged in the outer ring of the upper galleries beneath the Phoenix Tower, at the sign of the apple. We shall expect you this evening."

She drew back and Quentin's hand emerged from the billows of fabric. There was no hint of the opening, and it seemed no one amongst the other courtiers had noticed the incident, though in their condition this was hardly surprising.

Lady Alicia gave him a nod and a smile and turned away. For a moment Quentin started to stumble after her but then he regained control of himself.

Other courtiers waited for an introduction; to Quentin's right, Lord Laschan was quaffing a huge glass of wine in the company of two laughing women. Fifteen feet away, Lady Alicia was looking over her shoulder at him. . . .

Then one achingly familiar face detached itself from the swirling confusion. It belonged to a man in servants' livery, now struggling under the weight of two fully laden trays.

"Ho!" Quentin called out in relief. "Sandenin! Sandy!"

Heedless of the twittering lords and ladies, he made his way across the crowd to the young man, who stood gaping at him.

"Oh, it is good to see you, Sandy," Quentin laughed. "Put those down, will you?"

Sandenin obeyed after a moment's hesitation, laying his trays upon a table. As soon as his hands were free, Quentin hugged him in delight.

"God's teeth, Sandy. It has been too long since I clapped eyes on you!"

"Hello, Quentin," Sandenin answered in a choked voice. "Nine years you've been gone. I thought you were dead and I'd never see you again."

"Ha! We knights of Chrysanthe scoff at death. You thought I would be gone forever? With you still owing me ten bits? I have come to collect, you cheat. Hand it over at once!"

Sandenin did not reply to the affectionate gibe; Quentin realized many of the courtiers had fallen silent and were staring at the pair of them with faintly scandalized expressions. Apparently his reunion with his old friend did not win their wholehearted approval.

For a moment Quentin tried to frame an explanation or an apology. Then he stopped himself as his mind at long last caught up with his situation. No excuses need be made. The man who had rescued Princess Christine had no need to justify himself, not for anything, not to anyone. And none had the power to keep him captive anywhere.

"Please excuse me, milords," he said. "I am now going to speak with my old friend Sandenin. Thank you for the reception."

Holding Sandenin by the elbow, he exited the room. No one, not even Lord Laschan, spoke a word to hold them. Sandenin goggled at him as they strode out.

"What are you doing, Quentin?" he whispered as soon as they had turned a corner. "You can't walk out on the lords like that."

Quentin chuckled. "What will they do to me? Forbid me from attending future receptions? They would be doing me a favor."

Sandenin still looked uneasy, but he allowed Quentin to lead him well away from the courtiers' hall.

"I want to know what happened to you, Sandy," Quentin was saying. "Did you ever win Eldfrice?"

Sandenin made a wry smile. "Heh. I won her and then needed six months to get rid of her. Turns out all she cared about was shiny things and taunting other girls with her loot. I'm well rid of her. Three years ago I married the love of my life. Remember little Bronna, Kyral's daughter?"

"Bronna? Really? The one who followed us around and that we used to call Bug?"

"Oh, don't remind me of that. She's grown up to be a lovely woman. And we're expecting a child for early fall."

"Oh, this is wonderful news! Congratulations!"

Sandenin was shaking his head in amazement.

"Quentin, why are we talking about me? You're the greatest hero of the land now; why do you care who I married?"

"Because you are my friend still. That has not changed. I have not changed; I am still the same Quentin who left—in all essentials, anyway."

"Not on your life. When you took your vows, when you became a knight, already you were a different person. All your friends, that's when we lost you. It's not fitting for a knight to associate with servants, you know that. Even less for a knight who's just saved the king's daughter."

Quentin took him by the shoulders. "Sandenin, I do not care. I do not care what is fitting or not. You will not cease being my friend because courtiers are vying for my attention."

Sandenin's face was sad. "They're your people, now."

Quentin sighed. "Look, I will not discuss this further with you. I want you to find the others of the old group; tell them I want to see them all. Perhaps tonight, or tomorrow; whenever you can manage to get them together. You are my friends, and I have missed you terribly."

"Well, I'll see what I can do," said Sandenin. "I'll leave you a message when I can."

"You do that."

Quentin clapped Sandenin's shoulder in farewell, and watched him leave—returning, of course, to the feasting hall to retrieve his trays. Quentin hoped Sandenin would not be questioned or even harassed upon his return—but this was Sandenin's problem, and Quentin wouldn't humiliate his friend by intervening.

Reorienting himself within the castle, Quentin eventually made his way to Christine's apartments; there he learned that she was still sound asleep. He could have waited for her to awake, but the need for action simmered in his blood. Again inquiring of the servants he encountered, he went to Melogian's quarters.

He had expected to find guards at her door as well, or at least a footman. The sorceress's door was untended, identified only by a small painting of a blue-petaled flower. He was about to risk a knock when she called out from within: "Come in, Quentin!"

Melogian's quarters were those of a scholar: overflowing with paper and curios, though everything seemed tidily arranged, except for the main worktable. Melogian had been breakfasting on bread and cheese, and an herbal tea was still steeping in its pot over a tiny fire. She rose to her feet as soon as he entered; he started to bow but she went forward to him and kissed him on both cheeks.

"Good morning to you! Did you get your rest? You're still looking a bit worn."

"Oh," said Quentin, "thank you, Lady Melogian. I slept well enough, but I have had a busy morning so far."

"What, at eight in the morning? Don't tell me people are harassing you in the corridors? Well, that's the price of fame, you know."

"No, people in the corridors did not recognize me, in fact. I suppose I should feel lucky for that. But Lord Laschan found me; he woke me up and took me to a party of his fellow courtiers."

"That bunch?" Melogian rolled her eyes. "Leeches on the court. I can't believe Edisthen lets them slarge year-round at his expense. . . . Anyway, you escaped and sought refuge here. Good for you!"

"First I went to the Lady Christine's side, but she is still sleeping. . . . So I thought perhaps you would see me."

"There's no *perhaps* about it," she said. "Sit down over here. D'you want a cup of verbena?"

As Quentin sipped at his scalding infusion, Melogian added: "If Christine were awake, I would be there. The watch-web keeps me informed of her state. If you want to wait here with me, we can go see her together when she wakes up."

Her words brought to the surface of Quentin's mind something that had been bothering him almost since his return.

"Yes, that would be very nice," he said. "But still . . ."

"What?"

"Something confuses me. I would have expected someone else to have been with the Lady Christine by now: Orion. When we arrived in Chrysanthe, I sought to call to him, using a spell he had gifted me with, but he did not answer. He is apparently still not here in Testenel. If I may ask, where is he?"

Melogian's face fell. She put her cup down in its saucer and set it on the table, on top of a pile of parchments.

"Of course, you don't know. You left so long ago," she said. "I'm sorry. Orion is gone, Quentin."

Quentin felt his skin goosepimple. "God's teeth! Orion, dead?"

"No. No, not dead. If he were dead, then all the power he invested into you, into all the other knights who went questing for Christine, would have evaporated. You'd have been left stranded in the made world. That you came back is proof that he lives yet."

"Where is he, then? What has happened?"

Melogian took a deep breath. "Seven years ago, he went down into Jyndyrys, seeking Christine. But he never returned."

"Well then, it is merely a matter of time," said Quentin, striving to minimize the import of the news. "He is seeking for Christine as all of us were seeking; he will be back. . . ."

"No. He isn't seeking as you were seeking. Orion can travel very far in very little time. For him to be gone a month within a made world is possible; a year, ridiculous. And for him to be *lost* . . . is unthinkable. Yet he is lost. I've searched for him myself, and failed, when I couldn't possibly fail."

"I do not understand," said Quentin. "Do you mean that he is too far down in the world?"

"That would be irrelevant. Orion's mastery of the Art is such that he could distort the weft and reveal his location with a thought. To me, his presence, no matter how distant he was, would blaze like the sun through thin clouds. Now, I've gone down into Jyndyrys many times, to locate him. My spells say he is there; I perceive him—but I can't *find* him. There is no source to his light. I traveled through the made world until I reached the lees of nightmare; and then I went farther in still, until I came close to losing myself. I could feel him everywhere; I could find him nowhere. I no longer claim to know where he is. Maybe all that is left in Jyndyrys is an echo of his existence; maybe he has passed beyond the made world, somehow. 'Stranger the world is than even wizards know.' He's still alive, that I know; but he is gone from us, and I don't know when he will return, if ever."

Quentin reached for his cup of herbal tea and sipped at it, to offset some of the chill he felt. Melogian was doodling with a stylus on a wax tablet, inscribing notches in no recognizable pattern.

"He has been gone a long time," she said after a moment, looking up at Quentin. "We've gotten used to it; none of us talk about it much, that's all. And I'd rather talk about pleasant things. Like what you're going to do today."

"What am I going to do today?" asked Quentin.

"Well, aren't you going to tell Edisthen what reward you claim?"

"Oh, my. I had forgotten about that."

"I'd suggest you start thinking about it in earnest. It can't be all that hard, can it?"

"Yes it is. I have no idea what to ask for."

"Wealth. Land. A title. You could get a barony in northern Archeled."

Quentin pursed his lips dubiously. "The idea has merit, I suppose . . . but that is not my lifelong dream."

"What's your lifelong dream, then?"

"Hmm. It would help if I knew that. . . ."

Melogian chuckled. "You can always ask Edisthen for more time to decide. . . ." She started. "Ah! Christine is waking up. Let's give her enough time to get dressed, and then we can go see her."

🙞 Christine rose with a moan from the depths of sleep and a tangle of anxious dreams. She threw back the heavy coverlet and rolled onto her side; the back of her neck was slick with sweat.

She heard a discreet cough; instantly she shuddered and gasped. The fear had already died by the time she gave voice, however; memories had flooded back and she knew who it was that stood at the foot of her bed, even before she had opened her eyes.

She relaxed her hands that had clutched at the coverlet. Veraless was no more than a step inside her room, and he looked embarrassed to have disturbed her. She felt a mild dread at his presence, yet she had asked him to watch over her sleep, and relief mingled with her disquiet. Light filtered into the room through gaps between the drapes. It seemed white to her, with not the least tint of yellow: Morning must be well past. Reflexively, she glanced at the side of the bed, but there was no clock there.

"Hello, Captain," she said. "What . . . what time is it? How long did I sleep?"

"About fifteen hours, milady. It is half past eight o'clock."

Fifteen hours; and still she felt as if she could have slept till sundown. Christine ran the fingers of one hand through her hair.

Veraless asked her: "Are you hungry, Lady Christine? Do you wish to bathe?" but Christine was already asking her own question, as if in reflex. "Where's Quentin?"

Veraless inclined his head a fraction. "Sir Quentin asked after you earlier this morning. If you wish, I can go and fetch him."

"Ah . . . Yes, please. Thank you very much."

"Very well. Your maid is here, my lady. I'll send her in, and then I'll take my leave for the moment. It's been—" Veraless cast his glance down and his voice altered. "It's been a great honor to guard your sleep, Lady Christine." It seemed he wanted to say more, but instead he withdrew from her room; Christine heard the outer door of the suite open and close. A moment later a maid came in, a girl in her late teens or early twenties, with a pleasant square face and auburn hair.

"I'm Althea, Your Highness," she said with a bob of the head that must be a kind of curtsey. She was carrying a pair of silken slippers and a voluminous dark red robe. At her urging Christine threw the covers back and Althea fitted the slippers over Christine's bare feet with an expert motion. Christine levered herself out of the bed. The maid held up the robe and asked Christine to shed her clothes. Christine refused; Althea did not insist and belted the thick robe around her as she stood. It came down to her ankles and the collar rose nearly to her cheeks.

"There. M'lady is ready for informal occasions. Does m'lady wish to eat now, or go bathe?"

Christine felt an uncomfortable pressure in her bladder.

"The bath, please."

"Of course." Althea led Christine out, opening the outer door. Two guards, who had been waiting at the door, fell in step behind the pair of them as they walked down the corridor. The blue stone of Testenel glimmered in the light of oil lamps. Up ahead, past an intersection, a pool of sunlight came through an open door.

There was a guard at the intersection, and he held back two people, a portly man with a graying mustache and a plump woman dressed in deep red, wearing a ruffled scarf atop her blond curls. As Christine passed them, both bowed deeply to her and attempted to speak; the guard kept them well at bay. "God keep Your Highness safe!" the portly man called out after Christine, who flinched at the brassiness of his voice.

"Sorry, m'lady," said the maid. "The Demmerel Chambers aren't very private. When m'lady moves into a proper suite, she will find all she needs at her disposal."

They had reached the door from which the sunlight came. "Here we are," said

Althea. "We could have had a tub brought in, but m'lady's rooms were so small; m'lady will see this is much better."

The guards arranged themselves by the door; Althea and Christine entered a large room wreathed in rose-perfumed steam, like a setting from Romance Movie of the Week. A huge porcelain tub in the shape of a whale, filled with hot water, lay atop a dais. Sunlight came in through tall windows of frosted glass.

"Does m'lady want me to undress her?"

Christine shook her head no. She was looking about for a commode, and it came to her that in this land of castles flush toilets most likely did not exist.

The maid appeared to suddenly divine the cause of her unease. "Oh! Does m'lady wish to visit? It's through this little door." So saying, she opened the door into the conveniences.

Christine found them as luxurious as they were primitive. Though her instincts rebelled at the lack of any cleansing rush of water, the experience was not as embarrassing as she had feared. Still she came out blushing, yearning for the roaring that, though it announced to the world what you had done, also promised it had wiped the remains away from the face of the earth.

There remained for her to get naked in front of the servant. This she would not do; after a few awkward sentences she managed to get the girl to leave the room while she undressed and got into the tub.

The water received her gleefully. The bottom of the tub was padded by a woven mat, with a spongy cushion meant to sit on. A mesh bag hung down, tied to a hole along the rim, containing a cake of perfumed soap and a washcloth. Christine lathered up the cloth and scrubbed at herself, washing the sweat from her skin and the dirt from beneath the rim of her nails.

She lay back in the tub, resting her back against the inner forehead of the whale, her aching limbs soothed by the hot water's caress. She almost fell asleep again. She had not felt like this since she was a little girl and could lie back in the tub until the water came up to her chin. She felt a sudden, familiar urge to cry, a torn shred of her past fluttering in her memory, the mood she had lived with for so long: the keening of loss for something she no longer remembered. The grief was startlingly pure; she had been so young then, and the wound had been recent. She saw for perhaps the first time how it had festered in the following years, how her pain had worsened even as it seemed to heal. A tear escaped her; it burned down her cheek like a drop of blood from a cut. She felt beyond grief at this moment; it was the sweet pain of relief that ran through her. She dared hope, for a moment, that the wound was clean now, that she would at last recover.

She drifted off, dozing in the tub. Althea woke her; Christine reflexively covered herself under the water, but the maid was not even glancing at her body. Instead, she was taking a towel from a cupboard. She unfolded it, held it up past her head—it was ridiculously large, and thick as a pelt—and carried it blindly toward Christine, who rose to clutch it around her.

There was a very real risk of tripping in the folds of the towel as she exited the tub, but Althea guided her with a sure hand. Christine suffered the maid to help her dry herself. There were garments to put on after that: all-in-one underwear like a silken sleeveless leotard, and a long thick robe. Christine dragged the underwear on under the towel, had Althea fasten the clasps at the back, then finally wrapped the robe around her.

"M'lady is all clean now," said the maid. "We'll go back to m'lady's rooms, so she can choose how to dress."

They returned the way they had come; this time, at the intersection, five people waited, three men and two women. Three merely gaped at Christine; one woman swept her a bow with thinly veiled contempt on her face; the youngest of the men, barely out of adolescence, gazed upon her with the kind of adoration Christine had thought reserved for superstars of the screen. She kept her gaze away from them until she was safely back at the door of her suite.

Two racks of clothes had been wheeled into the bedroom while Christine was out; they barely fit between the foot of the bed and the far wall. Again Christine felt she must be on television, for these were like costumes from a historical drama— one heavy on both flamboyance and anachronism. Fantastically complex dresses trailing a dozen multicolored silk banners behind them, gem-encrusted bodices crisscrossed with strands of green pearls, a narrow sheath of iridescent metallic scales, a fur-trimmed velvet coat fit for a Varangian tsarevna in exile . . .

Althea busied herself showing them off to Christine, until the young woman cut her off. "I can't wear any of those," she said, vaguely outraged. "They're . . . they're silly."

Althea did not bat an eye. "If m'lady doesn't like any of those, I will call for more. There are at least two more racks to m'lady's size at present. Or if m'lady can tell me what she wishes, tailors will confection the dresses as fast as possible."

"But they'll all be like . . . like these, won't they?" asked Christine. "I just want something plain and simple. Jeans . . . I mean pants. A blouse, a jacket."

She gestured helplessly at a gape-mouthed Althea, who obviously found the request incredible.

"Trousers and a jacket? But . . . m'lady can't wish to look like an ostler's apprentice! M'lady is a princess of the realm: She must wear suitable clothes! M'lady must try some of these on: They were all made to her measurements. M'lady will see, they're perfect. . . ."

Althea broke off when Christine sat down heavily on the bed, shaking her head and sighing. All her life she had dressed as simply as she could manage, wearing the uniform of the anonymous. She couldn't put on any of these dresses. Despite what Althea claimed, they were not in the least made for her. . . . And yet she remembered the daydreams she'd had when very young, recalled blurred images of ruffled and ribboned dresses . . . dresses with real stars sewn onto them. But those were silly fantasies, fit for a young child.

Althea had carried back the rough clothes Captain Veraless had lent to Christine ages ago and left them in the outer room. Should Christine put them back on? They had been no more made for her than the court dresses. The only clothes she would have called real had vanished as she crossed into Chrysanthe; like the dreams they were supposed to have been.

Christine drew a ragged breath; her head was spinning, from the steam, from exhaustion, from the fear that all this was nothing, nothing but some psychotic breakdown. A retreat from the pains of real life into a fantasy land where she was the princess of the realm, where she got to put on fantastic dresses even the wealthiest woman could never afford and have servants wait on her hand and foot. . . . For a moment she was certain she was imagining all this; certain that in another heartbeat the real world would come clear in her sight once more, and she would be lying prone on filthy concrete, with a stranger's sex forcing its way into her, tearing her apart. . . .

She clutched at the folds of her robe, exhaled raggedly. Althea was saying, "Is m'lady well? What's wrong? Whatever m'lady needs, she just needs to ask!"

Christine mastered her trembling. She would not let herself go down this path again. She must focus her mind on something.

"Althea . . . I want you to tell me, ah . . . where you're from," she asked, as if challenging the girl to prove her reality.

"I, ah, I was born in Catulius, m'lady. That's close by Mount Sendan, near the Scyamander."

"And how old are you?"

"Twenty years next Harvestmonth."

"You're older than me, then," said Christine, and this somehow steadied her. "You were living at a time when I didn't even exist."

Althea looked at her with a mixture of incomprehension and concern, then nodded. "M'lady is correct."

"I'm sorry if I sound strange." Christine wondered then if Althea would start a rumor that she was insane; and did she care about it, or not? "I've had a . . . a very rough trip back from . . . where I was."

"M'lady never needs to apologize to me. I know m'lady has been lost in a made world most of her life."

"Yes," murmured Christine, looking into Althea's face, "yes, lost in the world." She shook her head. "I can't pick anything, Althea. You choose the dress yourself. Pick one that's appropriate, but please make sure I can walk in it."

After some more urging on her part, Althea chose a dress in shades of mauve and gold, with a hood of some filmy fabric that refracted light like a crystal prism. "This will suit m'lady very well. It's in the colors of the realm, which m'lady would want for her first day back."

Christine was doubtful, but the dress was neither a tight sheath nor an explosion of flounces, as others on the rack were, so in the end she let her maid persuade her into the dress.

Once they were done, Christine saw an apparition in the mirror. The refractive hood made her hair shimmer; the bright fabrics of the dress contrasted with her skin, making it appear not waxen pale as she had first feared, but glowing and flawless. And the dress did fit her extraordinarily well.

"M'lady is gorgeous," said Althea proudly, and Christine, though she almost corrected her, in the end remained silent. At that moment there came a knock at the outer door; Althea drew the inner door shut to shield Christine from prying eyes before going to the outer.

She returned directly, head-bobbed again to Christine.

"M'lady, the knight Sir Quentin and the Lady Melogian are at the door. Does m'lady want to receive them?"

"Yes! Yes, of course!" Christine went into the outer room and Althea let Quentin and Melogian in. Quentin's face broke into a wide smile, which Christine answered with her own. Melogian went up to her, took her hands and bowed.

"Good morning, Christine. How are you feeling?"

"Better. It's very nice to see you both. Please, sit down."

Christine's heart was beating strongly. Part of her wanted to go stand very close to Quentin, in the realm of safety his presence encompassed. The more rational part insisted being in the same room was more than sufficient for safety and got her to sit down so Melogian and Quentin could do so as well.

Quentin looked different to her eyes; he had changed his clothes for something much more festive, but that did not fit him as well, and his sword on its baldric swung noticeably at his side. Before, when he cloaked his garb in illusion, the sword had been invisible; it only showed itself in conjunction with Quentin's armor.

Christine asked Quentin how he had been; he told her he had spent a good long while at an impromptu reception some courtiers had thrown for him. Melogian made some acid comments about the courtiers, while Christine asked for details. They found themselves interrupted by the arrival of breakfast, which Althea had taken the initiative to send for. It came in a little gilded carriage on wheels. From a side compartment, Althea drew out a tray, which she set in Christine's lap. Grilled bread slices, butter, three kinds of fruit preserves, and thin slivers of cold meats were set in dishes on the tray. Althea unfolded a huge napkin that she tied around Christine's neck. Christine felt she was being treated like a sick child, but she reasoned Althea must know what she was doing, and ate her breakfast with as much elegance as she could muster.

With food inside her, in the company of friends, Christine found herself feeling vastly relieved, for all that the newness of her surroundings remained a source of anxiety. The return of Captain Veraless unfortunately acted to degrade her composure.

"My lady," he said as he came in, doffing his hat and bowing. Once he had risen again, he noted the other two occupants. "Oh, Quentin, lad, there you are. I went looking for you and never found you. Lady Melogian, good morning."

"Morning, Captain," said Melogian. "Christine tells us you guarded her well last night."

"The Lady Christine is very kind," replied Veraless with a pleased smile. "I did my best."

"Why are you still up, then? If I were you, I'd be in bed by now."

"Not yet, I'm afraid. I have been tasked to deliver a message from His Majesty."

Christine felt her heart speed up. "Yes?" she asked.

"Lady Christine, the king your father sent out messengers yesterday, to inform the people that you were back with us. The news reached Tiellorn first, of course. A huge crowd's gathered at the gates of Testenel. They're asking to see you."

"N-Now?"

Veraless shook his head. "The king was very clear that you may refuse. There is no obligation. You may take all the time you want to prepare. But if you are willing, certainly it would mean a lot to the people of the land. They've mourned your disappearance for thirteen years. I think some of them need to see you in the flesh to know that you're really back."

Christine looked down at her clasped hands. The temptation to refuse, to stay in her rooms, was very strong. But did she really want to become a self-imposed prisoner in her apartments? She thought back on the girl aboard the skyship, remembered the joy on her face.

"Well . . . how would we go about it?" she asked. "What does the king want me to do? Would they come in to my rooms, or—?"

"No, nothing so personal, milady, don't worry. The people just expect you to appear at a balcony and hail them. You'll be twenty feet up in the air."

Christine recalled sitting in clinic waiting rooms and leafing through magazines that were full of photos of such occasions, Princess So-And-So of Livonia waving to the crowds from a balcony, an entire royal family looking stiff and somewhat forlorn, their faces grainy from the enlargement of the picture. *I am one of those people now,* she thought. *Someone important despite her will, the focus of attention for thousands and thousands.* It was a chilling thought. Still, this was who she was.

"I'll do it," she announced. "I want . . . I want Quentin to be there. To guard me."

"You can have anyone you want, Lady," Veraless said. "I'll tell the king you've agreed. I think he'll have the event in an hour or so. Ah . . . he will be there himself, though."

Christine kept her head up. "That will be fine," she said.

It was Veraless who dropped his gaze. "I know that you find his presence difficult to bear; he knows too. His Majesty said he would take steps to make sure all goes well. He will be at one end of the balcony, and you at the other, each seated on a chair. There will be several people between you. Will this suit you?"

"Yes," said Christine quickly, "yes of course. It will be fine."

Veraless bowed and withdrew. Quentin looked at Christine, embarrassment on his features. "Lady Christine, I have informed the king and Lady Melogian of . . . of the precise reason you are troubled in his presence. Captain Veraless does not share in that knowledge; certainly I have told him nothing. But the king your father will have told him how upsetting your whole journey was. I am sure everyone will understand." He turned his head to look pointedly at Althea, who stood unobtrusively in a corner.

"I won't talk about it," said Christine softly, resolved to keep the matter out of her mind. "Let's change the subject. In an hour I'll go meet the people who want to see me; that's what a princess should do, that's what I'll do. Until then, I want you to explain to me about those courtiers, Melogian. There's a lot about life here I don't understand yet."

Three quarters of an hour passed, then a page came to deliver a message from the king, requesting Her Highness the Lady Christine to direct her steps to the Aulecine Gallery where she would greet well-wishers. With a measure of dread simmering in the pit of her stomach, Christine rose to go. Quentin and Melogian accompanied her, along with the pair of guards who had escorted Christine when she went to bathe earlier. They passed through a bewildering succession of corridors and rooms, down several staircases. The castle Testenel was ridiculously huge and Christine found herself lost within three turnings of the way.

They went down a final flight of stairs, at the foot of which a liveried servant guided them down a long corridor. Christine heard a roar like the sea, climbing in volume, as she neared the door at the end.

She had imagined a balcony like the ones in hotels, ostentatious but still decent in size; she stepped out onto a shining floor of white marble. It was so long and wide she was reminded of a skating rink. A number of people stood on the balcony, clustered near the center. A dais had been set up in the middle of the balcony, one large ornate chair at either end of it. The nearer chair was empty.

Christine made herself take a few steps toward the dais, drawing moral support from Quentin's and Melogian's presence a step behind her. At that moment the crowd caught sight of her and a bellowing cheer shook the air.

The balcony overlooked a wide courtyard, which was packed with people. There was a breeze: They were outside—but the mass of Testenel overhung the balcony and the whole of the courtyard; in fact it extended much farther, so that the effect was of a huge inner chamber with a ceiling of dark blue. It should have been sunk in shadow, but in fact it was softly lit throughout, from what source Christine could not be sure. Bathed in this light, the crowd gave voice enthusiastically. All of them were looking at her, pointing her out to their friends who saw her just as well as they.

A soldier in full livery had come up and extended his arm, inviting Christine to climb the three steps to the dais and the heavy ornamental chair, but she paused, transfixed by the scene below. The crowd was screaming her name. *"Christine, Lady Christine, Christine!"* She felt a compulsion to advance to the railing, balanced by an urge to flee. She turned her head to the left.

Across from her, at the far end of the dais, surrounded by a dozen people whose functions Christine could not guess, her father sat on the twin of her chair. He gripped its arms and sat back stiffly, as if he were reduced to a puppet.

Sunk in a haze of unreality, Christine stepped toward the railing; the people cheered her even louder. She could make out individual faces in the crowd; all shades of hair, all kinds of dress. Some of these people wore drab, rough clothes, and their faces were smudged with earth; others, cheek by jowl with them, were swathed in silks and heavily rouged. And all of them were shouting her name.

She turned toward her father, still sitting stiffly in his chair. And because she felt the crowd's need, felt it pouring through her, felt suddenly, with an intensity that could not be denied, that she was bound to these people in a way so deep it could never be fathomed, she extended her arms to him.

He rose from his seat, came down the steps. The courtiers between them parted to let him pass. He stood ten steps from her, then five, then one. Terrors spiraled in her, a hundred thorned memories, blinding pain and shame, but one image rose and blotted out the others: the first memory she had recovered in Dr. Almand's office. She was small, and her father held her tight at the rail of a ship, as she looked down into the shallow waters and saw the pretty fishes that swam there.

No matter that Dr. Almand had corrupted it almost immediately, *this* memory was real. She saw the fish with a hallucinatory clarity, remembered the turn of a tail and the flash of glittering fins. Remembered her father's strong, sinewy arms holding her close, and safe.

She had laid her head on his shoulder, put her arms around him, let his enfold her, and she held tight now, as the world spun around them both, as the crowd roared loud enough to shake the stars loose from the sky. And yet she could hear his heart as well, thumping against her cheek. His arms were as she'd remembered them, strong and lean and warm. She was home, and in exile, safe and in danger, she did not know who she was, though everyone else knew, but she was in her father's arms, and that at least could not be denied.

After a few seconds she had to break the embrace; the moment of grace had passed, and fear was rising through her again. She stepped away from her father, turned to the crowd who were still cheering themselves hoarse. Perhaps she should say something, though she could never be heard above the din.

Melogian appeared at her elbow, laid her hand lightly on Christine's arm. "Do you wish to speak to them?" she asked. "Allow me." She waved her fingers and muttered something under her breath, then touched Christine's lips. Something happened, though Christine could not interpret it. There was a sense of presence immediately in front of her face—as if some invisible object, or even a wall, had evolved there.

"Speak; they'll hear you now," Melogian urged her. Christine drew a breath and tried a few words.

"What should I say?" she said, and immediately her words boomed out, amazingly loud, echoing from the stone of Testenel above as if the castle itself spoke. The crowd fell almost silent. "I . . ." Christine was at a loss, cowed by the circumstances. "I . . . I'm sorry, I've had a tough time of it, and . . ." She paused, clung to Melogian's arm. She felt as though she were swimming—but she was *not* going to break down in front of everyone. She forced out the words: "I wanted . . . to tell you all . . . how glad I am to be back home. And thank you . . . thank you for welcoming me. Thank you."

The crowd started to cheer again. Hats were tossed into the air. Christine smiled and nodded; then she turned away from the railing, away from the chair that had been set up for her, away from her father. Still keeping a grip on Melogian's arm, trying to slow her steps, she made her way back through the door into the palace. Quentin was asking her in a whisper if she needed anything; she replied with a silent shake of the head, afraid the spell still affected her and that her least mutterings would thunder outside.

As soon as they were distant enough from the doorway, Christine stopped, pushed her hood back: She was sweating rivers. She fluttered her fingers in front of her mouth, trying to feel the presence.

"No, it's all right, Christine, I've quenched the spell," said Melogian. Christine allowed herself a long gasp.

"Milady, are you well?" asked Quentin.

"Yes. Yes, I'll be okay. I just can't believe what just happened."

Outside, the crowd still roared. Christine held to Melogian's arm, but her legs felt stronger than a moment ago.

"You've been extremely brave, Christine," the sorceress was saying. "You did wonderfully."

"But that's just it," said Christine. "It feels so strange . . . I'm not afraid anymore."

Out on the balcony, Edisthen was speaking. His voice was amplified as Christine's had been, and it rang clear in the corridor.

"My people," the king said, "I thank you all for your presence here this day. You are the first to have witnessed that my daughter has been returned to us. This is the happiest day of my existence, and I wish the whole of the realm to share in my joy. Starting tomorrow, the fifteenth of Summereve, the land shall know three days of celebration. None shall toil beyond the essential. Let there be feasts and dance, let there be laughter and drink!" The crowd roared once more. When it had calmed, Edisthen finished: "I bid you now return to your homes. Bear news of these celebrations. Go in the sight of God."

To further acclamations, Edisthen left the balcony, coming toward her. Melogian asked Christine if she wanted to return to her quarters; she shook her head.

"I told you, Melogian, I'm not afraid anymore."

Courtiers and aides passed through the doorway, hesitated, bowed to Christine and continued on their way. Then the king himself exited the balcony. Christine stepped up to him. She was filled with calm. "Father?" she said, sure of herself.

His face colored and he replied softly, "Yes, Christine?" It struck her then that this was the first time he had actually spoken to her since her return.

"I . . . Where are you going now?"

"To the throne room; I normally give audience at this time."

"Can I . . . join you? Would it be proper?"

Edisthen's face lit up. "Of course. Of course. Come."

Edisthen led the way through Testenel, and she followed. She did not walk too close by his side, but not far either. His voice had touched her like a balm: In the memories Dr. Almand had made her recover, she had never heard her father's voice; every word he spoke to her now seemed part of a spell of healing, proving the falseness of her nightmares. Quentin and Melogian accompanied her.

Passing once more through a maze of passages, they finally reached the throne room, whose polished marble floor and walls were geometrically patterned with a dizzying intricacy. Father and daughter climbed four steps to a high dais on which sat the royal throne, a massive affair of ancient carved black-brown wood. A hundred different shapes efflorcsced from the chair, heads of people and fantastic beasts, twisted turrets and fragments of impossible landscapes. "I—I remember this," said Christine. "I remember some of those heads! This one, and that one, oh . . ." She stood over the throne, abruptly crouched down, and looked on it from the perspective of a child. The light fell on a feline head blossoming from one of the arms, an image as familiar to her as the back of her own hand.

"Whenever you came in here, all you wanted to do was to climb up on the throne," said Edisthen. "I kept telling you it was forbidden but you wouldn't accept that. Until one day I got tired of the rigmarole and sat you down on the cushion. As soon as you found yourself surrounded by all these figures, you became terrified and screamed for me to get you off. Do you remember that?"

". . . No. I only remember the wonderful carvings." Christine rose to her feet.

"I trust," said her father, smiling faintly, "that you are old enough now to understand that it is still wrong for you to sit in the throne of Chrysanthe. But an appropriate seat will be brought for you."

An elderly chamberlain came through a door and addressed the king. "Majesty, will you be holding audience as scheduled?"

"Yes. It would not do to cancel the appointments at such short notice. How many do I have?"

"Four, Majesty. Lord Belthanus of Gladrien; Lady Mirwode is back to finalize her divorce; then two master jewelers from Tiellorn on a serious guild matter; and lastly, Denforth son of Lorvil—the pig-herder from Catulius."

"Thank you, Theorm. You will send in Denforth as soon as we open."

"As Your Majesty commands."

"Christine," Edisthen asked his daughter, "are you certain you want to remain here with me and watch me dispense justice? It might be boring."

Christine nodded. "I'll stay. I won't be bored."

A chair was being brought into the room, well stuffed and elegantly carved; in comparison to the massive throne it seemed almost miserly. There was ample room to set it on the dais at a slight angle to Edisthen's seat, so that Christine would see her father while she sat.

Melogian bobbed her head to the king and said, "If you don't need me, Edisthen, I will return to my quarters."

"You are dismissed, Melogian. Quentin?"

"Sire?"

"Have you given any thought to your reward yet?"

Quentin swallowed. "Sire, I beg leave for a further brief delay. But if I may make one small initial request, I would like a locked trunk to store my armor. My quarters are lacking in that one respect."

"An oversight. Olfane will take you to the chamberlain's office." He addressed a woman among the court functionaries within the room. "On my authority, Olfane, Quentin is to be provided with all the equipment he desires, including the services of a squire to take care of his possessions. Afterward, take him to the stables and have him choose a mount."

Quentin bowed deeply. "Your Majesty is too kind." He raised his gaze to Christine. "Lady Christine, do I have your leave to go, or do you require my presence?"

Christine felt a twinge of anxiety at his words, but still she granted him leave. "Don't worry, Quentin. I'm fine here. I'll see you later."

Quentin bowed again and left, and Christine remained with her father. He sat in the wondrously carved throne, and she sat in turn. She let her gaze wander from one fantastic shape to the other, amazed at her sudden recollections. When she looked up to Edisthen's face he was smiling at her. "Shall we begin the audience?" he asked, and she nodded her assent.

4. The Challenge

After the king's brief speech, the crowd began to disperse. Though commoner and highborn had been united for a brief while in the close confines of the courtyard, the groups swiftly separated. Commoners filed out through the smaller door at one corner, and from there they followed a path through the maze of outbuildings at the base of the castle to eventually find themselves on the road that linked Testenel and the capital Tiellorn. The highborn, for their part, exited through the grander gates at the farther end of the courtyard, and climbed aboard their carriages to be returned to their estates.

Among the crowd were several people whom one could not easily place in either category. Townsfolk, skilled artisans, perhaps one or two lowborn grown rich through some fluke of circumstance, who therefore belonged neither to one class nor the other. One man in particular appeared an odd bird: for though he wore clothes of a fine cut and carried himself with well-bred elegance, he did not mingle with the lesser nobles; he held himself apart, as if through excessive humility, or the certain knowledge that he did not belong. Throughout the speech, he had gazed intently at the king, occasionally breaking off to look all around him, as though he needed to reassure himself of something. One or two of the highborn had glanced puzzledly at him, failed to recognize him, yet felt that they should.

The man, rather than join them at the gates, rather than scurrying out through the narrow door with the commoners, waited until the courtyard was almost empty, then went to the guards who stood watch at a third door, just beneath the balcony, which led inside the main bulk of Testenel.

"I would like an audience with the king," he requested.

"Sorry, sir, you can't get in this way," said the younger of the guards. "Please go back to the Southern Gate and ask for authorization."

The man sneered. "I've never needed authorization to enter this pile of stone before; I won't have a soldier chasing me off."

"Nothing doing, sir." The younger guard took a defensive stance. Throughout the exchange, his companion had been staring intently at the stranger's face. Now, as the man put his hand on the younger guard's chestplate and began to push, he shouted out a warning: "Don't move, Jalek! Don't touch him!"

"Well, well," said the man, "have we learned some manners at last?"

"What the hell, Kurt?" said the other guard, bewildered.

"I recognize you, m'lord," Kurt told the stranger. "Though it's been a long while since I seen you last."

"Ah! So nice to be known in Testenel, if only by a lackey. Will you show me inside, now?"

"You know you're not allowed here, m'lord."

"But I've come for parley! Although . . . oh dear, I've misplaced my flag. But my word is good enough for you, surely? If I must speak with Edisthen, what choice do I have but to meet him in his home, since he never comes to visit mine?"

"Where's your carriage, m'lord? You shoulda gone to the main gates."

"Forget the carriage, forget the main gates. I am here now; let me in, before things get ugly."

Kurt hesitated a long moment, then he said, "Let him pass, Jalek. On my authority. I'll be escorting him."

Ignoring Jalek's protestations, he opened the door and let the man in.

"I assume Edisthen will be in the throne room?" asked the newcomer.

"Aye. He grants audiences this day of the week, but people must make appointments well in advance, sir."

"You're not actually claiming this applies to me, I trust," said the man, his blue-black eyes twinkling with amusement.

"I guess not, sir," the guard said stiffly. "This way, please."

They exchanged no further words. The guard led the man through corridors and rooms until they reached an antechamber to the throne room. Three people sat waiting for an audience; the door to the throne room was not shut and all were listening intently to the audience in progress. A chamberlain bustled up to Kurt and his companion.

"You can't come here except on business! You have no appointment, do you? I'm afraid I'll have to ask you to go."

The man took a step back, spread his arms as if in amazement. "Theorm? Is that you? My stars, but you've taken a turn for the worse, my good man. You used to be in such splendid shape; now you have one foot in the grave. How old can you be? Surely not more than threescore . . ."

The chamberlain gaped at the newcomer, and suddenly his eyes went wide.

"Your High—what are you doing here? Guard! How could you let him get here?"

"He asked for an audience; I didn't have the authority to refuse him."

"Your Majesty," a basso voice was coming from beyond the door, "I am so overjoyed, so thrilled at your daughter's return that I hesitate to bring forth the matter that preoccupies me. After all, given such happy circumstances, one cannot but feel somewhat foolhardy to soil, I mean stain, the atmosphere with less than radiant matters. . . ."

"Either get to the point or come back another day," said King Edisthen in a dry voice.

"Of course, of course. As Your Majesty may recall, it concerns the border dispute between Baron Malfric and myself, which has remained unsettled these past five years. . . ."

"It's been a pleasure reacquainting myself with you, Theorm," said the newcomer, "but I don't have all day, and I am *not* waiting for this buffoon to complete his business." He pushed the door open and stalked into the throne room.

Edisthen sat on the throne of Chrysanthe, atop a high dais. An armchair had been set not far from it, and his daughter Christine occupied it.

"Watch yourself, sir," Kurt warned, gripping his ax tight, but the man ignored him as he addressed the king.

"Edisthen! Hail to you, usurper!" his voice rang out.

The king half rose from his throne; the four guards who stood nearby drew their weapons and swiftly interposed themselves between the newcomer and the dais atop which the throne had been set.

"What is this?" sputtered the petitioner, looking more offended than afraid.

"Lord Belthanus, this business will have to be concluded another time. Please leave at once," said Edisthen, who slowly sat himself down. "Guards—you are to protect the Lady Christine in preference to myself, but do not attack him unless he offers harm. Kurt," he added, "go fetch me Melogian on the instant."

The guard left at a run, dragging Lord Belthanus out with him. The four other guards stood quite still, poised for violence.

The man burst out laughing. "What, all this tumult for me? Calm yourself, Edisthen, I haven't come to lay waste to Testenel, nor even to kick your gaunt arse." And he leaned on one leg, arms akimbo.

"What then do you want, Evered?"

"Well, I had planned originally to have a few words with you, man to man. But I see your daughter is present, and so before anything else, I would like us to be formally introduced."

"Perhaps another time."

"Hmmm; I think not. Besides, she looks desperate to know who I am. Why leave her in ignorance an instant further?"

Edisthen closed his eyes briefly, then complied.

"Christine . . . this is Evered. The eldest son of Vaurd, former king of Chrysanthe. Evered, you know my daughter far too well already."

&c Christine stared at Evered. He was a tall man, well formed, with a narrow face, deep-set blue-black eyes, dark brown hair. His posture, even more than his expression, was mocking, contemptuous. She could sense him throbbing with an energy barely kept in check; as if at any moment he might erupt with screamed imprecations or blows. Instead, he swept her a bow.

"Delighted to finally meet you, milady. Though I must say you're something of a disappointment. I've seen a fleshpaint portrait of yours, so I already knew you'd be no beauty, but you sit in that chair like a peasant on a manure heap. And from that glazed expression, I would assume you're as stupid as you're ugly."

Christine flinched at the anger in his voice, but his insults were delivered with such an excess of venom that they barely registered. What she mostly felt was bewilderment.

"That is enough," said the king in a cold voice. "You were exiled from Temerorn twenty years ago, Evered. Why have you returned? Have you anything meaningful to say, Vaurd's son, or are you here merely to spew bile?"

Evered paced before the dais, tossing his head and twitching his fingers.

"Oh, I have a few meaningful things to say to you, Edisthen. And to the Lady Christine as well. It's only fitting that she hear them, as your presumed heir."

At that moment Melogian burst into the room, then stopped dead, her arms wide. Evered jumped backward in a dramatic pose, affected an expression of sudden terror. "Oh! The Book protect me!" he wailed. "King Edisthen has summoned the court mage to his side. . . . Oh, wait, it's only the apprentice. Forsooth, Melogian, is Orion too busy to attend?"

Melogian bit her lip but said nothing. Evered tittered, sauntered over to the petitioners' chair, turned it around and laid a foot on its seat.

"Well," he said, "I guess everyone of importance is here, Edisthen, so let all present hear my words. I have come on this morrow of your daughter's return to deliver a formal warning to you, King Edisthen, because I am a prince of the realm and not the mad beast you would like everyone to believe me to be."

He rested his elbow on his knee and his chin on the heel of his hand before he continued, in a low, almost conspiratorial tone.

"You and I, Edisthen, we understand the situation. We are both party to the ugly little secret at the heart of your reign. For twenty years you've kept it silenced; for twenty years Chrysanthe has suffered under the rule of a wrongful monarch. Obviously, your poor daughter knows nothing about it; I daresay the mighty Melogian herself probably is as ignorant. What of it, Lady Wizard? Has your king told you what happened on that day, so long ago? No? Then shall I?"

Evered jumped up from his pose, resumed his pacing. Melogian had crossed her arms and stood frowning at him. Kurt had returned with her and now joined his four fellows, setting the butt of his ax against the floor.

"Christine, you poor little thing, try to follow what Uncle Evered is saying. I'll speak slowly, for your sake. Your daddy, that tall man over there, came up to my daddy, see, and he told him one great, big lie. And my daddy, who was an honorable man and a dedicated ruler, believed the lie, because it was so huge no man alive would dare utter it for the fear that God would strike him dead. Your daddy told my daddy he had to replace him, and Vaurd, my daddy, was to die—"

"Enough, Evered," said Edisthen. "I will not have you spit your poison here."

"Enough? Enough!?" Evered trembled from head to foot, took a step toward the throne, and halted as the guards blocked his way. The doors to the antechamber where the petitioners waited had been shut; from other openings in the room more guards poured in, including several crossbowmen. Evered spun on his heels in a full circle, sparing them a cursory glance, before jumping back to the chair and grasping its back with one hand.

"Oh, yes, more than enough. Very well, no need to dwell on the past. Let us instead talk about the future, yes? Because change is coming, Edisthen, whether you will it or not. For a long, long time, I have stood by and let the land rot. I kept hoping, I suppose, that things might improve. I let myself grow bitter, so bitter that I fell sick with outrage; yet I did not act. I kept to the charmingly rural prison where you had so kindly cast me and my brothers. . . . But now, here I am. I've paid you a visit, to deliver a warning. One last chance, Edisthen—see how chivalrous I am. I amaze even myself!"

Evered shifted his grip on the chair back, lowered his head, and coughed harshly twice. When he raised his face again, his eyes did not seem to be looking at Edisthen but at an abstract point above him. His voice was lowered in both volume and pitch, and his intonations muffled into a near monotone.

"I am here to warn you, Edisthen, that you are about to be cast down. My brothers and I will take back what is ours by right. Your hold on the realm will loosen and crumble; the land shall be placed into chaos; horrors shall walk the earth and scour the air; your armies will be slaughtered; Testenel itself will be razed. We shall shirk from nothing to utterly destroy your reign; for the power is ours, and the Law upholds us."

Animation was creeping back into Evered's tone; his gaze returned to Edisthen and he spoke on, his voice rising.

"But still I am merciful, as my dear father always was, to his ultimate grief. I give you one last chance: If you abdicate now, if you restore the crown to us of your own free will, I give you my solemn word that we shall spare the realm. Why should the people suffer even more than they already have? Give me your crown, Edisthen, give it up, and just leave, the way you came, a vagrant in a white surcoat. Take your daughter, take your little witch, take a servant to trim your toenails, and depart. I would like to see you suffer; but I'll forego that pleasure for the sake of peace. That circle of metal barely fits on your skull; it must be heavy at night. Take it off, hand it over, and we can conclude this ugly business in an instant."

Christine looked at her father, who had sat silent and stiff in the throne while Evered ranted. Edisthen remained silent for the space of three breaths, then he spoke softly.

"Evered, you made yourself my enemy twenty years ago, and thus the enemy of Chrysanthe. Because of you, and no one else, the land suffered a war. Because of you, and no one else, thousands died. Your concern for the realm is touching, but it comes two decades too late. I am the rightful sovereign by the force of the Law; it upholds me, and not you. And you took my daughter from me; you took her away and tried to break my heart. Don't expect any favors from me. Return to Vorlok and rot the remainder of your life in the hell you've made for yourself. Your father was—"

"Be silent!" Evered shrieked, his face twisted with fury, his eyes full of tears. "Be silent! To hell with you, then, murderer! I give you formal challenge: You shall have another war, to make the first one look like a summer outing! You shall be *cast down*, Edisthen, your reign will end in blood and fury! When the time comes, and all you love lies in ruins, don't look to me for mercy!"

The prince hunched over, as if preparing for a wild jump; the guards shifted their grips on their weapons, the crossbowmen brought theirs to bear. With a grunt of rage Kurt sprang upon Evered, ax raised to strike. Melogian cried out "Hold!" but the guard did not stop. An instant before he reached Evered, the prince winked out of existence; Kurt passed through empty air and ended his run by almost tangling himself in the chair's legs.

Edisthen had bolted from his throne. "Where is he?" he shouted. "Melogian! Find him!"

Melogian sighed and shook her head, her expression dejected. She stepped upon the lowest level of the dais.

"He isn't here, Edisthen. He never was."

"What do you mean?" Edisthen's eyes sparked with something like anger or fear. The guards were rushing about left and right, alarmed and bewildered.

"He was never physically present," said Melogian. "I sensed it as soon as I came in, but at first I couldn't believe it. What we saw and heard was an eidolon: an image of Evered, if you will, no more."

"That was no image!" protested Kurt, red-faced. "He moved the bloody chair around!"

"Yes, and that's why the correct word is 'eidolon': Evered was visible and solid, but he still was not truly here. Count yourself lucky, you fool: Had he been real and had you cut at him, you would be dead now."

"He was threatening the blood royal, Lady!"

The sorceress started to reply, but Edisthen cut her off. "Enough! Kurt is right, Melogian, and you're wrong. We will not pursue the matter."

A moment of silence followed, and Christine found herself saying, "You know, at times like this I feel I don't exist." Her father and Melogian turned their attention to her. She had not truly meant to say the words out loud, but now that she had she was compelled to complete the thought.

"This man comes in, says he's going to kill us all, then he vanishes and you just discuss what kind of an image he was. I'm sitting here in a f— a goddamned costume and magic just *happens,* and everyone acts as if they knew everything about it, and it feels like you're just putting a show on for me. . . ."

She had risen out of her chair. All the calm she had felt after her reunion with her father had evaporated; as if she had been briefly the person she should have been, and had now been cast back into her old flawed, inadequate, and terrified self.

"I'm sorry, Christine," Edisthen said, but she shook her head at him. His voice was no longer a balm to her ears, not after what he had said to Evered.

"No, I—I can't," she stammered. She stepped away from his throne, down one of the steps. Melogian climbed up to meet her. Christine suffered the woman's touch on her arm, but it barely calmed her. "I have to go," she said, desperate to leave this place.

"Come with me, then," said Melogian, and to Edisthen: "By your leave, Sire."

The two of them left the throne room in silence, the guards parting to let them through. Christine thought she could feel her father's gaze on her neck, but she dared not look back; all of her energy was focused on keeping her limbs under control. The gazes of the guards she noticed and almost cringed from.

They passed through the doorway and almost immediately through another. Christine followed the sorceress without paying much attention to where they went. Soon Melogian had led them into an empty, quiet area. The pressure Christine felt had lessened, but still she thought with dread of all the people back in the throne room: her father, the guards, Evered, who though he had gone had left behind the stain of his presence. "I wish I was home," Christine whispered to herself, half sobbing. "There are too many people everywhere, too many things happening." She felt as overwhelmed as she had arriving in Testenel, when Melogian had caught her in her flight; she wanted to lean on the woman's shoulder and cry.

"Breathe slowly, Christine. It will pass."

Christine took a deep, trembling breath. There were so many questions to ask—but it was better than collapsing or fleeing blindly.

"What happened, Melogian? What was that all about? Evered's father, and murder . . . ? Was he lying?"

Melogian sighed. "I had planned to explain those things to you soon, anyway. Now is as good a time as any. Let's go down a floor; there's a nice grotto there, and no one will disturb us."

Christine and Melogian walked down a curving flight of stairs and found themselves in a wide round room, whose walls had been plastered to imitate some unlikely limestone cavern. Fake rubies and emeralds glittered on the rough walls, and water issuing from an ornate spout plashed down a series of pools spanned by lacy stone bridges. Christine stood by one of the pools, finding a measure of calm in the flow of the water.

"Explain, please, Melogian. Was Evered telling the truth?"

"No, he wasn't. There was some truth in what he said, but mostly not."

"So, my father isn't . . . a usurper?"

"No. Edisthen took the crown from Vaurd, the previous monarch, but it was his by right. And no, he did not murder Vaurd."

Christine breathed out shakily. She focused on facts, chains of inference, to overcome her turmoil. "Okay . . . so this is a dynastic quarrel? I've read about those in history books. Vaurd claimed the throne through a given line of descent but my father's claim was better, is that it?"

"No. Things don't work in the true realm the way that they do in made worlds. There can be no question of a line of descent in the case of your father."

"Why?" Christine lifted her gaze to Melogian, who was waggling her fingers in apparent indecision.

"Christine . . . here, children are taught what I'm about to tell you from an early age; they believe in it the rest of their lives. You're not going to find this easy to accept, having lived so long in an imaginary world."

Melogian took a long breath and began.

"There is a Law that rules Chrysanthe. It is the way things are; one cannot argue with the Law, or flout it. We know, we have *seen*, what the Law is and demands. Are you with me so far?"

"Like the laws of physics, you mean? If I drop an apple it'll fall to the ground, because gravity pulls it down. That's a law."

"Yes, good, like that. Except that the Law of Chrysanthe is not about what you call 'physics.' Of course, it encompasses these 'physics,' but most of the time when we speak about the Law we speak about things that aren't as obvious as falling objects or the height of the sky."

"What are you speaking about, then?"

"The aspect of the Law that is at the core of this entire matter concerns you directly, as a princess of the realm. The Law says, '*No one of the blood royal may be harmed.*'"

"I don't follow you," said Christine.

"Neither the sovereign of Chrysanthe nor his or her immediate offspring may be deliberately hurt. This applies to your father and to yourself, and to Vaurd's sons as well, since their father was once a king. None of you may be harmed; the penalty is annihilation."

"Oh . . . that's why you said the guard was lucky. If he'd hurt Evered, you'd have been forced to arrest and kill him?"

"No, not at all. I am saying that if he had hurt Evered, the Law would have destroyed him: He would have died almost immediately, without anyone needing to intervene. In the same way that a dropped object has no need to be thrown to the ground: It will fall by itself."

Christine gazed numbly at Melogian for a few seconds. "That's ridiculous!"

"It's the truth; it's the way things are. It doesn't matter whether it offends your tastes; it is the truth."

"You're telling me that if someone wounded me, he would die?"

"If he so much as kicked your shin, he would perish within a minute."

Christine almost shouted in incredulity. "And what if you bumped into me without looking? Is that a death sentence too?"

"We don't know the Law down to the least detail; it is not written down in a book we can read. It *is* known that one must actively and deliberately harm a sovereign, by fleshly wound or bruise, for the Law to destroy him. There are recorded cases of monarchs being wounded by accident—the most famous one dates from seven hundred years ago, when King Rolume took an arrow through the shoulder. Lord Morsoch, who had shot it by pure mishap, thought he would be destroyed instantly; but in fact nothing ever happened to him. So the harm must be deliberate. Also, it must be bodily harm; anguish or sorrow don't count. I can insult you, terrify you, and the Law will ignore me. If I killed you by accident, I would be safe—at least from the Law. But a nick from a pen nib, as long as it's deliberate, means my death."

Christine was silent for a moment, struggling with this revelation. "What happens when people hurt a sovereign?" she asked. "They just drop dead?"

"No. The Law acts spectacularly in these cases. Anyone who harmed you would be destroyed in a way that spoke unmistakably of the Law's chastisement. He might be devoured from within by a boil of ants, or his bones might turn to ash. . . ."

Christine blinked, abruptly remembering Quentin's words in the train they had ridden through the made world. She understood them at long last. "That was what he meant, then," she whispered. "Quentin; when he said that no one who raped me could have lived to boast of it. If anyone had raped me . . ."

Melogian sucked in her breath. "Anyone who *tried* to rape you, Christine, would have been destroyed before he got very far."

Christine shut her eyes, shook her head slowly. The left side of her scalp tingled and she felt some of her hair stand on end. She opened her eyes when Melogian began to speak.

"I meant to ask you—eventually—if you remembered being abducted. You were four years old when you were taken away from us, and I expect the memories have blurred by now, if not vanished. . . ."

Christine shuddered. "I don't—I don't have memories of that time. When I was little, I cried because I'd been taken away from my father, but I didn't really remember him. . . ." And then Dr. Almand had come along and supplied her with a nest of nightmares to prop up her fallible memory.

"Evered was behind your abduction, of course," said Melogian. "The inference is inescapable, but at the same time, there never was any hard proof. It was nearly certain from the outset that you had been abducted out of reality, since otherwise a seeking-spell would have found you. To take you into a made world required magic; the only wizards, aside from Orion and myself, able to walk *beyond* had served Vaurd and now served his sons."

Christine gazed at her hands. She spoke softly: "I've known since Quentin came to rescue me that someone had stolen me away. But I never knew why; and I was afraid to find out. But I can't go on like this, not knowing. So . . . why did Evered want to get rid of me?"

"Because Evered hates your father and would do anything to harm him—but the Law protects Edisthen. Evered can't harm him physically; he cannot order someone else to do it for him, either, because in the eyes of the Law he would be just as culpable, and he would be destroyed along with his cat's-paw. But to torment your father with grief; *that* avenue was open to him. Orion always said that this had been Evered's main goal, beyond even cutting off the dynasty."

"I could see he hates my father," said Christine. "But it can't be just because he took the throne away from him. He said other stuff—"

"It's far more tangled than that. You see, Vaurd ruled Chrysanthe for fifteen years. Then, twenty years ago, your father came to claim the crown in the name of the Law. But when Edisthen showed up at the gates of Testenel, Vaurd refused to believe that he was the Law's champion. So they fought; and Vaurd died.

"Vaurd's sons—he had four—said that Edisthen had murdered their father. They claimed he was a usurper—a wrongful ruler. But in fact, it was Vaurd who was the wrongful ruler."

Christine forced herself to confront her automatic doubts over this statement. "Yes . . . except, anybody who was in favor of the new king would say the old one was the wrong ruler. That's how it always is. I don't want Evered to be right, but how do I know Vaurd was really a bad king?"

"Because your father appeared. But even discounting that evidence, Vaurd was not a fit ruler. I'll grant you I'm too young myself to know from personal experience. When I was a little girl I knew nothing of the king in the castle of blue stones. Later, when Orion took me as his apprentice, I came to Testenel, but I was still so young and so preoccupied by my studies I could spare no thoughts for Vaurd. . . ."

Melogian knotted her fingers in a complicated pattern.

"Still, by all accounts, he was inept. Under his reign, internecine conflicts were frequent. Barons formed militias and took to the field against one another, and Vaurd did nothing to stop them. People died in these skirmishes, but no reprimand ever came from court; Vaurd couldn't be bothered with the lives of peasants. In fact there was very little he bothered with. He was negligent about anything that went beyond his immediate circle of friends. He let the royal stores become depleted, and in the year of the great drought Estephor suffered famine. When Duke Théméo confronted him about his lack of foresight, Vaurd actually said to him, 'How am I supposed to guess what the next summer will bring?' People say the duke nearly had an apoplectic fit on the spot. . . . And yet, Orion always insisted that Vaurd was not a bad man as such, that he simply lacked the vision and purpose that all kings need. Vaurd's father, Alyfred, had been a tolerable sovereign, but he spoiled Vaurd as a child, and failed to cultivate the necessary virtues. He died young, barely two score and five; Vaurd ascended the throne much too early. These are the excuses you can find for Vaurd's misrule, but they don't change the fact of it in the eyes of the Law."

Christine nodded. "Okay, I understand. So my father just . . . just asked for Vaurd's crown? He was next in line for the throne, and he asked him to abdicate?"

"No. I said lines of descent were irrelevant in this case. When a monarch dies or abdicates, power is transferred to one of his offspring. If there are none, right of kinship usually prevails, and there are some complicated and not very consistent rules for special cases. But your father . . . that was another matter entirely. He was the Law's champion. By his very presence he demonstrated that Vaurd's rule was deficient, and that the crown should go to him. Vaurd should have yielded the throne at once, but he wouldn't accept the situation. So he fought with your father, and he died."

"Wait," Christine objected. "That doesn't make sense. You said the Law protects the royal blood. If my father had killed Vaurd, the Law should have destroyed him too."

"Edisthen never laid a finger on Vaurd. Vaurd attacked him, and died as a result."

Christine frowned as she puzzled out Melogian's meaning. "You're telling me the Law had decided my father was to become the new king, so it destroyed Vaurd when he tried to kill him?"

"Almost. The Law did not decide your father was to *become* king. Your father *was* the true king from the moment he existed."

"How did the Law choose him? Did he get born with a—a special mark? You're not saying he was like the Christus, with a new star in the sky to speak of his coming and all the angels in the field trumpeting it? How did he know he was the true king?"

"He wasn't *born*, Christine. Your father knew he was the true king because that was his entire reason for being. He is a Hero from the Book. He was written into existence."

There was a long silence; Christine kept her gaze fixed on the walls, noting the patterns of red and green stones. She crossed one of the lacy bridges in two steps, ran her hand across the rough-textured wall on the far side. The gems embedded in it looked very convincing indeed; and she had the sudden feeling that if she asked Melogian, the sorceress would confirm that they were genuine.

"Written into existence," she finally echoed as Melogian joined her. "That's not a figure of speech. You mean it."

"Quentin never mentioned the Book, did he?"

"The Book of Heroes?"

"No; the Great Book, from which Chrysanthe arose. The Words of God."

"Back where I grew up . . . that world that you want me to believe doesn't really exist . . . there are several religions that have a holy book. Septentrional America is mostly Christian. I went to Temple once in a while; we had a Byblos in the house, and I read from it. I never believed it was the true word of God, because it was written so long ago, and it was mostly full of stories about weird-named people fighting each other, or laws about what you couldn't eat or wear. I suppose you have a better Book here?"

Melogian sighed. "I guess Quentin didn't want to deal with theological matters; but I don't know that I can do much better than he could. We don't have a holy book claiming to contain the Words of God; that would be silly. When we speak of the Great Book, it's a way to envision things beyond our comprehension; it's the best image we have for the way the world is. We know that the world arose from nothingness, as did the First People, from whom the whole race of Man sprang. The way we talk about it is to say that the world arose from the Great Book."

"'In the beginning was the Word,'" quoted Christine. "The Byblos starts that way."

"Good. So the Book, the Great Book, holds the words for the creation of Chrysanthe, of the land and the sky and the sun, and the First People. There are also other Books, though some prefer to say they are other chapters in the Great Book. We speak of the Book of Heroes and the Book of Shades; the Book of Miracles and the Book of Plagues; the Book of Life and the Book of Death. From time to time things come to this world, miracles occur, plagues stalk the land: they are said to come from these Books. That is the case for your father. He comes to us from the Book of Heroes. We say he was written into existence because he arose fully grown into the world. . . . You don't believe any of this, do you?"

"Don't you think this is a bit over the top?" whispered Christine. "I mean, really! Terra is a planet in orbit around the sun. People evolved from apes over millions of years; only the fanatics deny it. . . ."

"The Earth orbits the sun where you come from, and Men may have been born out of animals. But Christine, that world isn't this one. Here, the heavens are a vault above us, and the sun swims in the upper air. In this world, people arose from the First, who emerged into existence from nothingness. . . ."

Christine was outraged. "You're just quoting legends at me!"

"No, I'm quoting their diaries. The First wrote books of their own, which have survived to the present day. They explain the details of their lives; that they were the First Men in Chrysanthe cannot be doubted."

"They could just have lied! Anyone can write lies in a book; why do you believe them? I mean, it would be easy for someone to make up a book and claim it came from these First. Anyway, how can you expect a book to last millions of years—"

"Six thousand and ninety-four. The world is exactly six thousand and ninety-four years old. The First wrote on sheets of metal with chisels and acid and their diaries are readable even now, though the spelling is somewhat archaic."

"Oh, that's just great. I suppose . . . I suppose they just wrote down 'First Day morning: We got created today, it's really exciting'?"

"Of course not. It took them over a decade to devise writing. As for the exact moment of creation, that is much debated; there are imprecisions in the diaries, so it cannot be pinpointed with accuracy. Assuming that mankind arose a matter of a few days after the creation of the world, it happened sometime in the spring."

"Better and better," said Christine. She strode across another pool, came to a hollowed-out space in the wall meant to serve as a seat, sank down in it, put her head in her hands.

Melogian rejoined her and put a hand on her shoulder. She said, in a compassionate tone: "During my apprenticeship, I spent months in a made world studying their knowledge. I was much taken with astronomy. For a long time, I learned the shape of their heavens, which were a vast, cold, and sterile expanse, peopled by lonely suns blazing in vain to warm rocky lifeless spheres. Until one day I grew tired of it all, because it was like reading a work of fiction that never ends and grows ever more pointless. There's an aging writer at court, Severn by name, who has penned twenty-eight volumes so far of *Sir Raven's Quest*. Every courtier claims to have read them all, since Severn still has the king's favor. Yet everyone knows that Sir Raven will never fulfill his quest, that Severn is just adding volume after volume of meaningless complications, and that the only way the work will ever come to an end is when that old fraud finally dies—leaving the story unfinished.

"The same goes for the knowledge of your world, Christine. It's like Severn's invented story; there's no point in it anymore. You are in the real world now, and things here are different. Your Terra was a round planet, yes? And it spun around the flaming sun."

"Yes, and that makes sense. There are equations that explain it, I read it. The distance from the sun determines how fast you go around it, and—"

"Christine. *This* world is flat, and the sun goes around it. The heavens are a vault above us and the stars are sparks. . . ."

"Where does the sun go at night, then?" shouted Christine in defiance. "Stars are just suns, seen from afar! *That* makes sense; your fairy stories don't."

"The sun sinks into the ocean at night, and passes beneath the land, and emerges at the eastern end of the world in the morning. Christine, I know because I have been there. I have flown into the sky and above the sun and I have touched the vault of heaven with my own hand. I have seen a star from up close; it was strangely bright and it nearly blinded me, but still it was a very small thing that sizzled and whined like a slab of meat in the pan. I have traveled to the edges of the world and I have seen the sun sink into the western ocean; its color changes to green and its glow lights up the waves for a while, until it passes beyond sight—heading east."

"I can't believe that, Melogian. I can't."

"I'm not lying to you. Why would I?"

"Maybe you believe it yourself, but you have to be wrong."

"If I took you with me, would you believe then? If I took you into the sky and made you touch the vault, would you believe?"

"I . . ." Christine shook her head. "I don't know. If I had proof . . . if you gave me proof . . . yes."

Melogian hunkered down and stroked Christine's arms gently.

"This world is as I've described it, I swear. In this world, Christine, people sometimes appear out of nowhere. They have no past; they have been created upon the instant. We say they have been written into existence because they can only come directly from the Book. They are Heroes, people shaped for a purpose, embodiments of the Law, of great forces. In olden days they were very numerous; one could say the First People were all Heroes themselves. Thousands of years ago, mighty magicians by the dozens walked the earth and performed miracles. Things have changed. In two hundred years only two Heroes have appeared: Orion, my teacher in magic, was one. And so was your father. Edisthen came into being as the rightful ruler of Chrysanthe. He was written because Vaurd was a weak king and the Law says that the throne of Chrysanthe may neither remain empty nor be filled by an unfit ruler."

Christine just shook her head.

"Poor little girl," said Melogian. "I can guess how hard this must be for you. I'm so sorry, Christine."

"Are you really?" Christine wailed in despair. "It feels like you're all playing a huge joke on me."

Melogian kept stroking her arm. "I swear I'm telling you the truth. We are all . . . very concerned for you. We want you to be well, and we can imagine how terrible it must be to be torn from a world and cast into another."

"No you don't! You have no idea, Melogian. You stand here, telling me the world is flat and the Law protects me, but you have no idea what it's like for me!" Her burst of anger was making Christine almost light-headed. "I traveled through the made world with Quentin, which was already bad enough. I was . . . His car . . . It tried to kill him, and . . ."

"He told us about that."

"Let me talk! Let me finish. . . ." She took a shuddering breath, and then shut her mouth and shook her head impotently, words failing her.

Melogian respected her silence, and after a hundred heartbeats Christine spoke again. "I'm not who I thought I was. And I'm scared of who I've turned out to be. I never wanted to be a stupid princess and have people want to make me disappear. I just wanted to be let alone. . . ." She looked up at Melogian. "I don't even know my mother's name. What was she like? She was just an ornament for the king, wasn't she? That's what queens are, just dolls for kings. I'll bet you're going to tell me she didn't even want me!"

"Your mother's name was Anyrelle. She was twenty-three years old when she bore you. She and I looked somewhat alike; there are portraits of her in various galleries around Testenel—you can go look at them, or if you ask, they'll be brought to you. Your father loved her with all his heart, and Edisthen's heart is larger than you can imagine. She was a very intelligent woman; next to her I always felt something of a dullard. When she died giving birth to you, your father was devastated. His grief shook the walls of the castle. All of his love he gave to you after that. He hasn't looked at another woman since Anyrelle's death, and I'm certain that he never will. She was glad to be pregnant; in fact she was radiant throughout, except at the very end, when her body betrayed her. We all mourned her when she passed away."

Christine had closed her eyes. "Thank you," she murmured.

"When you wish, I will tell you more. But I think perhaps you've had enough for the moment. I've had more excitement than I care for before noon. Do you wish to rest?"

"Yes. Yes, I guess I should. What . . . what do I have to do, after this? I mean . . .

what am I *supposed* to do? Just sit around all day? Go riding horses? Drill the army? What?"

Melogian half smiled. "When you were three years old, you were extremely willful. Your father could not refuse you much, and you almost always did exactly as you pleased. I expect things haven't changed, on his part. Tell him what you want to do, he'll agree."

Christine had risen to her feet. She asked Melogian to lead her back to the suite of rooms she had slept in. The sorceress took her back up a floor, and led her back toward the throne room. They were joined by a pair of guards who, on Edisthen's orders, escorted them through another series of corridors, keeping onlookers at bay.

Soon Christine found herself back in the stretch of corridor where the door to her suite opened. Two new guards stood at the door to the suite; they saluted Christine crisply and one of them opened the door. Althea awaited inside, dozing in a chair; as soon as the door opened, she was on her feet, asking what she might do. Melogian asked her to give them some privacy for a while, and Althea withdrew to the corridor.

Christine sat down in the chair Althea had warmed. She sighed. "You tell me I can do what I want. I don't know what I want; I'm not . . . prepared for anything like this. What should I want to do, Melogian? What is it I ought to be doing?"

Melogian shrugged. "Just . . . be there, Christine. The people need to see you; your father, more than anyone, needs to be reassured that you're well. I could tell," she said in a very low voice, "that once again it's hard for you to be near him. A hurt like the one you've suffered is never cured at once. You overcame the fear that was burned into you for a time, but it's perfectly normal for it to return. Things will be like that for a while: You'll get better, then you'll backslide a bit. You mustn't worry about it. In time, I promise, you will be healed. You've spent ages in a prison. Let yourself rest, now; you have all the time in the world. Learn to be happy here. Your life will be a privileged one. You can look forward to peace."

Christine looked at her, shaking her head.

"You're lying to me, Melogian. What about Evered? What he promised us hardly sounded like peace. He said he'd bring war."

"I wasn't lying," Melogian replied. "At least I didn't mean to. Evered has made threats before. He's sent letters to Edisthen over the years. . . . But he never showed up in person. This is the most explicit he has ever been. I do take what he said—and did—seriously. But it's still a madman's ranting. At the moment, your first concern must be yourself. For all our sakes. Will you do this for me, Princess?"

"Don't call me that, please!"

"Will you do this for me, Christine? I took care of you after your mother's death; some days I almost forgot you weren't my own little girl. Yesterday, when I caught you in your flight and you asked if I were your mother, I very much wanted to say yes. Will you get some rest, take time to think on all I told you?"

Christine nodded mutely.

"Duty calls me now," said Melogian, "but if you need me, send for me. The messengers in Testenel are swift and they will know where to find me."

"All right," breathed Christine. To her astonishment, Melogian bent down over her and kissed her forehead. The gesture left her misty eyed, and she saw only a blurred image of the door opening, Althea coming in as Melogian left.

Christine rose to her feet and went to the bedroom—Althea swiftly opened the door before Christine's hand could touch the knob. Christine wanted to protest that there was no need for this, but kept silent: If she was who she was, then Althea's behavior was only proper. Instead, she sat down on the bed and clutched one of the pillows to her, trying to let the turmoil she felt abate, trying to rest, dutifully, for everyone else's sake.

&c Evered shrieked at the empty air, "When the time comes, and all you love lies in ruins, don't look to me for mercy!" He hunched himself over, his face contorted. Through clenched teeth he murmured, "Out, out, get me out!" but Casimir had already guessed his intent and broken the spell.

"You are back in Vorlok, m'lord Evered," he said. The prince started and opened his eyes. He was panting and his face was mottled with red.

"The scoundrel," he said, "that murderous piece of *filth*! If I could just have wrapped my hands around his throat, I would have squeezed and squeezed. . . . God's eyes, Casimir, give me a knife and send me back. I shall put an end to him once and for all!"

Casimir kept his tone even as he answered. "That would mean your death, my lord, as well as mine. You wanted to challenge Edisthen, not slay him."

Evered gestured violently, in the grip of an emotion too powerful for words. Finally, he regained control of his speech. "He hasn't changed," he said in a strangled tone. "He looks the same as he did twenty years ago. I nearly saw my father bleeding in his arms . . . ! As if no time had passed. How? How?"

"My Lord Evered, you know Heroes are long-lived," Casimir said in appeasing tones. "You had to expect Edisthen would look little different from his past self."

Evered passed a trembling hand over his face. "Yes . . . yes, I know. Well, it was worth it. I wish you would send me back. I should like to haunt his daughter. . . . Touch her neck when she sleeps, whisper sweet poison in her ear . . ."

"We cannot, m'lord," said Casimir. "Remember our plan? Now that you have challenged Edisthen, I must finish my preparations for the next phase."

Evered looked at him, pouting like a spoiled child denied a toy. "If we must," he said.

"We must, m'lord. Don't worry, we have done good work. Your presence, even more than your words, will have made its point. Today you have cast fear again in Edisthen's heart, and he'll never rid himself of it."

"Yes . . ." Evered smiled. "Yes, that's true. I've cast fear . . . into his heart. . . ." He giggled at the words, uncontrollably; his breathing grew harsh and sobbing. His whole body trembled as his eyes began to roll up in their sockets. Casimir reacted swiftly and adroitly for all his bulk, pressing firmly at Evered's knees to make them buckle, while holding up his torso with one broad hand at his back. He maneuvered the prince to the floor and held him securely down as he began to scream and thrash. When he sensed the fit was growing too strong, the wizard unhesitatingly placed his hand inside Evered's mouth and let the prince's teeth bite deep into his flesh.

He called out the other's name, gently and repeatedly, but the prince was lost to the world for now. His body bucked and twisted; Casimir lay more of his own weight onto Evered, trying to hold him immobile. Evered's teeth sank farther into his hand and Casimir's blood slicked the prince's lips. Evered moaned and wept, his heels drummed upon the floor, and his erect penis pressed at the fabric of his breeches.

"Evered; Your Highness," Casimir called, holding his disgust in check. "Awake now. You are well again, my lord." He had no talent as a healer, but then no one had ever been truly able to help Evered's fits, which had grown less and less frequent over time on their own. Their duration had also markedly lessened: After a minute or two more, Evered's spasms lessened, his teeth unclenched, and his lids closed. Casimir withdrew his punctured hand, slimed by the other man's saliva mingled with his own blood. He resisted the urge to wipe it onto his trousers, went to rinse it in a basin of water and dab at the wounds with alcohol. Behind him he heard Evered coughing and trying to speak with a numb tongue and jaw.

Casimir turned to face him; Vaurd's son was struggling to his knees, trying as usual to pretend that the fit had not happened. For a moment the contempt the wizard felt threatened to break his loyalty, but sense prevailed. "Go rest, Your Highness," he rasped, pointedly displaying the bleeding punctures on his hand. "You are overwrought. Go rest, and I shall see you tonight."

Evered staggered to his feet; his mouth twisted but he could not utter a word. He turned away and left the workroom. Casimir watched him leave then went back to cleaning the bite wounds, hissing between his teeth in annoyance.

5. The Law

The sorceress walked swiftly through the corridors and rooms of the castle, her heart in turmoil. She remembered rocking the little baby in her arms, and playing with the tiny girl before she had known how to speak, clutching Christine's chubby little fists in her hands, making the princess giggle. She had never allowed herself to feel as though her own child had been stolen from her, and once more she took hold of that treacherous sentiment and forced it back inside her. The spells arrayed in her head stirred and tried to get themselves said; she felt a pang of temptation, strong as the stabbings of lust. At the core of her mind, the greatest spell she knew, the one she must never speak, beckoned to her. She allowed herself to consider it a moment, turning the words and gestures in her mind. If she had dared to, she would have sent a cry of defiance winging toward Casimir then. "You think yourself powerful, you fat toad. But if I said this spell, where would you be?"

She passed a hand over her face; a line of sweat had formed along the edge of her hair; a bead or two dripped down her temples. What must she look like to those who saw her; was her face scarlet, as she imagined? Sometimes she wondered that her own passions were not at all times blatantly visible to anyone with eyes. . . . By the time she had reached the throne room, she had regained her composure. Edisthen was still seated on his throne, and the chamber was full of nervous guards.

"I thought you would come back here," said the king when she entered. "How is Christine?"

"Doing well, my liege," Melogian replied. "I take it there were no further unexpected visitors?"

"No, everything is quiet."

"Not for long. The news will spread."

Edisthen shook his head. "I think not. I've taken steps to quell any rumors. Lord Belthanus has been suitably impressed with the need for silence, and old Theorm is under watch. I don't care for these events to spawn wild talk."

Melogian raised her eyebrows, then shrugged. "Well, you know your staff; I guess all will go as planned. For my part, I would like to speak with you—in even stronger confidence. May I?"

When Edisthen acquiesced, she climbed up three of the four steps, then turned to the rest of the chamber.

"Guards," she said, "I am casting privacy for the king and myself. You will not be able to hear us, and our images will be blurry. Don't be alarmed." She gestured and muttered a quick string of syllables. Sounds grew close as if thick curtains had dropped around them. The room all about them blurred as if viewed through sleep-hazed eyes.

"Why all this display?" asked the king, frowning. "We could have gone to the Griffin Room if you absolutely needed privacy."

"Even there, I would be concerned with spies," said Melogian. "Not so much people as spells. Perhaps all this is indeed excessive—but I have grown afraid, Edisthen."

"Why? Is something wrong with Christine?"

"No. Nothing new, at any rate. On the balcony, she overcame her fears, but one doesn't merely cast aside years of anguish. It will be some time before she is well. And of course, Evered's visit was hardly a calming occurrence.

"I've had to explain several things to her. Quentin never told her of the Law, nor did he describe the true world in detail. It's all been a shock. The made world where she was held prisoner was a very different place from what we know, and she still has trouble wrapping her mind around the truth."

"Have you had her taken to her suite?"

"No. She's still in the Demmerel Chambers. My spells are all in place and there are guards stationed there. In time we can move her to the proper rooms, but I thought it wiser to let her remain where she slept before. It will feel more comforting to her—and essentially, it is no less safe than her suite would be."

"Well . . . as long as she remains secure, I have no complaint."

Melogian sighed. "I said it was no less safe, but I cannot promise you she is safe in the absolute. I am outmatched in this struggle. Christine might still be vulnerable."

"Explain," ordered Edisthen in a cold voice.

"All the while I was talking to Christine, I was also thinking on what just happened here. Did you get the import of it?"

"I'm neither blind nor deaf. Evered has thrown down a formal challenge. And you . . . you think he meant it: You believe that he will go further than threats this time."

"I do, but that's not why I am afraid. I'm afraid because of how he delivered his message. My liege, raising a full eidolon has not been done since the days of Hundred-Handed Juldrun. Orion himself could never achieve it; but some mage in Evered's service can. Unless a Hero has come out of the Book to serve him, it can only be Casimir. Yet I never knew him to be able to work that spell before. Think about it: There was no need for such an outrageous expenditure of power; Evered could have sent a messenger. And to time his visit for the day after your daughter is returned to us? It beggars the imagination that it should constitute coincidence. This, all this, is Casimir *boasting*."

"Boasting? Let him boast all he wants. If all he's done is invent a new spell, is that so terrible?"

"A wizard's boasts are often deadly. And you don't see the point at all. I thought Orion would have explained it to you. Devising new spells has become a hard task in these latter days; for major workings, it's well nigh impossible. A wizard who buries himself too deeply in the search for new workings eventually goes insane. In practice, you learn what you can from your master; a great sorcerer might devise one or two fairly minor spells in the course of a decade.

"And now here comes Casimir, raising a full eidolon, for the fun of it. His mentor is long dead. So who is it that's teaching him?"

Edisthen was silent a while. "Do you think that some other mage could have arisen in the world?" he asked at last. "Another Hero, serving Evered and his clan?"

"How likely is that? I'd rather believe in a demon vomited from the Book of Shades. No, I think it is Casimir. I think that, somehow, he's gained access to long-lost spells. Even if we suppose that Orion was abducted, enslaved, and compelled to teach his arts to Casimir, it still fails to explain the situation: Orion didn't know the spells for eidolons; he cannot be the source of the knowledge. Are there then, somewhere, books from the Dawn of the world, spells inscribed on imperishable pages? And if so, which spells? Much of the magic of the olden days has been lost; some of the workings from the Dawn were so terrible they couldn't be wielded without courting annihilation. If some have survived and come into Casimir's hands . . ."

Edisthen frowned and clutched the carved arms of his throne. "Will we have to fight, then? I shall raise an army, and send it against them. The Lady Veronica is still hostage at this court; I'll use her as is necessary. In twenty years, Evered has never said a word about her; I am sure this means he is in fact deeply concerned. I can probably put pressure on him through her."

Melogian shook her head. "I doubt it will suffice. Ever since the Carmine War, force of arms has been the deciding factor in conflicts within the realm. But in this case, I fear it won't be. This will be a war of wizards. As long as Orion was by your side, there was nothing to fear: Your power could not be assailed directly. Christine's abduction changed nothing, but Orion's disappearance, that was a severe blow. My powers never matched his. And Casimir's boast is unarguable: He has now surpassed me."

"Then summon the other mages of the land to us. Get some aid, Melogian!"

"They would be more trouble than they're worth. Orion kept tabs on them, and I've continued to do so. In the past fifty years, there have been only six mages of any consequence in all the land. Most of them are now either dead or . . ." She winced at her own words and went on. "Or vanished and effectively gone from the world of the living. Besides Casimir and myself, none of the magicians that the land now holds are of any consequence: parlor conjurers, mountebanks, brewers of love-philters, stumbling amateurs who need a day's efforts to summon a working I can do in my sleep. The most promising of them is a ten-year-old boy with a knack for commanding to ants."

Melogian ascended the last step and knelt by Edisthen's side, gripping an arm of the throne, her hand nestled uncomfortably amongst the baroque carvings.

"I feel as if I'm just now waking up from a long nightmare," she said. "Evered's clan stole Christine from us and for thirteen years we've all been numbed with grief. Orion sank nearly all his time and energy in the search for your daughter. And I've come to think *that* was the real aim of the abduction: to burn out Orion's strength in a fruitless attempt to bring Christine back.

"But Quentin accomplished the impossible, and rescued Christine. This must have forced Evered's hand. He will attack us soon, before we've had a chance to rally our forces. Whether Orion was ambushed in Jyndyrys or whether something even stranger happened to him, he won't be coming back. I'm your sole magical defender, against whatever influences Casimir can wield. I've tried to ward Testenel against his probes, but I think today's events prove I've been unsuccessful. It may have seemed like Evered was delivering a challenge to you; in fact it was Casimir who was challenging me. I don't know if I can protect Christine or yourself adequately anymore."

Edisthen frowned at Melogian, then rose to his feet. Melogian stood up as well; though she was tall for a woman, she reached only to his shoulders.

"Go and gather the magicians who can be of help, Melogian."

"You didn't listen to me! They're no use to us, not if Casimir—"

"Melogian!" The sorceress fell silent. "You will calm yourself."

"I . . . Yes, my liege."

"I understand your concerns and I thank you for your frankness. But your task is to serve me, not to belittle yourself and tear out your hair. You are my court wizard, and you will follow my orders."

Melogian retreated down a step, eyes downcast, her face flushed. "I am yours to command, my king."

"You are forward and impertinent, Melogian, and I love you dearly for it, but what I need now is unquestioning service. You will go to these magicians and see which ones you can recruit to our service. I care little that their talents are weak, so long as I can make use of them."

"As you command."

Edisthen's tone mellowed slightly as he continued. "See to it that Christine is moved into her suite by this evening, and attend to the spell-web at that time. I will rest easier once I know she is where she ought to be. For your part, I shall expect you to leave tomorrow morning and to return within twenty-four hours; my daughter needs you by her side—and so do I."

Melogian looked up at the king, bowed, and stepped out of the enspelled region, which shattered apart as she passed, with the sound of a glass thread popping.

ℰℰ Christine remained sitting on her bed for a long while, considering what she had just learned, trying to still the whirling of her mind. After a while, she went to her window and drew back the curtain, letting sunlight into the room. The glass of the pane was uneven and slightly distorted the view. Towers of various heights and gauges rose across a chasm directly in front of her, built of blocks of blue stone. One squat shaft was a definitely paler shade; at the other extreme, a slim tower reaching much higher than its neighbors gleamed a deeper blue as well—could this be an optical illusion, an effect of their respective diameters? Or had their stone been chosen especially for a desired effect?

She looked down at the wall her window was set in. To left and right it spread, pierced with windows at regular intervals. Christine tried to count how many floors there were below before the wall ended at a peaked roof; five or six, she decided. Atop the spine of the roof a number of spikes rose; the one at the very edge was apparently a weathervane, though what it depicted she couldn't figure out.

The sun shifted in the sky, a sharp sudden movement. Astonished, Christine looked directly at it. She was used to a tiny solar disc so bright it spawned blue spots in her vision after a quarter of a second, a featureless coin of white gold. The sun of Chrysanthe was different: It had a perceptibly ragged corona, and its brilliance was somehow more tolerable. A ball of flame in the sky, Melogian had said it was; not a sphere of hydrogen fusing to helium a hundred and fifty million kilometers away, but a burning torch a few miles up, that swept through the air on its own. . . . Insanity. But why had it moved?

Christine's sight finally took in the whole of the view and she realized she wasn't looking at the sun itself, but at a mirror. A huge mirror, set between a pair of towers, pivoting on an axis that spanned a pair of metal struts. And that mirror was reflecting another mirror, beyond the edge of her view, which was reflecting the sun. Redirecting the sunlight into the core of the castle, which would otherwise find itself in perpetual shadow. It made sense, of a sort. The sun-tracking mirrors would need to be constantly adjusted; this was what had just happened. No doubt there were people here whose sole duty lay in gauging the progress of the sun across the heavens and ordering others to twitch this or that mirror half a degree farther. . . .

There were small dormer windows in the roof below her; now one opened and a youth climbed out onto the slope of the roof. The youth ascended casually to the saddle of the roof, then went to the weathervane, holding on to the row of spikes. The youth carefully examined the weathervane then pulled out a scrap of paper from a trouser pocket and jotted something down, double-checking, before returning to the window and vanishing from Christine's view.

Christine reflected that throughout this vast castle, life went on as it had before she was here, and would go on without her if she vanished. Being unimportant was a form of safety. She clung to the feeling, regardless of how uncomfortable it might be: It made sense that she was not the center of all things. She told herself she was just as negligible here as she had been before, and found a bitter reassurance in the thought, no matter that it was a patent lie.

Eventually Althea knocked upon her door and asked her if she wished to eat. Christine realized she was almost ravenous. She opened the door and took her second meal in Chrysanthe.

The knife and fork were gold-plated, the dishes polished silver, the serving spoons jeweled and spangled. At first she could not bring herself to use them. She thought of the youth she had glimpsed upon the roof, busy at some mysterious errand: She doubted that person ate with golden utensils. *This is plastic*, she told herself, a lie to reduce the outrageous to the mundane. *Plastic and steel and cheap plating. Anyway, what matters is the food; just eat it.*

The meat was a prime cut of beef; there were potatoes and carrots and some kind of tart celery. The other vegetable, thinly sliced and pale, she could not name, yet its taste was strangely familiar. She smiled when she finally realized she was eating some of Quentin's much-loved pickled abances.

She felt at a loss when she had finished her meal. She could have anything she wanted, Melogian had claimed. But what was she supposed to want?

She wanted Quentin. She needed his presence to steady her in this world, as it had throughout their travels. She should never have sent him away; how could she have been so foolish as to believe she was healed? She had lost her ability to see her own father without fear. . . . No, she must not think of that. She would only make herself feel worse. Somewhere within her mind, the knotted skein of lies Dr. Almand had made her recall twisted and shuddered, lashing her with all-too familiar revulsion.

"Althea—can you find Sir Quentin? I, ah . . . I would like to see him. I want to talk with him."

"Does m'lady want me to go myself? M'lady shouldn't be left alone; may I ask someone to go fetch the knight?"

"Yes; yes, of course, that's what I meant. And never mind the bib, I can take it off by myself!"

"Yes, m'lady." Althea opened the door and passed on Christine's request to one of the guards on duty. Christine meanwhile had untied the huge napkin from around her neck and placed it on the dining cart. As soon as Althea closed the door, Christine apologized.

"I'm sorry I snapped at you, Althea. I just don't want to feel like a baby."

"M'lady has nothing to apologize for. M'lady was right, I was at fault."

"No, no! Don't say that. I'm just not used to being treated like this."

"Of course, m'lady. As I said, there's no need for m'lady to apologize."

Christine would have suspected Althea of lying if the girl's face had not been so utterly guileless.

"It's not right for me to be angry with you, is what I mean."

"Oh, m'lady can be as angry as she wants with me; that's why I was chosen."

Althea's reply threw Christine off-balance. "What do you mean," she finally asked, "I can be as angry as I want?"

Althea's face betrayed the merest hint of anxiety. "I mean that m'lady can lose her temper if she wants, there's no danger."

"Danger of what?"

"Danger to m'lady, or to myself. I was first in line as m'lady's personal servant."

"What, you applied for the post and they picked you first?"

Althea lowered her gaze. "No, m'lady. I've been preparing my whole life for this service. There's very few of us. We're chosen from among all the staff, and only the best suited are picked."

"Who is 'us'?"

"Body servants to the blood royal. The stewards look for special qualities; it's a great risk and a great honor. I'm the one that was chosen to serve m'lady. Twelve years ago, m'lady, they made the first selection. There were five of us. Three made it through the second selection. I was the one chosen at the final selection, five years ago."

"The Law," muttered Christine, horrified. "Because of the Law. You can't have a temper of your own, in case you got angry at me and hurt me?"

"That's part of it, m'lady," Althea said, an innocently proud smile on her face. "We also have to be obedient and not repeat things we're told—I always forget the word for it."

"And you spent twelve years in training to serve me? I wasn't even here! What was the point?"

"I knew m'lady would return," Althea said, her eyes bright. "God wouldn't permit m'lady to stay lost forever. When m'lady came back, I was ready."

Christine couldn't meet the servant girl's gaze; she looked away, both embarrassed and frightened. "Well," she said uncertainly, "anyway . . . Just have the cart taken away, please. I'm going to take a nap, or something. Call me when Quentin gets here, will you?"

&ℯ Quentin diffidently accepted the bounty of Testenel's stores for himself. Olfane led him to the stables that lay under the huge main bulk of the castle, and there, after some persuasion on her part, he made a choice of mount. He had balked at laying claim to a squire, and insisted this formality be delayed. For a fact, his life was already complicated enough without taking responsibility for a squire in addition.

The main object of Quentin's desires had been a secure chest. He was immensely gratified that this could be immediately obtained. Once everything had been carried to his apartments, Quentin spent a considerable amount of time cleaning his armor and inventorying the damage that needed to be repaired. The list he drew up was discouraging, insofar as repairs would be expensive—and the imaginary coinage from his purse would never be accepted. Then he caught the flaw in his thinking and carefully laid the list on a table. If the smith even wished to be paid, Quentin could put the charges to the royal purse. Edisthen's generosity would no doubt extend to the maintenance of Quentin's armor.

There would be no more fighting for the foreseeable future, thought Quentin. No more hairsbreadth escapes, no more ambushing enemies, no more slaying metal wyrms . . . No more mourning the death of a faithful mount. The horse Quentin had picked was an ordinary one, somewhat slow even, hardly impressive. He would not lose his heart to it, would not writhe with guilt in his dreams at its loss should it die. Life in peacetime was duller but all in all, it was preferable. Less triumph, but far less grief.

Once the armor was as clean as he could make it, he put it away carefully in the chest. On the morrow he would locate an armorer and contract for repairs; until then this great treasure of his would lie under lock. Quentin turned the key and withdrew it, assured himself the lid was immoveable before he left for the refectory where he had used to take his meals, in that bygone era he had spent at court.

His appearance there caused a commotion: By now all of Testenel was buzzing with the news of Christine's return. Quentin was recognized before even he set foot within; a tremendous roar rose from the diners at his entry. These people were not courtiers but soldiers, servants, and tradespeople: Quentin's own kind. He'd never have thought to fear them, but their enthusiasm was far worse than the courtiers'. The morning's misadventure replayed itself, much to his chagrin. This time he was able to command some authority, however, and in due course managed to sit himself at a table and eat a filling meal—while remaining the focus of far too many eyes for comfort.

Sandenin found him there, told him that a gathering had been arranged for early the next morning. Of the band of eight whom Quentin had considered his closest circle of friends at court, one was gone to Waldern in Archeled, another had refused to join his comrades, a third had been evasive. Still, Quentin was glad to hear five old friends would definitely be present. Sandenin asked if Quentin would mind if Bronna were present as well; when Quentin told him he would have insisted upon it in any case, a smile mellowed Sandenin's naturally dour countenance and he left Quentin in apparently better spirits than before.

For his part, Quentin remained more or less a prisoner of the crowd for an endless while. He was offered further food and drink, which he refused, and when plied for the story of his deeds managed to tell a minimum. Unlike for the recounting he had given the courtiers, here he felt guilty at withholding the full truth; but he had had time to realize there were reasons both political and moral for discretion.

Eventually a messenger came in, carrying a summons from Christine. With some exclamations of wonder, the crowd parted around Quentin then and let him go to his lady's side.

The castle of Vorlok, to which Vaurd's sons had been exiled, possessed a chapel of sorts, an outbuilding in bad need of repair. In earlier times, there had been a chapel within the castle, but it had been converted into an armory seven decades before the present, twenty years before Vorlok's near abandonment.

Exiled in 6075, Vaurd's sons had come to a castle that had scarcely seen human occupants in thirty years. Its construction was solid enough that no significant architectural damage had been suffered, but repairs and maintenance still consumed most of the princes' stores of funds. Evered and his brothers had brought a handful of retainers with them, including the court wizard Mathellin; with time they had added to this sparse staff, recruiting help from settlements to the east, including an old priestess, Sharnas. Evered had hoped that her presence would improve the mood of his staff, many of whom wished to attend regular services. Evered and his brothers themselves seldom bothered, though at festival times one or two of them would always be on hand at the ceremonies.

It was thus a rare sight, perhaps a unique one, for one of the princes to cross the courtyard in the middle of an ordinary day and enter the makeshift chapel, having doffed his hat at the door.

Within, the smell of incense rose thickly, perhaps in an effort to combat an underlying reek of damp wood. Cobwebs festooned the corners of the high ceiling; the murals painted on the plastered walls were faded and flecked with mold.

Innalan made his way up the hall of worship, passing between the prayer benches and the four small lecterns on their daises. All this furniture had been built on-site and lacked the customary splendor of religious paraphernalia. A side door led to the priestess's quarters. The prince knocked, and was answered after a long moment by a frail voice bidding him enter.

It was amazingly hot inside the room; though this was a week before the beginning of summer, a small brazier was half full of glowing coals. The air was dry as a bone; it felt to Innalan as if an oven door had just been opened in front of his face.

Sharnas, the tame priestess his brother had summoned to them, reclined on a couch, her head supported by a huge pillow. Her face was wrinkled and pouched, her hair like milkweed fluff. She might have been dozing a moment ago, but certainly she was fully awake now: Her eyes glittered with alertness.

"Your Highness," she said in an even tone—if she was surprised by his presence, she did not show it. "What may I do for you?"

Innalan sketched a bow. "Good day to you, Little Mother. I have come because I . . . wanted to ask your advice."

"Sit." Sharnas pointed to a chair next to the hearth, which thankfully was not being used, so that in fact it was marginally cooler next to it. "Speak freely, my son."

Innalan sat and wiped sweat from his brow. How could the woman stand this heat? She was thin; probably her age made her always cold, and perhaps she feared the damp more than the heat. Once before she had been offered lodgings within the main keep, but she had refused, saying she must dwell by the altar. Evered would have had to rebuild a chapel within the keep to get her to move—hardly a budgetary priority.

Innalan could not get to the point immediately. "Are you well, Little Mother? I want to know if there's anything you require."

"I am fine, my son. People keep me fed, and worship keeps me busy. If I needed anything from you, I would have let you know. But that's not what you came to see me for."

Innalan settled himself in the chair. "This must remain a private matter," he began.

"God sees and knows all, my son. He will be included in our confidence."

Innalan repressed a sigh of exasperation. As always, his respect for the priestess was mixed with contempt for her endless banalities. He believed in God with all of his being; did Sharnas think her ready-made speeches plumbed the limits of that belief?

"Little Mother, I want to know how you feel about an undertaking we are, ah, contemplating."

"It isn't my place to judge. The Lesser Book warns us about judging—"

Innalan cut her off before she could start to quote. "I am not asking you to pass judgment. I'm asking you to tell me how you feel. I . . . We intend to move against Edisthen. My brother Evered is about to gather the barons of the marches, and sweep northward. I need to know how this strikes you."

"To move against Edisthen? What exactly does that entail?" The priestess's expression was bland. She kept rubbing thumb against forefinger, both digits trembling slightly.

Innalan sucked in his breath. Sharnas was *not* senile. In previous conversations, he had known her to be as elusive as water when she wanted to, which indicated intelligence. Obviously she wanted him to commit himself, because she was a woman of God and not a temporal power, and she must remain detached from worldly matters. The prince spoke to the point.

"We are going to make war on Edisthen; we wish to overthrow him and restore our line to the throne. We want to crown Evered king. We will bring war and death to the land, to bring back justice. *That* is what that entails. Now answer me."

Sharnas raised her eyebrows, the rest of her face remaining immobile, as if to mock him. *What, you thought I hadn't guessed at your plans years ago?* Or was her surprise too subtle for him to read? Nearly ten years she had dwelt with them in Vorlok, and Innalan knew almost nothing about her, no more than he did any of those who served him. The guards, the servants, they did not matter; it was as pointless to take an interest in them as it would have been to discuss philosophy with Casimir's golems. But this woman, God's representative, he should have made more of an effort to understand. Now, in a moment of need, he came to her, not as a master with orders but as a supplicant. He lacked the upper hand with her, when he had always assumed he possessed it.

For a long moment Sharnas was silent. Her eyes had half closed and her breathing deepened, so that Innalan became almost convinced she had fallen asleep. Then, just when he was about to shake her awake, her lids opened fully, and she sat up. "You will do what you will do," she said. "You come to me asking for my feelings, but it is my blessing on your enterprise that you want, nothing more. If Evered wishes God to smile on his venture he can ask me himself, though I will tell him what I tell you now: God sees all and knows all; God births Heroes and monsters, floods, plagues, and storms; God makes the grain grow and the sun shine. That is blessing and curse enough."

Innalan shook his head and protested. "That isn't an answer! I don't want your blessings, Little Mother, I want your opinion. You're just spouting cant at me!"

"You think my words are empty," said Sharnas, "but maybe it is you who are deaf, my son."

The reply stoked Innalan's dormant anger into flames. "More of the same! I came to ask you what God wants; but if you won't tell me, then to hell with you!"

And he rose to his feet and went to the door. Behind him Sharnas's frail voice rose.

"Prince Innalan: I'm fourscore-and-four years old, I've been a priestess nearly all my life; I have no idea what God wants. What makes you think anyone does?"

Innalan turned back to her.

"You're a priestess, you speak for God! Stop playing with me!"

She was shaking her head as if in sadness. "No, my son. I speak *of* God. God does not speak to us. We are separate, cut off. We are all alone, Innalan. Go out into the mountains and listen to the sky, and you will hear nothing. You do not understand what a priestess is, boy. I am here to *listen*. People must speak with a priestess, because praying to the silence of Heaven is too hard."

"Don't speak to me that way," Innalan threatened, but his voice was unsteady. Now Sharnas's words frightened him, so unlike her usual speech were they.

"Don't worry: I will not discourage your brother from his goals," she said. "I will not preach sedition amongst your servants. My branch of the sisterhood has always refused to meddle in politics. But I will speak to you as I see fit. And I tell you, Innalan son of Vaurd: Until the day you come to me as a mere man seeking the solace of God, stay away from my door."

Innalan wanted to rage at her, to strike her, at the very least to storm out in fury. He left in silence on trembling legs, to seek refuge in a drink, and another, and another, until his fear should doze at last, minutes before he himself collapsed face-first onto the table.

❧❧ Althea came into the bedroom and announced that Quentin had arrived; but in fact Christine had barely been dozing and had heard him at the outer door of the suite. She briefly suffered Althea to give her hair a few strokes of the brush before sitting down in her armchair in the antechamber. Althea opened the outer door and Quentin came in. As soon as the door had shut behind him, he knelt, bowed his head. "Lady Christine," he said, his tone more formal than it had ever been.

Christine was nonplussed. "Quentin? Why are you doing this?"

He raised his head to meet her gaze; his expression was slightly embarrassed.

"Lady, it is the proper form of address at court."

Christine shook her head. "No, no, no," she scolded Quentin. "I won't have it. Don't you start this with me, ever. Stand up."

Quentin obeyed at once.

"Ah . . . Well, sit down," she continued, pointing to a chair close to hers. Quentin sank down into the seat. As soon as he had crossed the few feet separating them, Christine felt a wave of relief, unexpected in its intensity. She could not hold back a smile as she gazed at the young knight. He had changed his clothes again, for something less flashy than this morning. The green hose and gray doublet suited him far better.

"I've missed you," she confessed. Her face felt warm; she shifted in her seat. "Where were you all this time?"

"On His Majesty's orders, I went to provision myself. I now have a secure trunk for my armor, and I have selected a new horse—we will see if he takes to me, but he seems a friendly mount."

"Well, that's good. You must have missed your . . . I mean, after what happened." Christine instantly regretted having brought up the death of Quentin's former mount. She recalled her terror, imprisoned in the shape-changed vehicle while Quentin fought with it; she tried to push the memory from her mind.

"I will always miss Thunder," Quentin was saying, his mouth bent in a rueful smile, "but it is not good for a knight to lack a mount. My needs are seen to; but what of yours, Lady? Is there something you require?"

Answers came to Christine's lips, pressing to be said. She needed him to protect her against Evered. To justify this world to her, the obscenity of the Law. Explain why he had never told her about her abduction, about the reasons behind it. Or did he not know, was he as much of an innocent as she was? She needed him to be at her side with his sword drawn, to take her away from all this, back to the glorious road, the nonplace that traversed all possibilities and committed to none. . . . But the road had also held dangers and frights; Chrysanthe was meant to be safe, this castle a refuge, this room a haven. She had to give it a try, had to be strong; she chose not to mention Evered's visit, not wishing to have to tell Quentin of everything else that had followed.

"Oh," she lied, "I'm fine . . . I really didn't have any good reason for calling you. I was just . . . well, bored. I mean, I don't know what I should be doing now. Melogian said to rest, but I've slept enough."

She couldn't restrain a nervous laugh.

"It's just, well . . . Part of me expects to get back in a car with you. To go . . . somewhere else."

"I have taken you to your destination, Lady."

"Yes, I know. But . . . I guess I miss traveling. Being nowhere in particular and seeing new things . . . I had never really traveled before, not like we did. I mean, it wasn't always easy, but . . . but some parts were nice."

Quentin smiled. "I am glad you can recall your journey with some pleasure, Lady."

"Don't *you* miss it?"

Quentin wouldn't meet her gaze. "It fills me with joy that you have been delivered safely to the true realm, Lady. And I am honored that I was the one to bring you back."

Christine blinked, not certain if she understood the unspoken reply. Perhaps to Quentin their flight through the made world could never have the significance it had for her; perhaps in truth all he felt was satisfaction at his accomplished duty.

"We'll never travel together again, will we?" she asked.

"You can certainly travel wherever you wish in Chrysanthe, Lady. Aboard a carriage or a skyship; there are a thousand beautiful sights to be seen in this land. And of course, if you . . . asked for me to guard you, I would be present."

"I wouldn't want to travel alone," she said. "If—when—I travel here, I'll want you to accompany me."

His smile reassured her: She wasn't alone in having at least some pleasant memories of their travels through Errefern. But this reassurance brought with it a pang of melancholy for her old life, forever lost.

"You know," she said, "when I was young, I dreamed of traveling in outer space. I used to watch a show on television, *The Cosmic Patrol*. I couldn't get enough of it. I wanted to be like Commander Seldar and pilot a ship between the stars and discover new planets and peoples. But here . . . nobody even knows what television is."

"Remember that I do, Lady," said Quentin. "Electric screens showing pictures and sound. Do you know, when I first encountered it, I believed it was a form of magic: dreams captured and blooming under glass. In Amarga I read a children's book about television. I could never quite make sense of it, but I remember the diagrams: the cameras with their scanning discs, the broadcast towers and the receptors. It is a wonderfully clever invention—but we could never bring it about in Chrysanthe."

"I know, I know. Pardon me for being dumb, but if you don't have television, what do your people do to entertain themselves? You have books, but is there anything else?"

Quentin answered instantly. "That would replace television? Plays; every week, there is at least one play performed in Testenel. Dramas from the classic repertory, comedies, all kinds of things. Television is very much like the theater. And there are other forms of entertainment, as well, more active ones. The nobility hunt, but it is mostly the men who enjoy it. We have various kinds of sports prized by ladies: Redball, Thief's Escape, string vaulting for the most athletic. Board games, also: Four Kings' War, Runaround, Seven Gates. People play dice, but gambling is not considered a refined pastime—still, if you wished to try your luck, no one would object."

Christine couldn't restrain a smile at the enumeration. Nothing on Quentin's list particularly appealed to her at the moment, but his enthusiasm proved that life within Testenel need not be dour.

"It's stories I always preferred," she said. "Television can't be as deep as a book, but it told so many stories so fast I couldn't resist it. It wasn't just *The Cosmic Patrol*; there were all these other shows, stories you followed from one week to the next." She shook her head ruefully. "I'll never find out now if Johnny Slate will ever get Chloe to admit she loves him." Her eyes misted. "Damn; I'm being stupid, but I mind losing that show. It's gone and it won't come back."

"You are allowed to have your feelings, Lady Christine. It is fitting to grieve for the place you have left behind."

"I can't help it," Christine said, wiping at her eyes. "I'm a child of television. I grew up with it. I had Tap to console me—" Her voice trembled at the mention of her imaginary companion, whose disappearance had triggered her slide into Dr. Almand's compassionate hell, and whose voice had been the same as Quentin's. "And he was very much like a cartoon rabbit—you know, animated pictures? If he had looked like a real rabbit, I wouldn't have trusted him the way I did. As a picture, I could believe he came from my own mind; until—well . . . I don't want to talk about that again."

Quentin seemed only too glad to change the subject. "I was a child of the fields," he said. "When I was very young, I kept wanting to run away from home, over the hills to the north of Lydiss, and discover something wonderful. When I was older, I made that journey north and found nothing but more hills, and trees, and the empty sky. Still, it made me happy enough."

"And then what? When did you decide to become a knight?"

"One must start training early. I became a squire in 6080, just after turning twelve. My parents did not like the idea very much: They hoped for me to become a trader like my uncle, perhaps even to inherit his business. But I have no fondness for figures and I hate to haggle. My eleventh year, he had me doing sums to 'help him' in his accounting. He wasted so much time correcting me he gave up after three days. . . . And for my part, I had heard one too many tales of bravery. I thought there was nothing finer than to be a knight of the realm, a defender of the crown. I was seven when the Great War took place; to me then, it sounded like a glorious adventure. So when I turned twelve, I was sent to Summer Hill to apprentice with Sir Glenn."

"What did you do?"

"What did I *not* do! Sir Glenn had me working chores morning, noon, and night. I had never realized how coddled I had been until I found myself cleaning the latrines with too short a brush. . . . But then, he also told me stories and taught me far beyond what the school in Lydiss had been able to. My parents had been sure I would give up after six months, I believe. I surprised them—I surprised myself, actually—when I stayed on, month after month, year after year. It may have been stubbornness at first, but as I toughened it became something else. I was fit to become a knight, you see. I had dreamed of it idly in my youth—Sir Glenn made it come true."

For some time Quentin went on, recounting anecdotes from his younger days. Christine listened to him speak, at times losing the thread, but caring little. It was his voice she had needed, the sense of him close to her, even though he was on the wrong side, to her right instead of her left. She closed her eyes a few times, imagining the scenes he described, raising her lids again if he stopped, to reassure him she had not fallen asleep and wanted him to continue.

Althea served them drinks and a snack; the twice-reflected sun kept shining through the windows of the bedroom, illuminating the whole suite. Christine's nerves were soothed by the passage of time, the quiet of the rooms, Althea's dusting of the rack of dresses awaiting Christine's pleasure. The sense of urgency that had been working at her had faded; she let Quentin's recollections carry her away, like a television show.

In this way a long while passed; there was no clock in her suite, so Christine could not tell just how long, but she did not care. This was like the good parts of their journey, when time became indefinite as Quentin shifted through the made world and the sun's progress in the heavens became almost arbitrary. Quentin's anecdotes kept jumping from his arrival at court back to his early childhood, and Christine was no longer sure if the girl nicknamed Bug had been Quentin's playmate in Lydiss or his friend in Testenel, unless it was both.

There came a knock at the door. Quentin fell silent; Althea opened the door a crack and reported Melogian sought admittance. Christine nodded, then rose to her feet to greet the sorceress, as did Quentin.

Melogian entered, bobbing her head at Christine and sparing a smile for Quentin.

"Hello, Christine. I trust you're well? Forgive me for interrupting," she said, "but your father has asked me to ask you if you wouldn't prefer moving to new quarters. These rooms aren't very appropriate for a princess, and you would be better lodged in the royal apartments."

Christine, reminded of the earlier unpleasantness in the audience chambers, was unwilling to be convinced to move, no matter that the king had insisted upon it and that the appointments promised to be literally palatial. In the end, it was the promise of a private bathroom that clinched the deal.

Melogian gently prodded Christine to proceed with the move immediately; when Quentin offered his help, Christine acquiesced. For a fact he did nothing himself: Servants would carry all of Christine's possessions. Quentin and Melogian merely accompanied her down the corridors of Testenel, Althea in tow and guards preceding and following them.

A sizable number of people turned up along the way, gawping at Christine, sometimes calling out, as others had done earlier in the day. Christine bore the attention stoically but was glad to finally reach their destination.

The apartments that had been set aside for Christine at her birth, and that had remained unoccupied for seventeen years, encompassed eight rooms situated high up in Testenel's core. Unlike the Demmerel Chambers, here the layout of the corridors and doors efficiently restricted access. It didn't feel like a prison, but it was hardly casual. When the inner doors opened, Christine was appalled at the splendor that lay revealed within. She almost demanded a return to her earlier quarters, but in the end she did not dare and accepted her lot.

It turned out there were many small matters to be disposed of and Christine had to be consulted. She seized the chance to busy herself with the precise arrangements of her furniture and possessions, as this gave her the opportunity to tone down the overwhelming luxury. Melogian once more quickened the magical web that watched over Christine, then excused herself, as she herself had much to prepare for the morrow. Quentin remained with Christine for a while, but he said and did nothing while she fended Althea's questions and insisted on helping her slide a gilt porcelain cat into a more inconspicuous spot.

After fifteen minutes of this, Christine realized with a twinge of guilt how quiet Quentin had become. Her initial fluster at her new arrangements had calmed down, and the necessary arrangements promised to occupy her and soothe her nerves for quite a while.

"Quentin," she said, "thank you for spending time with me. Maybe you'll come visit later? I mean, tomorrow?"

Quentin gave a little bow. "I would be delighted, Lady," he said.

"I don't know what I'll be doing. I guess you can just come whenever you're free. . . ."

Althea cleared her throat. "M'lady may be very busy tomorrow," she said. "M'lady remembers His Majesty has decreed three days of celebration? There'll be feasts, and dancing, and whatnot."

"Oh." Christine had for a fact completely forgotten this. "But these celebrations, they're for other people, not for me. I mean, I don't have to attend, do I? Not everything?"

Althea blushed. "Oh, no, m'lady is the princess, m'lady can do whatever she wants. . . . I wasn't thinking."

"It's okay," said Christine. "I'll figure it out tomorrow morning. Would it be all right if I sent for you, Quentin?"

"Whenever you want, Lady Christine."

Quentin took his leave; Christine was alone with Althea and the other servants who were still busying themselves in the other rooms of her suite. Trying hard to enjoy it and not really succeeding, she continued reordering things according to her tastes, still wishing for a plain wooden desk, her old chair with the vinyl cushion, and the magical box of dreams she had taken for granted all her life.

Like a struck bell, the whole of the castle had resonated to the news of Christine's return; and as with a bell, the initial peal quickly fell in volume. Quentin had dreaded crowds gathering in larger and larger numbers, besieging him in his quarters. In fact once he left Christine's apartments it appeared his fame would no longer trigger public hysteria. He was recognized again and again, but not assaulted by well-wishers. He did avoid the refectory, and prevailed instead upon the cooking staff to provide him with a meal in a corner of one of the great kitchens that served the inhabitants of Testenel.

Which of course meant that there was no insuperable obstacle to prevent him from sauntering over to the Phoenix Tower and seeking the door marked with an apple. His mouth went dry at the thought; Lady Alicia's promises made him feel like an overeager boy again.

And yet.

There was the chance that she had lied, or that she intended to put a liaison with Quentin to some embarrassing use at a later date. Assume these risks were negligible and that the courtier had been sincere—did he still want to go to her?

Chewing on a mouthful of bread, Quentin tried to order his thoughts. He knew what his body was saying; that took no subtlety to understand. He knew what the censorious part of his mind said: It said *no*, prissily, arguing from nothing in particular. Just *No, this is not fitting for you.* Because of the difference in their respective ranks? But Quentin's current status, unofficial though it was, put him higher than Alicia, higher than anyone in the castle save Edisthen and Christine. Yet might that not be mostly his lust talking?

Quentin sighed in exasperation. He felt as if he were caught in the middle of an argument between two blind, nearly senile oldsters. He didn't want to choose to obey one or the other. He needed to know what it was he himself wanted.

It was no easy task. He had lain with women, not a few times. The ideal knight of legend was a chaste servant of justice and honor, but in that respect Quentin was far from ideal. Once, in his travels through Errefern, he had spent a week in a warm world, a city full of gold and crimson flowers that reminded him of the unrivaled blooms of Chrysanthe. He had told himself Christine might be somewhere here,

that his hunter's instinct prickled. For a fact it was their women who awoke something in him. It had then been a year since his last, brief tryst; he found himself
overwhelmed by the local women, who wore very little, whose skin glowed honey-
brown and whose exotically slanted eyes sparkled with foxglove. Local mores placed
no restrictions on unmarried people. Quentin had spent days erotically embroiled
with a girl of twenty named Oru, in whose flesh he would lose himself time and
again, and who hungered for him with the same passion.

In the end he had realized that if the affair prolonged itself he might never
leave, might forget himself and his mission. He had left one morning while his par-
amour was gone to her job at the trader's market. He had tried to write her a letter,
a brief note, but he had given up the attempt, gone out, summoned Thunder with a
whistle. The horse, shape-shifted to a bone-white, chitin-plated mount, had sprung
into motion and by the time they had reached the end of the street Oru was worlds
away. Quentin had told himself many times that she was not real, after all, that as
soon as he passed out of her world she might as well never have existed. It had not
lessened his sense of betrayal.

There was no question of dalliance with an imaginary woman now, to be dismissed from reality with a step *beyond*; rather the promise of a very real affair with a
very real courtier—and her friend, if Quentin so wished. Lust whined and drooled
at Quentin's ear, while fear mouthed denials just as strong.

Quentin abruptly stood up and left the table, stalked across corridors and up
staircases, headed for the Phoenix Tower. He had nearly reached it when one of the
gibbering old men in his mind overcame the other and sent him back toward his
quarters.

"Good evening, Sir Quentin!" a young woman called out to him as their paths
crossed, her eyes merry. She also would yield to him, came a thought crackling
through his body. She would consider it an honor. He need not worry about Lady
Alicia; he could have any woman he wanted. Even if this one were married, would
she not gladly cuckold her husband with such a hero as Quentin was? Would not her
husband even praise her if he learned of it?

He turned toward her, unaccustomed words of command coming to his lips. No
seduction was necessary, only a crude prompting. She would do whatever he asked. . . .

He knew her face. "Bronna?" he asked. "Bug? Is that you?"

She shook her head, casting her gaze downward. "No, Sir Quentin. I'm Lynas,
Panille's daughter. We've not met before. But I heard what happened, what the king
said, and it's been told everywhere who brought Princess Christine back. People
said, a knight in green hose, with a flamberge at his side. I guessed."

It could never have been Bronna, who would be six months pregnant, a fact
he'd forgotten for a moment. But thanks to this mistake, his sanity had returned.

"My apologies, Lynas," he said. "I have been absent a long while and thought
to recognize an old friend."

"Oh, no apologies needed, sir. But if I may ask, how is she? The princess? I've
not seen her, but I've heard people say she was ill, that she was seeing no one. . . ."

"She is well," said Quentin. "She, ah, she does need rest, and privacy, but she is
quite well, I assure you."

"If— When you next see Her Highness, will you tell her— No, no, forget I asked."

"Tell her that you wish her well? Yes, I will, I promise," said Quentin. In his head, the argument had ceased.

Lynas thanked him, blushing. Quentin gave her a little bow then continued on his way, back to his quarters. He still had to inventory the necessary repairs on his armor and contract with an armorer: enough to fill his evening.

❧ Christine went to bed early, when the sun had barely set; she was still tired from her day and feeling not a little dread at the thought of what tomorrow would bring. Though her lids had nearly shut by themselves while she was up, as soon as her head hit the pillow she found she could not sleep.

The room itself was partly to blame. Her bedchamber was ridiculously large; it should have bred echoes, but there was so much fabric on the walls, so many pillows thrown about, such a thickness of rug that all sounds were deadened. Still, the sense of a vast space all about her awoke a faint unease in Christine's mind. A fireplace lay not far from the bed, flanked by braziers. This being early summer, there was no need for them, but Althea had explained in detail how they were used to provide a comfortable temperature, proudly pointing out the small compartment within the bed frame where a pan of coals could be set to warm the sleeper. That compartment stuck in Christine's mind as she tossed and turned; it mingled with Evered's threats and with Melogian's mind-bending explanations of the true nature of the world. The Law that all things followed, and that extended to protecting the bodily integrity of monarchs . . .

She dozed, dreamed of the compartment under the bed and of walking along the side of an asphalted street, past a row of closed stores, the summer sun beating on the back of her neck, as harsh as the Law, the Law that held the world in its grip. . . .

She came awake in a wash of sadness and dread. For a while it seemed to her a familiar thing, the feeling of unbearable sadness she had lived with for many years. She let it ride at first, then tried to fight against it, telling herself things had changed, that she was home now. Her attempts proved unsuccessful; in fact, they made things worse. It wasn't just sadness that held her, but fear, and a current of guilt. She tried to thrust the guilt away, but it only grew. More and more uneasy, Christine took a mental step back through the veil of sleep and gathered up her dreams. And memory fastened its claws into her.

For several minutes she remained motionless, clutching at herself, suffocated with horror. Then she made herself climb out of bed, took unsteady steps to the door. She remembered as she opened it that there was a bell-pull next to her bed, that she could have summoned help with a twitch of her hand. But she felt past all help in that instant.

The room beyond the door had been outfitted for quiet recreation: A refined lady of the blood royal might want to read books or listen to music, or play games, all in privacy. There was another door facing the one she had come through, and beyond that door she would still be within her domain, merely one level closer to the outside world. It was the door to the side she wanted, the narrow opening designed for the use of her staff, that led to the quarters where Althea slept.

She hesitated at that door; but she could not stay alone with her memories at that moment. She opened it; the short corridor beyond was lit by an oil lamp. Christine was still blinking from the unexpected light when Althea came to her, barefoot in a thin shift.

"M'lady? Is anything the matter?"

Of course there wasn't. How could there be? She couldn't ask for help. She did not deserve it, did not need it. But she was the princess of the realm, so much more important than anyone: She deserved to be capricious, to impose her whims upon everyone else. It was expected of her, wasn't it?

She stammered out Melogian's name, asked Althea to summon the magician to her side. Unquestioningly, Althea passed the request on to one of the guards at the outer doors of the suite—Christine hadn't thought for a moment that there would still be guards, but of course there were, there would always be, yet none of their metal could do anything about what threatened her now.

Althea fetched a robe and slippers for Christine, lighting candles as she did so. Christine sat herself down in an armchair in the game room and contemplated the circles and lines painted on the top of a small table until Melogian's arrival.

She knew it couldn't have taken very long, yet the wait was endless, made worse by the lack of a watch, another one of the things she had taken for granted and now would never see again.

So that when Melogian arrived, her hair in disarray and her clothes hastily belted on, it was the first thing Christine spoke of.

"Why isn't there a clock in here?"

"A clock?"

"A timepiece! Something to say what time of the day it is. Is this midnight or early morning? How am I supposed to know? I used to have a wristwatch, but what am I supposed to do now?"

Melogian approached and leaned against the edge of the game table, close to Christine. "I've seen mechanical clocks in made worlds, but we lack those here, Christine. People will often use hour-candles after dark: They're carefully made, so that when the candle burns down to the next ring, it marks sixty elapsed minutes. It would probably be better to install a clepsydra—a water-clock. They are nearly as precise as the mechanical timekeepers you recall. They are a bit noisy, though, so you might not want one in your room."

Christine said nothing. After a moment, Melogian added, her voice still gentle: "You didn't have me called to ask me what time it was, surely?"

Christine shook her head. She had belatedly realized she had not even greeted Melogian. "May I . . . please speak with you in private, Melogian? We can go in my room. Please?"

Melogian borrowed a candle from the game room to light their way. Once the door had shut behind them Christine sat down on the edge of her bed. She closed her eyes to ease the words out.

"I've remembered something, Melogian. When I was . . . seven years old, Katia, a girl living down our street, got angry with me; I don't remember why. Maybe I wouldn't share my doll, I don't know. She . . . she shoved me, hard, and I fell and scraped my elbow."

The memory possessed the vividness of a nightmare, every tatter of remembrance charged with an import it never should have carried. Christine went on, her voice breaking.

"I ran home. I didn't tell Uncle, I didn't tell anyone. There was no reason. There wasn't any blood; maybe just one drop. I'd scraped myself before; I just washed it and put on a plaster. It was just a small wound, so small! The next day, there was an ambulance at their house and long black streaks above a window. I asked Uncle what happened and he wouldn't tell me. At school I heard there had been a fire and Katia and her mother had been . . ." She opened her eyes, looked at the wall. "B-burned to death." She forced the next words out through a constricted throat. "She died . . . she died because she hurt me, didn't she?"

Melogian used a soothing tone. "Not necessarily, Christine. Children are not responsible for everything they do. An act of anger need not be one of malice. I cannot say how the Law operates in made worlds in cases like this. . . ."

"I can tell when you lie, Melogian! Stop lying to me!"

"All right," said Melogian, looking Christine in the eye. "I will not lie to you. Down in made worlds, the Law acts in ways less acute than it does in the true realm, but its rule extends there in full nevertheless. Anyone who hurt you in the made world would die just as surely as here, though perhaps not as spectacularly and immediately. There is historical precedent for this—I won't go into the details. The fact is if that girl meant to harm you, in fullness of intent, and if the innocence of childhood had left her, then yes, the Law did strike her down."

"So I killed them. Katia and her mother."

"No! You did nothing to harm her; what happened was none of your doing."

"She didn't know; she had no idea who I was or what would happen. . . ."

" 'Those who ignore the Law, yet are subject to it.' I'm sorry, Christine. I really am."

Melogian reached out to Christine, who shrank back. "Don't touch me! I don't want you to hurt me!"

"I'm not going to harm you."

"How can I take the chance?"

"The Law is stern, but not cruel. I don't mean to hurt you and that is enough. Even if I stabbed you through the heart, if it was not by intent, I would not suffer retribution."

"Tell that to Katia and her mother! But then, they don't exist, do they? Quentin told me that's how you people see things. Everyone I knew back home is just a dream to you, right? So you don't care; it doesn't matter what happened to them. Freynie can die tomorrow and you won't know, none of you will care!"

Melogian shook her head and sat down next to Christine. "The made worlds are real, and so is everything within them. They just aren't real in the same way you and I are. The philosophers say they are 'veracious yet absonant.' But they are real enough to matter. I truly am sorry about what happened."

"I never wanted . . . never . . . ," sobbed Christine.

"You were not responsible," said Melogian, spacing her words. Christine sank into despair.

"So what else is there to the Law? How many surprises like that does it have for me? How many ways can I kill people without wanting to?"

"The Law is a big subject. And we can't read it in the Book, we can only deduce it from what we see."

"What have people deduced, then? Tell me! I have to know!"

Melogian put out three fingers and rested her left hand on them, as if tempted to count. "Time only moves forward. The dead may not be brought back to life. None may sail beyond the sunset. None may soar higher than the sky. None may delve deeper than the roots of the mountains. The throne of Chrysanthe may not remain unfilled. Nothing tangible may be apported from a made world into the true realm. . . . There are several good books that deal with the Law; if you want, I shall take you to the library and you can borrow them."

"And what happens to people who break those Laws?" asked Christine. "I suppose they die?"

"There is only one Law and people seldom die of it. The frontiers of the world are just that, impassable bounds. Any fool can thrust herself off a cliff and fall to her death. It would be childish to blame the Law for her destruction. There is no way you yourself can kill anyone with the Law, unless you were to push him off that cliff."

Christine was crying, finally. "Oh God," she said, "oh God, I'm sorry for Katia. I didn't know. . . ."

Melogian reached out to her again and this time the princess allowed herself to be touched. She let the sorceress cradle her in her arms and stroke her hair, as she grieved for those the Law had condemned.

BOOK IV

The Book of Shades

1. Celebrations

With the dawn of the fifteenth of Summereve, the three days of celebration for Christine's return began. From Testenel the news had gone forth, carried by skyship to the capital cities, and spreading farther, though more slowly, from these points. The farther away from the center of the world one stood, the less relevant the news was and the less it was believed. There were anomalous regions here and there: a town of skeptics in Temerorn whose population grew furious at the fraud the king sought to perpetrate, a tiny village in western Estephor that burst into bacchanals of joy.

Tiellorn, oldest city of mankind, had draped itself in festive colors and prepared to enjoy the three days to the full. Even though the city itself offered entertainments aplenty, a steady stream of sightseers trekked from the city to the gates of Testenel, where they were obdurately refused admission. The more persistent of them made camp at the periphery of the castle, erecting a shantytown of enthusiasts. King Edisthen suffered them to remain, though soldiers were dispatched to patrol the area and prevent serious mischief.

For Christine, the first shock of this period was the change of quarters. To wake up in the suite she had initially slept in had been disturbing enough; this latest awakening was almost surreal. The princess's bedchamber was a treasure box of ornaments, dripping with pearls, crusted with jewels. An instant after this shock came the remembered guilt over Katia and her mother. She had unburdened herself of the worst of it in the early hours of the night. What remained had acquired a different flavor: ranker, reminding her of a cut that had become infected. But there was less poison to harm her overall; and after some painful moments she was able to rise and draw the curtains, willing to face the day.

Reflected sunlight filled her bedroom. As had been the case in the Demmerel Chambers, the light came from the system of mirrors deployed at the periphery of the towers. To look outside was to see in a mirror a patch of blue sky in which the sun swam, its glow mottled with red, a reminder that this was by no means the cosmos she was used to.

As soon as she had opened the drapes, there was a knock at the door of her room. Christine said, "Enter" in a hesitant voice; in came Althea, accompanied by another maid, whom she introduced as Rann. They carried a dressing gown, slippers, and a fistful of hairpins. Deftly, without a by your leave, they took charge of Christine.

She felt almost like a doll these girls were playing with. In a trice she was out of her bedroom, her nightclothes whisked away and the dressing gown wrapped tightly around her. The two maids led her to the bathroom, an extravagance of sea-green tiles and fish motifs, where the tub awaited her pleasure. Her hair was pinned up lest it get wet, and she was deposited into the water like a baby.

It surprised Christine how muted her reaction was. She should have been blushing furiously, sending the maids out of the room in outrage. But the previous day's events had left her numb. To go on, she must accept her status as a princess of the realm, and submit to this kind of treatment. Also, there was something in Althea and Rann's demeanor that insisted they were almost not to be noticed; that they were extensions of Christine herself. Doubtless Rann was also a graduate of the selection process that Althea had passed through. There was nothing forceful about their care, nor anything tentative. Rather, quiet competence that compelled cooperation.

Still, Christine felt some uneasiness. These maids were too much like what she had dreamed of being, once: inconspicuous, unnoticed, unimportant. She looked up at Rann, who was soaping her shoulder, and the girl's gaze slid away, until she looked at Christine only from the corner of her sight.

Christine felt a pang of fear. This young woman, older than herself, stronger, and probably much wiser, was a person in her own right. Christine might hold absolute power over her maids, yet it remained that the maids were controlling Christine at present. And they would for the foreseeable future. *They will know me in ways others won't,* Christine thought. *They could tell people anything, they could spread falsehoods about me, they could hurt me. . . .*

How could anyone entrust themselves to servants? The idea struck her that rulers were in turn ruled by those who served them most closely. How many princesses back in her world had been seduced by their chauffeurs, their bodyguards? Had there been kings in the Medieva who lived in fear of the power a simple butler wielded over them?

But no, Althea had told her the previous day: Both she and Rann would have been chosen with the utmost care. Discretion, an even temper, utter loyalty to the blood royal. It wasn't just the bloodthirsty Law that compelled it, but common sense.

Once Christine's bath was done, the maids led her out, dried her, and offered underlinen. The bra was a ghastly affair of lace that itched ferociously; Christine rejected it after ten seconds and demanded a plainer one, which was produced with some reluctance.

Now came the chore of choosing outerwear. Christine had racks and racks of dresses from which to choose, most of them, in her opinion, fit only for a wax dummy in a museum window. She picked a green dress that was encumbered with a minimum of lace and embroidery, hoping it would prove reasonably comfortable to move in. She dared not broach the subject of trousers: She had seen some women wearing them in Chrysanthe, but they had all been soldiers. She doubted the female nobility affected trousers. And this dress was a very good fit. Althea made to pull the laces in the back tighter; Christine stopped her, worried that the dress might be less comfortable. Althea informed her the dress had been made to her exact measurements, something Christine refused to believe until her maid pointed out the existence of several full-length fleshpaint portraits of her. The measurements had been taken from those. For thirteen years, dressmakers had kept Christine's wardrobe current, against the possibility of her return, modeling the clothes against the proportions revealed by the fleshpaint portraits.

Defeated, Christine let Althea tighten the laces to the intended degree, and was forced to admit the dress felt distinctly better fitted. When the girls proposed arranging her hair, she did not protest. The experience was rather soothing; the maids combed her hair gently and arranged it with a few further pins. When they were done, Althea held up a hand mirror. Christine could not restrain a smile at the face in the mirror, very much her own, but given a better balance by her hairstyle.

She was escorted back to the main chamber of her apartments, Althea promising breakfast. A third maid was present. "Messages for Her Highness," she announced, holding out two sheets of paper laid upon a tray, folded and sealed.

Christine took them with a pounding heart. The next-to-last letter she'd received had been from Freynie Long, two years ago and worlds away, when Freynie was at camp. She still remembered the ending, Freynie to a T: *Nearly drowned in the lake yesterday. Wish you were here. Love, Freynie.* And the letter after that had been Quentin's message, with its bright unreal stamp in what she now recognized as the colors of the realm, the letter that had turned her life around. . . .

The messenger had gone, but Althea and Rann hovered near her. "Give me a moment," said Christine, and they withdrew a few paces off, against the walls, like decorative statues. With icy fingers Christine broke the seal on the first message. She had to squint over the crabbed letters to make sure she correctly deciphered the words.

> *Lady Christine,*
>
> *Have left at dawn on orders from the king yr father. Expect my return by nightfall, or early tom. morning at the latest. Be assured that even though I am away, I remain aware of what goes on in Testenel & what befalls you in particular. You are quite safe; & I go to make you safer still.*
>
> > *Melogian std. Orion*

Christine reread the message, twice, frowning at the odd signature. Despite Melogian's reassurances, she felt vulnerable knowing that the sorceress was not within Testenel. She had sat down at a little table and remained for so long motionless that the maids began to fret. Finally, Althea could remain silent no longer. "Isn't m'lady opening the king's message?"

Christine set Melogian's letter down, examined the other's huge purple seal. She shone the reflected sunlight across it to better distinguish the relief: a crown of a dozen points over three parallel lines. Finally, she broke it and opened the letter. In contrast to Melogian's dreadful penmanship, the king's letter was scribed in a flawless hand.

> *My dearest daughter,*
>
> *Today begin the three days of celebration I declared in honor of your return. I can barely conceive of the pain you have endured in your journey back, and so I want this time to be a happy one for you. I understand that it is very difficult for you to be in my*

*presence; I shall not impose myself upon you. You are free to wander across Testenel as
you will, or remain in your chambers if this is your pleasure.*

*All my court hopes for a chance to see you and talk to you. Should you wish to oblige
them in this, there will be special occasions each evening. I shall not be present; if someone has the temerity to ask about this, do not reply.*

*I do not need to see you to be happy: Merely knowing that you are back amongst us
fills my heart with more joy than I can express. Whatever you desire, you may ask it of
me, and I shall grant it. I am*

*Your loving father,
Edisthen, King of Chrysanthe*

Christine put the letter down and sighed. She could feel the king's emotions
through his words, no matter how restrained his style. But even reading the letter
had sent shivers through her. No, she would not come into Edisthen's presence at
this time. She wasn't yet ready for it. In fact, she felt ready for nothing whatsoever.

She remained sunk in a reverie for a long while, until Rann coughed politely as
she delivered a third message, which had just come in. Christine picked it up and
discovered that in fact, it was a schedule of activities, detailing what was to take
place within Testenel during the celebrations. She was about to toss it aside when
she realized with amazement that it had been printed. Not neatly so: The dark-blue
ink had soaked the fibers of the sheet to excess and the letters sometimes blurred
into one another. But still, this was the product of a press.

She looked at the schedule again, and her initial rejection of its offerings softened. After all, she couldn't stay within this suite all her life. She had no interest in
the athletic contests or the noonday banquet, but there was a play this afternoon,
what Quentin had called the closest thing to television in Chrysanthe. To attend an
event where she would not be the focus of attention was a welcome prospect.

Until then, there were hours to be filled. She looked at the thick purple wax she
had broken into two halves, the line of cleavage striking through the crown diagonally, spoiling the lovely detail of the relief. She should at least reply to her father's
message. She asked for a pen and was presented with a gold-nibbed stylus and an
inkwell hollowed from a gigantic baroque pearl. For paper there was a stack of thick
sheets, so fancy she was loath to apply ink to it before she had organized her
thoughts properly. Once more she missed the pencil cup she had once told Quentin
felt like the most important thing in the world to her, the blue-lined cheap notebook
paper that came in blocks of three hundred sheets wrapped in crinkling plastic. She
shook her head to clear it. *Dear Father,* the letter would begin, of course. *Dear Father,*
with a capital *F*, yes. But then what? She couldn't hold it all in her head. One sheet
would absolutely have to serve as a draft. Remember: She was a princess, and could
waste however many tons of parchment she chose. . . .

❧ Quentin arrived at the site of his meeting a half hour early, too keyed-up to wait
any longer. During his stay at court a decade earlier he had spent many a pleasant
hour in one of the castle's myriad rooms: a strangely cramped hall with a high ceiling given over to cobwebs and dust, furnished with a litter of mismatched chairs and

a once-splendid table spoiled by a ruined leg. Ignored by the cleaning staff, it had become a favorite haunt of his and his companions'. There they had played endless games of cards, drunk cheap ale, and made grandiose plans for the future.

The hall had not changed: From the second he stepped inside, Quentin felt himself taken back in time. His assigned chair stood at its usual place; it made the same sound as ever when he scraped it away from the table. He was about to sit down when a sardonic voice rose behind him.

"Hail, Sir Quentin."

Quentin turned around to embrace his friend Kaldar and got his first shock: The years had not been kind to him. He had been the eldest of the band at twenty-three; now his hairline had receded most of the way up his forehead and he looked a decade older than he actually was.

"I brought something to drink," said Kaldar, hoisting a flagon bearing a shoddily printed label. When Quentin burst out laughing he continued: "Yeah, the same swill we used to quaff. Why break with tradition?"

Quentin had no taste for alcohol so early in the morning, but he did take a whiff of the beer's familiar sourish bouquet, for nostalgia's sake. The others filtered in one by one, greeting Quentin with a mix of enthusiasm and diffidence. In the end all were sitting around the table: "old man" Kaldar, little Felgun who had finally grown to a decent height, Faye who now—Quentin's second shock, far worse than the first—wore not even the pale gown of a novice, but the red habit of an initiate, Thellen looking scruffier than ever, and Sandenin together with a pregnant Bronna.

"Saw Dorith on my way here," said Felgun. "Said he wanted to come, but he didn't have the time. He says hello, Quentin."

"Right." Quentin nodded, at a loss. He knew himself to be the focus of their attention, but he wanted to shout at them that things were backward: They themselves should have been the subject of discussion, not him. All he had done was rescue Christine, the thing he had promised he would do; they on the other hand had changed, almost beyond recognition, and this was a far more radical development. . . .

"Did Sandy tell you why Radell didn't want to be here?" asked Kaldar. "It's really not his fault—"

"It does not matter. I am glad to see you all here," said Quentin. "This means a lot to me. Bronna, you look . . . well, not twelve anymore."

Bronna grinned at him, a hand on her swollen belly. "That's the first time in a long while you haven't called me Bug," she said. "Are you sure you don't want me to leave you grown-ups alone?"

"Don't you dare be rude to our Quentin," chided Faye. "He's all flustered to start with, you'll have him crying in a moment." She reached out to Quentin, took his hand with an easy familiarity. "And that wouldn't do," she added. "We're all very proud of him, and we should be celebrating him."

"Hear, hear!" said Kaldar, raising his flagon very high as if to drink a toast, then almost falling off his chair. It was an old, often-repeated stunt, but it still worked; there was general laughter, and the unease Quentin felt thawed somewhat. He asked a few questions, answered those of his friends. When they asked about his journey, he told the story as fully as he dared, though it felt as if he were unburdening himself of a shameful secret.

It was several hours before their meeting broke up, and on vastly better terms than Quentin had hoped for earlier, when faced with Sandenin's reluctance. With many promises of future gatherings, his friends went their various ways. Faye alone remained with him when he finally asked her what had happened.

"What?" she said. "I'm as you see me. Is it so strange, a woman taking God's way? I'd have thought you'd be proud of me."

"That is not what I mean," said Quentin, feeling himself blushing. "When I last saw you . . . when I left . . . you were not . . ."

"Quentin, I was fifteen. My jugs had sprouted, but I was still a tomboy. Some of us bloom late, you know that."

"So when did you . . . bear?"

"My little Rose is almost four. You can come visit us if you like."

"Oh, yes; of course, I would love to."

A frown pinched her smooth face. "So what is it, then? You're still upset."

"It hardly matters," said Quentin.

"Yeah, like God's nuts it does. Come on Quentin, it's me. You always could tell me anything, so tell."

Quentin looked away. "I was remembering . . . what happened long ago," he blurted out.

"What, that kiss? Oh, come on!" Faye burst out, incredulous.

"What do you expect?" retorted Quentin, his face hot. "We left on bad terms, we never settled things."

"Bad terms? Have you spent nine years thinking I was mad at you?"

"Well, you did not look happy!"

"I wasn't comfortable with it," said Faye. "I said I was still a tomboy then. But I never was angry at you. It's normal to want a kiss from a friend before you leave for a journey you might not return from."

"Well, it has always bothered me."

"Oh, Quentin, why does it always have to be about you?"

"What do you mean? It is *not* about me; it is about you!"

"You make it all about you: your betrayal of a friend. Your terrible secret! Come on, Quentin. You didn't rape me; you stole a kiss."

Quentin, flustered, said nothing.

"See," continued Faye, "that's why you became a knight: because it's in your blood to carry extravagant burdens. That's why I became a priestess, because it's in mine to just live my life in the sight of God." She took his hands. "I'm sorry if you hoped for more from me, but it wasn't in me to give back then. And even if I had been older, I would never have chosen you, not in a million years, and I'm sorry but that's just the way it is. I'll always love you and be your friend, and I want you to come see me and Rose and my husband and have meals with us and be our good friend Quentin, the great hero. Can you do that?"

Quentin nodded. "Yes, of course," he said, all his self-inflicted guilt in shambles. And it seemed unavoidable then that he should add, "Will you . . . will you bless me, Little Mother?"

Faye sighed, and said, "In the sight of God, Sir Quentin, may your sins be made light, may your deeds be acknowledged, may your soul be at ease."

She left him with these words, and he found himself alone, adrift in a room out of the past, bidding farewell to the youth he had been and had left behind all unawares these many years.

❧❧ Christine spent an endless time on her letter. In all her life, she had only written a few letters, always to Freynie Long, and then only to report on the ordinary drabness of her life. She began several drafts on the one piece of paper, changing her mind time and again. By the sixth draft she had reconsidered the salutation and could no longer even trust the first two words. How was a princess supposed to express herself, anyway? Especially when she spoke a dialect of the language, full of words no one understood? It had taken her until just now to realize that no one in Chrysanthe knew what "okay" meant, and that whenever she used that word with her maids they had guessed at its significance from context, not daring to ask an impertinent question.

It was a relief when Althea reported a visitor. Setting the letter aside, Christine was already preparing herself to greet Quentin when Althea identified the visitor as the priestess Bridianne. Swallowing down her hesitation, Christine agreed to meet the priestess in the sitting room of her suite.

Rann saw to Christine's comfort for a few minutes while Althea went to speak with Bridianne. Once Christine was arranged in a chair behind a table, Rann knelt at her side, much to Christine's surprise, and Althea showed the priestess in.

For an instant Christine considered the plump blond woman with puzzlement: Why should she seem familiar? But then she realized she had seen Bridianne before: On her first morning here, as she had left her rooms in the Demmerel Chambers, two people had looked at her from a cross-corridor. Then as now Bridianne had been wearing deep red. On this occasion Christine took the time to examine Bridianne's clothes and noticed that the apparent unbroken expanse of dark crimson was an illusion: There was elaborate embroidery on the dress, strands of beads dangling in a few places, but everything of the same hue.

The priestess dropped to one knee and said, "My Lady Christine." Christine started to rise, eliciting a startled look from Rann, then decided she should remain seated. "Er, welcome," she said. Bridianne took this as her cue to rise. Before Althea could indicate a chair, Bridianne seated herself with a simper.

"Your Highness," she began in a voice that aged her a good decade and a half past the midthirties she seemed, "I have come to your side at this time because I was sure Your Highness would have special need of me."

"I . . . I don't know what you mean," said Christine.

"Doesn't Your Highness want consolation for her soul? I have brought my counsel and the wisdom of the ancients."

Bridianne fished out a leather-bound book from a pocket of her robes and presented it with a flourish.

"I thought my lady might have wanted me to read excerpts from the Lesser Book in her company. I am spiritual adviser to several of the nobles at this court, and a second-tier priestess, below only High Priestess Ianthe. Perhaps you would like us to begin with a page from the *Fires of Day*? There is a wonderful passage I've always loved . . ."

"You're a . . . a priestess?" said Christine.

"Ah, yes, Your Highness, as I have just said," replied Bridianne.

"You don't mean a nun?"

"No, Your Highness." She gestured at her habits. "I am a full priestess, not a cloistered sister." Bridianne's smile had been replaced by a crestfallen gape of the mouth.

"Sorry, it's just that I've only met men priests. Never a woman."

Bridianne opened her eyes wide in shock. "But my lady!" she protested. "That was two thousand years ago!"

"What?"

"Chrysanthe has not had priests in two millennia, Your Highness," Bridianne explained as she would to a child. "To have men intercede with God breeds fanaticism; rival creeds sprout from quibbles over commas. For two thousand years only women have worn the habit."

Christine blinked at her. "Well," she said, "I've only met with male priests when I went to Temple."

Bridianne's expression grew almost tragic. "Oh, Your Highness, how sad. I know, of course, what you've been through. You've been lied to all your life, fed the twisted dogma of the made worlds. And from *men*!"

Christine had barely formulated a response in her mind when Bridianne went on.

"Thankfully, now that you've returned, you will be able to find solace in the Lesser Book. It has no equal in the world, and stands infinitely above all the lies of the made worlds."

Christine felt annoyed by the boast. She remembered many a fine book she had read in Errefern, and rose to the defense of her forever-lost library. "If it's so wonderful, why do you call it the Lesser Book? It sounds like a Byblos to me. . . . Shouldn't it be the Greater Book?"

Bridianne mastered the horrified expression that flitted across her face then set Christine straight.

"No, Your Highness, the *Great* Book is the Words of God, from which the world arose. This book is the *Lesser* Book, written by the wisest women and men of the distant past. Some of its passages go back nearly to the First."

"Okay. I mean, very well," Christine yielded. "There's no need to explain the Great Book, Melogian told me about it."

"But she did not, Your Highness, tell you about the Lesser Book? Well, I'm not surprised. Yet this book is what we turn to when we try to understand the ways of God. May I?"

Not pausing an instant for permission, Bridianne had already opened the book's gilt cover and scanned through the thin pages with a practiced flick of the fingers.

"Here. Perhaps after all the Third Descant of Rubeus is more appropriate. 'For what does it avail them to wonder at the pace of the world, whose life is blown by mighty winds? The greatest of us is like a mote in a gale, and our destiny is not truly ours to shape. . . .'"

Bridianne had much too fine a reading voice: Every phrase deserved its own rise and fall of tone, every punctuation mark its significant pause. The effect was to drown out any meaning inherent in the words, turning the written lines into a song as heartfelt and portentous as it was unintelligible. Christine recalled Uncle once getting a visit from a couple of itinerant proselytes who nearly had to be kicked out of the house. Bridianne went on and on while Christine hoped the next break would be the final one. Eventually, Christine was able to marshal her courage and cut the priestess off. "Excuse me," she said. Bridianne read on for three or four words, reached a punctuation mark, and looked up from the page, drawing breath for her pursuance of the recitation. "Er, no offense," hazarded Christine, "but I . . . don't want to be read to at the moment."

Bridianne gave her head an elegant shake and lowered her gaze.

"Your Highness of course may do as she wishes. I merely hoped to offer spiritual solace, and—"

"I appreciate it, I do. Please don't get offended. But I don't feel like reading this right now."

Bridianne inclined her head, the picture of obedience. "Of course, my lady. Now, I didn't know if this suite had been adequately furnished with reading materials as yet. I brought this copy of the Lesser Book with the thought that, perhaps, I could leave it here for Your Highness to peruse at a later time?"

"Sure. Just leave it, ah . . . give it to Rann, here, and I'll look at it later."

"As Your Highness wishes." Bridianne handed the book to Rann, who had risen up from her near invisibility by Christine's side, and who deftly went to put it on a delicate side table.

"Well then," Bridianne went on, "unless Your Highness has need of me, I shall take my leave."

"Thanks—thank you for coming to visit me."

Althea showed Bridianne out, and Christine looked at Rann, whose face remained guilessly impassive. She did not think she had handled that encounter well, but she had never liked attending Temple. And while a female priest was a novelty to her, who had never seen a Bharati in her life except in pictures, Bridianne seemed to her far closer to an importunate proselyte than anything else.

Sighing, Christine rose from her chair, intent on getting her letter done. At least this encounter had cleared away her hesitation; it seemed absolutely clear to her now how she was to write: directly and to the point. There was no way for her to ever match the courtiers' flowery turns of phrase or the stylistic elegance of the Lesser Book, and there should be no need. Let Edisthen read her words as she meant them; it should be more than enough to make him happy. Once the letter was done she would eat lunch, and after that, maybe she would attend the play announced in the printed program.

Casimir had been dreaming he was dead; woke up to find he was alive after all, and sighed in mingled pleasure and regret. His bedchamber was sunk in gloom as always: There were no windows, and sunlight never penetrated here. Casimir wiggled his fingers, spoke a short phrase, and motes of light emerged sizzling from his fingertips to hover in the room. This particular spell had not been cast in Chrysanthe in eight centuries; not since Red Affarian's death, upon which every last book of magic in his library had turned to a dust so fine it would seep through living flesh, and the secrets of his spells had been lost. Though not lost forever, as it turned out.

During the six months he had spent interred, Casimir had wandered a metaphysical space in which echoes of departed people perdured. This region of nonspace was subject to weird laws of distance and speed, and his first five months had been spent merely learning to move about. All around him, he could hear—though the verb was not truly appropriate—the spirits of Heroes. He yearned to reach out to them, to engage them in conversation. More than once he had felt about to give up and call for help—but he knew this would vitiate the whole enterprise; his will prevailed and he remained bent upon his task.

All the while his flesh was dying; the powers he had called up, that had buried him at his request, had taken no precautions to keep his body safe, nor could he have compelled them to do so. It was a gamble, but not so terrible as it might have been. Though death would have taken him irrevocably should he fail to be dug up after half a year had passed, his servants had been carefully instructed to come to him at the proper time. And as it turned out, his master Evered had panicked and disinterred him prematurely. When Casimir thought back upon it he seethed with frustration; better to focus upon what had gone right instead.

Over one hundred and fifty days in Chrysanthe elapsed before Casimir at last acquired control over his essence in the underground realm. Time passed for him in a different way than above, and the subjective span was both longer and shorter. He was nevertheless aware of urgency as he set out across the unlandscape that surrounded him.

The memories he had carried back from this place had decayed as soon as he returned to the flesh and the five mundane senses. When he cast his mind back to those days, he saw rolling hills in endless night, black on black, with here and there the golden crescent glints of wandering spirits: a feeble approximation of the reality he had experienced.

Through this realm he moved, his senses straining for what he sought. His passage roiled the very fabric of existence, and in his wake silvery lacunae arose, defects in the world, fingernail-paring gaps of nothingness. A trail of destruction that slowly faded away as the underworld reasserted itself. No others here moved in such a clumsy, destructive way, but Casimir at least could move, wherever he wanted, at adequate speed. His quarry flitted past like evanescent thoughts, but Casimir possessed vast resources of will, and on his third attempt achieved success.

The captured spirit twisted itself into fantastic conformations, sought retreat within itself, a snake swallowing its own tail into nonexistence; but Casimir knew the trick, and everted unspace even as the spirit attempted flight, so that its desperate thrust for freedom delivered it firmly into the wizard's grasp.

It was Casimir who entered into the spirit then; a ghost of the upper world bloomed into being all about him, as he merged his essence with the other's. He stood on a city street; after a second he recognized Tiellorn—a Tiellorn of the far past. All around him people walked about, though their faces were blank, devoid of intelligence. Their clothes were subtly strange, and the buzz of their conversation could not be understood. Across the cobbled street stood a man of uncertain age, tall and almost gaunt, wrapped in a thick purplish-black robe. A shock of mingled black and blond hair rose straight from his scalp; a wispy mustache reached down almost to the line of his jaw and fluttered in a warm spring wind.

The man's voice came to him very clear, as if the words were punching out holes in the air.

"Who are you?"

Casimir chuckled. "No, it is I who ask. Who are *you*, shade? Your name, if you please."

"Leave me be. Your presence here is an aberration. You are the thing that tried to capture me. Go away at once!"

Casimir took three steps toward the man, who retreated only two.

"You do not have the strength to cast me away. Your power may be effective against the other dwellers in this realm, but mine comes from the world of the living, old mage. And you, in case you didn't know, are dead."

"I am aware of that," said the spirit, who once again retreated as Casimir advanced. A town-dweller who was about to collide with him simply ceased to exist as he came too close. The walls of the buildings wavered, and they stood suddenly in another part of the city, at one of the entrances to the North Market. Above the rooftops, the towers of Testenel reared up, but their blue gleam was leached away as if by a huge distance. Casimir was another step closer to the gaunt man.

"You are the soul of a dead Hero," said Casimir, spreading his arms at his sides and hunching down his head on his bull neck.

"You are quite wrong." The man gestured and a swarm of angular gray shapes came into being, flew at Casimir, who simply batted them away. The man retreated again, his green eyes wide. "There are no such things as souls, or if there are, at death they rejoin God the Maker. I am not a soul."

"Tell me, then, what you are," said Casimir in a reasonable tone. "I am only here to learn."

The man climbed up a flight of stairs, his face still turned toward Casimir, who followed relentlessly. "I am an imprint," said the man, whose hands now trembled on the metal railing. "If an ink dark enough and abundant enough is applied to the page of a book, sometimes it stains the facing page, or sinks through the parchment. The letters may not be read; they do not fit the part of the story they find themselves in; yet there is something there nevertheless."

"A lovely analogy," breathed Casimir, who now stood two steps below the tall man. "The ink of Heroes is dark, then, and stains the pages of the Book in which they find themselves written—is this true of all Heroes? And ordinary men, such as myself—do any leave imprints as you do?"

Casimir stood one step below the man, who had reached the top of the stairs. A door to his right led into a building, but he could not open it.

As Casimir took the last step, the man whispered, "Perhaps, yes; all the Heroes, in likelihood." As the magician's hands grabbed the purple-black folds of his robe, the man gasped, "But ordinary folk—I am sorry, but I think not." As the thick fingers closed on his throat, he forced out, "Please—" Then Casimir broke his neck.

He tore the body apart, methodically. Bones snapped and ligaments parted; the flesh was hot in his mouth. Splatters of blood dripped on the wall and drew the name *Oschimald* in crimson. Casimir, a careful student of history, nodded in satisfaction that his initial guess had been confirmed, and continued his meal.

The spells came to him as he sucked the marrow from the bones; he was aware that this was no more than a small part of Oschimald's knowledge. Most of that knowledge lay embedded in the fabric of the ghost reality that surrounded them. Had Casimir been possessed of greater power still, or of a sufficiency of time, he might have consumed the whole of this place, and unlocked all that Oschimald, court mage to Queen Aillanne, eleven hundred years dead, had known. But here as everywhere there were limits; the Law extended to this nonplace as much as it did in the upper world.

Yet the harvest was enormously rewarding for all that. A large body of theory, abstract understandings that culminated in three summoning incantations of remarkable potency. Workings that altered facets of physical reality were the most easily understood spells, and their secrets could never be truly lost. But summonings were a different matter: In the early days of the world, it had been almost trivial to call things into existence, as the forces of Creation still stalked the world and the First People's wizards needed barely more than to express their wishes. In these latter ages, increasingly complex rituals were needed, and it had become infeasible to derive the necessary incantations. Unless one were a Hero oneself, like that buffoon Orion, and came into the world brimming with unearned knowledge, what had been lost in the arts of summoning could not be regained.

So it was with various other branches of magic, whose workings had become increasingly laborious and whose knowledge had been mostly lost after the Carmine War, in which the fifteen greatest mages of the land had died, leaving badly trained apprentices to carry on in their tradition. Casimir would not have risked his very life for anything but the richest of prizes—a hoard of spells long gone from living memory.

Oschimald had lived long before the Carmine War; his knowledge was delightfully fresh, almost pristine—it tasted to Casimir like ice shaved from an Estephorin glacier and flavored with syrup of mint, a coolness that filled his mouth and spread to his innards. He laughed aloud in pleasure, at the bright forms that pinwheeled through his mind, at the realization of what he could—would!—do with this new-found power.

And this was but the first of his captures; there were hundreds more flitting about the underworld, these ink traces, as Oschimald had named them, echoes of Heroes long gone. All there for him to sate his appetite. He had told Evered he would go looking for his father's soul during his quest, but he had guessed from the start that would be pointless.

Casimir withdrew from Oschimald's shattered, decaying ghost-self. The underworld returned about him, the pitch-dark unlandscape with its drifting motes of not-quite-souls. Before/above him what had been Oschimald's imprint quivered and fell/rose toward the ground. It did not vanish altogether; though its brilliance had dimmed and its shape wavered, as if it tore and remade itself on the fabric of space, it persisted. Casimir had expected to destroy the being utterly; here was an interesting development—but time pressed him even more now. He could not waste hours dwelling upon the fate of what had been Oschimald. He moved on, swollen with power, and behind/below him his trail stretched forth, a silvery, dotted wound in space.

He became better and better at the task as it progressed: To find, capture, and consume Oschimald took him eighteen days in the upper world; the next one, Weoll the Flame, he caught, raped, and ate in six; the next two he disposed of in three days. And even while Evered was digging him out of the clay with a gardener's trowel, Casimir snared Ilianrod, then took the leisure to bind and hurt her for subjective days, until in the extremity of torment she brought forth what he required. He decided to let her live in the end, because she excited some dim stirrings of pity in him, with her blond curls all in disarray, framing the gaping pits of her bloodied eye sockets; she looked like a child's abandoned toy, and Casimir found that thought very sad. And now words from the upper world broke through the nonspace and impinged upon him. Some barely familiar voice was calling his name. . . .

He had been back in the flesh for months now, and yet often still when he awoke he had some trouble remembering where he was. It would seem for long moments that the world around him was painted on canvas, a perfect trompe l'oeil, that in fact there was nothing around him but empty space and the flat images of things on a sphere shaped by his own mind, or that of a dead Hero. Sweet Ilianrod and her gouged orbits floated in back of him, he could sense her. . . .

Then the illusion would collapse, the primacy of his mundane senses reassert itself, and Casimir would sigh, at the same time relieved and cheated.

The motes of light swam all around the room, spreading a flickering light that limned every object in glowing edges. Casimir set his feet on the floor and rose, feeling gravity pulling his flesh toward the ground. So unlike the freedom he had won in the nonworld, where he could move in any direction he chose like a predator of the deep ocean. . . . Spells of flight did not figure amongst those he had forced from Ilianrod or Weoll the Flame. He could spin up a whirl as well as any other wizard, but it was the dreamlike power of self-levitation he would have liked. Yet another strike against Evered; in the week aboveground left to Casimir, what could he not have wrung from the shades of all the remaining wizards?

Casimir rubbed his whiskers. Get dressed, eat, and then to work. Seven demons waited for him within the earth, their locations wrested from Buell's docile spirit. The Archivist's mind had been like a desk of a thousand thousand drawers, all disorganized, storing a priceless treasure map within a heap of farming records; Casimir had tired of rifling it after a while and set the Hero free. Now he thought he should return to Buell's shade, take the time to pressure all the knowledge he could from it. Not yet, though, for he would not survive a second such journey so soon after the first. There were months, a year maybe, to wait before he could risk it again. By that time Edisthen's reign would be over, the land under the rule of Vaurd's line once more. Twenty years Casimir had spent in exile from the center of things, making his war on Orion. Events were coming to a head at last, and yet he felt almost a fear of the future. It would be over all too soon. There was no rush; it was better to enjoy events to their fullest as they unfolded. There were no greater delights than puppet shows, especially when the puppets were flesh; but they all ended too soon. The best part of a show was just before the curtain rose, the delicious anticipation of all the forces of story gathering. So it must be with this, his own show. Time to take some of the marionettes from storage and ready the strings.

&e Time passed by in fits and starts for Christine. She managed to finish her letter to her father—so much sweat and toil for so little, in the end, but she was glad to be able to send it off. She ate a light lunch, and finally, moved more by an apprehension of imminent boredom than by the actual sentiment, she risked venturing out of her suite. Quentin hadn't shown up. She was both dismayed and relieved; had he been with her, she would have felt invulnerable, but she might also have felt out of place, as if Chrysanthe were but another way station on their endless flight through the made world. She must get used to the presence of others besides her closest circle. So she gritted her teeth and walked about the passages of Testenel.

She was surrounded by armed guards, who kept people at bay with ruthless efficiency. There was ample need of their services, since gawkers and well-wishers gathered in her path wherever she went. She would have cut the excursion short very soon, but in fact she'd had a destination in mind. A play was being presented not so far from her chambers, and she would have liked to see it. Althea had assured her there was a royal box set well apart from other seats. And in fact the way to it was sealed behind a guarded door, so that Christine was able to escape the throng before its pressure grew unbearable.

The theater was surprisingly large, with ranks of comfortable seats framing a deep stage. The royal box was set high up, facing another such across the chamber. As Christine seated herself, the entire audience rose to its feet and cheered her; but, thank God, they relented after a few minutes and seated themselves again. Christine sensed their gazes as if they were velvety soft blows, but she knew that for an illusion, and eventually regained her composure. Meanwhile, the play began and Christine opened her eyes wide, ready to drink in the culture of an unfamiliar world.

The whole experience was appalling. The actors stood rooted to the spot, taking up extravagant poses, and shouted their lines in bombastic tones. Scenery was limited to a handful of backdrops, painted with skill but in garish colors. At the most awkward moments a minor character would burst into song to underscore a point that had already been made twice by everybody else. Meanwhile half a dozen bare-breasted coryphées darted across the stage. The first act ended with the main character getting his arse kicked by three different people in succession. The audience roared with laughter, and Christine wondered if the play had been meant as a farce, a parody of the theater.

She whispered questions to Althea during the intermission and was assured that this was in fact a great classic of the Temerorni repertory, one of the best-known plays in the world, and a deeply serious one. The second act opened with a sudden betrayal, immediate suspicions falling on the wrong party. Still protesting his innocence, the young knight Caldasce was soon dragged to the scaffold, whereupon his head was struck off in a fountain of gore, and Christine nearly lost her lunch.

It took her a good thirty seconds to manage to lift her gaze back to the stage. The audience was shouting itself hoarse in a mingling of horror and delight. For a moment, Althea had forgotten Christine and drunk in the awful sight; now she cuddled Christine in her arms and reassured her it had all been trickery.

"I know that," said Christine through clenched teeth, though in truth for a horrible moment she had doubted, ready to believe the worst. What did she know of reality, of Chrysanthe, after all?

Eventually she was able to sit upright again. Some in the audience must have seen her reaction, sunk in shadow as she was. At this moment she did not care. Nor did she desire to prolong the torture. As Caldasce's fiancée pounded the floor and shrieked her grief in a voice that could shatter glass, Christine rose from her seat and exited the box.

She was more than glad to return to her suite, and barely noticed the gauntlet of well-wishers she had to run. For a few hours, she quite enjoyed her solitude. Her internal clock still out of sync with the sun, she took a long nap, and avoided dreaming of the beheading scene, though she did have a dream about picking flowers whose intensity hinted at symbolic meanings.

She expected a visit from Quentin, and did not get one. She could have sent for him, but she remembered too acutely sending for Melogian the night before, and resolved not to act like a spoiled child. So she steeled herself to patience. Supper came, and soon afterward she decided to venture out again. There were gardens within Testenel, which Althea assured her were splendid. Notwithstanding her dream, she knew flowers would not offer the same risk of stomach-turning surprise as what passed in Chrysanthe for thespian pursuits. She asked Rann to tell Quentin, should he come calling at her apartments, that she had gone to visit the gardens, and prepared to go out. Althea insisted on a complete change of clothing; Christine let herself be talked into it. From the dresses appropriate for early evening, she selected one of the simplest. The skirt was dark purple, the bodice a saturated pink. She thought to recall watching a cartoon princess once wearing something similar. There was a hat as well, which she felt unsure about, but it did serve to complete the costume somewhat. The final touch would have been to be flattened into two dimensions, reduced to broad lines on colored cels, all her existence cut up into a series of frames that gave only the illusion of movement and life.

As she was about to leave, she recalled the book Bridianne had left her. In her earlier life, Christine had usually felt incomplete when she went somewhere without a book in her bag, to read at odd moments. In her flight with Quentin through the made world, she had not had time to feel that way, save perhaps in the second hotel room, when she'd looked at the glowing Byblos. She went into her sitting room and to the table where Rann had placed the book. It did not in the least resemble, either in binding or in contents, the paperbacks she used to tote around, but its heft in her hand brought a similar reassurance. And so she slid it into the woven handbag she carried on her arm. Althea, coming into the room with a piece of jewelry, gauged Christine's appearance, made a trifling adjustment to her hat, and nodded approval.

"M'lady looks gorgeous. And bringing the Lesser Book with her is a *very* nice gesture. People need to see their rulers be pious."

Christine did not tell her the true reason she had taken the book. Instead, she accepted the bracelet Althea wanted to add to her ensemble and swept out of her suite. Once more, she acquired guards at the door, and went forward into the vastness of Testenel. For a second or so she forgot her entourage and could imagine herself wandering the corridors alone, the way it ought to have been. But then people showed up, wanting to speak to her—she wondered how it was gawkers weren't camping on her doorstep, as celebrity hounds were wont to do in the life she'd known, but presumably here the guards and their blades would have dispersed such a crowd.

This time, among the folk were two young men dressed in an extravagance of clothes, carrying themselves with assurance and hauteur. Rich people, thought Christine, perfectly coiffed and dressed as such people were. She would have expected them to be tanned, but their complexions were in fact quite pale, the dabs of rouge on their cheeks making a sharp contrast. Unlike the others she'd met so far, who tended to gasp and proffer cheers, these two asked her questions, their voices pitched to carry over the surrounding hubbub. She was being invited to a nice little party up in the Tower of Owls, with all the trimmings, and surely she'd come? Bewildered, Christine didn't answer and eventually the pair were left behind as Christine and her entourage marched on.

They followed a completely new path, and soon Christine felt quite lost. All she could tell was that they were tending downward. They came to huge double doors that had been opened; and beyond them, a wilderness opened up.

The gardens were enormous; though they were perforce surrounded by the towers and buildings of Testenel, they had been landscaped with such a skill that their edges vanished from the mind's eye. All one was left with was a riot of flowers and plants, an explosion of colors, that after some minutes was revealed as carefully planned. The ground was anything but level, rising in hummocks all around pretty little alleys of crushed white stone. Some plants were familiar to Christine: evergreens, a weeping willow, peonies. But most of them astonished her. Here feathery leaves arched from the top of a smooth, slender indigo trunk; there a mass of vari-colored blossoms erupted close to the ground, the center of each flower an intense saffron, while the broad petals encircling it shaded from scarlet to deep purple. Tendrils corkscrewed from the center of a quintet of striped lanceolate leaves, their tips dusted with microscopic four-pointed flowers—unless they were enormous grains of pollen.

She wandered the alleys for a while, amazed at everything, barely aware of the gathering clots of people all about her. The sunlight was starting to dim, but it came from straight overhead, reflected by the great mirrors. Looking up, Christine saw blue towers leaning over her, about to fall; she couldn't restrain a squeak of surprise.

The sun was getting closer to the horizon and the mirrors were canted at such an angle that the surrounding architecture was also getting reflected.

By this time she had lost sight of the edges of the gardens all around; and trees provided enough shade that she need not deal with the sight of the phantom towers in the air. Still, she was feeling uncomfortable.

She stood close to a crossroads; and as she looked at the five paths meeting at that point she realized that all of them were full of people, all of them looking at her. This crowd was not as numerous as the one she had addressed on the previous day, but it was much closer to her, with nothing separating them.

Althea had noticed her unease. "Would m'lady want to rest for a moment?" she asked. "There's a pavilion right over there." Christine agreed without thinking about it. The guard escorted her across a stretch of lawn marked with a path of near-sunken stones, to a tiny rustic gazebo. Christine got inside, taking Althea with her, while the four guards stood at the entrance. And though more of the crowd had appeared—Christine could see them very well through the latticed walls—this seemed to hold the curious at bay. Christine ran a finger over her damp forehead; her hat was much too warm.

She felt almost like an animal in a zoo; she would rush back to her chambers if she could, but she was too deep within the gardens to just make a break for it. She would have to compose herself first, then gather her guard about her and walk, not run, back out of the gardens. She looked at Althea, who stood by the entrance, look-ing quite unconcerned; in fact, obviously enjoying the attention. Who could blame her? Her life's duty was to take care of the princess. Docile, trustworthy, not the sharpest tool in the shed, probably she couldn't understand why Christine should be so stressed by the circumstances.

Christine kept repeating to herself that she was safe, yet her instincts bristled. If only Quentin were with her now! She should have called for him earlier; she definitely wasn't ready to face the world on her own, not without someone she trusted at her side. Too late now; useless to scream out his name. She *had* called him to her silently once before, casting a spell, making magic without knowing it. She recalled it with a dry pang in her throat, the memory of that day still charged with dread and wonder. No, though there were flowers peeking here and there through the latticed walls, she doubted her improvised spell could work again in summoning him. It hadn't been just plucking the petals of the flower, had it? Much more had happened on that day, things much too raw that she could not really re-flect upon now.

And so she sat and gritted her teeth, wanting to calm down so badly it only tensed her the more. Eventually, she recalled the book she carried and took it out of the reticule, opened it at first at random, then carefully at the beginning. She had expected a title; in fact, it bore none. Presumably none was needed. The gilt leather covers weren't stiff as she had expected, but pleasantly supple. The book was di-vided into sections marked off by thicker pages. The very first section was titled "Analects": a series of brief passages not linked by any ordering she could discern. She paged through it quickly, found next a biographical sketch of an ancient king, who had been so pious that he praised God's mercy even as plague struck his people. Now why was she not surprised? With a sigh, Christine closed the book, still marking her place with a finger. She could never find solace in books of this sort. She needed blatant lies, stories so impossible they could not conceivably demand belief, to find a truth she could handle. The adventures of *The Cosmic Patrol* she could stomach; the heartfelt piety of King Ardech left her unmoved.

2. Wizards

From his vantage point, Quentin saw the crowd surrounding Christine ebb like water in a tide pool. Edisthen's daughter sat within a small pavilion, three of her guards blocking the entrance, the fourth circling the structure. The crowd kept its distance, barely.

It was obvious that Christine sat within, but the lattice granted her more anonymity than Quentin would have thought possible. All he could truly discern was the mass of violet fabric of her dress, the overlapping skirts so like the petals of a flower. Such a contrast to the way she had been dressed throughout their journey. It gave him a queer pang to think of it.

He recalled the pretty jacket he had purchased for her with imaginary money, and how happy and comfortable she had seemed in it. In her finery, she seemed to him no longer the same person he had rescued, but rather the incarnation of an abstract idea: the royal heir of Chrysanthe.

Quentin thought of going to her; but all around the pavilion stood dozens of people silently pressing their claims to her attention. Christine was back where she belonged now; she had become once more the princess she had forgotten she was. He could not see himself bullying his way through the crowd and gaining the sanctum of the pavilion. And so he turned and walked away, finding his task easier the further from Christine he got. She had not called for him today, and this was a good thing. More and more she would move within her own sphere, and he within his.

Quentin walked along a graveled path as it twisted and turned, and was soon surrounded by flowering hedges, with no idea where he was exactly. It reminded him of their return into Chrysanthe, and the memory brought another sharp pang with it. Coming upon a fork, he sat on a moss-covered boulder and sighed.

With the accomplishment of his quest, something inside him had vanished: The purpose that had driven him for so long was gone. Now his life, rather than fulfilled, felt pointless to him. He treasured the moments he had spent with Christine still, but he was not foolish enough to imagine there would be many more. Edisthen's promises of rewards would have brought joy to an avaricious man; yet Quentin could not consider them with any satisfaction. What was he to do? Request a demesne, a title to go with it, retire to a manor house in the marches of Archeled and brood over his past exploits? Ask to be made one of the Lady Christine's bodyguards, and spend years catching glimpses of her as she traveled from one place to another, while he aged inside his armor and grew stiff from carrying a useless weapon? Perhaps he should go in search of Orion; his power to move *beyond* still slumbered within him. He might enter Jyndyrys and cross the leagues into infinity, lose himself in another search, this one squarely impossible.

It had saddened him to see his old friends, to witness the work of time on his comrades. What they had been to each other, to him, had changed beyond repair. It wasn't that their friendship had gone sour; merely that things could never be as they had been. And yes, he was jealous of Sandenin, who was happy with Bronna, Sandenin who could with a clear conscience dismiss Quentin from his life, because he had a family now, and Quentin was still only a knight of Chrysanthe, as solitary as he had always been.

"I am lonely," Quentin confessed to the night air in a whisper. In his nine years among the made worlds, he had had time to make no friends; though he often forgot that none of these people were real, he could never thrust the knowledge out of his mind completely, making whatever companionship offered itself ring even more false.

No friends, only a few lovers, like Oru. He had been able to gain nothing better. Perhaps that was why in the end he had turned away from Lady Alicia's promises: Within the made world, he had known what it was to couple feverishly with a willing doxy; but that was not what he truly wanted.

And yet memories of Oru's burning passion still stirred his flesh; in fact, Quentin found himself uncomfortably aroused. But no, he would not go to the courtier's quarters, not after spurning her once, not even if he were sure she would forgive him. He shifted position and rearranged his clothing. The inconvenience persisted. Perhaps the best course of action would be to retire to his quarters and lie supine for a time, while replaying memories in his mind's eye. . . . At this thought Quentin felt a surge of anger; he was a grown man of twenty-six, who might long ago have been happily wed. His quest had deprived him of every opportunity for a normal life. Must he then behave like a boy? Or like an adolescent, seeking the fleshly favors of the first willing woman to come along?

Quentin shook his head to clear it of unworthy impulses, focused his will and thoughts onto ordinary things, so as to stifle the gallant reflex. After some time his lust subsided and he was able to uncross his legs.

But then the memory of a kiss came back to him, incongruously strong: His lips could feel again the pressure and the warmth of Melogian's lips, and he wondered once more at her feelings toward him. Her face mingled in his memory with Oru's face; his mouth went dry. Well then, and was he not a bold knight, handsome and strong? He had faced mind-twisting dangers to rescue Christine; could a woman's giggle of contempt be such a threat in comparison?

In the end he found her, more or less by chance, in the southwestern corner of the gardens. For all that he had spent nearly an hour tracking her down, audacity still sang in his blood; he had picked up an aracerulle blossom that had just fallen from a bush and remained yet pristine, and carried it in his hand, to warm it and let the red veins flush brighter against the pale green of the petals.

"Lady Melogian?"

"Oh, good evening, Quentin. A pleasure to see you."

Those courtesies were universal, and yet it seemed to him that in this case they were sincerely meant. Before hesitation could ruin his chances, he was handing her the flower.

"I thought you might like this," he began, then realized he had no idea how to continue. He had taken etiquette lessons, but they did not extend to courting magicians in the Royal Gardens.

Melogian smiled in surprise, took the flower from his hand, and considered it with a raised eyebrow. "Did you pick this? Douglas the head gardener will have you burned at the stake and use your ashes as fertilizer for the bushes if he hears of it."

"It . . . it had already fallen from the stem," replied Quentin with what dignity he could muster. "I would never . . ."

Melogian burst out laughing. "Poor Quentin; you can't tell when people tease you, can you?" He tried to keep a straight face, but he felt his ears might be burning. "Thank you," she continued with a smile. "It's lovely."

She tucked it into her long hair; Oru had worn the blossoms of her world behind her ear, and she used exactly the same gesture to tuck them in her dark tresses. Desire scalded him suddenly, the lash of a whip.

"You didn't course the whole gardens just to bring me a flower, though. What brings you?"

"Why should that not be reason enough, Lady? To find you here and give you a flower seems to me a perfectly worthy goal." He couldn't tell if this came across as a gallant compliment or a ridiculous boast.

"Well . . . thank you so much. Would a few minutes of my company be a bother to you?"

"Nuh—not at all. I would be delighted."

She led the way, following the low wall to an opening and steps leading down. Quentin strolled by her side, knowing now exactly the polite gait he should adopt, but she surprised him again by taking his arm as an old friend would. For a while they were silent. Quentin racked his brains for something to say, but dared not utter inanities about the weather, nor did he wish to ask her about wizardry.

"What is it like, being a knight?" she asked, surprising him.

"Well . . . I do not quite know how to explain it. One is trained in weapons and military science; disciplines of the body and some of the mind. I have never known anything else, not really, save for when I was a boy. But from the age of twelve I knew I wanted to be a knight. I became squire to Sir Glenn of Summer Hill when I turned fourteen. . . ."

"I was wondering about the armor."

"The armor?"

"Doesn't it chafe? All that weight of metal resting on your shoulders . . ."

"Well, we do use a padded jerkin, and ointment to prevent galls." This was turning to subjects unfit for polite conversation; Quentin stopped himself.

"Ah. You see, I never knew that. I always had this picture of raw metal resting directly on your underclothes. But that doesn't make much sense when you think of it. So the weight isn't too much to bear?"

"Plate and chain is very heavy; you do not run in it unless you have to. A simple mail-shirt is less of a burden. In my case, I had an unfair advantage all these years, as the armor was shape-shifted, so I felt only part of its weight."

"So it was a relief to hang it up for a while?"

"I would not say that. I tend to be uncomfortable without armor. At the least I can keep my weapon about myself."

"Is that how you see yourself, then? A fighter born and bred, a man of war and blood?"

"Oh no, Lady," exclaimed Quentin, all his unease forgotten in a rush of feeling. "I am not a soldier; I am a knight! I defend the realm, and of course I would lead others in battle if needed; but this is not the purpose of my life. I want to serve, and to serve I must be strong. I . . . I have not killed often. I take no pleasure in death. Oh, forgive me, I am being rude—I should not speak of such things."

"Why not? I started it. I'm the one who should apologize, not you."

Quentin stammered negation. After an embarrassed moment, he picked on the first available subject.

"I see we are nearly at the west wing. Perhaps I should take my leave now. It . . . it has been most pleasant to spend some time in your company."

"Where do you have to go?"

"I—ah—nowhere in particular."

"Then why won't you stay? I'm hungry; there's bound to be a collation laid out in the Blue Drawing Room; and if not, we'll ring and have one brought out, what do you say?"

They found themselves sitting down at a long table in the Blue Drawing Room, where, as Melogian had predicted, viands, bread, and fruit were laid out. She picked a plate, loaded it with bread and meat, and to Quentin's amazement tore the buns open and stuffed the slices of meat into them like a peasant girl would.

"Pass the mustard, please," she said with her mouth full. Quentin nibbled on grapes and bloodmelon slices while Melogian devoured her meal. She paused at one point, raised her eyes to his, and favored him with a wide smile; there was a yellow-dyed crumb at the corner of her lips and suddenly Quentin's desire was back. Their awkward conversation had buried it away; but the sight of her eating without restraint brought it back redoubled.

When she had sated her hunger Melogian wiped her mouth. She rose from the table and took his hand. He said nothing; she led him through Testenel until they came by roundabout ways to her apartments. She opened the door for him and he passed within, unsure of himself but unwilling to retreat.

She closed the door and he turned to face her. She took the flower out of her hair and brought it to her nose. "It has no smell," she said.

"Those flowers never do. I . . . I will bring you one that has a nice scent, if you want. . . ." He did not know what he was saying.

She shook her head. "I can conjure sweet-smelling roses any time I want. This is more precious, because I neither made it nor summoned it. It came unbidden."

She took a step forward and kissed him lightly.

"Do you want me, Quentin?"

"Yes, Lady." His hands had gone to her waist. He could feel the warm flesh beneath the layers of silk, the swelling of the hips against the edge of his palms. He was dizzy and words came out of his mouth without his willing it. "I love you, Melogian."

"Liar," she said, without bitterness. "It is not me whom you love." She kissed him again, ran her hands against his chest, pulled his overcoat off him.

"Take off your clothes and put away your metal, Quentin. Will you be naked for me? Will you lie with me, caress me, fill me with your own flesh?"

"Yes; yes."

"If you want, I will do things with you that you've never dared imagine . . . or perhaps you have. Your eyes say you have a wild imagination; and you've been among the made worlds. Did you have many lovers there? Women with blue-black skin and heart-shaped nipples? If one goes deep enough, one can find anything one wishes; had you traveled farther yet than you did, you might have come across a world where you were worshipped as a god, where women would kill each other for a chance to lie with you. Would have liked that, Quentin?"

"N-no. It is you I want, Lady. Only you."

He was half-naked; she had cast off her outer garments and loosened the cincture at her waist. He could see the soft curves of her breasts through the gap of her robe.

"Don't you fear me, Quentin? I am a sorceress. I know spells of unthinkable destruction. I might be cruel and wreak terrible transformations upon you if I became angry with you. I am outside all bounds of human law, for no one in this land has the power to punish me. I could harm you, or kill you, if I pleased, and even Edisthen could not punish me for it. Aren't you afraid of me?"

He considered for a moment that this might be a game she played, and meant him to answer yes. But he was too direct to bend to such a game; he had learned to speak truth when asked.

"No, my lady. I do not fear you."

She fell on him then and bore him to the ground. Her lips covered his and her bared breasts brushed back and forth across his chest. When he stood to take off his trousers, she rose in turn and dragged him to the bed in the next room.

Her lovemaking was as intense as Oru's had been, but without Oru's youthful enthusiasm; what stirred Melogian's passion was not clear to him, though in fact he did not much care at this juncture. She kissed and bit him lightly, ran her hands along his skin, drew fine lines of white along his flesh, using the edge of her nails. She straddled him and quickly brought him over the brink, then directed his fingers to finish the task for her. She collapsed on top of him, panting in the hollow of his neck. He stroked her back gently, ran his fingers through her hair, felt the stubble where she shaved it on the sides of her forehead and above the ears.

After a time she rolled onto her side, facing him. Her mouth was twisted as if in pain, or grief. Her eyes did not focus. "Lady? Are you all right?"

For a moment she did not answer; then she whispered: "'Lady.' Is that all I am to you still, Quentin? 'Lady Melogian,' indeed! Why don't you go, now that you have served your purpose?"

He felt a moment of confusion; then hurt. He forebore to reply, slid out from between the covers, and rose to dress. He was at the door when she called out.

"Quentin!"

He turned toward her; she was sitting up, the covers clutched around her, her face forlorn.

"I'm sorry. Please don't go. Please stay with me. I didn't mean what I said."

He hesitated, then went slowly back to the bed, sat down. She reached out a hand to hold his and squeezed tightly.

"Forgive me," she said. "It was my bitterness that spoke." She cast off the covers; her nipples were a pale pink, burnished gold in the lamp light. "Will you stay with me a while, please? Just to talk. And hold me if you want. Or if you really want to go, I won't keep you here."

He lay down next to her; she put her head on his chest and relaxed with a heave of breath. After a minute she whispered, "You're the only one of them all who isn't afraid of me. Everyone else treats me as a monster; and I guess I am, worse than the tarrask Juldrun of the Hundred Hands hunted down in the northern bogs and took three days and three nights to slay in full."

"You are not a—"

"I'm not asking for sympathy, Quentin. I *am* a monster, because I know things about the world people should not know. You all think magic is only about power, and the exercise of it. That is the least part. Magic is mostly hideous self-discipline; it is the accumulation of a colossal body of knowledge, all of it utterly arbitrary. Move your arms and fingers in such and such a way, meanwhile holding three words of seven syllables in your head, and when you say them backward—and only backward will do, while you hold them in mind forward—then flames will bloom in a line between your pointed forefinger and the object you have chosen as a target. Does this sound exciting to you?"

"I have used magic, Lady. It was simpler than that."

"You have just put your manhood in me, Quentin of Lydiss. I think that entitles you to call me by my given name."

"I . . . I am sorry. I will call you Melogian if you want."

"Yes, I want you to. And don't you tell me you know magic. What Orion did for you was to summon the magic but hold it in abeyance at the last possible instant, much as a man may hold back from the brink as he makes love. It is not easy—is it? It is even less easy to do it for a dozen spells, for a score of knights. This is what he did, giving each of you in trust a bouquet of spells for use in emergencies. You have no idea how much power he bound up in you, just so you could travel through the made worlds and hunt for Christine. When you shape-shifted your armor, all you had to do was to will it, and it gave you the illusion you were a mage of sorts. You are like a child who thinks, because his father has put him in front of him on the saddle and let him put his hands on the reins, that he controls the horse."

"I stand corrected," said Quentin after a moment. "Do not think, L—Melogian, that I am not grateful for all that Orion did for me, or that I do not appreciate it, even though I may not have understood the magnitude of the task."

She laughed at this. "Oh, the politeness of these well-bred gentlemen! You can't just say 'Piss off, wife' as if you were a peasant, no matter how much I insult you. . . ." She kissed his neck. "I'm sorry, Quentin. I told you I was bitter. Orion is gone and I expect never to see him again. I am all alone in the world, with no one to love me. It is a hard burden at times, and if I had not seduced you I would bear it in silence still."

He cupped her shoulder in his hand. "I think you are loved, Melogian."

"Not by you. Don't lie to yourself as well; I am not the one you love. But I don't mind, Quentin; I needed company, and kindness, tonight. I am glad you sought me out."

He insisted. "Does not His Majesty love you?"

"There are many kinds of love, Quentin. Edisthen esteems me, but even he fears me. He knows in his bones how much power I wield, even though unlike him I am no Hero from the Book. I'm a foolish girl still; I wish for deep romantic love, someone who would devote his life to me, as I would mine to him. Even when you know something is absurd, you may still crave it, you know."

"Surely, there is a man somewhere who could love you in this way. For everyone, there is someone else."

"This is not only childish, it is heresy. The Law orders the world, but our fate is not written. There is no single spell in the whole arsenal Orion taught me that deals with love; why do you think that is?"

"I do not understand magic. But you are a beautiful woman, and I am sure I am not the only man who is not afraid of you."

"There is one other. Casimir, Evered's wizard, isn't afraid of me. Do you think I should seek him out?"

". . . You are being deliberately stubborn. And I will have you know that I sought you out hoping to court you—not to lie with you, but to spend time with you. And while I did speak in the heat of passion, while I may not love you yet, if I had not felt I might one day, I would not have spoken to you tonight. I am not the kind of man who lies casually with a woman."

She half rose, leaning on her shoulder. "I am afraid I am the kind of woman who will lie casually with a man. God knows I've had too many lovers to count, down in the made worlds. Don't turn your eyes away from my face; I'm not a whore just because I indulge my sensuality. Will you tell me you never had lovers in imaginary lands as well?"

"Yes, I did. Not many, though."

"Don't look so hurt; I did not lie with you casually, Quentin. You're a handsome man; don't think I did not notice that nine years ago when you set forth. I wanted you then, and I wanted you again when you returned. But that isn't the only reason. I need a friend. Someone I can talk to all night. Edisthen is king over us all, and the burden of it eats him away. Now that his daughter has returned, he finds her soul is crippled, and he still knows no peace. I cannot afford to show him my weakness; I must be strong for him, now that my mentor has vanished. There were only ever these two in my life. There is space for at least one more. Will you be my friend, Quentin? Not just my lover?"

"I would . . . like that."

She lay against him, draping an arm over his chest.

"If we had time, which we won't, but if we had time, would you go for a stroll with me tomorrow? Would you go boating on the lake in the Royal Gardens? We could bring food and picnic on the Long Isle—have you ever seen it? It's very pretty. By the end of the road, the island is five miles wide, and there is a jetty there, where sailships moor. Traders who bring in spices and candy from more remote islands. We could go on a cruise, just you and I. The nights are always warm, and the stars burn pink and red and pale green in the sky. The ocean is full of the most wondrous fish, and the water is so transparent you can see them if you just lean over the railing. . . . Wouldn't it be nice?"

"Yes; yes, it would. I would very much like to sail with you."

"Kiss me. . . . And if we had time, if we could find an hour or two, maybe, would you tell me about yourself, when you were young? I've been to Lydiss; if we overflew it in a skyship, you could teach me to see it through your eyes. Tell me where you played as a boy. Did you ever visit Testenel when you were young? I did; I was twelve, you would have been, what? Five or six? Vaurd gave a party on the lawns, and I was invited, being Orion's apprentice. It was the first time I had ever drunk wine, it made me giddy and rather stupid. I've never told anyone this, not even Orion. . . ."

She brushed his eyelashes, once for each set; kissed him softly; drew him down over her. She had shut her eyes. "Lie to me," she whispered. "Lie to me once more. . . ."

&ε Mathellin slept through most of the fourteenth and fifteenth of Summereve, emerging at times from his slumber to stagger on uneven legs across the room to the jugs of water and wine set on a table. He would empty them both, piss a few dark drops into the chamberpot, then collapse back on the mattress. Servants came in as he slept, to replenish the drink on the table, and to replace the food that he could not bring himself to touch. His flesh roiled and bubbled on the bed, throwing out limbs at random, wrapping itself around the frame; the servants paid no heed, their eyes focused on their task.

In the small hours of the night, Mathellin came awake feeling clear-headed at last. He rose on trembling legs and tottered over to the table. This time he ate what had been provided and emptied the jugs as well. He felt faint still, hunger a thin whine in his ears. His body obeyed him, though, his shape flowing as he willed it to. The fever dreams that had tormented him had dissipated and he let go of the faint memories they had left behind. The man he had been so long had died back in transit through Errefern, leaving him once more he who he had been long, long ago. Even the man he had been during the hunt had died, he felt, a closer death, and more disquieting.

He adjusted his ears into great funnels, to magnify the sounds that came into the room. He heard stone creak, distant breathing, a drip of water. No one was near; his door had been left unguarded. He reached out to the handle and gently opened the door. He wasn't sure where he lay within Vorlok, but the castle was small, its floorplan trivial compared to the labyrinthine madness of Testenel. It was short work to orient himself and locate stairs going upward. On the upper floor, he passed two of Casimir's manikins, motionless, their unblinking eyes empty. He heard neither breath nor heartbeat coming from them.

He had discharged his duty to Evered, for the time being. While Vorlok still slept, he was a free man. Besides, had he not given enough of himself, for so long? Surely, the pangs of guilt he felt were excessive.

Coming to a window in the outer wall, Mathellin leaned in and shoved the shutters open. The land below was still shrouded in night; it would be some hours before the sun sprang out of the ocean in the east. Mornings in Vorlok were the best part of the day, by contrast with evenings, when the mountains to the west blocked out the declining sun long before it approached the horizon. Mathellin scooted onto the wide windowsill, then condensed his shape, let feathers sprout all over his flesh. He was a bird again, a pale raven. He flew out the window, rose into the dark, headed northeast. He set himself an easy rhythm for his wing beats; he could no longer afford to be in a desperate hurry, no matter the length of the journey he had to make.

Forty-six years before, the sorceress Udæve, on her travels through the made world Hieloculat, had lain with a half-man and allowed his seed to quicken in her womb. Upon her return to Chrysanthe some weeks later, the child had been solidly part of her and survived the passage into the real world; she had brought it to term successfully, and named it Mathellin.

He had shown, from a very early age, a talent for magic, which was, as his mother told him, what she had hoped for. The power to shape-shift, a gift from his father's blood, was an integral part of him, requiring no spell as such but a mere exercise of his will. His apprenticeship of it had been perilous, for to push himself too far beyond his limits would easily have meant death. On several occasions, Udæve returned to Hieloculat with her son and found her way back to the world of his father. There the boy was schooled for some months by elders of his paternal lineage, before Udæve brought him back to Chrysanthe.

Trained both by his father's kin and by his mother, Mathellin had grown up into a respectable sorcerer, in full control of his abilities. Unlike his mother, Mathellin was not satisfied by the pure pursuit of knowledge; he sought for a great enterprise to undertake, a word of his own to write in the book of history, in bold lettering. Udæve had hoped for him to carry on the bloom of her knowledge, to seek through the land for a child who had true talent, take it on as apprentice, train it. Too many wizards' lines had died out, too much knowledge had been lost. But to Mathellin such a task held little appeal, for it left no lasting mark.

Orion's achievements spurred his frustration: In 6066, the Hero joined Vaurd's service as court wizard, a post that had not been filled in half a century. Mathellin was seventeen, fresh from a visit to his father's world in Hieloculat, where he had been awarded the insignia that certified him as a shape-shifter of the highest native skill. Here he was, a man without peer in Chrysanthe, a mage of undeniable competence, able to alter his form to whatever he could imagine, strong and decisive; and all his mother thought to offer him was a life spent poring over books, hunting throughout the land for that one child in a myriad who might grow up into a wizard to succeed him. . . .

"Why him and not me?" he'd complained. "Why that graybeard with his pompous airs? The king is still a young man; why would he want a doddering fool?"

"Vaurd wants a Hero," his mother had replied. "In that respect, you can never compete with Orion. He was written into existence long before I was born; he's at least a hundred years old, probably more. For as long as anyone knows he's dwelled in Fargaunce. Now he's approached the king and offered to serve him. If I were Vaurd, I wouldn't trust him. He's a sly one."

"What do you think he wants?"

"To rule through Vaurd, likely. Heroes are drawn to power like flies to manure. In five years, we may have a mage on the throne of Chrysanthe in all but name."

Mathellin had looked to the west, imagining the towers of Testenel beyond the horizon. "I could serve," he'd said, with a sudden pain in his voice. "I could serve just as well as Orion; better, even. I don't want the damned throne. I merely want to achieve something commensurate with my abilities."

He had heard but paid no attention to Udæve's muted sigh, only listened to her words. "Well . . . I can't promise you anything. But if you want to serve the throne, I can at least help you get noticed."

For nearly two years Udæve had groomed her son as best she could, teaching him what she knew of life at court and what kings expected from wizards in their service. Her sources were utterly out of date and she harbored a raft of mistaken preconceptions, having never been within ten leagues of Tiellorn in her entire life. Further, she had spent so much time in Hieloculat that she unconsciously projected the lessons she'd learned in imaginary worlds onto the true realm. All this made for a somewhat lacunar instruction.

In 6069, at the age of twenty, Mathellin had traveled to Tiellorn, alone, his mother having elected to remain in Faryn. Filled with equal parts arrogance and insecurity, the young wizard had sought audience with the king, only to be told his name would be entered on a roll and he would have to wait three months, if not more, for an appointment with an adviser, the king being far too busy to entertain petitions from every bumpkin who traveled to Testenel.

"But I'm a wizard!" he'd burst out, astonished at his treatment.

"Oh?" The guard's tone was dismissive. "You know how many like you we see in a year? A score at least. Mighty wizards who just happen to have forgotten their book of spells, but who need to see the king at once, to show him their marvels. Oh yes, I know your sort. Now be a nice boy and go home, son. I'm sure your mother's worried."

Mathellin had thought he'd been prepared for anything, from immediate acceptance to a stubborn refusal; but to be dismissed as a lackwit! Humiliated beyond measure, he'd turned away without a word and walked a mile to the gates of Tiellorn, where he'd found an inn and rented a room for the night.

He had waited until the sun began to decline, then cast aside his clothing, thrown open the casement, and shifted into the shape of a bat. He'd flown back to Testenel, dodged the guard's attention, and entered the castle through the very door where he'd been refused admittance earlier.

He'd crossed several halls and corridors, unnoticed, before returning to a human shape in a deserted cloakroom, where he'd appropriated adequate clothing. Then he had set out to find King Vaurd—and become utterly lost within twenty minutes.

He had been retracing his steps for the third time, trying to remember where it was he'd made the wrong turn that kept leading him back to the same dim cul-de-sac, when a growl of a voice had risen behind him.

"What are you doing here, dream-spawn?"

He'd whirled around, a brief wave of tough scales forming themselves and dissolving away on his skin. Before him had stood a burly man, unkempt of hair, with a salt-and-pepper beard reaching to the middle of his chest. His features were somewhat coarse, his nose flat and his lips full. He wore a long dull-red robe suited to his considerable bulk, belted in white across his paunch.

"Who are you?" Mathellin had asked.

"I am Orion. What are you doing uninvited in Testenel?"

"I . . . came to see the king."

"For what purpose?"

"I wish to discuss something with him," Mathellin had said, rising up to his full height. "Please take me to him."

"I think not. If you have something to discuss, you may discuss it with me."

Deflated, Mathellin had blurted out: "I wish to enter into his service."

Orion had looked at him a long moment.

"Is that why you flew into the castle in a false shape?"

So he had been seen probably the instant he'd passed within. Mathellin felt disquieted at this demonstration of power: Udæve's teachings had not encompassed ward-spells of this potency. "The guard wouldn't let me enter; he thought I was mad when I claimed I was a wizard."

"Well, you shouldn't blame him too much. You know how few of us there are in the world?"

"All the more reason to treat my request seriously!"

"Hmpf. You're Udæve's made-world get—Mathellin. You'd be, what? Nineteen?"

"Twenty."

Orion had sighed. "I'm afraid King Vaurd doesn't need a second court wizard. Your offer was well intentioned, but matters are already complicated enough as it is."

"You won't even tell him, will you? You don't want him to know I was here! What, are you afraid, Orion?"

The mage's face had twisted into a scowl of disgust.

"Thank God in Her heaven I was never your age, boy. I don't think I could live with the embarrassment."

Mathellin had begun a confused and outraged protest, which Orion had cut short with a single word.

"Enough! Listen closely, Mathellin. You will not see the king. You will not be allowed to bother the king. If you choose to blame me for that, go ahead; your spite means nothing to me.

"I do not trust you—but even if I did trust you, I wouldn't allow you to petition His Majesty. Not now, with the land in the state it is in. In five years, if Vaurd is still on his throne, if the land is quiet, come back. Prove yourself trustworthy then, and we can speak again. But not before. Understood?"

Mathellin had felt a flush of rage—impotent rage, for he knew himself out-matched in power by the Hero.

"You think you can just send me away—" he'd begun.

"I don't think; I know. My wards burn at your approach; I feel your presence in the castle like I would feel a pin under my toenail. I let you get inside because I wanted to know what your intentions were. Rest assured, if you were stupid enough to try to get in again, in any way whatsoever, I would be aware of it instantly. And I would *not* be pleased."

Mathellin had stepped back, turned on his heel to leave . . . And stopped, at a loss what direction to take. Mortified, he had had to beg for directions, though he would not face Orion to do it. The court wizard had directed him step by step, hovering just behind him all the way to the exit; Mathellin's flesh had crawled from Orion's nearness, yet never once had he turned to face the Hero.

Once past the gate, he had shifted his shape abruptly, not caring whether Orion might take the gesture as hostile: He had to safeguard some modicum of his pride or he felt he could not survive the humiliation. He had become a leather-winged *drakk* from his father's world, and taken to the air in two strides. In his flight he had left Testenel behind, thinking it was forever.

Two years later fate had handed him his revenge; for Vaurd was not pleased at all with his court wizard, it turned out. With an uproar the king had discharged Orion from his post. News of this occurrence had spread throughout the realm, and in due course had reached Faryn. Mathellin had seen his chance then, and rushed to Tiellorn.

This time he had managed to obtain an audience with the king. He'd had to wait weeks for it, but he had learned patience in the past two years and spent the days rehearsing his arguments.

Again things had not gone as expected: This time, his success had been more complete than he had hoped for. Vaurd had appeared eager to replace his wizard, and more than willing to believe in Mathellin's usefulness. At the age of twenty-two, Mathellin had found himself the new court wizard of Chrysanthe.

For three years he had served Vaurd, faultlessly. What the king asked for, Mathellin provided without question. He had been entrusted many a time with diplomatic missions to convince recalcitrant barons on the margins of civilization; on solemn occasions Mathellin would use his talents for show, to add to the pomp of Vaurd's reign; once in a while, his spellcraft would be used to a more direct purpose. Throughout that time Mathellin had been happy beyond belief, secure in the knowledge that he served the sovereign of the land, in the highest post to which he might have aspired.

Then Vaurd had died at the hands of Edisthen. Mathellin, who had been away on a diplomatic task, had returned to Testenel to find the court in an uproar. Without a second thought Mathellin had attached himself to Evered's service, and in the years that followed had remained faithfully at his side, through the War of Usurpation, through the exile of Vaurd's line to the miserable refuge that was Vorlok. Although the royal decree theoretically compelled Mathellin as much as Evered and his brothers to remain within sight of Vorlok, the wizard felt no particular compulsion to obey it. Several times a year, he would leave the ancient fortress and fly home, to Udæve's house at Faryn in Archeled. He never spoke of the plotting that went on, and she in turn never questioned him about it.

But for thirteen long years Mathellin had remained Christine's guardian, forgetting who he was. He wanted—he needed—now to see Udæve, to hear his mother's voice, to remember who he had been.

His flight was a long one. The sun rose out of the eastern ocean and climbed high into the sky. Several times he stopped to feed himself, changing to a raptor's form and killing a small animal, devouring the carcass down to the bone before taking off again. Around noon he spotted deer beneath him. He alighted, shifted into a feroce and brought down a large buck, gorged himself on the blood-rich meat. At last, in late afternoon, he reached the town of Faryn, on the banks of the river Laurlied, which flowed into the Scyamander.

Udæve had had a manse built for her use, a spacious and attractive home, some distance from the town itself. Mathellin found it immediately and glided toward it. Something was wrong; he felt an unease he could not yet place. He landed outside the grounds of the manse, returned to the shape of a man, and advanced cautiously toward the gates.

They were open, rusted in place, and the path beyond was obscured by frail growths pushing up between the flagstones. Mathellin stepped along the path, noting the neglect of the grounds to either side. The garden to the side of the manse had reverted to wilderness, its once-trimmed hedges overcome by climbing vines.

Then he was at the front entrance, sunk in the shadow of a candlebush grown six feet too high, withered flowers crowding the stems so only a few live ones had space to bloom. There were locks on the door, both iron and sorcerous. Extending his fingers toward the wood at a cautious distance, Mathellin muttered a transposition of the pass-phrase and confirmed that the bindings remained inviolate, though the metal lock bore traces of tampering. One of the panels was stained at waist height by a splash of old blood—evidence that some fool had tried to force entry and paid dearly for it.

Mathellin's heart was pounding, and his mind shied like a frightened horse. He had no key, but a powerful enough spell would trip the mechanical lock as well. He spoke it flawlessly, felt the bindings loosen and the watch-spell go dormant. He pushed the door open with his bare palm and stepped into the foyer.

Inside the manse the air was musty and still. He trod the carpeted floor silently, along corridors until he reached the bedroom.

Her body lay on the bed, the coverlet drawn up to her shoulders. Mathellin remained silent on the threshold, hands clenched together. She had been old, of course. At Vaurd's death, she had been in her mid-sixties. In 6081, when Christine had been abducted from the court of Chrysanthe and Evered had ordered Mathellin to remain with her as a guardian, his mother had been seventy-two. For thirteen long years Mathellin had forgotten who he was, and hadn't thought once of the woman who had borne him.

He ought not to have been surprised: Though sorcerers tended to long life, their longevity did not compare to that of Heroes. But he had never really believed Udæve would die. He had been born of a man who did not exist; surely this meant that his mother must be more than real, to ensure some sort of symmetry. . . . It did not help that she had cloaked herself in ageless glamour, so that she appeared always young and vital.

So deep, in fact, had she cast the spell that faint traces of it still glimmered at the corners of her mummified lips. Mathellin went to the bed and knelt at her side. Her cheeks were sunk, her eyelids closed tight. Her body was scentless, uncorrupted. He brushed her face with his fingers; he had hoped to glimpse a last quiver of the glamour, a flash of the face he knew so well, but there was nothing; even the traces of the spell at the corners of her mouth went away at his touch. A strand of her hair caught in his fingers and broke off.

He rose convulsively, rushed out of Udæve's room and into his own, opened the wardrobe and brought out clothes, ashamed of his nakedness before his mother's corpse. He took the time to dress himself properly, to wash his face and comb his hair, before reentering the room where the body waited.

He pulled the covers back gently. There was no trace of violence. On the nightstand beside Udæve a tumbler might once have held water, though now it contained only dust. He found he was weeping, though the tears from his left eye were pale red. He had to focus on his self-image to repair the weakness in his eye.

Then he swept out of the manse, ran into town, to the temple and its chief priestess, a small woman clad all in crimson whom he had never seen in his life but who claimed to have known Udæve. When told of his mother's death the priestess bowed her head and expressed her sympathies. When Mathellin asked for an immediate funeral, she proved reluctant. Forms must be followed, the proper authorities notified. . . . She fell silent when Mathellin's clawed fingers closed about her head and began to draw blood. "Now, please," he asked in a quiet voice, and she agreed without further demur.

He chose a plain casket—what need have the dead for splendor? Wizards, whose wealth is power, deserve no ostentation when at last they are joined to the earth. A few people came with him back to the manse, though he begrudged everyone else's presence, even the priestess's. He allowed no one in beside himself, brought the coffin into the room carried on an enormous shoulder, laid the body within it and closed the lid, dragged the box out without looking behind him.

There was a spot within the grounds that was appropriate for the burial. He took all the others there with him, suffering four of them to bear the casket on their shoulders. Once they had reached the site, which thirteen years ago had been a quiet hollow framed by trees and now appeared as a glade within a young forest, Mathellin told them to dig. The work went too slowly, and to be done before the sun vanished completely, Mathellin had to take over the job himself, shoveling out the earth with broad flat tusks and adamantine claws.

Once the box with his mother's mummified remains lay deep in the hole, he barked at the priestess to hurry. She went through the rite at her own measured pace, and the sun had set before she was finished. Shovelfuls of earth rained upon the coffin as the sky grew darker.

"There will be a stone," Mathellin told them all. He might have done everything else himself, even to the oration, for he knew most of the words, but he lacked the skill to cut stone and had to rely upon an artisan within Faryn. "You will have her name put on it, and the date. Nothing else, no decoration, no other words. The job will be done as soon as feasible. It will be paid well, but it will be done tomorrow, or else your wives, your children, your parents will die. Now go; all of you. Go!"

They walked away from the grave, stumbling in the semidarkness. Mathellin watched them leave from enlarged eyes that drank in the starlight as if it were broad day. All around him trees grew, and weeds in the little hollow; in its center, the mound of disturbed earth beneath which lay Udæve in her little wooden box. Wind ruffled the leaves, insects disturbed the blades of grass, and the stars lanced the ground with their shine.

Mathellin brought a hand up to his face and brought it back red-stained: He was weeping blood again. He was still fragile, a broken toy badly repaired. He was forty-five years old, when a few days ago he had been thirty-two. Thirteen years of his life he had wasted, guarding a girl who had slipped between his fingers with the greatest of ease. All this time the true realm had gone on, while he lay trapped within the dream of the made world. He had awoken much too late, to a life in ruins. He had failed.

From the moment Casimir had joined with Evered's side Mathellin had known himself outclassed, but he had prided himself that none more loyal than himself could be found. He had served the prince without question, as he had served Vaurd his father. He had tried to forget his first failure, of being absent when Edisthen had shown up; tried to find absolution in irreproachable service to Vaurd's son. He had fought in the War of Usurpation, had seen soldiers fall to arms and to magic, had killed without compunction, had been swept off the field by Orion's superior skills. He had failed again. Exiled to Vorlok, he had plotted in earnest with the others, had accepted without protest the subservient role Casimir imposed upon him. He had agreed to ward Christine down in Errefern, to keep watch over her as long as it took—forever, was what was meant, and Mathellin had taken on the burden without demur, without a second thought, dutiful to a fault. He had sacrificed his life to his task, and failed to redeem himself. In the end, it had all come out to naught.

His fingers rooted into the earth, his back hunched, and his head lowered nearly to the ground. Alone under the pitiless stars, he wept for his mother, who had died and waited for years for him to come claim her, all her spells gone, all the design of her life faded out in an instant. It was not in him to fail, Vaurd had said to him once. Not in him to recognize failure. And yet here and now he had come upon a reckoning he could not avoid. What was left of his life, what was left of him, child of a dream and a dead woman, of his thirteen years of life as a rich merchant of Errefern, of Christine's warder, Christine whom he had loved and hated in equal measure, the pivot of his existence? Nothing. Dust under the sky, unseen, ignored, contemptible. He felt himself close up around the hard kernel of his failure, and his fever dreams returned, hovering on the fringes of his consciousness. He needed more than sleep; needed oblivion, nonexistence, an end to this litany of reproach that was his life. Broken, broken, and all he valued taken from him: his ward, his love, his service. And yet his idiot heart still went on beating.

3. Libraries

On the morning after the celebrations had ended, the eighteenth of Summereve, King Edisthen met with Melogian on a high terrace of Testenel, one of those which had hosted the dances. Although efforts had been made to tidy up, pieces of furniture were still scattered all about and detritus from the celebrations had drifted into corners. Melogian was feeling a dip of the spirits, if only through a repercussion of the previous rejoicing; the king's grim countenance did nothing to uplift her mood. He sat down on a bench shaped from the blue stone of the castle, his back to the enclosing wall. There was a warm breeze, which set a few hairs on his head aflutter. Guards stood at the entrances to the terrace; as Melogian sat down by the king's side, one of the guards admitted a portly, large-headed man in uniform. This was Fraydhan, general of Temerorn's armies: a veteran of the Great War who had gained his post by virtue of his exemplary service at the time.

Fraydhan crossed the terrace, approached his king, saluted, and remained standing until Edisthen motioned him to be seated. Fraydhan considered the bench for a long second, then dragged a wooden chair closer to his king, swept some confetti from the seat, and sat down. He darted a sour glance at Melogian, who was all too obviously enjoying the informality that made Fraydhan so uncomfortable.

"Your Majesty," said General Fraydhan stiffly. "Allow me to once more offer my congratulations at the return of your beloved daughter."

"Thank you," replied Edisthen, a frown of worry belying his words. "But after these three days of joy, I am afraid the time has come for us to discuss unhappy matters."

Fraydhan sat straighter; his eyes came alive. Melogian recognized the professional soldier's lust for action in his demeanor, and found it rather distasteful, like a carrion-eater's hunger.

"Yes. I have heard tell, Your Majesty," said Fraydhan, "that the deposed king's eldest son has been seen at court, that he came to offer challenge."

So much, thought Melogian, for Edisthen's quelling of any rumors; although she had to admit she herself had overheard nothing. Whatever information had filtered out had been contained; or else Fraydhan had directly asked one of the guards present at Evered's appearance, who had not been able to keep silent when questioned by a high officer.

"In essence, that is correct," Edisthen was saying. "Evered has indeed issued what can be interpreted as a formal challenge. I am prepared to take it seriously. Additionally, Melogian is of the opinion that the wizard Casimir poses a very real threat to us, far beyond what we could have expected before."

Fraydhan looked at Melogian questioningly. At Edisthen's request she explained the matter of Evered's eidolon and mentioned her fear of Casimir's new powers; Fraydhan pursed his full lips dubiously.

"Melogian, you talk of elder spells, yet so far all Casimir has done is to make Evered's image appear in Testenel, giving him an opportunity to vent his spleen. Forgive me if I don't consider that a mortal threat."

Melogian leaned forward. "The danger comes from what we don't know, General. Casimir might have some deadly surprises in reserve."

"Like fire coming down from the heavens, or a drowning wave on dry land, you mean?"

"I can evoke those effects myself; I mean far more terrible workings. In the early days of the world, when wizards fought, they could scar the land for a thousand years with the aftermath of their spells. I have access to history books that reach much farther back than you would think; there is ample reason to fear what Casimir may know."

Fraydhan made a tiny shrug and a dip of the head. "I'll accept your worries, Lady Wizard, though I find myself wishing they were more specific. It's hard to prepare soldiers to fight against perils one cannot even imagine."

Melogian was about to discuss the matter further but the king changed the subject.

"I sent Melogian to seek out the other wizards of the land," he said. "To rally them to our cause. I have not had a report on this matter yet. Melogian, if you will."

The sorceress swallowed once before answering.

"As you ordered, my liege, I left Testenel and traveled the land. I sought out all the mages that we know about, tested them no matter how unwilling, and identified those who have potentially useful talent. I took those back here, and quartered them in the Octagon Tower."

"And how are they doing?"

"Ah . . . Both of them are resentful and scared. Aliz worries about her granddaughter, who is due to give birth in a tenday. Coryn is excited enough about being in Testenel that he sometimes forgets to pine for his mother. You may have noticed them last night, during the Mascarene Dance."

"Two wizards! *Two?*"

Melogian, who still smarted from the king's remarks in their argument three days earlier, tried to placate his displeasure.

"I did warn you, my liege, that there would not be many. These two, I assure you, are both willing and able to serve the land. I don't doubt their loyalty to the crown. In my opinion, they would be best suited to defend Testenel, but the boy certainly can travel with an army, or aboard a skyship. The old woman is more delicate."

"What can they do?"

"Coryn can summon flame at will. With practice he might learn to cast it over far distances. He is a good pupil; I might take him on as an apprentice, though he is sharply limited in his potential. Still, he went far beyond what his mentor could ever achieve. Aliz has fairly good control of light and shadows; she can even manage the Mirrored Eclipse. If she can keep her head, in a battle situation this might prove handy."

"There is no one else?" asked Edisthen, almost sneering. "What of the boy's mentor, at least?"

"She's half mad, my liege, and masters only a handful of feeble workings. She would be nothing but a liability. I'm sorry. The world is old and almost all the wizardly lines are dead."

Edisthen threw his hands up in the air, an uncharacteristic gesture of exasperation. "Very well, then. Assign our recruits where you judge best."

"As you command."

Edisthen turned his attention to Fraydhan, his expression once more neutral.

"I take Melogian's warning seriously, General. But as we have found no new major ally to help us magically, we shall have to concentrate on military action."

Fraydhan nodded dubiously and spoke: "I mistrust too-obvious moves, Your Majesty. In this case, the obvious strategy is for us to bring forces to bear on Vorlok and pull Evered's fangs. But this must be what he wants—assuming of course that he is sane. His challenge is certainly a ruse, a way to lure you away from court."

"To what end?"

Fraydhan studied his knuckles. "Your Majesty, the Law is not the infrangible shield some sovereigns have believed it to be. Anyone who wishes you ill can strike at you, as long as he is prepared to pay the price. I am well placed to know that men can overcome their impulse for self-preservation in pursuit of a higher goal. Though you are unassailable in Testenel, during a campaign into northern Kawlend, you would be far less well protected."

Edisthen half smiled. "We think alike in that respect. Rest easy, General, I don't intend to budge from this place. If Evered expects me in Vorlok, he will wait a long time indeed. I rather think he hopes to bring the fight to me instead."

"Against the armies of all the land? They will crush him; even Evered is not such a fool."

"First these armies have to be raised, General," Melogian put in.

"I have five hundred men active, and I can have two thousand more ready in a week," snapped Fraydhan. "And even if I had a hundred only, I repeat: What can Evered do?"

"He can gather malcontents," replied Melogian, "swing the barons of the marches to his side."

"Of course he can. But even then, his chances of success are nil."

"What if a duchy flew its banner on Evered's side?" asked the king.

Fraydhan's eyes shut for a moment. "Ah. Your Majesty does not trust the Duchess of Kawlend," he said.

"Duchess Ambith might carry a grudge."

"That, my liege, is an understatement," said Melogian.

Edisthen pursed his lips. "You are far too ready to cast aspersions, Melogian. I would be a fool to trust Ambith, but I will not be such a fool as to assume the worst of her without any proof."

"But Your Majesty, weren't you saying just now that she might join Evered's side?" asked Fraydhan.

"I have to think of that risk. That is very clearly what Evered hopes for. He cannot swing Duke Archeled to his cause, and Corlin of Estephor is a young idealist who would never think of defying the Law. Ambith sided with Vaurd in the War of Usurpation; she might very well do so again."

Fraydhan had winced at hearing his king use this term for the war, which was frowned upon by loyalists everywhere. He now spoke in some haste.

"Kawlend was roundly defeated in the Great War. Their armies are strong and well trained, true, but no more so now than twenty years ago. Should the duchess rise against the crown, she would be defeated this time as once before."

"This assumes magic will not play a significant role, General," Melogian reminded him.

"But why should it?"

"Because Orion is gone, and Casimir's power, as I've been wasting my saliva telling you, has increased beyond the bounds of speculation. I'm well aware that modern military doctrine doesn't take magic into account. It wasn't so in the distant past, when mages were more numerous; then, their influence could be overwhelming. When we fought the Great War, Orion used his magic sparingly, both at your request, Edisthen, that soldiers' lives be spared, and because he was intent on counteracting Mathellin's efforts. In the end the wizards mostly nullified one another's influence. But surely, General, you haven't forgotten the rout at Lelderien, when Orion poured Red Ruin onto the vanguard of Kawlend's army and ended your war for you by slaughtering Ambith's finest troops?"

Fraydhan replied with a tight-lipped glare.

"Enough!" said the king. "I will not have you two bickering. I want the land to prepare for a possible war, General. And I believe it is possible for us to stand united against Evered's threat, Kawlend included. I want to summon the dukes to a conclave. Ambith can recognize sense when she hears it, and I will present facts as they stand. If she rebels, the whole land will suffer, but Kawlend most of all."

"I'd advise bribing her as well," said Melogian drily.

"I've already discussed the matter with Lord Halgund and Chancellor Melfay. A substantial amount of wealth will start flowing to Aluvien once we get Ambith's pledge of loyalty. Now, General, how stands the fleet?"

Fraydhan reached into an inner pocket of his uniform and withdrew a wax tablet on which several lines of information had been incised.

"The *Black Heart* remains at Testenel, Your Majesty. The *Excelsior* and *Llermand's Victory* are in Archeled, *Excelsior* being due back here in three or four days. The *Glorious Niavand* is due at Aluvien on the twentieth of Summereve, and will be in Tiellorn around the first of High-Summer. *Spindrift* is in transit from Korunn to Waldern, probably around Mount Gasphode at the moment. The *Nonpareil* and the *Winter Rose* are patrolling the northern reaches of the land; *Chiarron* is in the southern baronies."

Edisthen thought a moment. "Very well. *Excelsior*, when it arrives, will be sent back to Waldern to ferry Duke Archeled. I can send the *Black Heart* to Korunn for Corlin. Melogian, can I task you to find the *Niavand* in Aluvien and carry my orders to them?"

Melogian nodded. "Of course, Edisthen. In a whirl, I can reach the city in a few hours."

"I will have a sealed message for you presently. We will hold conclave on the third day of High-Summer. A free discussion. Let us have it all out in the open: If Ambith has grievances, I'll give her a chance to air them. In the meantime, General, I want you to start to prepare for a war. Come back to me with plans for various eventualities. Don't let rumors start; for one thing, keep the chancellor of the treasury out of it. Use whatever stale information you have at hand when forecasting the costs: All I want now is a rough estimate. If and when we move forward, then we'll obtain more precise figures. Melogian, in an hour's time meet me in the Griffin Room; I shall write the message for Ambith first."

Melogian bowed to the king and left. Though she walked in direct sunshine, she felt a chill of foreboding. *Prepare for a war*, Edisthen had said. She had been a girl of fourteen during the Usurpation War, and her apprenticeship to Orion had shielded her from it. Now she wondered fleetingly if it was the fate of every generation to endure a war, if it was necessary for everyone to learn in blood, again and again, the costs of madness.

❧ The three days of celebration had passed for Christine in a blur. After her misadventure in the gardens, she avoided too public surroundings when she ventured out of her apartments, and requested her guards to make sure that well-wishers were only allowed to see her in small groups. To be cast into the role of high nobility only worsened her feelings of unreality, and the strangeness of Chrysanthe kept her off-balance.

On the morning of the second day, she had sent for Quentin and kept him by her for most of the day. She needed his presence to cling to, an anchor in the flux of these times. With Quentin by her side, she was able to visit parts of the castle, and even return to the gardens for a very brief excursion, remaining at all times well in sight of the exit.

At long last the revelry of the third night had ended. There had been a dance, which Christine had witnessed from a distance. To her relief, it all looked very ordinary, and no one either dropped their clothes or started flourishing swords. It was less staid than she'd expected, the music surprisingly vigorous, with much rattling of snare drums and fiddle arpeggios, the male dancers lifting their partners into the air two or three times. Now that was an amusement she might take to; at least she'd watch it again with pleasure.

Still, at the close of the night, Christine was glad to retire to her chambers. She had hoped for a while that there might be fireworks to mark the end of the celebration, until Quentin reminded her that powder did not work in Chrysanthe. Vegetable oils and wax would burn, and so candles could be floated in tiny cockleshells on ponds in the gardens—she had watched from a high window the flickering flames dancing through colored glass, a distorting mirror of the constellations above—but there would be no rockets exploding in the air and casting their colored shimmer into the night.

Once back in her suite, Christine shed her dress—the most extravagant she had worn yet, and clearly a step too far for her in the direction of fashion—and put on the plainest nightgown she had managed to make Althea procure for her. She took to her bed and dreamed of riding beside Quentin in his red sports car, wearing the suede jacket he had purchased for her with imaginary money. In the dream the jacket was an infrangible armor that protected her from all possible harm. Quentin shifted gears again and again; each time, the car increased speed. Soon they were nearly flying along a road; then they entered a brightly lit tunnel, which curved

gently upward. As they emerged from the tunnel, the car bled its speed away insen-
sibly, until they were motionless, on a vast plateau, whose ground glowed whitely
underneath the whirling stars. Christine got out of the car; there was a chill breeze,
but her jacket kept her warm. Quentin came to her side, touched her shoulder, and
she woke with an unexpected sense of well-being.

From then on things improved. A day passed, and another, and slowly Chrysanthe began to feel more solid to Christine. She would wake in the same huge bed
every morning. Althea or Rann would be on hand, to bring her breakfast. She
could wander between the rooms of her apartments, be alone if she wished. Quentin would come by, early in the morning, in answer to her summons. She would take
brief walks about Testenel, escorted by her small entourage. They crossed paths
with many people, but not too many at a time. There were no scenes, no unpleasantness; and if ever any awkwardness arose, she was shielded from it. The routine
imbued her world with reality. She spoke with Quentin for hours; asked him about
the history of the realm, its geography. He knew much and was more than willing to
tell her. All those names and dates lay in a heap still in Christine's memory, but she
knew she would get them organized eventually, and thus gain a perspective of where
she stood in time and space.

Her father she encountered infrequently. Still she felt dread when they stood in
the same room; but she struggled with the feeling and made some progress in fighting it. They would speak briefly, then he would take his leave, always gracious. He
ran the affairs of the land, and was far busier than Uncle had ever been. Soon,
Christine promised herself—but she knew not when—soon she would gather
enough courage to seek him out on her own, to come into his presence unbidden,
perhaps to sit with him again in the throne room—but not yet, no, not yet, not for a
while. First she would wait until the world around her felt truly solid.

The season was early summer; the land around Testenel was warm and green,
and twice Christine went out of the castle, though remaining very close to it. Each
time she enjoyed the fresh air and the greenness; but the number of people by her
side disturbed her. She was especially vulnerable when she ventured out of the confines of the castle, and her retinue included a dozen guards along with both maids
and either Quentin or Melogian. In the past, she had envied the celebrities she saw
on television, the torch-songstresses whose long-players climbed to the top of the
charts; now she saw anonymity as a precious gift, and wondered why anyone would
want it taken away.

For a time Christine didn't read at all, save for the copy of the Lesser Book that
Bridianne had given her, and that volume could not keep her attention for more
than a few pages at a time. For most of her life books had been a refuge for her—but
all the literature she had ever known was gone from her existence, and she feared to
discover that Chrysanthe's books were as distressing as its theater. Still, when Melogian took Christine to visit the Great Library, which was housed in a squat outer
tower of the castle, she felt her love of reading stir back to wakefulness.

The library was much as Christine had expected: stuffy, full of shelves that
overflowed with books, sunk in a silence she knew came in large part from the muf-
fling effects of all the surrounding paper and cloth. Yet there were some differences:

most apparent was the lighting. She had expected oil lamps or candles; but the sole light came from outside, flooding through the palely tinted glass of the windows. None could bring their own light either: At the entrance to the library, a fussy warden frisked all visitors, to make sure that no flame could bloom within its walls. Christine experienced a very uncomfortable memory at this, but her rank exempted her from the treatment, and she was not about to complain. Melogian submitted to the search with good grace before ushering Christine among the stacks.

"It's an old prohibition," the sorceress explained. "Twice in history a fire damaged the library, the second time destroying a full third of its contents; Queen Guielle, at the beginning of the sixth millennium, set down a law that has been followed ever since. For nearly a thousand years the library has closed at dusk, and the dimmer stacks are seldom visited."

The entrance floor was pleasant enough: A number of tables set next to the windows awaited visitors, and the shelves loaded with large reference tomes were low enough not to impede sight. A staircase ascended to the upper floors. "There are hundreds of thousands of books in there," said Melogian. "Every kind you could desire to read, from romances to cookbooks, from geometry treatises to children's fables. Any one of the librarians will be glad to assist you; you certainly don't need my help there. However, there is a part of the library I think you should see, and without me you would not be allowed in. And I do feel you should see it."

The sorceress led the way down a long flight of steps. At the bottom lay a small square chamber. There was a door with a heavy lock, guarded by a bored-looking soldier who perked up at their approach. He prattled about half a dozen subjects in the time it took Melogian to unlock and push open the door; as the two women walked through, he loudly wished them to enjoy themselves, unwilling to let the conversation end.

The room beyond was low ceilinged; windows opened in the walls as in the floor above, but these were protected by a latticework of bars and their glass was very thick.

"What is this place, anyway?" asked Christine, looking at low shelves bearing still more books.

"The closed stacks. Forbidden—well, restricted—books are kept here."

"What kind of books? And why did you think I should see them?"

"It isn't the books that I wanted you to see. There is something in a farther room—unless you'd rather go back up?"

Christine felt a twinge of unease—the rest of her entourage had been left just outside the library. But when had she ever been afraid of books?

"No, let's go see it," she said. She passed close to a shelf, hesitated for a moment, then fetched a book from it. The cover was blank; she peeled it back and saw it was titled *The Torturer in Silhouette*. Melogian pulled it gently out of her hands.

"Pardon me, Christine, but I don't think you want to look at this. Even I lack the stomach for its etchings."

Christine frowned at the ranks of books. "So this is what you keep here? Pornography?"

"Pardon me?"

"Obscenity? Dirty pictures?"

"Oh, not at all. This is a historical work. It's just about a . . . very unpleasant subject. The history of torture during past millennia. There are ribald tales aplenty up above, and many with illustrations, if that's what one is looking for."

Christine was too embarrassed to comment. She followed Melogian through a doorway into another room, larger but less well lit. There were still more books here, and one tall case was filled with handwritten works, many bound with strings between leaves of cardboard.

"Blasphemous treatises," said Melogian, pointing to the bookcase. "People who can't get them printed may send them directly to the crown, and they are kept for the future. They are stored here to protect them from bigots, who've been known to tear pages into bits and actually eat them."

There was a door in the farther wall, also locked, and once more Melogian had the key. The room beyond was windowless. Some light came from beyond an archway, hanging lamps shining over rows of brightly covered books.

Christine, curious, moved toward the opening to get a better look; Melogian put a hand on her shoulder immediately.

"Don't. That way is dangerous. Stay here!"

The sorceress drew a vial from her robes and shook it with a flick of the wrist. The liquid within gave forth a greenish shine, bright enough to illuminate the near part of the room. This was shallow, and devoid of furniture beyond a closed bookcase and a lectern nearby.

"These are the only forbidden books," Melogian said, pointing to the shut bookcase. "Even the case is locked and spell-warded."

"What are they?"

"An odd lot. One is Talquen's autobiography, which was ordered burned. A single copy was saved from the flames and made its way here; officially, it doesn't exist. Another book is supposed to be magical, and cursed. For a fact it's sealed by some ancient spell, but it's almost certainly just a piece of old malice, like a pit someone would dig in the land and then cover with a thin crust of earth, just for the pleasure of thinking someone might fall in. That book should be destroyed, but successive sovereigns have kept it locked up in here and not bothered to decide any further on its fate. The other books are monstrosities banned by royal decree—far, far worse than the treatises in the previous room, at least in theory. They are kept in here as an example of what may not be committed to print; no one ever reads them, of course, least of all the kings and queens who like to forbid books."

"And all those books over there?" asked Christine, her gaze returning to the archway that Melogian had said was dangerous. Through it she could see shelves ranged to the limit of her sight. The vividly colored covers were stamped in gold characters, the leather dyed in reds and oranges and sometimes bright green or blue. The light from the hanging lamps was blue-tinged, steadier than any light she had seen so far in Chrysanthe. It felt familiar and safe, in contrast to the sorceress's warning—but that was, Christine realized suddenly, because the light reminded her of the cold glow of fluorescent tubes; an everyday part of her old life, but an aberration in Chrysanthe.

"Those are what I wanted to show you," Melogian was saying. "That is a made world, beyond the archway, Christine."

Christine's flash of insight dampened the surprise she felt, but still she looked at the sorceress with incredulity. "Here?" she said. "There's an opening here?" It felt wrong to her. Made worlds should open in remote wilderness; but in the core of this castle, at the center of the world? Yet hadn't Quentin said that some made worlds opened in civilized areas? "You have an opening into a made world in the middle of Testenel?"

"Yes. Not just one, in fact, but four. All other openings are distant from one another, except for two nearly adjacent ones in far Archeled, but here, within Testenel, there are four. Two have been sealed off for centuries. Two others are open. This is one, but it is well warded. There is a library within it, and in all the time it has stood here it has been but poorly mapped. The made world itself is strangely shallow; its gradient is imperceptible and walls constrict attempts at greater penetration. I . . . I searched for you there, when you were taken. I knew the library better than anyone alive. I spent a week at it, and got nowhere. The stacks go on into a peculiarly bounded infinity. I traveled for two days away from the opening, hoping to discern a better gradient, but there was nothing except more books."

"But why? Why is there a made world here? Quentin said they were opened by mages, right?"

"Yes, though we've lost the secret of it. The portal into this one was opened by Nikolas Mestech, one of the Heroes of olden days. As for what motivated him, histories report he found inspiration for marvelous schemes in his imaginary books. He is also said to have concocted several new spells working from these sources."

"If you knew the library well, you must have read the books yourself."

"Some of them, of course. I went into the imaginary library often in the latter years of my apprenticeship—but it was a complete waste of my time. I looked at every book you can see through the arch; even in that limited space there are more than in the whole royal library itself above us. And all of them are worthless. I think it's possible that Mestech carefully removed those few books he found useful and hid them somewhere. Perhaps he meant merely to protect them from harm, but in any case I never found them. As for the others . . . None of them is sorted, either by subject or by author. Some contain cryptic ideograms in place of words, others are written in complex ciphers to which no key is provided; over half, while plainly enough written, are in foreign languages. I found three short books filed together that were in the plain tongue. But they were written backward, letter by letter, so that it was impossible to read them naturally, even in a mirror, and I had to work out each word—which I did, out of sheer obstinacy."

"And what were they about?"

"The first dealt with symmetry, the next with palindromes, and the third professed to explain how to remember the future, but it actually avoided saying anything." Melogian chuckled. "I've grown to believe that this is all a colossal joke that Mestech played on future generations. I think that as a boast, or perhaps some sort of philosophical statement, he opened a way into a world of his making, filled with the most futile books he could conceive of . . . and he had a wild imagination."

"He imagined all those books, by himself?"

"Not individually, of course; but to open a made world is to cast a net into infinity. You don't have to know what a monster looks like exactly in order to catch one." At these words Melogian shivered and chafed her arms. "Speaking of monsters . . . The imaginary library isn't safe. Some strange things have been seen shambling among the aisles. If you ever want to visit it, I'll be glad to accompany you; but I'm loath to have you enter a made world again."

"I don't want to go there," said Christine. "I wouldn't have gone even if you hadn't told me about it, would I?"

"Not here, of course. But there's a fourth made world in Testenel, and you were never told about it. That one is wide open, and accessible to anyone, and you approached the opening earlier, while I was gone. I was upset when I learned of it. You were never in danger—but you were ignorant, and that isn't good."

"Where? Where is it?"

"In the center of the Royal Gardens. There is a ring of topiary around a pond, and the opening is at the center. The gradient is quite steep; within a few steps the gardens about you vanish, and you are walking along a forest path, down to a lake. There is no danger as such, and the way back into the real world is well marked. But still, you should be aware of the made world's existence."

Christine at last felt a chill at the thought of being so close to openings into made worlds. Even though she knew that nothing belonging to them could emerge into Chrysanthe, so that there was no risk of the monsters Melogian referred to crossing the threshold into this small room, still she felt vulnerable.

"I want to leave," she said.

"As you should. Let's go back up to the true library. We will get you books on the Law—Cartell's *Way of the World*, perhaps. And history books, if you want. Anything, really."

As they were making their way back to the outer door and its garrulous warden, Christine remarked: "You know, you didn't have to take me down here. You could just have told me."

"Yes; but showing is far more effective. As my master Orion used to say, it's always better to smell a flower for yourself than to read about its perfume."

Christine thought to detect a fallacy, but declined to argue. What did it say about her, she wondered, that as soon as the door had shut on Mestech's imaginary library, her thoughts returned to the books within, and that she found herself filled with curiosity about their nonsensical contents? Above her was a treasure trove of books about the true realm, its history and its nature; why did a part of her refuse to let go of what Melogian had shown her, the made world and all its weirdness? She was too eager for made-up stories, too little grounded in reality—especially, she supposed, when that reality had aspects that were hard to take. No, she must focus on the books above, and immerse herself into the truth they held.

❧ She did so, over the next few days. She cleared bare the shelves of her sitting room, moving aside precious gewgaws to make space for books, books of all kinds, which she was able to borrow from the library indefinitely, a privilege that made her terribly guilty but which she found she could not protest, though she made careful entries of each volume she borrowed, promising herself she would not let too much time lapse before returning each of them.

And she read, slowly at first, then with greater speed, once she had gotten used to some odd turns of phrase and typographical conventions. To sit at a table, to lay down a book and open it wide, always after burying her nose briefly into the pages and smelling the ink, was a ritual that brought back her room in the imaginary world of Errefern. It both soothed and unnerved her, so that her plunges into books were briefer than they had been wont to be in earlier times. There was much information to digest, also, a completely new geography and history. She saw names she had heard in Quentin's tales, traced out their lineages. A picture was emerging in her mind, a tangle of lives and strivings, across centuries.

She learned that the authority of Tiellorn had not always been paramount, and that there existed a much greater spectrum of attitudes than she had suspected among the populace. She consulted tomes that dealt with the Law, and was dizzied by some claims made therein. There was superstition, which was something she could recognize: claims that fetishes hung above a door brought good luck, and the like. There were sermons pure and simple: exhortations to good conduct wrapped up in threats of dire consequence. She had endured similar rants at Temple, dire warnings not to cast aside the salvation brought at the price of the Christus' blood. But there were also bald statements of fact, verified by what was claimed to be impartial observation. Cartell's book carried footnoted tales about the punishments visited to those who harmed kings. Melogian had said the Law never acted the same way twice, and indeed there was a wide variety of dooms meted out to transgressors: Death came to them swiftly, but it was never kind.

And, after reading that chapter for the third time, Christine decided that it could not be true. The thought was intoxicating. She was seeing more clearly now. When she had been young, she had believed nearly all grown-ups must be wise, and so when she had read books she had been certain what was written therein must be true. Having come across a whole series of volumes promising to reveal the new frontiers of knowledge, for a time she had sincerely believed that moonlight dulled blades, and that experimenters in Varangia were busily discovering the secrets of extrasensory perceptions and psychokinesis. That belief had drained away from her, not all at once, but bit by bit, as she began to notice how tenuous the claims happened to be, but mostly as she became aware that foolishness didn't stop at some arbitrary age, and that books were not published to uphold truth, but simply to make money.

Dr. Almand's theories had been nothing but foolishness, built on ideas seductive in their simplicity. Once people accepted some idea, they clung to it, and some were more than willing to lie to reinforce it. So it must be with the Law protecting royal blood. What else could it be but an ancient superstition, given credence out of a sense of decency? Cartell was merely repeating tall tales, stories that had taken place a hundred years safely in the past. There was no Law to protect Christine, no death sentence hovering over anyone who wished her ill.

But Katia? Here Christine felt a cold blade stroking her spine. She was dead, she had burned to death. Coincidence, then? Melogian had told Christine she was not responsible. All the more true if there was no Law to punish those who dared assault the princess of the realm. Christine was free of blame, the only one to see clearly amidst a superstitious nation who believed her blood was sacred to God. . . .

But she was in a realm beyond the world she had always known, brought here by magic, and the sun was a ball of flame in the sky, and people could cast their image across the leagues. Melogian believed in the Law, and was she a fool? Christine's certainty collapsed. She could not be sure, and there was certainly no safe way to test her disbelief.

She abandoned her study of the Law and delved instead into history. This was much safer, though at times less comprehensible. As in the history books she knew, much was made of the deeds of kings and queens; but there were endless references to earlier periods, to justify and explain those deeds. It was much as if King George's freeing of his colonies in Septentrional America had been explained as an inevitable consequence of Arnthor's pardon of his rebellious nephew: Unless you first learned enough about Arnthor's time, the explanation was opaque.

Becoming discouraged after some fruitless hours, she switched her focus to recent history; here at least, she hoped, she could get a sense of what had happened in the past few decades, never mind why it had happened this way. So it was that she was holding a very recent book on days barely past when Captain Veraless came to ask for audience.

She was sitting at her usual table, the book reverently laid on the wooden surface, for all that it was in no way fragile. Every book she had seen in Chrysanthe inspired the same respect in her. Printing had been discovered in the made worlds ages ago and the idea had been brought back to the true realm. Printing presses were an ancient technology here. In a darkened corner of the Great Library, protected by crystal domes and preservative spells, lay row upon row of two-thousand-year-old tomes.

And yet the books of Chrysanthe were still crude: Lines of print ran askew, letters were not uniform, typographical abbreviations were inconsistent, pages ragged and uneven. Their binding was often impeccable, but the process of printing itself was still terribly clumsy. Though the book stated it had been printed the previous year—in 6093—Christine's mind, fooled by the look of the pages, kept insisting it would fall apart at the slightest excuse.

She had been both excited and frightened when she had finally located this book: Titled *Chronicle of the Usurpation War*, it concerned itself with the events immediately preceding her birth. The very brief foreword was quite explicit.

In the six thousand and seventy-fourth year of Creation appeared a Hero at the gates of Testenel. Called he down challenge, & King Vaurd answered. Edisthen the Hero named himself, chosen of the Law, future king over the land. Vaurd fought ferociously with Edisthen, but in the end the Law's champion prevailed, and took on the mantle of kingship.

Though Archeled swore fealty to the new king, as did Estephor, Kawlend would not bow its head. Duchess Ambith raised troops against the man she decried as Usurper, & for six months a war raged, in which many were slain, until the lawful king's forces triumphed.

Althea had relayed Veraless's request, and Christine had accepted. Hearing his knock on the door, she raised her gaze from the book, rose, and bade him enter. Veraless walked in. He bowed to her, taking off his hat, and at the same time shut the door with a push of his boot—Christine found the procedure rather silly, but it appeared to be the current fashion at court, as she had seen several people perform exactly the same maneuver, admittedly with less elegance.

Christine replied with a nod of the head, then sat down again. She had learned that she wasn't expected to rise for anyone save for her father, but if she was already standing at the moment the guest walked in, etiquette wouldn't be violated. And Veraless still intimidated her, so that she preferred to be standing when he came to visit.

For a little while they exchanged courtesies. This was Veraless's third visit; unlike Melogian or Quentin, he wasn't someone she saw eagerly, but she didn't dare refuse him. At any rate, he was polite to a fault, and never overstayed his welcome.

Veraless himself directed the conversation the way Christine wanted it to go when he remarked that she was reading and inquired about the book.

"Well, as it happens, Captain, I would like to hear your opinion about it," she said, then carefully picked it up and displayed the cover so that the gilt letters flashed in the reflected sunlight. His face fell. "I'm a third of the way through," she said, "but so far it seems to be just about the fighting. I thought it would explain more about the reasons for the war."

"Oh, that's not a good book at all, milady," said Veraless. "Fershan's a pompous ass, and he was all of ten years old in the Great War. He's got most of his facts straight, but he's a hopeless dreamer, who thinks battle is something noble and beautiful. Besides, are you sure you want to read about the War? It's an ugly subject, and it cuts a bit close to the bone. . . ."

"And that's exactly why I want to read about it. The librarians found a lot of history books for me, but they never brought me anything about the recent past until I asked specifically for it. And even then, they didn't seem too pleased. I've been wondering why that was. But you just told me, didn't you? There's something ugly about the war, something nobody thinks I should know?"

"No, milady. It's just . . . Well, what's it like, reading about your own father taking the crown and having to fight a war. If it were me, I wouldn't be comfortable reading about it."

"I'm not. But it's mostly because I don't quite understand why things happened. Fershan just talks about who fought when and how. What I can't figure out is why people fought a war in the first place. I mean, it's more like what I grew up with. I understand civil wars can happen over a king's succession. But Melogian said my father ruled through the Law. I've seen in other books that duchies can be in conflict, and that people may not want to follow the sovereign. But how could people actually revolt against him? If he was really an incarnation of the Law?"

"The king doesn't rule through the Law, Lady Christine. Your father was chosen by the Law to rule, but he doesn't have any supernatural power of command. He can't just point at someone and make them do something against their will; only demons could ever do that, and some wizards in old times."

"I know that. I shouldn't have said *how*. *Why*, rather. Why would someone rebel against the king, if he was chosen by the Law?"

Veraless looked slightly embarrassed at this question.

"It isn't always so clear that a Hero has come from the Book. And even then, it's happened more than once that people have risen to oppose a Hero-king. Two thousand years ago, a Hero named Black Kelhorn took the throne and ruled for twenty years, until the whole land cried out in misery and he was finally, ah, deposed."

"'Deposed'?"

"Well, 'assassinated' to be precise. He was slain by one of his ministers; she died in agony as the Law took her. So did half a hundred others who had all been part of the conspiracy. They knew what would happen to them, but they were willing to pay the price. Kelhorn died, and his children were taken far away, to live out their lives in a hermitage. Ergenius took the throne; he was the first of the Luminant dynasty."

"Yes, I read about the Luminants," said Christine, unsure again whether to believe there could be a Law that killed so many people in retribution. Could this simply have been a self-serving lie for Ergenius and his offspring? "But why would Kelhorn be such a bad king, if he was a Hero from the Book? You'd say God had sent him to rule, after all."

"God doesn't send us blessings only, milady. There are evil Heroes. Some people claim that they come from the Book of Shades, like demons do. It's all the same, anyway. They have the powers of Heroes, and the destiny of Heroes. Nobody knows why God sends them to us; ask the priestesses and they'll tell you three different stories. Evil Heroes just come, like killer storms, like plagues."

Christine thought upon this for a minute. "So the people of Kawlend thought my father was . . . was an evil Hero?"

Veraless rubbed his chin. "No. Well, some of them, maybe. It's messier than that. You see, the duchess of Kawlend held a great affection for King Vaurd. When he died, she chose to back Evered's faction. I think even without all their stories she would have joined with them; she said she believed them, anyway. What's important is she tried to overthrow Edisthen, even though she had no real chance, not with Archeled and Estephor supporting the king. There was endless fighting, unbelievable slaughter. I lost many friends in that war."

"What stories do you mean, that the duchess believed?"

Veraless sighed. "It's all about Vaurd's death, Lady Christine. The way he died. You see, he wasn't destroyed by the Law. He was found dead in Edisthen's arms, stabbed with his own dagger. They buried him the next day, in the royal cemetery, with his ancestors. Evered always said that your father tricked Vaurd into stabbing himself. Nobody really knows what would happen if a sovereign designated by the Law tried to kill his predecessor—it's happened in the past, but there's no reliable histories for those times."

After a moment of silence, Christine asked, "*You* don't believe my father tricked Vaurd, do you?"

"No." Veraless's tone was flat.

"If he had, would it make that much of a difference? I don't want to offend you, but I keep thinking this is important. I have to understand."

"Milady, I know your father is a Hero. I've known him for twenty years; I know he wouldn't have tricked Vaurd into suicide, not him, not in a thousand years. That's not who he is. Duke Archeled has always said he saw them fight; he saw Vaurd attack Edisthen and collapse. Your father . . . well, he won't talk about it. I guess it's possible Archeled lied."

Christine was silent.

"There was no trickery, I know that," Veraless continued. "But Vaurd might have chosen suicide as a way out, rather than abdication. Do you understand?"

Christine recalled some instances of important personages in the news, dead by their own hand rather than face disgrace. She was forced to nod agreement. "But still," she asked, "suppose he had killed himself, why is that so terrible, so different from being defeated in combat?"

"Because that way Evered can claim Edisthen isn't a Hero at all, just a trickster, a fraud, who used Vaurd's fear of the Law to usurp the crown. You don't see it, milady? No one's ever attacked your father, except Vaurd. . . . But if Vaurd didn't actually fight Edisthen, then there's no absolute proof that Edisthen is the rightful king. The Law can only speak on his behalf if someone tries to wound him."

"You mean Evered won't believe my father is the lawful king until someone hurts him . . . and dies?"

"Aye. And so he's caught in a dilemma: If he orders someone to harm the king, he's just as guilty in the Law's eyes, and he'll be destroyed as well, if Edisthen is really the true king. So he doesn't dare put him to the test."

Christine pondered this, appalled.

"You say it's only happened once or twice that the new king fights the old one," she said. "But kings have been deposed more often than that. Heroes have been . . . sent by God to take the throne; it's happened several times, at least that's what the history books claim. So what happens when they don't fight? Why would the old sovereign just back down and leave? Is it just fear?"

"A sovereign of Chrysanthe, any sovereign, even an evil one, can hear the soul of the land. So if a Hero has come from the Book to replace him, a king of Chrysanthe will know it in his bones."

How convenient, thought Christine, *and how hard to disprove. Then again, it might be the purest truth.*

"And so we don't know," she said, "we can't be really sure who was right. That's it in a nutshell, isn't it?"

"Those who want to believe the worst can believe it, that's always true. But reasonable people understand what happened. Heroes can recognize another of their own kind. Orion swore Edisthen was a fellow Hero. But Evered just accused him of being behind the whole plan, of using Edisthen as his cat's-paw. You can't escape from that kind of logic."

"So how many people believe Evered? Do the people in Kawlend still want him as king?"

"God's eyes, no, milady! There's no one in the land outside of Vorlok who'll back Evered. Not even that old snake Ambith would be crazy enough to start another war."

Veraless managed to change the subject after that, describing some of the *Black Heart*'s travels over the land; Christine was lulled by talk of forests and distant cities, until the captain bowed and took his leave. But when he had gone she picked up the book again, and read some more of that tale of fire and death, trying to see the truth beyond the words, to glimpse the soul of this man who was her father, who had come into being to seize the crown and plunge the land into such turmoil.

4. The Usurper

It is sometimes granted the kings of Chrysanthe to feel the will of the Law, as a man may feel an impending storm by the taste of the air or the color of the sky. For months now King Vaurd had been feeling his destiny shaping itself. And much as a man may prepare for a storm yet is powerless to stop the wind and the rain, so it was with him, who spent hours unsleeping, sick to his stomach with worry, unable to halt the march of events.

He acted still in ways that befit a king, dispensed justice as needed, steered the realm he had been given to govern, passed edicts for the guidance of the populace. Yet the forces of the Law gathered themselves, irresistible. Was he being punished for some past misdeed? Or was this an arbitrary twist of fate, the birthing of some fiend to trouble mankind for years to come, a pestilence to harrow the land? Vaurd sat on the throne with a heavy heart and waited for the storm to break, but it never did.

Then one day he sensed a terrible easing within his breast; a lifting of the oppression that had dwelled there for so long. It had happened, whatever it was. The Law had moved at last, the hand of God reaching into the world. Vaurd wanted at once to laugh with relief and scream in terror. He did neither. His day went on as his days always went. That night, when he retired to his bedchamber, he took his wife the Lady Veronica in his arms and they made love. For a time he thought himself a young man again, forgetting his two score years. He lay in bliss with the woman he loved and she laughed at him, teasing him for this unexpected surge of desire. Afterward he rested by her side, brushing his hand lightly down her body, feeling under his fingertips the stretch marks on her belly; she had borne him four sons, and he found her as lovely as ever.

He did not sleep that night. He awaited further developments. Shortly after sunrise, his senses keyed up. He sensed an imminent presence. He rose and put on his clothes swiftly. Veronica lay in the bed, still asleep. He spared her one glance, then exited the room noiselessly.

At this hour few people were about; Vaurd evaded the notice of the servants as he left the royal apartments. He almost ran through the corridors and rooms of the vast castle, until he had come to a small oriel in the outer wall. He opened a casement and looked out.

It was a foggy morning. In this section of Testenel the overhanging mass of the castle was cut away, like a fjord amongst high mountains, so that there was a clear path to the gate set in the colossal stem of the base. From the side window of the oriel, which was barely fifty feet up from the ground, one could see far into the distance. But the surrounding land was indistinct; Vaurd felt as if the castle were adrift in some incomprehensible sea, as if the world itself had grown tenuous and meaningless. From the oriel he watched a man stride up to the gate, raise his fist and hammer it upon the doors; the blows, muffled by the damp air, sounded to him like the thudding of his heart.

He was a tall man, very thin; he seemed old: half again Vaurd's age. He wore no armor, only plain clothing. He should not have been able to come up to the gate unchallenged: There were sentries posted all around the castle, at all times. It was possible that they had not noticed him because he could move silently, and because the blanket of moisture was so thick as to block sight altogether in the early dawn. Yet it was also possible that the sentries had not challenged him because there had been no one to see.

The man's hammering had drawn attention. A slit opened in the door and a voice rang out, muffled as the blows had been by the atmosphere.

"Who calls? State your name and business."

"I am Edisthen," said the man. His voice was unimpressive; the chest from which it issued had no depths to give it resonance. Then he stated his purpose: "I have come to challenge Vaurd, in the name of the Law."

The guard's reply was an incredulous obscenity. Obviously she thought the man was drunk or mad. Vaurd had shut his eyes and his hands tightly gripped the edge of the balcony. He had to have known; all his worries about some demon abroad in the world, some plague that would strike thousands dead, were but a way to distract himself from seriously considering this supreme terror.

He thought, *I can refuse him entry. I can shut myself up in Testenel. What can he do then? Will he raise an army to ferret me out? He is only one man, an old man. Can he bring down the gates with a word?* But he shook his head. He could see that story unfolding before his inner eye, and it terrified him. He saw battles, a siege; people dying. And in the end, walls breaking open and the Hero striding through the breach. A man can hide from a storm until it passes, but only because the storm is not looking for him.

Vaurd shut the casement, took three steps back. For an instant he stood surrounded by the blue walls of Testenel, safe at the center of the world. Then he shook his head, and ran down a staircase to the gate below him.

He ran into a guard on the way; the man recognized him and snapped to attention. With a gesture Vaurd bade him follow. They reached the broad hall that led to the gate and Vaurd called out to the doorkeepers.

"You will let that man in," he said, marveling that his voice did not break. "Let him in and bring him to the throne room."

Kill him! The words were almost on his lips, for all that he knew what would happen should he utter them. There was nothing to be done, nothing.

He ran, then, desperate to arrive before the Hero. He ran through Testenel and arrived panting at the throne room, his saliva thick and salty in his mouth. He dared not spit it out, and swallowed it with a grimace.

He strode up the steps and sat on the great old seat, carved in fantastic shapes. He was breathing so loudly it sounded like sobs in his ears, but he couldn't bring his inhalations under control. He was still gasping when a side door opened, and his wife came in. Behind her, his eldest son Evered, and behind Evered, a moment later, Duke Edric of Archeled, who had been visiting at court. The duke, a florid man with a lion's mane of hair, scowled at Vaurd.

"My liege, what's this we hear? The servants have gone mad. They tell us Queen Adelline's descendant is here to claim the throne."

Vaurd paid him no attention. He was looking at Veronica, who should never have been here, whom he had left sleeping as she had been meant to. He opened his mouth to tell her to leave, to forget all this, that nothing, absolutely nothing, was going on. But he had no breath left in him, and now the main door to the room opened, and a confused knot of people stood on the threshold. Guards, servants, a courtier, all surrounding a tall gaunt figure with salt-and-pepper hair.

They meant to block his way, no doubt; and yet when he strode forward they broke before him as the sea before a prow of rock, until the Hero stood at the foot of the dais, with a single guard before him and the royal presence.

Evered held his mother's arm, in a gesture at once supportive and fearful: He was barely fifteen, not sure yet if he were a boy or a man. Duke Edric stood by Evered's side; he also looked indecisive.

Vaurd turned his gaze back to the Hero; he found his voice at last, reedy and thin though it was. "I am Vaurd," he said, "sovereign of Chrysanthe. You, sir, are a stranger at court, here without introduction. Still, I welcome you. If you would, I should like to know your name and your reason for being here."

"Your Majesty," replied the Hero, looking up at him with an expression so fresh, so innocent, he seemed a newborn child, "Your Majesty, I am Edisthen, champion of the Law. I have come to announce that your reign is at an end. I am the rightful king of Chrysanthe, here to depose you."

There was a moment of astonished silence, which Evered broke. "Scoundrel!" he shouted. "No one is allowed to make such jokes. Guards, seize this madman!"

"No! Don't touch him!" Vaurd shouted, horrified. The guards stayed motionless, none laying a hand on the Hero. Edisthen was looking at Evered and warned the boy before the king himself could.

"Be careful. I am the Law's champion, the king of Chrysanthe. Whoever harms me dies. Do not give such orders. The Law would hold you accountable as well, and kill you also."

Evered, furious, raged incoherently at Edisthen for a moment, until Vaurd stood from his throne and took one step down.

"Be silent, Evered!" he shouted, and mercifully the boy sputtered to a stop. His mother held his arm now, her fingers clutching at the fabric of his sleeve. She looked at Vaurd with a bewildered expression on her face. On the other side of Evered, Archeled's face was a mask. He understood, Vaurd thought, all too well.

He could not bear these gazes on him, especially not Veronica's. He gave a quiet command, that all should leave the room. But no one moved; at this, he screamed: "*Leave!* I, your king, command it! Leave at once!"

His command was finally obeyed. Servants fled like poultry scattering out of a peasant's way. Duke Edric ushered Veronica and Evered out of the room, the guards following them after Vaurd repeated his orders yet again. The doors were shut, and finally Vaurd and the Hero were alone.

Vaurd stepped back up to the throne, and gripped one of its armrests, his fingers curling around carven faces and limbs. He felt his pulse flooding his face with blood. Below him, the Hero had not altered his posture. Still he gazed at Vaurd like a child facing the sunrise.

"I am king of the realm by right," stated Vaurd. "I am Vaurd son of King Alyfred, son of King Gwynn, son of Queen Rovanne, of the Casthen lineage. This throne is mine."

"No longer," said the Hero in a quiet, reasonable tone. "As of this moment, you are deposed, Vaurd. I claim this throne by virtue of the Law."

"Who are you to make this claim? None may take this kingdom away from me. The people recognize me as their sovereign."

"You know who I am, Vaurd. You cannot deny it. I am the Law's champion, come into being to replace you."

Vaurd shook his head. Fear twisted in his gut, but he would not yield so easily.

"Any madman may claim to be a Hero. Do you take me for such a fool? There has been a single Hero written into the world in centuries. Am I now to believe a second one has arisen? And to depose me? What grievance can God have of me?"

"I don't speak for God, Vaurd. I know nothing of God. I speak for the Law. And you know very well that I speak the truth, even if you do not want to believe. Your face is naked to me."

Vaurd pulled the long dagger at his belt from its sheath. "I can kill you," he said. "One thrust of this shall prove you out." His arm shook. He was barely competent with any kind of weapon. He could not stand battle, could not bear to see someone die. He held the weapon as he would have a butter knife, then remembered to shift his grip.

"The Law protects me," said Edisthen. "Cut me and you shall be destroyed, no matter that you once were king. But if this is the way you want to end it, then let us fight. I have a sword; I will let you fetch one if you want."

Only then did Vaurd grow aware of the baldric over the Hero's right shoulder and the sheathed sword attached to it. Had it been with the pommel of his weapon, rather than his fist, that he had hammered at the gate of Testenel? Yet how could the guards not have noticed it?

"No," he whined, and then recovered his poise as he seized upon the flaw in the Hero's logic. "No; if you fight me, you will die as well."

"I would only die if I harmed you, Vaurd, which I will not. I will simply defend myself. Go on, fetch a real blade. Your death in combat will prove my claim beyond any doubts."

Vaurd said nothing, breathing heavily, his mind numb. The Hero continued.

"Several times before, sovereigns of Chrysanthe have been deposed by Heroes from the Book. Often they fought to challenge the claim, and died, but not always; twenty-five centuries ago, King Cwmedd chose instead to abdicate and fled into exile. I can offer you this, Vaurd: The Law does not ask for your death. Surrender the crown to me, and take your family into the margins of the kingdom. The Law will be content; you shall be allowed to live out your lives in peace."

Vaurd's mind rebelled at the words. There are some truths that may not be renounced without shattering a man's sanity. Vaurd was king and he would be king forever; on this principle his whole life rested. He could not yield the crown; and yet he could not deny Edisthen. The Law was crushing him like a kernel under a mill wheel.

For an endless time he stood at the side of his throne and stared at the Hero. He could feel Testenel all around him, sensed the buzzing of human activity within the shell of cold stone. And like the vast castle rooted in the earth and blossoming to challenge the vault of heaven, so did he feel his life stood, rooted deeply in the past. There flashed through his mind myriad memories, so intense that they seemed tangible. He held Veronica in his arms on their wedding night, saw his sons being born, swam in the river while his father Alyfred looked on and he cried, *Daddy look at me!*, played on the floor with the pink pebbles he preferred to the marbles he had been given, rode a horse toward Testenel, gazing at the edifice that would be his home forever, ate and drank at a feast and suddenly noticed a beautiful young woman, lay tossing abed with a fever through the night, received the dukes of the realm with the full pomp of the court, carried little Olf on his shoulders and turned round and round until the boy screeched with laughter, discussed philosophy with Duchess Ambith of Kawlend, opened his eyes and gazed at the ruddy flaming disc of the sun ascending through the sky, lay under the wheeling stars and felt the entire world breathe along with him. . . .

All of this was his, was himself, and for the Hero to overthrow him was to have these memories stolen from him, taken away—it was not something which could be borne.

Then he let go of the throne's arm, shifted his grip on the dagger, went down one step of the dais.

Edisthen stepped back, said, "We don't have to fight; we can bring this to an honorable conclusion." But he kept his hand near his sword, and his eyes darted left and right. Vaurd was comforted by this observation that the Hero was fallible, that he could not read minds. Vaurd could not really hate him; can one hate the storm that sinks ships and casts down houses?

Then he went down two steps swiftly; at the same time he brought his other hand to the dagger's hilt, raised his arms as one preparing to slay a pig. Edisthen drew his sword, his movements swift as a young man's, assumed a defensive posture. Vaurd had time for an indrawn breath of amazement. And strangely, in that moment he felt some pity for the Hero, overcoming his bitter envy for a man who could draw a sword for the very first time in his life and do it with such consummate, unearned skill.

Then in one smooth blow, Vaurd drove the dagger deep in the pit of his own belly. The point clove his flesh, tore open his heart. He would have screamed in torment; his mouth opened, but no sound came out.

He fell onto his knees; but before he could topple farther forward, Edisthen had caught him, turned him on his back. The Hero cradled him in his arms, his face bewildered. So clearly, he had never even conceived of such an ending. *You can't understand,* Vaurd wanted to tell him. *You were not born, you have never lived. To you everything is simple. One day, years from now, you will see the truth of things; if you take too much from a man nothing worthwhile is left of him. You have nothing to lose, but I have far too much. From the moment the crown descended upon my head I knew I would be king until breath failed me. . . .*

He felt his body tremble; a tremor shook his stomach, and a thin stream of blood overflowed his teeth to wet his beard. His lungs would not fill. There was a roaring in his ears, a cloud across his sight. He could feel himself falling, falling, or was it that he rose up in the air?

It did not take much time before the doors burst open, but by then Vaurd lay dead in Edisthen's arms. His blood stained the Hero's hands and clothing.

Evered ran toward the Hero, screaming, Duke Edric trying desperately to restrain him. Unable to risk harm to the prince, he could not acquire a firm hold. As the boy came at him, Edisthen twisted aside and avoided contact. Evered tripped on the dais and fell hard, slamming his head onto the edge of a step. Veronica ran to him, her eyes blind.

The duke's gaze met Edisthen's, and then Edric inclined his head. "I shall say you fought," he stated. "You fought, and King Vaurd was defeated, as the champion of the Law prevailed."

Evered had righted himself; blood poured from a cut on his eyebrow. His mother held his shoulder and tried to tend to him. "No!" shouted the boy, his mouth twisted. "I *saw.* I saw what he did!"

"I did not want this," said Edisthen to the boy. "It did not have to happen this way." Evered replied with an animal sound, the snarl of a caged beast whose mind is filled with death. He staggered to his feet, tried to launch himself at Edisthen once more, but collapsed in midstride and rolled helplessly onto his back. He clapped his hands to the sides of his head and howled, lost to the world.

More people were streaming into the throne room, halting to gaze at the scene. Vaurd's crown had fallen to the floor. Edisthen looked at it, then down to the twisted face of the corpse in his arms. For the moment he did nothing, spoke not a word. Not because he did not know what to do next, but because his spirit was filled with awe. He was like a traveler embarked on a journey to the next town, who reaches the top of a hill and sees spread before him a landscape vast beyond comprehension, and his destination at the far end of it, too distant yet to even be envisioned.

The earth rose in a mound that peaked and broke, shedding shards of rubble and clots of soil; claws rose to the surface, and between them a reptilian snout emerged. The beak opened, let forth a hiss of frustration. The ground shook rhythmically as the opening widened, cracks appearing in the earth. Another heave and the forequarters of the demon emerged. Its red and black eyes rolled left and right, maddened. Casimir could sense the pain that goaded it ever onward, its very blood aboil with rage. Its agony could never end, only lessen for a while. For ages it had lain within the earth, forced into quiescence. Not sleep, never sleep, for the perpetual

torment that flowed in its veins would not let it sleep. Its tiny mind forever sought
surcease, finding none.

Its back legs heaved and more earth erupted out of the pit. Its shell rose into
view, each scale topped with a fantastic spine. The demon screamed in frustration
and finally clawed itself free of its prison. Casimir shared its senses in part, and now
felt what passed for pleasure for the terrapin, a momentary lessening of its unending
torment.

Come, he bade it. A mere flicker of pain at the base of the tail and the terrapin
moved to escape it, its adamantine claws raking at the ground as it progressed. It
breathed stertorously, a faint cloud of steam blowing from its mouth at each exhala-
tion, and the grasses caught in that cloud withered. Casimir stood well in front of it
and walked briskly. The demon followed him, whining and snuffling, bigger than a
house and barely more sentient than the plants it crushed under its tread. There
would be leagues upon leagues of journeying through empty lands. But if, when
they crossed nearer to inhabited places, someone should happen to spot them—
well, the element of surprise counted for much in Casimir's plans, and human flesh
was one of the few things that moderated the demon's constant pain. One had to
treat one's soldiers well, if one intended to win a war.

King Edisthen sat in his study, blessedly alone for a time. The desk before him
was an antique, carved from dark griff-wood seven centuries ago for Queen Isolde.
The marble top had been changed once, two centuries back. His chair, unbelievably, was older still, a massive affair built to seat a titan. The cushion on the seat, at
least, seemed fairly new; but it still might be older than the king himself. Surrounded by these ancient furnishings, Edisthen felt his youth as a curse. Some days
it seemed to him that he could not possibly belong in eternal Testenel, though he
knew very well it was for the sole purpose of being here that he existed at all. He
wondered if other people ever felt something of the kind, but he dared not ask anyone. He could not afford to appear weak.

Edisthen looked at his hands: fleshless, the veins stark beneath the skin, the
hairs mingled black and white. Strong still, as strong as they had always been. They
might grow feeble with the passage of decades, but he did not know with any certainty whether they would. Orion had not known; Orion at two hundred years old
had expected to live for a long time still. It was very likely that Edisthen had the
same long future to look forward to. What would it be like, to live on and on, to
watch others grow old and die, while he himself endured? What would it be like to
watch his own daughter make her slow journey to the grave, to see her buried in the
royal cemetery—and to go on still, for another hundred years and more?

It did not bear being thought of. Absurd, really, this worry of his, when for
more than a decade he had tormented himself with the thought of never seeing her
again.

A fleshpaint portrait of Christine hung over the mantelpiece; she wore a dress
of purple and gold, sewn with beads of pure light, like stars. She had been depicted
looking over her shoulder. How often he had gazed at this portrait, his heart seized

by a dread too great for words. Through the years, he had watched his daughter grow, the dress altering its shape to match her body. He had seen the young woman bloom, her dark hair grow lustrous and long, her eyes like the mystery of the heartwood. . . .

Heroes so very rarely had offspring, Orion had taught him. Several times in history a sovereign had been written into existence, but never, as far as the wizard knew, had this sovereign founded a dynasty. What could it be like to occupy the throne for centuries, as his descendants multiplied, princes and princesses until their deaths, hoping for their children's children's children, perhaps, to rule the land?

No, he would not do this. He had thought to cling to kingship for want of a better solution, fulfilling his function until the day of his passing; but that had been when Christine had been lost to them all. In time, in a few decades at most—as long again as he had already lived—he would abdicate in his daughter's favor. He would let go of the throne gladly, start to fade from the stage of the world. Christine, he hoped, would have children, and one of them would become sovereign in turn. Perhaps, after that generation, Edisthen would follow Orion's path in reverse, away from the center of things into an isolated life of contemplation.

To speculate on these unborn times was strange to him; it left him with the aftertaste of a dream, as if he were about to wake to a much sadder reality. He put the fancies from his mind. There was time yet to figure out the course of his life, so much time.

He found his mind drifting from the future to the past, remembering Anyrelle and the love they had shared, remembering her dead on the bed where she had given birth to their daughter. After all these years that pain was almost comforting, the familiar shape of a mortal wound which still had failed to kill him. Had he been a born man, of more than middle years as he appeared to be, perhaps Christine's return would have driven him mad with joy. As it was, he had felt his mind twist and flex, but he was so young still that it had not shattered; he had accepted the turn of events, and been spared for the sting in the tail.

He wished more than anything for Christine's presence at his side, yearned to talk to her for hours, ask her all about her life, tell her of things here in Chrysanthe. But the very sight of him was hard for her to accept. When he had presented her to the populace, she had come into his arms then, and he had shaken with a happiness words could never contain. But the moment had passed. He saw her every day, but for very brief periods. Melogian assured him that Christine was hard put to adapt to her changed circumstances but was growing slowly to find her place in the world; that in the end, she would acknowledge and love him freely. Yet Edisthen doubted this. Her mind had been poisoned against him; how deep the scars in her soul ran he could not guess. She might well never be able to look him in the eye without quailing. And until she had grown able to tolerate his presence for longer than a brief while, he could never tell her all that he needed to.

Still, he had not been written as a passive man; he yearned for peace, yes, but not submission. He would strive, because in truth, he didn't know anything else but strife. He drew a stack of blank paper toward him, dipped a quill into an inkwell, and began to write. His hand was cursive, flawlessly elegant. Calligraphic ability is one of the proper attributes of a king—and it would have been hard to credit one who had been actually written into existence with sloppy penmanship.

He began to write to Christine, not a brief letter like the one he had sent before, but an accounting of himself and his life. Perhaps, if she could not bear his presence, still she would accept his words. And what else was he, in the end?

The sentences flowed from his pen at a moderate pace, but without hesitation. It did not enter his mind to lie even in the slightest; at best he would present the truth in the best order for his reader's comprehension, but he did not imagine holding back anything. He had no secrets: He hadn't lived long enough to amass any, and while there were certainly things about him no one knew, he did not know them himself.

❧ In his quarters Quentin awaited Melogian; she had promised to come visit him tonight, but the hour was advancing, and she failed to appear. He wondered sometimes how it could be that no one guessed at their relationship, or else if everyone knew but said nothing. It wasn't as if it were a shameful thing, or forbidden, or even tasteless. Yet he sensed the sorceress wanted him to remain discreet about it; so he kept all his feelings to himself when they were not alone. It pained him at times, in Christine's presence, to have to keep this secret. He felt as if he were betraying the princess's confidence. Surely, if she asked him, he would tell her the truth. But unless and until she did, he would carry that small weight on his heart whenever he stood before her.

Quentin's dalliances with Melogian followed no clear schedule; the sorceress was much preoccupied with various matters, and often at the end of a day, all she wanted was to sleep, alone.

There came a light knock on his door, and he went to open it. Melogian crossed the threshold and he shut the door behind her. Then he took her in his arms and kissed her; but she failed to return his ardor. He pulled away, looked at her with concern. She gave him a wan smile.

"Are you well, Melogian?"

"Yes, yes, of course. I'm just so tired. I wanted to see you, but I'm not very gay right now. Can we just sit down?"

"Of course."

They sat down on a small couch, where once—it was vividly clear in Quentin's memory—they had coupled savagely. He put his arm around Melogian's shoulders. She let him stroke her arm; she smiled again when he kissed her, but she was staring off into space, preoccupied with her thoughts. He tried to start a conversation twice, but she replied in monosyllables.

For a time then he stayed silent, and the longer the silence continued the more he got the impression he was being taken for granted. Eventually he could stand it no more and said, in a tone that betrayed his mounting exasperation, "I really wish you would talk to me, Lady Melogian. I am starting to wonder if I am your lover and your friend, or merely your . . . your pillow."

At this she turned to him, her eyes blazing suddenly. "Oh, no, not you too," she said. "I cannot have any more demands made of me, Quentin. Stop it."

"What demands do you mean? I—"

"I said stop it. Every time Edisthen asks my advice on something, I can hear him thinking at me, *You're not Orion.* Every time I look in the mirror I tell myself the same thing. Evered's brood sit in Vorlok hatching plots, and for all I know Casimir is taking magic lessons from Hundred-Handed Juldrun herself. I do *not* need you adding to the pressure; what I need is for you to help me loosen it. If you want to couple with me that badly, just throw me on the floor and be done with it. Otherwise, if I'm boring you, I can just leave you alone."

Her words stung him far worse than he'd have imagined they could. "You told me you needed a friend," he accused her. "Were you not aware that friendship goes in both directions?"

She turned her gaze to the wall before her, avoiding his eyes. "I don't want to quarrel with you!"

"This is not a quarrel. A quarrel is when people scream at each other. We are having a discussion."

"*Please,* Quentin . . ."

Vanquished, he threw his hands in the air. "Forget I said anything, Lady," he said, unable to restrain his bitterness. "I suppose I am making unfair demands. God's eyes, but you are harder to handle than any peril I have faced in my life."

"If you want a compliant wench," said Melogian, still looking away from him, "I gather you've had more than one offer in that direction lately."

Quentin suddenly saw things in a new light.

"Are you . . . *jealous,* Melogian?" he asked, astonished.

"Jealous! As if I had time for jealousy!"

"You are! You are jealous . . ."

Melogian ran her hands through her hair, her thumbnails scratching on the stubble at the sides of her head. Her eyes were tightly closed. Quentin moved closer to her.

"There is no need for this," he said softly. "I want no one but you. Forgive me for losing my temper. I should have seen—"

"Oh, God, Quentin," she groaned, "stop offering me that courtly love of yours. You're such a disgusting paragon of restraint. Why can't you just stalk off, go strump a baroness, and come back to me with a limp member and a feeble excuse?"

"Is *that* what you want from me?"

She turned to face him. "No, no, no, you idiot, I want you for me—but not to make *demands*! I can't measure up to you, Quentin, I can't be the high-born lady wizard with a pure heart and an empty head. You've read too many of Severn's romances; don't reduce me to a character in his fables!"

She was in his arms then, and he soothed her as she clutched at him.

"I can't be what you'd like me to be," she said, her teeth clenched. "I can only be Melogian. We're not made for each other, you and I. I became smitten with you because you were so perfect, because this is what my foolish heart wants in a man, but I cannot *stand* it when you ask more of me than I can give. The guilt burns in my craw like acid. And I can't cope, I just can't, Quentin!"

Quentin stroked her cheek. "I do not want you to be a lady out of Severn's books, Melogian. I do not want to be a burden on you. Forgive me."

"Don't think I don't want you. I do, even now when I'm so angry at you, I wish I could ride you until you made me scream, but I don't have the luxury. I can't focus myself on this moment and this place; I have to be everywhere at once, don't you see? If continence makes you unhappy, please find release with someone else, anyone. I won't be angry at you. I'll make no complaint."

"I love you. I do not want anyone else."

"I'm not the one you love," she sighed. "And it's better that way. But if we're going to pretend, then you have to take me as I am, the bad with the good. All right?"

He murmured assent and twined his fingers in hers. She rested her head against him; he felt the warmth of her breath on his neck. He was aware of her slender body in his arms, and of his reaction to it, but mostly he felt tenderness toward her, a plenitude in being there to comfort her, in spite of all his earlier irritation. He held her gently and after an eternity she began to relax, her limbs abandoning their tension. Still she remained in his arms, and he wondered if in fact she slept, or if she was weeping. But she suddenly broke the embrace; and when he beheld her eyes they were wide open, and dry.

"Sweet Quentin," she said, brushing her finger along the edge of his jaw. "I can't help how I feel about you, for all I wish I could. Tomorrow—I won't promise, but I will make time for you tomorrow afternoon. I'll find you, and we can do whatever you want. Yes?"

Quentin agreed and kissed her. He knew her offer was sincere, and that at the same time she did not fully believe in it. But he loved her all the same, and in the end that was what truly mattered.

5. The Shape of the World

On the morning of the twenty-seventh of Summereve, the sky was free of clouds. Christine went on her boldest outing yet, a picnic with her usual entourage for these ventures: one of her body servants, several maids and guards, not to mention Quentin. They traveled a short distance away from Testenel, along a well-tended lane that wound amongst low hillocks. The grounds about the castle were like a park: an immense lawn with here and there small clumps of trees. When the party had walked for half an hour, they paused and Christine turned her gaze back toward the castle. It was still shockingly large, a deeper blue than the sky, glistening in the sunlight from myriad windows. Quentin came up to her, holding a gourd of water with a jeweled stopper. Realizing that this was meant for her exclusive use, Christine recoiled.

"I thought this was a picnic," she said, and went up to one of the maids, who was drinking from a plain waterskin. "Isn't this water fit for me?" Christine asked. When the maid assented, blushing, Christine took up the waterskin and drank from it.

The others were staring at her; Christine gave voice to her sense of outrage. "Listen; this is a *picnic*," she said, "and I'm not an exotic pet. What's good enough for you is good enough for me. I'll eat the same food as you, and drink the same water. Is that clear?"

Everyone agreed emphatically, and the party continued its journey. Once they had reached their destination, blankets were spread on the grass and food was unpacked. True to her word, Christine ate the same victuals as the rest of the group and pointedly ignored the delicacies that had been brought expressly for her.

Afterward, some of the maids played a game involving three balls of varying weight, which had to be thrown and caught in a given pattern. They were neither skilled nor eager, and every missed catch was an excuse for laughter.

Christine sat in the middle of one blanket, watching them and the surroundings. Rann sat close by, her head shaded by a white lace hat. After a moment, Christine gestured to Quentin, who came and knelt by her side.

"I see the guards watching something over there," she said. "What are they looking at?"

"Gardeners, Lady Christine. A party of four, doing their rounds. All is well."

"I'm a bit scared, so far away from the castle. But what surprises me is how little I'm actually frightened. I keep telling myself I ought to be worried, but I can't manage it. . . ."

"You should *not* be worried, milady. Notwithstanding the guards, you are still protected by Melogian's magic. If she or I had any doubts as to your safety, we would not have approved this outing. It is a good thing, a good sign, that you are enjoying this and that you are feeling safe. It is said sovereigns can feel the Law; not only the part of the Law that protects you, but all of it. I believe you are feeling the health of the realm. How could you be frightened, then?"

Christine was unconvinced. "I wouldn't go so far. It's just nice to be out, and in the sunshine, and . . ." she heaved a trembling sigh ". . . I guess I'm getting used to this. This place, this world . . . I'm starting to believe. To feel real."

Quentin beamed at her, and said: "You surprised everyone about the water."

"Are you saying I should just have used my own water?"

"No, Lady. Not at all. What you did was a surprise, but not a bad one. The story will spread, and people—most people—will approve. Sharing your subjects' water and viands shows you to be close to them in spirit. A good sovereign is a sister and mother to her people. You will be admired for this."

Christine looked up at him, uncertain. "I keep forgetting everything I do is watched," she whispered. "The least little thing is a sign."

"No, it is not that bad, Lady Christine. And you just have to be yourself, as you have been so far. Your true nature will shine forth."

"If you say so," Christine sighed.

For a while they remained in a companionable silence. Rann tilted her head to peer at Christine over Quentin's knee, but her mistress wanted nothing and she settled back on her heels.

Presently Quentin said in a low voice: "There is one thing I wanted to speak of with you, Lady Christine. . . . I have a favor to ask."

"What favor?"

Quentin hesitated a moment. "I had planned to wait, but you have shown yourself confident today, and so I feel the time is ripe. My lady, I have not seen my parents in nearly ten years. I beg leave to visit them."

Christine felt brought out of herself by the request. She rose to her feet; Quentin followed suit.

"I . . . Oh God, of course you can. . . . Why do you even need to ask?"

"I am attached to your service. I cannot leave without your permission. I had to ask the king your father as well."

"I'm so stupid . . . I never thought of your parents. It's like they were dead. Of course you can go see them. Quentin, I'm not . . . I won't prevent you from doing something like that. Go, please! Just . . . Just how far away are they?"

"Lydiss is a four-day journey from here. I would be gone a fortnight." Christine felt a pang of anxiety twist her features. Quentin added immediately: "But I will not go, if you need me by your side."

"No. No!" Christine straightened. "I'll be fine. Quentin, I order you, you hear? I order you to visit your parents. When you're done, come back. Until then, I'll manage."

"If you are sure, then I will go. I would like to leave early tomorrow morning; then I might make the journey in three days instead of four, with a little luck."

"All right. All right." Christine turned her attention to the ball game, which had degenerated into a pursuit. She felt bereft at the thought of sending Quentin away for so long, but it was cruel beyond words to keep him here. Still, his request cast a shadow over the rest of the outing and she was hard put to enjoy herself.

By the time Christine woke up the next morning, Quentin was gone from Testenel. For all that she knew she was being childish to feel abandoned, her mood was sour. She tried to busy herself amongst her books, and found herself leafing through an atlas which offered numerous small-scale maps, but none at large scale as she would have wished, except a rather crude example on the first page. The maps were etchings, some quite nice, but all in black and white. Except for hand-illuminated manuscripts, none of the books in Chrysanthe displayed any color. A four-color printing process obviously lay beyond the technical proficiencies of the realm.

Frustrated by her circumstances, Christine was in a querulous mood when Melogian came to call around midmorning. As soon as greetings had been exchanged, she complained:

"Every time I think I'm fitting in better, something like this happens. I mean, I'd like to learn more about the world, but you people really don't make it easy sometimes!"

"What do you mean?" asked Melogian.

"It's all these stupid maps!" Christine leafed through the atlas. "I can go east to west just fine, but they all stop dead north or south. Shouldn't there be another atlas like this one? I couldn't find it; there's no catalog entry, even."

Melogian raised an eyebrow. "Christine, there's a good reason why there are no maps of regions beyond."

"Oh yes? Then what is it?"

The sorceress sighed. "When you and I talk about geography, it always degenerates into an argument, and I have had enough of that recently. I could tell you, but I might well upset you in the bargain."

Christine's irritation was overlaid by curiosity. She said, in a reasonable tone, "I know the world is a strange place. You told me before; and I accept that. So, whatever it is . . ." She felt a momentary anxiety, but forged on. "I'm ready to hear you."

Melogian opened her mouth then suddenly closed it and pursed her lips, stricken by a sudden idea. "Better yet; what if I showed you? You should see more of the world than Testenel and its grounds. What do you say to an outing through the air?"

At another time, Christine might have begged off, but today she was in no mood to remain cloistered in her apartments, feeling sorry for herself. Melogian went to her own rooms to fetch a few items of need, then returned for Christine. There was a bit of a to-do with Althea and her guards, when Melogian explained there would only be room for the two of them. Christine settled the dispute with a few words, finding authority came a little bit easier this time. Then she set off with Melogian, across corridors and up several flights of stairs. Away from her entourage for the first time in days, Christine felt a new sense of freedom.

Eventually they reached a short gallery that curved sharply, clearly following the outer wall of one of the towers.

This area of the castle was deserted, and seldom visited, as a thin layer of dust attested. Melogian knelt and swept an area of floor clean with her hands. "I am going to summon transportation of a special sort," she explained. "There is a balcony just behind yonder door; once I have made the summons you can open the door, but not before."

"I thought we were going to ride a skyship," said Christine, who had in fact been hoping to see Captain Veraless again.

"I hardly think so. We will be traveling two hundred and fifty leagues; a skyship would need a day and a half to cross that distance if it had favorable winds throughout and its crew needed no sleep. We need something a trifle faster. Please give me silence now."

As Christine watched, Melogian scribed a spiraling design on the floor with a piece of blue chalk, speaking slow syllables meanwhile. She finished the drawing crouching at its center; then she stood up, stabbed her left hand downwards, and spoke a single command. The chalk puffed out in a million particles and the design vanished. The door to the balcony trembled in its frame.

"You can open the door now." Christine did so, with not a little apprehension. Beyond the door was a wide and shallow balcony, with a low railing of chipped and cracked blue stone. The tower was at the periphery of Testenel and Christine was granted an uninterrupted view of the landscape beyond. The balcony was far, far above the ground, hundreds of feet. Floating just beyond the railing was a translucent, gray-blue, dish-shaped object perhaps ten feet across, which vibrated and emitted a low roar.

"This is a whirl," Melogian announced, standing at Christine's shoulder. "Barring instant transport, a spell lost to us four thousand years ago, there is no faster way of travel." She gestured at the whirl and it rose and drifted just next to the balcony. With an easy motion, she vaulted the railing and dropped down into the whirl. Christine was unable to match Melogian's negligence; even after repeated reassurances, the sorceress had to help her aboard, letting her clutch the railing with one hand until she was well settled. The whirl's apparent vibration did not affect its passengers; all Christine felt was a faint tremor, nothing compared to the thudding of her heart.

"Ready?" asked Melogian.

"No. No, not yet. Give me a moment."

"If you're too frightened, we don't have to do this."

"That's okay. I'm frightened, but excited too." Christine laughed nervously, keeping her gaze level, not daring to look down. "I've always wanted to fly, even though I was scared of planes. The skyship felt more like a boat than an aircraft, so that didn't really count. This, though . . . Is there any magic to make you fly by yourself, without being carried in something?"

"It's easy to levitate someone; far harder to actually make oneself fly, and the flight is slow and clumsy at best, since people are not birds and were not made for flight. This way is best: The whirl flies of its own, and it carries us in relative comfort. If you really want to feel like you're flying, I can tune it for complete transparency."

"No, no! This is already transparent enough for me, thank you."

"In that case, here." Melogian had brought a satchel with her and from it she now took out a small blanket which she spread on the bottom of the craft. "Sit yourself there; it's softer, and opaque. Now. Are you ready?"

Christine waited a moment more for her heart to settle, then she nodded fatalistically. The roar of the whirl increased and scaled up in pitch; with a breathtaking abruptness they were off, the walls of Testenel and the ground receding from them equally swiftly. "*Jesus!*" Christine screamed, clutching at Melogian.

"What was that?" asked Melogian, as she brought the whirl to a stop. She was repressing a grin. Christine panted for a few seconds before answering.

"It's, ah, the name of God's son. Your people would say 'by the Book,' I think."

"Well, that is the polite thing to say. One of our soldiers would be more likely to say 'God's balls.'"

"Fine. God's balls, Melogian, not so fast!"

The sorceress laughed. In that instant Christine saw clearly that Melogian was yet a young woman, with some of the wildness of youth still about her.

"All right, let us achieve our speed gradually, then. I don't know why you were so taken aback: Quentin told us your world had self-propelled mechanical vehicles that could attain great speeds."

"A car is a metal box that encloses you, and it's rolling on the ground. This is completely different!"

"I guess so. Once, down in Hieloculat, I rode a wing made of paper into the mouth of an extinct fire-mountain; once one has rushed in near darkness through caverns full of razor-edged stalactites, the prospect of a daylight journey through the upper air of Chrysanthe becomes positively boring."

"Are you making this up?" Christine peered doubtfully at Melogian, distracted from the vision of earth below her moving faster and faster.

"You say you can tell when I'm lying; am I lying now? I swear to you I did this thing. I won't deny I was so scared after the flight I vowed never to repeat the experience."

"Why did you do it at all?"

"Oh, it is a long story, and I don't want to get into it now. I was young and very stupid then, and I thought myself immortal. One day I'll tell you all of it. Right now I am more concerned with what I have to show you about the world. Can you stand to look down? I'll hold your hand. Good. See the river? That is the Scyamander, which is born in the chain of hills you see at the horizon, over there. Those hills mark the border with Estephor."

The abstract notions helped to settle Christine. "Yes, I know that," she said. "Two of the borders of Estephor are delimited that way: with Temerorn and with Kawlend as well. And the Scyamander forms the border between Archeled and Kawlend."

"Very good. How long is the Scyamander?"

"Nearly two hundred and fifty leagues."

"Over half the width of the land."

"I know that too."

"I have a point to make, but I don't want to say it baldly. Before I go on, are you ready for greater speed?"

"I suppose so. How fast can this thing go?"

"I've never pushed a whirl to its utter limits; that is risky. But we can easily reach speeds of two hundred leagues per hour."

"That's *six hundred miles*," said Christine, amazed, then gasped as the whirl shot forward and upward, its roar risen to a liquid whistle. Rising above her fear was a delighted giddiness; she found herself laughing and nearly screeching like a little girl. The land spread below her, tinted blue-gray by the whirl's hull as if it were the windshield of some marvelous plane. Testenel was a tiny dot; the city Tiellorn rose beyond it, on the banks of the Scyamander. She could see the patchwork of cultivated fields and scattered villages.

"Oh, my God," she gasped.

"Aye. When you tell yourself God can see Chrysanthe in this way, you start to understand Her better."

For over an hour they flew; the morning sun shone over the world and Melogian pointed out to Christine the various features of the land below. They were passing over the duchy of Estephor, the largest of the three outlying regions of the land, and the most sparsely populated. "The soil is thin nearly everywhere here," Melogian explained, "because the land rises higher. The climate is cooler also, making it much harder to grow crops. Estephorins are reputed a tough folk, proud and grim-hearted. This is both true and false, like all statements of this sort."

"What do they look like, the people of that duchy?"

"They tend to have dark hair and to be a trifle taller than the norm, but it's rather hard to notice. I frankly cannot tell an Estephorin from a Kawlendian, though Orion claimed it was an easy task to guess a man's birth duchy—I suspect he cheated through some spell he never told me of."

"Can you explain a bit of history for me? On . . . on Terra, there were constant wars, and this is how nations were shaped. A people would invade a region and carve out a country, or annex it to their own. In Antiquity the Romans built an empire that lasted over fifteen hundred years, but it changed shape completely several times. But the books I've read here seem to say there have always been Temerorn and the three duchies around it, and they've always been the same shape. Why is that?"

"Oh, that's not true. Archeled used to be larger, a thousand and a half years ago, but the region south and west of the Scyamander was transferred to Kawlend by royal decree."

"Because of a war?"

"No, because of a 'change of administrative practice,' which is a euphemism for taxation disputes. For fifteen hundred years, we've settled on reasonable boundaries for our duchies, which is only good practice. What your books don't dwell on is the real burning boundary issue, which is between baronies. That is in constant flux, and the duke's authority is sometimes insufficient to settle things. Ten or twelve times a year, the king himself has to adjudicate a quarrel between barons as to whose land a pond or field belongs. Edisthen hates it; he has a tradition of fining both parties simply for turning up for the adjudication, and sometimes their duke as well. Yet people still appeal to him."

"But people don't fight wars over land?"

"Not *now*; not anymore, I should hope to say. You've only been reading recent histories, I suppose, otherwise you'd have encountered references to the Conquest of Estephor, in the late fourth millennium."

"So no one feels their nation needs to expand? You don't have people in Archeled saying the part Kawlend was given should still be theirs, because their people live there?"

Melogian was silent a moment. "Because I've spent years in made worlds, I understand the sense in which you're using that word, 'nation,' but most people here would not. There is only one world, and one country, and both are called Chrysanthe. There is only one king or queen, and this is asserted and enforced by the Law. Edisthen's authority may thin out at the margins of the world, where petty barons rule over tiny scraps of land they can claim as utterly theirs, but anywhere close to the center, his power is recognized by all. When a sovereign is challenged, we have wars. But we do not have the kind of thing I believe you're thinking of, wars justified by the fact that the conquered are a different kind of men—what is the proper word: strain? A different strain of men."

"Race. Ethny. I guess this is what I was thinking. Everyone in Chrysanthe is the same in appearance, aren't they? You all have skin the same shade, and similar features? The Kawlendish aren't darker, or, or something?"

"Again, almost everyone would argue that we vary quite a bit. Some people will tell you Archeledians have big noses and Kawlendians drink too much wine. Others would point out how dark you are and how pale I am."

Christine laughed incredulously and started to argue, but Melogian was not finished.

"But I know what you mean. I've been to worlds where some people had skin nearly coal-black, noses like knife blades, and pointed ears, and others were ruddy pink, short, and round all over; your own obviously held a similar variety of shades and features."

"Not as much as that, but . . . yeah. We'd both be considered very pale over there. Why is it that there are no races here?"

· "I asked myself the same question nearly ten years ago, back from my first extensive visit of the made worlds. At first I had thought the question did not need asking: Things here are as they should be, while the made worlds are arbitrary. For every person asking why the dwellers in the true realm were so alike, I could find another who would ask how we could all be so hideously varied. But I had to admit after my trip that variety was the norm and sameness very much the exception; and in the end I figured out why. Which, as a matter of fact, brings us back to the topic I've been avoiding since the start."

Melogian sighed and pointed to the ground below them. Vegetation was thin in Estephor, but now the land could only be called barren. Here and there tatters of green clung to hollows of the relief; the sun glinted on the occasional streamlet cascading from the heights, which might water a small valley. But the overall shade was gray, the gray of rock and gravel. Though some part of the whirl's enchantment kept the wind at bay so that its passengers' breath was not torn from their lungs by the swiftness of their travel, still the air had been growing noticeably cooler.

"Whenever I tell you that the world is flat, Christine, it's clear from your expression that you just cannot believe me. The other day, when we argued about the horizon, you felt you'd scored a victory when I had to admit the world cannot be flat like the surface of a table. I let that pass because I knew sooner or later we would come here and you would lose the argument.

"In a way I'd prefer to just crush you under facts and get it all over with, but I don't wish to cause you distress. Also, a whirl will not reach to the vault of the sky, since the air at that height is so thin it cannot sustain lift, much less be breathed. There is a spell called Ilianrod's Chariot that would enable us to reach the sky, but it is a major undertaking. I've only invoked it once and I had to rest for a week afterward. So this time I will not be making you touch the vault with your own hand; your undermind can continue to believe I'm lying about that.

"However, it's time I laid down the exact truth about the size of the world. Because that is the answer to your question, Lady. There is only one strain of men in Chrysanthe because the land is too small for more. Made worlds tend to be larger than the true realm, and the larger the world, the greater the diversity of the people who dwell in it."

They were slowly losing altitude. Christine looked at Melogian with a frown. "You say that like it's something so dramatic. So this land is small; I have no problem with that. It makes perfect sense, now that you say it, that everybody here would be the same race. And in fact, this means people over the ocean might be very different from you. There might be another race of people to the south, you just never found them!"

"The *world* is small, Christine. There is nothing over the ocean and there is no one to the far south, because the south of Kawlend is just like the north of Estephor. Look at the sky ahead of us; do you notice anything? No? Look down to the horizon; from here, with good eyes, you can see the rim. Do you see it?"

Melogian gave the whirl a burst of speed while still reducing its altitude. "The sky, Christine. It is coming down. We're approaching the edge of the vault. Can you see it as a wall in front of us?"

Christine shook her head, disquieted. "It's just a lot of blue. I can imagine it as a wall; I could have done it as well back home, but it's still just a lot of blue, far away."

"Wait a while. Things will become clearer. Or I should say, murkier. You must notice the haze in the distance."

"That's always there. It was there in Testenel."

"Yes, but here it is thicker, isn't it? And look at the horizon; you must see it now, that ribbon of gray."

Christine squinted; she thought she saw what Melogian was referring to and said so.

"Right. We will reach the spot in a few minutes."

Christine peered at the tiny ribbon of grayness, saw it grow. The sky above was still the blue expanse she was used to; she had learned in a book that sunlight was scattered by dust particles in the air and that this caused the color of the sky. She remembered thinking that had she been born two thousand years earlier she would have believed the sky was a blue vault over the land, and she would have died in ignorance of the truth; and that had felt so tragic to her twelve-year-old self.

But here, the vault was the truth, so Melogian said. Christine tried to see the sky as a vault; at first, she failed, but suddenly her perspective shifted. There were no clouds before her, only a vast blue expanse, and a swelling gray margin at the horizon, which was getting closer and closer. The whirl lost altitude swiftly. Christine saw the sky as terribly near, curving down to meet the ground, and she shivered; the next instant, her old perceptions reasserted themselves.

The whirl slowed, its noise sinking down to a low growl; they flew a few feet above the ground. The gray border at the edge of the sky had grown huge as they neared it. Yet now that she expected to perceive it as a wall in front of her, it had faded into gray fog.

Melogian made them settle down lightly on the barren ground; she jumped out of the whirl and helped Christine off. The air was much cooler than it had been in Testenel and she almost shivered. There was a strange smell in the air—Christine thought of burnt rock, as if the thing were possible. The ground spread around them, flat and desolate, here and there sporting a cluster of rocks, a lone boulder. All color had leached out of the land; there were only shades of gray here. Christine looked to the north; the fog bank cut off her vision.

"What's beyond the fog?" she asked.

"There is no fog, Christine."

"Don't you see it?"

"I see grayness, as you do. But it is not fog. It is also a lot closer than it appears; we are near to the very edge here. Walk this way—and stay behind me!"

They took a few steps forward; the fog bank grew near with startling rapidity; it was as if it came boiling toward them. Melogian stopped, and Christine's perspective adjusted. There was no fog, no. The world . . . the world just faded into gray, twenty paces ahead. A boulder stood at the edge to her left; its proximate outline was clear and distinct. But beyond it . . .

"What is it? What's blocking our view, if it's not fog?"

"It is nothing. There is nothing there, literally. The northern and southern edges of the world are like this."

"Just . . . nothing? I can't believe it."

Christine tried to take a step forward; Melogian restrained her.

"Don't go any closer, please."

"What's the danger? This isn't like the made world under the library, is it?"

"Once I threw a pebble into the gray void. I did not hear it fall; and it never came back, because it had ceased to exist. I don't care for you to court obliteration."

Christine thought in silence. After half a minute, she asked: "And what if you brought a long pole, thrust the end into the gray, and brought it back? If you marked off the length we could determine its boundaries."

Melogian chuckled. "You speak like an architect; they too always have numbers on their lips. But I'd not risk it. Maybe the end of the pole would be erased, yes, and so we could say that this spot is so many yards from the end of the world. Maybe the pole and the one who wielded it would cease to exist, by contamination."

"The world doesn't behave—" Christine began, then stopped herself. "I guess the world *can* behave like that. It doesn't make much sense to me, but . . ." She shook her head.

"You aren't the least bit scared, are you?" Melogian asked.

"Scared? No. I'm too surprised. This doesn't seem real. I can't help seeing it as a kind of fog. Like a cloak-field in *The Cosmic Patrol*; I keep wondering who or what is behind it."

"'Blessed are the blind, for they see not the true terrors of the world.'" Melogian quoted. "*You* may not be afraid, but I have had quite enough of this. Come."

She led them away from the edge of the world for a score of paces. Christine kept looking over her shoulder; the grayness seemed to have condensed again, back to a low fog bank. Above them the sky loomed, a blue expanse dulled by a faint overcast of gray. "How high is it?" she wondered out loud. "It looks as far away as the real sky."

"Please sit down with me here," said Melogian, pointing to a spot close to a large boulder. The sorceress sank to the ground and leaned against the boulder's face. Christine sat facing her; the boulder cut off her view of the void.

"At this spot, the sky is about a hundred fathoms above us. However, if you returned here a year from now it would be much higher. And this place would look very different. You saw the other boulder, the black one, to our left? Half of it was clear, the other half just faded away. But a week from now that rock will be entirely clear and solid, and you might go around it in safety, for the edge of the world will have receded from it. This world in which we live grows larger, at the rate of about a foot a day, both at the northern and the southern margins. In the six millennia since Creation, the distance between the borders of the world has increased by nearly three hundred and fifty leagues.

"When the world was first made, it was a narrow strip of land running between oceans. The mountains that mark the border between Temerorn and northern Estephor, back then marked the edge of the world. Thirty years after Creation, an expedition tried to find a pass through the mountains; among them was one of the First, a man named Thillen or Tillen. They came upon the edge of the world, and were afraid to press any further, but Thillen was not to be denied. He stepped three full paces into the void, until he could barely be seen; then he faltered and staggered back out. His hair had gone white, his skin gray as lead. When the others asked him what he had seen, he could only shake his head and moan.

"They retreated some distance away, and made camp in a tiny valley. Thillen sat by the fire, holding out his hands to warm them. He had not spoken a word since his return. When his friends tried to comfort him he looked up at them and smiled; but all his teeth had gone coal-black—it was as if his mouth were a pit.

"None of them wanted to sleep that night, but one by one, despite themselves, they dozed off. In the morning Thillen was gone, but where he had been sitting by the fire they found thirty-two black pebbles and twenty pieces of chitin like the wing cases of silver-beetles. They dug a grave and buried these, and returned to Tiellorn with their tale."

Christine was silent a while. Once again, Melogian had confronted her with an absurdity she was nevertheless expected to embrace.

"And the world," she said, "just . . . emerges from the gray, like that?"

"Yes. At first it is nothing but rock and earth, devoid of color—like this area all around us. As the edge of the world recedes, life flows into the soil. It is a slow process, to be sure. Kawlend's capital Aluvien stands on ground that did not exist until the year twenty-five hundred, and only became fertile three thousand years ago."

"You're sure about this," said Christine, somewhat dazed.

"I'm no architect, but I can take my own measurements. I planted a pole near the edge of the world and returned there a year later, planting another pole farther north, since the edge had receded. I kept this up for five years and then measured the intervals between the poles. I obtained the same figure as others have in the past: The world grows larger by one mile every twelve years, to the north and the south both."

Christine was sketching in the gray dirt; her finger drew a circle then a wider concentric one. "So the world is like this." Melogian corrected her, drawing a wide squat rectangle then another one of equal length but greater height.

"No, more like this. Do you understand now the shape of the maps you saw? They depict all that there is to be depicted. The land reaches north and south and fades away into the void. East and west are the oceans."

"Those don't change? They have edges, but they don't move?"

"Well . . . that is what we presume. No one has actually approached the western or eastern edges of the world, save perhaps the adept Melcamanthil, who several times in his memoirs claims to have done so, but admits in the same breath to being a ruthless liar."

Christine blew out her breath. "This gets more complicated by the minute."

"It depends on your point of view. Made world geography can be attractive in its simplicity, I agree. Living on a sphere spinning on itself and rotating around another blazing sphere: It has a certain elegance. You cling to this when you want to see the true world as a disc, but the concept is . . . inadequate."

"So what about the oceans, then? What's the 'adequate' explanation?"

"The thing with the oceans is that their edges lie very far from land and the sea gets rougher and rougher as one travels outward. Did your 'Terra' have great ships? I've often seen them in made worlds."

"Yes, of course. Ships that could cross the ocean."

"Ah, what a sight those are; with their sails catching the wind and their stern-castles lifting a dozen turrets to the sky. . . ."

"Ah . . . the ones back home are made of metal and they have engines."

"Really! Well, it makes sense if you had self-propelled metal wagons; I should have thought of that. But even wooden ships of this kind are a fancy in Chrysanthe. We have fishing boats, and the greatest of them we call ships; but even those will not venture out of sight of land. To sail further out is to seek death. If one wishes to travel to the western edge of the world, one must use magic."

"Like a skyship," Christine completed.

"Well, no. Skyships can only sail over land. Their enchantment pushes against the earth; over water, they founder and sink. But a whirl will travel over the waves readily; and in fact I have made the trip myself."

"So did you reach the edge or not?"

"I could not. There is a . . . 'guardian' is probably not the appropriate word. There is something far out to sea that wizards cannot pass; those of us who've tried have all failed. I don't believe it was set there to repulse us, but that is a religious question; I don't believe that God puts everything in its place just so, to make the world move the way He wants it to. If a child playing in the forest is killed by a wolf, it is not a punishment from God, or a trial sent to its parents. It is just an accident. So I don't believe Leviathan is a warning; it is just there, for its own reasons. It so happens this is more than enough."

"You've lost me."

"I was two-and-twenty; that was in sixty eighty-three, two years after your abduction. Orion insisted I should attempt to see the western edge of the world; I knew nobody else ever had achieved it, and I suspected even then he had an ulterior motive. God may not play with us as a child with its toys, but Orion loved manipulating people. I guess he felt my going through the experience would help me; make me grow up, perhaps.

"So I traveled to Droadton; it's a tiny village on Forlorn Cape in Estephor, the westernmost tip of land of all Chrysanthe. Early one morning I invoked a whirl and set out over the ocean. I pushed the whirl to its best speed and I guided myself by the sun's course, always due west.

"I saw a hundred different colors of water; I saw currents swirling and fish leaping from the waves. I saw squales attacking whale pods and beds of algae miles in diameter. And at long last I reached Leviathan's realm, and it rose halfway out of the water to greet me."

Melogian passed a hand over her eyes and shook her head.

"Saying that Leviathan is a fish is like saying that Mount Gasphode is a very big pebble. In a way, it's true, but it misses the point. I don't know how large Leviathan is, really; I could not wrap my mind around its size. At any rate, it rose out of the water and . . . it spoke to me. I could see it, the back, the fins, the head, and those eyes, those eyes, by God! I had known it was there, and I had known its sheer size was frightening; I thought I had come forewarned.

"But it spoke to me. In my head, you understand. I could feel its mind in mine; it was . . . like a mountain bending down over you to have a chat. And then it spoke the three most terrifying words I have ever heard in my life."

"What words?"

"What do you think? *I see you.*"

Melogian shivered and hugged herself.

"You can't understand. To this day if someone utters this sentence within my hearing, ice goes down my spine. There was no threat in its words; it was . . . If God Herself had reached down from the heavens and spoken to me I would have felt less frightened, because God I could hold accountable for Her actions. Not Leviathan."

"So what did you do?"

Melogian paused and gave a rueful smile. "The exact truth? I screamed and shat myself. Then I regained enough presence of mind to halt the whirl, reverse its course, and fly back to Droadton. If I had gone on, you see, I believe Leviathan would have spoken again as I tried to overfly it. Its mind would have sounded so loudly in mine it would have destroyed it."

Christine was silent a moment. Then she asked, "And did you ever try flying east?"

Melogian's laugh was half outraged. "You never give up, do you? D'you think I wanted to risk my sanity once more?"

"But if Leviathan's in the western ocean—"

"It is also in the *eastern* ocean; either it has a twin there or else it knows when a wizard is about to fly too far and somehow travels beneath the roots of the world to emerge in the proper spot. Or maybe Mad Orlerin was right: Maybe the world is like a twisted ribbon and if I had passed beyond Leviathan, I would have arrived at the shores of Archeled, but my right hand would have become my left. I'll have to root out a copy of Thenuel's *Omnicon* and make you read it before we continue these discussions. You'd love him: He fills page upon page with fruitless speculations about the mysteries of the world."

"I was just asking a question," said Christine defensively.

"Don't look so hurt, milady. I didn't mean to get angry. I had just hoped to settle at least some things with this, and I get the feeling I will never make you accept things as they are."

"That's not fair! I *can* accept things as they are. It's just . . . I want proof, that's all. Solid proof. I can't afford not to demand that."

Melogian nodded and took Christine's hand. "Yes. You're right. If I imagine myself in your place, I grow very frightened. Did you get some 'solid proof' here?"

Christine rose and looked over the edge of the boulder to the end of the world. "I guess so. I wish I understood why things are this way, but it wasn't really different back home. Just . . . It's easier to accept a round planet spinning around a star. This . . . it feels wrong."

"Because you spent years learning dream-truth. If you'd spent your life here you would accept this state of affairs as proper and true. Give it time. Now, unless you have a burning desire to remain here, I'd like us to return to Testenel."

Christine acquiesced. She and Melogian walked back to the whirl and clambered aboard. Melogian impelled it skimming across the flat ground for a good mile before she made them rise high into the air again. As their craft sped southward, Christine looked over her shoulder to the edge of the world; already it was hard to distinguish. Soon it became merely a faint line at the base of the blue vault of heaven. They continued on their journey. Under their feet, the barren ground turned to earth, flecked here and there with green.

As they flew south, Christine reflected on what Melogian had told her and a detail itched at her.

"You said Orion urged you to try to reach the western edge of the world, right? But you could have been hurt badly. You could have . . . gone insane, if you'd traveled farther. Didn't he know the risks? Had *he* tried to go?"

"Oh yes, he knew the risks. I expect he had tried to go himself, in the past. He was already over a hundred and fifty years old; for all I know he'd tried it more than once."

"Then why send you? I don't understand. Why would he be this cruel?"

"I *was* very angry at him afterward, for weeks. In the end I forgave him."

Melogian sighed.

"You mustn't think I worship Orion, but he was—he still is, wherever he may be—an exceptional person. He is a Hero from the Book, immensely knowledgeable, and frighteningly wise. I forget how many times I've been convinced he was wrong and then he proved himself to have been right all along. After a few dozen repetitions of this, it is hard not to trust someone blindly."

"Maybe," said Christine, "but still, just because he's been right a hundred times doesn't mean he'll be right next time. Especially not if it's something where you risk your own life."

"That's very true. And as I said, I was furious with him. But I couldn't make myself forget what had happened before. The time in my fifteenth year that he spared my life when he should by rights have slain me. I will not speak of that. Suffice it to say that had I been in his shoes, things would not have gone so well for my apprentice. So, is Orion softhearted or ruthless? In the end, I decided to assume he was simply wise and leave it at that."

Through Estephor they flew, over the hills and into Temerorn, and soon the blue towers of Testenel beckoned. Seeing them appear, Christine felt a pang: This fairy castle was becoming home to her, ever so slightly. She ran her fingers over the blanket Melogian had laid out in the bottom of the whirl; lifted its corner to gaze through a thin translucent shell at the ground so far below. She was far less scared than she had been setting out. She was wondering how thick the whirl's shell was, and why it had to be this color, and how resistant it was. The real world could not be like *The Cosmic Patrol*, where details faded in the haze of the camera eye. She rapped the whirl with her bare knuckle, but could not hear the sound it made above the roar of the spell.

And now they were by the side of a tower, and she had to climb over a railing onto a balcony, which she only then realized was indeed the very same one they'd set out from, hours ago. Melogian threw her the blanket and the pack, and vaulted over the railing. Then with two words and a gesture, she made the whirl dissipate into nothingness. Christine felt an almost irresistible urge to ask a childish question: Where did the whirl go when Melogian dismissed it? But she guessed the obvious nonanswer: back where it had come from. Doubtless, from Melogian's point of view, no further explanations were needed. For the time being Christine would have to settle for partial answers. Possibly it was too much to ask for more, in a world set directly under the gaze of God, where land pervolved into being over millennia and titanic fishes warded the secrets of the ocean.

🙋 The skyship *Spindrift* was patrolling Archeled's forested northwestern reaches, on its way to the capital. Bored lookouts fore and aft swept their gazes across the land. One man was posted in the "mole's burrow," a cage of wooden slats and wire netting at the bottom of the long canted arm that extended below the keel. He hunkered down beneath a huge metal lid like a hinged shield, peering through the gaps in the floor at the land below. The sun was declining, though still a bright yellow; and so at first he thought it was a reflection of the sun he saw, thrown up by a small pond. Yet it could not be; the sun was to starboard, and he was looking to port. The land seemed to tilt up if he tried to interpret the flash of light as a reflection. Then what was it he had seen?

He sank to his knees, put his face against the wood, and looked through the metal mesh. He could not have dreamed the light; it had flared between two large trees, a searing yellow . . .

There it came again: It seemed to have a shape, though the watchman could not make it out. Something burning; a hut? It was hidden behind the trees again. He pulled the talking-drum close to his face, tautening the metal wire, and shouted into it: "Large fire sighted on the ground! Thirty grades forward from port, half a mile distant. A building, or something like it, burning." He wondered, as he reported this, why there was no column of smoke; but he had seen the flame. . . .

The membrane vibrated with another's voice, carried over the wire: "Logged, Rebis. Let me get confirmation from the fore watch."

Movement caught at Rebis's eye; he peered intently through a slit in the wall. Something had risen above the trees; something huge that flew without wings, that twisted in the air the way a snake coils itself through the grass. Golden fire bloomed from it in ragged clumps and flares. Rebis spent an endless moment looking at it, dumbstruck, then he was bawling alarm into the talking-drum.

The thing corkscrewed through the air, launching itself at the *Spindrift*. Under full sail, carried by storm winds, the skyship might have outrun it; instead, it was like a target in the path of an arrow.

Just before it would have rammed into the hull, the being reversed its course, whipping its body around and shedding flame. Clots of fire struck the underside of the ship, setting the hull aflame in a dozen places.

In the mole's burrow Rebis looked at the fiery being and screamed into the talking-drum. If the creature had been in truth like a snake, he would not have been

so scared, for Rebis was a brave man, and whatever came from nature he was willing to accept, even if it should kill him. But on the bronze-scaled flanks of the creature he could see twinned rows of children's faces, mouths distorted as if about to
open in a scream.

The monster swam through the air, skimming the treetops, curving around in
a wide circle. Broken curses came from the talking-drum, then nothing. Rebis
heard shouts from the men on deck, far above his head. He was watching the fire-
snake coiling itself beneath the ship, then rushing toward them as fast as a tornado.

Again the creature reversed its course abruptly, whipping off a barrage of fire
aimed at the hull. A clump of yellow flames struck the wooden enclosure; fire exploded upward through the slits. Rebis found himself burning, the very air he in-
haled aflame. Barely aware of his own actions, he pushed open the hinged shield,
tried to climb the ladder back into the ship. His pain-maddened arms, his seared
hands failed him; he lost his grip on the rungs and collapsed on top of the mole's
burrow. He was still burning, burning. All about him the hull flamed, gouts of fire
licking upward, fire spreading to the masts and sails. Flame ate at the arm and cage,
roared up all about him.

His mind was nearly gone; it was an animal that finally hurled itself out of the
fiery wreckage of the mole's burrow and launched itself into the air, rotating helplessly in its plunge to the ground, seeing against the blue of the sky a great mass of
flame that it still knew, dimly, could not be the sun.

BOOK V

The Storm Gathers

1. The Conclave at Testenel

Tiellorn stood at the center of the world. Outward from the city, fields spread, with their attendant villages. Beyond lay tamed wilderness, well-coppiced woods, and meadows where any traveler might refresh himself. Then villages again, and some modest towns. Human population had achieved a stable distribution here. Tiellorn had long ago ceased to grow; though its pull on the people of Chrysanthe remained strong, most of those who traveled to it did so merely as a sort of pilgrimage. One did not yearn to live in Tiellorn; one was either born to it or not.

Around the heart of the land the Hedges drew a sort of colossal maze, emblems of borders that had once, at the beginning of the world, meant much more than they did in this age. For centuries, the extent of Man's full rule on the world had stopped at the Hedges. To go past them was to travel into the unknown, and sometimes into mind-twisting peril.

In these latter days, the Hedges were no border at all. Temerorn, the central district of Chrysanthe, extended well past them and its borders existed only on maps. Three duchies divided the land beyond Temerorn: Archeled lay east, Estephor north and west, Kawlend to the south. At the outermost edges of the three duchies the land fragmented into ever-pettier baronies, until one reached the edges of civilization, where the rule of a single baron might extend no further than the borders of his makeshift castle. Though all of these regions owed ultimate fealty to the king on his throne in Testenel, in practice the power did not flow so smoothly. The petty barons' power might exert itself over a small area, but it was all the more fiercely bound to its native land, and its ties to the central authority tended to be weak.

Most of the barons of the marches cared little who sat on the throne. Whether the king's name was Vaurd or Edisthen, it all came to the same in the end. What they did care for was local power, and wealth. And that was something that the son of the deposed king might promise them, assuming he gained the throne.

So, when he approached the barons of the southern marches of Kawlend, Evered had found the terrain at first fertile: His cautiously phrased schemes had met with unexpected, instant enthusiasm. Support his cause? Well, of course the barons would. It stood to reason Evered had been defrauded of his inheritance. Nothing could be more important than restoring him to the throne that was his by birthright. Raise levies, of men and horses, to swell the ranks of their small military force? It was feasible. Indeed, a grandfather, a great-great-uncle, had done just that, in the olden days. That tradition had not been lost. Why, at a moment's notice they could be ready to move. . . .

But the more precise Evered became, the more evasive the barons. They could not commit to a date. Unexpected circumstances always arose: bad harvests, sheep plagues, insubordinate farmers. Hard and fast guarantees on their part were something Evered could never get. At times the Law was mentioned, almost idly. It was also remarked that promises of gold and favors were far cheaper than their actuality.

Though he tilled his field and sowed the seeds of revolt, Evered's crop remained disappointing. Still, he did not give up. Year after year he plowed the land anew and waited for a richer harvest. He got to know the barons, well enough to tell the rams from the sheep. But for all his patient work, he knew that he could not count on enough men to mount a viable attack on the center of things.

Chrysanthe's standing armies were small though well trained, and troop levies would greatly swell their numbers. Eight skyships plied the land under the direct command of the crown; these had proved significant in warfare in the past, useful both as scouts and as bombardment platforms. Even without the skyships to consider, to lay siege to Testenel, Evered would have to march through most of Kawlend and then the southern half of Temerorn.

When he was young still, Evered had imagined his forces sweeping north through Kawlend, under safe conduct from the duchess, protected from Estephor by the mountain range that formed the duchy's border—but always his fantasy faltered at the thought of Archeled. This was the most populous of the duchies, and one whose duke bore Edisthen an unswerving loyalty. From the day when Edric, Duke Archeled, had prevented him from flinging himself at Edisthen, Evered had borne him a very special hatred, as one holds fond memories of a former lover close to heart. And always in his dreams of vengeance Duke Archeled would appear, as if claiming primacy over Edisthen. Before even the usurper could be faced, his cat's-paw would defeat Evered, sometimes at the gate of Temerorn, sometimes before he had even managed to cross half of Kawlend.

Evered could not deny reason: Against Archeled the forces of the barons would never prevail. But several factors might be used to even the odds. For many years, Evered had cultivated his relationship with Duchess Ambith of Kawlend. She had been a favorite of Vaurd's, influent at court; in the Usurpation War Kawlend had thrown its lot against Edisthen. Though defeated in the bitter end, its duchess had scarcely been cowed. She had been a young woman barely out of her twenties during the war; she was now a mature woman at the height of her power. A man less idealistic than Edisthen might have seen the wisdom of taking her hand in marriage after the death of his wife. A man less of a fool would have seen the danger staring him in the face and had her assassinated. But the Hero, indolent ruler that he was, treated her with grave and absent courtesy. It did not take much brains to understand this enraged Ambith, who could not stand to be ignored.

Ambith had always been generous with Vaurd's sons; they had readily chosen Kawlend as the place of their exile, though the dismal castle of Vorlok offered no incentives of its own. However, Ambith had often graced them with visits in the beginning. Once they reached their majority, she allowed them to leave Vorlok to spend time in Aluvien, in direct contradiction to the peace terms Edisthen had imposed. Vaurd's sons remained discreet about these visits, even the slack-witted Olf, and their imprisonment became much easier to bear.

Shortly after the end of the Usurpation War, Evered had begun cultivating

Ambith, responding to her flatteries with some of his own, repaying every kindness as best he could. What passed between them was not sexual, much that Aghaid and Innalan liked to drop callow hints that it was. It was lust for power, pure and simple—though perhaps, on her part, there *was* some infatuation. Evered for his part felt no desire for her, who was fifteen years his senior, bony and dry. So he played a delicate game, scrupulous both to encourage Ambith's feelings if they existed, and to ensure that proprieties were always strictly respected.

In 6078 Ambith had wed a nobleman of Kawlend, an agreeable, spineless man ten years older than herself. This did not reduce the frequency of Evered's visits, nor their nature. Evered took precautions to be even more irreproachable than ever: Were the duchess's husband to become convinced he was being cuckolded, he would sooner suspect Talquen's shade of bedding his wife than Prince Evered. And as their odd relationship deepened, Evered won promises from Ambith, of men and money. Yet even with Kawlend's entire army on his side, history argued Evered could not win. The Usurpation War had seen Kawlend beaten and humiliated. A border action against Archeled might well succeed; seizing Waldern was remotely conceivable; an assault on the heart of the land would be met by forces from the three other duchies and fail. This war, however, was going to be a war of magic.

Magic had always been the key factor. Men fought with swords and bows, and there numbers were determinant. Wizards fought with spells that twisted the world, and there raw power was what counted. Troops at a numerical disadvantage could prevail given magical support, but since the Carmine War this piece of wisdom had been forgotten.

Casimir had joined Evered's service in 6079, after a long courtship, and swiftly proven his worth. The wizard, though younger than Mathellin by nine years, mastered many more spells and wielded them at a keener pitch of power. Evered now commanded two strong wizards; Edisthen had Orion and the latter's young apprentice Melogian.

One might think the advantage now lay with Evered's side. However, Orion's power was immense. During the Usurpation War he had mostly nullified Mathellin's efforts to help their side. Though at first the Hero had refrained from using magic of his own against enemy troops, in the end he had brought such harsh spells to the field that Kawlend was forced to surrender.

The way Evered saw it, it was thus imperative to remove the mage from the playing board. Christine's abduction had been a step toward this, rather than an end in itself. Orion had invested a large part of his power into the knights who had set out questing for the girl; and then had gone himself, time and again, striving to locate Christine.

Already this weakened Orion significantly. In fact, giving assault while he was absent was a temptation Evered had had to resist: Orion never remained gone for too long. It was a better strategy to use the power of the made worlds against him. Twice Casimir had raised imaginary armies in the made worlds and sought to capture him. The first attempt had failed. The second one also, almost catastrophically. Evered had ordered a stop then. For years the conspirators had made no move. Deep down in Errefern, Mathellin and all his spellcraft guarded Christine, while Orion quested for her in all the wrong places. Slowly, slowly, Casimir gathered new forces. He had always been impatient, hungry for power and mastery; Evered bade him learn the virtues of patience. Casimir buried himself in books, returned time and again to the made worlds to build a web of forces, much as Mathellin had done in Errefern. On the day the third and final trap was sprung, there had been no risk of failure. Casimir returned from Jyndyrys exulting in his enemy's destruction. And Evered's great plan entered a new phase.

With Orion eliminated, only Melogian stood by Edisthen—Evered felt nothing but contempt for the girl, most of it learned from Casimir. Yet he was not such a fool as to dismiss the talents of one whom Orion himself had chosen as apprentice. Casimir was confident he could best Melogian in a contest of magic, but Evered was not content with this. If the mages were to battle one another, leaving armies to take to the field, this would only be a replay of every major conflict since the Carmine War.

Then a new development had arisen, with Casimir perfecting a spell to enter an underworld and learn magics from ages past. For years the fat wizard had boasted of his plan to devise this enchantment, until Evered ceased to believe in the possibility. But it had come true. And what Casimir had learned from his explorations had transformed the conflict. His skills now surely exceeded Melogian's: He had learned spells humankind had forgotten for centuries and millennia. Evered began to plan for a bold assault on Testenel, supported by Casimir's elder magic.

His fortunes suffered a reversal when Christine was brought back to the real world. On the day he learned of this, Evered had affected indifference, though inside his head he could hear his own voice screaming inarticulately. For a moment of terror he had felt his old madness boiling up to the surface; but it was the realization that it had always been so close that truly terrified him. Yet he had overcome it; clenching his hands on the arms of his chair, he had regained mastery of his feelings. After all, Christine had always been secondary to his plans.

He had been ready to commit himself fully at that moment, to bring his forces together and attack, in sheer defiance over this caprice of fate. Casimir had convinced him to wait just a while longer, while the wizard exploited one more facet of his hard-won knowledge.

And at last it was done. Evered now bestrode the fields he had slaved over, and reaped his harvest, such as it was. Commitments were finally honored, some at the price of greater promises, some brought about by a trifle of inflicted pain—however forced, they were fulfilled. Men had begun to gather to him. Duchess Ambith was ready to raise her troops and place them under his orders. Soon the baronial militia would join with Kawlend's regular armies and Evered would stride forth at the head of a host that might well have lasted all of a week before it was torn apart by loyalist forces.

Except, of course, that Evered had a small surprise in reserve.

As he gazed down from the window, the prince could not suppress a shiver of primal terror. From adits sealed from the pryings of mankind, Casimir had drawn them. Six demons from the dawn of time, bound to a single man who commanded them with a word and a gesture. One by one they had come, crawling, flying, flowing at Casimir's behest. Now they stood arrayed before him; the wizard paraded them as if he were drilling a gaggle of boys with wooden swords. Evered did not know if it was the demons he feared more, or the man who commanded them—but this thought he buried in his mind almost before he had entertained it.

He did note that there was no one in the field behind Vorlok apart from Casimir and his horrors. Evered had walked among the men who had begun to arrive; had heard those who had seen the demons tell the others what it was that would be marching amongst them. Had seen more than one man grow pale and restive. Had challenged one such would-be deserter, drawing not blood with his dagger but shame with his words. Tomorrow, it would be necessary to force the men to get a closer look at the demons. It was vital that they understand the beasts would remain under Casimir's power. But once that realization had sunk in, it would work to Evered's advantage. Knowing he was being preceded into battle by Hell's very spawn, what man would fear opposition?

Still . . . Evered's stomach lurched. The most hideous of Casimir's demons was swaying back and forth, an affront to the sense of sight. This one did not have a body as such: The demon was a constant boiling of motes, sublimating into smoke at its outer edges, while nearer the center the motes thickened and clotted into a bulbous head-like shape, from which tentacles seemed to depend. But these were mere standing waves amongst the chaos of swirling flecks: Not one constituent part remained in place. The tentacles were no more real than the head, and yet one could *see* them, twisting and lashing the ground in a mad rhythm, as if the demon danced the way a flame burns.

Casimir's demons changed the situation completely. With them at the head of his troops, Evered could more than hope for victory: It was almost assured. His forces would sweep north into Temerorn, besiege Testenel, and restore the crown to its fated inheritor. The thought made him light-headed and sent sparkles at the edges of his vision; he had to lie down and breathe slowly, hoping that the fit would not really start. Even as he felt the cool floor beneath him, it seemed to him he could sense the six demons outside the walls, knots of malevolent presence, thankfully unaware of him. Terror and ecstasy warred within his mind, and he strove to contain them before one or the other overwhelmed him.

In the wake of Evered's challenge to the crown, King Edisthen had ordered a conclave be held at Testenel. He had summoned the three dukes of the land to his presence, along with some of their advisers and ministers. Delivered by skyship, the invitations had arrived promptly. The craft that had carried them remained at the ducal capitals to ferry the dukes and their entourages back to Testenel in as swift a manner as possible.

The most distant capital was Waldern, erected on the shores of the Eastern Ocean; yet it was Duke Edric of Archeled who arrived first, several days early in fact. He had started preparing to journey to Testenel as soon as news of the return of Christine had reached him. By the time the skyship *Excelsior* arrived at Waldern, Edric had already set forth; the skyship had to retrace its course and pick up the ducal entourage from an inn along the way.

Duke Corlin of Estephor was next to arrive. On the first day of High-Summer, the *Black Heart* returned to Testenel, ferrying him and his entourage. The duke was young—he had been born in 6071—and still bore himself in some ways like a child. Surrounded by friends of his own age, with only two or three graybeards to spice his delegation with an air of respectability, he greeted Edisthen with a minimum of pomp and a maximum of enthusiasm. Gaunt Edisthen accepted Corlin's effusions with stolid dignity; when the young duke asked to see the Princess Christine, he was informed she was resting at present and would meet him later.

Christine had spent as little time as possible at official functions, which both bored and scared her. Her father's presence she could bear, for a few minutes at a time, if he were not too close. But her tolerance varied from day to day, according to factors she could not divine; she sought not to press it, and kept her interactions with her father to the bare necessities. When Duke Edric arrived, she had been compelled to meet with him, but she found she did not like him much. He was too brusque, too haughty for her tastes; he was an old man, his hair mostly gone white, and Christine could sense in him a general annoyance at the world she associated with old men. And yet, her return to Chrysanthe had obviously delighted him; her presence made him blush pink and smile. Here was a staunch ally, it would seem. Perhaps in time, she thought, she would learn to like him.

She met with Duke Corlin on the afternoon of his arrival. There were rooms in Testenel specifically devoted to entertaining high-ranking guests of the royal family, and so Christine made use of one of these Presence Chambers. She would have liked Quentin to be by her side, but he had left for Lydiss three days before. She had promised him she would cope without him, and she did; still, she had come to depend upon him more than she'd realized. In the presence of a duke, warded only by ordinary guards, she felt herself on unsafe ground.

There were musicians in the Presence Chamber, bowing stringed instruments to make a music like an endless silvery sigh, fading into the background of one's thoughts. At Corlin's arrival, they struck up a sprightly theme, appropriate to the demeanor of the young man who came almost bouncing into the room. A guard at the entrance announced in a loud voice, "Corlin, Duke of Estephor, Warden of—"

"Yes, yes, thank you!" Corlin cut her off. "Her Highness knows who I am, I'm sure. Cousin!" This was said to Christine, in a jaunty tone of voice. Corlin strode closer, half bowed when he was within reach. He seemed to expect something from her, but Christine, not knowing what it was, remained immobile. Then the young Duke knelt abruptly and kissed the hem of her dress. His head rose up to meet her gaze: "I am honored to be in your presence, Your Highness."

Christine belatedly guessed he had expected her to extend her hand; but she wasn't willing to go that far.

"I'm, ah, very glad to meet you, Corlin—Your Grace," she said.

Corlin smiled broadly, the handsomeness of his face suddenly marred when a missing left premolar became revealed. "Corlin will do, Your Highness. Ceremony is for old people."

Someone cleared his throat behind him. Corlin glanced over his shoulder to the two people who had accompanied him, an older man in purple robes and a young woman dressed in hunter's breeches and doublet.

"Ah, yes. May I introduce my minister, Veldaunce, and the Lady Ysolde, a boon companion."

"I am glad to make your acquaintance as well," said Christine. Corlin's companions bowed deeply and murmured polite nothings.

There were chairs in place for visitors. Christine remembered just in time to tell her guests that they might sit. Corlin took his ease in the largest armchair and began a sprightly conversation throughout which he managed to cover two or three subjects at once, mostly referring to events and people Christine knew nothing about. Yet his energy made his speech most enjoyable and Christine decided she rather liked him. She attended the next evening meal in the company of her father and the two dukes, and spent a pleasant enough time. She worried, however, about how things would go once Duchess Ambith arrived. Her duchy had sided with Vaurd during the Usurpation War, and tensions had run high between Kawlend and Temerorn since then.

Conclave had been called for the third of High-Summer, but by late afternoon of that day, Duchess Ambith of Kawlend had not yet arrived. Near sunset, the *Glorious Niavand* finally appeared and docked at one of the tower berths. Duchess Ambith was aboard, along with her retinue. King Edisthen himself was on hand to welcome her; as soon as her feet had touched solid stone, Ambith called one of her guards to her. Holding on to the man's mailed arm and keeping her head very straight, she crossed the landing stage and reached the doorway where Edisthen waited.

"I am ill," she told him before he could open his mouth. "I wish to be taken to my chambers at once. We will speak in the morning."

Edisthen's nostrils flared. "Take the duchess and her staff to their apartments," he ordered in a quiet voice. Servants scrambled to obey; the Kawlendian delegation was taken into the heart of the castle, none of them so much as sparing a word for their king.

News of the snub traveled quickly throughout the castle and a hundred rumors bloomed. For his part, Edisthen simply sent word to the two other dukes that conclave was delayed until the morrow. That evening, Melogian went to spend a few hours with Christine, as she usually did.

Since their trip to the edge of the world, Christine had felt more adrift in reality. She was forced to admit now that her knowledge of the world was inadequate; the science she had learned, the explanations that had ruled her world, those were dream-lore. She could no longer dismiss the flatness of the earth as a naïve doctrine. Melogian had shown her the edge of things, and one day—not now, not yet—Christine would ask her to take her up into the sky, and see the sun from above, to touch the vault of the heavens with her bare hand.

When she did that, she had no doubt that something in her would shrivel up and die; but no matter how weird the truth was, still she would accept it. Logic, now, logic did not and could not fail her. The world was as it was; it was knowable, and so she would know it. She read works of geography, consulted maps, in an effort to memorize the shape of Chrysanthe. Not that the coastlines were complicated: one to the west, one to the east, each with some bays and capes. The interior was one contiguous mass, without anything remotely like a sea. There were many small lakes and an abundance of streams. The land sloped downward from the center toward west and east; there were some mountain ranges, and one extensive plateau to the north rose very high indeed, with Mount Gasphode at its center rearing its head to challenge the heavens.

Christine wanted to ask Melogian how a mountain so high could have arisen if the vault of heaven was low from the ground at the edge of creation. She wondered about rainfall, the effects of six thousand years of erosion on mountains and hills. Wondered if her questions would be met with shrugs or dodges, or claims that the Law worked in ways no one fully understood. Perhaps deep in the ground lay another edge to the world, and stone was born in those depths, pushing the land upward under Mount Gasphode. Faced with evidence of the miraculous nature of the world, it was easy to give up inquiry, or to invent fantastic explanations. Worst of all was knowing that the real answers might be even more fantastical than any she could imagine.

Christine wanted to take her time with her inquiries, both to avoid annoying Melogian and to pace herself. Too much dwelling on existential matters made her dizzy. Also, there was in the presence of the sorceress something very precious to her: companionship. She had learned not to fear Quentin, and now that he was gone, she needed someone familiar by her side. Althea performed her duties as loyally and cheerfully as ever, but Christine could not confide in her. The girl might be one of an elite circle of body servants; this did not necessarily make her a delightful companion. She was eager to please, impossible to upset, and fully competent at her tasks. She was also nearly incapable of initiative, incurious, and basically ignorant of everything beyond the castle and her duties.

So it was with genuine pleasure that Christine received Melogian whenever she came to visit. The sorceress always had interesting things to talk about, and lately Christine had started telling her about some of the episodes of her early life. It wasn't as if Freynie Long sat in Melogian's place, but still Christine could reminisce with someone who at least partly understood her.

That evening, Melogian came in bearing a distracted expression. She inquired after Christine's health then immediately came to the point.

"Kawlend's delegation has finally arrived, but Duchess Ambith claims to be ill; Edisthen has postponed the conclave till tomorrow. It worries me."

Though Christine disliked the subject, she did not ignore it. "Do you think he . . ." She forced herself to correct: "My father . . . made a mistake?"

"No, it's the duchess I'm worried about. Traveling aboard a skyship is hardly traumatic; Ambith is either lying to annoy the king, or she is really ill for some reason, and this makes her even more of an unknown. I expect the conclave will be stormy."

"You've said before that it would be hard. You're worried that Kawlend will side with Evered. But you said you thought things would be all right."

"Sometimes I do, sometimes I don't. My intuition says we are due for trouble, but intuition is just a mask our fears and desires wear. I wasn't even present at Ambith's arrival. Still, I have a request to make of you."

"What is it?"

"I believe, Christine, that you should attend the conclave. Hear me out; I know you said you didn't want to, but I'm asking you to reconsider. I thought at first it would be all for the better if you did not stay much in Ambith's presence. Now I'm not so sure; the duchess hates Edisthen, but she might not feel the same toward you. You're young, and a woman. Also, your disposition has greatly improved these past few days. You're no longer as fragile as you were when you arrived. You can take the pressures of the conclave; all you have to do is listen, no one will require you to speak."

Christine shook her head. "I . . . I don't think I could do it. You're asking me to spend hours at my father's side."

"No. Not at his side. That's just it. I've looked at the chamber, and there are several boxes; you can have one all to yourself. You wouldn't be present as Edisthen's heir and supporter, but as an independent observer if you will, come to learn statecraft. I've vetted it with the Master of Protocol and it's perfectly acceptable; he says there's precedent. You could show up at the beginning, stay for a while, and leave when you felt you'd had enough."

"You really want me to do this."

Melogian sighed. "Yes, I want you to do it. It will be good for you. It will be good for the realm. It will be good for your father. It might remind Ambith that Edisthen has an heir, a *female* heir. You don't have to do it if you don't feel capable. I will not force you."

Christine looked at her hands. "You told me the Law pushed Vaurd off his throne because he wasn't a good ruler. If I don't attend, if I just keep spending my time reading books and taking walks outside, I'll become a bad ruler, won't I? So I don't have a choice; the Law is a trap for me."

Melogian frowned. "It isn't that bad. You are who you are, yes, the princess of the realm, but you do have a choice in what you do. All of us are free. There will be many other occasions to learn. I would never think of compelling you; I am just asking you."

Christine heaved a sigh. "Yes, okay, I'll do it."

"Thank you," said Melogian. "I'll inform the Master of Protocol you'll be present. Ask Althea to choose something appropriate for you to wear. Someone will come for you just before the conclave is due to start."

Casimir had risen well before dawn and gone to his task. At his worktable were the sheets of parchment where he had scriven the words Nikolas Mestech had taught him; plans of Testenel; maps of Temerorn and Kawlend. In the middle of the table was a bowl full of fluid in which a ring of braided metal wires had been sunk. Two days ago, the ring had been so hot still that the fluid bubbled and steamed; now it had finally cooled. Casimir took up a pair of wooden tongs and dipped them cautiously in the fluid to fish out the ring. Three drops fell back into the bowl, then the ring was dry. Alloyed from gold, silver, and orichalc, its metal glittered yellow-white in the workroom's light. The wires had been perfectly fused at the point where the ring bent back upon itself: Now it had no beginning and no end, and what had been a pair of wires had become a single one, twisted with itself.

Scraps of knowledge he had salvaged from Mestech hinted at the immense potency of this talisman. Here was, Casimir thought, quite possibly the first and essential step to opening a made world. A ring that bit its own tail so seamlessly that the whole swallowed itself at the same time as it remained entire; had he known how to thread space between the braids and pass the ring thrice through itself without breaking it, he might have accomplished more than anyone in the past two millennia. . . . But the lore was too vague and fragmentary. Or perhaps, Casimir told himself consolingly, in these latter days the creation of made worlds had become an impossible task; perhaps at the dawn of time the mages of the First would have understood with the greatest of ease what was required, while the minds of the men of the seventh millennium could no longer encompass the underlying notions.

It mattered little, in the end. The ring could still be attuned to an existing made world, and Mestech's memories had yielded more than enough in that respect. Casimir had crafted the ring to resonate with a particular opening; in its final forging it had proven itself, and there had remained only the business of waiting for the enspelled metal to cool to a temperature that allowed its proper handling.

Casimir wrapped the ring in a square of silk and carefully wiped it, seeking the least bead of fluid remaining on the metal's surface. When he was satisfied that the ring was clean, he picked it up between left thumb and forefinger and put his right thumb through the opening. There was some resistance, but the ring slid over his thumb up to the second knuckle. Casimir let out a sigh of relief. He pulled the ring back up his thumb until only the tip remained within, then inserted the tip of the other thumb. Focusing his will upon the self-intertwined braid, he drew his thumbs apart; in his grip, the ring widened, remaining circular. Again there was resistance; again he overcame it. After two minutes, the ring had become a hoop as wide as his hand. The wizard grinned in triumph. He relaxed his efforts, and the ring shrank swiftly. Exerted his will again, and saw the ring expand once more, much faster than the first time. He let it collapse back to its initial size, laid it gently on the surface of the worktable.

He opened a cupboard door; there was a servant within, a small female that seemed ten or twelve years old. "You; attend!" said Casimir. The servant stepped out of the cupboard and looked at him with unblinking eyes. "Locate Evered within Vorlok," continued Casimir. "When you have located him, deliver the following message: 'Casimir has laid the trap.' Afterward, return to the nearest servants' post and assume availability for normal duties."

The girl shut her eyes for two heartbeats, then reopened them and said, "I understand." She exited the workroom and Casimir locked the door behind her.

There was a cask of water upon a pedestal, and next to it a commode. Casimir stripped off his clothes and clad himself only in a woolen robe. Then he went to sit on the commode, settling his bulk carefully onto the velvet cushion round the rim. A fine catgut tube had been tied at one end to the cask's spigot, at the other to a hollow needle welded to a metal grommet. Casimir checked the connections carefully, then he spoke a simple spell, grasped the hollow needle, and pushed it through his left cheek; the flesh stretched and stretched, and finally parted. His other hand reached inside his mouth and pulled the rest of the needle through, then gave it a quarter-turn; gearlike teeth on the grommet bit into his flesh and anchored the needle in place. The spell prevented any bleeding or pain.

Casimir turned the handle of the spigot very slightly; water began to dribble slowly down the tube. Presently a drop of water fell from the needle's tip onto his tongue; Casimir made a point of not swallowing, felt the moisture coat his tongue. The next drop came, moistening his throat.

There was a table to his right, within easy reach of his hand. Casimir tipped over the hourglass upon the table. A single grain of sand fell through the constriction at its middle. Then he brought his hands together in his lap, over the folds of the woolen robe, holding the braided ring in his palms. Days, perhaps a week, he could remain thus, a spider in the middle of his web, but then he would need to rest for a time; he was only human, after all.

He cast a final spell, to send his consciousness across the leagues, speaking with perfect clarity, unmindful of the sting of the needle on his tongue. Power gathered in the confines of the room; Casimir felt it coming to him in waves, and his heart sang with glee. He wanted this part of it never to end, the minutes when might flowed into him. He saw himself grow huge, huger than the world, so that he looked down upon it as God might, held it in his palm instead of the ring, to be molded according to his desires. Sweat beaded at his temples as he worked the magic; water dribbled into his mouth, unnoticed. The ring attuned to Mestech's made world lay between his fingers, singing with power torn out of the dead wizard's dream-flesh.

Casimir slipped the ring over his joined thumbs; one flexion of his will, and it enlarged. He was ready. He cast his perceptions toward Testenel, along the weft of force of the spy-spell he had laboriously threaded through Melogian's wards. From a hundred points within the castle inchoate sensations came to him. As he poured more of his power through the web, his apperceptions sharpened. Images came now to his sight, still dim and watery; sounds, echoing and muffled. His immediate surroundings faded; Casimir flowed into Testenel, until he seemed to become the castle itself. The vast majority of the edifice still lay beyond his senses; he was as a man stricken with apoplexy, most of whose body has betrayed him and now surrounds his soul as a dead burden. Splinters of sound and shards of vision coalesced in Casimir's awareness; he felt himself encompassing Testenel's expanse like strands of cobweb crossing a vast empty room. People moved within the reach of his senses; he saw and heard them. Servants of a dozen stripes, guards . . . He saw Ambith of Kawlend cross a corridor, with her minions in tow. Somewhere else within him Edisthen's daughter Christine slept in her apartments, but the wards were packed tight about this place and Casimir had not yet managed to wedge a strand of perception between them. . . . In a courtyard open to the morning air the Royal Gardens slumbered, the rising sun soon to kindle their life; no one walked their paths. . . . And in the core of the castle, where his adits clustered thickest, Edisthen's gaunt figure stalked the rooms and corridors.

Time passed. Casimir's bladder relaxed and urine plashed into the jug beneath the seat. On the wall behind him, a man's shadow was cast for a second, but it was as if it struggled in vain to be born, and the next instant it had vanished. Water dripped from the tube into his mouth. Another grain of sand fell.

It took until early afternoon before the conclave was able to start. Christine made her way to the council chambers dressed in full regalia. Althea had selected for her a gown beaded with gems as a spiderweb is beaded with dew in the morning.

Pale silk shot with yellow threads, it fitted her closely at the waist and belled out below, its shape maintained by a cage of wires. Her hair was knotted to a small apparatus that was in turn covered by a faintly ridiculous little pillbox hat, which Althea had spent ten minutes defending as the height of fashion to her skeptical mistress.

Christine entered the chambers announced by a herald; when her name was called, every head in the room turned to look at her. For a moment dread urged her to flee; she was saved by her dress, which so hindered her movements that she could not simply bolt out of the chambers. After a flustered moment, Christine regained her composure and allowed the Master of Protocol to direct her to her box.

The council chambers were circular, with tiers running up from the speaker's pit in the center to the walls. Seats in a variety of styles looked down at the central pit; low partitions set off several boxes. Christine took a seat in one of those, while two of her guards posted themselves at the forward corners of the box. Althea sat a row behind her and to her left, with an undermaid at her side. They had brought in food and drink for Christine, and Althea immediately poured a goblet of water that she put at Christine's left elbow.

Edisthen was there, with his advisers, not quite directly across from her. Between them were the Archeledians, a dignified group surrounding Duke Edric. The Kawlendian delegation sat to Edisthen's other side; Duchess Ambith looked at Christine with an absence of expression. Christine returned her look for a second before averting her gaze, intimidated. She knew Ambith was in her late forties, but she looked fifteen years younger—though the makeup was caked rather obviously on her face. Her prominent cheekbones and thin nose made her face harsh; her eyebrows were pulled down in a habitual frown.

Duke Corlin of Estephor was still missing; he arrived a few minutes later, his entourage contrasting with the solemn delegates from Archeled and Kawlend. As soon as they were settled in, to Christine's left, Edisthen rose from his seat.

The Master of Protocol gave a signal and a quartet of white birds, their wings dyed in contrasting colors, were let loose in the chambers. Flying each in a spiral pattern, they climbed to the ceiling and settled upon a gilded perch; an instant later, the perch ascended and the birds vanished. Christine watched the process with curiosity: Was this magic again? But a flash of light from above and a glimpse of a pair of hands guiding a panel shut over a circular hole proved that a much simpler explanation prevailed.

Edisthen had remained silent while the birds circled the chamber and left. Now he spoke, his voice clear and ringing. It was not very much the voice Christine imagined a king ought to have: a rich basso rumble commanding obedience. Edisthen's voice was rather high-pitched for a man's, and his long gaunt frame could not give it much bass resonance. Still, it had force and volume; Edisthen spoke, Christine thought suddenly, like one of those long and thin ceremonial trumpets.

"Cousins! Honored delegates! I have brought you here today concerning a matter of urgency. For the first time in the history of my reign, all three dukes of the land are gathered together under my roof. This is a memorable date and the annals of the realm shall preserve it.

"Thirteen years ago, my daughter and heir, the Princess Christine, was abducted from Testenel and vanished from our ken."

Most heads in the chambers swiveled to look at Christine, who felt herself wither under the attention. She clenched a hand on the arm of her chair and kept her expression neutral. To her relief, as her father continued to speak, the people's attention returned to him.

"On the thirteenth of Summereve of this year, my daughter Christine was brought back to us; this all of you know, as the news was sent all across the land. What you do not know is what took place on the fourteenth: I received a visit from Evered, Vaurd's eldest son. By royal decree Vaurd's offspring are confined within Vorlok, in Kawlend. However, Evered did not disobey the decree, inasmuch as he was not physically present: This was an eidolon, an image of him if you will, although possessed of far greater presence, evoked by his wizard Casimir."

A mutter ran through the assembly at this; Edisthen waited for it to subside before speaking on.

"I was surprised to see Evered, as you can imagine. More important, I was appalled by what he said. Evered spoke out in challenge: He threatened that I should be cast down from the throne, and that war should engulf the land. I have summoned you here because I take his words seriously, and I wish to engage all our energies to oppose him."

He turned to face Duchess Ambith, who frowned at him, her mouth a slit.

"Your Grace. Twenty years ago you and I were on opposite sides. I mention this not to embarrass, not to threaten, but because it must be addressed if this conclave is to move forward. I hold no grudge against you, none against your people. Loyalty is a virtue not a flaw, and you were loyal to the old sovereign. Our accounts were settled long ago. You are welcome here as a peer of the realm. I dearly hope that so much is clear to you."

To this speech Ambith made no reply, not even a gesture. After a time Edisthen turned his gaze away from her and addressed the assembly as a whole.

"I have brought you all here because I believe action must be taken, and I wish the realm to be united in this decision. I believe that Evered seeks to instigate war, using as his troops the armies of rebellious barons of the southern marches; but also, that he plans to make use of hostile magic, magic of great potency. You may well greet these words with skepticism; but I assure you there is cause for alarm, if only because the wizard Orion remains lost to the realm. I think it will be necessary for us to move against Evered, and even to fight a serious battle. We must prepare for this."

An old man seated two rows behind Duchess Ambith jerked to his feet and shouted in outrage. Edisthen allowed the interruption. "Your Grace," he addressed Ambith, "shall I let your counselor speak his mind?"

Ambith spared the man a glance; then she nodded once. The old man looked at the assembly, almost ignoring the king.

"We came here in good faith," began the counselor, "though we knew we would not be treated well. It has taken less than five minutes for His Majesty to start with calumnies and destructive innuendo. We are appalled, though I can't say I am very surprised."

Christine felt herself trying to shrink in place. None of the venom was directed at her, but every time she found herself in a situation like this, rather than feeling virtuously unconcerned, she would quail inside in unwilling sympathy for the object of the anger.

"When the Usurpation War was over, who was it who had to provide shelter for the deposed king's family? Kawlend! Who was it who suffered endless travails, who saw the flower of her youth slaughtered, who was over a decade stunned? Kawlend! Whose resources were strained by demands for reparations? Who was bled dry by weregild? Who has lost her status at the court? Kawlend! Twenty years of insult we have endured, and now this!"

"Och, that's rich coming from—" burst forth an Estephorin delegate, who was immediately bidden to silence by Duke Corlin.

The old man refused to acknowledge the outburst. Looking at Duke Edric now he continued: "For twenty years, Kawlend has done her duty and warded the sons of Vaurd, as she was ordered at the end of the war. For twenty years they have been watched, and for twenty years their behavior has been irreproachable. These men have spent a score of years within the walls of their miserable castle, peacefully resigned to their disgrace. The Law protects them, you say, but no Law compelled the king to imprison them, yet he did. And Kawlend has been their jailer."

The old counselor stopped there and crossed his arms. Edisthen waited after him, obviously expecting him to make a point, then eventually tried to give an answer.

"I should remind everyone present that Vaurd's sons chose Vorlok as the place of their exile, of their own free will. I am not casting any aspersions here, not on the duchy nor on any of its citizens. However, when we come to irreproachable behavior, surely threatening to cast the land into bloody chaos is not irreproachable. . . ."

Once more the king was interrupted by protests from Ambith's entourage. The tone was set for the remainder of the day. As Edisthen tried to make his point, various Kawlendian delegates would take the stand and offer protests. Nothing was acknowledged on their parts, no factual points debated. Instead they spoke of Kawlend as a victim of history; they listed injuries the duchy had sustained; they complained of generalized unfairness, financial imbalances, long-standing disputes never resolved. Archeled and Estephor replied to some of these accusations, to be countered by claims of favoritism. The Kawlendians demanded the floor, then poured out streams of recriminations that made Christine's head spin. She wasn't familiar enough with history to know if these claims were founded or not, but there were so many, and the delegates so vocal, that surely some fraction of their grievances was justified?

Tempers were rising; some of Corlin's delegation in particular were young and hot-blooded enough that they had trouble holding their tongues, and met some of the Kawlendians' claims with derisive calls. Edisthen tried, again and again, to bring the discussion back to the issue of Evered's challenge; he met with no success. The Kawlendians were now embroiled with the Archeledians over an abstruse reckoning of deaths suffered during a particular battle, which was apparently an emotional issue for both sides. Duke Edric had become involved in turn and was quoting official reports while the old Kawlendian counselor harped on his personal memories of the battle.

Edisthen, his cheeks coloring, gestured at the Master of Protocol, who rapped his staff on the floor repeatedly and shouted: "Order! Order!" The audience slowly fell silent. The Master of Protocol continued: "By command of His Majesty, a recess is called until tomorrow morning!"

Edisthen, his face hard and his brow clenched, rose to his feet; then, accompanied by his aides, he left the chambers. The audience had risen as well; once the king was gone, there was a moment of hesitation. Althea leaned forward and murmured in Christine's ear that it might be her turn to leave; but already Duchess Ambith was sweeping from her box, followed by her delegation. Duke Corlin was next. The Archeledians remained in the chambers. Duke Edric, looking very sad and tired, addressed Christine. "After you, Highness."

Christine in that moment lost some of her awe of him. She replied, "Thank you, Your Grace," and made a dignified exit. She retired to her rooms and ate a solitary meal, feeling glum.

Edisthen left the council chambers in a black mood. Kawlend had played him for a fool, and succeeded. His best efforts to debate the current situation had been in vain. As one man, every Kawlendian delegate had fastened onto a single subject and would not let go. It was as if, for them, the past twenty years had never been. Still they wailed at their losses, still they demanded reparations for every slight suffered in the war, while dismissing what others had undergone. Edisthen would have expected this line of argument from an uneducated commoner; coming from senior counselors of Duchess Ambith, it reeked of willful ignorance. Either that, or these men had spent two decades convincing themselves Kawlend had truly been the innocent victim of the war. Which was not beyond the reach of possibilities, after all: Nothing is so fiercely believed in as that which one wishes to be true.

Edisthen winced at the spike of pain in his left eye; his anger bred migraines. When he had given the order for recess, he had been on the verge of letting all restraint go and forcefully reminding Kawlend who it was had bloody well lost the war. Talquen would not have allowed such disorder amongst his vassals; he'd have had the Kawlendians cowering in terrified silence while he ranted his orders at them. . . . Then again, Talquen would have had Ambith beheaded upon her final defeat twenty years before. Edisthen was not cut of the same cloth; his way was softer—weaker, no doubt, less decisive, but it was his way. Less than any born man did he imagine he could change the core of himself. Some days he wished to be other than he was, but this was never more than a short-lived folly.

Still, for the moment he felt assaulted by despair and self-doubt. He needed a measure of solitude. At times like this the press of people all around him felt like a crushing weight. He wanted to walk alone among trees, with no sound but the sigh of his breath. He had heard many times of other people craving such surroundings; but in their case, what they sought, he knew, was merely peace. What he sought went further: He yearned to return to the moment of his origin—he would be wrong to think of it as a birth. He had come to consciousness almost all at once, walking in the forest, on his way to overthrow Vaurd and rule the land. Since that moment he had been driven, had driven himself, without cease. He did not mind it—how could he, since this was all that he was? Yet even he hungered at times for respite from his struggles; and he strove to return to the moment that had started it, or rather to the moment *before* that. He had been taking a step as he grew aware of who he was, but surely, since his leg was already coming down upon the ground, surely it had rested on the earth a heartbeat before? Surely there had been a time, so brief, less than a second, but a time when he had been in existence yet still innocent. . . . This was all the childhood he had had, that crumb of time before he grew into who he was. And he yearned for it at times, and accepted this yearning as something that was also part of him, that tied him to true humanity.

So he left the rooms and corridors of Testenel and came out into the Royal Gardens, and walked there alone. There were various gardens around the castle; most were situated around the edges, to be able to catch the sun directly, but some nestled close to the center and needed sunlight brought to them by the great mirrors that surmounted the castle, as otherwise the overhanging mass of Testenel blotted out all illumination. This was the case for the Royal Gardens, which were surrounded on all sides by the shafts of towers. The reflective panes of the mirrors sometimes presented an unexpected sky if one looked straight up; but most of the time the illusion worked and it was possible to imagine oneself outside of colossal Testenel.

The sun had set; the vault of heaven was cobalt blue though a smudge of pinkish brown still beat at the western edge of the sky. The stars were faint yet, not having fully awoken. Edisthen breathed deep of the evening air, savored the smell of wetness. He took a path close to the edge of the enclosure, lined by trees at either hand, a few of them old and massive enough to remind him of the forest where he had been written into existence. Beyond the trees, the highest towers of Testenel rose into the sky, blurred by dusk.

Perhaps, he allowed himself to think, perhaps one day soon Christine might walk this path with him. She bore his presence more readily now, as witnessed by her long stay in the council chambers; though Melogian insisted it was too soon to press her, still he could tell his daughter was healing. His heart swelled at this thought; hope was a fragile thing in so many ways, yet somehow it could not be crushed, could not utterly die. From its own ashes it rose, as Ilianrod's Firebird had in days long past.

Silence all about him; not even insects could be heard, only the breeze rustling leaves. The path turned left and meandered between trees set close together. The towers of Testenel could no longer be seen; for a moment Edisthen thought of the made world that opened at the very center of the garden, and which he certainly had no desire to enter, or even to approach. Yawning pits into infinity, Orion had once called them. In all the twenty years he had spent on the earth, Edisthen had entered a made world but twice, and then only briefly. One world was more than enough for him.

This path kept to the outer edges of the garden. Edisthen walked it peacefully, at one point closing his eyes and still striding. Was it a touch of memory he felt, or his imagination? It seemed to him he recalled an instant of time like this, his leg swinging forward, his eyes not closed but unseeing yet. . . .

The path went over a quaint wooden bridge over a dry stream; his boots rang on the weathered planks. At the end, he ran his hand over one of the knobbed posts, enjoying the grain of the wood under his fingers.

It was growing much darker. There were usually lights in the garden; why were they not yet lit? Were the gardeners aware of his presence, and respecting his solitude? Edisthen slowed and halted. He should go back: This section of the gardens was not very familiar to him, and the darkness made it even less so.

Ten strides did not bring him to the wooden bridge. Neither did ten more. Clouds were massing in the sky, and the gloom deepened. Edisthen felt his heart speed up, tension singing in the pit of his stomach. There had been no fork in the path; he could not have taken a wrong way back. He strode on, blinking furiously, and suddenly knew relief as the bridge appeared before him.

He was halfway across when he stopped; he could hear the liquid rustle of water beneath the planks—but the stream had been dry. He was sure, as sure as he could be sure of anything, that the stream had been bone-dry. It came to him then, as he stood atop the bridge in the darkness, that he had never known fear, never known what it was, until this very moment.

He shouted, his voice thunderous: "Guards! To me! Guards! The king calls! *Guards!*" Only the wind answered him.

Melogian had gifted him with a small spell, to summon her to him in emergencies. Edisthen brought it to the fore of his mind; it was like a bright insect, spinning and turning, waiting to be set free. He willed it loose, and with an inaudible snap it came free of him and vanished. Wherever the sorceress was, it would reach her and bring her to him.

He stood waiting on the bridge a long, long time, and no one came. A darkness nearly absolute had fallen, and still only the wind kept him company. He counted his heartbeats to measure time, and when half an hour had elapsed he stopped waiting.

He went all the way across the bridge; when his boots touched the path again it was sand they touched and not gravel. He wrapped his cape tightly about him as he sat down by the side of the path, leaning against the bole of an oak. He told himself he would sit here through the night, and when the sun had come up, he would try to find his way back. But there was a chill in his soul that said there was no way to be found, and he recalled that in time, even Ilianrod's magical bird had died.

❧ A gap, a hollowness, a sudden lack. Melogian started. Something was wrong. She sent her mind roaming among the strands of the web she had woven all about Testenel. Through intangible feelers she sped, back and forth, crisscrossing the castle and its hundreds of chambers, corridors, hypogees, anterooms, staircases, grand hallways. It took her three heartbeats, no more; finding nothing amiss, she shifted her attention to Christine. The protective tangle of spells she had set about the girl remained undisturbed. Immixed with the coils of defensive magic, the perceptive tendrils brought back the echoes of Christine and all nearby: the handpicked guards at the door of her suite, Captain Veraless on watch. Christine herself was sitting in a chair, reading a book.

Two heartbeats on Christine, then on to her father the king—Melogian stood up, a shout rising to her lips.

The web was severed around him, the strands of her spells evaporated to nothingness. Melogian had no sense of him. She sent a surge of power riding along the strands, to compel them to reconnect, but the effort was futile. She did shout then, and started running out of the room. *Where had Edisthen been?* Her question raged through the web, but the spells had little memory. From the swiftly fading impressions still extant within the strands, she gleaned a picture of the Royal Gardens drowning in the dusk.

She screamed for guards, and when she burst into the gardens it was at the forefront of a dozen soldiers with drawn blades. They were met by Corporal Keller, a grizzled veteran and member of the king's personal guard.

"What the fucking blazes is going on?" asked Keller angrily.

"Where's Edisthen?" shouted Melogian. "Where is the king?"

"He went down for a stroll, Lady. He's along that path."

"Alone? You let him go *alone*?"

"He dismissed us—but I'm no idiot. I've got three men keeping watch on him, he doesn't even know they're there."

"Edisthen!" screamed Melogian. "Majesty!" There was no reply. Here and there among the hedges and bushes, small lanterns glowed, barely able to overcome the darkness. Melogian shouted out a spell: yellow flames billowed out of her fingers, rose crackling up into the air over the center of the gardens, condensed into a ball of fire that shed a brighter and brighter light until it rivaled the sun's. Every flower, every leaf glowed in the glare and cast a quivering, bluish shadow.

"Find him," she told Keller, her tone equal parts command and supplication. "Find him!" From the shouts of the soldiers who strode through the starkly lit paths and met only one another, the situation became swiftly clear to her. Keller bawled orders, wrung replies out of the soldiers, went himself to verify. In the end he returned and confronted Melogian, disbelief plain on his face.

"We knew where he was, Lady. We fucking *knew*! Alfonse was twenty paces ahead of him, Anastasia less than ten to the rear. Ragels heard him cross the bridge; he says he was on the verge of revealing himself and offering a light."

"Where is he, then?"

Keller shook his head. "He's . . . he's not here, milady."

Melogian moved past, trying to shove him aside and succeeding only because Keller yielded to the weak thrust of her arm before it had even touched him. She walked stiff-legged along a radial white-gravel path, her shadow behind her growing shorter and shorter as she approached the center of the gardens above which her sunlet shed its light.

She stopped when she had gotten within ten paces of the inner bower. From here, it was no more than ten yards on a side, delimited by four rows of broadneedled shrubs, pierced by an opening at each corner. A basin of still water reflected the light of Melogian's sun. If she were to approach it, it would loom larger and larger in her sight, as the path grew wider and wider. Fifteen paces into the bower, fifteen paces into the made world Nikolas Mestech had raised, she would be walking a road through a clearing in a forest of pines. A quarter-mile farther in, she would reach a dock on the edge of a small lake where boats were moored. Across the lake was the Long Isle, and if she followed the road that threaded it, she would eventually reach a port where sailships from strange countries were docked. . . .

She had not been raised in a pious household, and being apprenticed to Orion since she was eight years old, she had scarcely ever gone to worship. Yet she found the words of ritual rising to her lips. "Sweet and gentle God, lay not this burden upon me. In the name of the Book, let this burden be taken from me. Heroes of the Book, lift this burden from me. . . ."

She started screaming like a little girl having a tantrum, her fists clenched at her sides, her face raised up to the blinding light, repeating "No! No! No!" until her voice failed her.

🙠 The sound of a commotion reached through two doors into Christine's bedroom, where she sat reading Alindor's *History of Chrysanthe*. She heard Captain Veraless open the door to her suite and then an exchange of raised voices. A knock sounded at her own door, and she answered it with a voice grown suddenly tense. Melogian entered, her face very pale. "I must talk with you, Christine. It is about your father."

"What about him?" The heavy book lay open in Christine's lap, her hands resting on facing pages. Captain Veraless was looking in over Melogian's shoulder, his face also in turmoil.

"He is gone. I mean, he has vanished. He was in the Royal Gardens when it happened, twenty minutes ago."

Christine could not rid herself of the impression Melogian was playing a joke on her. "What do you mean, he's gone? What happened to him?"

"I'm not sure. But I know he is gone from this world. I had woven spells all about him; they've been cleanly severed. If he had taken a secret passage, or even if he had been whisked away by magic to the northern edge of the world, still my spells would be bound to him. He isn't in Chrysanthe anymore; I believe he entered the made world at the center of the gardens."

"Why would he do that?" This still made no sense. The world had lurched out of true, without warning. Still Christine could only feel numb astonishment.

"He had no good reason," said Melogian. "And he disliked the made worlds, he only entered one once that I know of. So I have to assume that he was taken there against his will. Abducted."

In the silence that followed, Christine put the book very carefully on the table, marking her place in it with a ribbon of silk. She wanted very much to lie down and go to sleep. "If he's been abducted, then it'll be my turn next, won't it?" she asked Melogian.

"No. No, it won't happen. I will not let it."

"You'll really protect me?" asked Christine, her voice shaking. In reply, Melogian took her in her arms and hugged her.

"I will. I won't let anything happen to you," she said, running her fingers through Christine's hair. "I laid a much greater number of enchantments about you than about your father, and several of them are intended to oppose hostile spells. You're safe, Christine. Now listen: For the moment, stay in this room. Make sure that you are never alone. You're not in danger, but I just want to be utterly careful. All right? I have to go for now, but I will be back. If anything happens, scream. Call for me. I will come, I promise."

Christine shakily agreed. Melogian broke the embrace, stroked Christine's cheek in apology, and left the room with Captain Veraless. A guard came to stand into the room. Christine sat down, opened her book at the marked page, and stared blindly at the ink marks on the paper.

❧ Outside Christine's apartments, Veraless took Melogian aside.

"God's eyes, Melogian, you may have fooled Christine but *I'm* not a seventeen-year-old girl. She's going to go next, isn't she? What are we going to do?"

"She will not be taken, Veraless. I won't allow it."

"You won't allow it? It seems to me you pretty much allow anything to happen to anyone! You couldn't prevent Edisthen from being taken!"

Melogian held up her hands. She was fighting a sense of panic, and Veraless's ranting was making things worse.

"Reason this out with me, Captain, please. True: For the third time, someone from court has been abducted. But the circumstances have been different each time."

"What does it matter what the circumstances were?"

"It matters; it matters very much. Christine was abducted thirteen years ago, when she was four. One of her body-maids was bribed to bring her into a secluded room; the girl believed a minor noble wished to ingratiate himself with the royal family by giving the princess a special gift."

"I know the story as well as you do. The stupid cow was coshed the instant the door had closed, and Christine was taken away."

"Yes, by people who used both masks and spells of distraction so that they remained seen but unnoticed. They managed to conceal Christine, whether through disguise or just stuffed in a sack, or perhaps they convinced her they were playing a game. And they managed to take her outside of Testenel."

"Yes, and Orion himself couldn't help her!"

"You're being unfair to him. The instant Orion was apprised of the situation, he sent off a dozen benedictions in every direction of the zodiac, and then he prepared a seeking-spell. But a seeking-spell takes hours to cast, sometimes half a day. He acted as fast as he could, but even Orion isn't infallible."

"You're telling me! I've always thought it, and I'll say it to your face, Melogian: Your precious master was a fool; even the damned king was a fool. How could you leave the child in the hands of idiots, unprotected?"

"She wasn't unprotected! You have no idea, Captain, what the bringing up of a royal child entails. Grab her too roughly and you *die*. Maids have to be carefully chosen for placidity and mildness, and this means they tend to be . . . naïve. I'll remind you that abduction of a royal heir has been attempted only a handful of times in all recorded history; such plans had never succeeded before."

"At any rate, what happened happened. What good is it to rehash ancient history?"

"I'm trying to point out in what ways the abductions differed. Now consider Orion. What happened to him may not even be an abduction. Certainly it wasn't murder—he lives still. He was deep within Jyndyrys when it happened, and as far as I can discern he is still within it. A made world offers limitless potential for ambush. Whether he met with some horror from nightmares that overpowered him, or whether it was one of Evered's wizards who fell upon him, I don't know. But his disappearance was the result of direct physical attack, in an environment that was extremely dangerous. All right?"

"Fine! I'll grant you that. It was a direct attack. So?"

"And so, we come to this latest event," Melogian continued, forcing her voice to calm. "Edisthen has vanished from the Royal Gardens. Unlike Christine at age four, he knew what was happening to him. Like her, if he is so much as scratched, his assailant dies upon the instant. He was not heard to struggle or to call out. Three guards and Corporal Keller were keeping watch over him. Ragels reports having distinctly heard him cross the bridge. He saw him start across, then lost sight of him in the gloom, although he couldn't say when."

"One or all of them might be traitors."

"I've had them put under arrest and they'll be interrogated; but I don't expect them to be proved disloyal. Orion himself vetted each applicant to the king's personal guard. Also, what Ragels described is exactly the perceptual trick one experiences while traveling through a made world."

"Yes, you've said it before: You think Edisthen entered the made world at the center of the garden."

"And yet he was nearly a hundred yards away from the entrance. How then did it happen? How can one enter a made world without passing through the opening into it?"

Veraless shrugged exasperatedly. "How should I know? You're the wizard!"

"When I walked through the gardens and approached the bower where the made world opens," said Melogian, "I strained my senses to their utmost; and there was something overlaid on the gravel of the path, something over every leaf, every blade of grass. It was like when one washes a stone floor: the faint gleams as the last of the water evaporates from the surface of the stone. Even as I sensed them, they faded away."

Melogian took a deep breath. "I believe that the opening was made to expand, to gape hugely wide, for a moment. It caught all of them in its maw: the king and the guards who watched over him. Then it drew itself back to its natural size again. Like the surf withdrawing from the shore, it left them where they had stood, unaware that they had entered and exited a made world. Except for Edisthen; somehow, he was pushed farther in, and he remained inside the made world. Does that make sense to you, Captain?"

"I'm not a magician. It seems to make some sense, but I don't know the lore."

"I am not asking you to. Just tell me, do I sound insane, or am I making sense?"

"I think I can understand what you mean. You don't sound insane."

"Then help me make a decision. I must choose a course, and at once. The made world remains a dangerous trap, but there are limits to magic. I have no idea how an opening might be widened like this, but without a doubt the more it is to widen, the more difficult the task. I am confident it cannot reach beyond the walls that bound the gardens.

"So if I am right, then I must enter the made world myself and seek for Edisthen there. I'll have to cast a seeking-spell first, otherwise I might as well sift the sea with my fingers. The spell should sense him swiftly enough; surely—well, at least I hope—he can't be too far down into the world. . . ."

Melogian had been speaking very rapidly; now the flow of her speech slowed. Veraless put word to the very objections she found rising in her mind.

"You don't know how deep he is, do you? You just think he's close to the surface. And when you don't find him right away, are you going to do what Orion did? Are you going to summon all the knights of the land and send them down into the made world? How many years before the king is found? How many years will you spend looking for him and forgetting us here?"

"I won't abandon the king!" Melogian protested.

Veraless drew back his torn upper lip. "I'm not asking you to. Don't you dare put it in those words. You asked me to reason with you; well, now, you have to keep reasoning. You need to make a sane decision, not play along with Evered's plans. He expects you, he wants you, to bury yourself in the made world and never come out. He wants us all to panic, to stand there doing nothing except waiting for the king to return. The Book of Miracles gave us Christine back; I don't expect a second blessing to come down upon us so soon after."

"I don't care what you say, Veraless. I have to look for him!"

"One day, Melogian. That's all. I'll give you one day. Seek him for one day, and when the day is done, give up."

"You don't command me, Captain," she said hotly.

"No. The Lady Christine does, now. But you're not going to present her with that decision, are you? That would be sheer cruelty. So, have some presumption. Do what's needful, not what you think is right. The land has lost its king, don't let it lose all the rest."

"I didn't know you could be so callous."

"Then you're an idiot. I've commanded men in battle and sent them to their death; my soul is scarred aplenty, little girl. I spent over a decade mourning the loss of Christine, wishing I could have gone to find her myself. I won't have us start it all over again. We're going to fight Evered with our full strength. We're going to defeat him, slaughter his soldiers, put the traitors in our ranks to the gallows . . . and then I'll kill him. I'll slit his throat open; I don't care what the Law does to me after that. I've had enough of fear. We've been like Barkazan who wore an iron mask across his face for seven years after losing his right eye in battle, in fear that he should lose the left. You know the story? After seven years in utter darkness, when he finally mustered up the courage to remove the mask, he found his left eye had gone blind. One day, Melogian. Because even that is weakness."

She turned away from him and ran down the corridor, to her own apartments. Her mind was in turmoil; her power stirred within her, a dozen spells swirling confusedly before her inner eye. Once she had reached her workroom, she sat herself down at a table and forced herself to calm. To invoke magic in the extremity of passion was just as risky as swinging a weapon: The blow might be stronger, but it was less precise. And what she needed at this moment was precision.

She arranged implements for the casting of a full seeking-spell. Bowl, tripod, a seven-armed metal cross. It was the same spell Orion had used to hunt for Christine; the one he had laid upon a score of knights before sending them down into the made worlds. Of the twenty who had gone seeking, eight had returned fruitless; of these, three had gone forth again. Four had abandoned the search, three because they had sustained such injuries that they could never more pursue their calling, and one because of something that had happened to him, something he could not bring himself to speak of but which had withered his soul like a blade of grass dropped into a forge. And there had been that young knight, too, Reivin, who had thought to fetch a girl from the edges of the world and pass her off as the long-lost heir, and killed himself when his ruse had failed. . . . Fourteen knights of Chrysanthe still lost deep in the made worlds, hunting for Christine not knowing she had been found. How many of those would ever emerge again? Perhaps all were dead already.

Against her will, Melogian pictured Edisthen's broken corpse at the foot of a cliff of bone twenty miles high; saw him attacked by a swarm of winged horrors, huge flaccid-bodied insects with minuscule children's faces; then captured and enslaved by a race of blue-skinned giants. It was the worst parts of her own travels down into Jyndyrys she recalled, casting her liege as the victim of perils she had barely escaped. But these misadventures had occurred deep into the made world, where reality had shifted far away from the norm. Surely Edisthen must be close to the surface. He knew enough not to move down a gradient—though he might not be aware of its existence as such, the effects would be clearly apparent.

The final element of the spell must be a part of Edisthen's flesh; from a sealed box Melogian withdrew a single black hair she had plucked from his beard herself, laid it inside the bowl, and evoked a tiny flame to lick at the copper.

Then she cast the spell, wrapped it around herself like a tiny thread of power. It was a slow spell to cast, glacially slow, because its power must reach far: To hunt for a misplaced book amongst her shelves might take an hour, but to seek for a man who might lie miles distant, a world away, required half a day's casting. Slowly, slowly, Melogian kept winding the spell around her, thread on a bobbin.

Even this is weakness, Veraless had said. Melogian could not dispute it. She went from failure to failure in her life, unable to protect those whom she loved. Still she would try; she would go hunt for Edisthen, no matter that she doubted the point of it most of all. There were gradations of failures, and the failure to even make an attempt was not one she would allow herself.

◆◆ Edisthen opened his eyes and found the sun had risen, and a pale light now washed the garden. He levered himself to his feet, cast his gaze all around him. He was in a garden still, a garden that seemed very similar to the Royal Gardens of

Testenel. But where he would have expected to see walls and towers rise, there was only the sky and distant masses of foliage. If this had the same layout as the garden he knew, then there would be a bower at its center; and if the made world opened in that spot in Chrysanthe, did it not follow that this should be what he should aim for?

Slowly, he got into motion. The sandy path he followed ran straight and did not approach the center, which had lain to his left. Before leaving the path, he would see if he could find a fork that led in the direction he wished to go.

He went on for a while, and encountered no other path. Bushes and trees grew in tight ranks to his left: He could never make a straight way through. Still, this path led him nowhere he wanted to go; he had best attempt to thrash his way to the center. Just before stepping off the path, he was struck by a sudden thought and looked back the way he had come. Then a braying laugh escaped him, for the foolishness of his hopes. As far as his gaze reached, behind him, there were no footprints in the sand.

2. The Abyss

Evered was sunk in contemplation of the hearth flames. At these times he could feel a sort of peace, his mind taken up by the fire's dance and nothing else. It was as if the past dropped from his shoulders, so that he no longer needed to carry the crushing weight of all he knew and all he had seen; for a brief while he was no one, his identity dissolved away. Yet the trance never lasted long; soon he would feel the rage rising again, driven by the pressure of memory.

In the past few days he had been seeking refuge in the flames again and again, as a shield against anguish. Overuse of the technique seemed to lessen its effectiveness: His moments of peace became shorter and shorter. He had not had any fits, at least, though the tension whining in the pit of his stomach often seemed to promise the worst. Things needed to get into motion: He couldn't stand this endless waiting. Casimir kept promising him ever greater success, if he would only wait, wait, wait a while longer. . . .

Evered focused his gaze on a lashing tongue of flame, saw brighter ridges swimming up the body of the flame, ragged edges like bright threads fraying from a garment flapping in the breeze. . . . A particle of peace entered him, as small as one of the sparks from the fire. He could feel himself striving to hold it, a striving which guaranteed its escape. Yet for a moment more it held, and Evered drew breath, forgetting who he was and forgetting that he had forgotten it. . . .

Two thumps on his door, then it swung open of its own accord. All his hardwon calm shattered, Evered rose from his chair, angry words on his lips. He was brought up short at the sight of his wizard standing in the doorway, sweat running down his face, grinning broadly.

"It is done, m'lord," said Casimir.

Edisthen took a step back up the path, then another. The sand in front of him remained virgin of footprints. As carefully as he could, he retraced his path, but when he had returned to what should have been his starting point, there was no bridge ahead of him; instead, the path forked, nearly at right angles. He took the right-hand path, at the end of which he thought to discern a clearing of some sort.

But the coin-size spot of light did not grow any larger. The trees did instead. With every step he took, they rose higher, their boles ever more massive, until it seemed to him that it was himself who was shrinking. Shelf fungi grew from cracks in the trees' bark, and metallic-hued wasps built nests upon these ledges. Flowers sprouted from the ground: heavy blossoms, the color of fresh meat. The air held a spicy fragrance with undertones of rotting leaves. A rill flowed next to the path, and Edisthen went to it, filled himself with its cool water.

By now the light at the end of the path was a tiny dot: the head of a pin, no more. The sun's position could not be discerned; its light suffused the forest—why pretend? It was no longer any kind of garden he was in—and a sourceless viridian glow filled the air about him. From the trees' leprous bark more fungi erupted, electric blue and green, acid yellow. Wasps as long as his hand, striped black and silver, zuzzed overhead.

Fear drove Edisthen's steps now: Walking was the only thing he could do, distance the only enemy he might attempt to subdue. From time to time, he would forget who he was: In such a setting had he come into the world, and it seemed as if his mind expected his fleshly journey to be at an end, having returned to its starting point. He found no peace in the prospect, only the terror of annihilation that goaded him ever onward. He took to saying his name aloud, but in the increasingly humid, still air, the syllables began to lose their meaning, and he fell silent lest he exhaust their power completely.

In time he felt the overpowering need to sleep. He curled up in the crook between two tree roots that rose higher than his waist. The soil was bare between the roots, dark brown, dry and fine as powder. Edisthen shut his eyes. Unconsciousness fell on him like a bolster thrown over his head, and left him as abruptly.

Edisthen rose to his feet, found that the light had remained exactly the same. Had he dozed for a half hour, or an entire day? He bit his lip and felt tears coming to his eyes. He was hungry and thirsty. He must eat and drink, or he would die; and he did not want to die, although he could not be sure anymore exactly why that was.

He continued down the path. "I'm not supposed to die this way," he mumbled. "I am the king of Chrysanthe. I am Edisthen, the king. I am a Hero from the Book. The Law protects me." But he wasn't certain he still believed all that.

At first he did not notice the house; his gaze slid across it, interpreting it as a stump, or perhaps a huge scaly mushroom. Then he understood it for what it was, and stopped dead. Very carefully, he stepped off the path and toward the dwelling, keeping it at the center of his sight all the time. When he reached it, when his outstretched hand touched the wooden wall, he sobbed in relief.

There were no windows, but there was a door. It was its handle he had noticed initially, a regular shape, red with rust, which contrasted with the pale wood. A single hinge to the right marked the edge of the door. Edisthen reached for the handle, but before he touched it, the door opened with a creak; a young woman stood on the threshold, smiling at him. She was wearing nothing but a ragged off-white shift. Her hair was red-gold, her eyes huge. She beckoned to him in silence.

He stumbled inside. It was a very small house, hardly more than a shack. Light from the forest entered it from cunning openings in the walls, and a half-dozen candles were lit, set in wooden holders on as many shelves. Edisthen sat himself at a crude table. The girl poured him a goblet of water from a stone pitcher, which he emptied in one gulp. Another girl appeared from a room beyond this one, bringing a shallow bowl filled with berries, roots, and shelled nuts. She might have been twin to the first, save that her hair was raven dark. Edisthen ate voraciously. The black-haired girl had seated herself on the other chair, across from him. The red-haired one remained standing beside him, refilling his wooden goblet at need. Both of them watched him in silence.

Presently he had emptied the bowl. He lay back in the chair, brought his hands to his face. His mind felt vastly clearer. He looked at the girls, who were smiling at him.

"Ladies," he said in a voice once more firm, "I thank you for your hospitality. I was in dire need of both food and water. You have done me a great service; and again, I thank you. Is there any service I might do for you in return?"

Both of them shook their heads, and blinked their huge eyes quickly.

"Nothing at all? Will you not at least tell me your names, that I can know who it is who has rescued me?"

They shook their heads again. Edisthen noticed something that turned his blood to ice. He rose, picked up one of the candles in its holder, brought it close to the raven-haired girl's face. She did not pull back, only looked at him guilelessly. The candle flame was reflected not once but twice in each pupil. Her lips were full and pink, but they could never part: Her mouth was only a thin crease, a dimple in her skin. Nor did her chest rise and fall. Her red-haired twin stood by her side, her face set in a gentle smile, the pupils of her eyes dilated so far only a thin circle of dark blue showed along the rim. Edisthen took a step back, put the candle back on the shelf, and backed away and through the door.

Both of them followed him out, and as he returned to the path, they waved good-bye, each imitating the other's motions perfectly. When he had taken half a dozen steps down the path he looked over his shoulder: The house had vanished utterly.

🙋 The sun had risen but its full light was not yet reflected by the mirrors of Testenel: The Royal Gardens at the heart of the castle still lay in pearly shadow. Melogian walked down the gravel path leading toward the center. She was wearing loose thick trousers buckled at the ankles, and a short-sleeved coat over a blouse. Her hair was wound up in a bun and she had clapped a wide-brimmed hat down upon her head. Melogian had little training with physical weapons; still the leather glove on her left hand was spiked at the finger joints and a pair of knives were sheathed at her belt.

She had been right to fear Casimir's magic. From the moment she had seen Evered's eidolon, she'd had an intimation of the future. Somehow Casimir had found a means to push Edisthen down into the made world against his will. At the lees of the night, once her seeking-spell had been complete, she had gone to the library, shivering as she thought of Mestech's other made world so close below her.

In a section reserved for the oldest tomes she had hunted for information she dimly recalled having encountered once. She had found nothing definite, but the gleanings of knowledge she obtained strengthened her belief that mages of old had been able to work tricks with made worlds that were no longer known. Beyond their very creation, they could be manipulated in strange ways. As long, she prayed, as Casimir could not actually move the opening where he chose, for then they would all be swallowed up by infinity as they slept. . . . But if he could do this, he would have already.

At the threshold she paused and looked back over her shoulder. No one was allowed on the grounds; Christine had been forbidden a farther twenty-five-yard radius around the gardens, thus sealing off not only adjacent sections but several floors just beneath—Captain Veraless had argued for fifty yards, but Melogian had stood him down; not because she believed the precaution useless, but because one had to deny fear at some point.

It was hard to do so now. Melogian had imagined Christine would tell her to be careful; she'd had a bold reply all prepared. Instead, the princess had gazed at her soberly, looking suddenly very young with her brown hair combed back behind her ears, and said, "You won't be coming back." In that instant Melogian had nearly abandoned her quest. "I will look for a single day, Christine," she had said. "One day, and then I will return, whatever happens." But Christine had merely shaken her head miserably and turned away.

Melogian steeled herself, stepped forward, and passed out of reality. The alley widened hugely, the conifers rose tall on all sides. She struck out perpendicularly to the path then, leaving the gradient to remain at the same depth within the made world. The seeking-spell quivered within her mind, casting about for Edisthen's presence; it found nothing.

If Casimir had indeed enlarged the aperture, the question was where lay the rim of the made world as it had stood then. For if she tried to push outward through the pines, Melogian would emerge back in Chrysanthe, thrashing out of the hedge. Was it possible to strike out at a tangent, to tread an asymptotic path that remained within the made world while she traveled against the gradient? Melogian walked up to the pines, bent forward slightly. She summoned the power within her and took a step *beyond* then another. It took an enormous amount of effort. Pine trunks surrounded her: She was inside the made world still, but further from the center than she had been before. Ahead, the trunks grew closer and closer together. Another step *beyond*, and she reached an end: She felt as if she were a mite teetering on the rim of a glass, neither within nor without. The trees grew close-packed all around her, their branches bearing both needles and scaled leaves. She could sense a gradient on all sides, which would either tumble her back down the made world or throw her out into the true realm. She was unsure whether the trees repeated themselves identically or whether her sight was distorted as if gazing through a prism. "Edisthen!" she cried out. "Majesty!" There was no answer. She took a slight step to the side, no more than a shift of the foot, and reality flickered: For a moment she saw herself from the back; her other self was looking at the back of another Melogian, and so on down an endless tunnel of mirrors. Then she was back within the glade, the road at her left hand. She had to follow it; though Casimir would have enjoyed hiding Edis-then at the threshold of the world, she could not believe anyone could remain poised on that lip of chaos, even with a mage exerting all his power to pin him there.

And so she stepped onto the path and advanced down the gradient, watching the forest bloom wider and deeper all around her. If the mouth of the made world had been widened by fifty yards, it was not unreasonable to assume that she would have to go this deep into it to reach as far as Edisthen had gone. Once she had reached this distance, she halted and cast about. There was again no sense of pres-ence. She stepped away from the path and entered the domain of the trees. Looking for Orion, she had traveled through unspeakably strange realms, trawling infinity for a single man. Perhaps all the despair she had forbidden herself to feel then had come rushing back, for as she trod the fallen needles it felt to her as if she were walk-ing on her own grave, and the futility of her task nearly stopped her breath.

❧ Sobriety was no longer a welcome guest for Innalan. In the morning it hovered at the edges of his mind, kept at bay by a pounding headache whose misery was al-most comforting. He would go to the commode and void copiously; his bowels these days seemed to produce mostly water. Once the spasms of his gut had eased, he would totter back to bed, quaff a few mouthfuls from a flagon of cool water, and ring for breakfast to be brought. As he reclined on the sheets his mind, reeling from the blows of headache, would drift through lands both pleasant and not, until a servant arrived with his morning meal. Innalan ate lightly nowadays; he could not stand to stuff himself as once he had been able to.

He got washed and dressed by early afternoon; that was when he felt his worst, for by then his body had cleansed itself, and lucidity threatened. He would go for a long walk on the grounds of Vorlok, the fresh air bringing some relief; or else he would seek Tanyt, a girl from the staff he fancied, and bed her, finding himself rougher than he meant to be. Sometimes Tanyt would cry afterward and he would shout her out of his room, contentment gone sour in his soul.

By late afternoon he would at last allow himself some wine; he delayed the plea-sure out of perversity, he told himself, yet he also knew it was from fear. Nothing could match the kick of the first few swallows, and everything after that was a paler and paler shadow of the enjoyment he initially felt. Yet this only increased his thirst; he emptied flagon after flagon, feeling at last a glow rise within him, the potent magic of the wine, stronger than anything a wizard could evoke. He sang and laughed aloud at his own thoughts; at supper he would tell droll stories and pinch Tanyt's behind, winking at her and making double entendres. Evered was dour these days; he spent hours talking strategy with Casimir and Aghaid. Innalan found these meetings so unutterably boring he no longer bothered to make excuses not to attend, and Evered in turn no longer requested his presence.

By late evening the glow would begin to fade. Innalan would then stagger to his bed, helped by one or another of the servants, and there sleep like the dead, if he were lucky; if he were not, he would end up bent double over a chamberpot, puking up his guts. And when the spasms had stopped, he would recall, against his will, the words of the Priestess Sharnas.

God does not speak to us. Go out into the mountains and listen to the sky, and you will hear nothing.

God did not speak to humankind—save when He sent Heroes out of the Book. Innalan wanted divine blessing on their endeavor, and he knew it would not be forthcoming. If God had ever spoken in recent times, then it had been when Edisthen had come, and thus rebellion against him was tantamount to blasphemy. For most of his life Innalan had been able to dismiss this idea out of hand; he had known his family had been cheated out of the throne by Orion's cat's-paw, had known he was a victim of injustice. This certainty had now deserted him. His belief tottered like a deck set on rotten pilings. The thought that Edisthen was the rightful sovereign tasted sour and burning, like the vomit coating his mouth. And so he tried to wash it away; there was nothing else he could do.

℘ Lessons in magic are anything but simple. They are not like school lessons, in which the pupil might sit and be talked at; neither are they like lessons at arms, in which practice teaches the body. Each spell to be learned requires a new mind-set: One must first behold the words and gestures of power in one's mind, in such a way that they acquire the flavor of some higher reality, before a spell can be cast for the first time. To wield magic is to ride paradox as if it were a wild horse.

Orion taught Melogian, on her first day as his pupil, that willpower was key: A mage devoid of it could evoke nothing but the faintest of workings, pale shadows of power. On her second day, he taught her that knowledge was key: A mage who cannot learn the precise gestures and key phrases can work no magic. On her third day, she learned that imagination was key: A mage must be able to envision things that do not exist, that cannot exist, or else his magic will come to naught. On the fourth day Orion explained that discipline was key: A mage's mind must be ordered, all its knowledge available at need, in the necessary form, or else spells cannot be successfully cast.

Without the least concern over the contradictions in his teaching, Orion proceeded to train her in each of these four aspects, each time claiming the one he dealt with at that moment was paramount, ridiculing her when she thought to bring up the previous day's lesson. Day after day after day, she tried to catch at whatever small scrap of wisdom she was able to absorb, and despaired of ever learning anything of value.

After two weeks she figured out the flaw in Orion's presentation; it took her three more days to gather the courage to reveal it.

"Master," she said. "It's not willpower that's key."

"Don't be stupid, child! It is. Or are you going to tell me it's imagination again?"

"It's none of the things you've said it is."

"Oh?" Orion's tone was oozing sarcasm; Melogian almost lost her courage but went on.

"And it's not all of those things at once. It has to be something else. Many people have all four virtues, but none of them are wizards. There's another thing; that's the real key. You have to have it first. Maybe you need those other four things too but without the other one, you can't be a wizard."

Orion looked at her and mussed up his beard with his fingers. She was suddenly convinced he was about to send her back to her parents, and what she mostly felt was relief. She was eight years old, after all, and she missed them terribly.

"What is that other thing, then?"

"I don't know. But I know I have it, because you wouldn't have picked me otherwise."

He nodded his massive head, then, a half-smile upon his lips.

"Very good. You're quite correct, child. That thing you have, we simply call talent. Not one person in a myriad has it. I could see it in you from afar. That's why I chose you. I didn't want to let your potential go to waste."

"So that's the true key: talent."

"It's the first. The other four are important also, but they come afterward."

"So I still have to practice them?"

"You'll have to practice them for years before you can manage even a simple working."

"That's unfair," she complained. "Why can't I learn faster?"

"It's the way things are. All mages have to spend years of practice before they come into their power; well, except for me."

"What do you mean, Master?"

"I'm the exception. I was written into existence with all my knowledge already inside me. Don't you know Heroes like me aren't born? I was never young; when I walked into Chrysanthe from the top of Mount Gasphode, one hundred and fifty-nine years ago, I already looked like I do now."

She hadn't known, but she was young enough not to feel true fright at this idea: From her point of view all adults were equally ancient. So it was with this revelation that her apprenticeship truly began.

It should not be so surprising, given the perverse and arbitrary nature of the subject, that there is no set order for learning wizardry. Every mage plows her own path through the wilderness, and it is little use for anyone else to try to follow in her exact footsteps. As Orion's apprentice, Melogian was exposed to a vast array of concepts all at once, and as she struggled to make sense of them, her talent bloomed in unexpected ways. Though she often believed that Orion had no method whatsoever to his teachings, at other times she thought to glimpse a fantastically complex order to it all, which she would perhaps one day be wise enough to understand.

She made her way through exercises and disciplines, mastering one by one the various contortions of the mind necessary for spellcasting. Throughout her first two years of apprenticeship, she never learned how these elements were put together to summon power and shape it. She did try to figure it out on her own, and met with no success whatsoever. Impatient as any other child her age, she complained to Orion, who either turned a deaf ear or imposed further exercises.

But when he at last judged her ready, he offered to teach Melogian her first spell. She had been sensing the approach of this moment for a few weeks: When Orion made the offer, she was not taken by surprise. She still hadn't decided which spell she would ask to learn, though; pressed by Orion to make a choice, she blurted out, "Heartsick Yearning," almost at random. That spell made visions swim in the air, drawn from a person's feelings and aspirations.

Orion went to his spellbook then, and opened it at a specific page. Melogian watched him raptly: A wizard's spellbook was a very special thing. The pages where a wizard wrote down his spells held down a magic of their own. Indeed, though a mage's workings might outlive him, upon the instant of his death, his spellbook would decay to powder.

Though Orion's spellbook was hugely thick, he had found the page he sought instantly. He motioned for Melogian to approach and bade her look. With a fleshy forefinger, he traced the description of the spell. Melogian was astonished at the complexity of the required manipulations. She had believed spellcasting involved willpower and mysterious formulae. The spell she had chosen relied mostly on the simultaneous combination of six mental disciplines. She felt certain she had made a bad choice, and should have asked for something simpler. Still, unwilling to lose face, she gritted her teeth and set about learning to cast Heartsick Yearning.

It took her two months of effort before she could encompass the working; she experienced numerous failures and became so discouraged once or twice that she nearly gave up. And then, one day, understanding crystallized in her mind and she knew the spell was hers to command. Never again in her career was she to experience the same intensity of feeling.

The pattern of Heartsick Yearning was at long last clear to her. She flexed her mind in the six different ways the spell made necessary; then words rolled off her tongue, and she gave the proper twirl of fingers, so slight as to be imperceptible.

Power flowed into and through her, condensed and shaped itself. In the air in front of the ten-year-old Melogian floated a delicate flower at the end of a thorny stem. Its petals were dark blue shading to pale at the edges; the stem was black while the thorns were silver. She had shaped a rose from dreams.

For nearly a minute the image hung there, apart from her, yet hers. She even passed her fingers through it, and it remained undisturbed. She called to Orion in a strangled whisper; he came at last, a few seconds before the image dissipated as the power lost its cohesion.

"Did I . . . Did I do it? Master, you saw it, didn't you?"

"I did," rumbled Orion. She heard his quick footsteps then, and he caught her as she fell over backward. He lowered her to the floor, held her shoulders and neck as she trembled.

"Master," she breathed, "Master, it's . . ."

"I know. I know, poppet. You feel as if there is a hole inside you; as if the void beyond the vault of heaven has made a nest beneath your heart. I told you this would happen, remember?"

"My head hurts . . . ," she gasped, and retched weakly.

"Shh, shh, this is normal. The first casting is always unpleasant. And learning a spell bruises the spirit. Can you stand? I'll take you to your bed and let you sleep it off."

Just as no subsequent spell's mastery ever held the same impact for Melogian as that very first, so the consequent pain was never as intense, though she was never able to fully surmount it. As Orion had said, learning a spell bruises the spirit; unless one were to devise a way to steal knowledge of a spell directly from another mage's soul, there was no avoiding the aftershock.

It turned out Heartsick Yearning had not been such a bad choice, for as spells go it is a fairly easy one. The workings Melogian learned during the next few years were more taxing by far to master, though knowing that it could be done encouraged her no end.

But power is not tame by nature. Though a lifetime's discipline enables a wizard to ride it, it is not a beast of burden, and in some respects it goes where it will. In her fifteenth year, Melogian's talent fastened onto the Devastator and refused to let go.

It may seem strange that some hellishly complicated workings can be mastered almost without effort, while objectively simpler ones may elude a wizard for decades. Yet is it any stranger than a woman being born able to sing ravishing melodies, while her sister will struggle all her life to carry a tune for longer than a measure? Melogian had found certain areas of magical knowledge almost blocked to her: Though her grounding in the basics was impeccable, the makeup of the relevant spells ran counter to the grain of her soul. Rather than persist, she sought other domains more congenial. Orion never chided her over her failures but praised her successes; so she went for what felt easier, reasoning that it would always be time to return to the more difficult sections later.

Orion now allowed Melogian to peruse his book as she wished—it would be a decade before she realized what an enormous favor this was. She skimmed the book for hours, comparing her theoretical knowledge of magic with the practical reality of her master's list of spells, sketching future lines of investigation.

One evening, turning a page, she came across a spell that shattered her life as a hammer smashes a crystal goblet. From the moment her eyes alit on the words concerning the spell, it was as if she were suddenly reunited with a lover after a year's absence: She felt a thrill compounded equally of pain and pleasure, the shock of recognition and the delight of rediscovery.

It took her six months of training to master the spell, and for these months she worked on nothing else. Orion taught her without complaint, never venturing a single remark on her choice of studies. The spell was astonishingly complex, far beyond anything else she had encountered. Orion's notes were thorough but they did not spell things out at full length: She had to exfoliate their meaning three levels deep before she reached fundamental elements of spellcraft. Orion offered no help as such, but pointed out where she had made errors and helped her puzzle out the effects of the transformations he had notated.

The mental disciplines involved were an odd selection; the incantation itself was long and unusual in its requirements. Gestures and syllables of power were woven in an arrangement she had never seen before. She rehearsed them for weeks on end before she began to sense that her pronunciation was becoming adequate.

On an evening near the summer solstice, as she worked at the placement of her fingers, things at long last fell into the proper pattern. She became still, then straightened slowly, drew a deep breath and held it. Her mind at long last held the spell complete; she felt it sear itself into her soul.

Her mind moved in the necessary ways, like a butterfly unfolding its wings, again and again. Then she began to speak the spell, words loud and clear on her lips: Burning bright in her mind's eye, the pattern of the spell had commanded that it should be made actual, and Melogian complied without a moment's hesitation.

From the first instant, she could feel the air crackling with inrushing power, of an intensity she had never experienced. As she ran through the first syllables and gestures, a lattice of force formed all about her, spreading to the limits of her perception as if she could mesh all of Chrysanthe within the lacery. Strands extended in all directions, radiating from herself like cracks in a block of ice, growing thicker and thicker. . . .

Then she heard a deep voice, as if it came from far away. She grew aware that Orion was standing in front of her. She seemed to recall that he had been sitting at a worktable nearby, and that he had risen suddenly. The voice was his, of course, the basso rumble she was familiar with. But faint, so faint . . . and so unimportant: the spell, the spell burned within her, and it must be said.

Yet as she began the fifth word, something wavered in her perception of the world. The lattice she had sensed growing all about her was weakened; not unraveled, but thinned, each strand growing tenuous, sublimating to near nothingness. This was wrong; she strove with all her might to continue the incantation. She heard Orion's voice once more, noticed his gestures: He was casting a counterspell!

The ingathering power waned; Melogian's gestures slowed, slurred, and halted as the spell died on her lips. A shudder ran through her; she felt a terrible weakness, as if she in turn were dying.

Her legs gave way; she fell into Orion's arms, gasping for breath, drenched in sweat. It was as if she were waking up from some long bout of fever. Her mind, so long submerged, had regained sanity; the spell's hold on it had been broken. The old wizard stroked and soothed her until she no longer trembled.

"Master!" she wailed, still terrified. "What happened to me?"

Orion looked gravely at her. "When a wizard encounters one of the greater spells, Melogian, it sometimes infects him with a madness peculiar to our calling. Either it will destroy him or he will master the spell in the end. Even then, the spell will often carry a compulsion: It will attempt to get itself spoken as soon as it has been mastered. For six months I have lain in wait, knowing I would have very little time to stop you when you attempted it."

"But why stop me? The spell is only . . . It's only . . . for . . ."

"Yes, Melogian, tell me: Just *what* is it for, exactly?"

She shook her head, bewildered. She had spent the last six months learning this spell. She held it still in her mind at this very moment. Yet, she had not the least idea what it was. And she had never had.

Orion lowered her to an armchair, where she sat hugging herself, feeling a stranger in her own body. She wanted to cry, but to her surprise, though her eyes burned with pain, the tears refused to come.

"This is the madness, Melogian. The compulsion to master and cast a spell you know nothing about. You never asked me what it did, whether it was any use."

"But . . . it's been . . . half a year! Why didn't you stop me before?"

"I couldn't; not without breaking your mind, or killing you outright. Which I nearly decided to do, once or twice. But each time I stayed my hand, because I had faith in you, and in my own abilities. Still, I took a huge risk."

Melogian took in these words in silence. At last, she asked: "A risk? Why was it a risk?"

"If I hadn't been able to stop you, then you would have completed the casting."

"And then what? What is this spell about, what does it do?"

"Briefly put? It destroys the world."

Melogian stared at him, slack-jawed. "You must be joking, Master," she said after a long pause.

"Joking, no. I am, perhaps, oversimplifying. This is a working from the dawn of time. Of the sorcerers among the First, only one knew of it. It was passed on through the millennia, but was lost during the forty-fourth century, with the premature death of Albiendor the Green. It did not resurface until I was written into existence, with its pattern fresh in my mind. It has never been cast in all the history of the world. It is perhaps unique in that its power has grown in significance as the world has aged. In the beginning, it would have served no purpose to cast it. Later eras might have used it to greater consequence, but either the need for it was never encountered or the few who knew its secret did not deem it wise to use it. Now, its effects would be so far-reaching that they would amount to wholesale destruction of the land."

Melogian wiped her brow. "I don't follow you. This spell—what is it called, anyway?"

"I don't know its proper name, assuming it even has one. Call it the Devastator, if you must put a name to it. It ties into the secret of made worlds, although it goes far deeper. Those few mages who raised made worlds opened portals into infinity; to do this, as far as I can understand, they must have called upon forces that fundamentally reshaped the world. It is not as simple a business as piling stones atop each other and raising a castle, but rather of punching a hole in the fabric of reality, do you see?"

"But you said no one knows how to shape worlds anymore."

"Correct; even I don't know how it is done. However, I can guess at some of what is involved. And the Devastator is related to those workings. Imagine the world as a thin crust of ice, floating on the surface of a cauldron of boiling water. The boiling water is the raw force of Creation, which God shaped into the world. To raise a made world is to invoke some of that power and force it to extend outward, much as a thin thread of rime grows across a windowpane. What the spell you have learned does is similar but far more destructive: It shatters the boundary between our world and Chaos. It makes an opening through which the energies of Creation will pour in."

Orion had fetched a goblet of water as he spoke and now handed it to Melogian, who glanced at the water with thoughts of ice and steam in her head, before taking a sip.

Orion continued: "At the beginning of the world, everything was new and still partly unformed. Remember what I told you about Heovendil's journey across the Dead Marshes, which wavered between land and sea in the space of five steps. To unleash Chaos upon the world then would have made precious little difference. You might say that the ice which is the world was still warm. . . . But in these latter days the world has grown old: The Dead Marshes have become a plain, the Howling Castle has been silent for four thousand years, and if you spend the night on Mount Gasphode you will no longer see demons dancing in the flames of your campfire. If the world is ice in the cauldron, that ice has become so cold that if you were to pour the primal waters onto it, it would shatter at once."

Melogian shivered at the image. "But what good is such a spell? Why would anyone need to use it?"

"For the last time, girl, stop assuming magic is meant to serve us! Until the day you are cured of this illusion, you will never be a mage. If there can be said to be any service involved, then it is you and I who serve magic. It is there; the spells exist, we can learn them and cast them, but they are not meant to serve us. Magic is not an invention like the weaving loom, or a craft like iron smelting. Just be glad I happened to know the only possible counterspell to what you were casting, else you would be unleashing chaos upon the world right now."

"I'm sorry," she said. "Please don't be angry with me, Master. I didn't know. I didn't mean to do any harm."

Orion softened his tone. "I'm not angry with you. I've just been very scared on your behalf—and for the world in general."

"Then—you should have killed me, if I was going to put the world in such danger."

"That was the safest way. But I am a sentimental fool. I was certain I could stop you; nor was I wrong. As it was, you hardly put up a struggle, I'm glad to say. Spells benefit from being spoken by a strong and experienced wizard; you're still far too green to be a threat to me."

He put a hand on her shoulder, let it lie there for a moment. "Also, there are so few mages left in the world. Even if I didn't care for you as a person, it would be a sin to destroy you and rob the world of your promise. I took the risk because you are important to me in more ways than one."

"What am I going to do now, with that thing in my mind?" asked Melogian.

"Do you feel the need to cast the spell?"

She pondered this for a moment, looked inside her own mind and found the spell slumbering there, a thing of power craving the light. "It wants to be spoken," she said. "I can feel it; but I don't want it myself."

"Exactly. Your mental disciplines will serve to keep you safe from the compulsion. You'll never be completely free of it, but it will not cripple you."

She said: "I don't know that I should inscribe the Devastator in my own book, Master."

"Not yet," said Orion. "In fact, perhaps not ever. My advice is to wait until you have grown fully into your power, and feel the time has come to take an apprentice of your own. Then you will know. If you feel that the knowledge of the spell should die once more, let it remain only in your mind. I promise you that even if I take another apprentice, I shall not give him access to that spell. One near disaster of this scope is enough for me."

Through the years of her apprenticeship Melogian let the Devastator remain at the core of her mind; yet she did not leave it unattended. She returned to it time and again, and though it quivered at the touch of her attention and urged that it should, must, be spoken, she kept firm control over it as she pondered it.

Although she had grasped the pattern of the spell enough to successfully cast it, she could still sharpen her understanding of it. This was the way mages perfected workings they had already learned: They dissected the spell into its components, analyzed their interactions, reflected on other possibilities. Such work was exhausting and in fact damaged the psyche over time. The greater the working, the more severe the damage.

There was no question for Melogian to attempt a refinement of the spell, but she could safely consider its structure and meaning, helped along by the clues she found in historical accounts.

And so over the years the Devastator slowly yielded its secrets. As her understanding improved, the compulsion to cast it lessened. She grew convinced that Orion's view was inaccurate: The spell would not burst open the gates to Chaos. It would summon its wild energies, but it would shape them according to the mage's will. She had been well taught and recognized this for a trap: Spells that reached into the depths of their caster's soul were invariably dangerous. A working that evoked flame could set fire to a house if uncontrolled; a spell to bolster one's concentration might evoke unexpected resonances and distort the mage's psyche beyond repair.

The more she learned about the Devastator, the more she realized how subtle and how dangerous it truly was. By the time Orion recognized her as a wizard in her own right, her fear of the spell was greater than ever, but indirect, the way one fears an earthquake or a plague. She knew she would let the knowledge of it die with her; even the notes she had taken during her investigations she burned to cinders.

And still, from time to time, the Devastator stirred in the depths of her mind; when she felt exhaustion claiming her, or despair, the pattern of the spell rose before her eyes, terrifyingly pure. It promised a final relief from pain and fear, the same way that a man will overcome his terror of heights by throwing himself off a cliff, into the uncaring void below.

For three more days Edisthen traveled through the forest. He found springs and edible nuts to sustain himself. At the close of the second day he came across the remains of a camp; next to the ashes of a fire lay a discarded waterskin, which he appropriated and filled at a nearby pond. The path he followed remained straight and clear, though always deserted. At times a low, booming voice rose in the distance in mournful song, as if a giant were bemoaning his sad fate. The sun never set, the dim light that pervaded the forest never varied; Edisthen's periods of slumber served to delimit the days.

By the third day the relief had altered: Slabs of stone erupted from the ground at acute angles and the path, though it still did not curve, rose and fell in abrupt declivities. Edisthen clambered up and down these irregular steps. His fine clothes were grass- and earth-stained, his fingernails black-rimmed. He had no doubt he stank, though he had long since ceased to notice his own smell. Sometimes he would sing, nursery songs he had once sung to Christine as she lay in her cradle. They made him weep and he would dab at his eyes with the back of his hand.

Yet he no longer feared forgetting who he was, for he had found a potent charm against mental dissolution: He had started telling his story in his mind, as though he were writing a book for Christine. When he organized his thoughts this way, they became marvelously clear. He both heard and saw the words he must use, and their smooth flow gave him great peace.

My dearest Christine, began the book he was writing in his mind.

I, your father Edisthen, write this to you, for you and for myself as well. I lost you when you were yet a small child and you were returned to me thirteen long years later, after I had lost hope. You were too young to know me at first, and you returned soul-blighted, unable to let me hold you in my arms, so you have not been able to know me now.

Sir Quentin told me of what was done to you; of how your head was filled with false remembrances of my hurting you. I cannot imagine your pain; I can only grieve that you should feel it. There is no viler thing than to torment one's child; once I sent a man to the noose for that very offense. Though Quentin has assured me that you reject these memories, that you recognize them as lies, I quail at the thought that you might still hold them as true. I could never have acted thus; to harm you goes against my very being. And yet in saying this I betray that I am not perhaps fit to be a father after all, for there is in fact very little to me, who am less than three years older than you, a man of twenty, not yet old enough to rule by the laws of the land.

Oh Christine, you were born and I was not. There is such a huge gap between us, between myself and the rest of humanity, that sometimes I wonder if I can ever cross it. I was written for a purpose, that is all I am. I lay in bliss with your mother Anyrelle and she died bearing you, as if the Law were punishing me for my happiness. I dare not ask anyone if born men have such ideas cross their minds; I have never had a mother or father to tell me how life felt to them. All I have are books, the words of other men enfleshed in ink on paper; but even I know that people in books do not much resemble people in real life. And I worry that this is precisely the difference between Heroes and born men, that we are characters enfleshed and not true men at all.

And yet; and yet I can see and feel and hear like everyone else, and my heart beats and my bowels churn as any man's. And when the sun shines upon me I feel that I belong in the world as much as anyone else. Your loss cast a pall of despair over my life, but I took comfort in the thought that any other man would feel the same. That you came back to us even now gives me hope that my purpose is not a vain one.

Shall I tell you how I came to be? I do not, you understand, remember it exactly. My memory truly begins when I came out of the forest and saw fields of wheat in the sunset, and the houses of a village, and just over the horizon the towers of Testenel catching the sunlight and gleaming deep blue against the paler blue of the sky. Before that, I know I walked between the trees for a time, but how long? And what did I think then? Nothing, really. There was a time when I was not and then I was. I knew all about the land, about its weak king whom I was to replace. I knew much but I had never learned anything. When I looked at the fields I knew what grew there, and I could put a name to all the colors I saw, even though I had never seen anything but trees before, even though I had never beheld yellow or blue until I came out from the forest. I went toward the houses to get something to eat and drink, because my body required it. The people there welcomed me and asked nothing of me save my name. Perhaps they were afraid of the sword I carried at my side. Perhaps they sensed who I was. They fed me and gave me a place to sleep. That night I dreamed. I relived my day as it had been, down to the last detail; I had lived so little yet there was nothing for me to dream about. I woke up in the middle of the night and went to a window. I looked up at the sky and saw the stars. I went back to my couch and slept again, and this time I dreamed about stars, and wind, and the dark. I was far, far less than a man in these days; it frightens me sometimes to think of myself back then.

Edisthen climbed up one last declivity and saw that the path at last led out of the embrace of the trees; up ahead, brilliant sunshine fell onto a hilly country.

He increased his pace and finally emerged into sunlight. Behind him, trees towered to an astonishing height, growing in tight ranks; ahead the path grew sandy and led downward among broken terrain. He followed it, unsurprised to see he still left no footprints. The path curved and dipped, and Edisthen heard noises up ahead. Once he had gone around yet another tilted dolomite slab, he beheld a small town below him. It lay at the edge of a lake, and five or six ships rode at anchor there. The path led steeply downward to the town. By the time Edisthen reached it, it had swollen to a great city, shrunk to a squalid village, and expanded once more to reach its initial size. The lake had grown until its far shore could not be seen.

At a tavern he was given food and drink, for which he paid with the ring on his little finger. He asked for garments as well—requesting that they be brought to him, for he feared that walking to the clothier's would cast him farther down the gradient, to a world where he had never ordered anything, much less paid for it. After some delay, clad in traveling clothes and boots, carrying his soiled finery beneath his arm, next to the waterskin, he went out to the docks. He meant only to rest in the sunlight, which had so long been denied him. He found a bench to sit upon, a green-painted wooden affair with black wrought-iron armrests. There were metal tubes to the left and right of the bench, their single open ends pointed out to sea, resting on wheeled wooden trestles that raised them to an angle; their function he could not guess at. Edisthen sat on the bench and looked over his shoulder, to a town that had once more changed, its buildings mostly stone now, the great forest he had traversed decayed to a stand of woods atop a high escarpment. An atmosphere of hostility hung over the town, though he could not ascertain its source. Perhaps it lay in the sharp slope of the roofs; the narrowness of the windows, most of which appeared sealed, oddly, with dark-tinted glass; or the way the buildings huddled together, as if their walls leaned slightly from the vertical. Then again, it was probably within his own mind: The town he had first come to had looked like those he had known in Chrysanthe, and there he had been made welcome, fed, and clothed. This town was simply not the same, its architecture different from that he had seen all his life; small wonder he felt threatened by it. Still . . . he could not evade the disquiet.

He forced himself to grow calmer by continuing the mental recitation of his story; the words arrayed themselves on an imagined page and for a brief moment he forgot where he was. Edisthen sat on the bench and breathed in the mild air. From the salt smell he knew it was the sea he faced, no longer a lake. The docks were stone, the ships tall masted and bigger than any he'd ever seen.

He had been in this made world once before, over a decade ago. His journey this time, though distorted in comparison, still bore some resemblance to his first excursion: travel through a forest, to eventually reach a shoreside town. On that day, he'd been accompanied by a dozen of the court, including Orion. He'd brought Christine with him, and had carried her most of the way. Once they had reached the docks, they had embarked upon a small sloop and cast off, Orion guiding their descent into the made world. Soon they had achieved a lake brimming with brightly colored fish. Edisthen had held Christine tightly as she leaned over the gunwale and cooed at the forms swimming in the crystal-clear water. This memory was so very dear to him, for all that he had intensely disliked immersing himself in an imaginary land and had vowed never to repeat the experience. Christine had been delighted, and for her sake he imagined he might have broken his vow later. She had shrieked with excitement, in that piercing voice all little girls share, and he had known himself happy and fulfilled as her little body quivered in his grip. . . .

"Good shade, sir." A man stood before him, taking off his loose cap in what seemed a show of respect.

"And to you as well," replied Edisthen.

"I was wonderin' if you sought passage."

Edisthen hesitated, then equivocated. "And what if I do?"

"Well, we're castin' off within the hour. Captain asked me to ask you if you wanted to cross with us."

"Well . . . I had not decided yet."

"Sir, I can tell you, none o' the other ships are as good as us. I know, you'll say the others would say the same thing. But sir, the *Osprey* over there, her captain's ghost-blighted and her mate's a witch. And that Valentian tub at the end of the pier can't take another storm, she'll break apart the first sign o' wind."

"What about that one?" asked Edisthen after a moment, pointing to the fourth ship, whose hull gleamed from a fresh coat of black paint and whose gilded sterncastle glittered in the sunlight.

"Sir, if you're gonna make fun o' me, I got better things to do."

"Don't get offended; I only meant to ask you a simple question. Besides, I might not be able to pay for the voyage; I might decide to stay here for a little while."

The crewman scowled, turned on his heel, and stalked back to his ship. Edisthen watched him go, perplexed. After a while he rose and went to the black and gold ship. It did not alter as he approached it, nor did the other ships or the docks. Dare he hope this was the end of the gradient? Edisthen climbed a gangplank and wandered aboard. An odd smell greeted him, sour and sweet at once, with a harsh overtone; as if vomit or offal had been spilled on deck then the planks washed with lye. Crewmen were busy; they were using a crane to lift cargo from the holds. Edisthen had once been aboard one of Archeled's fishing vessels that plied the bays of the world's eastern shore, so the scene was familiar to him.

Less so was the sight that greeted him as a heavy net rose from the holds, bulging with bloated human shapes. An unbelievable stench rose from them, a chord of vile odors that went far beyond those of decayed flesh: He could smell spilled blood, feces and vomit, harsh spices, stagnant pond water, and some oily reek of fermented exudations. Edisthen gripped the rail with his free hand and felt cold sweat break out upon his brow. The crew, still ignoring him, started sorting out the corpses with iron implements that tore frayed clothes and mealy flesh before they hooked into the bones. Edisthen fled on trembling legs back to the stone pier; a quartet of burghers were arriving, pens and parchment in hand, wondering aloud as to the quality of the stock. One of them wore small panes of blue-violet glass held in gold wire on his nose, and he peered intently at Edisthen through these small windows, as if trying to see something that ought to be there.

Edisthen returned to his bench, but it no longer felt like a refuge. The stench from the corpse-ship, though the wind blew it away from him, had burned itself into his memory; he could not stop smelling it. Though the sun shone as before, it was as if its light had gone cold. He glanced at the town; its sinister aura chilled him further. A woman riding a black horse was coming in his direction. The horse did not have hooves; its four legs terminated in humanlike hands, which each clutched a heavy stone that jetted sparks as it struck the pavement.

Edisthen left the bench and walked as fast as he dared to the ship whose sailor had offered him passage. He was sure now he was no longer traveling down the gradient. Perhaps this had been his destination all along, in which case it was a trap. He did not need to be physically harmed; perhaps the townspeople would incarcerate him for no clear reason and detain him in a clammy cell for half a hundred years, or compel him into service aboard the corpse-ship. Then of course this other ship might be a trap as well; but Edisthen felt he would on the whole prefer to risk this. He climbed the gangplank, noting the prow bore a name in florid capitals that he could not decipher.

"Good shade," he said to a well-dressed man he took to be the captain.

"And to you, sir. Voule tells me you jested with him before that you meant to stay here. I told him not to take it personally—a wise man never commits himself too early. Have you made a choice now, though?"

"He warned me one of the other ships was not seaworthy, and the other's captain was cursed. You, on the other hand, have no such problems, I take it?"

"Sir, we're a fine ship, and well run, if I say so myself. Ten years now we've been making the crossing to Lewch-Head and back, and I've never lost a man to the corpse-ship. Can't say I've become rich, but none of my suns is ill earned. I can spend my gold anywhere I please and no shadow will cross mine. Not many other captains can say this."

"I have little to pay for my passage, I fear. . . ."

"Don't you jest with *me*, sir. A good joke is a short one, as they say. I have a berth for you if you want, otherwise I'll wish you well and let you return from Lewch-Head aboard someone else's craft."

"Forgive me," said Edisthen. "I spoke out of nervousness. I will gladly take passage with you."

"Very well," said the captain, nodding. "I could tell you're not yourself. First visit here, yes?"

"Indeed."

"I remember my first time. Couldn't sleep for a week afterward. I hope for your sake you were well served, but you don't have to tell me anything about it."

The mounted woman had been inspecting the *Osprey* farther down the dock; now she approached this ship, but the captain leaned over the rail and shouted at her.

"I'm done with trading, Voidness! Nothing left for you or me here!"

"I know you, Captain Quareltine," she called out. She was disturbingly beautiful, her features narrow and sharp, as if sculpted by an artisan who did not fully understand the shape of a human face. "I have an offer for you. Cargo too small and light to matter, worth over two thousand suns—"

"Nothing doing, Voidness! I'm done with trading this voyage; the *Celadon* is leaving anchor!"

"You're a fool, Quareltine. What captain turns his nose at easy profit?"

Captain Quareltine still refused; the woman started to turn away, then stopped herself and faced him once more, her mount shifting its grip on the four heavy stones. "Then what do you say to this?" she asked. "Carry this for me and I shall bring your wife back as payment."

Captain Quareltine shut his eyes and took a deep breath. "Sooner or later in every voyage the offer is made," he said to Edisthen though he did not look in his direction. "This time I thought I could avoid it. It grows harder every time to say no. . . ."

Edisthen took a step nearer to Quareltine. He was recalling Anyrelle and the grief at her death that had nearly driven him mad. The Law did not allow the dead to be brought back, this he knew from the core of his being; even down in a made world, where substance was as mutable as dreams, it must still hold. What the woman promised could not be delivered. Perhaps, he saw in a flash, she could leach out a man's memories of his lost love and shape a magical doll from them. Perhaps she could do this task so well the manikin would be undistinguishable from its model. The thought of beholding a copy of his Anyrelle filled him with horror, but he could sense as well a spark of desperate longing; if the offer were repeated to him, time and again, would his disgust and loathing still hold sway, or would he beg in the end for the deed to be done, since what did it matter whether it was truly Anyrelle or not, as long as he could not tell the difference?

"My wife," he said slowly to Captain Quareltine, "died seventeen years ago."

"You and I are counterparts, then," whispered Quareltine. "Mine has been buried for seventeen years as well. What was her name?"

"Anyrelle. And I did not tell you I am called Edisthen."

"Did you . . . did you come to Lewch-Head because of her?"

"Oh no. Not at all."

"If you were in my place, Edisthen, what would you do?"

"I think . . . I think I might throw myself into the water and drown," answered Edisthen, surprised at his own words.

Quareltine opened his eyes and smiled at him; two small tears coursed on either side of his nose. "Thank you." He looked at the woman and very quietly said, "Be gone."

She twisted her mouth into a sneer and rode off. Quareltine leaned on the gunwale and breathed heavily. Within the hour he gave the order to cast off and the *Celadon* left Lewch-Head. Edisthen had gone down to his berth, a cramped cabin belowdecks, which smelled of ginger and cinnamon. There was a printed image on a sheet of stiff paper pinned to the bulkhead: a crudely colored portrait of a young woman cradling a bared sword in her arms as she would a child, surrounded by a haze of tiny stars and crescent moons. A title was printed beneath the image and several lines of text, but Edisthen could not read the script.

When he looked at the image a second time, he felt puzzled: He could have sworn the woman's hair had been black, not the dark red he was now seeing. Then he understood. He climbed up on deck and found the captain, now pale haired and pale skinned, and fifteen years older. "Everything to your satisfaction, milord?" the captain asked, looking torn between deference and annoyance.

"It will do just fine," answered Edisthen. He went toward the prow, found a place to sit and look at the waves and the sky change colors, while the sun rose and fell in the heavens, and the seasons danced like drunks lurching through a gavotte.

3. The Regent

Throughout the fifth of High-Summer, chaos reigned in Testenel. News of the king's disappearance had flooded the castle. A mood of disturbance shading into panic had gripped most of the inhabitants. The rules and ingrained codes of conduct that regulated life in Testenel still held sway: Meals were prepared and served, living quarters were cleaned, the heartbeat and breathing of the huge castle continued. But its directing intelligence was gone.

Christine had sought refuge in her rooms. Had Quentin or Melogian been with her, she might have felt reassured; both were absent, and only Captain Veraless was a familiar face. She asked him to turn away importunates from her door; he accepted gravely and installed himself in the outer chamber of her suite to play watchdog.

But his authority could be overruled: On the sixth of High-Summer, shortly after the morning meal, Althea reported to Christine that dukes Corlin and Edric both stood in the outer room requesting admittance. Christine, steeling herself, went to meet with them.

Captain Veraless was present, along with three flustered-looking guards. When Christine entered the room, both dukes knelt to her.

"We crave your pardon for disturbing you, milady," said Duke Archeled. "Captain Veraless has indicated you wished for privacy, but the situation is imperative."

"I'm here now," replied Christine. She seated herself, and asked for her visitors to be seated as well.

Corlin smiled at her in a reassuring way. Edric cleared his throat then spoke: "Your Highness, it is known everywhere by now that your father is gone."

"He'll be back," said Christine in a trembling voice. "We don't know where he is, but he'll be back."

"I do not doubt it," said Duke Edric. "But until he returns, someone must be in command."

Christine understood what he hinted at. In the stories she had read, back in her imaginary world, vassals seizing power from a vacant throne were usually as devoid of scruples as they were ambitious. But how could she deny the duke—and did she even wish to?

"So you wish to rule instead of him?" she blurted out.

Corlin was shocked and burst out: "*Him?* No, cousin, you! You are the one who must rule in your father's absence. That's what we came to speak of."

"Me?"

"You are the heir," said Duke Edric. "You may not have come of age, but you are regent-designate by the laws of succession. You will not be granted the full powers of a sovereign, but that is not the major issue. The point is that someone must . . . stand for the king until his return. As his daughter, you are the only real choice."

Christine sat in silence for a while, controlling her breathing, though she still felt light-headed. "If I weren't here," she finally asked, "who would be the regent?"

The older duke frowned. "Ordinarily, a king has a family; if he does not have a child, then his siblings or their children are considered. Edisthen's situation is unique. No doubt a case could be made for one of us dukes to act as regent. . . ."

"That would be you then, Your Grace," said Corlin. "I certainly wouldn't volunteer. But that's academic, milady. You are the regent."

"It couldn't be Duchess Ambith?" persisted Christine.

Corlin's eyebrows rose. "If she tried that," he said, "we'd have a war all over again! Then again, all Kawlendians are hot-blooded fools; perhaps Ambith would be willing."

"Begging your pardon, Your Grace," Veraless intervened. "I apologize for my impertinence, but I'm a Kawlendian born and bred. Whether the people of my birth duchy are hot-blooded fools or not, they are aware this would be provocation of the worst order; even Duchess Ambith knows this."

Duke Edric frowned at Veraless but nodded. "At any rate, it is as Corlin said, milady: That issue is academic. No duke of the realm could claim the regency from you."

"As long as I'm alive," breathed Christine.

"I would die before I let anything happen to you," replied Edric, his face coloring.

"I stand by His Grace," added Corlin.

Christine forced her hands to unclasp. She wasn't sure if she believed these men. Still, what was the point of remaining cloistered in her suite? "All right," she said. "Fine. So I'm regent. Now what?"

"Summon the conclave," said Duke Edric. "This is the occasion for you to assert your authority and to complete the task your father began."

Christine gaped at him. She had barely given thought to the conclave, had
assumed it was suspended indefinitely or canceled outright.

"What do you expect me to do?" she protested. "If it's going to be like two days
ago, there's no point. What do I give to Kawlend? I don't know what it is they're
entitled to, and I can't expect you—well, I beg your pardon, Your Graces, but
you're not impartial—I can't expect you to tell me what I have to do."

Veraless intervened before the dukes could reply: "Milady, may I offer you my
advice? Tell the Kawlendians to shut up. They'll never be happy no matter what
you do for them. Duchess Ambith refuses to acknowledge her defeat from twenty
years ago. Don't listen to their complaints. Lay down the law, let Kawlend deal with
the consequences. Like all fools, they'll respect strength."

Duke Corlin harrumphed but said nothing further. Duke Edric pursed his lips
and commented: "Well, I would have phrased it differently, Lady Christine, but
Captain Veraless is correct. A show of strength seems indicated."

Christine pondered this for a long moment. "You're all in agreement, then?"
she asked. "You feel I should do this?" The three men assented. Christine's heart
was pounding in her chest. This was crazy—but she felt she had no other choice.
"All right," she said. "It's the Master of Protocol I should summon, I think? Captain, can you have him come to me?"

❧ Shortly before noon, Christine entered the council chambers once more. Althea
had helped her select garments suitable for the occasion: a pearl-encrusted gown of
sepia silk and a tiara of obsidian. Christine hoped that her dress projected an aura
of competence and sobriety—anything to hide her near panic. She had been introduced to Edisthen's array of advisers, none of whose names she could recall. She
had hoped for stability and comfort from them, but all of them were in shock over
the disappearance of the king, and they only worsened her anxiety.

The doors were opened for her; a herald standing on the other side cried out,
her head thrown back at a ceremonial angle: "The Lady Christine, regent and heir
to the throne!" All those present in the chambers rose to their feet and bowed.
Christine felt sweat pouring down the sides of her face. Gritting her teeth, she
walked to the box she had occupied the previous time. Some of Edisthen's advisers,
who had obviously expected her to choose the one her father had used, became
flustered at her choice. While Christine's entourage settled itself, she murmured to
Althea for help. The maid gave her a goblet of water to drink and dabbed her temples dry with a linen handkerchief.

There were no flying birds this time, no ceremony. The Master of Protocol
rapped the floor with his staff and that was that: Everyone turned their attention to
Christine, waited for her to speak.

She stood up, clutching the railing of her box to hold herself upright. Bubbles of
heat flowed along her limbs. "My friends!" she called out, her voice reedy. "My
friends! I've called this conclave . . . because we can't just sit and . . . and do nothing.
My father is gone." She had thought she would falter over those words, but they slid

off her tongue smoothly enough. "I don't know where he is, no one knows, and Melogian—" Now her tongue and voice did fail her, and for long seconds she could only croak. "Melogian hasn't returned yet. In my father's absence I am regent. This conclave must . . . ah, go forward. We must discuss what Edisthen meant to discuss."

She sat down abruptly, exhausted by the speech. At once Duke Edric rose to his feet and bowed to her. "Your Highness," he said, "all of us are grieved at this situation. Rest assured that we support you as regent and are at your service, for the good of the realm."

Christine swallowed a mouthful of water and struggled back to her feet.

"I . . . I am not as competent as my father is," she said, "but I have decided to continue with his business. I want to address Evered's threats. I want the duchies to commit to action."

A Kawlendian counselor—the same old man, in fact, who had first risen to speak when Edisthen had presided the last session—began to protest. "This is irregular! Our legitimate requests are being ignored, and—"

"You do not have the floor, sir!" shouted Christine. The old man fell silent, looked uncertain. "I'm not done talking. Sit down! When you wish to speak, you'll ask permission first."

The old man sat down. Christine could feel her pulse in the roof of her mouth. The power she had wielded felt like a huge, blunt weapon in her hands: ready to batter opponents into submission, but prone to slip from her grasp at any moment. She summarized the case for action, drawn both from her memories of her father's speech and the notes his advisers had tendered to her. "Evered, the son of Vaurd, challenged Edisthen—challenged the realm. The day after I returned, he was in the palace. He said that he would bring war to the land. He has magic behind him; Melogian thinks so. She feels there is cause for serious alarm. I . . . I'm not saying this is about me. It's about the land. You, none of you, want war." She looked at the dukes as she said so, and encountered Ambith's smoldering gaze putting the lie to her words. "I don't want war. But if Evered wants it and fights us, we'll . . . I mean, he mustn't catch us unprepared. King Edisthen was ready to summon the army—I mean to raise it. He wanted assurances from all three duchies that they would support him with their own forces." She paused, out of breath. Duke Edric made a motion to gain the floor. Christine said, "Duke Archeled, you may speak."

Archeled rose to his feet and his voice rose powerfully. "Your Highness, honored cousins, a conclave is a time for complicated discussions about details, but it is also a time for decisive statements of principles. Here are mine: Archeled is a loyal vassal of the crown, and Temerorn has our support in this venture. We can spend as long as my ministers want arguing over trivia, but our support is yours, Lady Christine."

"Cousin?" ventured Corlin, and when Christine had given him the floor: "The only thing I regret is that I wasn't first on my feet to say this. Now my cousin Edric looks like he is the most loyal of all dukes; I want to claim that honor for myself. My father fought for King Edisthen in the War when I was but a child; always I've dreamed of matching his service. My sword is yours, my Lady Christine." The Estephorin delegation approved this declaration noisily. Behind Christine, one of the royal advisers sarcastically muttered, "Oh, *well done.*"

Duchess Ambith rose to her feet now. She looked at her fellow dukes, then at Christine, turning her head slowly. With a slight gesture she clearly asked for the floor, and Christine granted it. For a moment Ambith seemed to study her hands, her long, thin, ring-encrusted fingers. Finally she spoke.

"Archeled and Estephor both jockeying for the right-hand place at Temerorn's side. What does this leave for Kawlend? Apparently I have lost this game before even playing it, since I did not jump up begging to be considered most loyal.

"From the start of this conclave I had hoped to present my people's case to the king. To reach an agreement that would offset some of what they have suffered. And now, what? Duke Corlin is ready to unsheathe his sword at the least word from our new regent. Duke Edric agrees in advance to any decision she may make. And if I speak with the voice of reason, I must be counted a coward at best, a traitor at worst. You have made it impossible, cousins, for me to say what I need without losing face. I can only assume this was your intent from the start."

Edric replied, looking annoyed: "Not so, Your Grace. I seek in no way to impugn your loyalty or your good faith. The regent of Chrysanthe has reminded us of the reason why this conclave was called; I have assured her that Archeled stands at Temerorn's side, no more. I have said nothing against you, nor do I intend to."

Ambith ignored him, addressed herself to Christine. "Your Highness, Kawlend has warded Vaurd's sons in Vorlok for twenty years. In all that time, they have done nothing actionable. They have remained within their domain and given no cause for offense. Their behavior, in one word, has been irreproachable. I can assure you this talk of war is sheer nonsense."

Ambith's intensity of speech shook Christine, who nevertheless replied, "But I was there . . . Your Grace. I heard him. He said to my father, *You shall be cast down. We will take back what was ours. The land will slide into chaos; horrors shall walk the earth and slaughter your armies.*"

Duchess Ambith heaved a long-suffering sigh.

"Your Highness, Prince Evered is mad. Do you understand what I am saying? His mind has been shattered by grief. He raves of vengeance. What else is there to his promise that 'horrors' will slaughter Temerorni armies? What does it matter if he has a tame wizard to conjure parlor tricks on his behalf? All he does is dream of retribution. Your father made sure it could never be more than dreams. Why else would he keep Evered's mother as a hostage for twenty years?"

This news stunned Christine. She had known nothing of this, had believed Vaurd's wife must be dead. How could Edisthen have done this—or was the duchess lying?

Ambith continued: "I do not doubt your word when you say that you saw Evered and that he threatened you. Call it undesirable, call it offensive; I stand corrected. Yes, Vaurd's eldest son has been foolish, aggressive, impolitic. Yes, to all these things. What does it matter? He's a child still, wailing for his dead father. He spins fantasies to soothe his chagrin. Words, Your Highness, mere words. Nothing more. And you wish for us to call up our armies, to tear thousands of men from their hearths. For what purpose? To assault a madman already a prisoner in his toy castle?"

Duchess Ambith took a deep breath. Before Christine could reply, she added, "But very well, of course, by all means, do what you will. It is your prerogative—while your father is absent. By all means, levy your armies, send them marching across the land, let them lay siege to Vorlok. What do you care, since it is not you who will pay the price?"

"I don't . . . don't understand," said Christine.

"My people will pay the price," replied Ambith. "As they did twenty years ago. You may not know this, Your Highness, since you've spent your entire life in a dream, but Kawlend is the poorest of the duchies, even though it is almost as populous as Archeled. His Grace Edric has his fields and his artisans, his river trade and his fishermen. I hear he eats dawn perch every morning! Corlin fattens on his mines and his inexhaustible forests—and meanwhile, my people tighten their belts. We never recovered from the War; now you plan to send your troops across our fields, to commandeer food from the mouths of my people. You put us in last place, as always. You hold private meetings with Archeled and Estephor, while Kawlend is ignored. How do I know that everything that you say here hasn't already been prearranged? How do I know all this talk is anything but a farce?"

There was a loud mutter of protest at this speech and various delegates from Estephor and Archeled made motions to speak. Christine would not let the conclave degenerate once more into chaos; she rose to her feet and called for silence.

"Your Grace," she said to Ambith, "you may think I don't care about you, because I don't know all the history I should. I know I still have a lot to learn, but I'm not blind. I know what it's like for people to be poor. In the world where I lived . . . before . . . there was a lot of poverty, and it's something I care about. I'm not going to give orders to make your people, or any people, suffer. I'll make sure that any cost you get—" Here she looked briefly at her advisers, several of whom were showing expressions of alarm and making urgent hand motions, presumably to get her to stop. But it was too late; she would show weakness if she halted in the middle of her reply, and besides, she wasn't going to make any ridiculous promises.

"Any cost to Kawlend," she continued, "will be repaid. You will not be penalized for this. No one is going to play favorites."

Christine sat down in silence. As soon as she leaned back in her chair advisers were whispering in her ear, and fighting with one another.

"Unwise, Highness, unwise! You promised to repay all costs, and now the duchess will refuse to pay for her own troops!"

"No, you idiot, this was the best way to shut her up! Ambith won't dare make a scene now that the throne has made such a generous gesture."

"She'll take advantage of it; give that snake a finger and she'll eat your arm. . . ."

Christine half turned and whispered furiously: "You're not helping me! I don't need people arguing with each other; offer me advice or just shut up!"

The advisers' whispers died off, and for long seconds not one of them had anything to say. Meanwhile, Duchess Ambith had been gazing at the regent with an amused expression. People in the chambers murmured among themselves, but quickly fell silent once Ambith spoke up.

"Your Highness, that is certainly generous of you, for all that Temerorn could afford it five times over without noticing. I thank you. At least we will be spared the worst of the insults of a new war. May I ask what your plans are for weregild?"

Christine's advisers urged her in contradictory whispers not to commit to any figure, to quote precedent, to refuse to answer. "But *what is it?*" Christine kept asking, faced with a word she had heard for the first time two days before and not managed to understand.

Either Ambith had sharp ears, or Christine had spoken far louder than she'd thought.

"Dear me, Your Highness," she said in a solicitous tone, "perhaps you are not familiar with the term. I keep forgetting your speech is not quite like that of the true realm. Perhaps, in the dream-world where you spent your life, there was no such concept. I meant 'blood-price.' Compensation for the death of soldiers in service to the crown."

Christine rose to her feet once more, shushing her advisers' discordant murmurs.

"Your Grace, I don't have the proper knowledge to decide on this matter now. I intend to consult with the . . . ah, the ministers, and we will establish something that is fair."

"You are aware, are you not, that weregild payments directly into the coffers of the crown nearly bankrupted my duchy twenty years before?"

This drew forth shouts of protests from two-thirds of the conclave and the Master of Protocol had to call for silence.

"Your Grace," said Christine, "there are a lot of things I don't know. I will do my best to learn what I need to understand, and to make decisions that, ah, that make sense."

"Ah, and this is supposed to reassure me, I take it? You shall do your best. You, a girl who has years before reaching her majority, shall *do your best*. Why is it, Your Highness, that I am not encouraged?"

More protests rose from the Estephorin and Archeledian delegations. Christine felt ice in the pit of her stomach.

"Duchess . . . Your Grace . . . ," she said, "what is it you want me to say? What do you want from me?" She was aware she was nearly whining; she felt her authority had completely escaped her grasp.

"You are the daughter of Edisthen, who claimed to have no parent save God Himself," said Ambith coldly. "A miracle walking amongst us, who pulled King Vaurd from his throne by virtue of this miracle, and who proceeded to wield a second miracle of his own by producing an heir. Quite a feat, considering the seed of Heroes is never potent."

To the roars of protest that burst out, Ambith reacted by qualifying her statement: "*Almost* never potent. I stand corrected. You see, Your Highness, I wonder if you appreciate your circumstances. You are the daughter of a Hero from the Book, and by virtue of this parentage you find yourself elevated to the throne of the land at a ridiculously young age. . . ."

Duke Edric shouted in reply: "Her Highness the Lady Christine is regent, not sovereign!"

"Ah yes," said Ambith. "Merely regent. Until her father returns from his mysterious vanishing. Is it not a wonder? Twenty years ago, a man claiming to be a Hero from the Book removed Vaurd from his throne. The land fought a bloody war over this event, and Kawlend paid the price of its loyalty to the king. For twenty years we paid that price. Two days ago, that Hero, Edisthen, brought us in to ask us to fight another war, on his behalf. But when Kawlend made its legitimate grievances heard, then Edisthen summarily interrupted the conclave . . . and vanished. Now, here comes his daughter, to replace him on the throne, until he should manage to reappear. Again, is it not wondrous?"

Corlin was on his feet, red-faced. "Calumny! Cousin, your words are poison!"

"I state facts!" retorted Ambith. "I imply nothing. I remark that it is astonishingly convenient that the man who stood at the cause of all of Kawlend's troubles is now gone, and that his daughter has been slipped into his place, ignorant of the history of the past twenty years. What conclusions is one expected to draw from these events?"

"You mock the tragedy befalling the king!"

"What tragedy? Edisthen has vanished. No explanations are forthcoming. He was there, then he was not. None know where he is. Magic of the highest order has snatched him away! Why should we be surprised? Did he not come into the world in this way? Are we meant perhaps to think that God has taken him back into the Book? I do not know; what I do know is that Edisthen is no longer ruler of the realm, but that he has been replaced by a youngster with no experience. The Lady Christine lived her entire life in a dream-world, and now she has been placed over all of us, without any consultation."

"Nonsense!" shouted Corlin. "We discussed—"

"Oh, *you* discussed it! Of course! Estephor and Archeled discussed it, but you did not feel it necessary to involve Kawlend, did you?"

Caught off-guard, Corlin stammered.

"And thus it always goes!" Ambith went on, her voice loud but controlled, her eyes glittering. "Thus it shall continue to go. Kawlend stands here, with no one to speak to. For twenty years we have been trampled; why should we expect any change in the state of things? My lords! Look at who you have set above all of us! This is a *child,* not even one-and-a-score, a girl pulled out of a made world like a golmina from a mountebank's pocket! And you want Kawlend to obey her whims, all in the name of her absent father, the self-proclaimed Hero?

"I have had enough of games and humiliation! I will no longer lend my presence to this farce of a conclave. The throne of Chrysanthe is empty once more; that is all I know. Until the day someone worthy sits upon it, I shall not again set foot in this court!"

With a snap of the wrist, Duchess Ambith made her entourage rise to their feet. She swept out of her seat and strode toward the door, followed by her entire delegation. A hubbub of astonishment floated throughout the conclave chambers. "Ware yourself, Your Grace!" Archeled shouted in a voice grown harsh, as the duchess reached the door. "Once before you made a fool's choice! Don't expect mercy a second time!"

Ambith turned around, glared at him, and spat on the flagstones. "Perdules!" she shouted in a tone of utter contempt, then vanished through the doorway, followed by her jostling delegation. Duke Archeled rose to his feet, his face crimson;

for a moment he looked about to rush after the Kawlendians, then he forced himself down in his chair.

Christine sat numbly in hers, horrified by the turn of events. What had she done wrong? Everything had collapsed on itself. She was just a seventeen-year-old girl, after all, just a stupid girl trying to impersonate a grown-up. She didn't belong here.

"Milady," whispered an adviser at her side. "Perhaps you should call for a recess."

Christine looked up at him, shook her head. She could not bring herself to give a command.

"Your Highness, may I speak?" Archeled had risen to his feet; his face had lost some of its frightening color but he still flushed a ruddy pink. When Christine said nothing, he continued: "I must extend the conclave's most profound apologies. What you have witnessed has left us all stunned. For anyone to show such disrespect to the regent of the land is unforgiveable."

"Och, unforgiveable? Premeditated, rather!" said Duke Corlin. Duke Edric shot him a surprised glance. "Come now, cousin," continued Corlin, "surely you don't believe that tidy little speech was extemporized? She's been planning something of the sort for a long time. The disappearance of our king served up the perfect opportunity, that is all."

"Your Grace, you are making a serious accusation," one of Christine's ministers warned him, triggering a hubbub of comments. Corlin's young voice rose over all others.

"The pardel cannot change its spots, as they say. Not a day went by without my departed father warning me against the bi— the duchess of Kawlend. I for one have always believed she was still in Evered's pocket. This only confirmed it.

"And so we are back to the Succession War!" Archeled concluded angrily. "Exactly like twenty years ago, with a renegade duchy and a pretendant to the throne; except that the king is vanished, as is his wizard, while a rogue mage has attached himself to Evered's cause!"

"Well . . . yes," said Corlin, rather deflated. "But at least we know where we stand."

"Duke Corlin . . ." Christine's voice rose. "You're saying this is inevitable?"

Corlin pondered for a moment, then he answered: "I think, my Lady Christine, that it is. Archeled is right. There will be another War of Succession. Unless the duchess changes her mind, she will throw her flag behind Evered's again."

"Or someone changes it for her!" interjected an Archeledian minister, her mouth twisted in anger.

"What is that, Loraly?" Duke Archeled scowled.

"You heard me, my lord. Why don't we get rid of the problem at the source? The duchess hasn't left Testenel yet; why don't we make sure she doesn't leave to spread her poison? Throw her in jail!"

"On what grounds? She cannot be imprisoned merely for speaking her mind."

"Then have her meet an unfortunate accident, my lord. The balconies of Testenel are dangerously high. If she slips and breaks her neck, that is the end of our troubles."

Shouts and jeers rose at the bald statement; there was much outrage, but a significant minority approved the sentiment. "I will not countenance murder!" bellowed Duke Archeled. "Loraly, that is beyond the pale!"

Christine stared around the chambers, horrified, as if this were some show put on for someone else's benefit. Chrysanthe was not the world she had known all her life; to speak of murdering a ruler, in public, seemed like madness to her.

Duke Corlin meanwhile shouted for silence, thumping a heavy pewter mug on the table until the chambers had grown mostly quiet. The Master of Protocol, overwhelmed, had stopped banging his staff long before.

"I was not raised to hold assassination as part of politics," he said. "I won't insult my father's memory by considering it. Estephor will not lift its hand against Kawlend's duchess in this way. If she declares war, then we will rise and quash her folly. But I will not have her throat slit as if she were a common thief."

"The more fool you, then, Your Grace!" shouted an Archeledian in the upper tier. Hubbub rose again, but this time both Archeled and Estephor slammed their fists for silence.

"Archeled also rejects this idea," finally said Duke Archeled, looking daggers at his minister. "My Lady Christine, do you favor assassinating the duchess of Kawlend? Or should we imprison her on imaginary charges, as Black Kelhorn so loved to do?"

Christine shook her head, relieved that at least the two dukes behaved in a civilized manner. She would never have been able to trust them if they had considered killing the duchess. "I won't . . . I won't have anyone killed," she croaked. "And no one will be put in jail on false charges." She felt a bit of warmth returning to her core as she said this. She might be a stupid girl, but at least she had principles.

"Then we must prepare now," said Duke Archeled. "Raise the armies and be ready to strike. If Duchess Ambith declares war, we will be ready. If she returns to reason, we will have lost nothing. Your Highness, what do you say?"

Everyone looked at Christine. She felt an almost physical pressure coming from the assembly. She could find nothing to object to in Archeled's speech, yet it was all going much too fast. "I . . . I call recess," she quavered. "Twenty minutes." She rose from her seat; as she did, the entire assembly stood up.

She turned; behind her, her advisers stood in a disgruntled clump. Althea and an undermaid clutched the backs of the seats in front of them, their faces impassive. Captain Veraless stood just outside of her box, hat in hands, his outrageous mane of hair miscombed so that one stark-white lock fell on the crow-black side. "Captain," she said, "you will ward me while I . . . while I'm gone. Come with me, please."

She walked down the steps, followed mutely by Veraless and two guards, exited the conclave chambers. As soon as they were out of earshot of the chambers, she begged him: "Find me a room where I can be alone for five minutes, please."

Rooms were never in short supply in Testenel and Veraless swiftly led her to a free one: somewhat anonymous, it had wooden walls and was furnished with low tables and chairs. One wall was stone, and Christine realized the room had been partitioned out from a much larger one.

"Guards, out," she ordered as soon as she'd entered. "No, not you, Captain!" She sank into one of the chairs, eliciting a puff of dust from the cushion, and put her head in her hands. "There's too many people about, but I can't stand to be alone," she confessed miserably. "I'm too scared now."

Captain Veraless said nothing. She continued: "Back home, sometimes I would be alone nearly half the day. It made me sad, in a way, but it was a comfortable kind of sadness. I was safe, then, Captain. I'm not safe anymore. What happened with Ambith? What did I do wrong? You said to be strong, I thought I was strong."

"You did nothing wrong, my lady. Ambith would have acted the same no matter what you said."

"That's not what you said this morning."

"It isn't, but I was wrong. I thought she had sense in her. Now we've seen she doesn't."

"She really wants war?"

"Aye. I didn't think she did; Kawlend suffered a lot during the Great War. She shouldn't have wanted to fight it again. But I guess she's so bitter she doesn't care."

"I can't help feel this is all my fault; I said the wrong thing, or I didn't say the right one. . . ."

"No, Lady Christine, there was nothing. The duchess meant to do this."

Christine was breathing too fast and too deep. She pinched her mouth shut, performed an exercise Dr. Almand—of all people—had taught her, forcing slow and shallow breaths through her nose. Focus on a detail, now, something minor.

"Captain, what did the duchess mean when she said 'perrules'?"

"Perdules, milady. A perdule is a . . . a small furry animal ladies of the court like to keep. You've seen some already. You know Lady Minderove? She always keeps a pair in her lap. Gold and black; they have huge bushy tails."

"Oh. Yes, I've seen them; I thought they were some kind of squirrel. But I don't see why Ambith used the term as an insult. . . . Oh, like 'lapdogs.' She was saying the dukes are like my pets?"

"Basically, yes. Also, herm, perdules become flatulent when they're fed too much. It's a very vulgar thing to call someone at court. Anything worse and she'd have lost face; a duke doesn't use gutter language."

Though she in fact did not find this at all funny, Christine could not restrain a giggle. "See?" she said when her nervous laughter had subsided. "I don't even know how to interpret insults correctly. I'm not competent to do this. I can't reign in my father's absence."

"Yes you can, my lady. You handled yourself remarkably well for a girl—pardon me, a woman your age. You have authority. And dukes Edric and Corlin support you."

She shook her head. "I don't know. I don't know."

For a few minutes she stayed seated, clutching the arms of the chair, until her dread had eased. "I'll give it a try," she said. "Let's go back; the recess must be almost over."

They were on their way back to the council chambers when they heard the rapid clatter of bootheels behind them. Christine, turning, beheld Melogian striding toward them. With a cry of relief she ran up to the sorceress, Veraless at her heels.

Christine stopped when she was within reach of Melogian. The sorceress's grim face spoke of failure. Christine felt the small flame of hope she had kept alive gutter out; yet despite her grief she threw her arms around the sorceress and hugged her with desperate energy. Melogian returned the embrace, running her fingers through Christine's hair. When they broke the clasp, Christine pulled back, saw Melogian's mouth twist and her lips quiver.

"I'm so glad you're back," Christine was saying. "I thought you wouldn't . . . I thought you'd leave me." Melogian shook her head, whispered a "no" with a sour smile. "Are you okay?" asked Christine. "You're okay, right?"

"I am fine," said Melogian thickly. For a fact, her attire was undisturbed: Except for a few mud stains on her boots, she might have come in from a brief stroll down the flower paths.

Veraless had come closer and drawn breath to speak. Looking at him, Melogian said without heat: "If I hear a single goddamned word out of your mouth, Veraless, I shall take you down to Hell and abandon you there."

Veraless held his tongue and looked aside while finger-combing his mustache. Looking at Christine, Melogian said: "Christine, I failed in my efforts to reach your father. I tried, believe me when I say that I tried. I could not do more. But it was an utter waste of time. I am sorry; I have to go get some rest now. When I have slept, we'll talk again. Forgive me."

She turned on her heel and strode off, her movements jerky as if she were battling exhaustion or rage. Christine watched her go; in that moment she wanted to ignore the conclave and run after Melogian. She was the regent, after all, she could do as she pleased. And it seemed to her Melogian needed someone by her side. She was reminded of that awful time she had come upon Freynie Long walking home stiff as a robot; how she had remained by her friend's side despite Freynie's repeated assurance that she was perfectly fine; how Freynie, at last, had wept on Christine's shoulder, but never telling her what had happened.

But Melogian was not Freynie; Freynie, after all, had never existed. And against the pain the sorceress felt Christine thought she could offer no bulwark. Once Melogian had turned a corner and gone from sight, Christine headed back to the conclave.

&ec; Every chapter in the story Edisthen was telling his daughter began the same way: "My dearest Christine." It was the tale of his life and a letter all at once; and some days it felt more like a confession, a litany of sins.

> I lacked the courage to go after you. Of course, there were reasons aplenty why I could not go: I was the sovereign and the land needed me; there were unknown dangers in made worlds; I had no way of knowing in which one you had been concealed and might spend a hundred years on a doomed search.
>
> But the truth is that I was afraid. I am not a born man, and to plunge within a made world disquieted me. For me, some days, it was as if my very substance were drawn from dreams; how then could I not fear I would dissolve into the fabric of the made world I entered?
>
> I have since lost that fear, at least. I sink deeper and deeper within this

made world, and I do not cease to exist in it; I go on, while the world around me grows ever stranger.

But at that time I still knew fear, and so I let Orion bestow the Quester's Gifts upon brave knights of the realm, and send them into the made worlds, to hunt for you until they found you, or perished. Some of them came back, after years of fruitless searching; and a few were brave enough to plunge back into the dream. These men and women whom I had barely had a chance to know sacrificed their lives for your sake, as I dared not do.

I know that no one truly lives up to the ideals he gives himself; but I had believed I was nothing but ideal, nothing but the embodiment of principles. I have spent my life finding out how wrong I was. Each such revelation takes away from me; I do not know what will be left at the end.

His voyage went on, day after day, days of storms and days of calm; he remained aboard the ship even when they made landfall, unwilling to step onto land and be forced to descend the gradient on foot. If he should find himself falling into infinity, then at least let it be aboard this craft, which granted him a measure of stability.

He traveled, and told his story, and the world around him changed, seasons passing as swiftly as breaths and sunsets stretching out forever. The ship sailed on into the east, under ever stranger skies.

One day Edisthen woke and felt a turmoil in himself: He knew that a boundary had been crossed. The ship by now was broad and tall, but absurdly shallow of keel; for the ocean was shallow too, a thin film of water over the rind of the world. Six or seven feet in depth, no more, it stretched out to the limits of vision in all directions. The water was translucent as a finely cut sapphire; schools of fish swam in it, while strange plants rooted in the sand and waved their bloodred fronds in the current.

Edisthen sat near the bow and watched their progress. The sun appeared strange; though it was the same diameter it had always been in Chrysanthe, its proportions were wrong. It seemed both small and close, as if the ship would pass beyond it in an hour or so. But this did not happen. They sailed on, and on, and the sun hardly crept up the sky. Wind swelled their purple sails and the bone-white man at the wheel nudged it a bit now and then, to an accompaniment of groans and crackings.

A boundary had been crossed: Edisthen had reached the end of the tale he had been telling, the story of his life. He could see it all neatly laid out in his mind's eye, as ink on parchment, every word he had shaped, page after page. At times he had wished to be rid of this weight on his memory. Now he had reached the end at last; had told of his abduction into the made world, his delirious flight through the forest, his descent to Lewch-Head and his setting sail with long-lost Captain Quareltine and the *Celadon*. He had told what had befallen him from that point up to now, the days and days stretching into weeks of voyaging, all condensed within a few sentences; now he was truly done.

A crewman brought him a flask of wine and a meat pie. The wine was weak as water, the dough tasteless and the meat within almost as pale as the crewman's flesh. Yet Edisthen ate and drank it all; his body needed sustenance and he did not deny its appetite. On and on he had voyaged, and by now all traces of civilization had long been left behind. Would he end up alone on this ship, tracing a meaningless furrow in the water, a line headed straight for infinity?

He stood up, cast his gaze at the mottling of clouds painted upon the heavens. His voice rose, rusty from disuse but still strong. "'Who raised the vault of Heaven above the Earth? Who cast life upon the void? Who stands above the Law?'" he quoted from Siladrin's Lament. For born men, real men, this was a famous poem the priestesses read to them; it was something schoolchildren were sometimes made to memorize and recite. Edisthen had come into existence with the words already inside him, along with tens of thousands of others. The entire text of the Lesser Book as well as that of other religious works lay in his mind, so deeply ingrained they sometimes recited themselves in his sleep, so well-known that he sensed only death could make him forget them. Perhaps he was in the end nothing more than these words: a man of words. Written into existence, cast into the world for a purpose, never knowing whether it had been fulfilled.

A spasm of rage shook him as he recalled the faces of all those whom he loved, faces he would never see again. He shook his fist at Heaven, then slammed it down upon the gunwale, a few bitter tears escaping his eyes. And from the depths of him the Lament rose again.

"'I do not thank You, for You have done nothing for me. I do not rail at You, for You have done nothing against me. I will not pray to You, for all life is prayer enough. I will not curse You, for all my tears are curse enough. . . .'"

Another's words, not his. The king of Chrysanthe fell silent. People of his court had never understood why he loved Severn so much; to them he was just an aging writer, spinning out a worn tale beyond its natural end. But Edisthen loved *Sir Raven's Quest* beyond all measure, because he never could expect what was to come next. And Severn's words were Severn's own, they were not quotes from books old before he was born. This made every sentence of his wonderfully fresh; Edisthen did not want the cycle to be finished, he wanted it to go on forever, one vista opening into another endlessly. The point of the quest was the quest itself, not its ever-elusive goal.

For a time he was pensive, then. Wondering if his life could be seen in the light of Sir Raven's; wondering if he had been giving too little credit to She who had written him. He went aft, to where the crew were mostly gathered. Corpse-pale men, yet well muscled and vital. They greeted him in the vulgate they spoke and which he could not comprehend beyond the simplest terms. Again, one offered him of their weak wine, and he drank it. The captain came out of his cabin, and sat down next to Edisthen. His only emblems of rank were a pair of metal five-pointed stars, nailed directly to his bare shoulders. He spoke; he used their high tongue, which approximated the language of Chrysanthe.

"A roseate wind, Liege. Currents deliquesce farther on, but we store enough effulgence to transect the glass-oases."

Edisthen could only make vague sense of what the man meant, but he had found it sufficed.

"And beyond?" he asked.

"Great poli, Liege. Challa-Harad, Muskadel, Ellourbanishpal. Bright specie, suns and moons embedded, six flavors of life, new principles to delight and confound."

"By the time you reach these places you speak of, I will no longer be on this ship. You are dreams and with every moment that passes I shift through the dreamscape. You are no longer the same man who told me of a roseate wind a moment ago."

The pale man shook his head emphatically. "Nay, Liege. Your innerance labors a lash-width false. In the extreme, the asymptote levels. Deep into existence the wise so travel, apporting minions, and waters spread a baulk over all modes."

Edisthen blinked. Had he understood correctly? Was the captain telling him he was bringing the ship along with him now, that this ocean stretched across worlds? It could be. He might have reached regions where such things became possible. It might also be nothing but lies.

And he realized at last that it did not matter. *It did not matter.* It became finally clear to Edisthen that the hand of God had been withdrawn from him long, long ago. He had been a purpose made flesh, a man shaped from words. He had overthrown Vaurd, fathered Christine, awoken the armies of the land to oppose Evered. But now all that was done. Whatever happened to him could no longer matter. He was free. His task was done, and having been trapped into the made world, he had been granted the life of a born man: to be a toy of circumstance, adrift in a life he did not control and that had not been shaped for him.

Relief and joy filled him, so strongly that he was blinded by tears for a moment. When he had knuckled his eyes clear, the crew were still about him, unchanged, and their half-naked captain with stars nailed to his shoulders was smiling at him. The pale man spoke words of sympathy which were complete gibberish but whose tone seemed to hint at comprehension beyond mortal sapience.

Edisthen turned his gaze to the east, to the sun toward which they sailed. He repeated the names of cities the captain had evoked: "Challa-Harad, Muskadel, Ellourbanishpal." Whether they reached them in a day, a month, a year, whether they ended up worlds away, it did not matter. Turning the pages of Severn's books had been like this: Never did the surprises slake his thirst for more. Delights and terrors always awaited him in the company of Sir Raven. From now on he would accept what his life gave him, and revel in it if he was able. He thought once more of the dear ones he was leaving behind forever. His love for Christine burned as strongly as ever, but he had let her go. Wind swelling its purple sails, Edisthen's ship sailed on into his new life.

4. Returnings and Departures

Leaving the council chambers in an uproar, Duchess Ambith and her entourage swept through Testenel's blue stone, back to the high tower where the skyship *Glorious Niavand* was berthed. If her captain was surprised to see the delegation from Kawlend appear without warning, she did not let it show.

The duchess demanded an immediate return to Aluvien; the captain calmly explained the ship wasn't ready for an instant departure and bade her wait a while. Ambith was left to fume and pace her cabin as the *Glorious Niavand* was made ready. It took over an hour for the bare minimum to be accomplished, at which point Duchess Ambith would wait no more. The captain did not see fit to oppose further resistance and the skyship set out from Testenel, heading south.

For three days they sailed, making at times disappointing progress due to contrary winds; whenever the duchess asked about the time remaining to their journey, she received a discouraging answer. Her fervid mood had cooled as soon as the ship had left Testenel, but she remained testy and her companions spoke with her as little as necessary. Half of them were pleased by her display at council; the other half were worried. She shrugged off the discomfort of the cowards in her entourage. For twenty years the whole of the land had endured the reign of an impostor, who had used fear of the Law against the people. Yet any inexorable force must be feared. Even she, though it rankled her to admit it in her moments of soul-searching, admitted there was a chance Edisthen might be what he claimed. And so she was caught in the same trap as Evered: To discover the truth was to risk her own destruction. The Law that protected the royal blood of Chrysanthe saw through obfuscations into the heart of everyone. If Ambith were to order that Edisthen be hurt, then no matter how many layers of underlings the order went through, she would be considered just as guilty as if she had wielded the blade herself.

For twenty years she had waited for the truth to be made manifest. Nothing happened. Ambith aged, while Edisthen seemed to remain the same. Some might have seen this as tentative proof of his claims; Ambith knew well that cosmetics might be used to give a much younger man the appearance of age. And that magic could not be discounted either, that it would be child's play for Orion to take a pretender to the throne of his own choosing and cloud him in glamour. There were hidden forces at play in Edisthen's coming, whatever they were, the Law itself or Orion's manipulations.

Throughout this time she had dealt with Vaurd's sons, forced to exile within her realm while their mother remained hostage in Temerorn. Edisthen had forbidden them to travel; while Ambith could not allow them to leave Kawlend, in practice she had entertained them discreetly many times at her summer palace. She had always been as fond of the sons as of their father. Even poor little Olf, the sweetest-natured boy she'd ever known. She had seen them mature into men, their souls shadowed by the tragedy of their house. Aghaid, she often thought, would have made the best king; he was born to command, forceful and intelligent, cool-headed. But Evered was the eldest, and his candidacy must take precedence, regardless of his raging temper. He ached to regain the throne that was rightfully his; Ambith's desires ran in the same direction.

And so, when events had suddenly taken a startling turn at the conclave, Ambith had sensed that the fulfillment of both their hopes was approaching. Yet her exaltation was not unmixed, and she viewed the coming days with a measure of dread.

So it was that the duchess's visitor on the evening of her second day aboard found her in a troubled mood. Seated in her cabin, Ambith had been brooding over old memories for hours. The skyship's progress was smooth enough that she could usually forget she was in movement at all; only a faint roll sometimes manifested itself. She had been lodged in the captain's own quarters in the poop deck, of course, and though the cabin was absurdly tiny it was at least reasonably comfortable. Some efforts had been made to increase its perceived size as well: Besides the square window that gave a fine view of the landscape outside, there was a large mirror affixed to the wardrobe door, which gave an illusion of space.

As she glanced at this mirror, Ambith noticed a cloud of tarnish in its center. Not fog on the glass, but an affliction of the silver backing. Yet she had noticed nothing of the sort previously. Under her eyes the cloud spread and sharpened, and soon the irreflective zones of the glass sketched the features of Casimir, Evered's wizard. Ambith rose to her feet and took a step toward the mirror, where Casimir's image now raised a ghostly hand. She waited for the image to speak; yet though its lips might have moved, she heard nothing. What was she to do?

After a long moment, she raised her own hand and brought it hesitantly toward the image. As she did so her features in the mirror seemed to coincide with those of the wizard, etched by the absence of reflection. The world all about her grew dark and vastly distant, leaving her floating in a void, her palm touching that of Casimir, whose appearance was still dim and silvery.

"Greetings, Your Grace," said Casimir, his voice muffled and buzzing. "I believe you have been thinking of me? I am here."

"I have not been thinking of you," said Ambith coldly. "I have been thinking of Vaurd and the Great War, but not of you."

The wizard did not appear to react to the distaste in her voice. "These subjects are very dear to me also; doubtless that is what I felt. In any event, I have come to speak with you, to carry any message you may have for my master Evered."

"You might have let me know before I set out that I should expect such a communication; I was taken quite unaware and this is unpleasant," said Ambith. Casimir muttered a patently insincere apology. In other circumstances, with anyone else, Ambith would not have let the matter lie; but she feared Casimir and his magic.

"I do have a message," she said. "Edisthen has vanished. I've heard it said he fell into the made world in Testenel's gardens and no one can find him."

"Indeed." Casimir grinned. "I was already aware of this."

"The land is now governed by a child, a girl not even twenty. The throne of Chrysanthe will remain empty until Archeled and Estephor acclaim Christine as queen. Archeled will wish to rule through her, and I expect Estephor will sue for her hand."

"Most likely true . . . but did you know, Your Grace, that the conclave debated whether to imprison you, or even, pardon my words, eliminate you before you had a chance to leave?"

Ambith felt a sliver of ice run down her spine. "You have seen this?" she asked.

"A spying-spell of mine carried the news back to me."

The duchess closed her eyes in reaction, and was startled to discover that this had no effect on her vision. Still she floated in black emptiness, facing a silvery image of the wizard. She struggled for a moment with speech and finally recovered enough of her composure to say:

"Well. I could expect no more of them, I suppose. I knew Kawlend was still hated after all this time, but I never thought the hatred ran this deep. So be it then. I know what to do."

"May I ask for explicit directives, Your Grace?" came Casimir's buzzing voice.

"'Explicit directives'? You may tell Evered I am declaring war. Let him gather his forces; Kawlend's armies shall stand with him when he moves."

"I will do so at once, Your Grace."

"Tell him also to be at the summer palace on the twelfth of High-Summer; we shall meet and discuss details."

"He will be there, Your Grace. I carry your words now."

Casimir's ghostly hand broke contact; light came flooding back into the world. Ambith found herself standing before the wardrobe, facing a mirror devoid of any strangeness. Yet in that instant, for a reason she could not have identified, the sight of her other self behind the glass became terrifying; she turned on her heel and went to stand in the furthest corner of the cabin, facing the angle of the bulkhead, her breath coming in harsh gasps. Like a child, she could not help but wonder if her image in the mirror had turned away also, as it should, or if it had remained in place, and if it was the gaze of its black eyes she could now feel boring into her neck.

In the council chambers of Testenel, discussion concluded after less than an hour and the conclave was dissolved. In the morning young Duke Corlin of Estephor left aboard the *Black Heart* and returned to his capital, thence to direct the levying of his armies. Duke Edric of Archeled sailed eastward, along the Scyamander, to do likewise.

Melogian came to see Christine shortly before noon, having slept through the morning. The sorceress asked Christine to recount what had befallen the conclave; she was so dismayed at the turn of events that her own account became even gloomier.

"I'm sorry, Christine," she said, looking forlorn. "I'm so sorry. I spent a day trying every trick I could conceive of to locate your father. I couldn't."

"You don't know where he is, then; not at all?"

"He's in the made world; the guards' accounts made that clear, and there were traces of manipulation at its entrance, visible to an adept. He was lured inside it. He ought to have remained motionless as soon as he realized he had left the true realm, and I would have been able to sense his presence so near to the mouth."

"So what went wrong? He moved? He didn't know what had happened?"

"There's a strong gradient in that made world, which is presumably deliberate. It is believed when Nikolas Mestech opened it, he sought for a pleasure-world. Move toward the center of the garden, and reality opens up like a blooming flower; the landscape gets huger and huger, and by the time you reach what you saw as a pond in the middle of the venue, you find yourself in a harbor town next to a lake."

"So he didn't know the town was there, and he got lost wandering?"

"He did know: He went into the made world once before, with you in fact. You won't recall it, but you took a trip on a ship with him, when you were three years old."

Christine's entire body shivered.

"He held me," she whispered. "He held me tight and let me look above the rail.

The water was shallow and I could see dozens of fish swimming. . . . Oh God." This was the first memory she had retrieved in sessions with Dr. Almand; one he had immediately twisted into a reminiscence of fear. She spoke up, anxious: "Were you there, Melogian? Did it happen that way, or did I dream it?"

"I think it did, yes. You recall the occasion?"

"He made me think I was deluded. I was afraid of falling, and my father held me, and Dr. Almand kept telling me I was afraid of *him*. . . ."

She wiped at the two tears that were rolling down her face.

"If he'd been there before, Melogian, he had to know where he was! Why wouldn't he go to the town to wait for you?"

The sorceress shook her head.

"If he knew where he was," she said, "not only could he have gone to the harbor town, but he might even have returned without my help. The gradient can actually be climbed, as long as you stay in the middle of the path. Under normal circumstances, he could have walked back out on his own."

Christine remained silent; Melogian went on.

"Casimir has been at work on the made world," she said. "I don't know how, but he altered it. He made the mouth gape wide to swallow Edisthen, but he also did something to . . . pull him down. Every made world is infinite, you know. No matter how it's been shaped, no matter how safe it can seem, you're jumping into endlessness when you wander in. This made world is like a shallow tide pool: Anyone should be able to climb back out of it. But it's as if Casimir made the ocean rise to the level of the pool, and your father was swept out to sea."

"You're telling me he's gone. Gone like I was gone. You can't find him."

"I don't know. I can't know; mages have forgotten much of the lore of made worlds. But I think he was impelled down the gradient, against his will. In order to find him, I would have to dive very, very deep. It would take me months, or years, to locate him."

Melogian looked away, her lips twisted.

"It's not that I refuse to do it. I would gladly search for him for as long as it takes. But the current situation in the land is dangerous. I don't dare leave Chrysanthe. Veraless was right: To seek for Edisthen would be weakness. I'm so sorry."

Christine felt numb. She asked, hesitantly: "The Law protects the king from harm, doesn't it? Why didn't it do something?"

"Because he hasn't been physically hurt. Pulling him down into a made world isn't the kind of action that will bring punishment."

"Of course. I'm being stupid. It happened to me too. You can go around the Law that way. So, what Casimir did to my father: He can do it to me as well, can't he?"

Melogian shook her head emphatically "No. No, it won't happen. For one thing, you will be kept away from the Royal Gardens. You won't be in danger from that made world. Likewise for the three others within Testenel. Also, I'm alert for the possibility of influencing made worlds, now, and I will emplace wards at their mouths. If Casimir tampers with them, I will know."

"But I'm still vulnerable. Something—anything—could happen to me."

"Christine . . . that has always been true. But that's why I won't leave. I will protect you."

"Right. Right, of course," said Christine, feeling very small, and chilled to the bone. None of Melogian's reassurances could ease her mood.

In the days that followed, she began to see herself as a prisoner of Testenel, forbidden certain areas of the castle lest Casimir wield his power over the made worlds. She was regent, standing in for the king, nominally in command of Temerorn's armies. In practice she made no decisions whatsoever. Her counselors and officers could handle the tasks at hand by themselves. No one asked her to dispense justice, no one sought her advice. Although to have to make decisions would have been a terrifying task, it seemed to her even worse to be consigned to uselessness. But then, she had had many years of practice at it; growing up, she had known she would never amount to anything, never matter to anyone else. She was back in the mental country of her youth now, once more the outsider, the ineffectual bystander who could only look at life passing her by and wish she didn't have eyes to see.

She withdrew into her rooms, turned them into a fortress against the outside world. Her days became set into a rigid routine of idleness: She slept late, spent mornings reading, ate at her desk. In the afternoon she sometimes received Melogian, listened to the sorceress speak but hardly ever uttered a word herself. Melogian never did more than brush against her defenses. Christine could safely let her speak on: She spoke like voices on the radio telling her of the unattainable world outside, where things happened which never reached within her desolate fortress. After the evening meal Christine would read again, almost at random. Prevented from going to the Great Library because of the made world that lay in the lower levels, she had had volumes of all kind brought to her room: histories, geography, philosophy, fiction. She plowed through them all, in a desperate hurry to finish every book, at a loss when she did. She read folk stories that seemed eerily familiar, she followed arguments between long-dead philosophers about trivial matters, she scanned map after map of Chrysanthe, the flat world above which the sun rose and set. She read Thenuel's *Omnicon* and couldn't recall a word of it afterward. One evening, disgusted with books, she instead thought of *The Cosmic Patrol*; she made a list on parchment of every last episode, with its title and plot. There were stretches of above a minute in length that she could bring to mind frame by frame: favorite lines, memorable characters. The Aphroditeans, from Terra's twin planet reshaped by human ingenuity, always so contemptuous of their brethren whom they so much resembled; Commander Seldar's flight through an alien ship, racing the clock to disarm a mirror-matter bomb; the glowing flesh of the man from the future, burning alive from temporal charge, delivering his message of doom in hopes of averting it . . .

There was no averting the doom that lay over her. She had trusted in herself too much, tried to assert authority when she never should have, and caused a disaster. Her father had vanished, he who had been the absent pivot of her life. She had spent all her life learning to hate him, to believe him a monster; in the past weeks she had discovered her life had been blighted by lies, had come to the true realm, had started mending her ties to Edisthen. Now he was gone, and with this anchor of her life missing, she had become the same frightened girl she had been before, let the reins of her life slip from her hands. She waited, but what she waited for she did not know.

se Quentin returned to Testenel on the fifteenth of High-Summer, having spent several days with his parents that left him emotionally torn. It is naïve to think that the world ages uniformly, when the truth is that parts of it stay young and changeless while other parts decay faster than would seem possible. Bits of his family home had remained untouched, linking Quentin to his earliest youth; they spoke to him and told him he had never left, had only perhaps been gone an afternoon, a day at most, and now he was back, at the eternal unchanging core of the world. And then he would encounter some new element, something that had not been there when he had left, and the gulf of time that had passed would yawn deep beneath his feet.

So, to be reunited with his mother and father had been bliss and heartbreak at once. They had changed; they had grown old, gray in their hair and a stoop in his father's back. News had reached Lydiss of his deeds; his parents knew what he had achieved. They had held some misapprehensions that he'd had to correct, but no more. And this disappointed him: He had wanted to reveal the truth to them, like a small boy overflowing with excitement at having dared to climb a tree. They already knew their son was a hero, and this new identity of his had erased whom he had been to them before. His father's gruffness was held in abeyance, his mother's warmth timid and stilted. They did not dare too much familiarity with this strange knight who'd ridden out of the made world bearing the name of their son.

They were pleased, naturally, by what he brought with them: the promise of a lifelong stipend, and the echoes of his own fame. Their status in Lydiss had increased, and now they need never fear for money. After a day or two, Quentin was able to bring into being a reasonable replica of the family life he had once known with them. Yet it was a replica only; there was too much between them now. He would have had to spend years at it for true familiarity to return. His place was no longer by their side. So after some days he took his leave. There were tears and awkward promises of future visits. It was a guilty relief for him to ride at last back to Testenel.

The first evening of his journey, he received appalling news—news that he refused to believe at first. That the ducal conclave had gone badly, he could well accept. That the king had died, as someone excitedly repeated in the common room of the inn, was patently ridiculous. The next evening he heard the king had vanished: still outrageous. By the third night, as he grew nearer to the source of events, he began to get a sense of deep dread. Something had indeed happened. Edisthen was not dead, no; but missing. Missing, as Orion had gone missing before him, as Christine, his daughter, had gone missing thirteen years ago. This he found himself almost forced to believe.

By the time he reached Testenel, his whole body felt icy, despite the heat of summer. He met with Melogian shortly after arriving. It took her three sentences to confirm his worst fears: Edisthen had indeed vanished, fallen into the made world within the gardens.

Quentin remained silent a long moment after the sorceress had spoken; then he felt something turn within him and purpose moved him again.

"I know what I must do," he announced. "I can be ready tomorrow morning." He felt almost happy. "Melogian, you will cast the seeking-spell on me once more. I shall—"

"No!" she cut him off. "You won't go after him. I tried it, and I failed. You won't go."

"I have done this before, Melogian," he said gently. "I can do it again. It is my duty."

"This is different, Quentin. When you sought Christine she was hidden in a fixed place. Edisthen is being drawn down the gradient, against his will. He is moving faster than you can. You can never catch up to him."

"Do you know this for a fact? If you have any doubts, then I must still risk it."

"No! I won't let you."

He took her hands in his. "I do not want to be parted from you, Lady. But I am a knight of the realm, sworn to my duty. Let me go look for him, Melogian."

"You stupid little peasant boy!" she said, her cheeks flaming. "Don't play the tragic lover with me. What about Christine? What about your duty to *her*?"

He hesitated for a second, then started to reply, "My duty to the king supersedes—"

"Your duty is to the throne, Quentin, not the king. And Christine is regent. It's her you must serve."

Quentin frowned. "That interpretation is incorrect, Melogian. The rules of chivalry argue that even in the absence of the sovereign, loyalty to his person must win over political considerations."

Melogian looked daggers at him. "Then will you at least for God's sweet sake go and speak to Christine? She's barricaded herself in her rooms. Since you don't have the slightest spark of love for her, go and tell her yourself you'll be deserting her in a doomed quest to seek her father. When you've done that, then fine, come back to me and I'll cast the spell for you. I'll shove you into the made world myself. You'll have a chance to do the right thing and desert your friends."

"I do not want to desert anyone," he said gently. "It is not like that."

She forbore to answer; he left her then, went to his quarters to wash and change his clothes before he sought audience with the Lady Christine. One of Christine's body-servants let him in as soon as he was announced.

Christine had been sitting in an armchair, reading. Her book fell from the arm onto the floor even as he entered the room. Christine stood two steps from the doorway, smiling tremulously. Quentin dropped to one knee, very briefly, knowing Christine disliked this much formality.

"Lady Christine, I am back."

"I missed you, Quentin," she said. "So many things happened. I have to tell you all about it. I've been so scared, I don't know what to do anymore. . . ."

He meant to tell her then that he knew the most important news and that he had decided what he must do. Then he looked at her, saw the joy and relief in her eyes as she gazed at him, and the words died on his lips.

He let her talk on, knowing that he would not do his duty to his king; that he no longer could. At some point in his life, though utterly unaware of it, he had shifted his loyalty. Perhaps when he had returned to Testenel with Christine, when Edisthen had ordered him: *Protect her.* Perhaps earlier still, down in the made world named Errefern, when they had been apprehended in the shopping mall and he had led Christine out, his arm around her shoulders. Or perhaps at the very instant he had located her after nine years of seeking, when Orion's spell had made his whole self resonate with such an intensity he had thought he was dying. She was the object of his quest, no matter that it was over; in his heart it would always go on. All his loyalties lay with her, now and forever.

He stayed with Christine the rest of the day, listening to her, offering the occasional bit of advice. When came the time for the evening meal they ate in one of the lesser dining chambers, in company with two of the royal counselors. Melogian dropped by unannounced in the middle of the meal and was made welcome. She sat at Quentin's right and looked at him with one arched eyebrow; he lowered his gaze. She patted his hand, gracious in victory.

⚬ Three days before Quentin's return, disturbing news had reached Testenel. The skyship *Spindrift* should normally have called in at Waldern, capital of Archeled, on the third of High-Summer. When it failed to appear as expected, no especial notice had been taken of the fact: The vagaries of the winds frequently delayed skyships. However, when it still had not shown up two days later, measures had been taken to locate the errant craft.

Shortly thereafter, the burnt-out hulk of the *Spindrift* had been found by *Llermand's Victory*. Not a single one of its crew had survived; some had been burned to death, others presumably killed when the ship had plummeted to the ground.

Although for most people the disappearance of the king overshadowed all lesser concerns, Melogian worried greatly about the fate of the *Spindrift*. Skyships did not spontaneously combust and crash. But what could have attacked the *Spindrift*? A squad of archers with flaming arrows could never have overwhelmed it in this fashion; and the reports insisted that the skyship's hull had been charred to the keel.

Another elder spell, then. But cast at this distance? Her mind reeled when she thought of it. Orion himself would never have been able to ignite the hull of a skyship fifty leagues distant. And if Casimir could do this much, then surely he could destroy the other skyships one by one; could, also, envelop a single person in flames. . . .

The protections she had spun around Testenel still held; she had believed they would shield the castle against magical intrusions of the coarser sort. They had been useless against the distortion of the dream world in the gardens, though. She could not be certain they would be of any help against a fire-spell of that magnitude. Her dreams were haunted by ghostly flames and charred corpses.

On the seventeenth of High-Summer, Duchess Ambith's declaration of war reached Testenel, delivered to Christine by a Kawlendian messenger clad in red from head to foot. The proclamation he read from a scroll in a stentorian voice managed to sound at once overblown and petulant, full of whereases and therefores, yet concluding on a whine about the rightful place of Kawlend in Chrysanthe.

Melogian had expected nothing else from Ambith; she was, however, pleasantly surprised at Christine's response. Dressed in formal robes, an unhappy look on her face, the regent looked at the messenger and delivered a reply worthy of a sovereign:

"Tell your mistress if this folly is what she wants, she may have it. We'll see what my perdules can teach Kawlend."

Looking at Christine, Melogian felt a warm glow of almost motherly pride. Edisthen's daughter was changing from the frightened girl Quentin had brought back from the made world into a capable woman. If she were given time, she would one day blossom into a fit sovereign of the realm. And Melogian felt a knife blade of fear at that thought: Edisthen might have chosen to abdicate in favor of Christine, but with him gone she could only be regent, until he should die; and Heroes might live for centuries. . . .

On the same day that the red-suited messenger brought the declaration of war, more welcome news arrived from Archeled: Duke Edric had wasted no time in readying his armies; his troops were already on the march. Furthermore, the duke himself would be returning to Testenel, to place his soldiers under the orders of the regent. Christine, who had been reeling from the day's earlier announcement, felt a disproportionate sense of relief.

Still, for all Edric's promises of haste, in practice it took him until the end of High-Summer to arrive. He did so at the head of a long column of men and supplies, over a third of Archeled's forces. Another third had been deployed along the border with Kawlend, and the final third were still in the process of mustering. The Archeledians swelled the ranks of soldiers that had been gathering for weeks at Tiellorn. Encampments spread outward from the city walls; from high windows in Testenel Christine gazed at them with a troubled fascination. The land she had barely begun to know was changing, descending into chaos. All her life she had heard about war, but it had always been something that happened far away: an abstract notion, deaths that did not truly matter, violence digested by television into a few seconds of barely coherent footage, sanitized and scrubbed free of blood and actual carnage.

And again, she supposed, this war would take place far away. Kawlend was much closer than the Orient where so much blood had been shed in the name of ideologies in her lifetime; but the real world was a very small place, she knew that now, and the war would proportionately still be distant, especially since there were no networks, no corps of journalists reporting the slaughter over the airwaves.

And the war would have to remain distant: because if Evered wanted her throne, then he had to be stopped, long before his soldiers came in sight of Testenel. That had been her father's original plan, so General Fraydhan had told her: to go to Vorlok and take down Evered's forces. There was no question of allowing him to enter Temerorn.

In the following days, Duke Edric became a regular dinner guest, whom Christine did not know how to refuse. She entertained him, as she supposed the regent should. The meals lasted hours, stretched out by spectacles and discussions. Melogian sometimes attended, Quentin always. There were invariably some of the royal counselors, but never more than two, as they tended to dispute amongst themselves over trivialities. Some courtiers filled out the table, although Christine kept their numbers small as well and insisted that the roster change every night. She tried to get to know these people, despite Quentin's disapproval of the entire lot of them. A few she found amusing and pleasant; almost all fawned on her to an extent she could hardly believe. It occurred to her that politics played a crucial role among her court as much as in the wider world. Here as well as there, facts were often secondary to feelings and social position.

By early Ripening, the mustering was complete. The main bulk of Archeled's forces had joined up with the Temerorni armies, which had been deployed at various key points throughout the land. The main force remained close by Tiellorn, awaiting orders that could not be delayed much longer.

Accordingly, one afternoon, Christine found herself in a vast chamber in one of the lower levels of Testenel, where General Fraydhan had put together a briefing that detailed known troop strengths and movement potentials. The chamber was devoid of windows and the walls hung with black drapes. A number of metal structures supported lit braziers at one end, while the other bore brackets into which translucent panes of glass had been clamped, five feet wide and three feet high.

On the glass, maps of Temerorn, Archeled, and Kawlend had been painted. Light shining through illuminated the features. Christine found the effect very pretty, but wondered why anyone would go to such trouble, instead of just painting the maps on ordinary canvases. Her question was answered almost immediately, as sheets of onionskin paper were draped in front of the glass panes. Arrows and various symbols had been drawn upon the paper, overlaying the features of the maps. As Fraydhan went through his presentation, attendants would remove one sheet of paper and place another one to illustrate the next point the general wanted to make.

Fraydhan was assured throughout his presentation. With brief gestures of a wand as he pointed out features on the maps, he explained how Evered had gathered rabble from the outer marches, how these undisciplined forces were now supervised by veteran Kawlendian troops, how the rebel army was moving from Aluvien northward toward Tiellorn, how it would have to be faced, sooner or later.

"I will not deny that I wish for an early engagement," he said in conclusion. "Point one: Our forces are fully ready as of today, and while we already have detachments between Tiellorn and the southern frontier, the main contingent remains here. Point two: We already outnumber the Kawlendians, even without counting Estephor's army, which is currently on the march but still many days away. Point three: The earlier the engagement, the lower the losses in lives.

"I must insist on this last point: A swift strike will pin Kawlend's forces within their own duchy and we can expect a clear and clean victory.

"The only alternative is for us to hole up in Testenel and wait for Evered's forces to besiege us. This will put the greatest pressure on his forces, since it will stretch their supply line to the utmost; and of course by the time they reach us we will have Estephor by our side. However, it also means that Kawlend's forces will be allowed to invade Temerorn; we can be certain of depredations among the civilian population along their path. I speak not only of the supplies looted from our citizenry, but also of torched farms and overrun villages. We will appear weak to the populace and Duchess Ambith will gain prestige in her people's eyes. A siege of Testenel would certainly fail, but the very fact of besiegement will put ideas in their heads we will be another generation getting rid of.

"We can, of course, try to play it both ways. Leave a strong defensive force here in Testenel and eventually send the rest southward. But frankly, I fail to see the wisdom in this. We gain the worst of both worlds. No, we have only two clear alternatives. You have heard which one I, as general of the armies, favor. What is your opinion, Your Highness?"

Fraydhan ought to have at least included Duke Edric in that last question, Christine felt, especially since he was sitting right beside her and had the experience that she completely lacked. Sensitized to currents of flattery by the last few days of dinner, she guessed Fraydhan was playing a mildly dangerous game, currying her favor while reminding Duke Archeled of his place. Christine was about to turn to Duke Edric and ask him his opinion but Melogian intervened.

"You make it sound so certain, General! You're trying to replay the Usurpation War, like one could replay a game of Horses and Wolves. You're pretending that nothing has changed since then."

Fraydhan scowled. "With all due respect, you were a girl of thirteen when the Usurpation War was fought, Lady. Are you telling me you remember how things were done at the time? I am not repeating history, but rather taking its lessons into consideration. When the Great War started, King Edisthen was hesitant; he wasted ages on diplomacy while Kawlend gathered its forces and advanced toward the capital. When it finally came to fighting, we had to engage Kawlendian forces on several fronts, because they had had a chance to position themselves to best advantage. An earlier strike on our part would have saved time and—most important!—lives." He turned to Christine. "I ask you to consider this, Your Highness. I am trying to make this ugly time as brief as possible. If we wait here for Estephorin reinforcements, we leave all the initiative to Ambith and Evered. And we appear weak, timorous. I understand that you recoil from violence. You're not a soldier; I don't expect you to relish the prospect of deaths. And this is what I'm trying to avoid, as well. I say we strike early and hard. We have the strength to do it."

Melogian was fuming. "And what of Casimir's spells? We neglect those, again. You won't even believe they exist!"

"I believe what I see, Lady Wizard. So far we've seen that Casimir can project an eidolon across a hundred leagues. Hardly a military concern."

"What about the *Spindrift*?" she retorted.

"What about it? We don't know what happened to it. It burned and crashed, yes, a tragedy. But we don't know why."

"Magic is the likeliest culprit!"

Fraydhan held up his hands. "The likeliest? So you admit there are others. Do you want us to build strategies based on superstition or unnamed terrors? I deal in facts. You've told me yourself that your magic can help our forces, and if you volunteer that help I'll gladly accept it; just as I accept that you won't commit yourself at this point because of your worries about Casimir. By all means, when you have hard facts to give me, I will listen. When you have concrete help to give I will take it. But I will not let you pretend you are a military commander. That is my lot in life. If the regent wishes to promote you in my place, she may do so. Until then . . ."

Melogian, speechless with indignation, turned to look at Christine, who avoided her gaze and turned to Duke Edric.

"Your Grace," she said, "I'm not a military strategist. I'd like to know what you think."

Edric smiled at her; in the dimness, his white hair tinted by the flames shining through colored glass, he suddenly reminded her of a Saint Nicolas doll lit by the colored electric lights of Christmas. "Your Highness, I came here to be by your side. I will support your decision, whatever it is. I will say that I don't like to remain passive. I favor action as a general course. I will say no more."

Christine returned her gaze to the maps over which the final trio of sheets of paper still displayed their arrows and lines, their carefully limned pictograms in red and blue ink that glowed in translucence. She rose from her seat and took a few steps toward the maps. From closer up, the magnificence of the display paled somewhat: The features of the maps were revealed as coarser than she'd thought and she grew aware of the surface of the onionskin paper as distinct from the glass pane. She sighed: She had no business making military decisions, but she was expected to render a verdict here and now, to commit thousands of soldiers to a course she chose. Even if she refused the responsibility, if she delegated it entirely to General Fraydhan or to Duke Edric, she would have made a choice, one born of cowardice or laziness.

She turned to face the others. "General," she said, "I greatly appreciate what you've done." She trusted Melogian far more than she did Fraydhan; in fact, she was a little afraid of him, if only because he was a man. But she could not make a decision based on this fear. And though Melogian had made Christine understand her concerns about Casimir's magic, Christine had to admit Melogian had no specific worries. She had seen Evered's eidolon, and it had frightened her as well. But should she let *that* fear dictate her decision? The fate of the destroyed skyship was worrisome, but it had been a month ago and nothing else of the sort had happened.

No; Fraydhan had spoken of lives saved. Mercy made more sense. Let mercy be her guide.

"And I have to agree with you," Christine said. "You're the military man. You have the experience. If you think we should strike swiftly, then let's do it. But! But, you should listen to what Melogian has to say. When she gives you information, you must trust her, as I do."

"But of course, Your Highness," said Fraydhan with a smile. "The Lady Melogian and I disagree about certain things, but we are on the same side, and I will never dismiss any fact she brings to my attention."

Melogian's jaw had fallen when Christine had made her choice. Now, hearing Fraydhan's smug reply, she gritted her teeth and stalked out of the chamber, without so much as a word. Fraydhan watched her leave then turned back to Christine and gave her a short bow. "Your Highness has chosen well. I am certain the Lady Wizard will see the wisdom of your decision soon. In the meantime, I shall give the necessary orders to get our troops on the move. Your Highness, Your Grace, if you will excuse me . . ."

Christine returned to her quarters in a subdued mood. She had never known Melogian to be angry at her before and the sorceress's reaction left her anxious. But how else was she to govern? She could not rule by making her friends happy and ignoring everybody else. That was how Vaurd had ruled—and he had been deposed by the Law as a punishment. Before Quentin returned from Lydiss, Christine would have welcomed a usurper sent by God to displace her from the throne. But she had made a different choice since then. Until the day her father returned, she would do her duty to the best of her ability. She had failed at this already, angering Duchess Ambith, and perhaps she had failed again just now, capitulating to General Fraydhan's arguments; if that were the case, then she was the cause of untold misery and death. And yet, and yet; could she blame herself when Ambith had been dead-set against the crown since before her birth? Could she truly choose a path that fear urged upon her without knowing she was betraying her stewardship of Chrysanthe?

On the tenth of Ripening the loyalist forces began moving southward, toward Aluvien and the rebel army. Regiments of infantry made up the greatest part of the soldiers, but a sizeable contingent of cavalry led the march. Mounted forces in Chrysanthe were lightly armored, favoring mobility over defensive capabilities. Christine wasn't sure she remembered correctly, but she thought to recall the late Medieva had grown disillusioned with mounted knights in metal armor after several battles in which infantry with pole-arms had thrown the knights to the ground and slain them. Still, among the cavalry there were a few who wore chainmail and heavy shields. Those were the knights of the realm, Quentin's peers. She had met some of them, briefly. They were all old men, and though they appeared greatly honored to meet her, they had avoided her gaze. She had realized later that there were no young men amongst them because the young knights of Chrysanthe were still in the made worlds, searching for her, unaware that Quentin had succeeded; and that these old men were the ones who had not gone forth, because they were too old, or too timid, to risk their lives in the depths of imaginary lands.

The loyalist armies would be supported by several skyships: the *Black Heart, Chiarron, Excelsior,* and *Llermand's Victory.* The *Glorious Niavand, Nonpareil,* and *Winter Rose* would remain behind as messenger ships, shuttling back and forth between the capitals to allow swift communication. Christine would have preferred the *Black Heart* to remain behind, so that she would see Captain Veraless from time to time; she had thought to request it, aware that her wishes might well be honored, but in the end refrained. Captain Veraless had been too eager to fight for her sake; she dared not deny him.

Still, his departure left her with few friends. In fact, if it were not for Quentin, she would have had none. Christine's world had settled into a new order, one that she deeply disliked. Melogian remained distant when in Christine's presence; she smiled as she had used to, but something was missing behind her eyes. If Quentin was also present then, Melogian would grow even stiffer and soon make an excuse to leave.

According to Quentin, she spent most of her time in her workroom; she had barred the door to her apartments and would brook no distractions. When Christine asked him what Melogian was doing there, Quentin made a gesture of ignorance.

"I cannot be sure, milady. I think she may be casting spells, trying to obtain information on Evered's strategies. Presumably it is not going well."

"And she's still angry that I sent the army south. She wanted us to wait."

"I think it is the king's disappearance that worries her most, Lady Christine."

"And me. She's worried something will happen to me, isn't she?"

Quentin looked down at the floor. "I believe she is," he admitted. "But rest assured nothing will. That is what the Lady Melogian is working to prevent."

"I wish she weren't so angry," Christine said. "I made the best decision I could."

"It was the correct one, Lady. The Lady Melogian is angry because she is trying to achieve the impossible and reproaches herself for her failure. You are not to blame."

Christine sighed at this. She wanted to believe Quentin, but her heart still stung from Melogian's anger. Still, what was done was done. The army was on the march, and when it met Evered's forces, then there would be blood and slaughter.

Alone in her workroom Melogian sat cross-legged in the center of a runed circle and tried to focus her perceptions across the leagues, to divine Evered's intent, foretell Casimir's next move. She failed, as she had failed so many times before; she would have wept in frustration had she still been able to cry. She had not felt this inadequate in years. She ached for her master's presence, knowing that whatever she found impossible he always could achieve with little effort.

Her eyes closed, all her senses turned inward, she felt herself drifting away from her purpose and remembering the years of her training. If she could not be with Orion in actuality, she would seek him out in memory, sate herself with a ghost of her heart's desire.

Orion had come into the world in 5910, in the early days of the Casthen lineage; he often told Melogian stories of this period of his life, dizzying her with casual mentions of people who had died a hundred and fifty years before she was born. But his memory actually reached much further back, for he had been written into existence brimming with a hundred times the knowledge of any mortal man. He knew the exact number of people who had died at the Battle of Chatter's Ford in 4008, and the way that their sword blades had been forged and tempered. He knew the name of every king and duke for the past three thousand years, and he could draw perfect likenesses of each one, something he would do when otherwise deep in thought. Melogian had spent many an evening studying her tomes, sunk in the leather armchair she favored, while Orion sat close to the fire and ruminated, his gaze far-off under his bushy eyebrows; at his elbow would be a dozen sheets of paper, a thin stick of sanguine gripped in his fingers. And as he pondered things beyond her speculations, he would draw, not even glancing at his work. Melogian would begin to steal more and more glances at him, forgetting her lessons. Face after face bloomed upon the sheet under Orion's hand, a gallery of portraits from the depths of time. The mage would come back to himself whenever Melogian began to pay too much attention to him. He would frown at her, reminding her of her duties, and she would sigh and bend her mind again to the runes in the book. When fatigue made her cross-eyed, Orion would pat her head and close the book, then lay his drawings upon the cover. She would point at one face, then another, and Orion gave them names and dates. It was a little like the way her father used to tell her stories at bedtime; she would not allow herself to think this, for it made her too sad.

She had known serenity in those days, the simple rhythm of a life lived with repeated effort bracketed by rest, a smooth progress toward a goal that need never be attained. Now she blamed herself for not having studied in the proper direction, wasting too much energy on lore that in the end would prove futile and neglecting important areas of knowledge, simply because she found herself unsuited for them. Why had Orion not driven her harder, pushed her to meet the difficulties head-on and overcome them? Perhaps he had believed he would always be there while Melogian lived.

Casimir, meanwhile, was coming up with forgotten spells from the dawn of time. She knew he had to be cheating, employing a subterfuge to gain this elder knowledge; but what difference did that make? As long as she remained ignorant of his methods, she could not emulate his prowess. And even without this advantage, Casimir's power would have been a match for hers. So she found herself pushed harder and harder against a wall: She must find ways of overcoming Casimir's spells, but she could not discover them. She had gone through books by the dozens, arranged her knowledge in lists and tables, sought for new insights and keys, all in vain. Devising new spells was a long and mentally damaging undertaking; had she had five years of idle time before her, she might have set out to perfect a minor working. She had days to discover Casimir's secrets, and she lacked the basic skill to cast her mind afar without a preexisting anchor to draw its perceptions. She could have probed Vorlok, if Casimir hadn't set up wards superior to her own, that completely blunted her percipience; she could not let her senses roam at will over huge distances.

The defenses of Testenel had not been probed in the past several days, which she believed meant Casimir was focusing his attention on the rebel army. No doubt Evered had ordered his wizard to accompany his troops. When the two armies met, Casimir would use his spells to upset the balance of combat; a child could have predicted this.

Which meant that Melogian should have accompanied the loyalist forces to counter Casimir's influence—save that this left Testenel insufficiently defended, open to a spell-borne attack. It was impossible to convey to others, to that close-minded Fraydhan, to the hidebound Duke Archeled, but also to Christine and even Quentin, just how much risk was involved here. Casimir could evoke an eidolon; had he also mastered matter transference? He could certainly summon a whirl and bring himself and a half-dozen soldiers to Testenel in a matter of hours. Could he then attempt an assassination, or simply another abduction? The made world in the center of the Royal Gardens had proven a gaping trap; and while the others were more distant and did not offer unimpeded passage down their mouths, still Melogian lived in dread that Casimir should make another attempt and bring Christine into the made world of the library. Its gradient was shallow, she reminded herself, the made world was somehow bounded. Even if Christine should be drawn into it, Melogian could fetch her out . . . as long as she stayed close by. So she remained pinned here like a moth to a corkboard, ineffectual, waiting for a disaster that never came.

❧ Twenty years before the present, the duchy of Kawlend had sided with Vaurd's line against the Hero Edisthen. Ordinary men have brief memories, and so they called it the Usurpation War, as if there had ever been only one, or even the Great War, as if it should outrank all earlier conflicts. Yet to one vouchsafed a longer perspective, it might seem more like a schoolboy skirmish. Gone were the days when mage strove against mage in displays of power that shook the roots of the mountains. A thousand years after Creation, the mages Chævold, Muspelmed, and a wizard remembered only as The Eyeless had fought a tripartite engagement at the margins of the world that had leveled hills and filled up valleys, changed the courses of rivers and poisoned the very ground for nearly twenty centuries. By the halfway point of history, the secrets of such mighty spells had been lost, yet when gathered to opposing sides in large numbers, wizards could still wreak large-scale devastation. The Carmine War constituted a turning point; afterward, wizards' powers were diminished enough from the heroic days that they found themselves at significant risk from common soldiers. Through a combination of folly, treachery, and plain ill luck, the wizards who had been drawn into the Carmine War were decimated and the majority of the sorcerous lines of the land extinguished forever. The history of warfare thereafter gave very little space to magic.

The Usurpation War had engaged two wizards: Mathellin on the side of Kawlend, while Orion defended Edisthen. Throughout the conflict, the wizards vied mostly against one another, each attempting to nullify the other's magical influence. Orion proved superior to Mathellin's efforts but refrained at first from bringing his power to bear against the rebel troops. As the conflict dragged on, he changed his mind and began to employ his spells to harass and demoralize the enemy, intensifying his efforts as time wore on. Finally, at the battle of Lelderien, Orion had unleashed such virulent magic against Kawlend's troops that they were broken and scattered, leaving them to be slaughtered by their opponents and precipitating Duchess Ambith's surrender a few days later.

On the purely military side, modern writers made much of the strategy and tactics of the Great War. Someone like Fershan might spend whole chapters on the subject, unaware that he was, for the most part, praising raw amateurs to the heavens. The sovereigns of Chrysanthe during the first half of the fifth millennium had exalted war as the greatest art, cultivated armies as a man might cultivate abances, striving to increase the population at the same time as they slaughtered it in incessant battles. Records of the time would have been dismissed as fiction by any sane modern reader; the early seventh millennium was a peaceful age, the population long since fallen back to a more sustainable number, the art of war still practiced but only as a last resort and not a holy calling.

❧ Evered's companies set out at dawn from Vorlok. Casimir rode near the front of the line, keeping a watchful eye on his demons, which formed the vanguard.

Circumstances had more or less forced their arrangement on him: The seven-limbed demon and the firedrake loathed each other so much that they constantly tested his control in their mutual lust to battle. He was forced to put them at each end of the line, and to send the firedrake flying into the distance at regular intervals. At the center, he put the terrapin, which advanced somewhat faster on the road than in open terrain. The men followed, keeping a cautious distance from the demons.

Duchess Ambith had promised them that regiments from the Kawlendian army would join up with the units Evered had gathered under his direct command once their march brought them to the great road that led directly northward, linking Aluvien to Tiellorn. While Vaurd's sons accompanied the army, Ambith however would remain in Aluvien; her generals would defer to Evered's leadership. This was more or less to Casimir's liking, since Evered might well lose his sense of perspective and command a foolhardy attack out of sheer spite. Gathering the demons was a more crucial part of the plan than he had expressed to Vaurd's sons. They not only ensured victory, but a swift one at that. A war of attrition, supported by Casimir's magic, would have been winnable in time, even with only Kawlend's forces against those of the other three duchies, as long as Evered's hotheaded leadership did not interfere. This frontal attack on the throne was unsubtle in the extreme, but it had a decisive advantage: Evered couldn't possibly spoil a strategy built on a lightning-swift advance into enemy territory.

When dusk came, Evered's forces halted. The men built fires and hunkered down to eat, turning their glances away from the demons. Casimir compelled the latter to take rest as well, though for a fact several of them did not require sleep of any kind. The firedrake slowed its flight, alighted softly onto the ground; then it swallowed the end of its own tail, arranged itself into a perfect circle, and closed its eyes. The flames abloom over its body quieted, until it merely sputtered sparks like a circle of burning cable. The faces on its sides shifted their features and opened their eyelids, revealing gaping empty sockets, and their mouths opened in soundless screams. A thin sulfurous vapor issued from these orifices.

Casimir went to each of his demons in turn, repeating in words the command he had already given mentally. There was no need for this, save that the soldiers badly needed the reassurance; Evered had insisted upon it. So Casimir went first to the firedrake, which was already sleeping; then to Egrevogn the ogre, who had terrorized the marches of Archeled three millennia before, and who was still remembered in fairy tales, though under the wrong name. Egrevogn was nearly twelve feet tall, with a massively-jawed head set upon sloping shoulders and no perceptible neck. He sat on his haunches and combed clawed fingers through the squirming serpents that were his beard. "Hungry," he rumbled at Casimir as the wizard came to him. "Feed now?"

"You're about to be served," replied Casimir. "Wait a bit."

"Wan' a nice juicy girl," said the ogre, "screamy and fat."

"You will eat what you are given, and nothing more," said Casimir for the fifth time, and ignored Egrevogn's displays of annoyance as he strode to the next demon. This was the terrapin, large as a fishing vessel, each scute of its shell boasting a spine shaped like some fantastic weapon. The demon's eyes were half lidded and it seemed not to hear Casimir's injunctions, though its foot-long claws quivered at his passage.

The cloud-demon was next, its body naught but a mass of motes whose swirling never slowed. Casimir touched its mind with the greatest reluctance, as its intelligence was so alien to his that communication with it was like trying to argue with a nightmare. It was no more capable of sleep than of immobility; the best Casimir could achieve was to keep it drifting no more than ten or twenty feet from a given position. For centuries it had been contained in a bottle the size of a thumb, sunk twenty leagues from the shore of the Eastern Ocean, under a thousand feet of water. It understood air and water, earth and fire, life and death; anything else it regarded with a blank incomprehension. Absent the compulsion on its will, it would kill, idly but without pause, reacting to life and movement the way a plant might bloom in response to sun and rain.

The fifth demon appeared pleased Casimir was coming to talk to it. This was the only one of his charges that could hold an intelligent conversation. Bound into stasis by a band of Heroes of the fourth millennium, it had remained aware the entire time. What would have driven any natural being utterly insane had been for it an opportunity for unparalleled cogitations. When Casimir had unearthed it and lifted the stasis, it had thanked the wizard gravely for freeing it and joined his service without the least complaint, gladly offering him the fruit of its two and a half thousand years of meditation.

"Good evening, Master," said the rider astride the pale horse. It cocked its head to the side, injecting the illusion of an expression on its face. "Bide a while. I would tell you more of Cipheris and the spells she wielded."

"Another time, Mehilvagaunt," said Casimir, looking not at the rider but at the horse. "You are to remain in this place and rest as the others."

"You already gave me that command, Master, and you know I have rested my fill in twenty-five centuries. If you wish to discuss your strategies with me, I might have some interesting contributions to make. Or does Lord Evered desire to converse? At least let me speak to one of your soldiers. . . . You there, the blond one! You look a bright lad; I can tell you tales you'll remember all your life. I can make you laugh like no court jester can—"

"You will not address, nor attempt to initiate a conversation, with any member of this troop, Mehilvagaunt; the prohibition is absolute and total, excepting only myself. Am I finally clear on this?"

The rider heaved a sigh like a deflating bellows. One hand reached up and pulled down the corners of its mouth and stretched the gray cheeks; sparse charcoal brows drew down over the withered eyes in their shallow sockets, producing a grotesque expression of sadness.

"I hear and obey, Master, and I remain ever at your disposal."

Casimir hurried away. Though it might appear by far the weakest, Mehilvagaunt was the most dangerous of his charges. It possessed genuine knowledge and its insights were truly profound; but every word it uttered built up a spell in whose net it could catch anything with ears to listen. Its mimicry of a human mind was perilously convincing, and in fact Casimir had been taken in at first, believing he had found an ally. He had grown aware of Mehilvagaunt's influence almost too late to order it to desist from its attempt. Had the demon succeeded, Casimir would have been little more than a puppet like the rider astride its back. Even now, when Casimir's orders appeared to cover every contingency, Mehilvagaunt sought and would doubtless find chinks in their logic, trying to escape its durance. More than once, Casimir had been tempted to get rid of it, to bind it once more beneath the ground and leave it for some other fool in the far future to find; yet in the end he always convinced himself Mehilvagaunt was too useful to abandon. The thought that the demon itself might be responsible for this reasoning had crossed Casimir's mind several times; once the campaign was over, the wizard firmly intended to rid himself of Mehilvagaunt for good.

The last demon was the seven-limbed one; like most of the others its name was beyond pronunciation and must be held in the mind as an abstract chain of symbols rather than sounds. Its hatred for its subjection was stronger than all the rest's put together. Casimir sensed that in some ways it was more intelligent even than Mehilvagaunt; but its mind was somehow blunted, either because of its long confinement or through some innate limitation. All it felt was an overwhelming hatred of all life save its own, with particularly searing rage directed at the firedrake and at Casimir. This demon constantly strove to break its bondage through sheer force alone; but on sheer force Casimir held the advantage, for the strength of his will was proportionately greater than any demon's. He was a man who never doubted himself, and on this base of serene arrogance his power throve, justifying ever-greater confidence. To Casimir, the world was a toy, meant to be played with; any game he played he could not but win, in the end. And so he held even the seven-limbed one under his power, with a bit of straining at times, but never more than that.

Done with his task, assured of the demons' quiescence until morning, Casimir went to Evered's tent and was admitted inside, to arrive in the midst of a scene.

"But I *need* it, Evered. I'm thirsty!" Innalan was pleading.

"You will contain yourself. I will have you sober while we wage this war."

"It's just one blasted cup I'm asking for!"

"Not one drop," said Evered in a tone that brooked no argument. Innalan was about to reply, then seemed to grow aware of his own trembling. He stared at his hands for a minute, holding his left in the right, yet unable to stop their shaking. He sat down abruptly, head hanging, like a puppet whose strings have been cut.

Casimir swept his gaze across the tent: Olf, seated in one corner, looked miserable, clearly wishing he could do something to ease matters and just as clearly having no idea what that could be. Aghaid had pursed his lips as if to contain a sneer of distaste. Evered stood in the middle of the tent, scowling down at his younger brother; then he turned to face Casimir and barked a question at him.

"All six are resting, m'lord. I will rouse them come morning," the wizard replied smoothly. He knew how to soothe Evered's temper, most of the time. There was an art to it, as one must not appear so obsequious as to be mocking Vaurd's heir.

"They won't bother anyone, then?"

"No, m'lord. They will remain quiet."

"Fine. I will go speak with the troops now. I can trust you to enforce my prohibitions on alcohol, can't I, Casimir?"

"Of course, m'lord."

"I expect Mathellin to return from his scouting soon enough. When he does, keep him here until I return."

"As you say, m'lord."

Evered gave Casimir a suspicious glance before striding out of the tent. His movements were ample and strong, but jerky all the same. Casimir guessed Evered was torn between ecstasy at finally marching to battle and utter frustration at having to deal with the vagaries of a moving army. For a fact, his hold over the baronial forces put under his command was weak. Casimir's demons served to prop it up. Once they had linked up with Kawlend's army, they would constitute a truly dangerous fighting force. Tomorrow, or the day after, no more.

Casimir sat himself at the table. He poured himself some water and sipped at it, while Innalan fidgeted and avoided everyone's eyes. God's balls, but Vaurd's sons were miserable company, thought Casimir, wishing in that instant he could return to that unworld he had gained access to, to find other echoes of Heroes from the long-gone past. He'd keep himself polite, refrain from any hostile actions, promise to grant favors back in the real world; anything for a conversation that did not consist of groans of dismay, inane chatter, or bitter ruminations over past injustice. Had he felt even a shade more bored he'd have left the tent at that moment to have a chat with Mehilvagaunt itself.

BOOK VI

The War

1. The Demons

The loyalist armies marched southward for ten days. Given the support of several skyships, they were assured of excellent scouting, and at first the leagues stretched past without notable incident. They passed through the lands at the core of Temerorn and soon reached the barrier formed by the Hedges. There were four openings in the mazelike corridors running through the Hedges, which allowed straight travel across the tall bushes without hindrance. The road south from Tiellorn naturally took the southern opening. The troops were slowed in their march only to the extent that they needed to funnel into the exact width of the road: The passage might be straight, but it was ten yards wide and not an inch more.

The road heretofore had been paved for its entire length, with flat stones set down ages before; as it reached the Hedges, the paving was interrupted and a grassy stretch of earth replaced it. It looked as if no one had ever walked there. Left and right walls of foliage rose to a great height, with great flowers blooming still, gold and purple. The armies advanced, a mere six men abreast, as if entering a canyon. Horses and soldiers, leaving the road, trampled the grass of the passage.

By the time the last men came through, the grass had been worn away and only bare earth remained. They walked through the Hedges; passages opened to the left and right, pristine and silent. No one took them, though there was no sense of menace coming from them. It was possible to become lost among the Hedges, but one had to be an idiot: The corridors did not form a maze as such, given that they frequently intersected and so did not much impede movement. Of course, the made world Errefern did open somewhere in the southern part of the Hedges: Crossing its threshold meant being lost in infinity. Even then, it was said clear warnings had been set in place, to make sure unwary travelers turned away. So an *illiterate* idiot might still be at risk. . . . Birdsong could be heard, and the blooming flowers wafted a heady perfume. Unmaintained by human hands, the Hedges slept on in mystery. At the end of the leafy passage, the paved road resumed and the elder magic of the Hedges was left behind.

There had been many villages on the way until now; as the armies entered the outer marches of Temerorn, settlements became rarer. Humanity was fairly thinly spread on the world and vast stretches of land were empty of habitation. Southern Temerorn had little relief: Occasional low hills rose in the distance, no more. This was mostly plains land, with many woods but no real forests. The duchy of Archeled, by contrast, was renowned for its three great forests. Its soldiers viewed this march much like a stroll through a well-tended park.

This was no forced march and the armies made steady, moderate progress, following the road. They reached the town of Darvien and spent a night there. In the morning, Temerorn's and Archeled's soldiers crossed into Kawlend. The border was unmarked, as exact delineations were considered irrelevant: Darvien was Temerorni, and the land beyond its immediate southern surroundings was Kawlendian. An hour's march south of Darvien, a token force of a dozen infantry bearing a flag in the colors of their duchy stood across the road. They challenged the loyalists, asserting Kawlendian sovereignty over the land and refusing them passage in the name of Duchess Ambith. With grave courtesy a mounted detachment went to speak with the Kawlendians, overruled their objections, and captured them. The enemy soldiers were disarmed, bound at wrists and waist, and taken to a wagon meant to carry prisoners of war. This development having been anticipated by everyone, the Kawlendians appeared more relieved than anything else. Unless an exchange of prisoners was to occur before the end of conflict, the war was over for them.

The loyalist troops well knew that Evered's forces, combined now with Kawlend's, were gathering to meet them. Twenty years ago, the engagements had started earlier in the campaign, as Kawlend's forces had moved north with some speed while diplomats dickered. General Fraydhan wanted this second war to be fought much nearer Aluvien, bringing to bear the power of the realm in a clear and memorable fashion.

Let Duchess Ambith attempt to replay history with a different ending! She would still lose. Temerorn's logistical situation would be more problematic given the greater length of its supply lines, but this mattered only in the long run. Fraydhan intended a bold, decisive strike, to shorten the conflict. Nevertheless, he planned carefully and took steps to allow fallback positions along the way. Four skyships patrolled the air above his troops, sometimes darting forward to scout for the rebel army. Fraydhan had requested a bolder scouting effort, but Captain Veraless, whom the regent had promoted to Air Strategist in Chief, emphasized caution, citing Melogian's worries about Casimir's magic. Despite Fraydhan's urges, Veraless had proved obdurate: None of the skyships would approach the rebel forces prematurely.

Still, Fraydhan was provided with enough intelligence of enemy movement that he could estimate where the two armies would meet. This estimation agreed so far with his plans; if all went as expected, his forces would reach their destination a full day before the enemy, giving him ample time to prepare for battle. Fraydhan keenly loved this orderly aspect to war, the marshaling of might, the planning and the execution; it was when chaos reared its ugly head, when the neat ballet of men dissolved into a screaming melee, that the whole experience became sour. He had drilled his troops as best he could so that communications would flow freely in battle, allowing for detailed orders. The Archeledians were to an extent an unknown quantity, as was their general, Leoch, whom Fraydhan barely knew and regarded as suspiciously young. Nevertheless, Leoch seemed willing to defer to Fraydhan as the more experienced of the pair, which should be good enough.

The loyalist armies reached Fraydhan's chosen destination on the nineteenth of Ripening, as planned. So far they had met with negligible resistance and the campaign had proceeded as smoothly as any exercise. Fraydhan gave well-rehearsed orders and arrayed the troops in good order. He was then taken aloft aboard *Chiarron* and was pleased to witness the near flawless execution of his directives from the air. Infantry and cavalry deployed themselves as per doctrine, in beautifully symmetrical patterns.

Fraydhan had planned flexibly and chosen a series of potential battlefields, spaced along the road, according to the relative timing of the opposing forces. This was not the southernmost of the list, but it was the furthest one he had expected to be able to reach. It stood a good distance from any significant settlement, and profited from favorable terrain. There was little cover, forestalling ambushes and other crude, ungentlemanly strategies. A stream ran to the east, then turned west and crossed the road not far to the south. This stream created a natural line of defense, though this late in the season the water ran quite low. The bridge over the stream was stonework, not something that could be destroyed though it could be defended. The terrain layout belonged in a military textbook.

To the west Fraydhan had set the Temerorni forces, Archeled's soldiery to the east. As the hours passed, the loyalists settled in and established a stronger defense, without losing their mobility. Wagons were set along the curve of the stream and some defensive pits dug, to channel attack from that direction into narrow corridors. Evered's army might well attempt to attack the loyalist forces from the west, where the terrain was more suited to a cavalry charge. He might even divert some of his forces to an attack while attempting to bypass the conflict with the greater portion of his army, hoping to bog down the loyalists while the rebels drove toward Tiellorn.

Fraydhan had planned for this eventuality, since it was the best course Evered could take. By contrast, to attack the loyalists head-on would put the rebels at a clear disadvantage, since the opposing forces were greater in number and better disciplined. This course of destiny what was Fraydhan hoped for: if mad Prince Evered overruled Ambith's leadership, then the rebel forces might well be crushed in a foolhardy attack. Even if Ambith's greater wisdom prevailed, still she could expect no miracles. At best for her, she would lose the war in a matter of weeks. Fraydhan dearly hoped it would take mere days before Kawlend was humiliated.

As evening fell, the skyship scouts confirmed the approach of Kawlend's army directly south, along the great road that linked Tiellorn to Aluvien. The rebels showed enough sense not to march on, and settled in for the night, as did the loyalists. The morrow would bring action.

ᔕ The twentieth of Ripening dawned gray and unexpectedly cool. The weather had been almost perfect during their march south; now rain threatened and an unpleasant wind from the east gusted.

By midmorning, General Fraydhan went aloft once more, aboard the *Black Heart*, to direct the fighting from the best possible vantage. Three teams of flagmen were at hand, to relay his orders to the ground troops. As the skyship gained altitude, he saw the rebel forces clearly: ordered ranks of soldiers now moving north at a determined pace.

Signals were sent to the loyalist forces on the ground; Fraydhan clutched the railing as he waited for the engagement to start. Veraless, for his part, had deployed the other skyships widely, covering the field of battle and beyond.

The skyship captain stood beside Fraydhan, at first silent; after a while, he spoke quietly into Fraydhan's ear.

"Doesn't it remind you of the beginning of the Great War, sir? I mean, this is basically the same as it was then."

"It does," said Fraydhan. "And I do take your meaning, Captain: I am well aware that this is not the Great War of twenty years ago. I do not expect Ambith to repeat the errors of two decades past."

"Of course not. She'd have to be insane. So . . . why is she doing it all over again?"

Fraydhan spared Veraless an annoyed glance. "I do not speculate about motives, Captain. Only strategies and tactics."

"Does a burned skyship fall under strategy, or tactics?"

"I would place it under the rubric of sabotage, Captain; you know my feelings on the matter."

"Yes, I do. But with all due respect, General, I don't trust them. I've learned that life has this habit of kicking you in the rear when you least expect it."

Fraydhan kept his irritation under control. "Whatever situation arises, I'm confident our troops will deal with it, Captain Veraless."

Veraless said no more, and both of them waited in silence for the battle to start.

The rebel forces closed in on the loyalist armies, then they slowed and halted. Men and women in the livery of Kawlend faced their counterparts in purple and yellow, or pale blue and white, and did not move. Veraless squinted at the ground below; but they were much too high to discern individuals.

"You don't think Evered's with these troops, do you, sir?" he asked Fraydhan.

"Hrm. I guess not. They all bear Kawlend's colors. It is reasonable to assume he is staying safely behind."

"That's showing great restraint for him."

Fraydhan shrugged elaborately. "He's been imprisoned in Vorlok for two decades; perhaps it has taught him wisdom, or at least caution."

The pause stretched out; the rebel army roiled slightly in back, while its forward ranks remained tightly ordered. Then suddenly bugles shrilled and Kawlend's army attacked.

Rebel archers let loose a cloud of arrows, which proved ineffective against the disciplined ranks of the loyalists, who protected themselves with their shields. Then a company of infantry moved forward, while the cavalry remained in reserve. With a ponderous motion, hundreds of soldiers came together in battle along the river line.

Fraydhan watched the battle eagerly. Veraless sent messages to the other skyships by flags. *Chiarron* and *Llermand's Victory* kept an overview from the air; *Excelsior*, meanwhile, advanced over the enemy troops and lost altitude. From its position, it began to drop pebbles over the Kawlendian troops. One could not aim at any specific ground target in this fashion, and there were limited supplies of stones. But a pebble cast from such a height would kill if it hit. A fistful of stones became a rain of death from above. The Kawlendian forces could do nothing in return, the skyship being beyond arrow range.

Fraydhan noticed the effects of the missiles, which were not as predictable as he'd have liked, given the difficulties the skyship had tacking against the wind, which wanted to push it westward. Still, it sowed confusion in the enemy ranks, while the loyalist forces engaged the rebels and not only held their ground but managed to advance, beyond the stream line.

The far left flank of the rebel army had crossed the stream to the west and now moved toward the engagement, but Temerorni cavalry countered the push and prevented the flanking action. The focus of combat drifted slowly westward, as if it too were being pushed by the wind. Fraydhan matched the progress of battle against his plans and found them still basically in agreement. This war had always been winnable purely from time and attrition, though the cost in lives would have been high and political considerations made such a future uncertain. Far, far better to strike deep and clean, like a surgeon lancing an abscess. Let them rout this army here and now, and Ambith would be forced to surrender.

An obscenity from Veraless brought him out of his momentary reverie. Veraless pointed to the west, where another skyship was making its way toward them, colored flags fluttering at its prow. And beyond that ship, a pencil line of smoke was rising in the sky, against the paler gray of the clouds.

"What is going on, Captain?" asked Fraydhan, disquieted.

"Flagman!" bellowed Veraless, ignoring the general. "Relay the message!"

A woman strapped halfway up the rigging replied in a stentorian voice. "Sir! Ship is *Llermand's Victory*; she signals 'Attack!' Enemy reinforcements . . . Overwhelming force. *Chiarron* is down. Repeat: *Chiarron* down! She signals 'Fire,' sir!"

Veraless turned his attention to another one of his ship's signal crew. "Order *Excelsior* back! Archers, get weapons ready! Dive, ten fathoms!"

Acknowledgements came from various parts of the ship.

"Get me more details!" Veraless demanded of the flagman, who unrolled and waved a series of flags of her own. After a while, clarification came from *Llermand's Victory*.

"*Chiarron* attacked by airborne enemy, sir! They say . . ." She was silent for a moment, reading the flags with disbelief, blinking her eyes and reading them again as *Llermand's Victory* repeated the message. "Confirmed, sir. Our ship says a snake, sir! A . . . flying snake . . . burned *Chiarron*."

Fraydhan protested: "You've misread, flagman! This is nonsense!"

The woman was already circling a purple flag in the *repeat* signal. "*Llermand's Victory* repeats, sir! 'Airborne enemy . . . S-N-A-K-E . . . D-E-M-O-N.'"

Veraless met Fraydhan's incredulous gaze. "Well, General," he said in a voice roughened by emotion, "now life gives us that kick I was talking about."

The warning from *Llermand's Victory* explained the fate of the *Spindrift*. Two skyships had already been destroyed by, of all things, a flying demon. Veraless had never dealt with supernatural threats before, but he was well read and knew tales of ancient battles with demons from the Book of Shades. Whether the accounts he'd read were accurate or not, he now had a good idea of their situation: The loyalists were facing a creature whose reason for existence was as an antagonist to humankind.

Obviously the demon possessed the power to ignite the wood the craft were made of; probably it breathed flame. Veraless ordered the *Black Heart* to lose altitude until it hovered just above the ground; if they were attacked, his crew would not have to face the choice of either burning alive or falling to their deaths. He waited for *Llermand's Victory* to reach them while General Fraydhan sent messages to the ground troops. From what Veraless could see, the battle had been going in their favor; with the arrival of a demon on the scene, things were about to change.

He tried to think matters through: This was clearly Casimir's doing. Melogian kept repeating the wizard had unearthed old, forgotten spells and wielded them now in service to Evered. A fire-breathing, winged demon, summoned from Hell, would cripple the skyships until it was brought down—if it could be.

Now assume the worst: What if the demon could indefinitely interdict the air to the loyalist side? Then their superiority was decreased, yet they remained stronger than the rebels. So today's battle could still be won, Ambith's forces compelled to retreat step by step toward Aluvien. This could not be the extent of Casimir's contribution to the battle. With an old trooper's pessimism, Veraless felt certain that the wizard still kept a few nasty surprises hidden in his sleeve.

Before *Llermand's Victory* could reach their own forces, Casimir's demon came to the attack. Veraless felt his stomach knotting itself as he beheld the thing. It was still distant enough that he could only get a general idea of its appearance, but that was more than enough. It was longer than the skyship itself, and a good six feet in diameter. The color of bright copper, it was swathed in flames that dripped off its flesh as sparks from a burning branch waved through the air. It had no wings: It did not fly so much as swim through the air, the way a snake would crawl upon a flat surface.

From everywhere aboard the *Black Heart* came shouts of alarm as the crew saw the situation. The demon caught up with the fleeing *Llermand's Victory*; Veraless thought it would now breathe out a gust of flame, or wrap itself around the craft. It did neither; instead, it reversed course abruptly, whipping its tail end about. A dozen clumps of flame detached themselves from the demon's flanks and were hurled toward the skyship.

Less than half hit; perhaps the gusting west wind had spoiled the demon's aim. Still, it was more than enough. The sails of *Llermand's Victory* caught fire, as did its hull. Its crew were prepared, however, and they appeared to keep the fires under control. In fact, the sails soon smoldered out, though the hull remained aflame. The skyship had been reducing altitude and it now increased its rate of descent, canting its outriggers.

Veraless had been so caught up in the drama unfolding in the distance that a cold touch upon his neck made him start and almost cry out. He tilted his face around and upward and was hit twice more: raindrops, finding their way around the brim of his hat.

He returned his attention to the airborne battle. The demon was attacking once more, lobbing flame at the skyship. Fire blossomed on the deck, to be swiftly doused. But the underside of the hull was still burning, threatening to damage the keel that kept the ship airborne. *Llermand's Victory* was now overflying ground troops as it reduced its altitude further. Rain was not yet falling in earnest, still only a sprinkle of drops. Veraless found himself wishing for a late-summer storm: What would a good drenching do to the demon?

Llermand's Victory tacked desperately against the wind, now well in back of the loyalist troops; it endured another attack from the snake demon, and this time it appeared that the fire could no longer be brought under control. The skyship now flew barely twenty feet above the ground; the mole's burrow beneath it had been cranked back up in its lodging, or else it would have been plowing up a furrow in the ground and capsizing the craft. As flames spread through the canvas of the sails, in spite of the drizzle that now fell from the clouds, the crew abandoned ship: Rope ladders were lowered over the railing, in spots that were still not at risk from the flames, and the crew swarmed down the rungs. One by one they jumped down from the ladders to the ground; and the snake demon attacked once more, shaking down flame from above. But it ignored the men scrambling away from their doomed craft, and hurled its flame only against the abandoned skyship.

Llermand's Victory continued on its course, now burning like a torch. Veraless bellowed to his crew to be ready to deploy full sail and rise. If the doomed skyship should collide with his own, both would end up destroyed. But long before this could become a real risk, the skyship's keel, weakened by the flames, broke in half. The hull splintered as its lift flickered like a candle in the wind. Then *Llermand's Victory* fell to the ground and collapsed into ruin.

Veraless now expected the snake demon to assault the *Black Heart* and *Excelsior*; but it did not. Instead, it swam back and forth through the air, as if it were at the end of an invisible tether. Indeed, after a minute or two more it retreated to the west, like a hunting hound recalled.

Veraless ordered the *Black Heart* to unfurl sail and head west, to gather the survivors of *Llermand's Victory*. Skimming low above the ground, they swiftly reached the downed ship's crew and took them aboard. The task was completed in fifteen minutes; last to come aboard, as she had been last to leave *Llermand's Victory*, was her captain.

She accepted Veraless's condolences woodenly and refused to meet his gaze. The left side of her face was smudged with soot and some of her abundant chestnut hair had been singed off. There was a bright red burn on her cheekbone she refused to let anyone attend to.

"We have to warn Fraydhan," she said, her breathing labored.

"We're headed back there," said Veraless. "We'll be able to talk to him in a few minutes. Please sit down, Captain Wallathin." And when she had at last folded herself into a chair, though she still swatted away the physician who wanted to treat her burn: "Warn him of what, exactly?"

"Of what's coming. We saw what's in the vanguard of the reinforcements. There are more demons headed this way."

Veraless suppressed a flinch and kept his voice even. "What did you see, Captain?"

She coughed wrackingly before she was able to reply. "About a thousand infantry, most in red and green livery. No marching formation to speak of, so they would be Evered's rabble. But they weren't alone. We saw things in the fore. There was an ogre; twice the height of a man, three times as broad. There was a beast . . . it moved like water flowing down a pane of glass; it had too many legs, and a head like a nightmare. I can't describe it. And there was something else, something bigger than a war wagon, round and spiky, farther back. We couldn't see it well."

"All right," said Veraless. "Please rest, Captain. You've done well. In a few minutes we'll inform General Fraydhan of all that you saw." For all that it promised to rob Fraydhan of his superior airs once and for all, Veraless did not relish the task.

༄ Fraydhan received the news from Captain Wallathin with dismay. He was reluctant to believe her, no matter that Veraless vouched for her utter honesty. He could not deny the existence of the fiery demon that swam through the air, but that more of them led Evered's forces seemed absurd. Veraless insisted that since Evered's wizard clearly commanded the services of one demon, it was possible he had bound more of them. Feeling like a fool, Fraydhan dispatched warnings to his troops to expect enemy reinforcements of an unexpected caliber.

Evered's forces now reached the site of the battle. While the Kawlendian host directly to the south had been able to contain the loyalist pressure, to the west they had dispersed themselves too much and so had shown less resilience. Archeled's troops, ably led by General Leoch, had pushed home the advantage and begun to bend back the rebel line. The irregulars coming to reinforce Kawlend's disciplined soldiery would by themselves have achieved little. But the demons that accompanied them were another matter entirely.

The Archeledians had received warning of incoming reinforcements; still, they were taken aback when Egrevogn the ogre strode into battle, swinging a six-foot wooden club sheathed in metal at its tip. Egrevogn's skin, green as the depths of a forest, was leathery and thick as a man's hand was wide; as if that wasn't protection enough, he had outfitted himself with a plastron of boiled leather, wooden greaves, and a composite shield hammered together from a dozen ordinary bucklers. Blows from his club stunned his enemies, crushed their shoulders, or outright broke their arms. He laughed a gargling laugh as he struck and slew; ropes of drool dripped from the corners of his mouth.

Some of the loyalist soldiers tried to engage him and failed; the rest decided to flee before the ogre, and found themselves attacked by a far worse adversary. From the ranks of Evered's forces the seven-limbed demon had emerged. It moved like quicksilver, impossibly fluid, uncoiling its length as its seven paws rested one after the other upon the ground, arching itself high over the heads of Evered's soldiers. Its metal skin reflected its surroundings so well that at times it became almost invisible, little more than a disturbance in the air; the next instant its claws would tinkle on a stone, its face would flex as it opened wide its jaws and it became so obviously present as to make everything else disappear. When a man met the gaze of its black eyes, his soul quailed within him and he fell insensate.

The seven-limbed demon wreaked havoc amongst the loyalist troops; in minutes their line became completely disorganized, and the Kawlendians were able to push back—cautiously, for neither demon was predictable in its movements.

Fresh troops came to the rescue, but the loyalist line had buckled so badly as to almost collapse; losses were heavy until the soldiers were able to retreat to the river line, scrambling down the banks, splashing across the stream, and climbing up the other side. There they proved able to hold back the enemy forces, at least temporarily. The demons seemed disinclined to press their attacks further for the moment. The bridge itself had been solidly defended from the first; the troops that defended the farther side retreated but the span remained clear.

The rain worsened, coming in larger drops, while the fitful wind strengthened and blew cooler. It now seemed that commanders on both sides wanted a pause; the loyalists clung to their defensive positions and watched the demons retreat within the mass of enemy soldiers.

General Fraydhan contemplated the ruin of his careful plans and tried to salvage what he could. He strengthened his eastern flank in prevision of the enemy crossing the stream farther to the east and set his best tacticians to devising means of overcoming the demons. Time passed without either side making a move; from the reports Fraydhan received he deduced the Kawlendians were strengthening their own position, but without observation from the air he felt almost blind.

He went to confer with Captain Veraless, who stayed near the grounded *Black Heart*. Both it and the *Excelsior* had been grappled to the ground, but could take to the air in short order. However, neither captain was willing to risk his craft and his crew. Veraless pointed to a brilliant form flying in circles in the distance: The snake demon still swam burning through the air.

"It could attack your ship at any time, Captain," Fraydhan pointed out. "If you let it destroy the *Black Heart* on the ground nothing will have been gained."

Veraless scowled. "It could, but it hasn't. As soon as my ship and *Excelsior* were grounded, it lost interest. Doesn't that suggest something to you?"

"That it cannot see things that lie on the ground?"

"No, that it was ordered to attack our ships while in flight. I don't know how demons think, or how wizards control them, but it makes sense to me that there are limits to their control. So maybe Casimir can force the demon to attack our ships when they fly but he can't make it bombard them when they're aground."

Fraydhan could offer no effective counterargument. He went on with the task of strengthening his positions as best as the limited intelligence allowed, sending out patrols to detect any attempts at flanking maneuvers. The day had darkened as the clouds grew thick; above the cloud cover, the sun progressed toward the horizon at the still-slow pace of late summer. It was possible Kawlend would try for an attack before dusk, but Fraydhan doubted it, unless the clouds should break.

They did not, though the rain stopped well before dusk. The evening remained gray under the overcast; the rebel forces stayed put. Fraydhan retired to his tent and discussed strategy with his officers as well as Leoch. They built up new plans from the ruins of the old, trying to foresee the contingencies presented by Evered's demons. But these were such radically unknown quantities that every strategy the officers envisioned was built on shaky foundations.

❧ Night fell. The air had grown cool, a foretaste of autumn. The cloud cover thinned and eventually rent itself; stars shone down from the vault of heaven. Soldiers slept uneasily. At a campfire Veraless sat down next to Captain Wallathin, who appeared to have finally gotten treatment for her injuries. The burn on her cheek slathered in ointment and protected by a square of gauze, she gazed morosely into the flames, chewing on a piece of marsh-root, every so often hawking a greenish-brown clot of saliva at the ground.

He sat silently next to her, and after some long minutes she began to speak. Muttered obscenities at first, then finally clear speech.

"I can't believe it, Veraless. God's eyes, demons leading an army. Three demons out of the Book of Shades, with men following behind. God has sent us an army straight out of Hell; what can it mean? Is He speaking against the king?"

"You're no priestess," said Veraless bluntly. "Don't you dare try to read the Book. That army wasn't sent by God. It's Evered's army, and whatever supernatural troops are in it, they only come from one man. Melogian warned us that Casimir controlled powerful magic. He's found a way to summon and bind demons to his service, that's all."

Wallathin snorted and spat.

"Wonderful. So it's just a wizard, not God Himself who has turned against us. What's our strategy, then, to deal with this mere man and his pets? Did General Fraydhan tell you what he intends to do?"

"I was at his tent with other officers earlier; there was a place for you but you didn't show up."

"No fucking ship left to command, Captain."

"But your crew are still alive, Captain Wallathin. You're still a competent officer; you don't serve your sovereign well by sulking in a corner."

Wallathin flushed red but wouldn't meet Veraless's gaze. He said nothing further and remained seated next to her, looking into the flames himself. He did not much blame Wallathin: She was beyond her depth, badly shaken by the loss of her ship. She had been a petty officer of twenty-seven at the time of the War of Usurpation, and her rise through the ranks had been achieved entirely in peacetime. The destruction of *Llermand's Victory* spelled the end of her career, but Veraless doubted she was concerned with that at present. Wallathin shared the worry of every loyalist commander present, and she had seen more closely than any one of them what Casimir's demons were capable of. Come morning, when the rebel forces marched to the attack, how were men of mere flesh and blood expected to withstand the assault of demons?

Fraydhan had ordered a double ring of sentries to ward the camp. All of them were fully alert, wary of enemy stratagems. Still, none of them discerned what passed between them, silent as the grave and near invisible against the darkness. One lone sentry did see it, for an instant, making the stars flicker; she blinked and rubbed her eyes to clear them of the film that she thought had settled there, and when she was done the stars were as clear as before.

In the light shed by the flames of a campfire the demon was more visible; but those who saw it took it for smoke at first. It hovered and pulsed, then settled upon a group of sleepers and slew them. Of the seven men caught in its grasp, two rose up, arms flailing, mouths open, their chests heaving, unable to draw breath. The other five never even woke up. The demon's constituent motes clustered about the standing men in a deadly filigree, as if some colossal spider had spun a web from their bodies. Cries of alarm from their companions aroused the camp as the struggling men collapsed. Three soldiers tried to enter what they still thought of as a strange patch of smoke; two were forced to retreat immediately, while the third reached a fallen man only to collapse in turn.

Panic spread; more fuel was thrown upon the fires, and in the increased light the cloud-demon became somewhat more distinct as it drifted across the ground, pulsing at its core, to engulf further victims.

Soldiers retreated pell-mell; the few who attempted resistance wasted their arrows, their sword thrusts, and their lives. The demon, however, did not chase its prey. It drifted serenely along and slew those whom it engulfed. It was enough to step out of its way to be safe. The whole camp was soon roused, and panic was avoided by the expedient of surrounding the demon with a ring of soldiers carrying torches. They kept pace with the demon, warning everyone of its approach. For two hours the cloud-demon wandered thus through the camp, drifting seemingly at random. There were no further deaths, but one or two close calls.

Then, without warning, the cloud-demon elongated into a tall column only to collapse back upon itself, accompanied by a chorus of alarmed cries. Yet this was no attack: The shrunken demon now moved back toward the rebel army. Its pace was quicker, but still no faster than a jogging man. Soldiers made way for it and its warders until it passed beyond the ring of sentries.

General Fraydhan had expected an attack would follow the cloud-demon's incursion and given orders accordingly; but in fact the rebel army remained quiescent and the loyalists' vigilance was unnecessary.

Standing close by the grounded *Black Heart,* Captain Wallathin remarked acidly to Veraless, "Yet another demon. No wonder we didn't notice this one at first. God's eyes! That's five of them. That wizard of Evered's is playing with us like a cat with a mouse, isn't he?"

"Yes. He's going to wear us down. The duchess could have attacked while the demon was sowing panic among us but that's not the plan, obviously. The rebels are resting until morning, and then we'll face them with our nerves unstrung. Whatever we try to do, they can loose a demon upon us to scuttle our hopes."

"So what do we do?"

Veraless chewed on the tip of his mustache. "We'll have to retreat. We can't push against Kawlend's troops now, they've got the advantage. We'll have to march back north until we can link up with Duke Corlin's forces, and even then we probably won't be able to make a stand. They'll drive us back to Testenel, harrying us all the way. Evered and Ambith are planning to win this war by attrition."

"So we do what they want, is that the plan? We just run north and they grind us down as we flee? Don't we have a wizard of our own, or is she just too comfortable in her apartments to bother coming down with us?"

"Don't badmouth the Lady Melogian, Captain. She would help us if she could. We can dispatch messengers to warn her of the situation."

"We're sixty-five leagues south of Tiellorn! It'll take forever to ride to Testenel.

By that time we'll all be dead! A skyship could make the journey in half a day with good winds!"

Veraless laid his hand against the hull of his ship, feeling the smoothness of the jointed planks. The *Black Heart* was beautiful, fast, dependable. Commanding her had been the crowning glory of his life. Now if he took her into the air he would ensure her destruction.

"If there was no demon to destroy it, it would; but there is."

Wallatin chewed her marsh-root energetically and spat another huge gob. "There's only one demon, Veraless, and we have two ships," she said.

"What do you mean?"

"You said yourself there are constraints of range involved. Evered's wizard has his demons on a leash, and it's not infinitely long."

"I'm no wizard. I *think* this is how things go. But assume I'm right; what's your point?"

"If we take *Excelsior* aloft, we'll draw the firedrake's attention. And while it attacks *Excelsior*, you can lift off in the *Black Heart* and fly for Testenel. If you make full sail north you should be able to slip beyond range before the demon is done with *Excelsior*."

"God's eyes, Wallathin . . ." Veraless felt his throat tighten. "I can't ask Captain Rober to sacrifice his command, his ship, and his crew."

"You won't, and he won't. I'll do it. I'll take *Excelsior* aloft and draw the drake's attention. I'll take volunteers from my crew; we know how to damp down the fires. We learned the hard way. We can protect the hull in advance, make us harder to destroy."

"You could get yourself killed. And Rober will never let you take command of his ship."

"Fuck him. I'll get Fraydhan to order him to surrender command to me. I should be dead now, anyway. If we don't try this, we'll have to retreat on foot and tow the skyships with us on ropes. What's the point? I'm going to talk to Fraydhan about this. Are you with me, Captain?"

Veraless swallowed, his hand still touching the flank of his beautiful ship. Then he broke the contact and nodded.

⁂ Dawn came. The loyalist army had endured no further harassment during the night, despite General Fraydhan's worries. Their situation this morning was not much better than it would have been anyway. To the south, across the stream, the main bulk of Kawlend's army stood fast. To the southwest were Evered's irregulars. Somewhere among the enemy ranks the wizard Casimir hid himself; his demonic allies by contrast were all too noticeable. On the eastern flank, Egrevogn the ogre had awakened from his slumbers and put on his armor. A tall man's head barely came level with his belt buckle. As he paced back and forth to warm his blood, Egrevogn chewed on a torn-off human leg that still dripped juices. His beard of snakes undulated and hissed. The seven-limbed demon remained coiled some distance away; its open eyes were like pits into the void. On the south flank, amid Kawlend's host, a new demon was now to be seen: It looked like a tortoise as large as a house, red and black in color. The center of each scute of its carapace sprouted a huge spike, shaped like some fantastic weapon, no two alike. Its head, wrinkled and ridged, swung to the left and right as it breathed. The steam of its exhalations had withered the grasses it bathed. Soldiers gave it as wide a berth as they could.

The crew of the *Black Heart* had taken its posts aboard ship and stood ready to cast off the moment Captain Veraless should give the order. Not far away, *Excelsior* had been crewed by volunteers. Captain Wallathin stood at her prow, in her stained and scorched uniform. Captain Rober watched her from a distance; Veraless could not read his expression. General Fraydhan had approved Wallathin's plan and given Rober an order he did not dare disobey. Had it been the *Black Heart* Wallathin had wanted to commandeer, Veraless would have refused and sacrificed himself rather than let someone else destroy his ship; Rober lacked the pigheadedness to do the same, or maybe he simply had better sense.

A breeze had risen, strong enough for decent maneuverability. But now the rebel bugles sounded and their forces went on the attack. On the south flank the terrapin began to walk toward the bridge with great thrusts of its legs, its movements peculiarly mindless. To the east Egrevogn trotted forward, a hundred soldiers on his heels as he roared and swung his club. The seven-limbed demon uncoiled and began a slow advance.

The loyalist host received the charge as best it could. Its archers sent arrows whirring at the attackers. Those that were directed at one of the demons were wasted: The terrapin's shell was impervious to the shafts, while the seven-limbed one was like liquid metal. Egrevogn, for all his size, was swift enough in his movements to bat away the missiles with his shield.

When the forces met, the rebel advantage became undeniable: The terrapin lumbered forward like a battle wagon, crushing any who stood in its path. Soldiers had to give way before it. It crossed the bridge, which was barely wide enough to hold it, in a few strides, smashing its defenders to a pulp. Rebel footsoldiers followed and spread out, no longer blocked from attack by the banks of the stream. Meanwhile, the seven-limbed demon proved nearly as terrible an adversary; it was able to stretch itself across the stream with ease, and once more soldiers followed in its wake. Egrevogn, meanwhile, waded across water that barely moistened his greaves and climbed up the bank like a man would climb a few steps. Gargling and humming, he smashed men's skulls with every swipe of his club. For all their careful preparations, the loyalists were outmatched.

As the situation worsened, Fraydhan gave the order and *Excelsior* took to the air. It headed toward the battle lines on the western flank, rising rapidly. Soldiers aboard whirled their leather slings and let loose their missiles at the enemy, letting gravity do the bulk of the work.

All this time, the firedrake had been visible in the distance, swimming loops through the air. Now it came forward, drawn by the skyship's presence. But at the same time, the seven-limbed demon broke off its attacks and retreated across the stream. It turned its head away from the loyalist troops and toward the incoming demon, which it watched approach as its entire body quivered.

The firedrake headed toward *Excelsior* and attacked her as it had her sister craft.

The crew aboard *Excelsior* put up a grim, efficient defense and the firedrake's initial volley of flame did no significant damage to the skyship. *Excelsior* continued on its westward course, drawing the firedrake away from the loyalist positions, its crew lobbing missiles overboard at the enemy troops below and readying their defenses against the demon's fire.

The *Black Heart* meanwhile had taken to the air and deployed its sails to best effect. The wind was not as fresh as Veraless had hoped, and he made them gain altitude as swiftly as he could, hunting for more favorable air currents. Steadily they moved away from the battle, from the doomed *Excelsior* that still resisted the firedrake's attacks. Three hundred feet up the *Black Heart* found better winds and picked up speed. The helmsman brought their course more fully to the north. The ship responded well, lightened as it was: During the night every unnecessary bit of equipment had been removed from the *Black Heart*, even to the mole's burrow and its articulated arm that had been cut loose from the lower hull.

They were leaving the battle behind. With every passing minute the distance between them increased. Veraless could still clearly see the firedrake engaged with *Excelsior*; the skyship was aflame in several spots, but still it fought on, and still the demon swam through the air around it, unaware of the other prey escaping.

He kept watching, as the scene shrank with distance, as *Excelsior* began to burn more and more. He saw her become a brand, saw her fall. But the firedrake did not come after the *Black Heart*. They had won free, at the cost of Wallathin's life and that of everyone else aboard *Excelsior*. And now they must fly north to Testenel, to report disaster.

❧ Melogian had gotten into the habit of wandering through Testenel. The exercise calmed her nerves, helped break her thoughts out of the rut into which they tended to fall. She still worried, still dwelled on her powerlessness, still wasted energy trying to anticipate and deny Casimir's strategies. But for a few hours each day, she could sink into the rhythm of her walk, she could ponder the intricacies of the corridors and try getting lost.

Lovemaking might have done an even better job than these walks, but she had vowed nevermore to approach Quentin. She knew he still did not understand his own heart, but to take any further advantage of his naïveté would have been wrong. But because she couldn't bring herself to state the bald truth, out of respect for Quentin mixed with wounded pride, their relations remained strained. She would have loved to stroll outside with him, or merely to sit by his side and talk; but he felt too much pain at their meetings, and kept himself irreproachably correct. Neither of them seemed likely to unbend at this point; and so she foresaw a long time of frost between them.

Her wanderings took her, as they frequently did, to the Grand Ballroom. In the middle of one of its walls was a huge fireplace, at present dead and cold, shielded by a foliate screen of silver-chased steel. Above this fireplace had been hung one of the two fleshpaint portraits of Edisthen; Melogian made a duty of viewing them at least twice a day.

The portrait was more than life-size; the Edisthen who lived in the canvas was nearly nine feet tall. He had been depicted standing before heavy crimson drapes, his left arm bent at the elbow. His clothes were plain: white robes embroidered with small touches of gold and purple at the hems. In contrast with Vaurd's sartorial flamboyance, Edisthen had always favored spare dress.

Whenever she visited one of these portraits, Melogian would spend minutes peering at it, trying to wring from it some information about her king's condition. Yesterday, she had thought to notice a difference; this morning she had not been so sure. Momentary changes were not reflected in the portraits, but long-term physical alterations were. Should Edisthen be significantly wounded, the portrait would reflect it. Were he held in durance, the marks of the fetters on his wrists would fade into being in the fleshpaint. And so Melogian inspected the portraits regularly, to check on her king's welfare as best she could, always hoping to divine a clue as to Edisthen's whereabouts within the made world.

This time, once she had come within three paces of the portrait, she was immediately struck that his expression had changed. A few heartbeats of staring confirmed it beyond a doubt. There had always been dourness in her king's face, and that had not changed. But the lines of strain and misery at the corners of his eyes were altered—subtly, yet undeniably. The man who looked back at her from the canvas was no longer so haunted as he had been.

And his face was darker than it had been before; this was the blush of sun on his cheeks. He was not imprisoned in some dank dungeon, then, but kept outside. Perhaps, dare she hope, not a prisoner at all? She thought of Quentin's proposal to seek after Edisthen as he had done for Christine. Now was not the time, but if it had been done once before it could be done again. If Edisthen had won free of captivity, then his flight into the made world would halt. He did not possess the power to move *beyond*; still, stopping his progress along the gradient would be sufficient. Given time, he could be located and brought back. The knights of Chrysanthe who still bore the Quester's Gifts could be sent into the made world in search of their king. Melogian herself would help them; the task was so much easier when one knew within which world to seek. . . .

And as she gazed at Edisthen's face, she saw a blue spiral appear on his cheek, coming into being between one moment and the next.

For an instant Melogian remained staring, her pulse painful in her throat. Then she called out, her voice loud but breaking. Guards clattered into the ballroom, weapons at the ready. Melogian motioned them to her side, then pointed at the portrait that looked down upon them from the wall.

"Lieutenant Dyann," she said. "Tell me, do you see something on His Majesty's cheek?"

"Aye. It . . . well, it looks like a tattoo, Lady."

"Exactly. A tattoo. But it wasn't there a moment ago."

"What's it mean, then, Lady?" asked Cotter, the other guard.

"It means His Majesty's just been tattooed," Dyann replied in an impatient tone. "That's how fleshpaint works."

"Except," murmured Melogian, "that it isn't. Fleshpaint does not react so fast. If Edisthen was tattooed this morning, then it should have taken days, weeks, for the image to change fully. There would have been a cloudiness on his cheek at first, then an outline would have become visible. . . . This spiral flicked into being as fast as a butterfly opens its wings."

A terrible thought crossed Melogian's mind then. "Cotter, go fetch me Sir Quentin of Lydiss, at once," she asked. She remained with Dyann, staring at the picture. "Is it changing, Lieutenant?" she asked. "Can you tell?"

"I don't think so, Lady."

She was breathing fast. They kept examining the picture. After several minutes, just as Melogian was beginning to relax, a matching spiral appeared on the other cheekbone.

"By the Book, no!" she cried out.

Quentin was just entering the room. Melogian called out to him; he ran to face the fleshpaint portrait. "What are those?" he gasped, and as he spoke more tattoos blossomed onto Edisthen's face, spreading so as to cover almost every square inch of it, like a boiling of snakes. Melogian gripped Quentin's arm tightly, her nails digging into his flesh. It was a foreign mask that looked back at them now from the canvas, coils and ropes of blue on darkened skin, framed by a beard that lightened to white, one black hair after another changing hue.

In the middle of the painted face, the pale blue eyes remained changeless, their gaze serene. Edisthen's hair became pure gleaming white; his beard first lengthened, then shortened. Though the fireplace was cold, Melogian could feel faint heat radiating on her face. She brought a hand closer to the painting: It was as warm as a fevered child. A subject's clothes in a fleshpaint portrait remained a fixed element, unless he were to be deprived of all raiment for weeks or months at a time. Yet Edisthen's clothing now grew blurred; the paint appeared to bubble, as if something were goading the fleshpaint beyond the limits of its inherent magic, forcing it to change, change, change again, faster than was possible.

The king's skin lightened, now creased by deep wrinkles. The spiral tattoos that had covered his face paled, then guttered out like spent candles. Throughout it all the clear blue eyes remained constant, until it seemed to Melogian the universe pivoted around their luminous gaze. Dirty yellow now the hair, absent the beard, the face a wizened apple. Still the eyes glowed, throbbing with life; for a moment of madness, she felt Edisthen would step out of the canvas, so vital were they.

And then the end came, as the heat from the portrait was starting to make the frame smolder. The paint blurred all over the canvas; with a crackling sound flecks of pigment dropped onto the marble tiles, a rain of blues, reds, and greens. What remained flowed and regrouped itself into stark new shapes.

The red drapes had gone from the background; it was dull black now, the darkness of a cave. A skeleton sat on the dusky ground, its white bones carefully arranged; golden ropes tied the arms and legs in ceremonial crossed positions. At each shoulder, a five-pointed metal star had been hammered into the bone.

Cotter let loose a limp string of blasphemies; Dyann halfheartedly ordered him to silence.

"He is dead," breathed Quentin. "But how? He . . . died of old age in front of us, in the space of a few minutes."

Melogian forced herself to relinquish her hold on him. "That is exactly correct," she said. Her voice was shaking. "He died of old age. We saw the passage of decades— of centuries."

Quentin looked at her, bewildered.

"You mean we are seeing the future? Has Casimir enspelled the portrait to show us what will happen?"

"Don't be daft, Quentin. Fleshpaint does not prophesy. It can only show the present."

"What happened, then, Lady?" asked Lieutenant Dyann.

"Isn't it obvious, you fool?" She couldn't contain the anger boiling inside her. "Our king was pulled into the made world. He was taken so far down the gradient that he eventually reached a part of the dream where time flows at a different rate. That was the trap Casimir had set for him from the beginning. Don't you see? Why do I have to explain it all?"

She was breathing in gasps; her arms shook. "Deep enough into a made world, all rules of nature are circumvented. All Casimir had to do was to pull him down there, ever farther down. He was never harmed. The Law extends to the farthest reaches of reality, and it protected him throughout his journey. You saw him, you saw what he became. He lived on and on in the made world, for five hundred or a thousand years—and he died of old age, while we stood here taking a single breath."

She was shouting now. "What are you all doing standing? Kneel down, dolts! Doff your helmets! The king is dead! The king is dead!"

Dyann and Cotter, ashen-faced, knelt, helmets under their arms. Quentin went to one knee, and Melogian collapsed next to him, turning her gaze away from that of the grinning skull in the canvas, sobbing dryly.

"The king is dead!" shouted Quentin; then he took a huge breath and bellowed at the top of his lungs: "Woe! Woe! Woe! The king is dead! *Long live the queen!*"

"Long live the queen!" echoed the guards, striking their fists against their breastplates.

Melogian had wrapped her arms around herself; she was staring at the marble tiles, her mind almost empty. She still sobbed, but had almost forgotten why.

"Lady," Quentin said gently in her ear. "Lady, we must spread the news. First and foremost, we must bring it to the Lady Christine. Will you come with me?"

She could not manage to speak and just nodded. But she resisted a moment more Quentin's gentle urging to stand. She felt if she could just untangle the rage and grief, the shame and the guilt and the obscene relief that moiled within herself, then perhaps her tears might flow. But her emotions remained in a hard, poisonous knot, and her eyes stayed dry as stones.

2. The Funeral of the King

The *Black Heart* fought with contrary winds and weak breezes and finally reached Testenel by early morning of the twenty-third of Ripening. As they neared the castle, Veraless became aware of the black gonfalons hung from the towers; his heart sank.

In a harsh voice, he gave orders to dock. His mind was boiling with speculations. Before even his ship had properly stabilized, he jumped onto the platform and strode to the entrance into the castle. Two guards stood there; they wore black veils over their helmets.

Veraless saluted as crisply as he could manage; the guards responded in kind.

"Welcome, Captain Veraless," said one of the guards, a stocky woman with a phlegmy voice.

"What . . . what news?" asked Veraless.

The other guard spoke. "The king is dead, sir. He died down in the made worlds. We don't even have a corpse to bury, sir." The guard's tone strove to disguise outrage; he was very young, and obviously felt the world owed him greater fairness.

Veraless closed his eyes in relief. He had feared for Christine's life. The horror of the guard's words was sinking in, but still, the heir to the throne lived.

"When did the funeral take place?" he asked.

"It hasn't, sir. His Majesty died yesterday. The ceremony is set for noon."

"Very well. Get the support staff up here and have them see to the ship. First Mate Redell will be in charge. I need to go."

"Captain Veraless, sir?" the female guard asked as he was trying to stride away into the castle. "You don't recognize me, do you? I'm Orlanthe. I served under you, in the War. I was a messenger on your staff."

She lifted the veil as she said so, giving him clearer sight of her face. Veraless nodded after a heartbeat.

"Orlanthe. Yes, I remember. It's . . . it has been a long while."

"Sorry to ask, sir, but how's the war going, sir?"

Veraless heaved an aggravated sigh. "Right now, it's not going well. I've come to report and get some help. Now I really have to go."

She held up her hand. "Captain . . . You'll hear some people say things. About the king, I mean. I won't repeat them; but I want you to know no one in the guard believes them. We all mourn for the king. He was good man and we loved him. We all believe he was a true Hero."

Veraless could find no words in reply; he nodded brusquely and turned away so that the guards should not see his eyes fill with tears.

Down through the corridors of Testenel he went; black-veiled soldiers saluted him as he passed. He replied to no questions and strode along so fast he could hear the breeze of his passage whispering in his ears. At the door to Melogian's apartments a guard told him the sorceress was within, but had given instructions not to be disturbed.

"Let me pass," Veraless ordered. But the guard proved obdurate.

"I'm sorry, Captain. The Lady left strict instructions."

"I'm overriding them."

"You can't, sir. Your authority is over skyship crew and ordinary soldiers. Not palace guards."

Veraless drew himself up. "What's your full name, boy?"

"Carl, son of Maude and Feyfnir, from Carhilion."

"Any brothers or sisters in the army, Carl son of Maude?"

"My older brother Threlgass, sir."

"Well, Carl, our forces are on the run from the rebels right now. They're being harassed by demons out of Hell. I need magic to succor us immediately. Now if you want your brother to live, you will let me talk to the Lady Melogian."

"Threlgass is in the Fifth Company, they're camped just outside Testenel, sir."

To be caught here arguing with that mulish guard when he should be mourning his king! Veraless felt a sudden fury seize him. With an oath he pushed the guard aside and kicked at the door, bellowing Melogian's name at the top of his voice. The guard attempted to grab him by the arms; Veraless screamed and struggled. Servants and other guards rushed to the scene, trying to break up the scuffle. Presently the door opened and Melogian appeared. With a few curt words she put an end to the wrestling match. Both men were panting and disheveled; Veraless had lost his hat. Melogian dismissed the guard with an imperious gesture of the chin, then turned her gaze onto Veraless. Though his blood was still aboil from wrestling with the guard, he could not fail to notice the haunted expression on her face.

"I have to speak to you now, Melogian," he said, but his tone was apologetic. She shut her eyes as if in exasperation, but compressed her lips and nodded, motioning him within.

He shut the door on the circle of onlookers and watched Melogian slump into a chair by the empty hearth. She buried her face in her hands. "In God's name, I've only gotten an hour of sleep in the last day, Veraless," she said. "Why couldn't you give me some peace?"

He leaned on the door, feeling his muscles tremble. He was so tired. *I am an old man,* he told himself. It was not the first time he had had that thought; but now he knew it to be true. While Edisthen had lived, Veraless had felt oddly eternal; the Hero's flesh did not age from year to year, so that he looked forever in his early fifties, even though he had spent barely twenty years in the world. In his presence, confronted by this paradox, the skyship captain had felt as if he had been vouchsafed a sip of eternity, a sense that time was a far more complex thing than a line, that since one might be at once old and terribly young, the yoke of future turning into past might somehow be thrown. Now he knew these fancies for what they were; knew there was much less time left before him than what had gone before; knew himself trapped by mortality. That this was the fate of all men brought him no comfort whatsoever.

And yet against this cold despair a part of him responded with heat and fury. He was a soldier; he had seen more death than anyone ought to, and he had come out of the experience hardened. His king might be gone, but he would never let himself desert his friends. He recalled the idiot guard's face and felt his anger return.

"You slept for an hour, Lady? Well, that's an hour more than I had," he retorted, putting sarcasm in his voice and finding his feelings followed the lead of his voice. "I can't spare any sympathy for you right now. Things are going very badly. Our forces ran into the rebel army sixty leagues south. Evered has irregulars from the marches, as well as Kawlend's legions. Not so much a problem on their own. But Casimir has also raised up five demons from Hell to send at us."

Melogian looked up at him in surprise.

"There's an ogre, and some cloud-thing that roams at will in the dark and suffocates men. And a fiery snake that flies. That's what destroyed the *Spindrift*. It took *Chiarron*, and *Llermand's Victory*; and *Excelsior* died with all aboard, so that the *Black Heart* could escape. We can't prevail against the demons. We need magic. I came to get you, so you can destroy these horrors and give us a fighting chance. The *Black Heart* will be ready to return as soon as you want."

"What makes you think I can help?" she said after a long silence, her gaze directed downward. "I'm just an apprentice, Veraless, just a stupid girl who plays with magic. My king died, and I couldn't do anything to prevent it. And now you think I can destroy demons with a wave of my hand? Don't be ridiculous. There's nothing to be done."

Veraless made no move, and she did not look up from her misery. After a time he asked, softly: "How . . . how did he die?"

"He was pulled down. Along the gradient, deeper and deeper into the made world." Melogian shuddered. "He was taken so deep that time for him ran faster and faster than for us, until in the span of one of my heartbeats he lived for centuries. He was murdered and yet he died of old age. I keep trying to imagine what it was like; by the end of his life, did he even remember us? All of us here who yearned to see him again, who expected somehow, one day, he would return . . . He was gone from us barely six weeks. But by the time he died, he must not have thought of Chrysanthe and all those who loved him in a hundred years."

Veraless sat himself on the floor, close by Melogian. "I'm sorry," he said to her, though she would not look at him and instead buried her face in her hands. "I was wrong. I should have let you seek for him longer. When I told you not to keep at it, it's because I was jealous. I wanted to go myself, and I was angry that only you could do it, that Orion hadn't granted me the magic to travel *beyond*. That's the ugly truth."

Her shoulders rose and fell once; still she kept her face shielded. "It wouldn't have changed anything. I hunted for him at the surface of the made world when he was already a hundred leagues deep into it. From the moment he was taken, it was too late. Even if I had been with him, I suspect we might never have found the way out. I think Casimir learned a spell that made it possible to compel someone to travel down a gradient even while standing still. Edisthen never had a chance to escape."

She lifted her head out of her hands, gazed at him. Her face was raw with anguish, yet her eyes were utterly dry. Veraless wiped at his own, which leaked unwanted tears. "I knew Edisthen well," he said, "and one thing you can be sure of: He remembered us. A Hero from the Book won't forget. I don't care if he lived ten thousand years: He remembered Chrysanthe and all of us until his last breath."

Melogian nodded glumly. Veraless continued: "But we can't let ourselves dwell on the dead. Not when the living need us. I know how you feel; but you have to let your duty guide you."

She shrugged again, her mouth twisted in self-directed scorn. "What do you want me to do?"

"Fly back in the *Black Heart* with me, or summon one of those flying discs you command, and bring your magic to bear against the demons. If you can keep his demons off, then Evered can't win by force of arms. As long as we're not crippled by the demons, we can take him. Estephor's armies are coming to reinforce us, they can hit him from the flanks—"

Melogian interrupted by blowing out a breath. "Captain Veraless, there's something you don't understand about this whole affair. Simply put: *No one can summon demons.*"

Veraless answered with a puzzled stare and a raised eyebrow.

"Demons cannot be summoned from Hell," Melogian continued. "Because there is no Hell. You know that as well as I do, but you let yourself forget it."

"'None know of the afterlife—'" Veraless quoted.

"'—because none can return.' I know! We like to believe the wicked are punished for ten thousand years after they die, and maybe they are. But even if there is an actual Hell where Black Kelhorn and Talquen are still roasting on a spit, how could one invite the tormentors of the afterlife to a jaunt upon the Earth? The Law says the dead cannot return; that is because nothing from the afterlife, whatever its exact nature, could exist within life. And there are no caves below the mountains where demons live and breed: Six thousand years of magic have failed to uncover such a region. No, demons are accidents of Creation, random outpourings from the Book of Shades. In the early ages of the world there were hundreds and thousands. Now they are all gone, or very nearly. Once or twice a century a demon might be written into existence; I can credit the odd monster emerging at the edges of the world, or crawling upon the beaches at the orient. But these beings still may not be summoned. This is a well-known fact. Believe me, it has been tried; but even when magic could still alter Creation like a hand wiping smooth a patch of sand, it could not be done."

"I don't understand," Veraless protested. "You're the one who told me Clever Niss was a real person!"

"So I did. Nissimandos really was the mightiest demonologist who ever lived. Demons *can* be commanded; they can be bound. The process demands enormous power, but once the compulsion has been laid, the demon can be commanded with a comparatively modest exertion of will. The point is that the demon has to be there to start with: You cannot conjure one from thin air, even with the full power of its name. And now here you are telling me that five demons are in the vanguard of Evered's army. . . ."

Melogian hiccupped laughter. "Did you ever hear the Clever Niss story about the king's gamble—what is it called, 'The Three Who Would See Tiellorn Before Winter'? It's a distorted account of how Nissimandos won free of his service to King Grynault, in 3576. What made the story so notable that all wizardly chronicles agree on nearly every detail, is that Nissimandos achieved his goals by commanding four demons simultaneously, a feat never before or since equaled."

The sorceress was staring at the back of her hands. "I'm very scared, Veraless," she whispered. "I'm terrified of Casimir. However he does what he does, he is the mightiest sorcerer the world has seen in ages—stronger even than Orion. He can take away the ones I love without effort, and there is nothing I can do against it. Did you ever meet him? I did, when I was twelve. He was fifteen years old, already tall and stout. There was something about him even then that I could sense. . . . It's easy to think it was just the normal fascinated dread a girl that age feels about older boys. For a long time I told myself it was only that. But I always knew there was more; there was something sick in his eyes. He had the gaze of someone who looks at the world thinking none of it is real, that he is the only living being in the whole cosmos.

"It goes beyond cruelty, you understand. A man may be cruel out of anger or a sense of betrayal. Such a man acknowledges the outside world is real and relates to him. Casimir treated the world as if it were a show put on for his enjoyment. . . . I can't quite put it into words. Maybe this way: I drank too much wine—it was the first time I'd ever drunk—and Casimir tried to take advantage of it. Now that itself is nothing; since the world was young, men have seduced through alcohol. What frightened me badly as I was fending him off is this: I had the feeling that he would enjoy forcing me, not even because he would take pleasure from my pain, but because it would make a nice entertainment to see me weep and bleed. . . . Oh, enough of this!"

She rose from the chair abruptly, went to a table and poured herself some water from a carafe, turning her back to Veraless who, sensing Melogian had confided far more than she had intended, rose to his feet and tried to ease her mood. He had barely gotten halfway through his sentence when the carafe exploded with a deafening report. Pottery shards whistled as they shot through the air and shattered against the walls. The door opened and a guard barged through, weapon at the ready; Melogian ordered him out with a harsh command; the guard withdrew. Veraless stood mute; none of the fragments had hit him, and it seemed Melogian was also unharmed. The sorceress at last put down her glass and turned to him, though she avoided meeting his gaze.

"Go away, Veraless. I'm dangerous. I'm losing control of myself. There are too many spells in me wanting to be spoken. I don't want to hurt you."

"If I leave you alone," he asked quietly, "will you harm yourself?"

"I don't know. I don't want to." Her voice was so forlorn he wanted to take her in his arms and rock her like a child. He stepped forward and gently put his hand on her elbow.

"Then come with me. Anger is something to be wielded like a weapon. Don't waste your passion on crockery! If you're going to unleash your spells, throw them at Evered's demons. You can make the difference between life and death for us all. Don't let us down."

Melogian raised her head and met his gaze, drew a shaky breath. "I'll come," she said, "but only after I have buried Edisthen. We will inter the bier at noon. As soon as the ceremony is over, I will come."

Veraless nodded brusquely. "Fair enough. You'll have to excuse me, but I won't attend, though."

"It is your decision to make."

"And . . . how is the Lady Christine?"

"In shock. How is she supposed to grieve for a father she never had a chance to know? I was with her for a while last night; she seemed to be bearing up well, considering. I left Quentin by her side; he is the one who can best comfort her."

Veraless nodded and made for the door, but stopped with his hand on the knob.

"One of the guards said I would hear things said about Edisthen that the guards themselves refused to believe. What is it that people have been saying?"

"Some idiots have been claiming Edisthen was no true Hero, since Heroes cannot die in made worlds. Head Priestess Ianthe issued a reminder that this is sheer nonsense, but denying the rumor has only helped it. Some of the palace staff are panicking; Christine doesn't inspire confidence in everyone, not that it's the poor girl's fault. One of the maids held forth such tripe the seneschal ordered her whipped, but it hasn't stopped her tongue from wagging. When I retired last night, people were muttering that Edisthen's fleshpaint portraits were fake."

"Fake portraits? What does that have to do with anything? Besides, they've been burnt now."

"No they haven't. Christine ordered they be kept hanging. Perhaps you should go see for yourself—but be prepared for a shock. Down in the made world, thousands of years have passed and very little is left of the man we once loved."

Veraless could find nothing to say. He left the room and strode through the corridors of Testenel, found himself approaching the Grand Ballroom. There was a crowd at the door and he had to shove his way in. The room itself was designed to hold hundreds of people; it was not crowded as such, but dozens clustered by one spot along the wall. There was no need to shove forward this time: The painting hung high on the wall and was lit by the reflected radiance of the morning sun. From twenty feet away he could see it very well.

For a few painful seconds he held the gaze of the browned grinning skull; in its empty sockets he felt the millennia looking back at him. He understood then why the rumors had started: This was not the way a Hero should die, though it was extraordinary enough. Edisthen should have fallen in combat, defeating Vaurd's lineage once and for all; he should have perished in slaying Casimir's demons; or in his bed, two centuries from now, survived by eight generations of descendants. His mind whispered to him that this could not be Edisthen he was seeing; it was some grotesque representation of Death itself, no more. The age-darkened bones of the skeleton seemed to mock him, and the tarnished metal stars hammered into the shoulders were like a parody of kingly attributes. Had there been a fire in the fireplace, Veraless would have pulled down the painting and fed it to the flames upon the instant.

He turned away, pushed through the crowd, and exited the ballroom through its eastern door, heading toward his quarters.

Mathellin flew out over the land, once more in the shape of a white hawk. For the first few days he had thus served Evered as a scout, helping to coordinate the movement of his troops. Then Casimir had convinced Evered Mathellin would be better used for another purpose.

And given a purpose, Mathellin always followed it. He had been a capable mage, more than capable; yet it was as a shapechanging monster that Vaurd had taken him on. He had been made a political operative, a task at which he excelled. With the coming of Edisthen, he had been forced into the role of a war-mage, in which he had acquitted himself but poorly. It was true his studies had not gone in that direction, as Udæve held battle-magery in very low esteem. It was also true Orion was the mightiest wizard the world had seen in centuries. Defeated and consigned to Vorlok, Mathellin had then been overshadowed by Casimir. He had conspired with the rest of them, but it was always Casimir's ideas that were chosen.

In this war, Mathellin would have been happy to take to the field beside Evered, even as Casimir led his demons as he would have led leashed hounds. To be made into an aerial scout was an implied snub; still, he had accepted it. But this wasn't enough for Casimir, Casimir who basked in the glory of his oh-so-clever mind. Casimir who served Evered, whereas Mathellin had served his father. No, Casimir had yet another wrinkle in the great plan, another task for Mathellin. . . .

It was a good idea, yes. Mathellin might have suggested it himself; Evered ought to have thought of it. But again, it had been Casimir's. Mathellin saw that he had become old and inconsequential: Strange how twelve years that had passed without his knowledge sufficed to turn him from a trusted, powerful ally to a doddering fool who was best sent away from the center of things. . . .

So now, away from the center of the war, out to do a daring deed, deal a great blow against the enemy that mostly involved skulking like a rat. Mathellin had once held the center of the stage of his own life; now it seemed to him that he had been pushed to the wings and almost off. Thirteen years guarding Christine, who had become more to him than life itself, until with her loss his story had become a tragedy. A return to the real world, to find that everything that had ever mattered to him had gone: his mother, his duty to the rightful king, his place at Evered's side. A sour anger filled him.

He would do what Casimir had asked. He would do it because it was part of his fight, because he was loyal, as Vaurd himself had said, up to and beyond death. Yet the dread was growing within him that he would fail at this, just as he had failed at guarding Christine, and that even should he somehow succeed, it would still amount to nothing. He flew on and on, recalling a similar, desperate flight recently, wondering if he would ever do anything other now than flee from one failure to the next.

There was a bit more than an hour left before the funeral. Althea and Rann both had been warning Christine it was time to come get dressed, but she paid them no attention. Instead, she sat at a table, playing a boardgame with Quentin. The game was similar to checkers, but the rules differed at key points, and Christine kept getting them tangled up in her head. Every time she made a mistake, Quentin patiently corrected her.

She felt what she was doing was blasphemous: Surely, with the king, her father, dead, she ought to be wailing and screaming nonstop, tearing her clothes; at the least, she should be sobbing quietly in a corner. But her body betrayed her, whispering treacherously that life went on, that *she* was not dead, and wasn't that a good and wonderful thing? She kept that thought at bay yet she recognized it, this surprising selfishness, as something she had not known about herself. Perhaps everyone felt this emotion in the face of death: this secret, shameful relief that they, at least, were still alive. Even so, what if they did? Should that make it all right somehow for

Christine to feel this way? She could not escape the guilt that rode on the heels of the emotion, and so she pushed it away from her thoughts.

How she wanted to grieve extravagantly; from time to time tears would spring from her eyes and she would welcome their arrival, hoping to dissolve into sobs, but they dried up after a few moments. Quentin had said something funny earlier and she had laughed out loud, unabashedly. At the end of her laughter, she had thought, very swiftly but very distinctly: *Wait, there is something I must remember, that will make me sad again—oh yes, my father is dead.*

As she recalled this moment, shame welled up in her; with a grunt of anguish she swept the pieces off the board; they clattered all over the floor and she began apologizing to Quentin, tears in her voice. What was she doing? The game had been a refuge for her, and now she herself had torn it apart. She buried her face in her hands and wailed, but again the distress died down before it could overwhelm her. She hadn't had long enough to know this dead man who had been her father, a scant three weeks until he vanished from her life again; how can you get to know someone in such a short while, when you cannot stand to be in his presence for longer than ten minutes at a time? She had thought she had the rest of her life to come to terms with him. Now he was gone forever; she could almost hear Dr. Almand clucking in satisfaction at her anguish, his eyes behind their lenses fairly quivering with interest as he planned his next article on the pitfalls of recovered memory among child victims of Ahrimanic rites.

Christine started beating her fists on the tabletop, clenching her teeth and groaning with fury at Dr. Almand, who had broken her and filled her mind with lies, who had cut her off from her father, so that she might as well have never found him again, the man who had held her close as she looked in wonder at the fishes of the shallow sea. . . . Oh, he had hurt her, had Dr. Almand; why couldn't the Law have struck him dead, cut his flesh to ribbons and bled him like a rabbit for the dinner table? She was appalled at her own cruelty and at the same time she kept seeing the parallel slashes into Dr. Almand's flesh, the wounds gaping red and the blood oozing and flowing. . . . The thought that she was insane was roaring in her ears. She was striking the table with ever greater strength, and she knew in a moment she would lash at her own face. Someone was begging her not to hurt herself; and then, unexpectedly, strong arms enveloped her, pushed her against a broad chest. Christine screamed but it was with relief; she clutched at her rescuer, digging her fingers into his back, her mouth against the fabric of his vest so as to muffle her cries.

She knew who it was; she knew it was Quentin who held her; but she would not fear his touch anymore. She hugged him to herself as a very small child might a stuffed bear, hiccupping with sobs. He raised a hand to her head and stroked her hair; she focused on the motion and let it calm her. She could hear Quentin's heart beating fast; her own had drummed a tarantella but it was slowing now.

After an endless time she broke the embrace, sat back in her chair. Quentin had been kneeling at her side; she saw the front of his vest was stained dark with her tears. She wiped with the back of one hand at her eyes; with the other she took Quentin's, to his obvious surprise. She was surprised as well, but something within her had broken; for the moment at least it felt the most natural and safe thing in the world to hold the young man's hand.

She had to swallow her saliva a few times before she could speak. "Will you help me get through this, please, Quentin?" she asked him. "I don't want to collapse like I just did at the ceremony."

"If you did, no one would object, milady. It is proper that you grieve."

"It's not the grief," she whispered. "It's the anger. This is so unfair I want to scream and break things. It's like it's all directed at me, to punish me for something. I know it's not, but I know what it feels like. I want to kill someone. . . . No, I don't. It's just . . . Oh, God, I'm not making any sense."

Quentin covered her hand with his. "More than you know. You are not the only one to feel so angry. Melogian also is furious. In your father she lost a man she loved deeply. And I am angry as well, and many more here. For you, it is the death of your father; for us, it is that of the rightful king. We cannot feel quite the same as you do; but we do feel some of your rage and grief."

She nodded miserably. Surprising her, Quentin went on: "And you are correct, Lady Christine, that this was directed at you. You are being made to feel punished. This is Evered's revenge on you. He has acted against all of us, of course, but I agree with you: It is a personal vengeance. You dared to resist the fate he had thought to write for you. Thus he hurts you, in the only way he is able to go around the Law: by causing you grief and torment. He tormented your father with your disappearance, he now torments you symmetrically."

Christine had expected reassurance, consolation, an avowal that she was merely a bystander to the tragedy. This plain and grim evaluation took her aback. But it did not damage her; to find that her rage and grief were not truly misplaced in fact calmed her. She felt a flame kindle at her core, something hot and corrosive: hatred. She was self-aware enough to recognize the danger in it, but she did not smother it as she would have done half a year ago; she let it burn on, small and controlled, filling her with its energy.

"Thank you, Quentin," she said, and rose from her seat to go get dressed at last.

Althea and Rann fussed over her as they helped the other maids draw Christine into proper mourning-dress. In deference to Christine's dislike of overelaborate clothing, the mourning garb was as simple as it could have been made; but still, for a princess of the realm, for the bereaved daughter of the departed, for the sole heir to the throne, it simply could not be made too plain. And so there were stays to lace, brooches to pin, a triple thickness of veils to array before her face. Christine let her attendants nestle her into the garments, letting her limbs be moved gently into position as needed. She was focusing on the little flame of hatred in her core, making sure it neither went out nor rose too high.

For the final touch, Christine was presented with black lace gloves; she usually refused any such accessories, but this time she drew them on, using more force than was wise. She heard a thread or two popping, but nothing disastrous occurred. Properly attired, she made her way out of her chambers and toward the burial grounds. Quentin did not accompany her; as she went to get prepared, he had retired to his own quarters to change. Melogian was not there either; though Christine would not have refused her company, the sorceress these days made no attempts to be in Christine's presence.

But as she swept out of her apartments, she encountered Duke Edric himself, who it seemed had been awaiting her. His funeral clothes, though austerely flamboyant, did not fit him well; not having packed the requisite items in his wardrobe when he had left Waldern for Testenel, he had been forced to beg clothes from someone else's closet.

Edric bowed to Christine and requested the honor of accompanying her to the ceremony. Not knowing how to respond, Christine merely nodded in reply. She and the duke made the rest of the way together; he was careful never to step ahead of her but always to be half a pace behind. Christine kept darting glances over her left shoulder, and every time his face bore the same grave expression of sorrow. Grief or worry had hollowed out his cheeks and his mustachios hung sadly down; his usually pink face bore an almost waxy pallor. He wore a black fur bonnet on his head, stamped with an escutcheon in the colors of Archeled; Testenel was warm enough that Duke Edric sweated freely under this burden.

Nearly four thousand years had Testenel stood in its place, close to the center of the world. Since it had been built, all the kings and queens of Chrysanthe had been laid to rest within the walls of the cemetery adjoining the castle. The passage of millennia had nearly filled the cemetery, which had never been huge to begin with: What had been a prospect of wide alleyways in the early age of the world had turned into a crowded necropolis where almost no scrap of bare earth remained. Everywhere the eye wandered it saw stone: stone walls of mausoleums, stone limbs of funerary statues, stone steles bearing the names of the illustrious deceased.

The cemetery had not been built close to the central stem of the castle, which would have left it in perpetual shade. For all that this might have been thought apposite, instead it had been built well outside Testenel's main radius. The funeral cortège thus had to walk in shadow for a while before they came into light. This light was grayish, weak: The sky was partly overcast, the air holding a breath of cold that presaged autumn and winter on its heels.

The cortège kept Christine at its head, and Duke Edric closely behind. Servants and guards accompanied the nobles and other distinguished personages who had won a spot in the procession. There was no sign of a coffin, which surprised Christine, who had expected one at the head of the procession.

She had not even caught a glimpse of the cemetery heretofore; once through the gates, making her slow way to her appointed place, she passed between a forest of funerary statues, many much larger than life, almost all of them standing, a few reclining. Queens and kings long since dust towered over her, atop pedestals and mausoleums. Some brandished swords or scepters; some gazed broodingly at unguessable sights; one king was depicted astride a rearing horse, whose clawed hooves still bore traces of gilt. One statue differed from all others; cast in time-dulled bronze, shaped with exquisite skill, it depicted a broad-shouldered man in cape and open-face helm, half-kneeling, bearing a whip in his hand. His face was masterfully rendered, twisted in either agony or rage, the lips drawn back in a harsh sneer. At the base of the monument was an engraved marble plaque; it read: *Here Lies Talquen King of Chrysanthe, Last of his Line. Let All Give Thanks to God for his Death.*

Christine realized she had paused to read the inscription, and was holding up the rest of the cortège; she got into motion again and reached her appointed place without further distraction. This stood at the edge of the occupied area of the cemetery. Beyond stretched a narrow grassy expanse, large enough for maybe another century's worth of monarchs or two.

Perhaps two hundred people were gathered in total. A hole had been dug into the ground and covered over by a black sheet. Amid the mourners and their servants, soldiers stood at attention everywhere Christine looked, armed and armored, a reminder of the war being fought far to the south. Careless of decorum, Christine turned to look over one shoulder, then the other, until she had spotted Quentin, who stood back and to her right, a lone familiar face in a sea of half-recognized features. Officials of the court and minor nobles surrounded her; Duke Edric, at her left hand, seemed more preoccupied by the tightness of his borrowed collar than anything else at present. An official whom Christine did not recognize bowed before her and spoke some orotund phrases. Christine had trouble following him and made no more than an absent reply; still, this seemed to satisfy everyone and the mourners rearranged themselves into a semicircle around the burial plot. There was barely enough space for them to do so. From beyond the walls Christine heard hushed voices; there must be some who had decided to attend at a remove, just over the walls.

Christine found herself near the head of the grave; Melogian stood across from her. The sorceress was dressed in an astonishing gown of a thousand pleats and drapes. The fabric was the proper black of mourning but it shimmered silver and gold in the pale sunlight; it was incongruously lovely. Behind the veil, though, her face appeared flat and pale, and the flesh beneath her eyes was bruised, making them at times look like pits into her face.

Sounds came from the core of the cemetery; heads turned to look. A procession was making its way among the monuments. At its head marched Ianthe, Great Mother of Tiellorn, in her wine-dark robes. Then came three hierophantas, followed by four men carrying a coffin on their shoulders; each man's face was hidden by a dead-black cloth mask and he wore a long cape, but otherwise they were naked, shorn of every trace of body hair. Their bare feet came down upon the gravel of the path with ponderous deliberation. A dozen musicians followed, blowing silver pipes of various sizes and shapes. The instruments raised a shimmery chorus without discernible melody, in which notes seemed to endlessly fly up the scale. Five more priestesses closed the march, each carrying a small thurible aloft in her gloved hands, from which rose a thin smoke that smelled of flowers. The procession arrayed itself in the other half of the circle left free by the mourners. The four bearers let the coffin down onto the grass then sat folded beside it, legs crossed and head dipped between their arms, draping their capes on themselves so that they effectively vanished from sight. The sun now stood directly overhead, visible as a disc through the overcast, its rim noticeably ragged with flames.

The pipes raised a crescendo then faded away. Mother Ianthe stepped forward and addressed the crowd, her voice lilting and formal.

"From the void we arise and to the void we return. Thus speaks the Law: It is given to all but one life to live, and all life must end. We who stand here today have come to honor and grieve for the king of Chrysanthe, the Hero Edisthen. Like us all he was born, though from the words of God rather than the womb of woman; like us all he strove and struggled, laughed and cried, loved and grieved. And like all men at last he died. For Edisthen the Hero, the king, no less than for the least of us, it is so. We are all God's children, whether Hero or man. The love of God our Mother is boundless, but in Her infinite wisdom She did not grant us eternal life. Thus we grieve, and fear, and despair, overwhelmed by this terror at the core of our existence."

A late arrival made his way around the priestesses, to stand finally at the rear of the crowd, a few paces from Christine: It was Captain Veraless. He spared her a momentary glance but then focused his attention on the ceremony, which had proceeded undisturbed. Mother Ianthe spoke louder now, her voice warm and strong, as if she intended to banish all sadness in her hearers.

"Yet in your grief be you comforted; in your fright be you calmed; in your despair be you reassured. We who stand within Creation must revere He Who created it, for in His infinite power He answers our prayers. For all life that ever was shall endure; all thought that ever was shall endure; all that ever was shall endure! As words in a book endure, to be read ever anew, so do all things stand eternal in God's sight. Our beloved King Edisthen is dead, yet he lives on forever in God's mind, to be recalled entire, throughout all of time, and beyond its end."

The silver pipes blew a discord that first wavered then resolved to triumphant harmony. From this simplest of chords a melody at last blossomed forth, mingling sadness and joy.

The bier was lifted up and borne down into the grave, and now tears were at last rushing forth from Christine's eyes, as if the music had wrung them out of her. She let herself sob as the empty coffin was laid to rest, aware that this was what she was supposed to do and dimly astounded to find some comfort in this knowledge.

Ianthe came up to her; men in black livery were bringing her father's two flesh-paint portraits in their gilded frames.

"My Lady Christine," said the priestess. "It is traditional that the portrait of the deceased be burnt. At first you ordered that these should remain hanging. Now I ask you again: Do you wish for King Edisthen's fleshpaint portraits to remain?"

Only a token attempt had been made to cover the portraits: a simple black sheet, which was lifted by the wind. Christine looked at the portrait thus uncovered and shuddered. The bones of Edisthen had darkened; the stars at his shoulders were lumps of rust and the cords that had bound the bones together had rotted away, so that the skeleton was losing its shape. She foresaw that soon it would be nothing but a tumble of moldering brown sticks; what would be the point of the picture then? "Burn them. Burn them!" she said, turning her face away. She closed her eyes for the remainder of the ceremony. The pipes played on and the priestesses sang. The assembly recited responses from the Lesser Book. Dirt was spaded into the grave and clattered as it rained down upon the lid of the bier. Wood and canvas were burning nearby with a crackle; when Christine turned her face to her right she thought she could feel a touch of the flames' warmth.

And then it was over. Silence had fallen. Christine opened her eyes, wincing at the daylight. Both Duke Edric and Captain Veraless were offering her their arm. She knew she should take Edric's, she knew she dreaded any man's touch. She took the arm of Veraless, surprising both of them. Once beyond the cemetery, Veraless bowed to her and disengaged himself. "I must leave you now, milady. Duty calls me back."

Christine nodded absently at him and watched him walk away. Duke Edric now took her other arm; she let him do as he pleased, numb to her core. She wanted Quentin, but couldn't see him in the crowd that pressed all around her. They were walking under the overhanging bulk of Testenel now, and she clutched at Duke Edric's arm as she passed into shadow.

3. The Battle of Darvien

Melogian watched Christine with a heavy heart: The girl's face was tear-stained under her triple veil, her steps short and hesitant like those of an invalid. Veraless had left Christine's side and now came to Melogian. Mourners were still filing past as he whispered, "Are you ready to go?"

"I'm not about to go into battle dressed like this, Captain. I'll go change and gather whatever apparatus I may need. In an hour, meet me at the stairs that lead to the Ice Tower."

She took her leave of him, and walked briskly out of the cemetery. There was a lump in her throat when she allowed herself to think of Edisthen, but no tears, never any tears. Back within the confines of the castle, she made her way to her apartments where she rid herself of her mourning dress and put on clothing more suited for battle: thick trousers, a coarse shirt, and heavy laced walking boots. She bound her hair with a leather thong and washed what little paint she had applied to her face. In the mirror, it was a tomboyish figure that looked back at her, a scout in the army maybe, or a smith's apprentice; nothing like a powerful sorceress. It felt appropriate, somehow. She saw a smile halfway to a sneer bloom upon her lips.

Now that she had decided to leave Testenel, she felt relieved of a great weight. Nevertheless, there would be no shirking of her protective duties. She considered the array of warding-spells she had woven about Testenel: She could not maintain a full link with them at a range of more than sixty leagues. Even should she be warned that her spells had detected danger, she would be too far away to be able to respond in time. Someone else would have to be linked with them. One of the two mages she had recruited would have been the simplest choice, but she trusted neither of them: either too young or too old, and certainly untried under pressure. In fact there was only one man she felt fully confident could carry the weight.

She sought him out, and finding him as she expected in the company of Christine, she was made to feel even more awkward as she requested the regent's permission to take him briefly aside.

When they were alone together, Melogian found herself unable to speak for an instant. Quentin watched her guilelessly, his handsome face registering nothing but concern: for the realm, for the outcome of the war, for Melogian herself. She loved him still, she found. No matter that she had tried to break off their relationship, still he had the power to melt her heart. She wanted to take his hands, to feel the warmth of his fingers in hers; instead she crossed her arms tightly.

"Quentin, I have to leave very soon."

"I know. Is there anything I can do to help you, Lady?"

"There is. In fact, I have a big favor to ask. I need to link the warding-spells to someone; I can't oversee them from so far away. Someone must be there to react if they sound the alarm. Will you accept the burden?"

Quentin's expression hardly changed. "Of course. What must I do?"

"Nothing. It'll be like when you received the Quester's Gifts. All I need is your consent."

"That you will always have, Lady."

She cast the link then; with a few words and passes she shouldered off the burden of her spells and passed it on to him. He shuddered involuntarily when the watch-strands hooked into him.

"Not pleasant, I know," she said, "but the sensation will fade in a few minutes. Now listen: You've taken on the link to the watch-spells, but since you aren't an adept, you can't make use of it. You cannot look through the spells as I could; you're only a passive observer. Above all, don't try to exert your will through the spells: you'd fail, and there would be a backlash. If anything untoward happens, then the spells will inform you. You'll feel a—let's call it a pull, a compulsion. You will know where the wards have been triggered; that will be more than enough."

He nodded, his mouth set. "I understand. And I wanted to say . . . You were right. We should all have listened to you. You were wiser than any of us, but we did not see it. I should have sided with you and convinced the Lady Christine to follow your lead instead of General Fraydhan's."

Melogian sighed. "It doesn't matter now. You all did as you thought best. And I don't have time for more of this discussion."

She leaned forward quickly, kissed his cheek, unable to resist any longer. Before he had time to decide whether or not to clasp her in his arms, she had pulled away and left the room, saluting Christine crisply as she passed by her. Edisthen's daughter, sunk in gloom, did not seem to notice. Melogian gnashed her teeth as she strode away, once more torn between guilt and anger.

Back in her quarters, she filled a small satchel with necessities, then went to meet Captain Veraless at the foot of the Ice Tower. She took him up to the spot where she had summoned a whirl to visit the edge of the world with Christine, in the distant past of two months ago, when she could still laugh. She drew the invoking diagram once more, a spiral of chalk, speaking the syllables of the spell meanwhile. Veraless watched her in respectful silence. When she was finished, standing at the center of the design, she felt the successful meshing of forces as her invocation gathered energy. She stabbed a hand downward and spoke the activation command; the design erupted into dust as the forces ingathered and the whirl pervolved just beyond the wall. She threw open the door and revealed the whirl: a translucent disc three yards across, groaning and vibrating, floating three hundred feet in the air with nothing visible to bear it up.

Melogian vaulted over the railing of the balcony and stepped onto the whirl, then sat down on it and motioned for Veraless to join her. Veraless gave a nervous laugh, but bore himself much better than Christine had, though Melogian did notice him clutching the strap of his baggage tightly as he sat down next to her.

This time she was in no mood to tease, and so she accelerated gently away from Testenel, letting Veraless get used to their mode of travel. The whirl responded smoothly to her will, banking gently when they turned, then settling once more level as soon as they resumed a straight-line course. She made them pass close by the *Black Heart* before they left Testenel, setting off a chorus of startled hails from the skyship. Veraless bellowed in reply to his crew, then the whirl sped away.

"You'd think people who spend their lives aboard a magic flying craft ought to greet a whirl with less turmoil," commented Melogian.

"That's a sorceress talking. A skyship is a ship, with a rudder and keel, and sails; it's something you wrestle with to coax out a mite more speed. It's hardly more magical than a fishing boat. If you were a fisherwoman, how would you react if you saw your captain and a she-wizard floating in the middle of the sea, seated on nothing at all?"

"No doubt you're right. I can never understand how normal people see things," said Melogian gloomily. For a while they were silent. Then, shaking herself out of her mood, she put more power into the spell: The whirl gained altitude and speed and they arrowed southward, toward the front.

𝕏 Veraless, looking down at the landscape below them, sighed in exaltation. The *Black Heart* could fly as high as Melogian's disc, but never as fast. The ground beneath them moved at a wonderful pace.

"This is incredible," he said. "Why can't we have many flying discs like this? They're perfect scouts, far better than skyships."

"Because you'd need a squadron of wizards for that," replied Melogian. "A whirl must be actively impelled by magic to fly, it isn't a spell that someone else can be imbued with; not to mention that it burns up much more energy than any other mode of travel."

"Well, could you make it larger? With a half-dozen archers at your side and some stones and gravel, you could rain death from above."

"Don't think it hasn't been tried. Larger whirls fling themselves apart, though you can link several in a sort of train. The fifth-millennium battle-mages evolved a variety of magical weapons, including a pyroclast intended to pour fire from the sky upon the enemy. It was used only once, with a team of mages lofting it into position using a six-whirl train."

"Did it work?"

"Not really. While still over their own forces the bearers were attacked from the air and their whirls shattered by counterspells. The pyroclast fell, along with two of its bearers. Legend has it this disaster reshaped the Blasted Hills near Abridosh, hence their name, though I personally doubt it."

They flew on and on, and the landscape spread itself below them, like a precious board carved for some splendid game. Veraless recalled the hours he had played war with his brother, moving their metal soldiers about maps he drew himself, of imaginary countries; landscapes full of bridges and fortresses, mountain peaks and crevasses that made labyrinths for the soldiers to explore. Perhaps, if he were to watch armies fight from this height, he could delude himself they were toys, and find childish joy in their clashes, forgetting the ugliness far below. How convenient that leaden soldiers did not bleed. . . .

The speed of the whirl was such that they reached their destination well before Veraless expected it. From the air it was evident that the loyalist forces were in full retreat, marching north at haste. Veraless rose to his knees and scooted forward to look over the edge of the whirl. "Don't grasp the rim," warned Melogian, "you'll burn your fingers." He kept his hands flat on the surface of the whirl and peered intently at the ground.

Evered's forces, joined with Kawlendian soldiery, were advancing north along the road. Small cavalry detachments rode in the fore, harassing the loyalist rear guard, goading them to greater speed in their flight.

"Damn! They're driving our troops back like a flock of sheep," growled Veraless. "Evered doesn't even need his demons at this point, if all we're doing is running away."

"I see one of them," said Melogian. "That burning snake you described; it's flying over the rear of the rebel forces."

Veraless looked in that direction and felt a sting of panic at the sight of the firedrake, for all that it was shrunken by distance.

"What of the other ones?" Melogian asked. "You said Casimir kept them at the head of their troops? I think I see something, but we're too far up."

"I'm certain they're there."

Melogian had slowed down the whirl to a crawl; she rubbed her mouth briskly and frowned.

"What do you say we get a closer view, Veraless?"

"Of course. We can't stay in the middle of the sky forever."

"Then do as I do." She stretched out prone against the surface of the whirl and waited for Veraless to copy her. Strangely, looking straight down through the translucent substance of the whirl made him feel far less secure than when he peeked over its rim into a half mile of air.

"You have to remain flat, now. Don't worry: You can't possibly fall off the whirl as long as you don't move. Keep your head straight, and look down. Let's go."

And then they dropped like a stone; Veraless felt his stomach lift within him and his body shivered to a primal terror. The whirl shrieked with a brazen voice and began to tilt forward.

"Melogian—!" he shouted above the noise, lifting his head to look at her.

"Look *down*, Veraless! Remember everything you see! I won't be making another pass!"

The whirl was horrifyingly close to the ground when its trajectory at last flattened and it shot forward over Evered's forces. Veraless, splayed against its translucent surface next to Melogian, saw troops flash by. Rank after rank of heavy infantry and archers, all bearing Kawlend's livery. Then he saw the demons: the colossal tortoise with a spiked shell, and walking next to it the twelve-foot ogre. His sight flickered back and forth, trying to drink in the whole scene in the instant he was vouchsafed; he saw the seven-limbed demon, gleaming blue and silver through the whirl's hull, rear up on its many legs and coil itself, staring at them as they flew past. Then more troops, Kawlendian archers and irregulars bearing Vaurd's colors; and now he was being pressed down as the whirl ascended, the rebel army shrinking beneath them.

After a while the crushing weight on his back eased; once they were at their former height it vanished. The whirl was once more level. Melogian rolled onto her back then sat up, panting. Veraless followed suit.

"All right," said Melogian, wiping her forehead. "All right. That was the most foolish thing I have done in years, but I'm not sorry. For months—God's teeth, for *years*—I've swatted at shadows. Hunting for Christine in illusory worlds, waiting for Evered's brood in their distant castle to hatch more plans, trying to imagine what spells Casimir will come up with, sitting in Testenel listening to third-hand reports of troop movements . . . God's heart! For the first time in my life, I've seen my enemy."

"We were never really in danger," Veraless reassured her. "Not a single archer below us even had the time to think of shooting at us."

"Oh, I wasn't worried about archers, or even demons. It is simply that now Casimir knows I'm here, I've lost whatever advantage of surprise I could have had against him. But as I said, I am not sorry."

The whirl descended, gently this time, toward the retreating loyalist army.

"Did you get a good look at the demons, Lady?" asked Veraless.

"Yes. Good enough, in fact, to recognize one of them."

"*Recognize?*"

"Yes, recognize. I know one of these demons. And I think now I know at last how Casimir was able to bind the demons to him. That monstrous tortoise with the spiked shell; it was fought and defeated nearly three thousand years ago. It had crawled ashore from the Western Ocean and plowed a path of destruction inland; no weapon of wood, metal, or stone could prevail against its flesh. It was like Hundred-Handed Juldrun's tarrask: Even if you cut off one of its legs it would grow it back in a few heartbeats.

"In the end a wizard was able to bind it to her will. This is a common story, you understand. When the world was young, demons by the hundreds had to be battled; but some could not be readily killed. Those were imprisoned, usually in sealed adits deep beneath the ground and put under an eternal sleep. So it was with this one, whose name is as lost to us as that of the wizard who bound it. It was sealed under the ground, to sleep forever.

"Casimir must have discovered the locations where some demons were buried; he dug down to them, broke the enchantments that kept them dormant, and bound them to his will. I am terrified that he could do this, not once but five times; but at least I understand what he did. It is something any sorcerer with the proper knowledge could attempt."

Veraless seized upon this last statement. "So, since you know that tortoise-demon, you could control it yourself!"

Melogian shook her head.

"Not in the least. I have no experience with commanding demons and precious little theoretical grounding. I'd need to know the demon's name to be able to make a serious attempt, otherwise Casimir won't even have to clench his grip. No, I don't think I can do anything of the kind. Oh, don't look so gloomy, Veraless; I haven't given up. Let us go down, find General Fraydhan, and see what we can do."

Their arrival among the ranks of the loyalist army drew much attention; as they floated above the heads of the retreating soldiers, some set up a ragged cheer. Melogian was unsure whether she could fulfill their hopes, but at least her presence seemed to galvanize them.

They found General Fraydhan soon enough; with enormous relief Melogian lowered the whirl to the ground, climbed out of it, and allowed it to dissipate. Their flight had taken a toll on her.

Fraydhan greeted the sorceress's arrival with more annoyance than pleasure. Melogian chose not to notice his demeanor and forced him to talk of strategies.

The days since Veraless had left the battle aboard the *Black Heart* had been spent retreating. Loyalist forces were unable to mount effective counterattacks and the rebels simply drove them northward. The demons made infrequent excursions, always to devastating effect. Discipline was still maintained, though morale was low.

General Fraydhan, at least, did have a plan: He was driving his forces to the town of Darvien, still a day's march away. The town was large enough to be used defensively. This had been envisioned as a contingency option should the raid into Kawlend meet with too strong a resistance. Of course, demons had not figured in the original forecasts.

"I can assist you in the defense of the town," Melogian said. "I have spells that may hold the demons at bay, at least for a time. We can make a stand in Darvien."

"So glad to hear it from your own lips, Lady," said Fraydhan sourly. "I was afraid you'd have other ideas for our troops."

She had to be content with that exchange. She asked for a mount, and was assigned a gelding far closer to a packhorse than to a destrier, which suited her just fine; she also received, almost as an afterthought, a pair of bodyguards whom she put to good use, questioning them to learn what she could of the state of the troops. She devoted the rest of the day to morale-building efforts, surprised at the range of reactions her presence evoked. Orion had taught her at length about his experiences in the Great War, and mentioned that the presence of a mage amongst the troops was a positive force, once the soldiers learned of it. She found out that this was less of a certainty than Orion had told her, as some soldiers proved almost contemptuous of her. To be fair, she had not yet demonstrated her powers to any practical effect; or perhaps it had been different for a Hero from the Book.

They spent an unquiet night. Melogian learned that the cloud-demon no longer haunted the campsite, now that the loyalists took measures to reveal its approach. Still, the efforts they made to ward themselves with light were not without cost. To do her part, Melogian spun a simple warding-spell that would react to a demon's presence and laid it around the perimeter of the camp. She did not sleep well either, keyed up as she was for the approaching confrontation.

Nights in the month of Ripening were still fairly short; with dawn the loyalist army prepared to march again, before the rebels could harass them further. And before noon had come, their situation improved immensely, as they drew in sight of the town of Darvien.

In the distant past, Darvien had been a frontier town, little more than a village at the margins of civilization. As the edges of the world receded, the land south of Darvien became fertile and humanity moved to colonize it. Darvien grew and thrived. Centuries passed; the country to the south expanded until it became impractical to see it as part of the central realm of humankind. There were no dukes yet, but already Kawlend existed, in an inchoate manner. For a time Darvien served as its capital, and palaces rose atop its gentle hills, their windows gleaming from the light of candelabras.

The palaces had long ago been abandoned; their walls had tumbled down, their floors lay buried under the soil. Now the hills of Darvien appeared pristine, and only trees rose atop them. The town had shrunk and reverted to Temerorn, whose southernmost border it now marked.

The loyalist army, reaching Darvien, had also reached home; in the battlefield of the mind, where symbols matter more than the tangible, this made a profound difference. Asked to fight and die in the hills a league south, Fraydhan's army would have obeyed disheartenedly; but now that they fought on the land they came from, they would be vastly more ferocious—and symmetrically, Kawlend's army would feel itself more at risk.

Fraydhan arrayed his army to take advantage of the town's defenses. This would be no siege, as Darvien lacked walls. At worst, it would be a holding action; at best, the loyalist forces would stand firm long enough to repulse Evered's troops. General Fraydhan did not seem to believe in this scenario; Melogian forbore from raising his hopes, but she knew her presence would affect the outcome of the battle.

As the loyalist army began to prepare for an assault, Melogian wandered a short distance away from the town. Her two bodyguards, Ewayne and Grethe, a pair of experienced soldiers, accompanied her without comment. They made their way to the summit of a low rise a hundred yards east of town. The true hills of Darvien rose to their left; to their right the town lay quiet. A column of people was winding its way north along the road: those who had chosen to flee the town before fighting broke out. It astonished Melogian how many had chosen to remain. War was an imposition of chaos onto the quotidian, and faced with such a disruption of routine too many people buckled down and chose to believe they could go on with their lives as before. If Melogian were a simple town-dweller, she thought she would have fled screaming at the first glimpse of a soldier.

She sat down in the grass, cross-legged, and closed her eyes, gathering her energies, arraying the spells within her mind. Orion had taught her that when using

spells in war, subtlety was best, as long as one was adequately supported by experienced troops. If not, then brute force would have to do. This was said with some
irony on his part, as his main contribution to the Usurpation War had in fact been
in the realm of overwhelming assaults. Melogian did not have as much power as
Orion did, nor was she so broad in her knowledge that she could use every warlike
enchantment ever devised. Still, she had a decent repertoire and intended to give
Evered a wide sampling of it.

All too soon, Evered's forces neared. Part of the loyalist army had positioned
itself immediately before the town. The strategy called for them to stand firm at first
then withdraw within the town, where ambushes could be laid. Melogian had not
discussed this, nor had she volunteered to be part of the strategy. Fraydhan did not
understand all she could do, and if she bound herself to a specific action she would
be hampered. She remained a free agent: Her help would be unplanned for, a way to
equalize chances. The tactical simplicity of the situation made it even more appropriate. This was no time for clever plans. She would not slip through enemy lines
under a spell-cloak, locate Casimir and assassinate him; she would not sow confusion among the soldiers and start them fighting one another. She would wait for
Casimir's demons to appear and then strive to hurt them any way she could.

The enemy drew nearer, then halted their advance. Kawlendian troops stood
at the wings, while the center was occupied by Evered's irregulars in the colors of
Vaurd's line. For a time they stood motionless, then their ranks parted and demons
came forth. The terrapin crawled at the fore, its spiked shell bobbing from side to
side as its stubby legs lifted in turn, while beside it a quicksilver many-limbed horror
flowed back and forth.

As Evered's troops followed, trotting to battle behind the demons, Melogian
shouted out one of her most powerful spells and threw one hand forward. The air before her flickered and trembled, blurring sight; waves of density raced from her fingertips toward the demons. As she poured energy into the working, the air began to glow
a soft buttery yellow; after another moment, the working reached its critical point. A
huge cone of flame flowed forth two hundred yards to engulf the two demons.

For three heartbeats they were bathed by the flames. The grass around them,
the very soil under their feet, caught fire. Yet they were not harmed; the terrapin
kept advancing stolidly, while the seven-limbed demon hissed, either in pain or anger, and scuttled out of the reach of the flames. Melogian kept the focus of her spell
on the terrapin, hoping to at least discommode it and make it turn, but it did not
even seem aware of the fire.

With a gasp, Melogian relinquished the spell. The enemy soldiers had not been
close enough to the demons to be affected, but certainly they had noticed the working and reacted. The infantry ranks had stopped their advance and milled confusedly. In addition, the ground still burned where the spell had caught it, a long
swath of flames that would serve as an obstacle for Evered's human forces until it
guttered out in half an hour or so. Otherwise, the effort had been a complete waste.
The quicksilver demon had danced away from the spell and was now approaching
the loyalist troops from a different angle. The terrapin plodded on, panting.

Melogian cursed in frustration. She had expended far too much power in this first attack, to no practical effect. She should not have used this spell from such a distance. In fact, she should not have been here at all. She should have remained with the troops. She wasn't used to fighting alongside others; in all her wanderings within made worlds she had always made her stand alone. "Let's go," she told her guards. "I need a vantage point closer to the center—"

She felt a sudden thrum of power under her skin as one of her wardings ignited: A link-spell was striking at her. Despite her warding's resistance, the link bound itself to her, like a noose closing around her body. Melogian shouted out a warning to her guards as she turned to face the direction of attack. The link-spell firmed, like a line snapping taut, and Casimir's true attack surged through it.

Agony coursed through her body, in streams raying out from the crown of her head, flowing down her limbs to lose themselves in the earth at her feet. Her sight was filled with a rush of images: a palimpsest of grinning skulls and withered flowers, unsheathed blades and red running blood. Her heart struggled to beat, its every pulse a dry crackling of tindersticks. It was not air she tried to draw into her lungs, but stone. Her blood turned to steam and seeped out from within the gaps of her flesh. Her nerves were stretched until they snapped, her muscles dried to twisted strips, her bones were rubbed away to grit and powder.

For an endless time Melogian stood in the grip of the death-spell, keeping herself alive through sheer force of will, drowning in morbid hallucinations. At long last the hostile force ebbed and she regained her senses. She was unharmed: Her will and her carefully layered wards had prevailed. Even the emotional shock of the attack had faded. Ewayne was holding her by her elbow and waist, halfway between concern and fear.

"Are you all right, Lady? You were screaming like a stuck pig. . . ."

"Never mind. Let's leave, now." She let him help her climb astride her horse. "Just be grateful that spell was targeted for me alone," she whispered too low for him to hear. Their mounts galloped toward the town. Melogian wanted very badly to send the guards away; her wardings did not extend their protection to others, and if she were attacked by a wave of elemental force rather than a death-spell her escort might well perish.

Still, they would be safe for a while. They had to be. Surely Casimir was not strong enough to cast another spell of equal power immediately after this? The effort must have left him sweating and gasping, weak and confused; a death-spell put a terrible burden on its caster. By the Book, the man could not be such a bottomless pit of power!

The loyalist troops had retreated within Darvien as soon as they saw the demons were leading the attack. Archers within houses, atop roofs, drew and aimed, ready to let fly. Yet the demons did not press on; they slowed and halted still some distance from the town. The terrapin collapsed upon the ground and let out a braying bellow, twisting its long neck. The seven-limbed one rose tall on its hindmost limbs, its head swaying left and right, then it coiled itself fluidly into a tangle of legs and claws.

Yes, yes! Melogian exulted. *He's reeling and mumbling, rocking back on his fat arse, and for the moment he couldn't add two and two. He can barely keep his hold on the demons; he dares*

*not continue the attack, so he makes them stop! You overconfident bastard, Casimir, how does it feel
when your body betrays you?*

They made their way into the town and Melogian lost sight of the enemy. Past the
second row of buildings, Melogian dismounted beside a three-story house that had
been old when Hundred-Handed Juldrun was born. She ran inside, climbed stairs,
and at last gained the flat roof. Three Temerorni archers were stationed there, claiming the cover of a low parapet. One of them hissed furiously at her to get back down.

Ignoring him, Melogian went to the edge of the roof and knelt. For the nonce
there was no movement on the part of Evered's army. The soldiers had gathered just
behind the immobile demons and assumed defensive positions. The swath of ground
touched by her spell still burned. If General Fraydhan had wanted to launch an assault, the opportunity was there. Melogian wished she could find him and urge an
attack, but how long the demons would remain quiescent, she did not know. Let
Fraydhan decide for himself whether the loyalists should strike, she resolved.

For a few minutes nothing happened on the rebel side. Within Darvien, Edisthen's troops frantically worked to improve their defensive position. Melogian focused her mind and considered in turn every spell in her arsenal. Even had she
mastered a death-spell on a par with Casimir's, she did not doubt he would be able to
shrug off its effects: To attack the enemy wizard directly was hopeless. Still, she was
able to unleash destruction on a wide scale; against ordinary soldiers she would prevail, whether through flame, murderous cold, insidious acid, or subtler effects. Demons whose very existence proved them near unkillable, she could only hope to fight
to a standstill. But this would prove enough, if Evered's army could be demoralized,
if its men and women could be attacked and slain.

Buried deep at the root of her memory, the spell she must not speak beckoned
to her, as if hinting that it was the key to victory. She pushed aside its urges with the
ease of long practice. She thought instead of a working that would evoke billows of
acidic smoke. The acid would burn flesh and corrode metal; it would not kill unless
one were to remain within the cloud overlong, but it would put any soldier out of
action. Conceivably it would sear a demon's flesh badly enough to anger it, to make
it buckle against Casimir's commands. Wishful thinking, to hope that the wizard's
control could be broken by this; and yet wishes were all she truly had.

Melogian cracked her knuckles, then began to twist her fingers into the proper
mudras; but before she could begin the invocation itself she saw a fiery form approaching from the south. Casimir's firedrake was swimming its way through the
air toward them. From closer up, she found it terrifying. Its coppery flanks were
burnished to brass and gold by the light of its flames; all along its length huge child-
like faces set amidst its scales frowned as if in tormented sleep. Its sharp-toothed
mouth clashed its triple jaws spasmodically. As it passed above the town's buildings
it was pelted by arrows, none of which seemed to cause so much as a scratch. It
shook itself, a sharp undulation traveling down its length, and clots of flame dropped
from its body. They struck below, setting buildings ablaze, killing those whom they
hit directly.

Melogian's heart sank. It seemed Casimir still had enough control to send at
least one demon toward his enemies. From a refuge, Darvien was about to turn into

a trap. Melogian halted her casting; she had to respond to the immediate threat. She reviewed her spells once more.

The firedrake spun in a lazy circle; it shook itself again, and again death rained down. Deep within Jyndyrys, Melogian had once faced a creature that likewise produced flame: reptilian, four-limbed and winged, red as blood, belching fire from its mouth, it bore little enough resemblance to the demon that swam through the air above her. There was no compelling reason to expect the firedrake to be vulnerable to the same forces as that imaginary monster; logic would lead one to believe drenching it in torrents of water would be far more effective. Still, anything was worth the attempt—and Melogian did not know any spells that would drown a flying enemy.

Melogian brought to mind the spell that had prevailed against her imaginary opponent. Its formulas ran through her mind; she spoke their syllables in a ringing voice. She felt the forces gather from the air surrounding her, energy pooling in the joints of both her shoulders. She repeated the secondary pervulsion three times, bringing the spell to its keenest pitch of power. Pain lanced her teeth and eyes from the effort of keeping the spell under control. As the firedrake swung closer and closer to her position, incandescent slaver dripping from its jaws, she released the forces she had gathered. With the sound of a hundred thousand silken sheets being ripped apart, a swaying, branching line of lightning erupted from her hands and sped to strike the demon's head.

The result far exceeded her expectations. The firedrake shrieked in pain; the children's faces on its copper flanks opened their eyes, revealing gaping pits glowing from its internal fires, and their mouths unsealed, dribbling cinders. The demon wavered in the air, began to drop down. It recovered itself just above the roofs and began to twist away, but this time arrows found their marks in the open mouths. With desperate speed the firedrake flew off toward the rearguard of Evered's army.

Melogian sagged in relief. The archers on the roof with her were stammering in amazement. Ewayne muttered an obscenity that Melogian took as a compliment.

Briefly, Melogian allowed herself to think the battle was won, that Evered's forces might retreat at least for today. Then she saw the seven-limbed demon uncoil and shake itself. The terrapin, which had withdrawn its head into its shell, now poked it out and began to advance once more. Behind them, the vanguard of the rebel army marched to the attack.

Melogian cast the working she had originally intended as quickly as she could manage; just in time, clouds of thin, acidic smoke erupted from the ground just beyond the buildings of Darvien. The demons charged blindly through the cloud; behind them, the advance faltered. Evered's irregulars broke ranks and retreated, but Kawlend's disciplined troops pressed on. As they breathed the smoke, as it seared the skin of their faces and the lining of their lungs, men began to scream and panic. In horrified triumph, Melogian watched dozens of them, rather than fleeing, fall to the ground and clutch at their eyes, cough blood, and die.

Still, the demons had passed through the cloud without noticing it; and all the ambushes Edisthen's forces had laid availed them nothing. The terrapin lumbered forward, striking with its limbs at any obstacle in its path. With three blows it could bring down a house; archers shot at its neck and face point-blank and still their arrows bounced off its hide. Swordsmen rushing to the attack were swatted away before they could swing, their bodies rupturing like overripe fruit. The seven-limbed one flowed through the streets, killing with swift blows of its claws. Its gleaming hide was soon marred in a dozen places by the impact of weapons, but to strike it was like striking a wall of living steel, and men's weapons flew out of their grasp if they hit.

The first ranks of rebel soldiers had been decimated, and still billows of acid rose from the ground. Faced with the grim evidence of their dead comrades, even the Kawlendian troops refused to advance. The demons wreaked slaughter, but they fought alone.

Come on, Casimir, thought Melogian, *your precious toys are unprotected. That nasty Melogian has hurt your flying snake. Maybe she can find a way to do the same to the others. Can you take that chance? What is Evered telling you now? That his men don't want to go through that killer smoke? But it's Kawlend's men who've died, not the rabble from the marches he gathered to himself. How do the Kawlendians feel about this? You're all arguing now, I know it. I can keep the acid going for a long while. . . .*

Her side's bugles were shrilling retreat; Grethe was at her side, speaking urgently.

"We've got to go, Lady. We're pulling out. Can you hear me? We can't stay."

Melogian protested: "I'm maintaining the spell; the soldiers don't want to cross the smoke, it's all that's keeping them from attacking."

"Look to the south, Lady; can't you see they're moving out to flank us? Unless you can surround the whole town with that death-cloud of yours, they'll just go around it and attack us from the sides."

Melogian repeated Ewayne's earlier obscenity, this time in consternation. She could not do as Grethe had suggested; once more she felt like a fool for not grasping what was obvious in retrospect.

There was no way for her to defend the town against an encircling attack; she lacked the power to evoke protection over such a wide perimeter. Melogian made some additional passes, imparting momentum to the spell so that it would continue on its own for a few minutes, then broke off her casting. The three archers had already fled the rooftop and only her two guards remained, Grethe by her side and Ewayne halfway down the ladder into the house, urging them to follow him. Swallowing a curse, Melogian rose to her feet and ran to the hole.

&& In the end most of the loyalist forces escaped Darvien. The rebels chose to occupy the town rather than pursue, which gave the loyalists the opportunity to retreat. Melogian told herself her magic had bought them this respite, but it had hardly been worth the expense: The loyalist ranks had been noticeably thinned, whereas the rebel losses were insignificant.

And still the army fled before Evered's forces. They were two or three days' march from the Hedges. Behind them, to the south, columns of smoke rose from Darvien. The buildings struck by the firedrake's flames were burning still. As they marched on, they passed refugees dragging handcarts piled high with their belongings, old men and women who could walk but slowly and whose families had abandoned them, a child crying for its mother.

Melogian, riding on her horse, felt ashamed. Yet she rode on, ignoring the pleas for help she could read in every eye. She had to find General Fraydhan and confer. Once she finally located his entourage, she was brought to him immediately. Fraydhan proceeded to give her a public tongue-lashing that severely strained her self-control. Once his torrent of invective and reproaches had run dry, she tried to respond.

"You are correct, General Fraydhan," she said, her ears burning. "I *am* undisciplined. I did not inform you of my plan and thus we could not coordinate our actions. Of all this, I am guilty. We wizards are all reckless and incomprehensible, anyway. But it was my spells that drove away the firedrake, and that halted the rebel infantry. I won you a reprieve, when Darvien might instead have become a death trap."

"And what new surprises of the sort should I expect from you, Melogian? When we camp for the night, will you raise walls to protect us? Or is that beneath your dignity?"

"I can work no such spell," replied Melogian, gritting her teeth.

"You cannot? But how was I to know that, since I am not worthy of being informed of your capabilities?"

Melogian opened her mouth to yell a stinging reply, then regained her composure.

"Enough, General. I cannot remain here. I will return to Testenel, to report to the regent and Duke Archeled. I will ask for orders, and return here. Once I am back, we can discuss strategy all you want and I shall act in concert with your directives. For now, I must leave. Good-bye."

Fraydhan, furious, ordered her to remain by his side; Melogian paid him no heed. Subordinates might have attempted to detain her, but they apparently feared her more than they did Fraydhan; no one laid a hand on her.

Captain Veraless found her as she made her way out of the flow of troops; she greeted him with a tired wave.

"Didn't you see me before, milady? I heard your discussion with the general. I thought the old man would die of apoplexy. I've never seen him so humiliated."

Melogian merely shrugged.

"You did well, you know, Melogian. It's true, you're not a soldier, so you don't have military discipline. But Fraydhan was wrong to blame you; you helped us immensely today."

"I'm glad someone thinks so."

"Can I return with you to Testenel? I want to rejoin the *Black Heart*. In fact, I was thinking, since you can deal with the firedrake, you could fly back with us. Fraydhan won't be able to refuse your help if you stand aloft, throwing levin-bolts at Casimir's demons. You wouldn't have to tire yourself flying on a disc."

"Perhaps," said Melogian. "First we have to get back."

She found a secluded spot some distance from the road, flat enough for her purpose. She took a piece of chalk out of her satchel and began scribing the circle onto the grass. As she did so, she felt a rush of weakness engulf her. For an instant, she feared another death-spell, then realized this was no more than fatigue taking its toll, now that the emergency was past. Her eyes burned, and she trembled, but the release of tears was as ever denied her. Gritting her teeth, she completed the pattern, recited the invocation, and summoned the whirl.

She climbed aboard and Veraless followed. She focused her power and they rose into the air, then set off north. Their return journey was much slower, the whirl's pace almost torpid. She found she lacked the energy to impel it to greater speed. Though she had shrugged off Casimir's death-spell earlier, she suspected she was now paying for that bravado. Once she had reached the castle, she promised herself, she would sleep. The world would look less bleak to her after a few hours of rest.

Captain Veraless did not speak and she felt no inclination to converse. She should feel triumphant: She had pitted her power against Casimir's and he had not defeated her. She had won a precious respite for the army, which might have been crushed if not for her intervention. Yet a black despair, borne of exhaustion, had taken hold of her soul and she returned to Testenel as if for another funeral, this time her own.

4. The Assassin

Mathellin flew into view of Testenel as a bird still, but this time a sparrow. This was close to the limit of smallness he could manage: His substance was condensed and cramped within the tiny bird's shape so that he felt a constant urge to change back into his natural shape, or even better, a far larger one. Dreams of bat-winged drakes and sea monsters flitted through his mind and he had to bring himself to focus more than once.

He flew around the castle, seeking an open window leading to an inconspicuous area. There was an overabundance of towers of all sizes and heights, all of them pierced with many openings, so he found himself in the situation of a hungry man at a buffet table—one on which most dishes turned out to be fake. For a fact the windows were too often sealed off by glass panes, and those he found that were not invariably gave onto occupied areas. He landed on windowsill after windowsill, only to leave rebuffed. In his quest he found a few birds' nests in various corners, some of whose occupants twittered at him. When he was very young Mathellin had foolishly imagined that taking on a creature's shape would make him able to understand its language; he soon enough found out all but the crudest displays remained as opaque to him in a metamorphosed state as when he was human.

Ignoring the sparrows' advances, whatever their nature, he at last managed to locate a small casement that had been wedged open a crack, behind which lay an empty room. He hopped through the triangular gap and found himself inside a small storage room, on top of a table set just below the window. The water stains on the dust sheet covering the table attested that the window had been forgotten open for weeks. Mathellin jumped to the floor, where there was just enough free space to resume a man's shape.

With a sigh of relief he allowed his form to expand; in reaction to his long confinement, he grew to a height of seven feet, elongated his arms to thrice their normal length, and grew a pair of antlers on his forehead. After holding this shape for a few heartbeats, he pulled in his flesh and took on human form. Nor did he remain nude: He had early on learned the trick of altering his substance into simulated clothes, though it made him feel like a crustacean just after a molt, before its shell had hardened. He shaped buskins, trousers, and a loose tunic from his flesh, then concentrated on setting his face to one much different from his own—if he were not careful, his self-image would impose his features on whatever humanlike shape he took. Once his appearance had firmed in his mind and he felt at ease keeping it, he opened the door and calmly strode out, shutting it behind him. Then he set off through the corridors of Testenel, as if he had lived there all his life.

He had in fact lived in this castle for nearly three years, as court wizard to King Vaurd. But that had been over twenty years ago; and he had never at that time made much of an effort to memorize the castle's floorplan.

It took him a few hours of work to get a decent idea of the lay of the land: The castle's interior plan had been complex when it had been built and it was further recomplicated by partitions added in latter days; certain areas were mazelike and only experienced dwellers could tread them with ease. Avoiding spaces delimited by wooden walls and keeping to the main walls whenever he could, Mathellin was able to refresh his faded memories. During this time, he was twice challenged by guards. On both occasions, he kept his calm and displayed just enough dull-wittedness to defuse the situation. It had been his experience that most people were inherently stupid and that the smarter segment of the population must learn to cope with them. He never claimed that he had lost his way: Instead, he insisted he was headed exactly where he should be, according to the instructions he had been given. Once he had been disabused of this notion and properly chastened, he was sent on his way, and the incident no doubt vanished from the guards' minds. To ensure this, Mathellin each time altered his appearance once more, so that the mooncalf who had blundered too close to the council chambers could not be identified later.

Once he had grown confident he could once more find his way around Testenel, Mathellin started a proper search for his quarry. In this he met no success at first, every likely spot he investigated proving to be the wrong one. In the end, it was by bluntly asking where Duke Archeled resided that he got his answer. The blue-liveried servant who answered the pretty little maid's question was so eager to impress her that he revealed everything he knew about the duke, including that His Grace liked a small glass of brandy before bed. Mathellin simpered and batted huge eyelashes and otherwise displayed suitable awe, then took his leave with a saucy twist of the hips. He was forced to keep this latest shape for a long while after that, unable to remain alone and unobserved. He got lost once in trying to return to his point of ingress but swiftly recovered his bearings and in fact found a shorter and quieter way back.

Once within the storage closet he leaned against the door and let out a sigh as he let the maid's form drop from him, resuming his own naked shape. He would wait until night, until he was certain Duke Archeled had swallowed his brandy. He knew the way now to the duke's quarters; the only task left was to strike. He flexed his left hand and willed it to compress and collapse upon itself, into a sharply pointed length of barbed steel. He swung this implement left and right, thrust it hard, driven by enlarged arm muscles. He practiced the transformation again and again, until it felt as natural as breathing. Then he set himself to wait. This proved a more unpleasant duty than he had expected; he was too keyed up to sleep, and could not manage to empty his mind. If he let his thoughts drift they would come back to Casimir, and Evered, and Mathellin's own diminution of status. And then, with a sensation as if slipping off the edge of a cliff, he would recall the long years of his vigil over Christine. That span of time he perceived as if through a veil of gauze: He had shaped himself into someone else, so powerfully that he had for a long time nearly forgotten who he truly was. The preoccupations of his other life came back to him now as if out of a dream: buying and selling, the amassing of wealth and influence, the ever-present dread that anything should happen to his charge, the little girl he loathed so much but could hardly say why . . . Mathellin shuddered and brought his mind back to the present. But there was nothing to gaze at here and now, except the random clutter inside this tiny storeroom, and the sky through the window. He remembered the sky of the made world, the dreamland deep within Errefern, and the terrible wonder of its moon, a bone-white luminary of the night sky that went through phases of light and darkness. In the course of its near-monthly cycle, it spent a night or two at the full; whenever this time came Mathellin had felt an odd turmoil within himself. He would come home very late, after Christine's bedtime, and open the door of her room a crack to verify that she slept. At those moments he sensed something dangerous within himself and would close the door almost as soon as he had opened it. There had been some summer nights, starting in Christine's twelfth year, when he had not come home at all. . . .

Mathellin felt a drop of sweat at his temple. The memory was like a decomposing beetle at the heart of a cotton boll, an ugly thing masked by pure white threads. He remembered the girls whose flesh he had purchased on those nights; but they were not the same as the other girls, on other nights. His manhood on those summer nights of the full moon was a weapon, a club of flesh that forced its entry and would not be denied. Whores were well used to penetration, but his roughness had made even them protest. And one night he had finally crossed the line, and allowed his member to exfold inside the whore's belly, to grow protrusions and horns, and force itself in ways her body was not meant to allow. . . .

He had had to kill the whore's pimp as well, and leave quickly after that, in the shape of a feline. The papers had spoken the next day of the grisly murders and mutilations, and he had hid them carefully from Christine. There had never been any chance that he would be traced, of course, since he never went to a whore without changing his own face at least, and usually his entire body. And so he had been able to utter outrage at the state of the world to his colleagues at work, and live his life as before; until the next time the moon swelled to a disc of pitted argent and he felt the urge once more to change, to forget who he was, to become a beast, a monster.

He had killed. He had raped, and killed, and eaten human flesh; fifteen or twenty times, on summer nights of the full moon, he had yielded to the madness inside him and allowed it to erupt. Autumns, winters, and springs had never been so contaminated, and throughout those seasons he would forget, he would hardly ever feel the need for the flesh of a woman. He traded and busied himself, and kept a watch on Christine that was at once close and disinterested. Then summer would come, and the moon swell, and the night call to him.

They had been dreams. Those women had been dreams, as the whole of Errefern. Only he and Christine had been real in the midst of the made world. Death and joy meant nothing in dreams; he had always known this, and it was because he knew it in his bones that he had done what he did. Mathellin wiped his forehead; his skin puckered with gooseflesh, his hairs sprouting thick and white, like the pelt of a hare, while his half-erect cock and his scrotum withdrew inside his pelvis. He shuddered again, resumed his normal shape with a grunt of anger at his weakness. Flexed his hand, shaped it into a weapon, shook his wrist and sprouted thorns and blades all the way up his arms.

He stood up, cast his mind back before all the ugliness of these thirteen wasted years, back to his youth and training at the feet of the masters of his dream-father's tribe. He forced his mind into the state his teachers had called *zarend*, began a routine of advanced exercises. He had not practiced these techniques in ages, had known or believed himself far past them, well into the realm of a master. He had let himself grow slack, overconfident. Even in all the days since his recovery he had neglected to practice.

Left arm straight; let it become a cylinder of flesh and bone, handless, elbowless. Let it compress, shorten, keeping it rigid. Now the right arm. You are a stick-figure man, your head is a sphere, you have eyes everywhere and nowhere. How simple can you make yourself before your shapeshifting power reaches its limits? How small? Hugeness is easy: to be a storm is nothing. Can you be a single drop of water?

The image of a woman's torn body pulsed through his mind and he broke from the trance, unfolded his shape halfway back to human. With a strangled moan of frustration he emptied his mind again and focused on his exercises. He assumed shape after shape, alone in this tiny room, striving for a purity of form he had once embraced easily. He sweated and felt a burn in his flesh, and banished it from him with the power of his will. Shape after shape; all of them sloppy, marred. Their lines were not smooth, they trembled and betrayed irregularities.

At last he stopped, as beyond the wedged-open window the sky darkened and dusk enveloped the land. His anger had been burned away with exertion, but still he knew himself diminished. He had once been a master of his power; though he still could shape himself as he pleased, though his flesh still obeyed his will, he had fallen from the pinnacle he had once achieved. The masters of his father's tribe would have seen it at once. Something in him was still broken: His mind was wounded, bruised, and battered from his long confinement in the role of Christine's uncle, deep inside the dream of the made world. The flaw in his mind revealed itself as flaws in his shapes.

He would return home, then. Once this task was accomplished, he would return, sit once more at the feet of the masters, relearn the peace of *zarend*. Or else he would dive into Errefern and find again the world where he was worshipped as an avatar of the Godhead. He had been mighty; but he had invested much of his magic in the made world, recruited allies and threaded his power through the worlds. What had he sunk to? What had happened to him? He had left too much of himself behind. He had grown a shell around himself, and then become the shell rather than the man inside. The shell belonged to Errefern, and in losing it he had lost himself. He had extended his power too far, and damaged it. He recalled hunting for Christine in her dash through Errefern, and casting himself into the munken, worlds away, in his final bid to capture her. Recalled his battle with the knight's mount for control of its shape, and how he had nearly died . . . Still, the memory brought trauma with it. He needed to forget, needed some peace, some order in his life. . . .

Mathellin focused himself, wiped the bloody tears from his left eye. He still had a duty. He would perform it. He would strike in Vaurd's name, once more, one last time. Once he had reported success to Evered, then he would be able to hold up his head, and tell him that he was going away for a time. Let Evered fight the remainder of this war without him; Mathellin had done his part, far more than his part. He had sacrificed too much already.

The sun had sunk into the western ocean; the stars now became visible through the rents in the clouds. Testenel grew quiet. Finally Mathellin eased the door open and slipped out. On swift and silent feet he sped through the corridors of the castle, having resumed the shape of the girl who had been so full of innocent questions about the mighty personage still resident in Testenel.

Presently he found himself near to the duke's quarters. The passages ahead were guarded and he would have to be careful. There were spells aplenty he could use, ranging from the blatant to the subtle. A burst of noise and flame could generate confusion enough for him to approach his quarry unnoticed; or he could try to implant a suggestion in the mind of a guard that he saw a fleeting shadow up ahead, which he must investigate immediately, telling no one about it. . . . But Casimir had warned him that Melogian had spun a net of wards all about the castle; surely they would be sensitized to the casting of magic.

In the end he decided on simplicity, trusting the element of surprise. He hardened his tegument to form a carapace both hard and flexible; now a sword thrust would scarcely do him more damage than a paper cut. Keeping the girl's shape he approached the duke's chambers.

To the first guard's challenge he replied that he was bringing His Grace some more brandy, and displayed a small flask which in the dim light the guard could not see was in fact attached to his hand rather than held within it. He was allowed to go up a staircase and into a corridor leading to several sleeping chambers. At one door a young guard stood watch, obviously very full of himself and his duty. Mathellin tried the same approach; the guard would have none of it. "His Grace said nothing about this. I can't let you pass."

"Oh please, sir, he'll be ever so cross; he's asked especially for this. I got my orders from Floresm the steward. . . ."

However the guard's suspicions had been aroused, he proved obdurate and ordered Mathellin away. Assuming a bewildered expression, Mathellin instead came closer and when the guard made to physically push the importunate visitor away, stabbed him below the breastbone.

The guard made little noise, what with Mathellin's hugely flattened hand clamped over his mouth and nose, sealing off all breath. After a few seconds he lost consciousness and Mathellin removed his hand as the man went limp. The guard's armor clanked, but no more than if he had leaned against the wall. Mathellin slid him down to the floor; the guard was breathing shallowly and blood was staining his livery. Mathellin left him where he lay and went to the duke's door.

❧ At the moment of Mathellin's attack a spell-strand that had been woven at the threshold of the duke's chamber was ignited; a flare of force propagated along the web Melogian had spun, passed through four nodes and thence straight to Quentin's brain. The knight awoke, his whole body spasming. Where a wizard would have received clear knowledge of what had happened and even been able to cast his senses back through the web and look upon the hallway, all Quentin could feel was a nauseating pang of distress, an urge to run at all speed to a certain point of the castle that he could not even identify.

For a few seconds, he remained confused, standing up in his nightclothes, feeling the tug of the spell-web but unsure whether he was still dreaming. Then he snatched up his sword in its scabbard and ran out of his room, shouting out the alarm.

❧ Mathellin had needed less than half a minute to defeat the door and enter the duke's rooms. They were dark; he adjusted his eyes to drink in a different light and he beheld the apartments through the dim glow of heat, which he had long ago discovered was a form of light in itself. He swiftly oriented himself and went to the door of the bedchamber where Duke Edric of Archeled lay sleeping. In the heat-light the duke was a monster, as were all men, the features of his face a complete contradiction to their appearance by normal radiance.

The duke was no heavy sleeper; he awoke as Mathellin approached him and opened his glowing lids to reveal the even brighter eyes beneath. They were featureless balls of light, neither iris nor pupil discernible. Duke Archeled muttered a word, perhaps, "Who?" Mathellin leaned over him and drove a barbed sword-hand into the duke's belly, then with a grunt disemboweled him. Archeled's entrails poured out of him, so, so bright.

The duke uttered a strangled scream, which his assassin swiftly cut off, clamping the duke's mouth shut. Through Mathellin's brain, as his fingers clenched on his victim's jaw, passed a fearful thought: that he had been unbelievably stupid, that he should have strangled the old man, broken his neck. Why had he done this gruesome deed? Evered—Casimir, in truth—had ordered Archeled killed; yet had he wished for butchery such as this?

But no; Mathellin had done what was proper. There was life still in the duke, a few seconds of comprehension left to him. And so Mathellin called out to him, a voice out of the darkness—how he wished he had light at hand, to show himself to the duke; and yet was this not more terrifying still?— a rasping hiss devoid of humanity: "You die in the name of Vaurd, in the name of Evered his son and heir, the rightful king of Chrysanthe!"

The duke was not moving, nor breathing. It was a corpse upon which Mathellin gazed, its blood spattered all about the sheets, already dimming as it cooled. Had he heard Mathellin's message before his soul fled? Had he known, or died bewildered?

Mathellin was breathing fast; he heard a dull roaring in his ears and his legs trembled. The horror of what he had done filled him; it was like when he came out of the moon-trance and beheld the dismembered corpse of a girl.

He fought to overcome the weakness in his spirit, to master his emotions. What was done was done; he had to leave now. But his customary techniques failed him and he remained standing at the dead duke's bedside, sick with loathing. Why did this sick dread, this crushing guilt, continue to fill him? He had killed before. He had killed in made worlds, and the imaginary man he had shaped himself into had suffocated at his own deeds, but swiftly regained his poise. Now that he had killed a man who was more than a dream, it seemed his true self could not stomach it.

But he had been following orders, had he not? Had he not acted at the behest of his king? In his mind's eye he saw the form of Vaurd, to whom he had sworn over his loyalty and his life; and Vaurd was long dead, and to his son Evered Mathellin had transferred his loyalty. Forbidden thoughts echoed inside his mind: that the son was unworthy of anyone's loyalty, that Casimir had harnessed the prince's rage to his own ends, that perhaps God had truly spoken twenty years ago and cast Edisthen into being. The pillars that upheld his sanity were being pulled at, and in their shifting they sent Mathellin's mind tottering toward prospects he had never allowed himself to glimpse before.

He turned to go; a kernel of his self was insisting it was past time to leave, urged him to transform, become a dog, a stoat, a rat, anything small that could slip away unseen or unnoticed. There was a stamping of feet and shouts at the door to the duke's quarters; two heartbeats later armed men poured in, carrying torches and lanterns, whose glare drowned out the heat-glow, nearly blinded him.

Mathellin shifted into an armored shape, all horny plates and spiked limbs; he gaped wide jaws garnished with steel teeth. Yet he did not feel the fury he should be feeling, not with the core of his being, which still reeled and trembled. And when he had adjusted his eyes to regain his sight, Mathellin recognized the one at their head—and terror swamped him.

This was the one who had killed him, down in Errefern, as he tried to recover Christine. This was the knight who rode a car, whose sword had smashed his entrails and shattered his eyes, who had brought him to the very edge of oblivion and still haunted his nightmares.

In panic Mathellin turned to the wall and bashed it with his fists; he thought only of crumbling the stones and escaping. Though he broke off great shards of blue rock, the wall was thick and remained standing. The guards were screaming in rage; one of them cut at his leg. The blow should have bounced off; instead it sank deep into his flesh, jarred the bone. Screaming in turn, Mathellin pulled away and turned to face his assailants. In his turmoil, he had been losing his grip over his shape; what ought to have been infrangible tissue had softened to ordinary meat and skin. The wound in his calf was a huge slash, bleeding copiously. Mathellin focused himself and stanched the flow of blood, letting the rest of his shape melt and re-form, expecting to disconcert and frighten the guards.

The knight had unsheathed his sword and was advancing upon Mathellin. He wore no armor, no shield, in fact he was in his nightclothes and barefoot; yet he seemed utterly fearless, his face set in a grim mask. Mathellin, transfixed, watched him approach. Hideous memories welled up in him; seared with a hot needle of pain, his left eye began to bleed.

The knight thrust at his chest; Mathellin opened a hole in his substance and the sword passed through empty air. Undaunted, the knight swung back and up; Mathellin tore himself nearly in half to avoid the blade. In a blind terror, he made himself melt and compress down into a flowing tangle of limbs, a flattened armored thing like a gigantic centipede, which darted out between the assailants. One sword blow thudded into him, nearly severing his endmost segments, but Mathellin was too fast and he emerged from the duke's chambers before more damage could be done. He ran up the wall and the ceiling, hurried down the hallway and let himself fall down the stairs, coiled up like a ball of chitin, bouncing off the heads and shoulders of confused retainers. At the bottom he changed into a dog, whose right hind leg dripped blood and whose tail was chewed ragged. He was noticed but obviously not recognized; and as a hawk he finally escaped Testenel, flying through the night sky and seeking refuge up a fir tree, in whose branches he regained human shape, clutching naked at the trunk, bleeding from right calf and left eye, the lower part of his pelvis broken and blazing with pain. He whimpered and wept, trying to make sense of it all. He was the one who had killed; he was the murderer. Why then did he feel as though he were the victim instead?

It took the whirl hours and hours to reach Testenel; by the end of the journey, Melogian felt her strength waning dangerously. In the past, she had often met with dangers down in the made worlds; but there, it had been easy to take a step or ten *beyond,* to seek refuge in a safe corner of reality. She had never had to use so much of her power at once. Whether it was because of these unaccustomed exertions, or a delayed reaction to Casimir's death-spell, she felt exhaustion rising up to claim her.

Half dreaming, she saw her power as a handful of pebbles covered with a thin film of water, fast draining away. When there was no water left the stones would begin to dig into her flesh and make it bleed. The stones were the spells she had cast and left active: the web of wards throughout Testenel, her personal armory . . . She toyed with the idea of letting them all lapse, recuperating the strength she had invested. A lot of it would go to waste if she did this, and she would have to cast the spells once more at any rate: Surely she could leave neither herself nor Testenel undefended in the circumstances. She wasn't at this extremity yet.

The whirl was slowing down and losing altitude; she gritted her teeth and made it climb higher, increased its speed to a tolerable level. It was past midnight now. She had recently passed over two sleeping villages; she ought to find herself in familiar territory soon. . . . A film of water over sharp-edged pebbles . . . There, at the horizon, she saw light from Tiellorn; the great castle would be to her left. She swung the whirl in a lazy curve and flew on.

When she reached Testenel she dared not make the whirl ascend to the gallery she had used before; instead it fluttered under the colossal slope of the castle's upper floors and settled before the southern doors, in front of a pair of startled guards. Once Veraless had disembarked, she climbed out of the growling whirl and let it spin away into nonexistence.

"You know who we are," she said to the guards in a broken voice. "Let us in." The guards unlocked and opened the doors; she and Veraless entered. Veraless was eager to speak with the *Black Heart*'s crew; they parted with the promise that they would meet the next morning. Melogian went on alone, hoping only to creep into her bed and sleep. She had not reached halfway to her apartments when the turmoil surrounding Duke Archeled's assassination caught her in its grip.

Somehow she found the necessary strength to remain awake throughout the time that followed. The news was unstoppable; soon the entire castle was thrumming with it. Melogian went up to the duke's apartments and beheld his body; Quentin was by her side, though she did not remember when he had arrived. She nodded dully at all that she saw. At one point she heard a counselor asking someone what should be done; curious, she waited to hear the answer the counselor would receive, and only after a long minute did she understand she was the one being asked. But she had no ideas anymore.

She left the duke's chambers with their stink of blood and offal, staggered down a flight of stairs, wandered along a corridor and pushed open a door at random. She entered the room beyond; she was still accompanied, though she knew not by whom. There was a settee against a wall; she lay down upon it. "I am going to sleep here," she announced, slurring every word as if she were dead drunk. Her eyes closed; someone was talking at her but blessedly his words had ceased to make sense.

🙒 She came awake with a lurch; her head was spinning and twin pulses were throbbing behind her eyes. It took her perhaps fifteen heartbeats to remember she was in the midst of catastrophe. She swung her legs down and stood up. She would have gladly returned to sleep, but feared it was already late. In darkness she stumbled to the door, unwilling to use the least iota of her power even to shed some light. She opened the door and squinted against the light from the corridor. Sunlight was streaming in through windows in the distance, reflected by the great mirrors that overhung Testenel. There was a guard posted at the door, a freckle-faced young woman barely of age to bear a weapon. She eagerly informed Melogian that morning was well advanced, that this room was three floors up from the Porphyry Court, and that Sir Quentin of Lydiss himself had asked that Melogian meet him as soon as possible.

Melogian told the guard she would go to Quentin immediately, then went to her chambers and took the time to eat, drink, void, wash, and dress before anything else. The duke would be no less dead if she hurried madly, and she had had enough of mindless precipitation for the nonce.

Food and drink did wonders for her, and sluicing the dust of her travels from her skin was sheer bliss. She held herself back from eating all she could, not wanting to become torpid with digestion. She drank two glasses of wine, one more than was prudent for her, who very rarely imbibed, but she had always heard alcohol helped steady the nerves and now was as good a time as any to test the saying.

Only when she was feeling nearly herself again did she leave her apartments and go to find Quentin. Even then, as she was going down a flight of stairs, the knowledge of Archeled's death stabbed through her anew, as though she was just learning of it; and it was in a state far removed from the calm she yearned for that she at last met with Quentin.

She did not know him well enough to discern the traces of exhaustion or anguish on his face; always he held himself rigid, the discipline of his training keeping him at all times an image of the dutiful knight. Even in the throes of lust his expression had remained guarded. Still, she thought he betrayed something in the way he moved, the shallowness of his smile. He had been standing at the window of a seldom-used dining room he had commandeered as a makeshift headquarters: There were remnants of food on the table no one had been by to clean up, and several floorplans of Testenel spread out with knucklebones placed here and there as if they were the pieces of some complicated boys' game.

"I have heard the news through Captain Veraless," he told her when she came in, and it took the sorceress a moment to remember that she had been meaning to inform Christine and Duke Edric of the situation at the earliest opportunity. "But I would appreciate it, Lady Melogian, if you told me your own take on matters as they stand."

"Well, you know the news isn't good," she said. "Our army tried to make a stand in Darvien, but we failed. I used magic against the rebels, with mixed results. I have discovered that I'm probably not cut out to be a military wizard; maybe I'll learn from my mistakes. Casimir used a death-spell on me; obviously, I survived it.

"I know how Casimir got hold of his demons, though that doesn't help us. The tortoise and the silvery demon appear immune to fire and acid; the flying demon I know I can hurt, using lightning. Veraless suggested I could fly back with him aboard the *Black Heart*. Since I can keep the firedrake at bay, I can attempt to deal damage from an aerial platform."

Quentin's nostrils had flared when Melogian mentioned the death-spell. He spoke slowly.

"I am glad you are well, Lady. Veraless tells me the army is three days' march from the Hedges, and that the rebel forces are running them ragged. Estephor's army is moving southward; our estimates suggest they should join up with them in two or three days."

"That can't hurt, but I really don't know what it can accomplish," said Melogian. "Steel won't hurt Casimir's demons any more than fire. I'll be heading back to the front as soon as I can; Fraydhan might be able to come up with a strategy where I can be of use, or else I'll just go along with Veraless's suggestion. But I'm not sanguine about the outcome. You'll need to consider how to withstand a siege, I'm afraid."

Quentin sighed. "We were fools. Casimir may slaughter our army before it can return home. And meanwhile, Duke Edric of Archeled is murdered in Castle Testenel by some supernatural beast. This is not a made world, Melogian. We are not supposed to suffer this sort of travail. You were too wrought to answer me last night, but I am asking again: What was that? What in God's name are we supposed to do about it? I have ten men warding the Lady Christine day and night, but what good would they be against *that*?"

Melogian rubbed her face, recalling all that had transpired after her arrival last night. "That, Quentin, was Mathellin. I told you last night—unless I dreamed it. It must have been the wizard Mathellin who killed the duke."

Quentin's jaw dropped. "One of Chrysanthe's own wizards? Were you not supposed to keep tabs on all of them? I cannot believe you left us undefended from him! How could you—"

"What the hell do you want from me?" she shouted, stung. "If it's miracles you require, petition God in Her heaven!"

Quentin stammered: "But could you not have set wards against him? Protection of some sort?"

"There *are* wards all about this place; they alerted you, didn't they? I've scattered spell-interdictors, force-inverters, and dread-sinks as if they were salt grains, but I can't cover every square inch against everything!"

"But why did you not put a simple watch-spell on him to start with?"

Melogian held up her hands. "Because, Quentin, there are no such things as 'simple watch-spells'; especially if you're trying to keep tabs on a wizard, who can easily cloak himself with counterspells. Also, Mathellin vanished years ago; we had every reason to think he was lost at the bottom of a made world. I heard rumors, a month ago, that a wizard claiming to be Udæve's son had been seen in Faryn. I never had the chance to corroborate them. But it would seem the likeliest prospect."

She had started pacing back and forth before Quentin; each time she turned, she felt an urge to backhand him across the face, in hopes of getting some sense through his thick skull.

"Of course, there is another explanation. We could be dealing with a sixth demon. If Casimir can locate and control five forgotten demons, I'm sure he can manage six. So we'd be facing attacks from a shapechanger straight out of the Book of Shades rather than the dream-spawn wizard who replaced Orion twenty-three years ago. Would that be better, do you think?"

Melogian's headache had returned. In exasperation, she put her clenched fists at either side of her head and pushed her knuckles into her temples until that pain distracted her from the other one.

"Melogian . . . Melogian, please," said Quentin. She let her arms fall limp and drew a ragged breath.

"Forgive me," said Quentin. "You had a harrowing experience yesterday and I have been putting additional strain upon you, when you have not had a chance for proper rest." He reached out a hand to hers, brushed his fingers along her wrist. Melogian shrugged. The pain, at least, had let some of her anger bleed away. Quentin was right that she hadn't yet recovered from her ordeals.

"I never meant to blame you," Quentin continued. "Let us suppose for the moment that it was indeed Mathellin. What does this tell us? What can we do?"

"I don't know. Why should I know?"

"Tell me about him; Mathellin. I have heard the name a few times. He was Orion's rival, did you say?"

Melogian sighed; the request brought out the teller in her and she could not deny Quentin. Many times in her apprenticeship Orion had made her retell a long story, distilled into something that could be easily understood; to bring the skill forth once more granted her a measure of calm. "Not his rival. Orion became Vaurd's court wizard nearly thirty years ago, but Vaurd did not like him—or more accurately his advice. I imagine Orion never tired of pointing out the proper path for Vaurd to take; after all, that was the only reason he'd joined his service, because he could feel the Law straining about the throne and wanted to put things right."

"Orion could feel Vaurd was not a proper ruler?"

"My master was a Hero who had been granted perceptions much beyond the human norm. I don't doubt he was able to sense Vaurd's outrages to the Law. And please note that he did not have to do what he did; he might have remained in his retreat and waited for the Law to restore the balance, as Weoll the Flame waited two score years for Queen Fyrith to lose the throne. Instead, he tried, he really tried, to save Vaurd from his fate; tried to make him a fit ruler.

"But Vaurd was a member of that race of men who cannot stand to be told what to do. Warn such a man that he shouldn't put his finger in a candle flame lest he burn himself, and he will hold it there until his flesh blisters. Vaurd ignored all of Orion's advice, and after five years he dismissed him from his service. He'd have done so earlier, but I suppose he feared losing face in casting a Hero from him—and perhaps Orion would simply have refused to leave. He was a very stubborn man.

"What Vaurd did was to hire another wizard to his service, which allowed him to release Orion without damage to his reputation. By then, Orion had given up on him. He had myself to deal with as well; he had taken me on as his apprentice in 6069, when I was eight years old. At ten, I was about to embark on the difficult part of the apprenticeship."

Quentin nodded. "So Vaurd hired Mathellin to his service. But where had Mathellin come from?"

Quentin had sat down. Melogian sat in turn, aware that he was attempting to calm her anguish; she hoped his transparent plan would succeed. He gazed at her with those long-lashed eyes of his, utterly intent, and her heart melted within her. How she wished he truly loved her; yet though he still lied to himself about his feelings, she knew a bond had been forged between them that would endure come what may. She had been half in love with Orion most of her life, enthralled and scared at once, as if the Hero were a flame that could consume her should she venture too close. Edisthen she had worshipped in much the same way, though he had set himself clearly beyond the reach of any such feeling after the death of Anyrelle. She had loved both the Heroes of this age; now she found herself loving a too-mortal boy, frail and boundlessly strong at the same time. This time she was the one who could destroy him. And yet, though he held no fear of her, this would no more work than her previous loves. Still, there had been a small measure of joy in his arms; and she felt this joy in her now, a tiny kernel that she had thought vanished without hope of rescue, that she now believed—equally foolishly, perhaps—could never be lost, only briefly misplaced. She cast her mind back to what Orion had told her of his replacement at Vaurd's court.

"Mathellin is the son of a sorceress from Archeled, named Udæve. She passed away eight years ago—at least, she vanished and is presumed dead. Her house is sealed and Orion never found it worthwhile to battle the sealing-spell. Perhaps we should have . . . but she was nearly fourscore; it was reasonable to assume she had passed away. Mathellin would be now in his middle forties. His father is unknown; Orion told me that Udæve had conceived in a made world and managed to bring back the child within her body into Chrysanthe. This makes Mathellin what we call a dream-spawn. There have been a few throughout history: Hundred-Handed Juldrun bore a girl whose father was a king of some desert land deep within Errefern."

Quentin looked at her wide-eyed. "How is that possible? When nothing from the made worlds can pass into the true realm?"

"When you eat food in a made world, doesn't it sustain you? Think how long you spent hunting for Christine; in that time much of your flesh and bones absorbed matter from Errefern and you lost an equivalent amount of substance from the real world. If the Law were as harsh as you think, when you tried to come back into Chrysanthe most of your body would have been left behind, and I rather think you would have perished on the instant. The Law allows a living being from Chrysanthe to return from a made world; what counts isn't the matter you are made from but the pattern you've imposed upon it."

"You are correct, of course; pardon the digression," conceded Quentin. "So a woman of Chrysanthe may be impregnated by a man from a made world, and then return home to deliver the child."

"Right. But since the father is imaginary, his seed is not quite human, and so the results of the pregnancy can be surprising. Dream-spawn will sometimes diverge very far from the humanity we know; Juldrun's daughter, for instance, had a third eye in the middle of her forehead. Mathellin's differences are not so blatant, but they go deeper."

Quentin frowned. "But was this origin widely known? I know I was still a child during the Great War, but I never heard much of import about Mathellin. He seemed a colorless character from what little I know, completely at odds to Orion."

Melogian sighed. "Compared to Orion, we are all pale sketches of people. Mathellin, from what my master told me, was totally devoted to Vaurd—I guess that would make him somewhat drab. He was often sent as an 'ambassador' of sorts when Vaurd wanted to compel some noble to his point of view. Mathellin would intimidate his host with displays of his special magic, and to Vaurd's mind this crude threat constituted effective diplomacy."

"His special magic?"

"What you saw in the duke's bedchamber. Mathellin is a shapechanger. This isn't some spell he has to cast, it is an innate power; like the tree-lizards of eastern Kawlend, which can change from brown to green."

"Can he change into any shape he pleases?"

"I don't know. I suppose so."

"So could he be the chair you are sitting on?"

Melogian shook her head. "No. I have some wards about me that would flare at his presence: Being a dream-spawn, he's not entirely of this world."

Quentin looked down at the patterned rug. "Last night I asked you what we should do, but you did not seem to hear me. Do you have an idea now?"

"Well, I can add to the wards I have already put into place. Knowing Mathellin is a threat, it may be a good investment of power to tune the web specifically for his presence. Beyond that, I'm out of clever plans. I can still hope to discover weaknesses in Casimir's demons, but I'm not counting on it."

"But why not, Lady? You told me you were able to vanquish the firedrake; surely that is a good sign?"

Melogian gave a wry chuckle. "It was sheer dumb luck, Quentin. You're forgetting that these abominations were sealed beneath the ground thousands of years ago precisely because they could not be destroyed. Why should I succeed in defeating them when mages in the past could not do so? If I could wrest control of them from Casimir, that would seem the best attack. But I do not know their names, I am no demonologist, and Casimir is more powerful than I am. It would be like a child trying to wrest the reins of a team from a grown man."

She sighed. "Still, I will do what I can. I shall fly back, and try to find the means to repel them. If I can hold the demons at bay, then our troops will be able to engage the rebel army. If I cannot . . ."

Quentin avoided her gaze. "If there is anything I can do to help you, you need only ask," he said. "Will you leave soon?"

"Not at once. I have to reinforce the web, and I need some more rest. In my present state, I'd be no use at the front."

They had both risen from their seats. Hesitantly, Quentin asked her, "Will you come see me before you leave? I would not have you go without saying good-bye."

Something in his attitude betrayed he was about to embrace her; fearful of her reaction, she retreated a few quick steps. "I will, I promise," she said, and left the room without further discussion, unpleasantly aware of her powerlessness in every phase of her life.

She sought out Veraless next, informing him that they would be returning to the front shortly, as soon as she took care of a few necessities. Much to her surprise, Veraless shook his head at the news.

"I'm not going back with you, Lady."

"Why not?" she asked. "Why would you want to stay in Testenel?"

"I am going back to the *Black Heart,* Melogian, and I'm going to use it to do what needs to be done. I'm going to hunt down Mathellin and kill him."

Melogian held up her palms. "You can't hunt him down. He can become anything he wants, Veraless. I can show you his portrait and you can memorize his features, but do you think you'll recognize him as a dog, a bird, a bush? And doubtless he's gone back to Evered's side now."

"Stop making assumptions; they've cost us dearly in this war. Wherever he is, I want to locate him and destroy him. He's not Casimir; he doesn't have elder spells to defend himself. He's mostly a shape-shifter, and even though he murdered Duke Edric, when the guards faced him they wounded him, and he fled. I'm tired of watching good men die trying to hurt invulnerable demons. I'll settle for getting rid of one of Evered's perdules."

"How do you want to find him, anyway?" Melogian asked, then answered her own question: "Oh . . . you want me to cast a seeking-spell and bind it to you."

"Aye. You can do it, can't you?"

The sorceress sighed. "Yes. Orion taught me the skill. I helped him bestow the Quester's Gifts for several of the knights who set out to find Christine, and they were using just this kind of seeking-spell. But we'd need some of Mathellin's flesh . . ." She fell silent.

"Will some of his blood do? There were splashes on the walls of the duke's chamber that were Mathellin's . . ."

"No need. Orion was a very pragmatic man. His chambers hold what we need."

Indeed, Melogian's master made a point of keeping samples of the flesh of many people, for use in casting should it prove necessary. In a locked and warded cupboard in his chambers stood an array of glass vials etched with names and symbols. Most held only dust, the mage or noble whose scrap of flesh they'd contained having long since died, but in a few Melogian had seen bright red slivers of meat; Orion had even shown her her own vial and the flesh within—which puzzled her no end, since she could never find any wound on her person from which Orion might have taken it.

On the verge of leading Veraless to Orion's chambers, Melogian hesitated: "When Edisthen disappeared into the made world, Veraless, you told me spending even a day looking for him was a mistake. You were right, for all that you spoke out of pain and spite. Isn't what you're proposing to do now even worse?"

"I don't care if it is. What have we been doing so far, except make one mistake after another? Do it, Melogian. I order you."

"You *order* me? You can't give me orders, Captain. I'm not one of the *Black Heart*'s crew. No one is left on this earth who can tell me what to do!" As she spoke them, she grew aware of the pain in these words. How she wished there was someone to whose authority she could defer; but Edisthen was dead, Orion vanished, and Christine had lost her way.

"Fine. I'll beg, then. Please, Lady Melogian; give me a chance to avenge the duke's murder. I'll seek out Mathellin even without the benefit of your spell. I'm not sending the *Black Heart* back to the front to be burned to cinders and I won't let it stay here idle. I want to fight in a way that makes a difference."

How much of our lives is spent making excuses for others to do what we wish of them, Melogian wondered. And how much is spent acquiescing to the folly of others because it is the easier path? She motioned for him to follow her.

❧ Melogian had rarely entered Orion's quarters since the wizard's disappearance. Devoid of his presence, the rooms seemed to seep wrongness from every surface. Conceivably this was the effect of some subtle spell Orion had not told her of, aimed

at keeping intruders away, and to which she was barely subject by special dispensa-
tion. Yet when she brought Veraless into the antechamber, he appeared undisturbed. Perhaps it was only her dread manifesting itself.

She motioned to the heavy black-wood table that occupied a third of the room.
"Sit here, and remain seated, please," she told Veraless. "There are wards almost
everywhere and you could get killed by an importunate touch. Avoid staring at the
painting on yonder wall: It can feel your attention and will retaliate in unpleasant
ways. You may look into the crystal ball on the table if you wish; the light patterns
it displays are harmless."

Muttering under her breath the safe-words Orion had taught her, Melogian
opened a door into another chamber, very small and low ceilinged. There was a sort
of attic above the ceiling, accessed by a trapdoor at either end of the room, which
Orion had warned her never to open under any circumstance. As she crossed the
room, she heard a familiar noise, a rapid patter of claws or hooves, coming from the
ceiling, following her movement through the chamber. She ignored it as she always
had and pulled on a heavy ring to open the other door. This led into Orion's main
workroom, which though large was so crowded with tables, benches, chests, shelves
overflowing with curios, and heavy magical apparatus, that it felt far more cramped
than the previous room. Melogian unlocked and opened a cupboard, increasing the
pitch of her incantation to keep the warding forces that protected the cupboard at
bay, and took out a glass vial containing a sliver of Mathellin's flesh. Then she be-
thought herself of something else, and spent a few minutes hunting for a specific tome
in the bookcases. She brought both items back to the antechamber, where Veraless
fretted in his seat, uninterested in the tiny blooms of light that swirled within the
crystal ball and manifestly trying not to look at the painting on the wall to his left.

"I have what I came to get," she announced, "and while we're here I thought
we might look at whatever Orion wrote about Mathellin." She sat across from him,
laid the book upon the table and opened it. Veraless raised an eyebrow as she leafed
through the manuscript pages.

"I always thought wizards' books would be huge affairs, with iron locks and
silver ink," he said. "This almost looks printed."

"Ah yes, well, we keep the vellum made from flayed infants for the really important matters," she deadpanned. "Likewise the demons bound into the pages and
the invisible ink. At any rate, this is hardly a book of spells; it's a chronicle from the
seventies, starting just after my master was dismissed from his post and replaced by
Mathellin. . . ." She paused, turned a page, and glanced through Orion's flawless
calligraphy, hunting for a reference she knew must be there.

"Yes, I remember when that happened," said Veraless. "So Mathellin actually
moved into these rooms for a time?"

"Oh no. When Orion left, he sealed the doors behind him. On the day he returned, he verified the seal had remained undisturbed. Mathellin never even tried
to enter these rooms; I suspect he feared a trap had been laid for him. He may well
have been right, too. There is an old, wicked spell in that corner of the ceiling; I can
sense it festering, biding its time, like a lurk-snake lying in ambush. It might well be
Mathellin it's waiting for."

"You're joking again, aren't you?"

"Not this time. . . . Wait, I've found it. Why did he take twenty pages before saying anything about the mage who'd replaced him? Oh. *Oh.* God's teeth . . ."

"What?"

"It would seem Orion knew much more about Mathellin than what he told me. Look at this."

She turned the book so that Veraless could read it, but he frowned in puzzlement. "I can't make out more than a few words. Is it in cipher?"

Melogian snickered. "Hardly. The vowels have just been rotated. *E* means *a, i* means *e,* and so forth. And some consonants have been shifted in the same way. 'Thriem-sbewn' means 'dream-spawn,' see? Anyway, my master appears to have known exactly where Mathellin was conceived—I wonder how he learned it; I can't believe Udæve would merely have told him, although she did fear him—and he went down into Hieloculat to learn about Mathellin's parentage. Give me the book back, I can read it much faster than you."

She ran her finger down the page until she found the passage she sought, then began to read aloud: "'These Men bear our likeness in their natural shape, though they can alter it at will. The talent is innate but takes half a life to master. An adept may take on the shape of any living thing; a master can assume any shape he envisions as long as it exhibits sufficient 'inner patterning,' what their language calls *phrawn.* Thus no one may become a simple boulder, but Grandmaster Vielos was able to assume the appearance of an efflorescence of rock crystal two inches in diameter.

"'With the ability to metamorphose into raging beasts encased in impervious armor, one would expect their wars to be fantastic slaughters, shaking the earth to its core. Yet they are a peaceful people, owing not to any moral superiority but to their great vulnerability. Regardless of their shape, in contact with the metal *gevroin* their flesh dissolves as flower petals dipped in lye. Every town keeps a stockpile of *gevroin* weapons; the most terrible assailant would wither and die under a hail of arrows. So they practice their talent for spying, for contests, or for sheer art. . . .

"'It took me two weeks to ascertain an equivalence for *gevroin.* I cannot bring so much as a speck of it into the true realm, of course, so utter certainty is not possible. Yet I am as confident as I could be that the earthly counterpart of *gevroin* is—'"

"Yes?"

Melogian snapped her fingers in frustration. "I'm not sure what he meant. He uses alchemical symbols I'm not familiar with. . . . Oh, that's an inverted tau! So that glyph would mean . . ." She raised her eyes and met Veraless's gaze. "Cold-forged orichalc."

Veraless was silent a long moment. Then he breathed: "Are you telling me that an orichalc blade will destroy Mathellin, no matter what shape he's taken?"

"If it is cold-forged, and if Orion understood the correspondences correctly. But yes, it should."

"Well; I'd call this a sign from destiny, Melogian, wouldn't you?"

Her retort was immediate, and heated. "No, I wouldn't. There is no destiny: Our will is our own, and the future is not written."

"Fine; not destiny, then. Call it fate."

"Spare me. Both words mean the same thing: God, reduced to an insensate force. A wizard's training changes one's outlook: I believed in fate when I was little, but I will not now believe in a God who constantly intervenes in our lives. There is enough chaos and blind chance in the world as it is; we don't need to explain every occurrence as coming from the Book of Miracles. When you work with wizardly forces, it's sheer folly to assume God is standing over your shoulder to help. Magicians who trust in fate tend to wind up dead at an early age."

Veraless spread his hands in a gesture of surrender. "All right; no need to quarrel over philosophy. Can we agree to say this is good luck? Now we just have to get ourselves some orichalc and someone who will cold-forge it. I've only seen it used for candlesticks and the like; there must be a few artisans in Tiellorn who have a quantity on hand."

"Don't bother," said Melogian. "Bide a moment." She returned to Orion's inner sanctum. Though it appeared a rat's nest of oddments, there was an underlying order to it; and she had been trained to decode it. What purpose it served Orion to so clutter his belongings she did not understand, though she guessed the core of him rebelled at neatness, as if an excess of order somehow denied life. At the back of one huge trunk she found an index of her master's possessions, once more as hideously disorganized as it could be, entire pages crossed out, with annotations scribbled in the margins. Yet armed with the understanding of the method behind Orion's madness, within two minutes she had found what she sought, inside a hide pouch nailed to a high shelf. She made her way back to Veraless, clutching a pair of daggers in their sheaths. She drew one of them: The blade was the grayish green of lichen, rough-surfaced. The edges and point were keen, though, still sheened with oil after many years.

"I guessed Orion would already have had weapons made should the need for them arise," she explained. "You might say fate has spoken again—if you wanted to make me really angry. Now let us go eat something; a seeking-spell is slow casting."

It took hours for Melogian to lay the spell upon him; Veraless almost nodded off in a mixture of boredom and exhaustion. He felt the magic being worked as a faint tingle: Melogian was spinning the spell around him, imbuing him with its power as she was casting it. It awoke parts of his mind he had not known he possessed, something he found deeply unsettling. He had been afraid his dislike of the magic might make him resistant to it somehow, but Melogian had brushed off his qualms, explaining that even the dullest-witted dung-sweeper in Chrysanthe could receive her seeking-spell. Aware of her growing annoyance with him, he had forborne from pressing his point. The sorceress had to know what she was doing.

The sliver of flesh in its tiny bottle had been placed on the floor a short distance from Veraless's feet; Melogian wove a complicated path about these two points, crossing between them at times, as she waved a seven-armed cross and muttered incantations. Toward the end of the process Veraless began to feel the spell more and more strongly, as if it were a coil of thin rope that encircled him and strove to bind itself to his flesh. The last few circuits Melogian made charged him with a mixture of pain and excitement; then it was done at last. Melogian spun the cross in her hand and tugged sharply as if to snap an imaginary thread. Veraless felt the windings tighten about him and into him, merging with his fleshly self, reaching the axis of his spine before they vanished. He moved his limbs cautiously, expecting to find their movement impeded, but all seemed as before.

"You feel it," Melogian said.

"Oh, yes."

"I told you even a lackwit could be sensitized."

"I'm glad I took to it. Is there anything left to the preparations? How do I use it?"

"Think of your target. Close your eyes if you want, it may help. Turn to face all directions of the compass; you will know when you face in his direction. The closer he is, the stronger the pang will be. And remember: If he flees into a made world, you can no more track him than you can follow. Even if I gave you the power to walk *beyond*, you could not sense him across worlds. So you will be unable to locate him if he escapes into Jyndyrys or Hieloculat."

"But I can sense him now, if he's still in this world?"

"You ought to be able to, yes."

Veraless closed his eyes and thought of Mathellin; having never met the man, he had to rely on a painting he had found in the archives, that showed a court scene during Vaurd's reign, with his court wizard half obscured behind the king. He filled his mind with the face in the picture, the brush of light-brown hair, the uneven nose, the tight-lipped mouth. . . . He felt something: an urge, a disturbance, like the sense of someone's presence. He spun slowly in place; the feeling waxed, then waned as he continued to turn. He stopped, spun in reverse, felt the pang increasing to its previous level. He opened his eyes and nodded.

"Yes! I can sense him. The spell is working."

Melogian smiled grimly.

"Good. Now listen: The ability will improve with practice. The more you concentrate, the stronger the effect. But be careful not to overdo it. Make sure not to spend more than an hour at a time hunting; it's possible to work yourself into a frenzy otherwise, especially since you're completely untrained. This is a hard spell to contain; you may find it difficult to sleep, and if it takes you more than three or four days to find him, you will begin to suffer physical ailments: heart flutters, sweats, blurred vision, and ringing in the ears. The Quester's Gifts were wrought with greater subtlety; what I've imbued you with is a coarser grade of magic."

"Four days? I'll be flying the *Black Heart*, Melogian. I'll find him long before then."

"Let's hope so. I have to leave now. Good hunting, Captain."

Veraless clasped her forearm, unwilling to take a formal leave but not daring a more personal demonstration.

"Good-bye, and thank you, Lady. I'll see you when all this is done."

"Of course," said Melogian, gently breaking his grip. She turned away from him and left. Veraless thought of Mathellin, and once more felt the spell tremble within him. Time to hunt.

By the time the eastern sky had begun to color with the imminent arrival of the sun, Mathellin had regained enough control over himself to leave Testenel behind.

For hours he had crouched on a branch, naked and trembling, gazing without sight at the vast bulk of the castle. Troops had been billeted in the area surrounding Testenel, and patrols ran a circuit of the walls on a regular schedule. He had stood even odds of being discovered, but no one had come near him. With the passage of hours some calm had returned to him. His mind was still reeling, but he could focus on essential tasks. He had healed himself, repairing the rent in his leg and his broken pelvis. His left eye no longer bled, although its sight was still blurry.

When came the time to leave, he could not make himself take on a bird's shape; so he dropped to the ground as a feroce, and loped through the trees to the southeast. All too soon, he emerged into the clear, as only small patches of woodland existed near Testenel. He was noticed shortly thereafter, and pursued by a pair of overzealous mounted sentinels; lengthening his legs, Mathellin ran with desperate energy and finally outraced the horses.

By that time he was lost; he assumed Tiellorn lay to the north, but he thought this close to the city he ought to have encountered cultivated fields. He slunk through a copse of trees, located a stream and drank his fill. He felt weak with hunger. There should be hares close by; but he felt discouraged at the thought of chasing them. Instead he became a ruminant, and lowering his head to the ground he began to crop the grass. Once he had stuffed his first stomach he lay on his side and let himself process the food, chewing his cud and swallowing it again.

The rebel army was still far from here. He would have to fly; he could not walk the distance, neither as a feroce nor as a horse. He found himself wishing for a fabulous mount like those he had commanded within Errefern. He could return there; there was nothing preventing him. Did it matter whether or not he reported to Evered? Vaurd's sons would receive soon enough the news that Duke Edric was dead; in fact, Mathellin suspected Casimir had learned of it moments after it was done.

So why return? To take new orders, undertake some new degrading task? He had already resolved he would not. Did he want to confront Casimir, then? For a fact he did not. Before, he would have considered such avoidance a sign of shame; but the man he had become held somewhat different opinions. No, he had to return home, to the only home he had now: the made world of Errefern. Not as deep as the land where Christine had been held, with its corrupting moon, no. But in other worlds closer to the surface, where he had found, or dreamed up, allies and helpers, built an invisible empire that pivoted around him. He would immerse himself in the made world, recover the remains of the power he had left behind there. And afterward visit the land of his father in Hieloculat, regain his place amongst the masters. The entrance to Errefern, indeed, was much closer than the gate into Hieloculat. Going in that direction brought him nearer to the front; still, he would vanish into the made world long before battle even came near the Hedges.

He rose to go, still in the grass-eater's shape. With an annoyed grunt he gaped wide his jaws and vomited forth what remained of the grass he'd been digesting. Then he reshaped himself into a white feroce, sleek and swift. He felt stronger now, but grass remained poor food; he'd have to eat again soon, a better meal. Even in the feroce's shape he still felt unease at the thought of hunting and shedding blood;

he promised himself he would find a village and either steal a fowl from the run or just a cooked one from the fire. In the meantime, he would head south and a trifle west at an easy lope. Soon enough, he told himself, he would encounter signs of civilization and get his bearings back.

❧ Veraless had ordered that the *Black Heart* should remain at Testenel while it underwent repairs. With his return, he had charged its crew to be ready to leave at an instant's notice. He had thought at first to use the skyship to ferry medical supplies to the front, or else to convince Melogian to use it as a platform to attack Casimir's demons. Now he had a better plan. As soon as Melogian had left him, he went aboard his ship and informed his crew of his intentions. If some of them felt guilt at once more abandoning the loyalist armies to their fate while they hunted Mathellin, they said nothing.

As soon as the *Black Heart* had left the immediate vicinity of Testenel, Veraless went to the forward deck and stood immobile. He closed his eyes, and put his hands over his ears. He imagined himself in a dark, silent prison, wrapped in layers of cotton so he could touch nothing. *Mathellin,* he thought. *Mathellin.* He prayed the wizard wouldn't go down into a made world. Perhaps he had returned to Evered's side, and the *Black Heart* would be led back to the front. Perhaps his next target was Duke Corlin of Estephor, in which case it was imperative that he be found. Veraless filled his mind with darkness and silence. *Mathellin!*

In the depths of his imaginary prison the spell-borne sense awoke in him once more; like a tugging, a pain, yet an arousal also. The presence of his quarry. As Veraless immersed himself in his search, blind and deaf, he felt ice needles in his vein break apart, melt and freeze again, now all pointing in the same direction; a sharp metallic taste blossomed upon his tongue and sent fumes of ecstasy into his brain when he faced that way. He opened his eyes abruptly, pulled away his hands. The pang ran through him, harsher still; he leaned forward, as if teetering on the edge of a pit. He raised a hand, extended his arm—it was as if someone else was pulling it: He was unaware of any muscular effort.

"That way," he breathed. And then, in a roar: "Thirty degrees to port! Full sail! Full sail now!"

The *Black Heart* set forth at a good speed, south-southeast. Veraless leaned forward in eagerness. There was something liberating in this, in behaving in an irresponsible way. Perhaps he was being an utter fool; perhaps the acquisition of power in the end becomes merely an excuse to do exactly as one wishes. Perhaps he was seeing clearly, taking an adversary more to his measure than invincible demons. He was too old to care.

The *Black Heart* sailed on, and his sense of Mathellin sharpened still. Soon he perceived the wizard's direction changing, and corrected the skyship's heading. The sun traveled through the heavens as the *Black Heart* ran down Mathellin. Toward sunset, as they came into view of a village, Veraless began to tremble. He felt every vein in his body crackling with Mathellin's presence.

"Drop sails; dive, dive!" he commanded. The *Black Heart* slowed its course and dropped toward the ground, coming to rest at the outskirts of the village. Taking a half-dozen crew with him, Veraless climbed down. His blood was roiling in him, the spell's pang echoing still.

The inhabitants had noticed the skyship coming aground and several had left their homes, chattering in excitement. Veraless tried to sense if Mathellin was among them, but the shapechanger was too close: The spell no longer allowed Veraless to discern his precise direction. He only knew his quarry was present. Almost groaning in frustration, he ran among the houses, followed by his crew. He thought to hear bells in the distance, felt his heart stutter in his chest.

There was an inn at the center of the village, and behind it a large fowl run. In the orange light of the setting sun, Veraless saw an old man leave the run, carrying a chicken by its wrung neck. Something burst in him and for an endless second he thought he was dying. Then with an inarticulate yell, he ran forward.

&& Mathellin's mouth was overflowing with saliva as he left the fowl run. He heard a sudden yell followed by pounding steps. Damn! He'd been noticed. He snapped his head up, excuses on his tongue, making ready to shift back into animal shape and run away with his prey in his fangs.

The man running toward him wore an unfamiliar uniform. Half his hair was stark white and the other raven black. He held a blade in his left hand; though the metal was out of his body's shadow, it did not gleam and sparkle the way it should have. Instead, to Mathellin's eyes, it appeared to smolder like a dying coal.

"Sir, sir! What's the meaning of this?" Mathellin called out in an old querulous voice, as the muscles of his arms bulged, as his feet grew clawed, as a mouthful of razors replaced his teeth.

The man stopped himself a few steps away. Mathellin's eyes enlarged, drinking in more and more light, so that the man now appeared to him haloed in glory, every plane of his face blazing with the ruddy glow from the western edge of the world. He did not recognize the stranger's face. Villagers were coming toward him, and in addition to them there were six men in uniform.

The old man with the particolored hair spoke in a voice reedy with passion. "I know who you are, Mathellin. I have come for you." And then, in tones of command: "Surround him! He mustn't escape!"

At the mention of his name Mathellin had gone cold with dread. He was aware of the soldiers making a ring all around him, but for an endless moment he did not react. A bird. He should become a bird, and flee. So simple, really, to be the hawk again. He was tired, so tired, but he could fly if he needed to. . . .

"Murderer!" shouted the old man, brandishing his blade and rushing for him.

Mathellin dropped the dead fowl and let his forearm bloom into a shield of bone, straight in the path of the man's weapon. In his imagination he sensed already the blade bouncing off his flesh, his return blow felling his opponent to the ground.

Instead, the dagger buried itself into his flesh, and *burned*.

Mathellin screamed as he tore himself away from the blade. It was a scream no human throat could have formed. His forearm folded back to human shape, scored by a gaping wound running from elbow to wrist. Though he clamped his right hand on the wound, still it dribbled fluid both clear and red.

With cold horror Mathellin at last identified the metal of the blade that had glowed so bright in his vision: *gevroin*. How did the man know? How could he have availed himself of *that*? Mathellin's flesh, which he could shape so as to withstand immersion in molten lava, was seared by the merest brush with *gevroin*—the obverse side of his imaginary father's legacy. But *gevroin* was a substance of Hieloculat; it could not be brought into the real world!

The six other men had drawn swords and tightened their ring around him. Mathellin gazed at their blades: Their metal did not smolder in his sight. Only the old man had the deadly weapon, then.

Mathellin focused his self-image and regained a fully human shape. He felt the lips of his wound close and the flow of his blood and lymph stop. Only a few seconds had elapsed. For a moment longer he delayed, moved by conflicting impulses. He was no fighting wizard, with an array of battle-spells always on his lips; it took him a few heartbeats to bring to mind an incantation that would serve him against this opponent whose blade he dared not face.

But as he began to cast it, he was assaulted by two of the soldiers. He was unable to finish the spell, forced to defend himself by further shapechanging. The soldiers' swords clashed against the metallic scales that had sprouted over Mathellin's back, drawing sparks. He thrust out his left arm, slamming the spiked club of his hand against a soldier' chest with terrible force. He heard a satisfying *crunch* as the soldier's rib cage stove in.

Then the old man, feinting past his exposed guard, drove the *gevroin* dagger into Mathellin's heart. The pain blinded him; he contorted his body desperately, feeling the fibers of his heart dissolving in contact with the blade. Raking at his chest, Mathellin managed to hit the wooden haft and dislodge the blade.

He found himself on his knees, head down, his arms crossed over the crater in his chest that still poured blood. Mathellin's heart hammered erratically, its fibers almost unable to reknit themselves. He focused his self-image with a desperate intensity, healed himself even as more men rushed him, stabbing at his flanks.

Their swords cut him deep, but these wounds hardly mattered; Mathellin snaked an arm up one blade and ripped the man's flesh from his bones, from the elbow down. He rose to his feet, stanching the flow of his blood from his stab wounds. Four men faced him with drawn swords; another lay on his back, dead; the sixth clutched at his nearly-severed arm and screamed. But where were the old man and his *gevroin* blade? Mathellin had thrown it away from him blindly. Had the old man found it?

Then he saw the old man, who had indeed recovered the dagger, moving toward him. Time to end this. Mathellin sprouted blades between his fingers and lengthened his arms. One swipe and he would decapitate any enemy.

Two soldiers rushed him, one on each side. Mathellin struck, and the right-hand one died. Then the *gevroin* blade, flung through the air, slammed into his bowels. Mathellin bent double, screaming, tried to remove the blade. The surviving soldier grasped its haft and forced it up toward his heart; Mathellin's flesh parted like gauze at the touch of the caustic metal.

He grasped the soldier's hands in his, bent back the man's arms to pull the blade out of his flesh. Once it was free, Mathellin squeezed, crushing tendon and bone. The soldier's fingers opened nervelessly; Mathellin saw the hateful dagger drop to the ground, even as the blood dripped from his wounds onto the blade and sizzled.

Mathellin threw the soldier away from him then rose up, his bladed hands held forward. The old man faced him; he had another *gevroin* dagger in his grip. He stroked it across Mathellin's hands and peeled off both fingers and blades, as if scything grass.

A soldier stabbed Mathellin from the back; the wizard fell forward, against the old man. He rebuilt his ruined fingers, extended venomous claws to rake his opponent's flesh to the bone. As they collided in a deadly embrace, the man drove the *gevroin* blade into Mathellin's right eye.

Mathellin twisted, fell onto his back. His arms still clutched his opponent, who fell atop him. Mathellin's head swung back as his neck lengthened, trying to evade the dagger's further blows. The man stabbed him in the heart; the *gevroin* blade shattered his ribcage as if it were cork, rammed into his heart and burst it. Blood spewed onto the blade and boiled up into steam.

With desperate energy, Mathellin twisted and bucked. The dagger slipped out of his ruined flesh as its wielder was thrown off. Overcoming the agony that battered at his soul, Mathellin held his true shape pristine in his mind and compelled his flesh to assume it.

The pain left him; he was healed, whole, if exhausted. He opened his eyes in time to see the old man raise the *gevroin* blade with a trembling arm and bury in the middle of his face. Mathellin heaved his body away, sprouted blades on his hands, swung blindly. The claws of his right hand bit into bone; he grabbed for the old man, fell on top of him. The blade rammed itself into his left ear and pain blotted out reality.

It hit him again, crushing his chest once more, searing his heart to a cinder. Mathellin rose up on his knees, swung his arm—buried his claws into the earth. It seemed to him that he was adrift on a tempest-tossed ship, anchored by one hand to its deck. The ship rose up on a wave, and he no longer knew which way was up and which was down. His right ear was his only portal upon the world anymore—should he not protect it? But his heart had been destroyed, he must repair it, now, now! He reknitted his flesh, and as he did so a burning spear slammed into the right side of his head.

All that was left to him was touch then; his head had become a useless appendage and he sank it down between his shoulders, making a cage of bone for it. And as the *gevroin* stabbed him again and again, as his flesh bubbled and charred, Mathellin grew a dozen arms and groped for his adversary. He found him; his fingers lengthened and wrapped themselves around him and squeezed, squeezed. . . . He felt bones break and his enemy's blood wet his flesh, but the blade was lodged deep in him, so deep, at the very core of him. His heart was ashes, his blood drained from him as if he were a ruptured bladder.

He was dead. It came to him, in a moment of pain-birthed clarity, that he had been dead for years, ever since he had shed his identity to guard Christine. He had fought on, as Vaurd had foretold, long after death. But now, he was so very, very tired. He did not want to fight anymore. He could not make himself believe he was still alive; could no longer keep up the lie by which he had existed for so long.

❦ Veraless lay on his back, crushed under Mathellin's weight, enwrapped by a dozen arms that had gripped him like bands of steel. His right hand still gripped the orichalc dagger, held it inside the shapechanger's chest. Mathellin's flesh sizzled on the blade, his own weight driving it deeper and deeper.

The arms loosened their grip on Veraless, then went completely limp. Barely able to breathe, Veraless felt Mathellin become a dead weight on top of him. His monstrous shape shifted, condensed; and now it was a man who sprawled on top of him. A light breeze had risen. Veraless saw a cloud of flecks rise from the corpse's back.

As Veraless lay helpless, his bones broken, his muscles torn and envenomed, Mathellin's flesh darkened, dried, and crumbled to a dust that the wind carried away. The weight on his chest was gone, but he could no more move than before. His bones had been snapped and his muscles crushed. He felt a strange hollowness inside him; every internal organ must be bleeding.

He thought he saw someone bend over him, one of his crew, face dripping with blood. But Veraless's sight was growing dim: He did not have long left.

He remembered the words of Great Mother Ianthe, her promise that God held all His children eternal in His sight. In this moment it did not comfort him, and he thought it was a reassurance meant for the living, for those who went on. What did it matter to him that his life could be seen laid out like an opened book? What mattered was that he had lived it. He felt no fear; it was too late for that. He had come to the end of his life, and before this simple fact everything else fell away. His eyes closed and he slipped serenely into darkness.

BOOK VII

The End of the World, and After

1. Testenel Besieged

On midday of the twenty-ninth of Ripening, Estephor's army joined up with what was left of Temerorn's and Archeled's once-proud forces. They had been run ragged, forced again and again to turn and repel sudden thrusts from Evered's pursuing army before resuming their speedy retreat. Melogian's spells had won them a narrow escape twice more, but she had exhausted herself as badly as the men and women she was trying to protect, and none of the demons had been more than briefly discommoded by her magic. They were still two days' march away from Testenel.

That morning the armies had crossed the Hedges through the southern passage. The grassy sward their feet had worn down to bare earth was green once more. Once more they trampled it; this time, some of the soldiers darted into the side passages, on whatever transparent pretense suited them, whether scouting or a call of nature. A hundred feet in, the passages bent at right angles; the soldiers vanished from sight. No pursuit was given: In these surroundings, desertions seemed to lose their importance. The late-summer flowers bloomed still as thick as before, and scented the air as if with incense.

To emerge from the green passage into the central plains of Temerorn was to return to a desperately grim reality. The loyalists trudged on, only to pause when they made contact with the Estephorin outriders. The columns slowed down but still marched on: They could no longer afford to rest unless exhaustion demanded it.

Two hours later the armies joined up. Estephor's troops were led by young Duke Corlin himself. An enthusiastic student of war, he had been dreaming of battles since he was a mere child. He immediately sought out General Fraydhan; the old soldier greeted him with the merest trace of deference. Corlin spoke loudly of his plans: His men would make a stand, allowing the Temerorni to retreat at a less punishing pace. Anyone who was still fit and willing to fight would of course be more than welcome. Fraydhan regarded him with an expression mixing fondness and a faint disgust. There would be no help forthcoming from his own men, he said in a flat voice. They would make for Testenel and wish him the best of luck. And with that he turned away, leaving Corlin somewhat bewildered.

The young duke thought to call Fraydhan back, but then he understood how the general was feeling; his heart melted with pity, and his determination to save the day through his people's valor only increased. He spent liberally of his own men and supplies to tend the Temerorni wounded; he arrayed his soldiers in defensive positions and discussed tactical plans with his colonels, moving painted blocks of wood on a map, before marshaling their flesh-and-blood counterparts.

The Estephorin were well fed and eager to fight; the sight of their exhausted brethren was disquieting, but very few of them lost heart because of it. Toughened by their life in a harsh land, they were a people who did not shy at difficulties and indeed took a grim pride in succeeding where others would fail. They prepared themselves for battle with a quiet efficiency.

❧ Melogian was aboard the *Glorious Niavand*. They had been scouting to the south of Temerorn's army, a task they could undertake without fear of being downed, as long as the sorceress was present to hurl levin-bolts at Casimir's firedrake.

For what little good it did them. For days now the situation had remained the same: a panicked flight by the loyalists, while Evered's army pursued. Casimir's demons appeared indefatigable; time and again the wizard would send a pair of them ahead of his main force, to harry the rearguard of Temerorn's forces, or merely to terrorize them into faster flight. Melogian had tried to strike at the demons on these occasions, so far with almost no effect. She could target Evered's men instead of the demons, of course; against them, her magic was quite effective. But not only did her stomach turn when she unleashed death at people; it also left her more vulnerable to an attack from Casimir. He had not attempted another death-spell, which she had proven she could resist. Instead, Evered's wizard had assailed her with a working so bizarre she had almost refused to believe in it, even as it was battering her wards and nearly tearing the life out of her. Invisible to any eye but hers, it appeared as a tarry boiling of hooks and barbs, cleaving any obstacle as it attempted to reach her heart. Her wards could barely hold it at bay; she had tried to null its force, but her spells slid from it like water drops. Still half-thinking this was yet another demon, not a spell-making, she had dredged an exotic counterspell from her memory, geared to oppose workings in a style Orion had decreed long obsolete. This counterspell worked at last, paring Casimir's sending down to nothingness, one barb at a time.

When the attack was over, Melogian had hugged herself and panted, drenched in sweat. It was as if the past itself were attacking her, dawn mages from the First unleashing their forgotten secrets, reaching through the millennia. . . . She wondered once more how Casimir could have gained this knowledge. Had he opened a window into time, to spy upon elder mages as they cast? Was it a miraculous book of spells he had unearthed, scribed upon imperishable metal?

There was no point in wondering. Feverish with discouragement, she guarded the *Glorious Niavand* and did what little she could to help the loyalist armies. Now, as they made their way back to the troops, she beheld Corlin's army with a dull emotion, too worn and frayed to be hope.

The skyship was hailed as it approached; it decreased altitude and Melogian was lowered to the ground in a gondola, to be brought before Duke Corlin.

"Your Grace," she said with a simple nod of the head.

Corlin took her hand in his. "Lady Melogian; I am very pleased to see you. I have been hoping to discuss strategy."

He led her inside his hastily erected tent and offered her wine, which she declined. She listened as he moved his wooden blocks on the map, found herself lulled by the music of his voice. When he asked her opinion, she struggled to find her words.

"Your Grace, I don't understand military strategy. All I know is that General Fraydhan is a lot older than you, and a lot more experienced, and that he has failed to halt Evered's advance; that he left you to run for the shelter of Testenel, where he does not expect us to survive a siege. I feel that this does not bode well for our chances. But your understanding may differ from mine."

Corlin looked crestfallen for a moment, but appeared to shake off the feeling.

"Estephor stands strong, my Lady Wizard. We can and must prevail. I understand your exhaustion, and I shouldn't have pressed you when you clearly need rest. All I ask is whether you will fight by my side."

Melogian smiled at his words, managing to draw some valiance from Corlin's own fire.

"I will fight with you, Corlin. I can do little against the demons, but I can harm Evered's men. I'll go back aboard the *Glorious Niavand* and use it as a platform. When you attack, I'll use my spells to support you. I've learned to do that a bit better now."

Corlin thanked her gravely and let her go. Once more aboard the skyship, she watched the loyalist armies retreating toward their still-distant goal, while Estephor's troops deployed themselves below. She went to the prow of the ship and waited for the rebels to arrive.

⁂ Evered's troops had been little delayed by their crossing of the Hedges. Rather than filter through the relatively narrow southern opening, the human troops stood by while Casimir's demons opened up a much wider passage. Egrevogn could batter the bushes to bits with only a moderate exertion of his strength. The terrapin pushed through slowly but surely, clearing a wide swath; the firedrake shook off flames onto the bushes just before it, aiding in the destruction. By the time the rebel forces had made it through, the southern passage through the Hedges was almost thrice its previous width, a smoking strip of bare soil. Flowers by the hundreds had fallen to the ground, burnt and trampled. Those few that had not been destroyed curled up their petals and wilted. By the morrow they would have matured into pods; in three days' time these would rupture, pouring seeds upon the devastated ground. In a week the first shoots would emerge from the soil, and before winter the new bushes would be six feet high.

The rebel troops continued their march at a good pace; in the early afternoon they met with Estephor's army. When the rebel army appeared at the rim of the shallow vale where Corlin had decided to make his stand, it paused and hesitated. For a time the soldiers milled in apparent confusion, as the demons took a few mincing steps down the gentle slope then retreated. Before the rebel forces could decide on a course of action, Duke Corlin gave the signal for a charge.

The vanguard of the Estephorin army flowed up the slope, to be met by the seven-limbed demon. It struck again and again, impaling men on its claws, cleaving horses in half with a single bite; but the soldiers ignored it, and pushed onward. It was the human core of Evered's forces they sought, and as more and more Estephorin soldiers pressed to the attack, they found it.

The rebel soldiers, even Kawlend's troops, had grown complacent, their campaign become little more than a late-summer's outing. The Estephorins' furious attack took them ill prepared. Even as dozens of their fellows died under the attacks of Casimir's demons, Corlin's soldiers tore into the rebel forces and wreaked slaughter of their own. More and more Estephorin soldiers poured into the breach; the battle turned into a confused melee, in which Casimir's demons now proved far less useful, as their attacks would kill both friend and foe.

Casimir was forced to withdraw them from the thick of the fighting; and so, for a few minutes Duke Corlin was able to believe in his dream. Even Melogian, from the vantage of the *Glorious Niavand*, steeling herself and invoking a rain of flames onto the rebel forces, allowed herself to hope. Evered was panicking, it seemed; his army convulsed and thrashed like a huge living thing, caught unawares and badly wounded by a single thrust.

A detachment of mounted soldiers found itself cleaving Evered's ranks too easily: Suddenly, they were facing Egrevogn the ogre, who swung a metal-shod club and roared in a voice so deep it threatened to shatter bone. Possibly the soldiers had heard the tales of him that survived to this day; possibly some of them knew terror at being faced by a child's nightmare made actual. Possibly, though, others were heartened at seeing his flesh scored by a dozen smoking wounds, proof that this skin was no more impervious than theirs. They rode to the attack, shouting their company's slogan.

Egrevogn's club pulped a man's head and struck another one from his mount with the same swing. The backstroke killed one more, but a spear had lodged itself in Egrevogn's hip, another in his knee. He turned, and that leg betrayed him; Egrevogn slipped and fell to one knee, dropping his mattock. With his bare hands he reached out, unhorsed two men and crushed them to death; but the others were on it, striking desperately. With vast, dull-witted surprise, Egrevogn the ogre went down under a tide of men and did not rise again.

This moment of glory was the crowning of Corlin's attack, and the beginning of its failure. The Estephorin assault would have wrought utter carnage, had it been able to continue at this pace; but it faltered from simple lack of men. Evered's forces rallied and began to push back the attackers, while the redeployed demons wreaked ruin on the flanks. In half a minute, with the majestic inevitability of the tide, what had been triumph became disaster.

Aghast at the failure of his dream, Duke Corlin committed the remainder of his army in one last thrust. He led that desperate charge himself, and for a brief moment he recaptured his heart's desire, as Evered's forces once more trembled.

But still he failed; his assault gave his vanguard a few more minutes of life, but they were still as doomed as they had been from the start. And their would-be rescuers found themselves surrounded, with an enemy army before them and demons at their backs.

From the air, Melogian had seen Corlin's dream draw breath, live, and die. She used up her reserves of strength now, invoking enspelled death on Evered's human forces, killing men by the dozen with fire and acid. Her efforts could no more prevent the disaster than a child's sandcastle could hold back the ocean.

The *Glorious Niavand* was already at some risk from enemy archers, since it had to reduce altitude to bring the enemy troops into range of Melogian's spellcraft. With Estephor's attack in shambles, Casimir now sent his demons back in. Melogian saw the firedrake approach them, gingerly. Clearly the demon remembered the pain she had caused it. As it undulated closer and closer, Melogian marshaled what was left of her power and gasped out another spell.

The levin-bolt she hurled at the firedrake lacked its full strength; still, it hurt the firedrake badly enough that it retreated, though not before lashing out and pelting the *Glorious Niavand* with flame. As her crew worked frantically to extinguish the blaze, the skyship fled from the battle, as did a few Estephorin stragglers on the ground.

Of Estephor's army nearly nothing was left; those who had been the hope of Chrysanthe lay dead upon the ground in their thousands. Duke Corlin survived, but he had been gravely wounded and captured.

Still, the rebel army had been hurt. In another kind of war, this damage would have been minor; paradoxically, it was much worse in this case, precisely because Kawlend's army and the baronial rabble had not really needed to fight heretofore. What they had perceived as an invincible vanguard had proven to be an imperfect protection—and certainly not invulnerable, for Egrevogn the ogre was dead. His gashed corpse lay steaming at the center of a circle of dead men. The snakes that were his beard had parted from his body and fled into the grass. His green flesh already swelled and crawled with rot. Pores on his abdomen opened and spewed out clouds of purulence. A swarm of viridian wasps was emerging from his mouth and nose; already they had stung two men, who had died from their venom.

And so Evered's army found itself reluctant to press onward. Though it moved forward and out of the vale in which Estephor's dead and its own lay scattered, it did not get much farther before stopping for the night. Corlin's suicidal attack had in fact bought the loyalist forces time enough to withdraw to Testenel. Over the next two days, Evered's vanguard never got within sight of Chrysanthe's army.

Melogian returned to Testenel aboard the *Glorious Niavand* on the twenty-ninth of Ripening. Exhausted and demoralized, she withdrew herself from the fighting, to recover her strength before Testenel was besieged.

She met with Christine and reported the situation. She spoke with Quentin in private for a time; they found themselves quarreling, albeit without much heat, and eventually made peace. She went to visit Orion's quarters, looked for the vial that had held the scrap of flesh from Mathellin, and found only a blackened tatter inside. Her relief at this development was cut short when the *Black Heart* returned to Testenel carrying the corpse of her captain.

She spent an unpleasant night, and in the morning began unweaving part of the web she had spun about Testenel, to recover some of the strength she had invested there. From a short distance, she did not doubt Casimir would be able to cast his perceptions within the castle as he wished, regardless of her own counterspells. No need then for the barriers to vision she had labored so hard to erect. She verified the wards she had set about the openings of the made worlds, even the two that had been sealed off for centuries, and double-checked the protections she had spun about Christine.

Having completed these preparations, she spent some hours pondering the courses of action left to her. Presently she reached a conclusion; it filled her with dread, and yet there was also calm to be gleaned from it. With the paring away of choices, there was no more reason to waste energy pondering what might be. She thought of discussing her plan with Quentin, then rejected the idea. Better to present him with a *fait accompli*. When the time came, he would do what was needful. That night she slept soundly and woke more rested than she had been in weeks.

⁊⁊ Testenel stood some distance from Tiellorn; it had been built at the summit of a low hill, which had been in the long past extensively reworked so that it presented a better defensive position. Over the centuries, the purity of the initial arrangement had decayed. Erosion had dug gullies in the slopes; bushes and trees had sprouted, and the incessant labor of worms in the soil had slowly buried stones. For a time the land immediately surrounding the castle had been tilled fields. Then the fields had been paved over, with pathways marked and statuary erected at the corners, so that the castle occupied the center of what might have been a colossal gaming board. The paving stones had cracked, broken, and slowly been washed away for nearly a thousand years. Then they had been all removed, the land returned to a semi-wild state. During the early fifth millennium, when the whole of Chrysanthe was torn by war, Testenel had been no more than an architectural ornament, of no strategic value: The sovereigns had dwelled in Perfenel, the ancient dour castle within Tiellorn itself, nearly as old as humankind. When the world returned to a more peaceful state, the court had emerged from the crumbling redoubt and returned to the blue spires of Testenel, a home better fit for the rulers of Chrysanthe than the haunted and sweating gray stone of Perfenel. Testenel then lay at the heart of a small forest, carefully tended and coppiced, as if attempting to rival the great gardens of Tiellorn, which were still maintained by the same dawn magic of the First that kept the Hedges eternally pristine.

Three hundred years before the present, that forest had been mostly cleared away, and since then the windows of Testenel had gazed over vast lawns featuring the odd clump of trees.

Over these lawns the remnants of the loyalist armies had staggered back home. The wounded and the unfit had been conveyed to Tiellorn, where they might regain their health behind the city's walls. The others, a fraction of the number that had set out, made their way up the slope of the hill and entered the castle, bringing with them an aura of gloom and defeat.

The next day, the first of Harvest, brought Evered's forces to Testenel. As they had during the Usurpation War, Kawlend's forces ignored Tiellorn, which in turn ignored them. To assault the city would have consumed enormous resources and gained little; this was not a war of conquest, as few of Chrysanthe's wars had ever been, but a challenge to the crown. Evered's forces were well fed, being supplied from Kawlend and having looted the towns along their route; they had no need as yet to extort food from the city, and consequently left it alone.

To besiege Testenel, Evered must perforce cut off its link with Tiellorn, a scarcely defended road running from the castle to the western gate of the city. It should have been the first order of business of any determined general, yet the rebel forces deployed themselves to the south of the castle and there halted.

It was near midmorning. Melogian stood on a south-facing balcony and gazed at Evered's host; and she wanted to laugh. Not from irony, nor from despair, but because of the tininess of this war. In her travels through the made worlds she had witnessed battles of immense scope. Once she had stood at the crenellated summit of a mile-long wall, and looked down through driving rain at an army that numbered ten myriads, each warrior seven feet tall and clad in gleaming black steel. When the signal for the assault had been given, the helms had flowed forward like the waves of the ocean in a storm. . . . And Melogian had taken one step *beyond*, and found a different army assaulting the wall, red-liveried, stoop-shouldered manlings carrying torches that burned despite the deluge. And another step, to feel the stones under her feet already trembling from the blows of a hundred battering rams; and another, to witness defenders tipping cauldrons of magma onto their carapaced and winged assailants; and another, and another still, and now the mountains that had channeled the assailants fell away and a vast plain stretched to the limits of vision; a plain filled with soldiers in numbers she could barely conceive of, so that the patterns of their attacks mirrored the rush of the storm clouds above.

Compared to what she had seen, Evered's and Chrysanthe's armies were jokes, a gaggle of children playing war in a forest clearing. She should have felt unconcerned with the paltry hundreds or thousands who might die today, for had she not seen millions condemned to the slaughter? And for a few seconds at a time, she could make herself cease to care, could achieve the cool detachment of one who had seen it all. But she could not sustain it, and did not truly wish to: This was Casimir's way of looking at the world, not hers.

Like a flower of blue stone, Testenel blossomed from a central stem, so that the upper floors of the castle were three or four times as wide as the lower. From this stem radiated spines of outbuildings, like thorns. Three concentric walls ringed the stem, the diameter of the outermost one somewhat exceeding that of the upper stories. From her vantage point, Melogian could not see the foot of the wall below, but she had seen a detachment of their remaining forces exiting through the gate in this section of the wall, to establish a line of defense outside the castle.

A portion of the armies of Temerorn and Archeled had remained to guard Testenel; these fresh troops had arrayed themselves before the castle, with a significant force already hunkered down between the concentric walls.

They might have made a brave stand against Evered's men and women, might even, conceivably, have broken the siege, given enough time, since Archeled and Estephor both could muster more and more troops and send them to the relief of the besieged castle. But against the demons there was no true defense. They stood there now, in the front ranks, towering over the human troops; Melogian was reminded once more of very young children playing at battles, using toys grossly mismatched in size. Why were they not moving to the attack? Had a reprieve been called for bath time? If only these could be toys left abandoned in a sandbox, to molder in the rain. . . .

❧ General Fraydhan himself came to see Christine. She had not yet met with him since the return of the loyalist armies. She was struck by the change in his appearance: not so much physically, although he certainly looked quite tired, but in his bearing. The serene confidence he had shown in himself and his appraisal of the situation had vanished. He was a man haunted by his failure to predict the disaster that had befallen his troops. When he presented himself, he walked in with a hesitant step and spoke in a low voice.

"Your Highness . . . A delegation from the rebels has delivered a message," he said. "They request parley. Prince Evered wishes to speak with you, out on the field."

She felt chilled at the request: To venture outside of Testenel was to expose herself, and every step taken would bring her closer to the demons. She had been looking at them from a distant vantage point, and even from afar they filled her with horror. But what was the alternative? To remain immured within these walls and wait for Evered to launch an attack?

Quentin was by her side, as he had been almost constantly since his return from Lydiss. "Sir Quentin," she asked, "what do you think? Is this parley a good idea? I'd like to hear what Evered has to say."

"You should not expose yourself to harm, Lady Christine!"

"Doesn't the Law protect me?"

"Demons don't know the Law," Quentin objected.

"Your Highness," interjected Fraydhan. "Don't forget, Casimir would be seen as guilty in the eyes of God if he sent his demons to attack your person; surely the Law would destroy him. But still, let us demand the demons be withdrawn from the fore of Evered's troops. You would be inarguably safe then."

Quentin made further objections. Christine was on the verge of agreeing with him when Melogian entered, so abruptly that Rann hadn't finished calling out her name before the sorceress reached Christine's side.

"Did I hear correctly?" she asked. "General, did Evered offer parley?"

Fraydhan's dislike of Melogian could not have been plainer writ upon his face. "Indeed, Lady Wizard, Prince Evered has requested parley," he said stiffly. "The regent was debating with us whether or not to agree."

"Please, Christine," began Melogian. She was very pale, except for twin spots of color high on her cheeks. What she said next was a complete surprise. "You should go. You must agree."

"What?" Quentin was scandalized. "Lady Melogian, why?"

Melogian looked at Christine eye to eye. "I will go with you. Quentin should probably come, and as many soldiers as you want. We should take the opportunity to speak with Evered. It could make a difference—a huge difference."

"You really think this is so important?" Christine asked.

"I do." Christine had always been able to tell when Melogian lied to her; there was a shift in the sorceress's eyes that betrayed her untruths. She saw no such sign now. Melogian seemed in utter earnest.

"But why?" asked Fraydhan.

"It will help me," the sorceress said after a moment's hesitation. "It will help me know what to do to protect us. It will help you, Christine, but I admit it will help me more."

Christine looked at Quentin; he nodded. "The Lady Melogian was right once before, and we failed to pay her enough heed," he said. "And we have suffered from this error. If truly this meeting makes such a difference, then we probably should do as she says. I will come with you, milady, and we will have a score of soldiers to guard you."

A message was sent back to Evered's camp. After some back-and-forthing, arrangements were agreed upon by both sides. An hour later, Christine found herself at the core of a delegation, crossing the walls that surrounded the stem of Testenel. The soldiers stationed along the way watched the delegation pass intently; Christine felt a familiar unease at being the center of attention, and tried to ignore it.

The gates of the outermost wall opened for them, and they walked out upon the lawns surrounding Testenel. The rebel forces seemed farther away to Christine than she had guessed, watching them from a high vantage point within Testenel. Casimir had withdrawn his demons. Only one of them could be seen: the firedrake, which was flying far to the south, a burning curlicue.

The rebel delegation now approached them. They were somewhat fewer in number, a dozen or so. It had originally been proposed that the parties should meet within the outermost wall, but Evered had rejected the conditions and eventually a meeting just outside the gates of Testenel was deemed acceptable.

The rebels walked along the graveled path that led to the gates. Christine knew that archers were training arrows upon them, and she wondered what would happen if one's thumb were to slip and an arrow hit Evered. The regent of Chrysanthe held herself very erect, but her fists were painfully clenched.

The rebel delegation came close; Christine recognized Evered—his face had branded itself in her memory. Aside from soldiers, he was accompanied by a portly man with auburn hair and a fringe of reddish beard along the line of his lower jaw. "Is that Casimir?" she asked, and Melogian breathed "Yes," like a lover in the throes of passion.

The rebel party came to a halt while still a few yards distant. Evered, however, strolled forward. The soles of his boots scritched on the gravel. The sword at his side stayed in its sheath; his arms swung loosely, reminding Christine of the carefree stride of a young child. Casimir had remained behind and smiled benignly at the scene. Christine found it hard to believe this man was able to hold five demons under his control at once: He looked like a television repairman who spent his evenings drinking beer. Now he flexed his wrist and lifted a hand from his paunch, fluttering his fingers as if in a discreet greeting. "*Fuck* you, you cur," whispered Melogian through clenched teeth, all too close to Christine's ear. She glanced at the sorceress, astonished, and saw Melogian biting her lip, trying to look away.

Evered stopped a pace or two from the guards, who had all drawn their swords. Christine sensed his presence acutely, as if he were somehow exerting pressure on her skin. Quentin stood to her left, his hand at the pommel of his blade. For several seconds no one spoke, until Melogian broke the silence.

"So, here you are, Evered."

Evered tilted his head and sneered. "Oh, here I am, indeed, apprentice. The last time I was in this place, I lacked the means to fully appreciate it. Now, though, my feet are truly on the soil of my rightful home. I must say, it is a delight. How about you, my dear? Are you enjoying this moment?"

"Well, I enjoy knowing your metamorph is dead. Captain Veraless slew him before twenty witnesses. He won't be coming back for further orders."

Evered's expression froze long enough for him to blink twice in quick succession. Then he replied, "I am sure I don't know what you mean."

"Don't mock us! You've wrought so much evil—"

Evered cut Melogian off. "I take responsibility for no evil; not before you, not before the Law. I have fought desperately to restore Chrysanthe to a rightful rule. History will recognize the value of my life. My name will be praised in future decades."

Melogian drew breath to reply. Christine intervened, unwilling to let this verbal sparring continue.

"Cut to the chase, Evered. What do you want?"

Evered pursed his lips and whistled soundlessly. "You still betray the speech patterns of the made world where you lived, you poor little girl. Fortunately I can guess at your meaning. What I want, my Lady Christine, is your surrender. I will not speak of abdication: You are not queen, merely regent. So yield to me; give up the crown. I had been planning to have you exiled to the world of your childhood, but now that I see you again, I am moved to pity. If you insist on remaining in the true realm, I will allow it."

That threat sent a cold chill down Christine's spine. Her voice faltered as she said: "Oh? You were less clement the last time we spoke."

"I am hot-tempered, Christine; I won't deny it. But I have a soft heart; I do. I enjoy being merciful, when I can afford to be so. Give me a chance, milady, and you will not regret it. After all, how could you ever wear the crown? You are barely a woman, inexperienced, ignorant of the world. How can you expect to rule? You are merely your father's child, while I am mine, and that, strange as it seems, makes all the difference to the Law. The throne of Chrysanthe is mine, by birth and training; never yours."

As Evered spoke of the Law, Christine found herself recalling Tap Fullmoon. A childish fantasy; a benediction Orion had cast for her and that warded her as she was taken down into the made world; an embodiment of hope; whatever he had been, she could almost see him again at her side, next to Quentin, the devoted knight who spoke with his voice and who had rescued her from her bondage. She became aware of herself standing in the courtyard, of Testenel behind and above her, of the land extending in all directions until it reached the borders of the world, the oceans and the gray void north and south. . . . She saw herself, not *within* Chrysanthe, but part of it, at long last. In that moment it seemed to her she stood at the fulcrum of the world, and she felt the touch of an outside wisdom. Her heart had been pounding in fear; now its rhythm steadied, and it was anger, blossoming into rage, which pulsed through her veins. Her voice shook still, but so little only she could register it.

"You're half right, Evered," she said. "Maybe I am unfit to rule Chrysanthe. If I am, I have you to thank for it. All the filth Dr. Almand poured into my head, all the misery I suffered, came from you. You and your pet wizard, you're responsible for all the hurt I have ever known."

Evered's features twisted into a mask of incredulity. "Such ranting, my Lady Regent! You truly seem unstable; I'd be doing you a favor taking the crown from that ugly little head of yours. . . .".

Casimir had stepped forward to stand at Evered's side. Vaurd's son noticed him with a start and hissed at him, "I thought I told you to stay behind!"

"I'm not your golmin, m'lord," Casimir replied in an easy voice.

"If it were only my pain, Evered," Christine continued, "I would yield to you now." Those words got their attention: Both Evered and Casimir looked at her, surprised. "If it were only me, only my hurt, I would forget it. But there's something more. There is the matter of the Law. And the land doesn't want me to yield. Do you hear me, Evered? *I can feel the Law.* And the Law rejects you."

She took two steps forward, nearly shouldering her guards aside.

"You are not, and you will never be, the rightful ruler. Your father Vaurd was deposed; your dynasty is over. I am the daughter of Edisthen and the legitimate successor to the throne. I am the regent, I shall be queen, and I refuse to yield to you, now and forever."

She caught her breath; she was quivering in every limb, but she felt more right than she had in ages.

Evered slouched dejectedly and heaved a huge sigh. "Dear me, what a tantrum. Little Christine claims she can feel the Law, like every good sovereign should. How convenient. Like her father before her, how can one verify her claims? Poor girl; you'll play through this charade to the bitter end, won't you? Well then, we shall have to unseat you by force. Let me make my condolences for the additional thousands you are sentencing to a needless death."

He turned on his heel abruptly, though not fast enough to hide the spastic sneer that distorted his features, and started striding away. Casimir made to follow him, when Melogian called out in a loud voice, at the threshold of a scream: *"Hold!"*

It is so much easier to reach a decision in one's heart than to announce it. Throughout the parley Melogian had waited for the proper time; and perhaps, truth be told, she had hoped to find another way out of their predicament. What sealed her decision had been that momentary dispute between Evered and Casimir, the ludicrous digression that interrupted the most important discussion of the entire war.

Casimir had moved forward, of course, because the events interested him and he stood at the center of his own private world. Melogian had seen that deadness in his gaze the very first time she'd met him; it was still there, that glassy reflection that hinted at a void at the core of the man. She was convinced, meeting the gaze of these dead eyes, that in Casimir's sight nothing truly existed but Casimir himself, and when he gazed at the outside world he merely allowed himself to get absorbed in the fancies his own mind generated. It occurred to her then, with sudden clarity, that there lay one of the keys to his power; and it only reinforced her decision.

Still, Melogian let Christine finish speaking, both because Christine needed to say her piece, and because her words were fitting for a future queen of the land. When Christine announced that she could feel the Law rejecting Evered, Melogian felt a rush of pride and love. This must be how mothers felt when their children grew up, she thought.

Evered spoke in reply, almost clownish in his exaggerated posturings. Here was madness of a different order from Casimir's: Evered believed in the outside world, but he was trapped within it, unable to accept the way things lay, endlessly waging war against reality. Another might have pressed his claim to the throne and been content to win it; even if he deposed Christine, Evered would spend the rest of his life in anguish, finding new targets for his wrath since he could never assault his own past. And so it was time for Melogian to act.

As Evered turned away, as Casimir prepared to follow him, Melogian called out, "Hold!" The wizard looked at her, a smug smile on his lips. He lifted an interrogative eyebrow.

"Casimir!" Melogian shouted, making her way through the guards. "I call challenge!"

As she stepped forward, closer to Casimir, her gut twisted within her and shivers chased themselves down her spine, so intense was her revulsion. Evered she could despise, hate, perhaps even pity. Casimir she could only loathe.

She stopped when she stood two paces away from him, raised her head a trifle to look him in the eye, and spoke the words of an old tradition. "Through the turning of the sun and within the arms of Ocean, I call challenge. Our blood shall bear witness; our lives shall stand in the balance. Challenge is called!"

The wizard grinned from ear to ear, his eyes wide, his face alight.

"What was that?" he purred. "Did I hear you aright? Have you just called challenge, sweetling? How deliciously archaic!"

At her back, Melogian heard Quentin's choked protest, an indrawn breath that could be Christine's. She finished the recitation: "Your puissance against mine, before the eyes of God, Casimir. I call challenge!"

No formal duel of magic had been fought for three and a half centuries, but Melogian had learned the ritual formulas, and she had no doubt Firlow had taught Casimir as well as Orion had taught her. As a young girl, she had repeated these very words to herself dozens of times, imagining herself overcoming some vague rival through sheer mastery and power. How thrilling it had been then, when nothing was actually risked. Now that she had truly spoken the words, she felt like running away and hiding under a stone.

Evered had turned back; his scowl betrayed his uncertainty. Then he assumed his habitual mantle of contempt and sneered. "In God's name, what cant are you spouting, apprentice? Go back inside; go practice turning pebbles into turds."

Casimir stepped toward Melogian, so that she was forced to take a half-step back. She caught a whiff of his smell, a rankness of unwashed flesh and soured sweat. "Under the sun, amidst Ocean, I hear you, Melogian," he intoned. "My blood and yours to stand witness, our lives at stake, under the gaze of God. Challenge is accepted."

"Casimir!" Evered shouted in a furious tone. "Enough of this!"

His wizard pivoted to glare at him. "Pardon me, m'lord, but this is a wizardly matter between the girl and myself, and none of your business."

"It's a trick, you fool! Your duty is to me; I order you to leave here at once."

Casimir's mouth twisted in a grimace of disgust. Seeing his expression so clearly, Melogian shivered. She and Orion had always entertained strong suspicions about Firlow's passing. Now she wondered how they could ever have been less than certain. She understood, chillingly, how it must have pleased Casimir to dispose of his mentor in such a fashion, once he felt Firlow had become more of a hindrance than an asset; and that the only thing that held Casimir back from eliminating Evered was the sure knowledge that the Law would obliterate him in retribution.

The wizard let his breath hiss between his teeth before replying.

"I am not a fool, my Lord Evered. And this is not a trick. Melogian is far too nice a little girl to joke about a formal duel—are you, love?"

She said nothing. Casimir looked behind Melogian at the royal delegation and smiled.

"I see this is as much a surprise for your friends as it is for me. When exactly did you expect us to contest, sweet Melogian? Or is it my choice as the challenged party?"

"The time and place are yours to choose, within reason," she answered.

Casimir pursed his lips like a little boy savoring a stolen piece of candy. "Well, then. Shall we say that low knoll yonder, the one with a ruined fountain? In an hour?"

"I shall be there."

"And I, love, shall be awaiting you. Now, my Lord Evered, we can go back."

The rebel delegation strode away, back to their own lines. The loyalists, meanwhile, remained motionless. Both Quentin and Christine were looking at Melogian, bewildered and appalled.

"Melogian, what did you just do? What was that?" Christine asked.

"I've given challenge," the sorceress explained. "It's a very ancient ritual, going back millennia. Casimir and I are going to engage in a spell-duel, one against one."

"Lady Melogian," Quentin asked, intently, "what kind of duel?"

Melogian wanted to lie; had Christine not been present, she might well have, but she always betrayed herself to Christine.

"It's to the death," she said.

"God's teeth, no!" Quentin was outraged and grasped her arm with painful strength. As he started expostulating, Melogian began walking back as swiftly as she could toward the castle. The rest of the delegation followed her. As soon as they were within the outermost wall, Melogian led them to a sheltered spot and dismissed their escort, who grudgingly moved some distance away. Then she cast a spell of silence to surround the three of them and shield their conversation from other ears.

Quentin had kept up a steady stream of protests, while Christine remained silent, her face white. Melogian held up a hand, shouted above Quentin's loud voice.

"Enough! Listen, both of you! Listen to me, in God's name!"

Quentin fell silent. Melogian, breathing heavily, looked at Christine's frozen face and had to close her eyes.

"I know what I am doing. I have been planning this for a long while," she said. "Fighting Casimir in a spell-duel is my best hope of overcoming him."

"But you keep telling us how powerful he is!" objected Quentin. "Why a direct confrontation?"

"You're thinking in military terms, Quentin. In magic, it's more effective for the weaker mage to engage in direct combat than to work through intermediaries."

"But you are gambling with your life!"

"Yes, I am. Because there is no other way out. What makes Evered's army irresistible are the demons Casimir has raised, and the elder spells he manages to wield at the same time. He is more powerful, more knowledgeable, and more skilled, than I am. If I expend my strength supporting our army, he will eventually wear me down and Testenel will fall."

"No," said Christine in a small voice. "No, Melogian, don't do it. No!"

"I have to."

"*No!* I forbid you! I order you; I order you as your sovereign! Stay here with us."

"I won't obey you, Christine."

"Lady Melogian! This is your queen speaking!" argued Quentin. "You will do as she says. . . ."

"I won't. It doesn't matter who she is. No one under God's gaze has power over me anymore. I've served Orion, I've served Edisthen, and I still serve you, Christine. But I serve you best by doing what needs to be done."

She spoke on, raising her voice again, ignoring their words.

"You need to prepare for what will happen during the duel, and afterward. I have advice you need to hear!"

Both Quentin and Christine paused in their protests and she took advantage of that lull.

"My most important piece of advice is that you should get wed; if not now, then soon." As they gaped at her in astonishment, she drove the point home. "Christine, you're young enough that you have a right to be confused. But frankly, Quentin, a man of your age should be able to know his own heart better, and recognize love when he sees it in a girl's eyes."

Christine flushed, followed by Quentin, and Melogian felt a grim amusement at the two youngsters' discomfiture.

"I don't have time to enjoy debating this with you, Quentin. I can anticipate all your objections, and the fact is, you've earned Christine's hand a dozen times over. Furthermore, crass politics says a regent who hasn't reached her majority will benefit from a marriage to an older man. Especially now, with both dukes dead, the land will welcome this union."

She drew breath and went on. "Secondly: You must prepare for flight. If I lose the duel, then Evered's forces will soon overwhelm our defenses. Quentin, you will have to take Christine away into exile. The hinterlands of Estephor are your best choice: The Estephorin will never let Christine be taken. I know Quentin is skilled enough that both of you can hide as long as needed. Casimir may still use a seek-spell against Christine, but remember any attempt at forceful restraint would be fatal: You can use the Law to your advantage and evade capture. I wouldn't recommend seeking shelter in a made world, but Quentin still bears the Quester's Gifts. I trust his judgment if he decides you need to vanish into Jyndyrys or Hieloculat for greater security. One day, it will be time to return, and reinstate the rightful reign. Remember, the Law will not allow a madman to retain the throne indefinitely."

Quentin, still blushing, stammered a question.

"But—but even then, Lady, why are you doing this? We can still follow your plan without you going into battle against Casimir! What can you gain by fighting him directly so he can just burn you to cinders?"

She shook her head. "He can't, Quentin. It isn't that simple. I'm warded more thoroughly now than since this began. He's attacked me directly twice, with extremely strong workings, but I've survived. He may be stronger than me, but that doesn't mean he can crush me without breaking a sweat. And he's already tired. No one can have limitless reserves of energy, and Casimir has been driving his demons for weeks. Don't you see what this means?"

"I see it means we can remain in Testenel and fight him from a distance!"

"It means that even if I lose the duel, we can still win. I am going to exhaust Casimir, make him expend so much power he won't have anything left in reserve. And once he's reeling, I'll snap the tether with which he holds his demons in thrall. If he loses control over them, it will turn the tide of the war."

"*If* he loses control?" gasped Christine. "You don't even know you can do it!"

Melogian shrugged. "I believe I have a good chance. Perhaps I'm wrong. We'll soon see."

"Don't do it! It's insane!" Christine protested. Quentin opened his mouth as if to scream and berate her, then cast his gaze down and simply begged her: "Stay with me, Melogian, please."

She felt her eyes burning, but as ever they remained dry. "I'm not brave, Quentin," she said. "Don't make this any harder than it has to be."

"Then stall for time! Ask for a delay. Allow us some chance to better prepare; ask General Fraydhan for his advice. . . ."

He was clearly flailing, but his words set Melogian's mind on a sudden new tack and an idea burst into her head.

"Of course," she said. "What an idiot I am! I'll never learn to be a proper battle-mage. Thank you, Quentin."

She kissed him, briefly, on the lips; then turned to Christine and took her in her arms as she had so often wanted to and never dared. Christine struggled in her grasp; she was crying and sobbing, and Melogian felt a pang of guilt to be inflicting so much sorrow on someone she loved so much. "Forgive me," she breathed in Christine's hair, then broke the embrace and strode away at a near run, ignoring Christine's and Quentin's desperate words. She had to see General Fraydhan before anything else; every minute now counted.

2. The Duel

Nearly an hour had passed when Melogian strode out through the gates of Testenel. She had arrayed herself for battle and wore garments of a striking cut: a deep-cleft vest and loose trousers, reinforced with patches of woven silver strands and studded with bronze medallions. She had twisted her hair in a pair of braids and tied gemstones at the end of each one, and bound a sash across her forehead; an onyx scarab shone upon her brow. Glittering feathers, purple, green, and gold, rose in stiff fans from her shoulders. She looked like a barbarian princess from deep within a made world; all that was missing was the requisite sword, though she had brought a dagger sharp as a surgeon's knife. There were nasty bits of metal hidden within the fabric of her clothes as well, and a full array of wizardly implements sewn to the lining of her vest. The duel might run in an unforeseen direction, and she intended to be ready for all eventualities.

Wordlessly she passed through the ranks of soldiers massed between the walls. She saw some of them salute her and gave a few nods left and right. Fraydhan had assured her he would be ready when the time came.

When she had reached the gates of the outermost wall, she paused and looked up to the window behind which she knew Quentin and Christine were standing, watching her. She raised her hand in a subdued salute then walked through the opening gates.

Across the wide, carefully tended lawn she slowly strode, down a gentle slope. Evered's army massed ahead of her, the thousands of soldiers in the colors of Vaurd's line and of Kawlend. The demons had returned to the front ranks. She saw the terrapin and the seven-limbed metallic horror standing amidst soldiers who had almost lost their dread of the demons; the firedrake flew to the rear of the rebel army. The green ogre was dead, at least: Melogian had seen him fall. The cloud-demon she could not discern and assumed it had been kept in reserve.

Evered could have laid an ambush: It was risky, what she did, crossing the sward alone, vulnerable to a sudden rush of men, or a demon's attack. Yet she understood Casimir to that extent, that he would never stoop to treachery to defeat her, not when he could use his magic alone to destroy her utterly. Evered wouldn't have the same scruples—she hoped Casimir had warned his liege against any such trickery.

At last she reached the low knoll Casimir had indicated. The wizard was already there, waiting for her. He appeared composed, almost bored. He hadn't changed his garments and wore the same reddish robes as before. There were mud stains on the hem and she couldn't decide if they were a sign of absentmindedness or a gesture of contempt toward her.

She reached the flat top of the knoll and stopped, fifteen paces from Casimir. She had made plans, careful and complicated; chains of spells to be evoked, branching according to possibilities, looping upon themselves. . . . It made a weird design in her mind, almost a spell in itself. Her skin felt stiff with wardings and counterspells already cast; she would almost welcome their piercing by Casimir's magic: At least she would feel freer of limb before she was destroyed. . . . She caught the morbid thought and extinguished it. Her heart was pounding; she felt blood drumming at the back of her palate.

"I have come to this place of challenge," she said, following the ritual words. "My blood and my life are in the balance."

"My blood and my life are in the balance," replied Casimir. "Here in this place, let our challenge be fought."

"So be it," she said. "Ready when you are."

"Oh, I'm always ready for *you*, girl," replied Casimir.

He spoke the spell that delimited the area of the fight; it was a twin-spell, one which needs to be spoken by another mage in tandem if it is to hold. Melogian spoke her half of the spell and together they brought it to completion.

A blurring of the air now encased them as in a colossal egg, a trifle over fifty yards long and two-thirds as high, encompassing most of the knoll itself. The world outside could no longer be seen except as washes of blue, white, and green; its sounds were muted into inaudibility.

Although the barrier was only sensory, to exit the arena would be to admit defeat and so to lose one's life. In the past, some duels had been fought with even sterner isolation: According to half-legendary records, Nissimandos had battled a mage named Greinecher within an infrangible bubble of space linked to reality by the thinnest of threads, and indeed at the duel's bloody conclusion had nearly lost his own life as well, being barely able to reexpand the thread before the air within the bubble grew so stale as to suffocate him.

"I'm going to kill you, you know," Casimir announced placidly.

"That remains to be seen," she answered. "Assuming you are, though, I was wondering if you would honor a condemned woman's last request?"

Casimir raised an inquisitive eyebrow. "What request would that be, m'lady?"

"Would you tell me what you did with Orion? I could never figure it out."

Casimir chortled at this, ran his thumbnail along the fringe of beard at his chin. "Oh, why not?" he said, and in this also she had judged him correctly: He was eternally a boaster and could not resist telling her of his accomplishment.

"Yes, I imagine the puzzle must have tortured you quite a bit over the years," he said. "You could pick up his scent everywhere, so he couldn't be dead; and yet he was nowhere to be found. . . . I would have killed him if I could, you understand. There is no Law to protect him, after all; but dear old Orion is very stubborn about dying."

Casimir heaved a nostalgic sigh. "We laid an ambush for him, down in Jyndyrys. He was hunting for Christine in all the wrong places. From the depths of the world I had raised nightmares, and I brought them down upon him at a place we had carefully prepared for months, seeding rumors for hundreds of leagues up and down the world, so that all signs pointed to the castle where he would think the king's daughter was held—and where instead our forces waited for him."

He smiled dreamily. "Orion was alone against hundreds of opponents, taken by surprise in a place of weakness—and still that Book-spawned shit-eater almost won the battle. But in the end, we defeated him. There he was, trussed with ironweb and gagged with pitch. I struck his head from his shoulders myself—and then it hopped back into place and glared at me."

Casimir chortled. "I knew Mathellin could do that trick, but I never dreamed Orion had the talent. And in fact, he had it in a greater form than Mathellin, because even when we hacked him apart and burned the pieces, his self-image was so cogent his flesh rose from the ashes the moment the flames faltered. He almost escaped us then, too, since his bonds no longer held him. God's eyes, what a fight! I hadn't had this much fun in ages."

He was silent for a long moment, until Melogian forced herself to prompt him: "And then?"

"And then? Well, I found a way out of the dilemma and we got rid of him. So, are you ready for our little duel? . . . Oh, ho, ho, the expression on your face! All right, all right, I will tell you the end of the story.

"See, I had a brilliant idea: I took Orion on a little walk through Jyndyrys—bit by bit. We cut off one of his arms and I traveled *beyond* with it, worlds and worlds away. I severed the tip of his little finger and left it in the dust; then I took a few steps *beyond* and dropped off another little piece. And so forth, walking and paring off tiny bits, every one worlds away from the others. Then I returned to the ambush site and carried off a leg. Seven days it took me to scatter ten thousand pieces of him every-where. So he's alive, still, because something in him refuses to die, but not even Orion's powers can reassemble him across the boundaries of worlds."

Casimir shrugged. "Now, once you've defeated me you'll want to go look for him, of course. I have no doubt that if you collected all of him, he would revive; but with a myriad pieces to find, it might take you a while. Now, I'll tell you something to get you started. Let's see . . . it was a slice of nostril I dropped down that erupt-ing caldera, yes. As for the lens of his right eye—I'm very proud of that one—I added it to a ghibbelin's hoard of lenticular crystals. If you don't feel like sorting through them, I guess you could just take the whole chest with you, though that's hardly an elegant solution. . . . And as for the rest, I'll confess I don't remember it in much detail. It is a very tedious job, dismemberment of that kind. And anyway, time is passing, and we do have a duel to fight. So, when you're ready, just let me know."

Against those who hurt us for their pleasure we are ever defenseless; to hurt them back is seldom possible, and even then it will not lessen our grief. All we can do is endure, grin through the pain, hope that it will all be over soon. Melogian did not doubt that Casimir was telling her the truth; the explanation fit too well. But even if it was all a lie, she had to accept that Orion was gone and would never re-turn; that the man who had molded her into what she was, whom she had wor-shiped for his power and wisdom and loved for his frailties and quirks, was gone from the world, from her. She grew aware that she had fought a delaying action all these years, that part of her had waited for Orion to return, had believed all it had to do was to hold things together until her master came back from wherever he had been, and set all aright with a wave and a word of power.

All the forking paths of spells she held in her mind began to fade; her plans had been made with this fatal insanity at their core, that if she could but fight bravely enough, somehow Orion would know, would see what she did. Would return, as if her sacrifice held the power to bring him back from infinity.

Casimir might be tired, but so was she: She had expended too much of herself recently, and she lacked the stamina for an extended spell-battle. She saw how mad she had been to hope that she could somehow tire out Casimir, could duel with him long enough for Fraydhan to risk his last gambit. How stupid she had been to ask for news of Orion, when all the answer brought her was despair.

There remained one spell she could use: the one she had spent her life deny-ing. She had learned—perhaps—what it was. Had understood its words were not agents of wholesale destruction, but rather summoners of a power so caustic it could, in theory, burn away the foundations of the world, but need not, if properly wielded. Or perhaps she had deluded herself, and it was indeed nothing more than a working of ultimate destruction that could never be controlled. She did not care any longer.

"I'm ready," she whispered, and in the next moment brought the spell that had burned so long in her mind to its fore, and began to cast the Devastator.

᳂᳂ Quentin stood at Christine's side within Testenel, behind a window that gave a good view of the duel site. They had not spoken to one another in nearly an hour. Melogian's words had overwhelmed him and his first impulse had been to leave Christine's presence. But she had commanded him to stay, and he had obeyed. As they stood by the window she had reached for his hand and held it tight in hers. He wished this were another time and place, where they could discuss the situation, where he could reassure Christine of the purity of his intentions, reassert his former relationship with her. But she held his hand with the same trust and intensity as that imaginary girl whom he had tried to bring into the real world and who had vanished between one step and the next. He could no more move away than he would allow himself to take her in his arms.

In the distance, he saw Melogian and Casimir approach each other, stepping slowly and carefully, like marsh birds in their courtship dance. He saw them cast a brief spell and disappear from sight behind a shimmering curtain that delimited the bounds of their arena. He felt Christine shiver, her hand trembling in his. "She mustn't lose," she muttered. "She can't afford to lose."

And looking down close, Quentin saw now that Fraydhan had launched the sortie Melogian had called for. While Casimir dueled, he could not actively control his demons. Given their demonstrated narrow-mindedness, Melogian had urged Fraydhan to make the best of the occasion: While the duel went on, Evered's only usable troops were human.

He heard the shrill of bugles; saw the gates open, saw the loyalist soldiers pouring out, charging at the rebel ranks. The demons in the fore stood stock-still. While Melogian and Casimir fought behind the enspelled barrier, the remnants of the loyalist troops gave the attack.

The rebels were slow to react; then, as they grew aware that the loyalists were charging with desperate energy, and that the demons were inert, they braced themselves to receive the charge.

The armies met and clashed. Once more, the rebels' too-easy campaign had betrayed them, made them complacent. The loyalist charge staggered the rebel army; men and women fell, wounded or dead, and the besieging forces began to yield ground.

And then, as the battle intensified, as the loyalists began to know hope, as the rebels once more lost confidence, the world came to an end. Neither with a bang nor a whimper: In the space between one instant and the next, a force took hold of everyone on the battlefield, everyone in Testenel, every living thing the whole length and breadth of Chrysanthe, and froze them into place, as if a spike had been driven through them, pinning them to the undersides of space and time.

For an endless instant every being granted awareness within Chrysanthe knew a sense of absolute finality. It was as if the world had become flat as a sheet of paper, then crumpled into a ball and thrown into roaring flames. Time held its breath; thoughts froze; Creation stuttered.

All these years, the Devastator had waited to be spoken. Melogian's mind unfolded itself as the spell's pattern burned bright before her inner eye. The necessary mental disciplines were finely honed in her: It took less than five heartbeats before she was ready for the invocation. As she held the first word in her mind, then spoke it, she felt the scream of power in her bones. With the second word, that power began to beat in time with her pulse. The third word burst forth from her lips, and she felt a lattice of force form all around her, threading through space itself.

As they had before, her perceptions extended outward. This time, because of her greater experience and skill, she was able to integrate them into a coherent picture without losing her focus on the spell. Even the walls of the arena did not hinder the effect: She could have, if she had wanted, examined every room in Testenel, or just as easily scanned a back-alley in Waldern, on the shores of the Eastern Ocean. She did neither of these things, but she did bring Casimir's image before her, clear and sharp.

He was casting a spell of his own, of course. The one thing she had feared was that he would have known the counterspell Orion had used to inhibit her first invocation of the Devastator. Anything else he could assault her with, she was confident she could repel long enough to finish invoking her spell.

Casimir spoke a word which she recognized; and to Melogian's horror, she saw a lattice of power growing about the wizard, that overlaid her own. She spoke the fourth and fifth word. Casimir was two syllables behind her.

Melogian felt panic rising within her, so strong it threatened to interrupt the flow of her casting. Casimir knew all she knew, and more. Even this ultimate spell she had believed a secret only Orion shared, even the Devastator, he knew.

And yet, and yet: He was not casting the counterspell! This thought steadied her and she spoke the sixth word of the spell, flawlessly.

He does not know the spell Orion used to stop me the first time, she thought. *Which means he has nothing at his disposal to counteract the working. Instead, he is trying to cast my own spell himself, in an attempt to wrest the power from me.* The seventh word thundered on her lips. Casimir was echoing her perfectly, yet still a second behind.

She brought her hand in front of her face, slowly, fingertips pointing upward, then curled her little finger. She felt as if she were moving mountains. The lattice around her grew and grew and grew. . . . And she felt still more power rushing into and through her. The preliminaries of the spell were over, and she was moving into the main sequence.

She spoke further syllables, and made a single movement of her left arm. The power scaled upward; her skin was puckering and golden sparks chased themselves along her arms. The next step was not a word so much as a moan, guttural and rasping; she had not yet ended it when Casimir began his. *He is catching up,* she thought, appalled. *He is going through the spell faster than I can!*

As she drew breath for the next word, her sight flickered and she plunged into darkness for a moment. When light had returned, she found herself in the presence of Orion.

She tried to call out his name, to run to him in warning. Instead she found herself speaking in a conversational tone. "I don't understand, Master," she said. Those were not the words she had meant to speak. Around her the walls of a familiar room had asserted themselves. She was back in Orion's manse, deep in the forest of Fargaunce in Archeled.

Her limbs moved of themselves; she sat down next to the fire and looked at her mentor. "We of the arts travel down many strange roads, Melogian," Orion rumbled. "Many of those are of the mind rather than of space. At times, shelter along these paths may mean the difference between life and something far worse than death. What I've done for you now is to build you a shelter. A few minutes of memory into which you may retreat in dire straits. Should you come close to disaster in the future, you will find yourself back here, in memory. It's not a big shelter—only a few minutes deep—yet it might prove precious beyond imagination."

"Have you . . . ever had to use a shelter like this, Master?"

"Twice," he said, stepping closer. "But this is not the time for this. Look at the fire. I want you to breathe out, slowly. Relax—no, don't close your eyes, keep them open. Look at this room, which you know so well. Here is shelter, Melogian. There is no need to fear."

She felt her chest rise and fall; her eyes wandered across the room, of their own accord. All the sights she was vouchsafed were dearly familiar. Even that greenish stain on her right hand, which had taken years to fade . . .

Orion spoke again. "Now listen: These words are intended for your future self who may find her way here. Understand, Melogian: I have used a spell to carve a hypermemory for you, a pocket of time where you are safe. You cannot stay here long, but these few minutes will be enough. Center yourself. Feel the talent within you. We are keys in the locks of power, and there is no door we may not open. What lies behind these portals may be terrifying, but you must rise above your fear. There are fates worse than death, my child. If you must choose extinction, do not be afraid to. Remember that whatever happens, the past will always stand."

Orion knelt by Melogian's side, took her hands. She felt again, through a recall so perfect it could not be distinguished from experience, the warmth of his big hands, their strong fingers. He looked at her, his dark eyes twinkling, a fond smile upon his lips. "I love you, child," he said. "Fear nothing."

Then the hypermemory faded, and Melogian found herself plunged back into the Now. Not a tenth of a heartbeat had elapsed; her lips still vibrated with the last echoes of the moan. But the shelter had served its purpose. Her fear had abated. She felt the talent within her, and with surety spoke the ninth word of the spell, raised one elbow a fraction of an inch.

Power moved through the lattice, but now she could sense its flow was impaired, as Casimir's own spell resonated with hers. She was familiar with this effect. Many times she had done this with Orion, both of them casting the same spell at the same target. The spell's focus would swim from one mage to the other, usually cleaving to one mage in the end, but sometimes shattering itself apart. They had done it as a game, but the lesson behind it was profound: In the absence of a coun-terspell, of a magic stronger than an enemy's working, then one might cast the very same spell as a form of attack. Casimir was trying to either wrest control of the Devastator from her or shatter the spell completely.

Both of them had reached the same point now, and Melogian felt the focus of the spell fluctuating, going one way then the other. But this was not a lesser cantrap to levitate a pebble; this was one of the greater spells, and by its very nature trying to make it exist in two places at once was hideously dangerous.

She should have been afraid, but she was not. The art she had spent her life mastering held her in its grip. The tenth and eleventh words had been spoken. It was becoming harder and harder to continue. She might stop, she might interrupt the incantation, yield control to Casimir. This far along into the spell, the backlash would probably kill her. *There are fates worse than death,* Orion had said.

She saw her opponent, her enhanced sight piercing through the washes of light that now bloomed from the lattices. Casimir's plump face shone with sweat; his lips trembled. Both of them were now speaking the spell in perfect unison.

Rotate the right hand palm outward, holding the arm straight. The gesture was measured, slow, and Casimir copied it. Melogian felt the spell waver and pulse; pain blossomed at the base of her skull. Fire began to lick at the edges of Casimir's silhou-ette. She saw similar flames around her own body. They did not consume her, but they did burn. Both she and Casimir had risen in the air, freed from the pull of the earth.

She spoke the twelfth word, her voice rising and falling in pitch as prescribed. Pain ripped through her, worse than Casimir's death-spell. A sword was thrust into her bowels; claws slashed her back open along the spine.

Power massed inside her, drawn from a source she could not quite perceive, as if it lay in a direction no fleshly eyes could discern. She imagined a dammed river and herself picking at the stones of the dam one by one. She bent her right elbow and pivoted her wrist, spoke the thirteenth word. Her lips burned with acid; hot lead was poured into her eyes.

She understood then that this agony was not caused by the spell-battle, but that it was an effect of the spell itself. As the fourteenth and fifteenth words rose in her mind, she saw that to finish speaking the Devastator would be to kill herself.

Floating in the air, she and Casimir had been drawn closer and closer to one another. The lattices pulled at one another, then repelled. Casimir was barely five feet away from her. Their gazes met and she thought she saw in his eyes the same realization that she had just had. And she saw something else, something so very strange, in back of the flames that bloomed all about him. . . . Shadows not his own, a dozen or more, twisting and swaying, darting about him.

They both said the fourteenth word. Melogian felt a long needle thrust into her ear, and the pain nearly robbed her voice of its strength. Casimir was leering evilly at her, his eyes bright despite the pain he must also feel, as if he were actually enjoy-ing the experience.

And then one of the shadows flickered more substantial and stood in front of him, between them. It had the shape of a man, in torn raiments; darker patches in his hair seemed to speak of grievous wounds—even a crushed skull. The apparition raised a hand and made to claw at Casimir's face. As soon as it touched the bloom of flames about him, it vanished.

Melogian saw incredulity on the wizard's features; his eyes widened in something that might even have been fear. They said the fifteenth word together; Melogian felt the spell's focus fluctuate between them, faster and faster. The marrow of her bones was on fire. Another shadow now flickered into being. This one she saw in profile: a hawk-featured woman, with a dark mane of hair pulled back into a knot. The shadow raised her arms and began mouthing words and gesturing as if casting a spell.

The flames that surrounded the two wizards bloomed fuller; they touched the ghostly woman and she was gone before she could complete her working. As they began the sixteenth word, Casimir looked at Melogian and this time undeniable fear registered on his face.

He must think Melogian was somehow summoning these apparitions, even while she cast the Devastator. For her part, she had no thoughts to spare and wonder at what those shades were; pain filled her almost to the brim now. And the spell was far from ended. What if she abandoned the casting, took her chances with the backlash? Casimir would almost certainly be forced to complete the spell, sealing his own doom. . . .

No. This was not the answer. She would not let pain divert her path that way. She must try to win this battle. The seventeenth word rolled on her lips and it was like giving birth to a coil of razors.

I will die, she thought. *But I shall not fear death. I will speak the spell to the end, and die.* She surrendered to the magic, and spoke the eighteenth word in a chorus with Casimir.

Three, four, six shadows took momentary shapes around the wizard, threatened him impotently, and vanished. One last shade appeared; a woman whose eyes had been torn out of her face, whose bloody sockets still dripped, whose mouth still twisted in a scream of pain.

And Casimir faltered.

He slightly slurred one syllable of the nineteenth word and moved an arm outward by the width of a thumb, as if in a reflex to ward himself from the fugitive presence of the eyeless woman. Now, even in casting a greater spell, minor imprecisions were not fatal. This far along the course of the invocation, such a slip would have been irrelevant—had it not been that Melogian was casting the same spell, and had made no such mistake.

The fluctuation resolved itself. The focus of the Devastator clove to her, like a dead lover risen from the depths of the ocean. Casimir's invocation was shattered; the lattice anchored to him dissipated into nothingness.

The wizard himself was hit full on by the backlash; the release of force tore him apart before he could even scream. Every scrap of his body was flung outward, his flesh sliced into ribbons, his bones ground to powder, his blood boiled to steam. In a heartbeat, nothing was left of him except an expanding cloud of pink mist.

The power flowed now sure and strong through Melogian's lattice. As she had expected, this only worsened the pain. The full power of the Devastator was focused on her now. She continued with the casting, speaking the twenty-first word, then the twenty-second. The flames were truly burning her now; she was past the point where she merely felt the agony and now her body was actually being destroyed. Blood flowed from gashes in her side that her gestures had opened. Though her sight persisted through the agency of the lattice, her eyes had withered in their sockets from the heat of the flames.

A few more words and gestures . . . Melogian could feel the spell's end coming, beheld the pattern of it in her mind once more. It was as lovely and compelling as it had ever been, like an assassin's gold-chased blade. Her world had shrunk now until there was only the Devastator, and the pain.

She spoke the final word, and it tore out her throat and mouth. Her hand closed into a fist, then opened, and with this uttermost gesture the dam broke. Power surged out through her and blasted her to cinders.

3. Harvesting the Dead

In the first few instants, the torrent of power was so intense that what survived of Melogian was unable to react, could only feel it passing on and on, through her unresisting essence. Then it lessened slightly, and she could regather herself to herself.

I am dead, she thought. *The Devastator destroyed me. Yet—I exist still. How can this be?* She thought of raising her hands to her face, but she had neither hands nor face. Gone her body, gone also the agony. She grew aware then that she existed as a ripple does in the surface of a pond—she was a frail pattern imposed on the rush of energy. Yet it did not bear her away; she held on, safe and secure. The spell she had cast had summoned the power, but it seemed to protect her as well.

And in fact, it went further than this: for she *was* the power. She had shaped it in her destruction, and what poured outward into the world bore her imprint. She could shape it further still, impose the patterns she wished onto the raw power. She stood at the cusp of spell-casting; she sensed a near-infinity of possibilities, like a wild wind blowing through her.

She turned her attention outward, and her perceptions expanded dizzyingly, borne by the lattice of force that still spanned the whole of existence. She saw the armies frozen in battle on the field before Testenel; she swept her attention through mankind's oldest city Tiellorn, through the dukedoms and provinces, into the remote hinterlands, the cold marches where no one dwelt. Her gaze ranged everywhere, out to the ocean where the sun drowned each night and where Leviathan swam. And this time it was she who said to the fish, with a voice not of sound, *I see you.* Had it not been held frozen in time, it would have cowered at her words like a fingerling.

She encompassed the whole of Chrysanthe, the land and the rivers and the seas and the vault of heaven above; she saw the openings into the made worlds, portals into infinity. She felt the whole of the world, ringing like a bell at what she had wrought. Dammed-up magic, held back since the Creation, had been let loose. Orion had likened Chrysanthe to a snowflake upon the surface of a kettle of heated water; he had feared that chaos from outside the world would infuse it and boil it away. But this was nonsense. There was no outside, not as Orion had imagined it. What Melogian had let loose had always been part of the world. The furious magic that erupted through the rent she had torn was not alien to existence; it was no threat as such to the foundations of the world—though it would not leave them unmarked.

And the torrent had crested already. There was a limit to the power her spell had summoned: It was running out even as Melogian grew aware of its existence. She could not hold the magic back, could not store it for future use. The dam had been breached, she must seize the moment and draw on the force of the inrushing water, or else it would be gone for no purpose but its own.

She had no time for doubts or remorse; she let her heart speak. She drove her gaze through the portal into Jyndyrys; called across the borders of worlds, in a voice that could not be denied: *ORION!*

And every fragment of him, every last scrap of flesh, responded to the call. His self-image, shattered into ten thousand pieces, blazed across the made world. Melogian sent power hurtling through the worlds, reaching out into infinity with a myriad arms, and brought every last iota back into the true realm.

He gathered himself before her eyes: Orion, her mentor, hale and whole. Yet frozen in time, as all the world still lay.

She turned her attention to Evered's army then. She exerted her will to destroy the demons, to strike down every standing soldier . . . and found she could not. The power that moved through her was creative in its essence; when she tried to use it to destroy, it fled from her grasp. She brought herself in consonance with it once more, understanding now that she did not, could not, really control the magic, but only divert a fraction of its force to her ends. And it was running out faster and faster.

I don't know what to do, she thought for a fugitive unsecond. In hesitation and dread, she called out an empty phrase from the rote. *Heroes of the Book help me!*

In her present state, the least stray thought bore grave consequences: As if she had implored it, the wild magic of Creation complied. Out of the torrent of power, she saw them come into being, summoned by her call: six Heroes from the Book, come to save the land in the moment of its need.

She saw them, knew them, and named them. Clever Jayren, always awash with a hundred plans, who could fight a giant armed with a pin. Phæda of the coal-black skin, head full of elder spells. Cantorble the dwarf, strong as the earth, wise as laughter. Scandassil with his metal left hand, gold and silver fingers and iron thumb, who ran fleet as the wind. Nyradë the archer, whose arrowheads of green obsidian were sharper than memory. Kliphtoth of many colors: tireless warrior, sweet-voiced bard, master tactician. The six of them ringed her, still frozen in the instant of their creation.

Melogian knew a strange sensation now; not weakness, but dimness, the sense that the power that bore her was running so low that it could not do so much longer. Was it time for her to die again, a final death?

She could let it all go; this would be the easy course. She had a dim intimation that if she did, she would not in fact cease to exist, but find herself growing slowly less and less real, less and less present, from here until the end of time. It promised an eternity free of suffering and strife; but it was not what she wanted.

Let me live again, she thought. *I wish to be enfleshed once more. Please, let me live!*

Her body rose into being, filling out empty space. It was like putting on a suit of clothes after years spent naked. The rush of wild magic was nearly spent; she felt time about to resume its forward progress. Already her memories of her former state were dimming into incomprehensibility. Fleshbound once more, she could have wailed in mingled grief and joy.

And while a few unseconds were left to her, out of utter, perfect selfishness she shaped the power of Creation one last time and crafted something gloriously useless, something hers alone, repaying a debt to a younger self in a way no one had ever been able to. Rooted in the ground before her, a blue rose grew, her heartsick yearning given at long last substance. The magic ran out; the world moved forward once more, and Melogian fell to the ground in a faint, at the foot of a perfect flower.

The battle before Testenel flagged, as every man and woman felt the world, having trembled and lurched at its core, regain an equilibrium. Soldiers on both sides now gazed upon the world as one does upon a picture long since grown invisible from familiarity and suddenly brought into sharp focus. Those who were mystically inclined let their weapons drop from nerveless hands, overwhelmed by the haecceity of the land, filled with a terrible peace that left them unable to strive anymore. But mostly the reaction was fear, shading into terror. Had the forces been solely human, the lines would have broken and both sides would have immediately routed. But five horrors from the dawn of the world stood amongst the human soldiers. Five demons no longer enslaved by Casimir's will; all five of them unable to feel fear, and now filled with an all-consuming rage.

With a brassy shriek, the terrapin demon swiped at the nearest soldiers with both front feet. Adamantine nails ripped through armor, flesh, and bone; the rebels fled screaming from its attack, running blindly toward the enemy lines and Testenel. The demon lurched after them, bellowing still, its breath steaming from its mouth.

The cloud-demon had spent the past several days in compressed form; it now expanded its shape into the size it favored and drifted across the rebel lines, its constituent motes boiling in rapid waves. Soldiers caught in its grip clutched at their throats and fought to draw breath. One after the other, they fell; the demon continued its gentle drifting, leaving a trail of dead men behind.

Mehilvagaunt, freed from Casimir's orders, immediately called out to the soldiers that surrounded it. It had been laying the groundwork for the past several days, letting stray remarks drop that could not be construed as attempts to communicate. One by one, it had attracted the attention of various Kawlendian soldiers. These had found themselves staying close to the demon and experiencing most curious dreams, of wealth and power. "Reynard!" Mehilvagaunt called to a soldier. "Faithful friend! Terrible magic has been used; you are in danger!"

Reynard had been looking around in fright. "What was that?" he wailed. "What happened?"

"Listen; I can help you. But will you help me?"

Reynard gasped acquiescence and ran in a panic to the rider astride the pale horse. When their hands met, the soldier's face went slack and his eyes glassy. He positioned himself ahead of Mehilvagaunt, weapon drawn. Already the demon was calling out to another soldier, to add to his personal guard.

The firedrake swam through the air, burning. From the beginning Casimir had been forced to keep it well away from the seven-limbed demon, for the two creatures loathed each other and could barely be induced to focus on his orders when they were close. Now, freed from Casimir's coercion, it arrowed toward the seven-limbed demon, which for its part was also making for its enemy, oblivious to the surrounding human rabble.

The two demons met toward the rear of the rebel army. The quicksilver demon reared high, limbs spread out, its claws shining in the sun. The firedrake dove down; the faces on its copper-scaled sides opened their eyes and their mouths dribbled sparks.

The two demons collided with an explosion of flame, wrapped themselves around one another. The seven-limbed demon's claws gouged its opponent's scales, punctured the child faces and sank themselves deep into their eye sockets. The firedrake fastened its three jaws around one of its opponent's limbs and coated it with flame as if with slaver. The two demons became a single tangled mass, bleeding fire, rolling blindly atop human soldiers and crushing them to death. The quicksilver demon clawed and bit, tearing open the firedrake's flanks. Molten ichor flowed from the wounds as the firedrake tried to bite its opponent's throat. With a heave of its entire body it vomited clots of fire that stuck to the other demon's metal skin. The two kept twisting and rolling, shaking the ground with the force of their conflict.

The wizard Orion drew a deep breath; though the air that entered his lungs reeked of blood, brimstone, and demon ichor, it was as water to a man dying of thirst. How long had he spent torn in myriad pieces, all thoughts driven out by agony? He had known himself alive still, and with all his being had tried to re-form his shape, but he had been scattered across worlds, unable to reach *beyond* and unite himself. Days, months, years, millennia, he could not tell. Suffering erased his sense of time; all he could feel, beyond the pain, was regret and shame that he had been trapped by his enemies.

But then release had come at last: a rush of sweet power erasing all barriers. From everywhere his scattered pieces had converged back to the true realm. In the instant of his return he had reintegrated his shape and had resumed existence. For a moment as he looked around him, the carnage in the near distance, the sight of his apprentice lying perhaps dead at his feet, the screams of men and demons, the stink of blood and offal, all were to him beautiful beyond measure. Then, in the next heartbeat, his sanity returned and he felt flooded with horror.

"There is little time for introductions," said someone at his shoulder. Orion focused his attention and grew aware of the presence of six people, all of extraordinary appearance; he recognized them as being of his own kind. "I am Kliphtoth," continued the man, who had one blue eye and one red, one ear pointed and the other round, and whose armor was particolored green and gold. "We are all six Melogian's shapings. I understand you to be her mentor Orion, long lost in a made world."

Orion did not bother to reply. He knelt by Melogian's side, half-certain she had died. "Fear not; she lives," said the woman with the coal-black skin and the white hair. "But she will be insensible for a time; she has passed through a unique ordeal."

"Understand this, Orion," continued Kliphtoth. "You have been missing for

seven years. King Edisthen is dead. The heir Christine has been found and returned to the land. Evered's army, allied with Kawlend, assaulted Testenel aided by
demons. Melogian dueled with Casimir and won; he is gone. Mathellin is dead as
well. The demons are left unshackled. Evered and his brothers yet live."

Orion absorbed the news with a sharp nod. Now that he was whole again, he
felt his power flooding back to him. He had invested much of it in the knights he had
sent questing for the king's lost daughter, but what remained was still great.

His gaze ranged across the battlefield. Chaos reigned; demons slew men left and
right. Soldiers in the liveries of Vaurd, of Kawlend, Temerorn, Archeled, and Estephor, fought side by side, trying to contain the demons' attacks, failing and dying.

Having been written into existence, his head was full of elder knowledge; sometimes it seemed to him as if he had been alive millennia ago and actually remembered
it. Looking out now upon the scene, it was as if old enemies had returned to battle one
last time, though they had brought unknown allies with them. . . . He recognized the
terrapin horror that lurched across the field, leaving a trail of mangled bodies in its
wake; the seven-limbed, metallic demon he could even put a name to; and the roiling
madness of the cloud-demon seemed as familiar as the melody of a children's song.

"We must first destroy the demons," he said. "If Evered still wishes to fight afterward, we will deal with him then." He looked down at Melogian, who lay supine
next to a tall bush bearing a half-dozen blue flowers. "But I will not leave Melogian
here unprotected."

"Of course not." The one who spoke now was a youngish man with a sharp
face and forked beard. "None of us would dream of it. Can you remain by her side
and call magic to our aid, or are you still too weak?"

"Give me a minute and I will bring the sky down around Evered's ears,"
growled Orion. The Hero smiled and turned to the others, speaking rapidly. "Then
here is what I suggest. Nyradë, you can remain here with Orion and shoot your
lovely darts where you please. Scandassil and myself can help finish off the pair that
are fighting. Phæda and Cantorble can cover the right flank, where the cloud-thing
rampages. Kliphtoth, you can decide better than I where you should go."

Kliphtoth grunted. "Let us not divide our forces to excess. I will go with you
and Scandassil; three of us are not too many to destroy two demons. Orion; if you
are threatened, call out to my colors and I shall hear."

The five Heroes instantly set off. Cantorble and Phæda went to the right, the
dwarf moving swiftly on his bandy legs. Phæda summoned her magic as they went;
armors of filigreed light enclosed them both and power sparked between her opened
palms. The three others ran toward the area where the seven-limbed demon and
the firedrake fought.

"I will take the terrapin," Orion told Nyradë. "It moves slowly enough that I can
sunder it with Red Ruin. But I'll need a few minutes before I can summon the full
power of the spell."

His power awoke; he began the proper invocation, gesturing and reciting the
spell. He was still dazed by the change of his situation; he sensed a colossal anger
coming to a slow boil inside him. When he was done with this fight, and only then,
he would allow himself to give it free rein. If Kliphtoth was to be believed, Evered's

two wizards were dead already, so he could not avenge himself upon them; but he could still find someone who would pay.

❧ Nyradë nocked an arrow to her bow and scanned the battle, squinting to focus her sight, noting possible targets. She considered the two demons who fought one another: They had broken apart, the snake-thing shaking itself partly loose from the other, which held on with three of its limbs as its opponent tried to gain the sky. Experimentally, she sent a shaft flying to the metal demon, five hundred yards away; it impacted its body and bounced off in pieces. She tried another shot, this one at the snake demon: The shaft ignited, but the point still appeared to strike home, although even she could not discern its impact through the flames that surrounded the demon's body. The cloud horror she did not even bother with: Obviously, missiles were not the proper form of attack.

The movements of troops were becoming clearer to her hawk's sight. Those who fled from the terrapin ran toward the walls of Testenel. The rebel forces close to the cloud-demon had first routed, but were now being brought into a semblance of order. The demon itself was moving randomly, preying on wounded individuals who lacked the wherewithal to move out of its way. This one seemed to have very little for a brain; Phæda and Cantorble should have no great difficulty disposing of it.

Scandassil, Kliphtoth, and Jayren were approaching the fighting pair of demons cautiously. Those were surrounded by a ring of men, obviously trying to contain them and perhaps slay them if an opportunity presented itself. They bore the yellow and purple of Chrysanthe and Evered's green and red both; their enmity had vanished in the face of a far greater threat. For now, that situation would appear contained.

She spotted an anomaly in the flow of troops: a concerted movement of soldiers, coming in their direction. A tight knot of rebels surrounding a mounted figure, shields raised, moving with single-minded purpose. Could they be escorting Evered? wondered Nyradë. If they were, she could do far worse than shoot him through the eye. . . . A pang of distress came after the thought. To kill Vaurd's son meant her annihilation. She was new to this life yet, but already she was starting to care for it. And she might be needed later in the battle. Besides, it did not seem to be a normal man who led the forces. . . . Her gaze sharpened still; her field of vision seemed to narrow until it was a sea of meaningless colors, with the rider's face the sole speck in focus. She saw it clearly, then, and across the distance her gaze locked with its eyeless perception. It opened a ragged slash of a mouth, shouted out some order, and the rebels headed directly for them.

Orion was still casting his spell beside her. She did not wish to interrupt him; she drew back on her bow and let loose an arrow straight at the demon's face. It flew true, but was deflected at the last instant by a raised sword blade. Nyradë cursed, shot again, then three times in swift succession. The last arrow found its mark and buried itself deep in the demon's empty orbit—to absolutely no avail.

The sky was becoming overcast; the edges of the clouds were limned with red, as if the sun were already setting. A faint rumble sounded. Thunder? Nyradë knew what that was in the abstract, but she had never heard it before; for a moment, distracted, she wondered what rain might feel like.

The knot of men was approaching at a run. Orion's spell was yet unfinished, and Melogian lay insensate at their feet. Where was Jayren when she needed him? He would have a good plan already laid out in his head. . . . Nyradë shot more arrows at the demon, to its face, neck, and chest. Several found their marks, but still the thing urged its soldiers onwards. Was it already dead, and thus unkillable? Its followers wore slack faces, as if their will was not their own. . . .

She did not know this demon. She knew the history of the land by heart, she could sing every ballad written in the past thousand years, she could midwife a birth, she knew how to plant and raise a dozen crops. . . . But no Hero was omniscient. This dead thing she could neither name nor understand.

"Orion," she warned him, "you must finish your spell soon; we will be attacked shortly."

Fitting arrow to bow again, she shot at the men surrounding the undead rider. They, at least, fell when hit; even though their shields were raised, they were not large enough to form an effective wall against her arrows. Once or twice one of her shafts caught on wood or metal; otherwise, it buried itself into flesh and a man died.

Still, it was not enough. The front rank of soldiers was thinned but there were a good thirty men still standing; the undead rider croaked out imprecations and waved its two slim swords in the air. Nyradë glanced about. To her right, Cantorble and Phæda were engaging the cloud-demon, apparently finding it a tougher battle than they'd thought. The seven-limbed one had defeated the fiery demon, which lay disemboweled on the ground, its incandescent entrails disgorging smoke and sparks. The quicksilver demon had lost two of its limbs, which hung withered and charred at its sides, but did not appear otherwise discommoded. It now turned on the three Heroes, weaving and bobbing, its reflective body half-invisible in the dimming light. The terrapin, meanwhile, had altered its course; no longer laboring toward Testenel, it seemed to be headed for Orion and herself. She could not prevail alone against two demons. In desperation, Nyradë sang out, "Green and gold, red and blue, come to our aid!"

As he battled the seven-limbed demon, Kliphtoth heard the call of distress Nyradë had sent. A thrill of fear shot through him, at the thought that Melogian should be threatened. He stepped back, his attention distracted from the fight: For a moment, his defense wavered.

The demon coiled forward and one of its paws seized Kliphtoth's blade; it flexed its limb and twisted the weapon out of the Hero's grasp. Kliphtoth brought up his shield, which was seized by another paw. Unbalanced, the Hero took several steps to his right, struggling against the demon's attempt to rip his shield away.

The demon bent down over him; Kliphtoth found himself staring straight into both of the demon's eyes. His mind nulled; the blank roar of the void filled his ears. Claws smashed through his armor and tore him open from crotch to neck.

As the demon coiled in attack, Scandassil had ducked inside its reach. The demon's flesh appeared basically impervious, but the firedrake's fiery slaver had cracked and weakened it in several places. Scandassil aimed under the shoulder of one battered limb. When the demon bent forward, he thrust home the attack, smashing through the metal skin and burying his blade up to the hilt.

The demon reared and twisted about like a drop of mercury. Scandassil clung to the pommel of his sword and was lifted high into the air. He braced his feet on the withered limb; the demon's head was snaking toward him, its daggered teeth flashing as its jaws gaped wide.

Undaunted, Scandassil saw his opportunity: Flexing his legs, he jumped up toward the approaching head and landed atop the brow ridge. The demon's skin was slick as polished metal, warm as living flesh. Scandassil clung to the brow ridge as the demon lifted its head. Its eye was a black sphere as big as a man's head. Scandassil stiffened his metal fingers and drove them like a wedge into the demon's eye.

The cornea yielded under the blow and split open. Black humors flowed out of the rent. The demon screamed and shuddered. Scandassil drove his arm elbow-deep into the eyeball. His silver and gold fingers closed upon a nerve at the back of the eye and squeezed with crushing force.

The quicksilver demon screamed again; it twisted and whipped its body, battering Scandassil against its metal snout. But the metal hand would not loosen its grip; the Hero tightened it still and twisted his metal wrist.

The demon's body grew rigid. It quivered under the Hero's touch. Scandassil twisted his wrist again, felt the nerve grow scalding hot. A tarnished crust appeared on the demon's skin, spreading outward from the eye socket; hairline cracks scored themselves on the surface. Molten beads dripped from the rim of the socket, charring Scandassil's clothes and blistering his skin. From the ground, fifteen feet below him, he heard Jayren's voice urging soldiers to dig into the ground next to the demon's lower limbs, to try and overbalance it. A tear of molten metal burned Scandassil's right, fleshly thumb, sending up a whiff of overcooked meat; he shouted in pain and let loose a string of obscenities. The demon's head was slowly pivoting to follow the twist in the nerve, which meant Scandassil would soon lose his clutch and slip off, to dangle by his left hand.

There was a deep rumble all around him, and he felt a warm wind lift his hair. Calling down curses on all unnatural beasts and their refusal to die politely, Scandassil folded his knees up against the demon's head to give himself leverage. Then, straining with all four limbs, he pulled and twisted at the nerve.

The nerve snapped; the demon's body instantly shattered, like a pottery urn struck by a hammer. Scandassil plummeted to the ground, amidst a welter of metal fragments.

Phæda had felt confident that she and Cantorble would soon prevail. Her head seethed with spells; with calm assurance she unleashed them against the demon, but none of them seemed to affect it. She dropped curtains of flame upon it, but it did not burn. She raised winds to scatter its substance; it only seemed to gain energy. She drenched it with water, but only the earth grew wet. She hammered the ground with a pulse of force, and though corpses were thrown about like ninepins, it did not disturb the demon in the least.

Then, with sudden, unexpected speed, the cloud-thing advanced upon them.

Its previous behavior had led her to assume it had no mind to speak of; now she thought to perceive a malign intelligence within its unbody.

"Fall back, fall back!" she shouted to Cantorble; but the dwarf was not as fast as she was. The demon reached him and engulfed him. The dwarf flailed about with his ax, encountering no resistance. His motions already grew slower, enfeebled, as his lungs sought air in vain. Phæda screamed out a spell, reached into the swirl of motes with glowing arms of force. The demon's substance seemed to shrink back from the spell's manifestation. She caught Cantorble and pulled him out, then ran with all the speed her spells could give her, clutching the barely-conscious Hero to her side. The demon pursued, but Phæda was faster by far. Once she had reached a comparatively safe distance, she lowered Cantorble to the ground. The dwarf coughed and spat out a thick thread of saliva. "Thank you, witchsister," he gasped. "That was nearly the end of me."

She looked at the approaching demon, desperately trying to think of a suitable attack. Had she learned anything from her failures so far? "We are still in danger. I do not know how to affect the demon; it appears immune to elemental forces. And not even your ax could slice at its substance. It did not like me reaching into it when I plucked you out—but that is not much of a fighting spell. If I only had Juldrun's hundred hands, mayhap I could work something to greater effect."

Cantorble scratched at his temple with blunt fingers. "I can't very well dig a pit under it, or crush it with a boulder," he said. "Running away is undignified, but I don't see what else we can do at this time. I'm afraid now that it's had a taste o' dwarf, it won't leave us alone until it finishes me."

". . . A taste? Of course; that is brilliant!"

"Beg pardon?"

"It feels; it has senses. Most likely it sees and hears. . . . Close your eyes and cover your ears, Cantorble!"

Phæda summoned yet another spell from her mind and flung it toward the demon. There was a deafening burst of sound, like a giant's hammer slamming onto an anvil, and a violent flash of light. The demon halted its advance and roiled in place, its substance disorganized, quivering to a hundred different frequencies.

"Progress at last!" said Phæda with a grin. "Let us see how much it enjoys Oschimald's charming little invention from even closer at hand. . . ."

⁂ No help was coming; the phalanx led by the eyeless demon impeded Nyradë's view of the battle against the seven-limbed horror, but Kliphtoth would have reached them already were he able to. Still Orion spoke his spell, long rolling syllables, unhurried as the tides. Her arrows killed two more men, but there were too many left. Nyradë knew fear, fresh and new-minted. And shame that she was unequal to the task.

The demon had urged its men into a ponderous charge; its mount was cantering now, held back by the press of soldiers. *Its mount!* At last Nyradë guessed the truth, and sent a shaft whirring between two shields, through a crack between armor plates, into the feral horse's knee. It stumbled, and the eyeless thing atop it screamed, flailing its swords about at random, beheading one of its own men. The charge lost momentum and cohesion. The rider bawled more orders, just as Nyradë's second arrow found its mark in the chest. The hell-horse screamed in turn, brimstone dripping from its mouth; the third arrow clove its tongue to its jaw.

It turned about to retreat. The rebel soldiers were slow to react; it had to fight against them to move. She felled two of the soldiers to get a clear shot at the demon's rump. In quick succession, two shafts buried themselves in its left leg, at hock and stifle: The leg gave and the demon fell on its side, throwing off the rider like some huge gray leech.

Thunder gave voice again, a loud thrumming as of taut kettledrums; a crimson flash filled the sky, and Orion's spell reached fruition. A cataract of ruby fire fell from above directly onto the terrapin, drenching it in flames.

The Red Ruin seared the demon's exposed parts: Clumps of scales fell off, revealing the raw red flesh beneath. Bellowing in pain, the terrapin halted, withdrew its head and limbs within its shell. The Red Ruin kept falling from the sky, splashing onto the shell. Everywhere the ruby drops fell, they seared the ground to ashes; armored corpses caught in the deadly rain melted into nothingness.

And still the terrapin's shell withstood the virulence of the Red Ruin. For five, ten, fifteen heartbeats, it seemed impervious. The demon cowered, safe, at the center of a crater full of steaming ashes. Then Nyradë saw the grotesque spines at the center of each scute were drooping, like wax melting under gentle heat. The scutes bulged at their centers, and the seams between them started bubbling.

The shell cracked open like a nut bursting in the flames. The demon's flesh erupted, flinging scraps and boiling ichor over scores of yards. Dozens of soldiers were splashed with ichor and poisoned. Where the drops fell on the ground, grass bleached and withered.

Nyradë turned her attention back to the hell-horse, which was vainly attempting to bring itself to its feet. Its rider still thrashed around on his back; he had lost his grip on his swords and could not coordinate his movements. The men who had accompanied the demon had come out of their daze. Most of them had fled; those who remained, Nyradë slew with grim efficiency, taking no chances.

By her side, Orion sagged in exhaustion, hands on his knees. "God's eyes," he panted, "I wouldn't have believed it could survive a direct blast for so long. Give me a minute, friend, before I attempt another working. . . ."

She recognized Jayren approaching the fallen demon, mounted on a horse he had gained somewhere, leading a dozen soldiers, rebels and loyalists alike, wielding pikes and halberds. Three spiked the rider to the ground, while the rest busied themselves hooking the armor away from the demon and swiping at its legs every time it threatened to regain its footing. Dear methodical Jayren, who liked a job well done when he could; once the hell-horse was fully vulnerable, it was butchered by a sextet of blades, its entrails laid out in a triangular pattern and then set aflame. Jayren stood by, watching his handiwork with grim satisfaction.

Nyradë called out to him and waved; after a moment, he acknowledged her hail and rode to meet her.

"Nyradë! Orion! Is all well?" he shouted out when he reached the top of the knoll.

"We are unhurt, Jayren. What of you? I couldn't see what was occurring; is the demon fallen?"

Three loud bangs made her wince and a distant flash of light left a black spot in her sight. Shielding her eyes, she peered through her fingers. "It's Phæda! She seems to have found a way of dealing with . . ." She broke off and buried her face in the crook of her arm against the renewed assault of light and sound.

"She obviously has," commented Jayren. "Let us face away from that direction while we talk. Yes, the seven-limbed one and the firedrake are both destroyed. In hindsight, Orion, we should have dealt with the terrapin later and used your help against the two demons."

"There was no time for a strategic meeting," replied Orion, frowning. "We did as best we could."

"Forgive me; I am not blaming you in the least, only myself. I grieve at the loss we suffered; it could have been avoided had I been less of a fool."

"The loss? What loss?" asked Nyradë, shocked.

Jayren's voice softened. "Kliphtoth fell in battle. Scandassil avenged him by slaying the seven-limbed one, though in the process he broke a leg and an arm. Metal shards cut him in a hundred places and he's lost quite a lot of blood, but his wounds heal quickly. He promised me he would be dancing in celebration tonight."

"Where is he? Did you leave him alone?"

"Of course not. He is in the care of several soldiers of the crown. And I saw Cantorble heading his way as I was leading the attack on our mounted friend; I have no fears for Scandassil."

Nyradë was weeping. And though sadness filled her, a part of her guiltily rejoiced that she was here to feel it; that *she* lived. "But Kliphtoth!" she wailed. "Now we will never sing . . . I know, I *know* how our voices would have sounded together; but now I will never hear it! This is . . ." Words failed her. She looked at Orion, asked "Why?" in a strangled voice.

He took her hand and said, "Bootless to ask. You're less than a child, Nyradë, and the world will make even less sense for you than it does for me. And still, after a hundred and eighty years, I dare not ask myself that question too often. Allow yourself some time in the world before you start trying to fathom it."

His words brought her no comfort. She closed her eyes and felt tears rolling down her cheeks; they reached the corners of her mouth and she marveled helplessly at their salty taste.

❧ When the end of the world had come Innalan had buried his face in his hands and collapsed in the saddle. His whole body had shaken like a tree leaf in a high wind as he awaited whatever awful events were now inevitable. Any moment now, God Himself would tear open the sky and reach down to earth, to gather the wicked in His hand and send them all to Hell.

After a moment, Innalan regained enough courage to raise his head and look up: He saw chaos on the battlefield, Casimir's demons out of control, attacking each other or the rebel soldiers next to them. Evered, near him, screamed out curses and orders, then urged his mount to the west, toward a wing of his army that was still in good fighting order. Unthinkingly, Innalan followed. Evered was paying no attention to him anymore, but Innalan felt drawn to his brother as if connected by a cord.

This is wrong, he heard himself think. It could not be right that Evered still fought now. Their demons had slipped their tethers: What could it mean but that Casimir had lost the duel? Even now the beasts he had summoned from the depths of the earth were slaughtering their army. The very world had shuddered in revulsion at what was happening! How could Evered fail to take notice? They were passing through ranks of their own soldiers, a third of whom were kneeling and praying, sobbing, or laughing like children. The others moved like men in a dream, their officers unsure of where to lead them. Many were following Evered, no doubt as Innalan was doing, out of instinct.

Innalan clenched his hands on the reins. God had spoken as clearly as She could: She did not approve of Evered's venture. She never had. He had tried to wrest this admission from Sharnas in Vorlok but the old priestess had resisted. Perhaps, he thought, she had been meant to. Perhaps it was fitting, was *necessary,* that Evered attempt to wreak his evil and fail. But fail he must: Vaurd their father had been cast down by a Hero from the Book, and that had been just and proper. It was not proper that Evered defeat the house of Edisthen. Tears leaking from his eyes, Innalan sensed what it was he must do.

He urged his horse to greater speed and caught up to Evered, who spared him barely a glance. As they galloped westward, Innalan drew his sword from its sheath. His hands no longer shook; after days without a drink, his head was finally clear of the fug of wine. He felt as if he had been asleep all his life and only now was he at long last awake. The dread that had filled him had escalated into icy calm.

Innalan brought his horse close to his brother's until they were almost touching. When the moment came, he slashed at the girth that held Evered's saddle and severed it in one blow. Evered shouted in surprise and turned toward him, to be met by Innalan's backstroke. It slammed into the back of his head and stunned him. Another blow came; Evered clumsily dodged it while his mount shied and danced away; the saddle slipped off and he was thrown to the ground.

Innalan dismounted as Evered got shakily to his feet. All around, soldiers mounted and on foot, their liveries either green and red or ivory and brown, had halted their course and were rushing toward them. But they were too far away to intervene. Innalan's naked blade rose high in the air then came down upon his brother.

In their entire lives Vaurd's sons had never feared violence. It was easy for them, never having fought, to believe chainmail armor was an impervious shell. Innalan knew this was not the case. His blade came down on Evered's armor and severed the links. Evered shouted in pain and stepped back; he ordered Innalan to halt this madness. There was no fear in his face, only bewilderment.

Evered took one more step back and tripped; the weight of his armor unbalanced him and he crashed onto his back. Innalan came at him, roaring, and drove the point of his sword between the bars of Evered's face guard, cleaving his skull.

Innalan stepped back, almost falling himself. His sword, freed from his grip, remained vertical for a second then slowly tilted forward, to rest diagonally against the edges of Evered's helmet, still buried in the ruin of his face.

Soldiers now surrounded the two brothers at five paces' distance. Incredulous shouts rang out; some of the men took to their heels, looking back over their shoulders in a panic. For a few endless seconds Innalan looked at the faces all about him; his lips trembled with words unsaid, explanations, justifications. But then he raised his face to the sky and screamed out to the only one to whom he needed to speak.

"I have done Your will!" he roared, his voice flayed raw. "My ears opened; I heard Your voice and obeyed! Holy of Holies, God our Father, Who art in Heaven eternal, have—"

His flesh ignited like kindling in a furnace. A single flame rose blinding, a tongue of pure silver. Innalan's screams contained no words now. His armor glowed white hot, then melted away. Still his flesh burned; it ran from his bones like tallow, until all that was left was a skeleton, burning argent. The bones slowly curled and darkened, yet still the flame rose, unchanging. When all that was left of Innalan were a few thin blackened sticks, it began to dim, to wink out as the last ashes sublimated. Those soldiers who had not yet fled did so now, to spread the word that the Law had avenged Evered's murder.

 On the eastern flank Prince Aghaid tried to lead the tattered remnants of a company in combat. Enraged, refusing to accept defeat, he drove his men against the loyalist forces with desperate energy. Had all of them been as determined as he, their charge might have succeeded. As it was, half his troops either deserted or simply paid no attention to his orders, and he found himself charging at the head of a pitifully small band. Their Temerorni opponents were far too numerous. Their pikes held firm against the mounted assault; mounts were gutted, riders thrown off. Undaunted, Aghaid charged into the ranks of the enemy. He wore the plumed helmet of royalty and a shield bearing the Casthen arms, emblem of Vaurd's lineage. On the battlefield, this garb had always meant absolute protection; and so it proved again, as loyalist soldiers melted away before him. Aghaid felt a grim exultation: No one would dare strike at him, protected as he was by the Law! He swung at an enemy soldier and slashed open the man's side. He laughed at his own invulnerability.

When he turned his mount around, he saw the enemy had re-formed ranks behind him. He had been cut off from his own men, who were getting slaughtered. Snarling in anger, he tried to make his way back. Pole-arms pierced his horse's armor and a mace blow shattered its leg. The beast collapsed; Aghaid was able to vacate the saddle and gain his feet.

A dozen men surrounded him, weapons drawn. Aghaid took a step forward, fearless. "Make way, churls!" he challenged.

"You won't pass, Highness," said one of the soldiers, a stocky, grizzled woman in half-mail, blood besmirching her face.

"Stand back, or I shall kill you!"

"If you're going to kill me anyway, then I'll fucking well bash your traitor's head in first. What difference does it make to me?"

"I said *stand back*!" Aghaid screamed. His troops had abandoned their attack;

the few of them left hale were fleeing the field. All around him, soldiers in yellow-and-purple livery faced him with bloodlust in their eyes.

"Go fuck yourself, Highness. You're a prisoner now. Throw down your sword. If you don't I'm gonna lose my patience and cut your fucking head off. Haven't you heard? Your brothers are dead, struck down by God's own fist. You've lost the war. Now give yourself up or we'll have your head on a fucking platter for Queen Christine."

The ring of enemies tightened around him; Aghaid swung his blade and they halted their advance. He pivoted to his right and charged. A man met him head-on, parried his sword thrust and struck in turn. When their blades rang together a second time Aghaid's sword arm was numbed by the violence of the impact. Shouting a war-cry the soldier moved in and dealt him a blow to the chest, the blade crushing the links of his mail and driving them through the quilted undercoat to bruise his flesh. Aghaid staggered back, appalled by the pain he was enduring. For a second or two no one moved; Aghaid struggled with the enormity of what had happened, and what had not. Had it all been a lie? Was there no Law to protect him after all?

The soldier who had struck him stood immobile, a savage rictus stretching his features. And then he moved to attack once more. Aghaid parried his blows, one after the other, dread rising within him. He struck back, slicing through the soldier's light armor and cutting his flesh open. Drops of blood glittered as they dripped from his sword. The soldier stepped back, his face gone pale, his eyes wide. His mouth opened and his lips drew back until they bared the roots of his gums. His armor fell into ribbons, revealing his bare torso. There came a series of popping sounds and blood spattered from his mouth; then the soldier's torso blossomed open and everted itself, flinging out his entrails. He collapsed onto his back, the snapped bars of his rib cage framing his still-beating heart.

"There *is* a Law," croaked Aghaid, "and it protects me. All who harm me shall die. Now let me go!"

But they would not. Three or four of the enemy edged away, but the others merely tightened the circle yet again; like a noose. He realized, astonished, that they were not willing, even in the face of the Law's punishment, to let him live. They were going to cut and batter him, as long as they could before the Law took them, one after the other. And these were experienced soldiers: Before the last of them fell victim to the Law's fury, he would have suffered a fatal wound. He understood for the first time the limits of the Law's protection: It did not prevent, it only avenged.

He was going to be slain by common churls, in an anonymous corner of the battlefield, unknown and unnoticed. Rage shook him at the thought of such an end. So when the grizzled woman stepped forward, weapon at the ready, he cheated her, he cheated them all, of their prize.

There was very little pain. The Law that punished the slightest harm to those of royal blood did not rule against suicide. It affirmed, rather, that his life was his to do with as he chose, and ultimately to take. When their hands came down upon him, when he was seized and hoisted aloft and carried across the battlefield, a bloodied misericorde driven beneath his breastbone, it was a corpse they bore: no longer the youngest son of Vaurd, no longer a man protected by the Law, but a piece of dead flesh, which could not be hurt anymore. Whatever soul or spirit had resided within this envelope was fled, to an afterlife of which nothing may ever be spoken, for none have ever returned from it.

☙ Casimir's last demon had fled, like a storm cloud blown by a hurricane wind. Phæda pursued it, running on enspelled legs, harrying it with actinic flashes and deafening bursts of sound.

Across the battlefield, no one was left who still wanted to fight. Exhausted soldiers let themselves collapse to the ground, rebels alongside the regent's troops. Those most affected by the end of the world still wandered in a daze, indifferent to the fate of others.

For her part, Christine had experienced a moment of transcendent terror then a shock of understanding: In the seconds that followed the change in the world, she had felt that she had grasped the meaning of life, had gained a revelation that put her entire existence in order. And in the next heartbeat, it had drained away, leaving wonderment and frustration in its wake. Something profound had occurred; not just in her, but at large. She did not know what it was, but she felt she had to find out. And one thing she was sure of, was that it had to do with Melogian's spell-duel against Casimir.

Atop the knoll in the near distance, the blurring of the air that had shielded the wizards had gone. There were several people there now, instead of two. Most of them had run toward the army lines, where the demons had gone wild and started attacking at random. By this clue Quentin had deduced that Melogian must have won the duel, that Casimir's death had freed his demons from their tether. But who were those additional figures, and where had they come from?

Standing at the window, both of them saw the demons fall one by one. They saw clouds boil up in a pristine sky, they heard thunder roll and witnessed a rain of flames obliterating the terrapin. They saw the quicksilver demon slay the firedrake. They saw the violent pulses of light that repelled the cloud-demon, and could no more explain these than they could explain the sudden disappearance of the seven-limbed demon.

Throughout it all, Christine worried about the fate of Melogian. She ordered messengers to bring back information and waited in vain for news: The situation on the field was so chaotic that no intelligence could be gathered.

Now things appeared to have settled somewhat, yet Christine still had no news.

"That's it," she said. "I'm going down there. I have to know."

"Lady Christine," protested Quentin, "you must not! It is too dangerous. Wait here, and—"

"Is it true?" she asked him, cutting him off. "Is it true you love me?"

That silenced him; he blushed red and said nothing. She had trouble speaking, yet she pushed on.

"I never . . . I didn't . . . I have to know, Quentin. I love Melogian, and I need to know what happened to her."

"She must be alive; where else would the rain of flames have come from? Surely she has gone pursuing the last demon."

"I'm not staying here and waiting to be brought news. If it was me down there, you wouldn't wait for news; you'd go get me yourself. So let me go, please . . . if you love me."

She had never in all her life used this gambit; had always found it ridiculous when she encountered it in television shows. *If you love me, you will let me do what I want.* It was arrant stupidity. And yet it worked on Quentin, who lowered his gaze and assented to her wishes.

They went down the levels of Testenel to the ground. All along she was thinking that Quentin loved her, and she wondered at her own feelings. She had always been sure no man would ever love her; even now she felt Melogian must have been wrong, had lied to get them to do what she thought was best. The sorceress had seen into Christine more than she'd have liked, but surely her feelings were normal, inevitable, and meant nothing. It was normal to want to be with the man who had rescued her, normal to feel safe in his presence. It did not mean love in the sense Melogian had meant. She certainly wasn't going to marry him.

But he did not deny loving her, and that was . . . beyond belief. Inappropriate. Courtly love; she'd read about courtly love during the Medieva. It had to be that. What else could it be? Yet she hadn't found any reference to this concept in the books she'd read in Chrysanthe. If Quentin truly meant he was in love with her, well, that was ridiculous. For her part, she was not in love with him: She had spent most of her life knowing such feelings weren't for her.

At long last they reached ground level and left Testenel. Troops still milled in the enclosure between the central stem of the castle and the first perimeter wall; most of them appeared attentive to their duty. Medical supplies were being ferried out of Testenel. Quentin shouted for the regent to be given a horse and a mounted escort and it took only a few minutes before Christine found herself riding out astride a horse. She had only tried riding a few times since her arrival in the land and found the experience intimidating. Her mount's military saddle was far more uncomfortable than the riding saddles she had used before and the beast itself was of a large and heavy breed. Its hooves were clawed. Still, the soldier who had lent the horse remained by Christine's side and held the bridle tightly; the horse, for its part, appeared docile enough despite its fearsome size and walked at an easy gait.

They went out upon the battlefield; one of the soldiers held up a banner with the royal arms on a field of yellow and purple, broadcasting Christine's presence when she would have preferred to remain anonymous. But those were details, when what mattered was Melogian's fate.

So far, the battle had been almost like a television show. Even though she knew people were being killed, the physical distance, her uninvolvement in the action, made it easy for her to view all this as a spectacle staged for enjoyment. Seeing the demons destroyed, she had felt a stirring in her heart, almost a euphoria. And even now, she thought of Melogian, not of the wounded and the dead.

As the royal entourage entered the battlefield, Christine could not sustain the illusion. Bodies were strewn about, inert flesh stained with its own blood. Christine glanced at them then turned her gaze away, horrified. The battlefield was still chaotic and groups of soldiers in rival liveries stared at one another with distrust. Rebel soldiers were in the minority so close to Testenel; most of them were in the process of surrendering. A few fled south, and none appeared inclined to pursue. Here and there soldiers wandered at random with a blissful smile on their faces, still in the throes of a mystical experience.

She heard a voice call her name; startled, she clumsily reined in her mount. Her company swirled to a stop about her. Christine dismounted, hurried from among the horses, trailed by the company and preceded by Quentin, who had also left his horse.

Three men had fallen here, one loyalist and two rebels. One of the rebels was still alive: a boy of her own age, with a face that seemed never to have been burned by the razor's kiss. He wore only light quilted armor in Vaurd's colors; there was a dark red crust on the fabric at the height of his navel. He was lying on his back, but his head was tilted to the side and upward; he had seen her riding by and called out.

She reached his side; he said again, in a boy's cracking voice, "Queen Christine . . . I'm sorry, Lady. Water, please. Water . . ." His head fell back.

She wanted to kneel; Quentin held her arm and kept her upright. "Milady, no," he said. "There is nothing you can do."

"Quentin, he's hurt! He has to be helped."

Quentin shook his head. "He is dying, Lady Christine. He cannot survive his wound."

"Give him some water!" she urged.

Quentin took a flask from his hip, knelt by the young man's side, and moistened his lips. The boy swallowed convulsively and begged for more, but Quentin had pulled the flask away.

"Let him drink, Quentin!"

Quentin had risen and was shaking his head again. "If I did, it would only bring him more pain. He is bleeding to death, milady. There is nothing more to be done."

"Bandage him, help him! He's *dying*!"

"Yes, Lady Christine, he is dying, as hundreds have died here today. There is nothing we can do for any of them."

She ran blindly away from him, ran toward where Melogian had fallen. There were corpses everywhere she looked. Here a man had been gutted like an animal in a butcher's shop; there a dozen had been crushed by the terrapin-demon into a mangle of bone and flesh. A middle-aged woman bearing the livery of Chrysanthe lay on her side in a hollow of the ground. She was unmarked, intact; it was as if she'd merely lain down to rest. As Christine glanced at her, the woman's body jerked once, as if from internal pressure, and collapsed into a mound of ashes.

Christine's escort surrounded her, and she was at last prevailed upon to remount. She let herself slump forward in the saddle, dazed. For a moment she stopped knowing or caring where she was going.

Then they reached the knoll where Melogian had fought Casimir. Quentin shouted in astonishment. Christine raised her head, aware of her surroundings once more.

Four people stood before her group. Behind them, Melogian's form lay supine on the ground, at the foot of a large bush, tall as a man, covered with blue flowers. One of the four was a bearish man with a huge salt-and-pepper beard, wearing brown and black hooded robes. He approached until Christine's guards barred his way.

"Christine? Lady Christine?" he said. "Oh, by God's tongue, girl, but it is worth it all to see you again!"

"Do . . . Do I know you?" she asked, knowing how inane she sounded.

Quentin exclaimed: "That is *Orion*, Lady! Orion is back with us!" He dismounted and ran forward to clasp the man's arms. "Where were you, Lord Mage?" he asked. "What has happened? Is the Lady Melogian . . . ?"

It was another of the four who answered him, a woman who bore an articulated longbow on her shoulder. Her face was lovely despite a definite oddness of features. "Melogian is alive," she said. "She won the duel and obliterated Casimir, after which she called for us. But her travails have exhausted her. She sleeps."

Christine attempted to dismount and once more nearly fell from the saddle. The soldier caught her as she had the first time and very carefully set her down on her feet. After a moment's hesitation, she stepped forward. Orion was an intimidating presence, but she had never heard anything about him except praise. He was even taller and fatter than Casimir, but where Evered's wizard had looked like an alcoholic lowlife, Orion looked . . . well, he looked crazy, she had to say. Like someone's eccentric bachelor uncle; or rather, like an anchorite just released from a decade of contemplation. And yet Quentin trusted him, and she in turn trusted Quentin; so she stepped forward, and greeted him.

To her astonishment and alarm, he came forward and hugged her, with a fierceness obviously held in check. She had feared he would smell of must and rank sweat; his clothes in fact reeked of wood smoke, cinnamon, camphor, and patchouli, a mix of smells that scoured the back of her throat. She could not suppress a sneeze as he released her.

"How you've grown!" marveled Orion. "You would be fift—no, seventeen. Oh, my child, I've searched for you for so long. I can't tell you how happy I am that you've returned."

Christine was stammering something in return when Quentin's voice rose. He had been kneeling by Melogian's side, under the large bush, and pressing his head to her chest.

"She barely has a pulse!" he cried out in alarm. "I cannot even tell if she is breathing!"

"She's breathing, and she'll be quite all right," said the dwarfish man who stood next to Quentin. His red beard reached to the middle of his chest, barely three feet from the ground. He carried a double-bladed ax as tall as he was and wore black armor that shimmered silver in the sunlight. "In fact," he added, "I'd be willing to bet that at this instant she's actually invulnerable. I could try to chop her head off and my blade'd bounce back."

Quentin looked at him in bewilderment. "Who are you?" he asked. "Master Orion, who are these people? Are they trustworthy?"

"They are Heroes from the Book, Quentin," rumbled Orion. "Melogian brought them into being after calling me back from exile. They came in the moment of the land's need to defend its rightful sovereign. You can trust them as you trust me."

He turned back to Christine. "My condolences, Lady. I am very sorry. I've been told of your father's passing. I will mourn him."

Christine looked at the assembly and felt her mind reeling. "Heroes?" she said, looking at the three others. Besides the archer and the dwarf, there was a young man in pale clothing, at whose belt a profusion of small bags were hung. He looked more ordinary than even Orion; slim and supple, like a dancer, but not otherwise remarkable. "And did you say Melogian called them?"

The young man spoke up: "She did, Lady Christine. She called us into being from the void. And we have been remiss. It is time we showed proper respect for the sovereign."

As one, all three Heroes knelt to her. Orion, for his part, curtseyed ponderously.

"Don't . . . Please, stand up," said Christine. "I don't want this."

They rose. The young man continued: "I am Jayren, milady. This is Nyradë and this, Cantorble. There were three more of us. Phæda is off pursuing the last demon; Scandassil is recuperating on the battlefield. Kliphtoth, I regret to say, fell in your service."

Christine closed her eyes and shook her head. This was too much. She had wanted to know the fate of Melogian, and now Heroes from the Book were distracting her from her concerns.

She went to Melogian's side: The sorceress lay on her back, shielded from the sun by the leaves of the flower bush. She smiled faintly; her eyes were closed, her hands crossed at the wrist, in the traditional pose of the newly dead in their coffins. Christine touched Melogian's throat, felt a faint, slow pulse under her fingers.

"Don't worry, milady," came Cantorble's gravelly voice. "I have the sight; I can tell you she's in no danger. It's just that she's passed through the fires of Creation; it takes a lot out of you. She'll wake in time."

"Can't we do something to help?"

"Nah. We can bring her indoors to rest on a proper bed, sure, but she'll come out of the trance in her own good time."

There was a commotion; Christine heard her guard call challenge. She rose to her feet, Quentin close by her side. The three Heroes immediately stood in front of Christine, Nyradë with an arrow nocked in her bow. Cantorble unlimbered his ax and began swinging it threateningly.

A group of mounted rebels were approaching; one held high the standard of the Casthen lineage with its field of red and green. Christine's guard formed a line and drew their weapons. Orion, just behind them, had raised one hand to shoulder height and was muttering under his breath: The air crackled around him and bluish sparks flew from his fingers.

The rebels drew to a halt; a single man dismounted and approached with his arms in the air.

"Parley!" he shouted in desperate tones. "Parley, in God's name!"

"God's teeth! That is Prince Olf," said Quentin.

Olf stopped some distance from the group. "What do you want, Olf?" called out Orion, his voice dripping with menace.

"I've come . . . I have come to surrender," said Evered's brother. "I will swear fealty to the queen."

"Where is Evered?" asked Quentin. "What are your brothers doing?"

Olf shook his head. "There is only me now. Only me. The war is over. Please, I want to surrender."

Christine stepped forward; the three Heroes guarded her advance. Olf, catching sight of her, smiled and cringed at the same time; he dropped to his knees, his arms still up in the air.

"We won't harm you, Olf," said Christine. "Tell us where your brothers are."

"Dead. All dead, Lady; I've seen it." His voice caught and he struggled to continue. "When he was drunk, Innalan said the Law would punish us. He didn't want to believe, but he knew it in his heart. He was right. He killed Evered, but the Law took him too. And Aghaid's men saw him kill himself. I don't want to fight anymore, Lady. Please, take my oath. I promise I'll serve you well. Please!" He was weeping like a child.

"I—I accept your oath of fealty, Prince Olf. Rise." Christine hesitated, flustered; spoke to Quentin in a low voice. "Quentin, can you have someone . . . I mean, take care of him? I don't want anyone capturing him if he's joined us. I just don't know how I should go about this. . . ."

Quentin was already directing two of their soldiers to escort Olf away. The prince kept grinning inanely, babbling to his captors with a light tone, as if in an extremity of joy or terror.

Orion, standing at her elbow, murmured: "That was perfectly put, child. Now let us go back to Testenel. You should not remain here."

She turned to him; the horror of her surroundings, for a moment disregarded, asserted itself with full force. "Why?" she asked. "Am I in danger? Are any of the enemy left? Olf just surrendered. Are you telling me there's more killing left?"

"No, but you should be in a safe place, Christine. Come, I will summon a whirl and we will fly back to the castle."

At the thought of flying above the carnage, like a VIP touring a war zone aboard a private plane, Christine's gorge rose. And her numbed mind finally realized just who stood before her in his hooded robes. "No!" she shouted. "You're a wizard! You're the most powerful wizard in the world, that's what Melogian always said. Then do . . . *something* about this!" She swept her arm at the corpse-strewn battlefield.

"The dead cannot be brought back to life, child. It's the Law."

"I know the Law! But the wounded! All those people who aren't dead yet. Use your magic; save them!"

"You don't know what you're asking for," said Orion quietly.

"I don't care. I'm the regent, aren't I? Then I *order* you, Orion. Save the wounded. Do it! Now!"

Jayren ventured to interject. "Lady Christine, look there: People are tending to the wounded already. Some will be saved. If you wish, I shall go help them. I have skill as a healer. Cantorble and Nyradë could assist me."

Christine would not listen to him, nor to Quentin who sought to intervene. She stared at Orion and felt her anguish mount as he refused to drop his gaze.

"Christine," he rumbled, "I don't have the magic you imagine I have. I can summon all my art and save maybe a half-dozen of the dying. You want me to chant a spell and make all their wounds vanish? No one in the history of the world has ever been able to effect that. Destruction is easy, healing is not. I have enough power left to save a few people, if they aren't too far gone. If you command me, very well, I shall do it. Just tell me whom I must save and whom I will let die."

He held her gaze, his mouth twisted sourly. Christine felt herself tremble. She wanted to ask Orion to save the blond boy, and realized he might be dead by the time she located him again. How could she decide to grant life to someone and death to another? She clutched at Orion's robe and shouted. "It's not right, it's not right! They're in such pain. . . ."

"I can help with that," said Orion in a subdued tone. "I can ease their passing. Do you want that, milady? I can take away their pain, all of them. They won't suffer anymore."

"You'll make them die faster, is that what you mean?" She had a fugitive thought of fatal drug injections given to the terminally ill.

"No; I mean it will ease their suffering. I can cast a working that will numb their pain; it will do no harm otherwise. No one will die from it, I promise."

She nodded violently. "Yes. If you can do that. Take away their pain."

"Very well." Orion took a few steps back, dug out a handful of soil which he kneaded between his palms while muttering over it. As he kneaded it, the ball of dirt seemed to grow smaller and smaller; when he finally pulled his hands apart they were spotless. He turned his palms upward; from the ground at his feet a sweet-smelling vapor arose. With a resonant string of syllables Orion spread the effect outward, to encompass the entire battlefield. From every clod of earth, save those blighted by Red Ruin or the terrapin's ichor, the same vapor issued forth. Breathing it in, Christine was dizzied by sudden brief dreams; her whole body felt numbed, uncoordinated, as if she moved underwater, tossed by currents.

"It is done," Orion announced.

"Thank you," said Christine. She let her shoulders slump. "If we have to go, let's go." Quentin helped her mount her horse, atop which she swayed slowly. Orion cast a brief spell and levitated Melogian's supine form, which followed him as if borne on an invisible litter. Nyradë said, "Go without us. Cantorble and I shall go dig a grave for Kliphtoth. Less than one hour was he given in the world. Weep for him, those who can. Of all the Heroes from the Book, none had so brief a life."

Jayren had already left, to tend the wounded as he had offered; and so none of the newly written Heroes returned with them to Testenel. The company made slow progress back to the castle, everyone, including the horses, being affected by the vapors which still rose from the ground in sweet-smelling clouds.

Christine's attention was disconnected from her feelings; and so perhaps it was not so surprising that she was able to find the young rebel again. In a half-daze, she led her horse to him, dismounted, and knelt by his side. He was still breathing; there was a smile on his face. She stroked his brow. After a second's hesitation, in a soft voice, she asked him his name. But he made no reply, lost in Orion's spell-borne dreams. Within a minute, he shuddered and died. Christine rose to her feet, took a few steps away, breathing fast, her limbs tingling.

This, all this, had to be real, she reflected. The rapes she had imagined recalling were not one tenth as hideous as this carnage, these pointless, absurd deaths. Someone she had never known had died in her arms and she could not even learn his name. Her mounting horror finally overcame the spell's daze; she fell to her knees, her gut twisted and she vomited, splashing her clothes as well as the ground. Already that earth had been soaked by the gore and lymph of fallen soldiers; she felt ashamed to defile it even further. She sobbed, drawing flecks of her own spew into her lungs, and suffered a violent bout of coughing. Orion came to her side; she staggered away from him. She could not bear the thought that he should use magic to help her. Her saliva, thick with acid, dribbled from her mouth in long strings. She coughed again, her lungs burning, and retched.

She would not remount after that. They made their way back to Testenel, a ring of mounted soldiers surrounding Orion, with Melogian floating behind him unconscious, Quentin by her side and the regent of Chrysanthe next to him in her vomit-stained finery, tottering and lurching, still coughing from acid-etched lungs, wiping bile from her lips.

4. Ever After

Melogian drifted in and out of fugue; the world about her seemed less constant than the flicker of torchlight. She fought to anchor herself in reality; her fingers clenched on random objects, but she could not discern their shapes. She longed for the focusing experience of pain, but whenever she flailed her limbs about, they were restrained. Would no one understand what she needed? She needed . . . she needed . . .

For a moment, lucidity returned. She was in her apartments in Testenel, lying in her bed. Her whole body ached, as if she had just swum a hundred leagues. A young man sat by her bedside, holding her hand; she recognized the Hero Jayren, recalled with an astonishment too vast for words that she had summoned him out of Chaos.

She forced words out from between her lips. "Jayren. What's—happened?" Her voice was a strangled croak, as if her vocal cords had never known use.

"We've won the day," he replied. His lips twisted in a smile she found strangely familiar. "All is well, Melogian."

She blinked. The events of the duel were coming back to her. "Casimir . . . He failed to win control of the Devastator, and the backlash killed him. But Evered? The demons?"

Jayren shook his head. "The demons are gone, even to the last one, which Phæda managed to stun and bottle up in a clay jar. She just returned with her prize; I put it inside a triple chest in the Hypogeum Apotropaic. We'll see later about sealing the chests in molten lead and dropping off the ingot in the ocean, or maybe getting Leviathan to swallow it. As for Vaurd's sons, they are no longer a concern. Innalan murdered Evered before his own troops; then the Law turned him to ashes. Aghaid committed suicide rather than allow himself to be captured. Olf had never had the stomach or the brains for a war; he surrendered and swore fealty to Christine on the field of battle. He's with the Lady Veronica now. They've both been weeping themselves dry; it's quite touching."

"Not prudent to leave them alone. You are . . . overconfident, Jayren," she gasped. She could not understand why talking should be so exhausting. She wanted to warn him that the Lady Veronica was no dolt, that she had been kept as hostage because she had it in her to lead her sons to a successful revolt, had she chosen . . . She could not push her reasoning forward, found herself hearing again Jayren's words, which he had spoken a moment ago.

"I guess overconfidence is a consequence of always having a plan. Don't reproach me too much. I am as you made me."

"As *I* . . . made you?"

"Yes. You shaped me as you shaped all of us, when your need reached out through the raw energy of Creation. The six of us that you drew from the void are embodiments of your hopes and dreams. You are the only mortal to ever have seized God's quill and written on the page of the world. We are the first ever Heroes who can actually boast a parent. We've been fighting amongst ourselves for the honor of being by your side. I chose this shift because I thought it was the earliest time at which you might awake. . . ."

Melogian felt she was floating upward; yet Jayren still held her hand, and the other clutched at the covers. "I think I'm dying," she whispered. She was a fulcrum, and the world revolved around her; she felt its colossal momentum in her bones. A parade of grotesques crawled across her field of vision, lopsided limbs dragging along the ground, emitting moans and musical cries. Some of them bore her face, hideously distorted.

"You're not dying," Jayren was saying. "You're delirious. You've passed through the fires of Creation and you still require some time to reinhabit the flesh. We've been giving you some febrifuge. You just need to sleep some more, Mother."

"No! If I sleep, you will just go away. I have to hold you in my mind, all of you, or else you'll die. . . ."

Someone else had come into the room; she felt a small, icy-cold hand on her brow. Water was poured into her mouth. She felt it go down her throat. *I am absorbing it,* she thought with a vast wonder. *The water is becoming me.* It was like the deepest mystery of the universe.

"God's beard! Is she still apporting pests, or did we overlook these two?" a voice rumbled.

A thud, a strangled squeak, then scurrying noises. Melogian tried to speak, but her mouth would not obey her. Her sight had gone beyond the surface of things and she gazed uncomprehending at a tangle of enmeshed shapes and colors she could never describe in words. Incarnate names of long-gone Heroes drifted past; eidolons of force bore up the world as pillars of time might uphold causality; and beyond/ below these she glimpsed a whiteness so absolute it seared her gaze. . . .

"Sleep," a voice kept telling her. "Sleep now." She was too tired to fear any-more; she let oblivion claim her.

⁊⁊ In her apartments Christine threw off her soiled clothing and begged Althea for a bath as soon as humanly possible. She thought she smelled foul, even after the vomit- and bile-stained dress had been taken away and she wrapped a robe around herself. There was a small washbasin in one of her rooms; she used it to wipe her face, then scrubbed at her teeth with one of Chrysanthe's pathetic substitutes for a decent nylon toothbrush and gargled with lavender-scented water, trying to rinse off the aftertaste.

As soon as Althea brought the news that her bath was ready, Christine rushed to the tub and immersed herself up to her chin. She even held her breath and dunked her head down all the way, as if she could thereby lave herself of every wicked deed done in her name. When she emerged, she did not feel any different: She was still the same person as before, still sickened by the slaughter on the lawns before Testenel, still afflicted with guilt that Evered's madness had led to this out-come and that she had done nothing to stop it, still grieving for all her dead, still frightened by the prospect of dealing with Duchess Ambith.

And yet, and yet: Orion was back, and Melogian had defeated Casimir, and the war was over. And she, Christine, at last had gained the sense that she belonged here. She harbored no illusions about her fitness as a ruler: She might very well prove incompetent, as Evered had claimed. If so, then the Law would remove her from the throne, as it had Vaurd; and she would go quietly, without protest. She lathered herself with lavender soap and scrubbed at the rim of her nails where blood and vomit had caked. Under the rough caress of the sponge, her nipples perked up, and when she stood up to rinse off the lather from her crotch, she found she had aroused herself. She stood there for a moment, naked and chilled from the evapo-rating water, uncertain and wondering. Then she finished sponging herself clean and stepped out of the tub.

Wrapped in her bathrobe, she padded barefoot to her bedchamber. In the silly romance books she had read, Quentin would be in the antechamber right now, and she would use a discreet passage to have him come to her bed; she would greet him and mutely doff the robe, to reveal herself to him. . . . Instead, her every move was subject to witness by her body servants. If Quentin were brought to her, the whole of her staff would know, and how long before all of Testenel buzzed with the gossip?

Far, far safer to remain chaste; in years to come, she might be courted by no-bles. Perhaps one of them would meet her fancy; they would marry, and only on their wedding night would she find out whether he was a wondrous lover out of the Rosy Hearts Library, or brutal as a rutting bull.

She dressed quickly; Althea by now knew her preferences and had been able to assemble a whole wardrobe of clothing that did not require two other people's assis-tance to put on. As soon as she was presentable, Christine went out into her receiving room. Through Rann, she requested that Quentin pay her a visit; when he arrived, she begged him accompany her to her study, where she dismissed both body servants. The two girls curtseyed and left without protest.

Then she led Quentin down the corridor to her bedchamber, closed the door behind him once he had entered. She kissed him, on the lips, and took off her clothes. He did not put up much resistance; soon they were both naked. It was surprising; messy; a bit uncomfortable at times; but it did not hurt too much, nor too long. It bore no resemblance whatsoever to her induced memories of rape. When she felt Quentin inside her, she wanted to shout for joy at this victory over her past.

When they were done, she started laughing. She couldn't help herself, and seeing his bewildered expression only made her laugh the harder. She lay her head on his shoulder and stroked his chest, still giggling. When he asked her what the matter was, she said he would never understand. She wasn't sure herself, but she thought, after all this time, it might be joy.

Melogian slept a long time; there were no more dreams to trouble her. Her heart beat on and on, her lungs drew in air, in defiance of her extinguished consciousness. At last her mind rose from the nameless depths it had sunk to and she awoke.

This time, there was no one by her bedside; for half a second she had the thought that everyone had vanished from existence save herself. Then her hold on reality returned; chasing the grotesque idea away, she stirred her limbs and tried to climb out of bed.

The door opened and Orion walked in. Beholding him, Melogian felt her heart pound in her chest; she tried to speak, but could not force the words out.

His voice was the smooth rumble she remembered so well. "Oh, daughter, it is good to see you awake at last! Here, let me."

He put an arm around her shoulders and helped her sit up. Melogian brought a hand to her face, touching her cheek in wonder. Her limbs felt new, slightly stiff in the way of just-washed heavy fabric.

"I came as soon as the spell warned me you were awakening. How are you feeling?"

"I . . . I brought you back," she said, unable to state anything more than the obvious. Her voice had returned to its normal state.

"Aye, you did. You called every last piece of me back to the real world. I have not yet been able to thank you properly for rescuing me, but I will soon. I did bring you a little gift, to start with. Isn't it pretty?"

She looked at what he had pulled from within his robes and started. "My rose!" she shouted in outrage. Orion held an opaline vase in which a single blue rose had been set. Her eyes met his; her face was undone by a sense of awful betrayal. It had been alive, and he had cut it. . . .

"Not your rose, Melogian," Orion was saying. "One of its many children. The flower you brought into being has grown into a bush, eight feet tall and covered in a hundred blooms. Since this morning it's been putting out runners; it's like one of the walls of the Hedges. I've had to detail a squad of gardeners to trim it, lest your flowers overwhelm the entire kingdom."

"But I just . . . I just made the one flower . . . I'm sorry . . ."

"Come now, I was joking. I don't think we're at risk of being drowned in roses just yet; if the bush doesn't stabilize its growth on its own, Phæda knows how to contain it by sorcery."

Melogian was shaking her head, her eyes lowered. "Phæda. She's the one who knows elder magic. I know this . . . I knew it at the moment they all came into being. I know all about them. Like a gift from God. But Jayren said . . . he said they were my own creation. Was he correct?"

"He ought to know, I suppose. At any rate, this is what they've been telling people, that you brought them into being. You're being hailed everywhere as the savior of the realm."

"Savior?" Melogian knotted and unknotted her fingers, ran them on the fabric of the covers, feeling the fine weave as if for the first time. "Well. If you want to see it that way. I wouldn't."

"Why not? Your plan worked. You defeated Casimir and broke the rebels' back."

"What plan? How could I plan what happened? It was a desperate improvisation, nothing more. I had lost all hope; I gambled."

Orion frowned. "You risked bringing about the end of the world to defeat Casimir?"

"No. I . . . I did have a plan at first. I remembered the story of Merolind's duel with Riam; I wanted Casimir to expend his power trying to destroy me. I hoped it would weaken him enough to loosen his grip on the demons. And General Fraydhan thought of the obvious: to launch an attack while Casimir and I dueled, since the demons would no longer be under Casimir's active control."

She took a deep breath. "I had never intended to resort to the Devastator. But when Casimir told me what he had done to you, I understood . . . I understood myself all too well. I lost hope. I no longer believed I could prevail against him, or even hold on long enough before he destroyed me. And I just . . . I let the spell speak itself, because at that moment there was nothing else left to me."

And to her astonishment, Melogian felt two large tears roll down her cheeks. She put her hand to her face once more and felt unfamiliar moisture on the pads of her fingers.

"Don't cry, child. I'm not blaming you; how could I?"

"I knew the spell was not as you feared it was, Master. It wasn't something that let the outside chaos loose into Creation; I knew it wouldn't destroy the world. It would change it, by summoning raw power, at a keener pitch than anything else we can evoke."

"And you were able to control this power?"

"Barely. I could harness a very small part of it, but most of it escaped my control completely."

"I had gathered as much. Pardon the question, but how is it that you survived?"

She raised her gaze to meet his, smiled tremulously.

"I did not survive, Master. I died. When the power broke out, it destroyed me. Merely casting the Devastator would have killed me; the power itself vaporized my corpse."

"Strange; for a woman dead and gone, you appear quite tangible, Melogian."

"Well, something of myself remained; I think by becoming the doorway for the wild magic into the world, my pattern was preserved. I'm not sure; I can't really remember what happened. It made sense at the time, but now it's faded as a dream fades. I do know that I found I could shape the flow of Creation. I used its power to bring you back from Jyndyrys; I called the Heroes into being. And then, before the power ran out, I . . . I grew my body back."

She sighed. "In a way, this is not me; I mean, I am not Melogian. I must be nothing more than a copy of her."

She hugged herself, shivering. Orion took her arm and squeezed, a gesture she recalled well, which he had used when correcting her during her apprenticeship; it was both friendly and slightly painful.

"Nonsense! You are Melogian; no less so than I am myself. Would you deny I am Orion, on the grounds that I was hacked into ten thousand parts and only your magic reassembled them?"

"I . . . You *are* Orion, of course, Master . . ." She tried to wiggle out of his grasp, but his hand was both large and strong, and could hold her as well as a vise.

"Every morning," he continued, "I wake a different person from the previous night. What happened to you was not qualitatively different."

"Master, you don't know what you're talking about! And let go of my arm, damn you!"

He complied with a smile. "See? You grow angry in the same way as you've always done. Your appearance is unchanged. How can you not be Melogian?"

"I can tell casuistry when I hear it!"

"Really? Then you must be Melogian, since she's the only person in all of Chrysanthe who could be so impertinent toward myself. Here's casuistry for you: Remember how Thenuel's *Omnicon* claims that memory defines identity? Well then, what do you recall of your life? Can you tell me how we first met?"

Melogian sought for the recollection—and was so astounded that she gasped. Marshaled in perfect order, every moment of her past life lay within her memory, pristine and complete. She riffled through them in a blur, one instant a little girl, the next a grown woman. She knew then both that she could not be Melogian, who had never possessed recall one hundredth so perfect, and also that she could be no one else, for every deed she had ever done lay forever at the core of her soul.

"God's eyes . . . I remember . . . I remember everything," she said in a small voice. "But . . . has anything like this ever happened before, Master? For a wizard to be destroyed and reborn in the next breath?"

"Every time a Hero has come into being, my child, something similar has happened. Born men regard the moment of their death with terror, but I can tell you, we who have been written into existence look at our own beginning with the same dread. I don't wish to belittle what's happened to you; but in a way, it's an old story as far as I'm concerned."

Melogian nodded. "I want to stand," she announced after a moment. Orion lifted the covers from her legs and she swung them out. When she tried to stand up, she felt slightly dizzied and reached out for a staff to support her. She took two steps with its help and then stopped, staring in stupefaction at the wood in her hand. Orion's eyes had widened.

"This wasn't here . . ." she breathed.

"No, it wasn't. We've noticed that your experience seems to have imbued you with some new powers. You had some surprising bedside companions while you suffered from fever."

"Did I just summon this? It feels . . . like I willed it into existence."

"Interesting. Can you do it deliberately?"

She tried, hesitantly, to pervolve something in her hand, a pink and blue marble; the effort made her nauseated and weak, and Orion had to catch her in his arms.

"I'm so sorry, child. I shouldn't have asked you. You're still barely able to move."

"No, it's all right," she replied, still clutching the new-made staff in her hand. "I feel better already. Tell me what's happened. Jayren said we had defeated Vaurd's sons and the demons were slain. What of the armies? How many did we lose?"

"Most of the troops survived the battle. Duke Corlin is alive; he was found in Evered's tent. He's sorely wounded, but he'll be able to return home in a few weeks. Those rebels who didn't surrender have fled. We've received further levies from Archeled. As far as military matters go, the Second Usurpation War is over and done. We may have to organize a punitive expedition into Kawlend, though I suspect Ambith's star has faded. She's led her people into disaster twice; the ducal moot will probably demand she surrender her scepter. Meanwhile, if they thought the last war's weregild was onerous, they've seen nothing yet. We can probably scare them to death with the proposed reparation payments, then Christine will show herself to be magnanimous, rescind most of the debt, and win broad support. It's elementary demagoguery, really."

Melogian tottered over to a chair and sat down. She worked her shoulders and neck, trying to get rid of the stiffness.

"So the news on that front is good," continued Orion, "but there is something that concerns me. You see, there have been quite a few changes in the world, Melogian. Last night, I counted nineteen new constellations blazing across the heavens; several of their stars shine in green and red. I summoned Ilianrod's Chariot and rose up to the vault; but I couldn't reach it. There appears to be a distortion of space just within the shell of the heavens. I'm not sure yet if the stars are both farther away and larger than they were, or if it is a simple case of an impassable barrier springing into existence."

"The Devastator?" she asked, but she already knew it could be nothing else. She had wrought miracles by diverting only a small portion of the raw power she had summoned; the majority of it, therefore, had gone out into the world and changed it. But she had never expected effects of this sort.

"Of course. It apparently inverts the usual rule of effects weakening with distance. At the point of irruption, nothing appears to have changed at all, except for the rose you shaped; but the further away one goes, the more evidence of change there is. In Tiellorn, there are half a hundred instances of base metal objects being transmuted into solid gold, clay pots sprouting legs and running away from home, and flour spontaneously shaping itself into cakes."

Melogian could not restrain a chuckle.

"It does get uglier, though," Orion continued. "As soon as the *Black Heart* is ready, I will take a company of soldiers with me to inspect the marches of the realm. I'm rather worried about what we'll find there. Yesterday I flew to Aluvien aboard a whirl, to spread the news of the defeat. I found many who didn't care about the war's outcome, being more preoccupied by an invasion of their own; invisible things that drain a man's blood in the night and leave needles of glass embedded in his flesh. There were reports of unspeakable things stalking outlying villages—though how much of those was mere rumor I don't know."

Melogian realized with horror that her invocation might overall have wrought far more ill than it had done good. "I . . . I will accompany you, Master," she said. "I brought this onto our heads, I will help to correct it."

"You will remain here and rest. Don't think I blame you for what the spell wrought; and by God, I forbid you to blame yourself."

"I don't need to rest; and I did cast the Devastator, and—" She stopped herself. As she spoke the spell's name, she realized she no longer recalled it; its deadly pattern, which had lain so long at the core of her mind, was gone without a trace.

"Gone," she said. "The spell's gone."

"No wonder there," commented Orion. "It's vanished from my own mind as well. It's still inscribed in my book, but now the writing makes no sense. All power has fled from the words. This is not a spell you can cast a second time, once you've entered the new world that it's made."

Melogian sagged back in her seat; her initial anguish-borne burst of energy had flagged and she now found herself almost out of breath.

Orion put his hand on her shoulder. "Stay here and rest. There'll be plenty of time for brave deeds later. Scandassil and Phæda are just outside the door, and they're desperate to meet you at last. Shall I let them in?"

It was almost half-past Nineteenth Hour; Carl Almand forced himself away from the screen. He'd worked more than enough for today and his eyes were wearied from so many hours of staring at green letters on a black background. He saved his work before quitting the typing-program, then keyed in the backup command. He pushed in the cartridge labeled with his book's title, *Notes on an Ahrimanic Disappearance.* It had taken him a long time to draft, but he was at last nearing the end. His publisher had been dropping hints with increasing frequency that he was starting to get impatient.

Over the grinding sound of the file writing itself to the cartridge, there came a knock at his office door. Frowning, he rose from his seat and went to open the door. Two men in uniform stood there, holding a huge package wrapped in brown paper and thread.

"Good eve, sir. Here is your deliverance," said the one who had knocked.

"What?"

"You are Dr. Carl Almand, are you not, sir?"

"Yes, yes. I'm Dr. Almand."

"Well, then, this deliverance is for you."

"He means *delivery*, sir," said the other man, a youth barely out of his teens with a pointed goatee. "He's foreign."

"But," objected Dr. Almand, "a delivery at this hour? And I didn't order anything. . . ." His surprise gave way to sudden comprehension and fear. These obviously weren't delivery men, but robbers. He tried to keep a level head. If he remained calm, he wouldn't be hurt. They would want to steal the computer, of course. His insurance would pay for that loss, but what he couldn't afford to lose was the cartridge with his book on it. Fine; he'd beg them to let him keep the cartridge, he'd offer money, he'd give them the personal code for his bank card.

The men's uniforms bore no markings of any kind: they were plain, chocolate-brown clothes. At least he'd show them he wasn't an utter fool. "What company are you from?" he asked. Robbers this bold should be willing to play fair; unless they were the kind who maimed and killed for the fun of it, in which case he had nothing to lose anyway.

"We keep only the best company, sir," said the older man as the two began to bring the package into his office. It was over six feet in length and three in height, but less than six inches deep. Once they'd gotten it in, they stood it up on its narrow side against the filing cabinet. Dr. Almand expected them now to end the charade, to draw weapons and begin their threats. Instead, the younger man nodded and the other touched his left hand to the brim of his cap. He was wearing a metal glove of some sort, all four fingers glittering gold and silver, the thumb gray iron.

Both of them turned on their heels and left his office quietly. After a moment of incredulity, Dr. Almand rushed after them. When he looked out into the corridor there was no one to be seen, and he heard no footsteps on the stairs leading down to the street.

He closed his door and shot the bolt, then went to examine the package. The front of it bore his name and the address of his office, in neatly calligraphied letters, written directly onto the paper, rather than on a label. He got a pair of scissors and cut the threads. The paper had been folded and glued together, instead of using adhesive tape; it proved easier to slide one of the scissor blades along one side and peel the package open.

It was a painting; a life-size portrait set in a heavy frame. Dr. Almand finished removing the paper, stood back to get a clearer look.

He recognized the subject at once: He had spent the past two and a half years writing about her. This was Christine Matlin, who had been abducted by her stepfather in 1981 and whom he had believed dead. In the painting, she wore a dress of purple and gold resplendent with jewels; on her dark hair was a crown of twelve points. The painting was a remarkable likeness, almost photographic in its details.

For a minute Dr. Almand scrutinized the portrait, amazed and bewildered. Then he noticed a splash of white at the base of the painting, which was in fact a folded piece of paper wedged between the canvas and the frame. He plucked it out, unfolded it and read:

To Dr. Carl Almand:

There are two rival factions in my court. The first are those who argue that you do not really exist, and that my sending this message to you is thus a complete waste of time. The others are emphatic that you do exist, and that therefore, in retaliation for the damage you have done me, you deserve to die.

Whether or not you are actual is irrelevant: Imaginary man or not, I will forever bear the traces of your meddling on my soul. Still, I have no desire to exact such retribution from you, no matter how ill-guided your efforts were and how much pain you have caused me.

This, instead, is my vengeance upon you. I beg you to keep it by your side, and to look at it once a day, without fault. Know that I am alive and well, and that my father, whom I met before he passed away, was never the monster you made him out to be. Know that, despite all your efforts to discover horrors in my past, I was never abused. I should not blame you too much: My enemies sought for a world in which a fool such as yourself would exist, and within infinity anything may be obtained. I can only hope that dwelling on the mystery of this painting will instill such doubt in you that you will never again dare force your paranoid preconceptions on vulnerable children such as I was.

Farewell, Dr. Almand. Our sessions are at an end.

Dictated by Christine, Daughter of Edisthen,
by the Book and under the Law, Queen of Chrysanthe,
in the six thousandth and ninety-eighth Year of Creation.

A Lexicon for Chrysanthe

abance: A tubular vegetable, gathered when barely ripe, and pickled.

Aluvien: Capital city of the duchy of Kawlend.

Ambith: (b. 6044) Duchess of Kawlend. Sided with Vaurd during the War of Usurpation.

ansognia: A kind of flower, with broad fleshy petals.

Anyrelle: Christine's mother (6054–6077). Married King Edisthen in 6076. Died in childbirth.

aracerulle: A variety of flower that lacks perfume. Petals are long, thin, and green.

Archeled: The eastern duchy of Chrysanthe, rich and populous. Ruled by Duke Edric.

Book, The: Chrysanthe's main theological metaphor. Refers to the miraculous core of Creation, the will of God made tangible.

Buell (the Archivist): A Hero from the Book, consulted by Casimir during his travels through the underworld. Buell served as a living repository of knowledge for an entire dynasty of kings; his memory was flawless and extended far into antiquity, though it became more fragmented the deeper into the past one went. He had the mind of a docile child and would answer any questions put to him by a person in a position of authority. He was eventually murdered, presumably to conceal some dangerous piece of knowledge Buell would sooner or later have disclosed.

Carmine War: A long conflict during which most mages of the land were killed. Wars henceforth were decided by force of arms rather than magical prowess.

Casimir: (b. 6058) Wizard tutored by Firlow. Joined Evered's service in 6079, four years after the end of the Usurpation War.

Christine (Matlin): (b. 6077) Daughter of Edisthen. Abducted at the age of four and taken to the made world Errefern, where she remained for thirteen years, warded by the wizard Mathellin and ignorant of her true parentage, until rescued by Quentin. Her name as given is an English transliteration of the original: literally, "daughter of the anointed one."

Corlin: (b. 6071) Duke of Estephor, son of Théméo (6020–6082).

Edisthen: Hero who overthrew Vaurd and replaced him on the throne of Chrysanthe, leading to the War of Usurpation.

Errefern: The made world within which Christine was imprisoned for thirteen years. Its entrance is within the Hedges, south of Tiellorn.

Estephor: The northern duchy of Chrysanthe. It possesses a relatively cold climate and is not very fertile; its population is spread thin.

evening sweet: A small bush bearing many small dark-petaled flowers. Their nectar is notably rich in sugar and attracts various insects.

Evered: (b. 6059) Eldest son of Vaurd. His reason shattered upon his father's death in confrontation with Edisthen.

Firlow: A wizard, Casimir's former tutor. Murdered in late 6079, for reasons unknown.

First, The: Collectively refers to the Men created at the beginning of time, and sometimes also to the generation after them. Among the First were many Heroes of great prowess, but most of them were the same as contemporary Men. The First are generally numbered one hundred and forty-four, though their chronicles do not give a numerical census of the population and there is some doubt about twenty or so of the people mentioned in the chronicles, whether they were born of woman or of the Book.

Fraydhan: General of Chrysanthe's armies.

Freynie (Alfreyna) Long: (b. 1963) Christine's closest friend in Errefern.

Gasphode, Mount: The highest mountain in Chrysanthe; approximately three miles in altitude. Sometimes referred to as "God's Stair," it stands in the middle of a plateau in Estephor, about four hundred miles north of Tiellorn. Orion walked down into the world from the summit of Mount Gasphode.

golmin, golmina: A little paper doll. Mountebanks in Chrysanthe often perform puppet shows in a tiny theater. The paper dolls they use are called golmins when male and golminas when female. Used metaphorically: a cat's-paw.

Hedges, the: A labyrinthine structure made of dense flowering bushes growing in straight lines and forming twisting corridors, the result of ancient magics from the Dawn. The Hedges make up a rough square one hundred miles on a side and one mile thick. Their growth is regulated by an enchantment almost as old as Chrysanthe.

Hieloculat: The made world from which Mathellin's shape-shifting father came.

Juldrun: Often called Hundred-Handed Juldrun. A famed wizard from the distant past, renowned for many heroic deeds.

Jyndyrys: The made world where Orion vanished while seeking for Christine.

Kawlend: The southern duchy of Chrysanthe. Colder in climate but still provided with abundant soil. It supported Vaurd's sons during the Usurpation War.

Lelderien: A town close on the border between Archeled and Kawlend.

Lesser Book: The standard religious text of Chrysanthe. Synthesized out of a variety of preexisting texts, including extant journals of the First, around the turn of the second millennium, it evolved (mostly through additions) for the next two and a half thousand years and was fixed in its current form around the year 3500. It should be noted that none of the writings therein are considered to be of divine or divinely-inspired origin. The Lesser Book itself affirms "God does not speak to us with the words of Men." The Lesser Book is mostly concerned with Man's relationship with God and the world, and contains very little historical information.

made worlds: Realms of existence consisting of stacked parallel realities, created by magic, which open into Chrysanthe. Made worlds differ from one another but all are by their essential nature infinite in extent. Adepts may travel through made worlds and experience the limitless spectrum of possibilities they offer. Though beings or objects from one reality of a made world may be freely brought to any other reality, they cannot pass into the real world of Chrysanthe; this leads most philosophers to conclude that made worlds are incarnate dream-stuff and that the individuals that seemingly live within them are not truly real. Gradients may exist within made worlds, that make travel for nonadepts amongst realities possible. Much as all dreams hold the possibility of turning into nightmares, so made worlds are best reckoned to be intrinsically dangerous.

Mathellin: (b. 6049) A dream-spawn wizard, Udæve's son. His father was an imaginary man of Hieloculat, a shapechanger. Mathellin inherited his father's metamorphosis abilities as well as his mother's gift for magic. Became court wizard to Vaurd in 6071 after Orion was dismissed.

Melogian: (b. 6061 in Archeled) Orion's apprentice.

Nikolas Mestech: A Hero from the Book, one of the great wizards of the fourth millennium. He opened three portals into made worlds within Testenel itself, a feat that ensured his name would live in history. His motives for so doing are unclear and his personality remains ambiguous.

Orion: A Hero from the Book. Written into existence in 5910. A wizard of immense power, he lived in the forest of Fargaunce, away from the travails of mankind, for a century and a half, until he decided to enter king Vaurd's service in 6066. Of this early life very little is known; there is reason to suppose his exploration of several made worlds occupied decades on end. Popular tales attribute all sorts of miracles and secret deeds to him; it is doubtful if the true story will ever be revealed.

Oschimald: A wizard and Hero from the Book.

Quentin: (b. 6068) A knight of Chrysanthe. Sought for Christine within the made world Errefern from 6085 until 6094, when he found her and brought her back into the real world.

perdule: A small handsome furry mammal native to southeastern Archeled, usually russet or blackish-brown, bearing a long bushy tail. Easily tamed, perdules are affectionate but also rather stupid and indolent. They tend to gluttony and become flatulent when overfed. They are nevertheless popular with the female nobility of Chrysanthe.

Scyamander: The longest river in Chrysanthe. Flows from the mountains to the northwest of Ticllorn all the way to the Eastern Ocean. The Scyamander accounts for the fertility of Archeled.

slarge: Pejorative middle-class slang: to laze about, accomplishing nothing. Often directed at the nobility.

Temerorn: Central duchy of Chrysanthe, under the direct authority of the sovereign. The core part of Temerorn is surrounded by the Hedges.

Testenel: A huge castle built a mile or so outside of Tiellorn; home to the sovereigns of Chrysanthe for the past several millennia.

Tiellorn: Capital city of Chrysanthe, the oldest dwelling place of humankind.

Udæve: A sorceress (6009–6086), mother of Mathellin.

Usurpation, War of: The conflict sparked immediately after Vaurd's death and Edisthen's seizure of the throne of Chrysanthe. Kawlend sided with Vaurd's offspring in declaring Edisthen a usurper and his claim to the throne baseless. Ended in defeat for Vaurd's line. Though a small conflict by the standards of past millennia, it was reckoned by contemporaries as a bloody war that would scar generations to come.

Vaurd: (b. 6034) Elder child of King Alyfred. King of Chrysanthe from 6058 to his death in 6074. Vaurd married Veronica, a minor noblewoman of Kawlend, and produced four sons: Evered, Innalan, Olf, and Aghaid.

Veraless: (b. 6038 in Kawlend) Soldier; rose to command of the skyship *Black Heart.*

Veronica: (b. 6039 in Kawlend) Wife of King Vaurd. Although a minor noble, the daughter of a baron, she was related to Duchess Ambith, her father being Ambith's cousin. She was kept a prisoner at the court of Chrysanthe after Vaurd's passing.

Waldern: Capital city of Archeled, built at the mouth of the Scyamander.